WAKE UP.
WE'RE ALMOST THERE

ALSO BY CHANDLER BROSSARD

FICTION

The Double View

The Bold Saboteurs

Who Walk in Darkness

PLAYS

Harry the Magician

The Man With Ideas

NON FICTION

The Spanish Scene

The Insane World of Adolf Hitler

CRITICISM

A New Approach to American Culture (editor)

WAKE UP.
WE'RE ALMOST THERE

Chandler Brossard

♈

Richard W. Baron

New York

1971

FOR
Daniel and Toby Talbot

WAKE UP.
WE'RE ALMOST THERE

I I'M JUST AS SICK AS THE NEXT GUY. BUT NO matter how hard I tried, I couldn't stand those arguments with Sylvia. They left me feeling like a dirty sock. What an awesome talent she had for destroying God's finest work! With one obscene word, or a gargoyle sneer, she could undo millions of years of evolution. I've never fallen for those spooky Bible stories—I always felt they were meant to be read by people recovering from some awful disease—but living with Sylvia has made me think twice about the Devil. Now I know that he wasn't just some bad Jewish dream. And I'll tell you something else. Those hairy Bible penmen don't know how lucky they are. They would never have written that book if Sylvia had been around. She could make birds forget how to fly.

"Why do you have to play that crummy music all the time?" she would ask from her traditional position on the sofa.

"That's Boccherini."

"He ought to be deported."

"He's a wonderful composer," I would say, making my way slowly up the wall. "And besides, listening to him relaxes me."

"You know what I think would really relax you?" (A smile like a snake head.)

"What?"

"A good jump off the George Washington Bridge."

I reach the ceiling and hang there upside down. "You obviously don't care what pleases me. As far as you're concerned, I don't exist."

"That's the most intelligent thing you've said all week."

"Why did you marry me then?" I have slipped back into the warm, questionable comfort of my mother's womb.

"Obviously I was suffering from brain damage."

"Why don't you find someone else then?"

I am now breathing through gills and taking up with a couple of sea worms.

"As soon as I can get a few decent clothes together, I will. You can be sure of that, Buster."

"My name has never been Buster."

"Change it then. Might bring you luck."

Like that. Many days I go to the zoo for comfort. It is fortunate that I live within walking distance of it. Other times, before the zoo is open to the public—even the animals must be given time to prepare for humiliation—I buy a pint of Thunderbird and sit with the bums on the corner stoop. This can be quite lovely. We don't consider ourselves bound by time or space or the tight-mouthed rules of logic and manners that stifle the lives of middle class citizens. We cavort freely. Alcohol taken in the morning sun can save the world's sanity, believe me.

"I taught Joe Louis how to jab with his left," one troubador with an old sweat shirt says. "It's all in the shoulder, Joe, just remember that."

"A lot of those people who were supposed to go down on the Titanic are still living on an iceberg," sings another, a small castoff with a mushroom nose. "They've begun to breed with the penguins. Damn smart idea."

"My brother George and I slept in the same bed until we were old enough to join the Navy."

I breathe in the carefree stink of unwashed bodies and let my eyes glide over whole countries of uncircumcised face stubble.

"Eighty percent of the people who read comic books are potential child molesters."

"Here comes the hot dog man. That'll cost everybody twenty cents each. I recommend the hot onion sauce. Comes right from the island of Cyprus and won't get in your hair like that sauerkraut will."

The trusting youth of the nation march by us on their way to the educational abattoir. Their mothers grin like apes at them from the apartment windows. They try hard not to look at us dribbling away there on the brownstone steps. But we all know what they've been told: "Those men are dirty and dangerous and a crime in the eyes of God. Don't take any candy from them."

What these aging somnambulists don't realize is that their dumplings will be joining us sooner than they think. Why is it, I ask myself, that the human race would rather close its arms than open them? I must take this up with a biologist friend. So many answers are to be found in the lab these days. Alas, why not in the human heart? Has that been demoted too?

Don't knock the life of the stoop. Fight off your natural inclination to feel superior, and you might learn a little something. For instance, you can be both the viewer and the viewed, the participant as well as the spectator, you can feel immeasurably distant, and yet so intricately there as to be as essential as the tick of a clock. The big trouble with people is they look at themselves as a mouse would look in a mirror. That kind of a situation can stop you in your tracks. There is more to life than an ache for cheese.

I know what you're thinking! Who is this gourmet philosopher? Does he have eyes so blue he thinks they're sapphires? Did he study under Montaigne? Is he on speaking terms with Spinoza? How does he presume? Or is he a weightless cod with cradle cap, who wets himself at the mere thought of Tempest Storm? None of these! I am just an ordinary American boy trying to make his way. Give me a hand and I'll probably eat it off. And then berate you for having no Dijon mustard on it. I learned this from my mother, who bought and sold children at country fairs.

From time to time, as much out of loyalty to my companions on the stoop as from simple boredom, I panhandle to get up the money for morning lubricant. (I wish I could break the boys of their addiction to the heavy strong wines—muscatel, white port —and introduce them to a Moselle or a Pouilly Blanc '36. It is so much nicer to the skin and besides it goes well with food. Can you imagine washing a fine goose paté down with warm Gallo sherry?) I collect change or not depending on how I happen to be draped. Things go poorly when I am wearing my English shetland jacket and soft grey flannel slacks with suede shoes. People think I am putting them on, and they often get quite exercised. Like the upper class dandelion who was walking her neurasthenic French poodle (my city has become one gigantic shit house for animals).

"Oh! What a disgusting thing to do!" she screamed, pulling her dog baby close to her for protection. "You're a disgrace to your class!" She acted as though I had suggested we fornicate in a tree, instead of merely asking for seven cents. (Odd amounts break through their defenses.) "You must be mentally ill or something. Begging! Look at you. Why, without even looking at the label, I'm positive that you're wearing a Brooks Brothers jacket. Really!"

I adopt a Zen expression, combined with a fifth-century wood-cut body gesture, and reply, "Mother, we are all beggars in this world. What mortal does not need another's help?"

At this point in our dialog, the good lady was having her first psychotic episode symptoms. In deference to her condition, I bowed—a bit I have always admired in others—and saying I hoped I would see her Sunday in church, moved on down the street and toward an overflowing, gelatinous black woman who clearly spent her days cleaning up after sloppy white folks. She was wearing a bright and utterly unashamed Indian prayer rug for a dress. We smiled, looked into each other's eyes, and no explanations were neccessary. We were above such vulgarity.

"You lookin' real sharp today, poppa," she said slipping me a fine greasy dime. "I can tell this gonna be your day alright."

"I hope to hit mah stride 'long about midday," I said in a southern way. (Whenever I primitively love people, like this mountain of black jello, I assume their speech mannerisms. I don't want my own keeping us apart. At that soft moment something came back to me, something my friend Levi-Strauss was telling me just the other evening's dialog—

"As the night went on we could see that the effect of poetic creation was accompanied by loss, the chief's loss of consciousness. The characters were going beyond the performer, as it were, and his different voices took on so strong an individuality that it seemed unbelievable that they all belonged to the same person. . . .")

My black lady smiled and I disappeared into her huge mouth. "I wish I was gonna be there with you to share it. But I gotta lotta cleanin' ahead."

"We have our whole life ahead of us, sweet lady," and I floated on in deep euphoria—my goal of fifty cents having been reached: pennies, nickles, dimes—these delicate and absurd small coins made me a sweaty child again, heading for the yum-yum store.

The boys on the stoop welcomed me back from my torturous journey. Truly, each panhandling trip was implicitly regarded by us as something quite daring and perilous, a separation from each other and the mother steps—akin to an expedition of old, with cries and murmurs of admiration and pleasure, and wild grins that you ordinarily see only in mad houses.

"Daddy boy," said Blaster, a pock-marked retired killer, "You haven't let us down, as usual. You have brought the True Word. They would have worshipped you in Damascus."

A skeletal little fellow—he should be on exhibit in a wire factory—who used to be a chauffeur for Irish politicians when he was younger, howled as he saw the bottle, just as if he were a baby seeing his momma's big tit. "Never seen anything prettier in my life! Makes me feel sweet and squeezy all over. Swear to Christ it does. Now give it to me, you greedy son of a bitch!"

I felt like cradling him in my arms, but I was much too self conscious and still too bourgeois for such a decent gesture. Somebody might think I was a queer. Sylvia, for example. Naturally, being a magician of anti-logic, she would forget the Darwinian fact that what brought us together in the first place—squid hugging squid—was my uncontrollable desire to hump and pump her night and day. Even when she was sleeping. It didn't matter to me as long as I could sink into the lunacy that is her body and thus into my own self-destruction. Out of the millions upon millions of women available to me—women of character plus insatiable sex urges, women who smiled instead of spat—my demon forced me to choose Sylvia as a life partner. What a vile commentary upon my character, that I, a man whose chords respond only to the higher sounds of life, should require, as some weird price for being a person of intellect and sensibility (a veritable field of taste buds), a woman who loathed me and who did not allow a day to escape without dramatically showing this! Aye! Why did I ever crawl out of Bosch's brush!

Getting Sylvia to make love was a calculated descent into the most treacherous of labyrinths, but I could no more hold myself from making it than I could command my heart to stop beating. From the very moment the song of my loins was heard, the gates of hell opened for me. God only knows what fragile thing would provoke this deadly music: a suddenly exposed shoulder strap, a faint smell of perfume, or even the careful way she would munch a piece of cake with her after-dinner coffee. Trembling inside myself with apprehension, I would begin my advance. It was never a direct one; the more circuitous my approach, the less chance my quarry would sense what I was up to. Of course, the longer my route, the more acute was my suffering, and when I ultimately reached the threshold of confrontation, that beginning point for most people, I was ready to disintegrate.

"Don't do that!" Sylvia would say as I touched her belly, or grabbed her from behind and put my hand between her legs.

"I want you."

"I don't feel like it," and she would twist away from me.

"Oh come on," and I would embrace her again and put my tongue in her ear and my hand on her surly tit.

"No! I don't like that."

"Just relax. You'll love it."

Again, she freed herself and sat down at the far end of the room. "You just won't understand, will you?" she said, her face tightening up. "I'm not in the mood and you're trying to force me."

"But once we start, you do like it," I whined, creeping, cringing over to the couch from where she had left me standing empty armed and trembling.

"That's beside the point. You're too concerned with your own selfish desires to consider my feelings."

"But you never seem to feel like having sex. I can barely recall the occasions when you openly expressed a desire to make love. Maybe before we were married."

"You ruined whatever spontaneous urges I had."

"And just how did I do that?"

"I couldn't possibly enumerate the ways you have of killing feelings in people, of alienating them. It would take days to catalog them."

"You were alienated long before I came along." By now my desire had turned to poison and my whole being was contaminated by the foul mismagic.

"Go to hell, you unpleasant son of a bitch!" And she got up from the couch.

I yelled after her retreating figure. "One of these days, you'll realize that you have obligations to me as a wife."

A bark, a snort, a sound of the deepest contempt issued from her mouth. "My only obligation is to myself and to keep from being driven insane by the presence of a psychotic like you."

Lovely, isn't it? Exactly the sort of human exchange that is required to build civilizations. A religion-worshiping hatred. Too much love can ruin the mind, make it swampy. Makes you more than understand old Pascal when he said, "The natural misfortune of our mortal and feeble condition is so wretched that when we consider it closely nothing can console us. When I consider the short duration of my life, swallowed up in the eternity before and after, the little space which I fill, and even can see, engulfed in the infinite immensity of space of which I am ignorant, and which knows me not, I am frightened, and am astonished being here rather than there, why now rather than then."

But all is not lost. My instinctive animal cunning—some people would simply call it my urge to survive—directed me to other gardens of delight, one in particular being an extraordinary example of womanhood in full flower, a former Puerto Rican teen-ager named Lola, who lived just a murmur from my own spike-lined nest. Lola was a complete child of nature; there was not a single cuckoo, abstract, unnatural idea in her head. Mother Nature had created her in the hopes of counteracting the Sylvias of this world. Quite early in life, Lola had grasped the essentials of reality—elements that have eluded the establishment mind since the beginning of time, I might add—and selected the highest and most demanding of professions, or really, philosophic positions. She became a prostitute, and she was to this noble calling what Mozart was to music.

At least twice a week I worshiped at the shrine of her endless ingenuity, and thus not only kept myself from going to the funny farm, but also restored my belief in the human race and in particular the majesty of fucking. A mere call on the telephone and I entered another world. She always greeted me at the door in a most superb costume: (I don't believe she had worn a dress since childhood). She never wore anything that covered more than a few inches of her astonishing body. Each item was a master work of the imagination and surely was designed in heaven. A mere rumor of transparent cloth supported breasts that made you hate your mother; and hiding each nipple was a tiny black rose that had never dreamed of ending up in such a garden. Being the most limited of mortals—though I have read Shakespeare intensively—I couldn't possibly do verbal justice to the scene that started at her belly button and ended between her resonant thighs, so I will content myself with scientifically recording only the facts: black mesh arched and curved around that dense delta, no haughty attempt being made to stifle the auburn moorish pelt that spread generously over its edges, and around her lewd, sleepy buttocks —Reubens, I can hear your screams of joy!—it fitted so precisely as to become part of the skin itself. Looking too long at those delinquent cheeks was surely to risk complete gibbering blindness.

"What took you so long?" she would ask teasingly, with a heavy Spanish accent. "I've been so excited waiting for you, I thought I would tremble to pieces," and she stuck out her tongue and then slowly licked her lips. I kissed her, gorging on that tongue, and she grabbed my bishop.

"I crawled here on my hands and knees," I said, barely able to get the words out. "I was too hot to walk."

She laughed. "You always talk so funny. But I like it. You don't sound dumb like the others." She put her hands on those rolly, half naked hips and turned slowly around in front of me. "You like my new clothes, baby?"

(Her perfume must have contained some rare drug, for my senses began to flip out.) "Oh boy. I sure do." And I showered her ass with kisses.

She murmured with delight. (Oh, that sound! Nasser's ancestors destroyed entire villages for it.) "Are you a little hungry?"

"Famished."

She unloosed her bra and her breast leaped at me. "Would you like a little taste?" And as I stammered something in a strange language, she lifted one of those wild beauties and put it in my mouth. My sucking noises must have aroused the neighbors. "Mmm. Oh yes," she whispered, putting her hands inside my shirt. "That feels so great, baby. Bite me a little. Like that. Ohh. Hurt me, baby, Hurt me! Oy Dios!" And she began to moan and shudder under my ravaging teeth and tongue.

Now, only a fool would think that that kind of messing around could go on indefinitely. It didn't. "Uh, listen, Lola honey," I stammered, pulling my mouth off for a sec. "Let's . . . uh. . . ."

She read my thoughts. "Yeah," she panted. "Sure thing." And she slipped off her panties. I was about to but she did it for me: she unzipped me (I was more or less back on a tit now) and yanked out my ringing cock, and sat down on it jucily.

"That's better, huh?" she murmured.

I would like to handle this whole thing in a sane manner if I can, but it's going to be difficult. To say that what she did was "better" would be crass understatement. To say that it was quite a bit "more comfortable" would be lunatic. It was heaven, goddamnit! Do you hear me? Heaven! My parched pecker had been dragging itself across miles of desert for this bath of joyous twat quench, this murmurous loin creamery, this. . . .

"Thatababy!" I shouted, grabbing her roiling ass and plunging into her breasts once more with my mouth.

"Don't let me slip off . . . whatever you do," she advised me, sucking on my ear. I would rather have shot myself.

I'm not quite sure how I managed it, considering the extreme pressures I was working under, but several minutes later I was diving on her as she stretched back in a red velvet armchair with her legs spread and held high. I suspect I carried her as she continued to sit and squirm on my immobilized cock. I must have been beside myself with strength, because ordinarily I'm not much for lifting anything. Anyway . . . there I was on my knees with my tongue in the till, completely indifferent to, but quite conscious of, the admonitions of civic moralists against performing such a degenerate act. Hardcheese, I say. I would have kept my mouth sucking and licking away down there indefinitely, but while my tongue and lips were willing, my neck was beginning to break. Her howls and shrieks of pleasure, and her well-timed compliments—"Glory Jesus what a tongue you got! You don't . . . . oooh . . . miss . . . ahhhh . . . a thing." And, "Ayyy! Do it so good and slow. . . . I'm going to drown,"—distracted me from my pain for a while (and of course there was my own disgusting pleasure), but I had to get up and get her on the bed where the main events were scheduled.

"I can't stand it anymore, sweetheart," I moaned. "I mean. . . ."

I didn't carry her to the bed. We both crawled.

"You sure do it, baby," she babbled. "I'll never be the same down there."

Lola's genes and character were formed in the skirling days of the whip and the torture chamber, when the demonic Arabs were fusing man's ecstacy with pain, and to see God was to bathe in blood, so it was quite natural that her surging lust should cry out for the lash. Under her whimpering, savage guidance I was transformed into the divine scourge. I tied her writhing nude body to rungs she had in her bedroom wall and as she prayed and screamed and sweated with passion and need, I flogged her, flogged her until red streaks covered her back and trembling ass and she reached climax again and again. Afterward, on a bed large enough for an army, she threw herself upon my own sweating, tormented body and licked and bit me from top to bottom. She was a consummate master in the lost art of toe blowing. Before meeting this oceanic sex box, I had thought feet were only for stepping on. It seemed hours before I got around to the orthodox act of mounting her— I had experienced a world history of sexual logistics—and when I did it was like riding a wave, from the more challenging behind situation (where I qualified for the Venice rodeo championships) to the relatively easy front one, and throughout the entire cavalcade Lola and I kept up a frenzied commentary.

"Harder, baby! Harder!" she shouted. "Drive it home!"

"Raise your legs higher! Move your ass!"

"Tease me with it. That's right. Right there. Oy!"

We left out only one thing—the filming of it. What an enormous cultural waste

"Big boy," she said, wiping the glistening happy sweat from her face, "you got it. You really got it where it counts. And I'm not kidding."

I cleared my own vision of the vestiges of madness. "I owe it all to you, lovebud. You and Buddha are the world's great teachers."

"I never heard of that other sweetheart, but if you like him, he's got to be okay. You know, when you make love to me, I go to places I've never been to before. You're a magician or something," and she gave me a big bonus tongue kiss that tasted cunningly of cinnamon.

Our sex carnivals were always followed by a big feed. Black

beans, rice, fried plantains, roast pork, crunchy hog tails, onion slices, spiced shrimp, cold Peruvian beer—her table competed admirably with her bed. Whereas Sylvia (that anti-Christ haunts me even when I'm happy), her bed is filled with chasms and snow storms and her table is more suited to the Ganges River scene. Someday, perhaps my last hour, as I prepare to start my dialog with The Big Man, I will understand what drove me to her deadly night shack. (Is it possible that I, in another's form, killed Christ and must do penance eternally?)

"You've got to keep your strength up," Lola, said, interrupting my dreary digressions. Out of a modesty most becoming to her, she had slipped on a pair of bikini panties for her kitchen work. "You're getting too skinny." She laughed that indescribably Alhambra laugh. "If you don't watch out, you'll disappear on that bed one of these days."

"It would be my ultimate climax," I said, and kissed her spicy quiff as she served me a steamy helping of soul beans. Her left breast brushed my face as she did so, and the beans were immediately elevated to caviar. The first spoonful was borne to my mouth not by my own absurdly mortal hand but by Lola's, crossing in front of my raised arm, and this sudden juxtaposition of actions and identities, in this simple yet sensitive moment—after so many previous moments, when whatever the rigid components had been of my own character structure, were dislodged and reordered by our extraordinary love making, preparing the groundwork for utter human newness—changed time and place and person.

And she was saying, in a voice of feather and morning breeze, "What can one say of another's death?"

"How can one understand the water?"

"Precisely."

"And to ask the ducks why they fly north?"

"It is to court the absurd and make the stomach wince."

There were so many people around us, swarming, you might say, but nonetheless sweetly and without rancour. I felt that I knew them intimately but this was not the time to speak to them. I smiled, and this quite humble gesture journeyed effortlessly from known face to knowing face. One man, who seemed to be in charge of all the people but who at the same time had the sad, soft expression of their prisoner, said, in a voice I immediately felt was coming from a radio, "It's in your own interest. Don't forget that."

"I'm sorry," I said, and squeezed Lola's hand for support.

"He meant something else," she whispered, "but he didn't have the heart to say it."

"I understand." I did not know whether to feel good or cheated. "All's well that ends well," I shouted.

"You learned that at your mother's knee!" a gray old crone howled, and threw a bag of potato chips at us.

"She's just feeling her oats," Lola said, and winked at me. I quickly felt very sexual but I knew I would have to hold this in. "You put it so well," and I put my head on her bosom for a moment.

"Four score and seven years ago . . ." she began.

"Yes, I know. Please leave it."

We were in a cafeteria. Hundreds of people were seated at long tables. No one was eating. At one end of the room a small fat man dressed all in white was presiding over huge quantities of rich foods. The smells of meats and sauces made me feel that I was a child, and I wanted to cry a little.

"What you don't know won't hurt you!" the man shouted, full of confidence and purpose, and put a huge piece of meat in his mouth.

"Don't eat it all!" said Lola, but while I'm sure she meant it for him, her statement came to me as a secret code that I knew I should spend much time studying when I was ready for it.

"He's the owner," I explained, but I could not hide from myself the fact that I made this up for the moment.

"You should keep certain things to yourself," a tall thin woman said, rising from the table nearest me. She looked like an old friend who had lost weight.

"I'm sorry," I murmured and kissed her lightly on the shoulder.

"It isn't that easy," Lola said, and before I could explain myself she was sitting down on the lap of a young, extraordinarily handsome boy.

I kicked at her but I missed by a mile and fell oh so gently to the floor. Hundreds of throats poured out a symphony of laughter, and I wanted to pee pee I felt so silly and against the grain.

"There's so little to go on," I yelled, and held my knees in an old rocking position.

"Possession is half the law of gravity, you know that," the boy carefully explained to me, and began playing with Lola's breasts. I thought she had been wearing a dress but I was mistaken, for she was now in a red topless bikini. I was oozing with a rare sensation of sadness and pride. Across Lola's back someone had written, in bold but straggling letters, the words, "Give a little, take a little."

I sighed and tears rolled down my face. "I only wish I could." An old lady was fixing my trouser legs and I stood up. "But I've had trouble with my back lately."

Everyone knew this was not so but they all banged their tin plates in appreciation. It seemed to me that I had uttered a profound scientific formula that could help many people in their life struggle. And before even I knew it I was standing on the shoulders of two squat and hairy men and was singing a long, trilly song about the infinite joys of childhood. I knew my mother was somewhere in the crowd, laughing, but I could do nothing about this.

"You care nothing for men's cultural efforts," I cried.

She cackled like a giant bird in a zoo. "That shows how much you know," and breaststroking powerfully, she swam out of the steaming throngs. She always was a strong person against currents.

Now Lola and I were in the subway. In the lovely fens of misty remembrance I sensed that we had just emerged from days of extensive conversations about very important world problems. I could not recall exactly what they were, but a tingling euphoria told me that we had agreed upon everything. I was dressed in a sailor's uniform and she was wearing a black dress of major consequence. Her face had changed, and now it had the look, at once penetrating and reassuring, of a retired detective. "What have you been doing to yourself?" I heard myself inquire.

She stuck her thumb to her nose and wiggled her fingers naughtily at me. "Nothing that you would like to know about."

I nodded my head wisely, because I really did not know what else to do. "Perhaps you're right. I've never been much for exposures."

Her only response to what I considered a careful and irresistable ploy, was to start playing on a Jews' harp. I wasn't certain, but

I suspected the tune was *Pennies From Heaven.* A blind old man smelling of turnips tapped his way by me and when he had passed I saw that he had slipped a note into my free right hand. I thought this was presumptuous of him, for I had never seen him before, but I read the message nevertheless: "Follow your own neurosis." What a very lovely gift to come from one so blind, I said to myself, and began kissing my own hand. A fight had broken out at the far end of the train, near an old bagel cart, and two splendid looking Negroes, both laughing richly and intelligently, were slicing each other up amidst a gushing of blood, but I did not react with any visible distress.

Lola now opened my fly and was peering into the shadows of my manhood. "I don't think you got your share of the gravy, sonny boy," and she giggled but not without brains.

"I make up for it in other ways." (A sea wind was blowing in my face and it was evident that another part of me was on the Atlantic.)

She gave my penis a telling, classifiable squeeze. "You'll have to tell me all about it sometime. I was brought up to listen to reason."

I wanted urgently to scream out against the cruelty of life, but in another moment a storm was lashing at our port side and all manner of men and beasts were clamoring onto the deck. The sails were torn and bleeding heavily, and a heavy sinking blackness in the mother sky let everyone know that the end could very well be near. Naked children were being swept overboard by growling waves and fat wives were clinging to their frightened lovers and moaning old lies told them years ago by cynical baby sitters. Then a magnanimous, all pervasive voice was issuing from the hatch. It was a familiar voice that I now realized I had been hearing all my life but had never really listened to.

"Only the deaf can truly hear and the mind steals more than it gives. Who among you knows where home is? And how many of you wouldn't scream in horror once you truly found where you belonged? Oh, blackmailing blackbirds! Mouse-thinking elephants! Lily-livered lobsters! Look under the rock and read your destiny. Cease upon this midnight of self-deception. When you're asleep you are really awake but you don't have courage enough to accept this. You wear your stars like stones and the heavens cringe at the sight of you."

An immeasurable silence held us. Lola put her head on my shoulder and I could feel her tears of reflection on my skin. I looked up and discovered that all of the people were gone. Lola and I were the only remaining humans. "What a way to treat a friend" I said, and shook my head as if I were a very old man. The boat was now dissolving under our feet.

I AM, AS YOU HAVE CERTAINLY OBSERVED, A universal type, quite at home in the marshes of Southeast Asia, absurdly comfortable in a giant redwood tree house, more than in my element in the leering salons of Paris, wing happy in the eerie reaches of Greenwich Village. I draw the line at no place or human being. In fact, I've got eyes for everybody. I'd dive on King Kong if he gave me the nod. Nuclear physicists invite me to all their parties and drug addicts call me their brother. Even the Black Muslims have been sniffing around lately looking for my patronage. Well then, it will come as no surprise to you to learn that one of my closest companions was a faggot thief. (I am tolerant of all forms of poetic expression.)

"A girl has to live," Cedric would often say to me when he was on the defensive about his criminal activities. "Besides, I didn't do this sort of thing out of choice. I'm forced into it by the unfair employment policies in our society. Management thinks homosexuals aren't humans and therefore not to be trusted with so much as a rubber band."

"This culture is doomed, Cedric," I would say to comfort him, and as often as not I meant it.

"The day will come when our government realizes what a terrible mistake it has made in not harnessing all the vast homosexual energy in this country," he continued delicately fussing at his hair, which was dyed red and teased. "It's a great natural resource, like water and oil."

"I would write to the Department of the Interior if I were you."

He reallocated one of his bobby pins. "As soon as I find a free moment, dear. Right now I'm up to my palette in work, if you know what I mean."

Cedric was a second-story man, and he used the jimmy with the same intimate skill with which he used his own sensualist body. And he had a marvelous gimmick—one he adored using, of course—that allowed him to perform his work without any suspicion: he always dressed as a woman when he went out to separate people from their worldly possessions. "Who would ever dream that a dear thing like me was up to no good?"

He robbed during the day—when his victims were busy taking dictation or concocting wild lies about toothpaste or soap—and patrolled the slavering streets of sodomy at night costumed in chic women's clothes, or dressed simply in a normal swish way—tight, tight pants, so that both his sex departments, front and back, would be exhibited to best advantage; French Riviera tie shirt (which means that it was designed by Brigit Bardot) and girl's sandals, perhaps of lapis lazuli, or of hand painted shells, or merely an everyday fireman red patent leather. If you were drunk, or confused, Cedric could very easily fit into your fantasy even if you were not a homosexual like most of his customers, he was that successful a show. You had to give it to him: he really threw himself into whatever he did, heart and cock. He gave the customer his bum's worth all right.

"I don't understand these girls who pull that I've-got-a-headache, half-way shit," Cedric said one evening as we sat in the city's most delerious homosexual park on Broadway. "They act like they got the rag on, or that some big evil daddy in the sky is making them do all these naughty things. Oh Mary! Kiss my sweet blue ass! Why, my own dear mother, bless her schizophrenic soul, often said herself you can't make blood run backwards, and that's a fact." He delicately adjusted some discomfort between his legs, smiled understandingly at two very gay sparrows twitting by, holding fingers. "They've just discovered each other in the same tree. Anyway, I may not know history, my friend, but I sure as shit know the human heart and it can beat in all kinds of ways, believe me, and it's a plain worm who says one way is better than another. All water is wet when you get down to it, and that's what counts. The color of it comes second."

There was a full house at the park now. Pushing their way in and out of the wavering, irridescent throngs of faggots were the bullish swaggering lesbians. They shouted to each other across the benches and intimidated shrubs (nature was certainly taking a beating here) and in voices and accents that were intended to make you feel you were in a steamfitter's orgy or at the fights. Wandering hesitantly but hopefully at the edge of the scene were the male buyers, the normally dressed men looking for a queen for the night. Here and there one would see them negotiating with a perfumed, swish faggot whore. Cedric said he wanted to do the park a couple of times, to see what was on the menu—after all, these were working hours: he couldn't sit around all night chewing the philosophical blubber with me. "Who knows," he said, smiling, "there might be a Broadway producer waiting out there for me." He giggled and swished his hips. "They say the theatre is due for a revolution, right?"

And the tremulous vibrations there absorbed him. Cedric's walk was an undulent filigree of seduction, not a functional device for getting from one place to another; and each gesture, from the timing of an arched eyebrow to the caressing of his own neck, pollinated the eager fantasies lying on call in the park's richly planted denizens. Every nerve ending and brain cell in Cedric calculated the moment by moment response on this journey. My legs feel light as feathers tonight, he mused, much in suspense. I'll bet I could take twenty Johns between them and not even feel the burden of it. Who's that fat one over there with the soft shoulder suit? Trying to act like he really isn't here for a little meat and gravy, just waiting for the bus which he very well knows stops two blocks down. Small sneaky eyes under the chic straw lid of his. He's got a wife and kids in Fairfield County as sure as my name is Cedric W. Whitely. And he's just a little bit more than average lushed for somebody like him in a vile tabu situation such as this. Wouldn't at all surprise me if he is on his town's board for the imprisoning of pederasts. These closet queens all are. He and the wife make it maybe once every week or ten days with the lights absolutely turned off so that not even an owl could make out who he was having or doing. He looks so mean and unhappy too, like I'm to blame for his being gay. Ooh! Just look at these two aces of spades up ahead. One of them looks like she tried to go three rounds with Ray Robinson. My, how some of these girls love to be knocked around by rough trade. "Good evening, ladies. How's business?"

"I don't believe there's ten dollars in the entire place."

"These are hard days for all of us."

The one with the spaniel eyes looked remarkably like a negro boy Cedric had been in the army with in Vietnam. A tough, endlessly delighted boy named Edmund who thrived on Batman comic books and whose wallet was luxurient with pictures of the Beatles. "That Ringo cat is really something. Too bad he ain't the President," Edmund would say bouncing along in the transport truck carrying them into the savage hallucinated Viet highlands in pursuit of mortal combat with the Viet Cong, who, they all knew, were watching them this very moment and smiling through their leafy hiding places in expectation of the moment when their traps would spring and the white skin (though sometimes black) of this absurd invader would split and spurt blood all over the somnolent jungle foliage. The dozen or so other soldiers in the truck gave no sign of discomfort or even interest as they bumped against each other in this grotesque ride.

"Tell me something," Edmund asked, grabbing onto the seat to keep from falling. "What do these Cong cats think about?"

"Food, and when they're going to get laid, if ever," Cedric replied, and scratched at his stubbled dirty cheek where something had bitten him.

"No, I mean do they really like killing us GI bastards because we're imperialist mother fuckers—or do they think the whole damn thing is just a lot of crap that some smart-assed government people thought up?"

Four American jets screamed above them, angel high in the soft, inaccessible blue where Cedric wished he could flee forever. "My guess is they don't feel one way or the other." The soldier next to him spit tobacco juice onto the floor of the truck. "They would just as soon be here as anywhere else. Things aren't that different to them." The sound of heavy mortar explosions a couple of miles ahead. Strange thick jungle smell, almost like a toilet.

"Uh huh," said Edmund. "Just the way some people feel washing dishes in a restaurant. Things so dumb and tough all around, it don't matter much what you do."

(Two butch dikes in tight pants began kissing each other under the statue of Kosciusko. A fat old lady shouted to them that she was going to call the police.)

A boy sitting in the front of the truck was calmly examining his forty five automatic. A boy across from him began talking to himself as he stared terrified into the passing jungle.

"Somebody told me Ann-Margret and George Hamilton are coming to see us," said a red-faced southern boy to no one in particular.

Another laughed, "Why in God's name would anybody want to see a miserable bastard like you?"

Then the truck hit the mine. Someone screamed. Cedric felt something metallic hit his face as he fell from the overturning truck, and at the same time machine gun bullets, making that horrible whistling sound, began spraying all around them. Now he was on the ground, crawling frantically into the brush to get away from the bullets and the burning truck. The young lieutenant was shouting hysterical orders to them. Moans and cries for help were coming from the overturned smoking truck. Cedric began firing his rifle into the dense growth around him. "Where are they?" he yelled to Edmund up ahead. "I can't see the bastards!"

"Who the fuck can?" said Edmund, crawling over a dead tree trunk. "Just keep shootin'!"

A boy crouched a few yards away from Cedric raised himself up a little, and drew back his arm to throw a grenade. His face was suddenly blown apart by a machine gun spray. Cedric moaned, and threw up, and the blood from the deep cut in his face poured into his gasping mouth.

"Oh mother! Oh mother!" he kept saying. Mountains were collapsing inside him. He could not feel Edmund dragging him to cover.

He strolled by the glum heavy standing suburbanite, swishing and smiling as elegantly and whorishly as he he knew how. "Lovely night, isn't it?" he ventured.

"Sure is," the man replied, a sick little smile opening the thick sullennes of his face.

"Too lovely to waste, I'd say. Wouldn't you?"

The man sort of giggled.

"You looking for a party?" Cedric went on, touching at his lovely hairdo that had cost him ten dollars.

"Why not? Are you real good?"

Cedric laughed softly with a very mandarin superiority. "Honey, I'm the very best. Don't you worry about that." First looking around, as if at this stage of his involvement, both physical and spiritual, he thought he still might get away with it without being observed, or known, the man took Cedric's arm roughly. "OK. Let's go."

Cedric didn't move. "Wouldn't you like to discuss price?"

The man let his arm go. "Oh, yeah. Oh. What's the tariff?" He giggled again like a sneaky little boy.

Cedric felt deliciously powerful and wanted. "It starts at ten." He winked lasciviously. "And it's a bargain at twice the price."

The man looked Cedric over, seeming to speculate on what varieties of sexual pleasure were pegged at what prices, and then said, "That sounds Okay."

"You won't regret a moment of it, dear," said Cedric, and led the way through the grinning underbrush.

HOW ABOUT A CHILDHOOD STORY, JUST FOR THE record? I'd like to douse those rumors that I didn't have a childhood and therefore must be some kind of freak. Then we can forget about the damn thing. Okay?

Frank Lipscomb and I had a pretty good time of it together for a while, even if there was something kind of funny about him. Frank and I went to the same class at school, and that's where we got to know each other. Frank and I somehow didn't seem to give much of a damn about that old school. I once heard our teacher telling another teacher we were "problem children." I guess Frank and I did make a few problems for them at that, what with not doing our lessons always and sometimes coming and going from school pretty much as we pleased, staying away for maybe two or three days at a time, without even caring one bit what they were thinking in that school. They could go on thinking it, that's the way Frank and I felt.

As I say, Frank was kind of funny. I never could exactly figure out what was going on inside his head. Like sometimes he would say let's do something, and I would say all right let's do it, and then the next thing you knew he was saying let's do something else, entirely different. I didn't really mind this so much because I didn't care what it was we did. You know the way it is with a fellow when he has a lot of time lying around. Sometimes Frank would look hard at me, staring into my face, and say, "buddy,"— and his eyes would then start running all over the place like a couple of beebees—"buddy," he'd say, "I've. . . I'll tell you what. I've got us an idea." And then maybe for no good reason I could see he'd smile as though he was going to break out laughing, and while I was waiting there for him to tell me this idea of his, why, suddenly he might look up at the sky and say, "You know, buddy, maybe it's going to rain."

I'd look up and say what I thought about the weather, but I wanted to know what his idea was, so I'd ask him what about this idea he had, and then maybe he'd laugh funny or maybe he'd look at me surprised and say, "Why, what idea? What idea you talking about, buddy?" Sometimes I'd tell him what he had said to me, but after a while there I'd just let it ride. Seemed he forgot so easily sometimes. Or maybe he just wasn't ready to say what he was going to say.

There was the way Frank dressed which made me almost laugh the first time I saw him. I don't know where in the devil he got it, but he had an old chauffeur's cap that he wore tilted real far down on his head, and besides this he wore some riding pants, black ones, shiny slick in the seat. These riding pants didn't fit him any too well, but he didn't seem very troubled by that.

I guess it's pretty strange when you think about it, but even though Frank was two years older than me—he was fifteen but in the same grade I was—I felt in a way I was a little older than him. I think he felt this way too. It was something between us, you see. I was about the only friend Frank had in that school. Nobody else seemed to like him very much.

The two of us would walk around the city looking in the store windows when we played hookey, or sometimes we'd go to the zoo and lie on the grass there and talk and watch the animals. We both liked this very much. We got along fine. Our people, they didn't care a hell of a lot what we did.

Frank was crazy mad about two things: girls and automobiles, especially fast automobiles. I don't know what he knew about the girls—he talked about them plenty—but I can tell you he knew just about everything there was to know about automobiles, how to work them, and what to do if something went wrong with the motors, and all that. And he knew how to steal them, too. Why, some cars he could steal just by putting a quarter somewhere under the driving wheel, without any keys. Just think about that for a while. And with other cars all he had to do was twist a couple of wires together and the motor would start. Oh he knew about cars all right. And he taught me about them too.

Frank and I were out late one night, messing around, and we passed a parking lot and there was a car there all by itself, a Chevvie. I looked at Frank and he looked at me, understanding each other right away, and then he got in the car and fooled around with it a little. Then the motor started, and before I got in with him I looked around but nobody was in sight, so I got in too. We had a swell time driving outside the city. We must have been gone nearly three hours. After we'd been out for a while, I took a turn at driving, doing it the way Frank had showed me. It went all right, but I was kind of nervous at first before I started really enjoying it a lot. Then Frank took over. I could see he got a different kind of kick out of driving than me. He didn't talk much when he drove, and he kind of bent over the wheel and he drove very fast, and all the time his eyes had a shiny steady look in them. We took the car back when we finished with it.

After that we stole a car nearly every night, a different one, and every now and then we were lucky and found a car that already had the keys in it, so Frank didn't have to fool with it any. But I was sorry about this because I liked to watch Frank work his magic on a car. Something about it really excited me. A couple of times I tried working a car without the keys, and once I was able to do it.

Then one night I got the idea that while we were driving around we might as well look in the parked cars to see if they had anything we could take. Frank thought this was a fine idea. This is the way we worked it: I would drive the car we had taken, drive it slow, while Frank walked along the sidewalk and tried the doors of the parked cars. I'd drive ahead of him while he looked in the cars, so we wouldn't attract any attention, you see, and when he finished looking in a row of cars he'd meet me at the corner and we'd put the stuff he'd taken in the back seat. If he saw something in the seat of a car, but the door was locked, he'd bend one of the windows open with a screw driver. If he came to a big expensive looking car that was locked, whether he could see anything inside or not, he'd always bend the window open so he could look in the inside pockets. I guess he felt that a big car like that just had to have something good inside it. Sometimes he would drive and I would look in the cars. This was always at night.

Maybe you'll think I'm crazy, but we never were worried about the police. We thought about them, sure, but we weren't worried, which is different. We just didn't think they'd catch us. If we'd worried about them, then everything we did at night would have been ruined by it. You can understand that.

We used to get a lot of stuff, cameras, cigarettes, coats, blankets, watches, liquor, books, and stuff like that. Frank knew some boys in the neighborhood who'd want this kind of stuff and he'd sell it to them, nobody asking any questions about things that did not concern them. What we couldn't sell, we'd let pile up in the basement of the place where I lived. We couldn't see throwing anything away, nor leaving anything behind in the cars.

Frank and I went on like this for about a month or more, making some money and getting a whole lot of fun out of it, secretly between us, you know. We stole all kinds of cars to ride and steal in. Then something happened to Frank. He began to show up at school driving these cars we had taken at night, or ones he had taken himself. Maybe one day he'd drive up in a big yellow Packard, or maybe it was a Lincoln convertible, or a bright snappy looking Ford. Well, he'd drive up as though the car was his, and everybody looked at him a lot, wishing they could be sitting in a car like that. A lot of kids who had never even bothered to talk to Frank before this now talked to him, and he would take them for rides around the school. He didn't do so bad with the girls either. I saw him take two out at once one afternoon in that yellow Packard, and he drove away from the curb like he was Barney Oldfield himself. And Frank acted kind of strange now too, like he was a little drunk or something.

I was angry he was doing this, and sorry too. I'd thought Frank would feel the way I did about what we had been doing. You know, that it was a secret between us that nobody else knew about. We'd do what we did at night, but when we were at school we were kind of like different people entirely, not letting on anything at all. That seemed to me the way to do it and that's the way it was for a month or so. But now Frank was this other way. He seemed to be in it all by himself, and he didn't seem to care what people thought when they saw him driving those cars he had stolen in the broad daylight, and acting excited in that funny drunk kind of way I said. I hinted to him what I thought, but he really didn't pay me any attention. Sometimes he acted like he didn't even hear me talking to him. I felt embarrassed now about him, and I had honestly never felt this way before.

I minded it most when we went out at night to get the stuff from the cars and to ride around. Frank now made too much noise opening and closing the doors of the parked cars, and then he drove so loud and in such a way you could hear us a mile off, I'll bet. I told him one night to take it easy, but he just laughed.

Well, one night when we'd made a date to go out looking for stuff he came by for me in a big long green Cadillac sedan. I didn't like the whole thing right away, because we had taken this green Cadillac out twice before (it had the keys in it) even though putting it back just the way we found it, and because we were supposed to walk far away from where we lived before we got in a car. It was safer all around that way. I felt bad now. Then when Frank opened the door of the Cadillac and I looked in, I got a quick funny sad feeling all inside myself. He had brought a girl along. I'd seen her at school. Her name was Betty something. She was fifteen or so, I guess, and she had a reputation at school for being pretty much something. She was kind of good-looking, but I'd never liked her much, to tell you the truth. She thought she was pretty big stuff.

"Hi, buddy. I brought Betty along," Frank said to me when he saw me looking kind of strange at him and the girl.

"Hello," Betty said, but I looked at her and did not say anything.

"Betty's okay, buddy," Frank said. "She's my girl now." He smiled at her and then he reached over and grabbed her and kissed her. She giggled when they finished, and Frank kept on looking at her and smiling. I was standing in the open door.

Then, looking in at them, thinking about the way Frank had been going on lately, and now this girl supposed to be going with us, I knew the whole thing was over. I felt very bad.

They sat there waiting for me to get inside. I stood where I was. Frank said, "Come on. Let's go. We got things to do." He certainly was ready to go.

I didn't want to tell Frank that I saw it was all over, that we couldn't do it this way, so I said, "I think I'll stay home tonight, Frank. I don't feel so hot."

He didn't seem to understand me at first. "Come on. This is going to be a swell night, buddy." Then he looked over the hood of the Cadillac and whistled soft and said, "Man, isn't this some bitch of a car. She'll do a hundred and twenty, I bet." Then he said, "Well, get in, buddy."

Betty tried smiling at me.

I said, "No, Frank. Let's make it another night. Honestly, I don't feel good at all."

"You sure you don't want to come?"

"Yeah, I'm sure. You go ahead."

He looked at me for a moment, then he smiled wide and said, "Okay then. See you tomorrow."

"Okay," I said. I didn't see any reason to talk to Betty.

"Take it easy, buddy," Frank said, but looking as though he was getting excited about driving on.

"I will," I said, and I closed the door of the Cadillac for him. They drove away very fast, the gears making noise when he shifted quick.

I didn't see Frank after that. A couple of days later, at school, somebody told me Frank had had an accident in that Cadillac and the police caught him. I was very sorry to hear it, but I could not do anything.

I didn't desert Frank or anything like that, I want you to know. It was just that, well, he had one way to go and I guess I had mine. We had a good time together for a while there.

II A MAJOR QUESTION: HOW DOES ONE MEA-
sure the crimes of another? Against one's own? Or as absolutes?
And what is crime? Can any of us truly say? Of course, this sort
of thing attracts our cleverness, but are we willing to employ the
wisdom of our heart?

Whenever I am seized by a calm, exploratory mood (I would
like you to know that I am not always paddling in the sewers of
this world, or watching reruns of atrocity films), I ring up a friend
of mine, Zachary, a Zen master—unlike so many others, he did not
quit the game when he was ahead—and, breaking out a jar of
guava shells and a slab of cream cheese, we have a go at it. (He lives
in a converted water tower.)

"What we must first establish," he suggests, "is that war exists
within the self. That the self is divided against the self."

"This would never go over with the unity groups," I said.

He threw a handful of birdseed in my face.

"That man is living a double, if not triple, life," he continued.

"We have not yet established that man is indeed living."

More birdseed into my face.

"What are these divisions? How did they get there? And what
must be done about it if man is to exist as a great totality, a truly
throbbing oneness?"

Holding a book before my face—the pushers often cut the
birdseed with gravel—I ventured, "How can we assume that man
has a self to begin with?" He fooled me by lashing out at my belly
with his foot. "Isn't this self a necessary composite of all these
warring factions?" I went on, pushing myself off the floor. "The
assumption of the self is that it is some pure and static thing that
is virginal hiding somewhere in man's body. I don't see this." I
thought for a moment. "In fact, I would say that the self is merely
the breathing of man. The rest is up for grabs."

He stroked his beard (his one indulgence out of many possibilities). "Man has been taught too many rules, too many direction
finders, too many ideas about life. This body of nonsense oozes a

poison that destroys man's essential organism. It makes him contradict his vibrations with nature."

"Would you say that this alien body, a substance in man, separates him from his fellow beings?"

"More than that. It is killing off the flowers and the fish are drowning in the seas."

"Would you say there is no such thing as right or wrong?"

"I believe you are finally approaching a satori."

"Why is man always judging himself?"

"It is a game he plays while he awaits death."

"Is there anything he can do to save himself?"

He closed his eyes and did not speak for a full minute. I was tempted to take the last of the guava, but I wasn't sure I could get away with it. "Yes," he finally said, his eyes still closed. "He can force himself to sink into complete silence for one year. Float in universal nothingness."

"How does he do this?"

For a fat man, he is extraordinarily quick; he had wacked me over the head with a bamboo pole he kept next to his chair.

"There you go again! Asking idiot questions! Next you'll be asking the water why it is wet!"

"Forgive me. It's my lousy upbringing. I guess that what we can conclude with is that man is simply man, no more and no less."

He scratched his foot, "Let him find the true way by going in, not out."

"The Great One is waiting there for him," I said, changing my tactic.

"You are a perverted degenerate!" he screamed. "The Great One isn't waiting for anybody. The Great One is oneself!"

"Yes. Of course! How ungrateful of me!"

"Now go out and get some more guava."

You couldn't see me for my dust.

When I returned I found my seat had been taken by an elegant white-haired man whose face, while handsome, seemed devoid of reality. Or rather, that it was *refusing* reality, like the fathomless face of a statue. At the far side of the huge room two women were putting records on the hi-fi set. One of them was in her forties; the other looked about twenty-two or-three; both were quite good-looking. Though they did not resemble each other, an unaffected intimacy betweem them told me they were mother and daughter. The girl was a grown up candy bar—perniciously voluptuous, long blond hair that had never, in its fierceness, given sanctuary to a hat; a body of half slumbering depravity, a mouth of divine and insatiable cruelty, for it knew of nothing but its own will. And her eyes . . . leopard, sheer leopard. The mother—how can I describe her except to say that when she looked into a mirror she did not recognize herself. Now the room began to sob with Indian sitar music, and the girl danced slowly like a somnabulist to it. I wondered to what enchanted scene she had transported herself in her mind.

"When I was in Calcutta," the man said—he could have been making a recording—"all I saw were the vile bodies of the dying." He turned around and stared at me. "Why do we keep giving money to a country that worships death?"

"What is money?" said Zachary, taking the cream cheese from me. "Merely another form of death, my friend."

The mother tip-toed over to us and sat down next to the man who I guessed was her husband. "Let's talk about something pleasant," she said, straightening her skirt. "People are always talking about money or death or venereal diseases—awful things. What's happened to all the pretty things in life?" She looked toward me and smiled, but I was the last person to answer such a question as hers. "This used to be such a lovely world."

"When?" I asked.

"When I was a girl."

I felt something brush against the back of my head. It was the girl. She smelled of Chanel No. 5.

"I didn't know you ever were a girl, Moms," she remarked, and something like a laugh came from her. She put a finger under my collar.

Her father stared over my shoulder at her. "There used to be respect for one's elders in this world," he stated.

She laughed, and as she did so she put her hands delicately around my neck and poised her body against the back of my chair. "You ought to give speeches at the United Nations." She leaned over and whispered in my ear. "This place is a graveyard. Let's split."

Zachary sat up now—he had been lying on his back without

saying anything, just staring at the walls and stroking his red beard. "Man is his own worst enemy," he muttered. "Life should bathe him as the air permeates the leaf, but he cultivates conflict as a farmer cultivates his crops."

The thin, wavy Indian music was entwining and manipulating all of us, as if we were hypnotized snakes.

"I was hoping we could have a Zen lesson today," the woman said to Zachary. "I've come all prepared, so has Eli," and she smiled in a harmless way.

Zachary grunted. "Have you cleansed yourself of superficial things?"

The girl whispered to me again. "If she did, the poor thing would disappear entirely." This time her lips gently touched my ear.

The father came forth now. "I spent the entire night reading Buddha." He gave us each an intensely meaningless look. "What I am puzzled about is why he left India to go to China."

Zachary lay on his broad naked back again. "It makes absolutely no difference. The point is he got there." A silence followed him. "Do you ask how the shrimp got to your plate?"

The girl snorted softly into my neck. "That's telling the old bastard."

The mother got up from her chair and tip-toed to the center of the room. "I'm going to assume the lotus position."

"Oh God," the girl breathed. "Let's blow." and she put her hands under my arms and urged me up.

"See you later," I said to Zachary.

"Think of Buddha and his sufferings," he advised me.

The girl pulled me out of the place.

She had been accustomed to pulling people, especially men, out of places all her unimpeded life. No was a word that, when addressed to her, became ashamed of itself and its mission enroute, and simply expired. As a child she upset the sweaty equilbrium of the boys, making them behave in a frenzied, seriously disconnected manner. And as a girl of thirteen, as naturally as objects fall toward the earth, she assumed the throne of her womanhood by so exciting an up-to-that-point chaste and responsible Sunday School teacher that he raped her in a backroom of the church and immediately afterward fled the city to become a desk clerk in a series of small, completely lewd hotels in the aching, zonked-out middle west. That was nice and crazy and I loved it, she said to herself after he had run off and left her alone and she was putting her totally stunned pink panties back on. They did not fit quite right, it seemed. I wonder what he ran away for? And why was he crying so? Do all men do that after they take a girl? Mm. I hurt but I don't care. I don't even want to go back to school again. That's for kids. I'm not going to tell anybody. They'll only try to make me feel bad, and they'll take me to a doctor to see if I'm sick. Mm. Wipe this blood and runny stuff away with the kleenex mommy gave me this morning. New kind of blue kleenex. I love blue. I'll ask mommy to buy me a blue sweater to go with my gray skirt.

During high school, after her father had made a small fortune by rigging a stock sale with some close and loyal friends, the family moved to Hawaii (disposing of everything, down to two pieces of Wedgwood, so that there would be nothing at all to come back to Cleveland for), and no sooner had her mother installed the wall to wall carpeting and joined a health food club, than April, by this time an encyclopedia of experience and self expression, walked down the beach and into the forest to take up residence with a young Hawaiian chief in his thatched, pig and chicken populated, village.

"We are going to be sublimely happy," he said to her one evening as they lay together on a thick woven grass mat near a small waterfall. "None of the corruptions and diseases of Western society will reach us." He had been educated at Princeton and had come back to the islands only because it was a question of taking over the tribal reins from his ailing father, whose sole reason for living was drinking large quantities of Courvoisier while sitting on his boat. His name was Bosworth.

"I'm particularly glad there are no phones around here," April said, playing with the black curly hair on his chest. "My mother would be ringing up every half hour to see if I'd gotten yaws or been sacrificed to the noon goat."

"We won't be doing that for another month," he said, delicately and thoughtfully sucking on her finger. "And besides, we already have three girl volunteers who are dying to throw themselves into the volcano."

Far away someone began playing on a drum, and nearby them two jungle-hidden birds started calling to each other in a most unusual way. April thought they sounded just like Yma Sumac.

"What do you suppose they're saying to each other?" April asked.

He disengaged his hungry mouth from her right boob and said, "It has to do with the basic ingredients of animal survival, love and security." And he want back to sucking her boob and squeezing the nipple of the other one.

"Wouldn't it be wierd if birds and animals had the complicated times human beings do?" she suggested softly, her body beginning to respond now to his various activities. "Wonder how they avoid cracking up. Somebody ought to study that, don't you think?"

But her chieftan lover was fathoms deep in the ocean of her endowment and being. April watched him, sidelong, for a few seconds, then she closed her eyes and, disengaging herself from all thought and other placeness, abandoned herself utterly to the urgent and unusual talents of his hands and tongue. He explored and cultivated each part of her, twirling his wet tongue in her unshaved armpits, down her side, onto her now heavy belly, tickling softly her button hole, where as a child, she had often stuck pieces of gum, pausing in the sacred matting between her thighs (upon which white field many a fantastic presumption had met its match and defaulted the tourney), down her thighs and calves to her toes, where to her squirming and multi-dimensional pleasure (the birds and animals were sounding through the water-rushing night, so why shouldn't she?), he licked and sucked and chewed each member so superbly that her feet, heretofore earth bound, achieved an erogenous status and life on a par with her breasts and mouth: they were feet no more. Then he returned, actually slithered, back to the divinity of her crotch matting, and here, where all human pain and pleasure begins and ends, performed such tongue wizardry that April, screaming and writhing, thought she was simultaneously being created and destroyed with the wonder of it all. Eventually, he mounted her, and once again, having rested for seconds on a plateau of orgasmic realization, she soared to sky-high peaks. For at least an hour she lost her memory and mind and sense of being anywhere, and merged with the entire ageless universe. Every piece of her flesh sang its song most ecstatically. Every part of her body said yes to every other part. She became the unharassed resonance itself. A total come swell.

After light years she returned succulently and softly to the both of them. (They were both naked naked.) "I can't tell you how great that was," she murmured, kissing his warm quiet face. "I mean, it was the best thing that's happened to me since, golly, I don't know when."

"It was my happiness," he said, smiling without any guile.

"So I think I ought to do a little something for you."

"Whatever you have in mind will be okay by me," he said.

"I'm very glad to hear that. Some people draw the line at the kind of presents they'll take."

"Not me."

"That's swell," April said, rubbing herself around on him. "Because if there's anything I hate, it's being made to feel shy." Her hand went to his basket and began communicating quite a bit of interest in and plans for his sex, and it responded by getting quite hard again. "You know what I mean?"

"I certainly do," he said, closing his eyes.

Pretty soon her mouth was where her hand had been, and she was kissing his member with undivided devotion. "I'm not a doctor or anything like that," she said after a few moments, "but it seems to me that your, uh . . . " She kissed it on its tip, " . . . your penis-cock is quite a bit larger than is normal."

"Well, I . . . " he mumbled.

"Oh listen," she said hurriedly, giving it another tongue kiss, "Please don't apologize. I'm not criticizing by any means." She put her mouth over it and let it sink utterly in there for a second. "Golly no. I was just . . . " She had to put her mouth over it again. " . . . just making what I guess you could call an academic observation. You know?"

He made some kind of a sound that was not quite able to develop itself into a word formation.

"Academic . . . " she went on juicily, and swallowed as much of him as she could without choking. "Because I would be plain silly to complain about a thing as fantastically big and . . . oh Lord!" And she abandoned all discourse and began gorging herself on his outsize organ with insatiable frenzy. She did everything but chew it off. She wanted to do this at one unbearable, tasty point (when his rapturous writhings were making it necessary for her to grip him firmly by the arms so that she would not be heaved into the nearby bushes), but she realized that she would live to regret it something awful, so she didn't. When he finally made her the gift of his consummation explosion, she thought she was gulping down half of Mikoko Bay. But this did not in any way distress her. Quite the contrary.

"Wow," she said very softly before they both slipped into a combination swoon and very deep sleep. They did not rise until dawn (a light dew had settled on them).

"I'll never be the same," she observed in their grass palace later on, where they were dining on a variety of meats and fish and exotic fruits and vegetables. No forks or knives, just fingers. They were being waited on by several of his female relatives, among them a willing but disenchanted older sister who had majored in anthropology at Vassar. All of these helpers were dressed only from the waist down and were barefooted, which creeped April at first because she couldn't hear them approaching her from behind.

"Ortega says we change our identities with each new idea we assimilate," Bosworth said, stripping a barbecued spare rib in one motion and throwing the bone to the matted floor, where it was instantly dived on by two miniature Dobermanns he had brought back from the east.

"I'll remember to say that the next party I go to," April said. One of Bosworth's aunts, a Princess Fatima Jane, slipped another fried banana onto his plate. "That is, if I ever go to another bash. I'd just as soon sweat out the big scene here." For a few seconds she tried to remember what her old crowd looked like, but they had become vague and faceless.

Bosworth allowed his sister to wipe his face with a hot towel. "We must discuss Ortega," he went on. "He's a veritable fountain of insights."

"Let's save him for later," mumbled April between morsels of shrimp. "After the water god rites tonight."

"Just as you say, my almond cookie, just as you say. Philosophy must wait its turn." And he grinned at her across the knolls of food. He was a beautiful boy and he had perfect white teeth. April realized she never seen her father's teeth because he never smiled. For a few seconds she tried to imagine her father and mother making love, but no reasonable picture would form. The best she could imagine was a shot of her mother in bed with a bathing suit on.

Someone was breathing down her neck. "Can you lend me some eye shadow?" It was Princess Fatima Jane. "This berry stain is blinding me."

That night the entire village reached new frontiers of pleasure. Even the children and the senile cripples experienced breakthroughs. The teen-aged girls competed wildly with one another in nude dances around the hugh bonfire on the beach, while drums beat and the people clapped and chanted, and when the last one drenched in pagan sweat, collapsed in front of April and Bosworth, April leaped up and, whipping off her sarong, put on a show of her own that was so original and provocative that three men threw themselves into the foaming surf to keep from throwing themselves upon her (a misdemeanor that would have resulted in their being blinded with hot coals). Nothing was gained by this gesture, however. All were so smashed on punch that they drowned in a matter of minutes.

"Where did you learn *that*?" Bosworth asked when April fell panting into his arms.

"Nowhere. I just made it up as I went along."

"You're better than Martha Graham," he went on happily.

"I should hope so."

Firecrackers and rockets were set off and no one noticed or cared that two huts caught fire and burned down. (Later one of the more civic-minded elders said a building renewal plan had to begin somewhere.) All manner of contests broke out now, mainly around the gigantic punch bowl, which was being bartended by two large breasted women standing inside it with ladles. Four young warriors engaged in a team sword duel, shouting traditional obscenities and challenges at each other, and three decapitated, mutilated bodies left no one in doubt as to the winner.

"That's some game," April remarked.

"It is fun, isn't it" said Bosworth. "And it's so good for the general morale."

April couldn't figure this one out, so she didn't pursue it. In

between the performances the happily abandoned drunken villagers made their way among the many roasting and steaming pits, where pigs, chickens, fish, birds and snakes were being served up. From time to time April's attention was diverted from Bosworth by the sound of a screaming child falling from one of the many palm trees. Their parents let them drink on these occasions so they would not feel left out and consequently develop severe separation anxieties. Since no one else seemed to notice these fatal accidents, April assumed that they must have no meaning or importance. She remembered reading somewhere that some islanders eat their children, and this comparison comforted her. Besides, Bosworth was kissing her on her neck and back, and saying quite original things to her, and this cut down on her outside attention span. She could not have recited the Declaration of Independence to save her soul. The next show was an exhibition of fucking techniques. The village sex historian, whose revered position had been passed down from father to son for thousands of years, kept up a running commentary, as the couples or threesomes went about their tasks, in which he pointed out the excellent execution of various styles, positions, and climaxes. The exuberant viewers struck one another with sticks and shouted whenever something especially pleased them.

Bosworth's sister, Mimi, who had been lying down a few feet from them, sipping from her own supply of martini mix, leaned over to April. "I made a movie of this once for my anthropology course," she said, slurring her words a little, "but the faculty wouldn't let me show it, the prudes. So I sold it to an art movie house. Made a thousand bucks"

"That's good money," April suggested.

The girl took a big swallow of iced gin.

"It's simply amazing how white people resist real art." she continued (several people near them began shouting loudly as the performers, a threesome, pulled off a beautiful synchronizing trick). "Makes you wonder how they manage to survive."

Bosworth kissed April's ear, and blew into it ever so sweetly. "The trouble is Aristotle. Aristotelian logic has ruined western man." He chuckled a fine, cultivated Princeton-Hawaiian chuckle. "Everybody except April. She escaped."

April returned his ear kiss, only she put a good deal more

tongue in hers. "I didn't escape, Bos honey. I was born free."

"If you're going to grab any of this spectacle," Bos' sister began, slurping her gin, "You've got to look at it from a structural-ist point of view. Myths and rituals and all are models productive of social cohesion. Cassirer put it this way (she partly stifled a gin belch) 'Each participant constructs for himself a shared world of meaning within the medium of the ritual action.' You see?"

"Mm," April murmured, her entire self covered with swell feeling. "The whole thing sounds creamy."

"Scheffler of Yale," Mimi continued, licking the last of the martini from her upper lip, "wraps it up beautifully. 'Most of the supposed irrational or illogical behavior of so called primitive peo-ple has, on closer inspection, proven to be no more than behavior which differs from what we would expect in a given situation, and the behavior differs because the participants define or conceive of the situation differently than we would.' Therefore. . . ."

A squealing and a scurrying, and April for moments thought it must be one of the overwrought performers heading for the jungle. But she discerned it was only a pig when it ran over her bare legs. Another stoned child plunged out of a tree behind her. She didn't care; she was quite smashed now herself. He's playing on my body as though it's a harp, she mused. When I think of all the years I wasted wearing clothes. Phooey. They numb the skin. He smells so good. Like somebody rubbed flowers all over him. Nice girl, that sister, could use a few more pounds on her. Proba-bly worries too much. All those schools and tough subjects. She's got eyes for Bos. Hope she doesn't get any funny ideas while I'm here. Blood's thicker than punch and all that but I'd have to let her have it. What in God's name are they doing up here now? Can't make out. . . . Wow! Four of them. Looks like a trapeze act. That one girl's got two guys. Sitting on one and chomping the other, and the other girl, a little chubby but that long hair is fabulous, she's doing something to the guy standing up. Boy, these natives are going off their chump they like it so much. They're all beating each other with sticks and yelling. Oops. Somebody fell in the bonfire. Looked like an old guy though. Those nuts in Viet Nam. Wonder if they took drugs before they burned themselves up. Who was it told me you could think yourself out of pain? My old man? Sounds just like him. Hmm. Shouldn't have eaten all that white gooey stuff. Tummy hurts. Mm. He's got his hand just in the right place. Hope he never takes it away. That's right. Move it gently. Ah. Does he know how good that feels? Jesus. The way he does it. Ooh. Wish I had his big cock in my mouth.

"This is going to be quite remarkable," Bos was saying amidst all the shouts and laughter and drums and chanting (and blood excitement he was stirring up in April). "Our champions later are going to have a tournament. Have you ever seen an 'eat' before, April sweetest of all pies?"

"A what?" Her voice was understandably a bit remote. All her concentration was below her navel. Neither could she hear too well.

"Aggressions in gluttony," he continued. "One assumes, and certainly the contestants do, that they are lovers of food and just can't get enough of it. Actually, they don't like food at all. This is a case of savage transference. They are taking out all their anger and hatred on the food, when really they want to take it out on the human race." A wild shriek of pain pleasure. Two giggling, lushed young men threw another howling old man onto the bonfire. "Just think what it would be like if all such cases of neurotic obesity were turned away from the table and onto their real objects, the human race. Lord!"

April heard his words through oceans of softness and satisfaction. She was completely spent now and very very happy. She was smiling. She had a funny vision of three immensely fat men cooking and eating her mother and father around their swimming pool.

"Let's go down and look at the water god float," Bos' sister suggested. "I blew up three-hundred balloons for it yesterday so naturally I have this maternal concern about it."

Bos, in his majesty and superior strength, carried April to the beach. April admired him for the way he nimbly hopped over the naked bodies lying in their path. Three praise-singing women kissed his calves on the way. One of them, whose hair was down to her feet and who wore a darling necklace with animal skulls strung on it, mistakenly shouted Merry Christmas! but Bos took it in his stride. He's got such a great cool, April thought. He's really the most, no matter which way you want to slice it. On the beach another party was in full swing. Two giggling women, whose rich-breasted, heavy-thighed bodies were glistening with unfettered native pleasure, were having a gay time rolling the passed out drunks into the angry surf, where they were captured by the strong outgoing tide and taken to bye bye land.

"Funny thing is, nobody misses them," remarked Bos' sister, lighting up a cigar.

Out on the water a dozen huge canoes were bobbing in the waves. They were all lit up with torches, and decorations of all kinds, among them Mimi's balloons. They looked enormously gay and attractive and crazy, like something concocted for visitors' day at Boys Town. Loads of happy young warriors were singing and drum beating in the boats. It struck April after a few moments that there was something different about them.

"Isn't there just a little something odd about all these guys, Bos honey?" she asked, still cradled in his bulging weightlifter's arms.

He smiled in a kingly way and gave her shoulder a little bite. "Yes, my mother of pearl. They are all painted white."

"Oh yes. But, uh, why?"

"Because they're all faggots," Mimi said. She took a swig of gin out of the army surplus canteen hanging on her shoulder. "We discovered—don't ask me how because it's a tribal secret—that the water god is a homosexual. So you can imagine how inappropriate it would be to sacrifice girls to him."

"Sacrifice?" said April..

"Roger," Mimi continued. "In a little while the lucky ones will be tossed to the sharks, or eaten by the water god. Clever, eh?"

April reflected for a moment (one of the white faggots on the boat was singing something like an aria from Butterfly.) "How are the, uh, lucky ones chosen?" she asked carefully.

"The ones with the longest dongs qualify," Bos explained. "It's appropriate and eminently fair that way, don't you agree?"

"Oh eminently," she replied. "I mean, you can't win 'em all, can you?"

Something plopped down from a palm tree to April's left. She just assumed it was another blotto kid and not a coconut.

"Well, everybody," Mimi announced, "what do you say we swim out to the boats and start the old ball rolling?" and she made for the surf.

Bos noshed a little more on April's ear. "I recommend the breast stroke in this particular water, sweet orchid."

"Thank you, Bos baby." And out they went. April was glad she had taken that summer swimming course at the girl's Y on Grand Avenue.

COURSE, I COULD GO INTO SCOUTING. SUDDEN secret handshakes. Closeness under the stars. Good clear singing. Row Row Your Boat and Old McDonald Had a Farm. Stuff that keeps a fellow straight. Makes him feel that to fiddle with his whang under the sheets, or in his pup tent and sleeping bag, that's what dirty guys do who have Greek names and wind up as busboys, half asleep on their feet all the time. Burnt meat and warm soda from cans. Poison ivy on your ass from taking a dump in the woods. Reek of solid good kid. (Perhaps he'll be a police chief or work for Methodist solidarity: "Now look here, friend. I just know we can iron out our differences. We'll win with God, I just know that.") Jesus. Sweaty kids. Toe jam contests. Push the kid who eats his boogers into the lake. Clean him out. Pimple squeezing. Freckles in fields of blackheads. Lots of salutes and standing straight, cause no scout with any kind of decency wants to be a hunchback. Friendship and slaps on the back. "Gosh, Mr. Abernathy. It sure is swell to be out camping. I mean I feel real good all over. Honest. I just can't wait to tell my Dad." Swell tussling after morning church services under the dripping pines. Several grips and holds. Just hope that pretty little Gibson kid doesn't go and blab to his mom that you sucked his weenie after a real deep scoutmaster talk about manliness and friendship and the Spartans and the fine tough way they lived without such dirty things as broads. 'Cause they will give you five years in the state pen. After which you will have to change your name and resumé again and get a job in the Chinese Youth Corps. Tracking. Sniffing of rabbit shit and skunk piddle just like the old Injuns before they got their red asses blown out of the game by the white brother. "Boy! This sure beats hangin' around on the corner and plannin' bad things to do against people. Look! I'll betcha a big elk or somethin' just left that thicket there!"

"That ain't no elk. That's a fuckin' bull." Have to talk to that boy. Discuss his unhappy home life and why scouts don't talk dirty. He's the one who doesn't understand why it's bad to cheat even if you win all the time. Merit badges and good citizenship awards and tugs of war and bugle practice without wiping off the other person's spit even though you want to because you might throw up. Loyalty oaths and catatonic looks of firm purpose and sincerity. So many grannies being tied that the old age problem is on the verge of being liquidated. "Mr. Abernathy, sir. You know what my dad says? He says that anybody who won't die for his country on the battlefield is worsen a yellow gutter dog."

And after the long march home or bouncing for six hours on the back of a Greyhound bus (somebody puking, of course), you come in and your flat chested wife is on the phone getting other flat chested wives out to vote for Hitler. She has been out all day with her bowling team—the gals, as she calls them—and she is still wearing those obscene black bowling shoes. And you make yourself a peanut butter sandwich instead of smacking her brains out.

Sure, I could go in for Scouting. But by the same token I could sign up for volunteer night duty at the county mad house, or test parachutes for the air force.

Instead, I have become an enemy of my government. I support the National Liberation Front in Vietnam. More than that; I send money and clothing to the people of Hanoi. And my treason does not stop there; I support a VC kid. That's right. Through my very good connections with the Ho Chi Minh government, I located a child whose family had been burned to death by napalm bombs, leaving him totally alone in the world, and I send money to the enemy authorities for his support and general well-being. Part of the money is put into a special college fund; I want him to attend a Moscow spy school. I'm sure he'll get a scholarship; my contribution will take care of extras, girls, vodka, good eats (they tell me that cabbage soup turns mean on you) and an occasional trip to one of those swinging Black Sea beaches, where it is against the law to wear clothes. Sylvia doesn't know about this of course; if she did, I know she would get right on the phone to the F.B.I. "Communist traitor punk bastard!"—I can just hear her shouting at me. One of these soft days I hope to discuss Sylvia's brain with a biochemist. Maybe he can illuminate me. I'm sure the microscope can explain her.

At this very moment I am sitting in a large irresponsible room with a dozen or so badly dressed people, mostly frauleins in their twenties; though there is a sad, heavy, middle-aged fellow in a corner who seems to be melting slowly away. I don't know whether despair is doing this to him—the world is such an un-gratefulness these days—or whether it is something in the way of regressive genes. Perhaps his great-great-grandfather was a Camembert. Or perhaps he is protesting the wrong war. I would not be surprised if it turned out that he had come to discuss the sending of American troops into Nicaragua. To my left, seated under a huge mural cartoon of Superman strangling a talking tiger, a chaste bald-headed man and a warty woman in her fifties are munching on peanut butter sandwiches and drinking from a thermos bottle. Glowering over them in an epiphany of rage, is a huge poster portrait of Trotsky.

But as I noted before, all the others are in their righteous twenties. Let me show you a liberty loving few of them: a lovely, Botticelli boy with shoulder-length hair, raven-colored, is seduc-tively debating the merits of bringing China into the war with an adorable flashing-eyed young mulatto girl. (Oh what breathtaking cominations and products lie waiting for us when the races are free to blend unquarelledly!) Her hair is a contoured black velvet. "I think China will never feel self-respect or a part of the world power community until she drops her bomb on an enemy," she is saying, holding his hand with one of hers and gesticulating with the other.

"I can't say I blame her," the boy replies, with a loveliness of smile that makes me think he should really be talking about music, not war. "But she will have to be forced into it. It will be in self-defense."

"Oh, yes," the girl says sweetly. "She will have to be driven to it by imperialist threats. No question."

A tall young lady, her femininity seccessfully disguised in slacks and sweater, is reading a copy of *Madame Bovary*. She looks up from time to time and scans each face there as if she expected them to disappear when she wasn't looking. I know that suffering beneath those raunchy clothes is a supple, giving body full of games and compliance, but right now I cannot come to its aid. Two young men with an aurora borealis of acne and furtive, giggly expressions reciting assaultive lines from President Johnson's speeches and nudging each other (why do they make me think they are refugees in the hold of a ship at the turn of the century?).

"We will not allow the freedom lovin' people uv Asia tu be entimadated bah communis' aggressors!" mimicked one, and they both broke up.

A very somber and very clean-faced unpimpled boy—blue eyes that have often faced the suicide waves of hysterical mother love—sits by himself against the side wall (dominated by another poster portrait, this one of Batman; and underneath it is a miniature photograph of President Roosevelt with that long cigaret holder in his mouth). He is not so lonely as you may think. He is sustained by a beatific vision of the triumph of will. He is wearing the same button I am. Hey! Hey! L.B.J! How Many Babies Have You Killed Today? Two beards and a pair of earrings huddle up front. One of the beards is authentic; he is in the full glow of his youth and strength and everything he does is backed up by the power of innocence. But something is fishy about the other, something at once ingratiating and calculating in his eyes. Now it hits me: he is an agent for the F.B.I. The girl is a jelly doughnut. If you squeeze her, jelly squirts out of her mouth and ears. It is delectable. She is talking about her trip to Italy last summer. "The Italians are so much warmer than the French," she says. "They don't want you to tip them for having a generous feeling."

"I grew up in an Italian neighborhood," says the spy, putting everything he had into the good chum act, "and I think they're wonderful. Boy! What great spaghetti feasts we used to have! Mamma mia!"

I'll have to keep a close watch on him. A matter of fact, well-integrated fellow comes in and checks out our plans for the morning. We are going to picket the U.N. He gives me a sign to carry. In big red letters it demands that American troops be withdrawn from Vietnam. I would prefer a more inflammatory one, something showing a hydrogen bomb killing God, let's say, but I keep this desire to myself because I am trying to cultivate selflessness. "Now remember," our leader is saying—he is a director of the Young Socialist League and he has well thought out political career plans—"don't let the hecklers get to you. Practice the Gandhi methods we studied last week. Okay. Let's go!" The melting man claps his hands.

Outside, we all climb into a fruit pickers' truck and head for the U. N. building uptown. A youth smelling of sleep leans over to me. "Didn't I see you in Memphis last spring?"

"Afraid not," I reply, observing that the government spy is listening. "I always spend spring in Canada, at my folk's hunting lodge."

"I could have sworn I met you at a SNCC rally," he goes on.

"Wrong again," I say.

"Well, I'm glad you're with us," and he gives me a soft hand that knows no borders, no ethnic qualifications, no religious rituals.

The bounding and jiggling of the truck, its smell of fruit and vegetables, the wood plank seats along the sides, the names of José and Carmelita carved in the wood, all this is disengaging me from this identity as an anti-war marcher, and luring me into the California fields, into a pair of blue overalls. The sun is abominably hot but I keep on picking, picking. The salty sweat is running down my face, into my eyes and mouth.

"Hernandez! Hernandez!" the boss, Peters, is shouting from his scaffold perch. "Stop daydreaming! Get a move on."

"*Si! Si!*" I reply, and go at the avocados with greater zest. I am afraid of being laid off.

"You greasers!" he shouts again, laughing loud and hoarse, the laughter that only a victor has the prerogative of employing. "All you think about is fucking and drinking!" He laughs some more and in spite of myself I laugh too, I am that afraid of defying his contempt for me and my contrymen.

"*Si! Si!!*" I shout. "*Veramente, mi Capitan.* Tacos and tiquillos and jig jig!" Much laughter from the fields. In my mind, I can see my wife Vera watching me with deepest hatred because I am acting like such a clown and helping them make fun of me. She wants me to be a man, but we all know that is an impossibility. Birds will bark before that happens. My finger is bleeding. I have cut it with my knife in fury.

"You guys ought to be happy," Peters roars again. "Back in Mexico there ain't no work at all. You'd be starving." He laughs. "We're tryin' to help you bastards. But you ain't grateful."

Tonight I am going to get drunk at the cantina. I know I will get into a fight. I love to fight. I feel like a man. Perhaps someday I will kill somebody. Then I would feel like God. Maybe. Some day I will go back to my village and buy a good house and make wonderful things grow and play with my children in the evenings. And drink.

"Fernando, when you go to the store I want you to buy me a new Virgin." This is Vera talking to me. "Paco dropped the other one in the well." I tell her my plans for the future. "You will have to win a lottery," she says, and she calms herself by giving her breast to the baby. I sometimes think she likes to hurt my feelings. Jesu Christu it is hot. That son of a bitch Peters sure is big. You would have to hit him from behind to get him.

Bend like a willow, Zen (through Zachary) advises me, and that is exactly what I am doing. Otherwise, I'd break into pieces in this bouncing, banging truck. I feel that I am escaping from somewhere, desperately eluding the police, rather than going to the United Nations to protest for peace. The lonely girl is refusing to recognize this condition; she continues to read *Madame Bovary*, never taking her eyes off it, even when she rises high off the board seat when we go over a bump. I admire her concentration—or her psychotic disengagement. She will make an excellent guerilla fighter in the highlands, in the war against the imperialist warmongers. I see her wearing only the smallest amount of camouflage; she is quite above looking like a bush.

In a few minutes we are walking up and down in front of the world peace building. The big blue policemen, who, ironically, are there to protect us, are hiding their contempt beneath masks of everyday boredom. The hecklers are in splendid form. They are writhing with patriotic hatred.

"Dirty commie skunks!" an old charwoman shouts, shaking her umbrella.

"You oughta be whipped!" screams an old man with a drunkard's bloated purple face. "You're not clean enough to breathe American air!"

But none of us is deterred. The government spy least of all. He is walking ahead of me, carrying a sign which says Allow Free Elections in Viet Nam, and his shoulders are so straight, his head so high, you would think he belonged to the D.A.R. The two young beards flank the chubby girl, as if to protect her. They could not be happier. (I had not noticed before what a first-rate fanny she has—robust, saucy, full of unusual ideas.) I wonder how long it will be before they discover their true destiny in the suburbs. The two old people are admirable in their fearlessness. They march as the Christian martyrs of old must have marched. The old lady has just passed an apple to her husband. He must keep up his courage.

The anger of the crowds is mounting (the receptive and passive docility of the single individuals is merging into one). Many of them have been drinking and their eyes are aflame. A boy in his twenties, clearly from the lower classes, his profession a trucker's helper perhaps, darts past a policeman and swings at me, hitting me in the shoulder. "You lousy sons a bitches!" he howls, as I push him away and a cop grabs at him. "You want me to hate my mother! That's what you want!" and he begins to sob wildly. The cop pushes him back into the crowd.

Someone throws an egg that hits the Negro boy in the face. He makes no effort to cleanse himself; the slimy yellow and white mess slithers down his black face and onto his shirt, like an obscene sea worm. "Nigger queer!"

That voice is familiar. I look closely. My God! It's Cedric. He's dressed like a woman and is in a frenzy of indignation. He looks right at me and makes a dirty gesture with his finger. He doesn't recognize me, perhaps because I am wearing dark glasses. He is with a young sailor who is smiling with a vast idiocy. I'm sure he is so dumb he will never discover that Cedric is a woman.

"They don't know what they're doing," a young fellow marcher behind me whispers. "They've been so brain-washed by the reactionary press."

"You're right," I say, but I don't mean a word of it. These yellers have never been so clear headed, so sure of anything. Their blood is speaking and acting for them. They want to exterminate us.

"They need to be re-educated," he countinues.

"I agree with you," I said, dodging a coke bottle. "That's where we come in." It is difficult to carry on any sort of reasonable conversation, the hecklers are making so much noise. All of us are being pelted with garbage and newspapers, and the cops are smiling about the whole thing. An especially doltish-looking man, whose hairy arms were covered with girlie tatooes, is making dirty suggestions to one of our girls. He is going at it with his mouth and with his body, like an ape in the zoo. The crowd adores him, of course. He is telling our girl how he would take care of her and show her what a real man can do. She is clearly dying of embarrassment, but her Gandhi training helps her restrain herself from responding.

A heavy policeman manages to bump into me, knocking me off the pavement and into the gutter. "You fuckin' bums," he said half under his breath, "I'd love to see what our boys in Vietnam would do to you punks. Boy would I love to see them work you punks over!

"We're against war," I say, picking up my sign and brushing off the gutter dirt from my suit. "That doesn't mean we're cowards."

He just spits at me, hitting my shoulder with a huge gray-green phlegm blob. Marching parallel with us are about a dozen hefty-breasted, very aggressive and well-tailored members of the Daughters of the American Revolution. They hate us, too, of course. They are also carrying signs. A giraffe type lady is holding one that says "Thomas Jefferson Betrayed!" Right behind her is a steely-eyed, huge-assed granny, half-covered with a sandwich board, "Beatniks should be jailed!" one side says. "Keep America strong!" is on the other. At the very end of of this gray-haired, tight-assed line is a mad-eyed bony hag who is dressed up as one of the minutemen of the revolution. She even has a blood stained —catsup, of course—bandage around her head. She is a one man-woman band. She is holding a harnessed harmonica in her mouth, and strapped around her shoulders and waist is a drum. Suddenly she strikes up her music. She is playing *Mine Eyes Have Seen the Glory of the Coming of the Lord.* All the crones join in. The audience applauds wildly.

That's not all. The Nazis are out. Those marble-eyed, flat-faced young maniacs who mourn the death of the world's most awesome killer. They are dressed in Nazi uniforms and one of them is holding a big swastika flag. Two others—they are in their teens, these devotees of death—are holding signs: "Kike Corrupters! Christ Killers!" They are talking about us. "Draft fairy peaceniks! Bomb Red China Now!" The crowd adores them too. These growling shouting blobs are getting very restless. A beer can hits our leader in the back, and a roar of pleasure explodes from the masses. I recognize the marksman. It is my stoop friend, the retired killer, Blaster. He is crazy drunk. I hope for his peace of mind he doesn't recognize me. A plastic bag filled with water hits one of the girls. The DAR women clap their hands with delight. Now the crowd is kicking over the wooden barricades that are supposed to keep them from us, and the police do nothing but laugh.

"That just shows you how corrupt the police are," the melting man says to me. "They're on the side of mob rule."

"I know," I reply intelligently, dodging an orange. "It's terrible." I make up my mind to send two more pints of my blood to the Vietcong every month.

Our leader bravely starts singing, *We Shall Overcome,* and we all join in. The classy-looking Negro boy has a penetrating soprano voice that goes right through me. The opposing groups are not to be outdone. The sound of the club striking his head is a living, breathing thunk. It does not disappear as other sounds do, joining the timelessness of the air. It becomes part of my body and spirit like a growth. I will never be able to disengage myself from it.

The DAR grannies begin shouting the Star Spangled Banner. They sound like a demented church choir at a chicken dinner social. The Nazis now swing in with the *Horst Wessel* song. Someone in the crowd starts blowing a bugle—and the hecklers, half of them stoned, suddenly go screaming nuts, and attack. The three girls in our crowd are pulled to the ground. Their clothes are ripped off and the madmen are trying to rape them. Everybody is fighting everybody else. The grannies are wrestling with the hecklers and the Nazis in absolute joy and confusion. A huge naked granny is sitting on top of a Nazi boy and pounding him with her sign, while a snob type is grabbing her from behind. The cops are wantonly hitting everybody with their clubs. Two men jump me and we collapse together slugging and kicking.

"Don't fight!" shouts our bleeding leader. "Remember Gandhi!" He is clubbed down by a grinning, swollen-faced cop.

I am trying my best to choke my red-eyed assailant to death while the other one is kicking me in the head. One of the beards in our group screams with pain as a granny, clad only in a torn bra and a girdle, bites him in the leg. The old man is bleeding from a smashed nose. Police sirens wail madly, and just as I shout,

"Down with fascism!" I am smashed on the head by what feels like a beer bottle, and as I slide into stunning mother-soft oblivion, my wrecked brain produces a sharp color picture of Sylvia taking a shower with her clothes on.

I WAS IN A FOUR-STAR, SEVEN-NOODLE PLAY last night. Where? At the Open-Fly Theatre in Paris, of course. Where else would a chap of indecent identity be beguiling himself these days? Anyway, it was one of the truly dazzling, blood-changing experiences of my life. I'm going to do my very best to reproduce the osmotic vulnerability of it for you right now (if only you will stop lying to yourselves for a few minutes and face the fact that you may very well be the center of the universe.) Here it is, friends. Judge for yourselves what part I play:

SOME DREAMS AREN'T REAL

A PARK. TWO OR THREE BENCHES. TWO TRASH CANS. A YOUNG GIRL IS SITTING ON A BENCH. SHE IS OBVIOUSLY DEPRESSED AND IS PLANNING SOMETHING TERRIBLE. IN A FEW MOMENTS AN OLD BUMMY LADY COMES ON STAGE. SHE IS A SCAVENGER. SHE IS PUSHING A BABY CARRIAGE WHICH SHE USED TO HAUL HER "COLLECTIONS" IN. SHE IS LOUDLY SINGING "ROLL OUT THE BARREL."

SCAVENGER

(Passing the girl enroute to the trash can at the other side of the benches.)

Evening, dearie.

(Girl does not respond at all. The scavenger pauses for a moment and looks up in the air.)

Just look at those swallows. *(Pause.)* Crazy as they can be.

(She goes to the refuse can and begins rummaging through it, tossing a few choice items into the baby carriage. Then she turns and faces the girl.)

You know, a lot of people feel sorry for me because I do this sort of thing. But the poor dears completely miss the point. They don't realize how glorious it is to pick at humanity's castoffs. Why, only this morning I found a baby bonnet that I just know belonged to President Harding!

GIRL STILL DOES NOT RESPOND. SCAVENGER GOES BACK TO PICKING IN THE TRASH CAN, HUMMING "ROLL OUT THE BARREL". A YOUNG COP STROLLS ONSTAGE, SWINGING HIS BILLY CLUB. HE PAUSES IN FRONT OF THE GIRL.

COP

Isn't it a bit late for you to be in the park alone?

GIRL

(very shyly)

I'm . . . I'm expecting to meet a friend here.

COP

(dubiously)

It's a strange friend who would keep a nice girl waiting.

SCAVENGER

(in a stage whisper to the girl)

Don't believe a word he says. His mother was a Vanderbilt.

COP

(staring at the girl a moment longer)

Well, miss, I certainly hope your friend has shown up by the time I make my rounds again.

GIRL

(haughty, hurt)

You don't have to worry about me. I can assure you that my friend will show up shortly.

SCAVENGER

That's telling him.

COP

Just make sure you don't try to make any friends here in the park, if you get my meaning.

SCAVENGER

I wonder why it is that all authorities have dirty minds.

COP

(laughing, walking over and tickling the old lady lady with his stick)

Ah there, granny. What tattered little goodies have you reclaimed today?

SCAVENGER

(putting her hands on her hips)

You tell me your secrets and I'll tell you mine!

COP

(laughing wildly)

You're a naughty one, you are. *(He begins to move off stage.)* Be good now, granny. Be good. EXITS.

SCAVENGER

Oh go chase a pickpocket! *(She turns to the girl)* You've got to be firm with people like that. Otherwise, they're apt to take liberties with you. *(She resumes her picking. She finds something nice and takes it over to the girl.)* Here's a little something for you, lovie. A choo choo train, brimming with memories of happiness.

(The girl does not respond at all. The old lady sighs.)

Well, it's getting late. I have to trundle home. I've got a pig's foot on the stove.

(She begins to wheel off stage, then she turns for a moment.)

I know "the friend" you're waiting for, sweetie. But it isn't right. Not for a dear thing like you.

SHE SLOWLY GOES OFF SHAKING HER HEAD. ALONE AT LAST, THE GIRL LOOKS ABOUT TO BE SURE SHE ISN'T BEING WATCHED, THEN SHE PULLS OUT A GUN FROM HER POCKETBOOK AND IS ABOUT TO SHOOT HERSELF, WHEN A YOUNG MAN COMES ON STAGE. HE IS WALKING IN HIS SLEEP, HOLDING HIS ARMS OUT IN FRONT OF HIMSELF. JUST AS THE GIRL COCKS THE PISTOL HE DROPS HIS ARMS, AND WAKES UP.

YOUNG MAN

Wait! *(the girl reacts stunned and hides the pistol.)* You've broken my dream!

GIRL

I'm sorry. I didn't mean to. Really I didn't.

YOUNG MAN

(grabbing the gun from its hiding place)

Another good dream gone to hell. All because you decided to blow your silly brains out.

GIRL

I was desperate.

BOY

So was I!

GIRL

(indignant)

But I didn't ask you to wander by my bench.

BOY

And I didn't ask you to put a pistol to your head. *(He sits down sadly.)* Gosh, the things that keep a fellow from getting the most out of life. Would-be suicides!

GIRL

A girl has a right to take her own life if she so desires. Nobody can force you to go on living after life has become unbearable.

BOY

(jumping up angrily)

Where did you learn such rot! In the Japanese Army? *(He begins to pace.)* Holy God—the very idea! Makes my blood run cold. What makes you think you're any better than the rest of us? *(The girl acts aloof but scared. He now draws close to her and whispers loudly.)* Besides, it's against the law.

AT THAT MOMENT THE COP STROLLS BACK ON.

COP

What's against the law?

BOY

(surprised and ruffled)

Uh . . . hatred.

COP

No, it isn't.

BOY

Well, then, uh, self-abasement.

COP

(patronizingly shaking his head)

No my boy. You are completely mistaken. I'm afraid you're living in a dream world. *(He smiles and whirls his stick. Then he turns slyly to the girl.)* Is he the chap you were waiting for?

GIRL

(nervously)

Well, not exactly . . . .

BOY

What she means is . . . .

COP

Oh, so he's some dirty sex maniac who came along and tried to get fresh with you, eh?

GIRL

No! No! Quite the contrary . . . .

COP

You don't have to protect him, miss. *(He turns to the boy and looks him up and down.)* Say, you look familiar, didn't I see you in a nightmare I had last night?

BOY

What was I doing?

COP

You were sitting way up in a tree and barking like a dog.

BOY

(shakes his head)

No, that wasn't me. I've never been in a tree in my life. They make me dizzy.

COP

This fellow was the spittin' image of you. Maybe you've got an identical twin who goes in for nightmares.

BOY

There has never been a twin in my entire family.

COP

(returning to girl)

Well, as I was saying, miss, it's my duty to protect the innocent, and any time . . .

HE IS INTERRUPTED BY THE OLD SCAVENGER, WHO RACES ON STAGE PUSHING HER CARRIAGE.

SCAVENGER

Whoops! Just listen to him!

COP

(behaving like a child, stamping his foot)

It's the truth! Don't you dare say it isn't!

SCAVENGER

The innocent don't need protecting, you silly bastard. *(She laughs and heads toward the ash can. As she gets to it she shouts at the young couple.)* Don't let him interrupt anything you were doing. He's got the crazy idea that he has to be working all the time.

COP

(becomes a whimpering child now)

You're trying to destroy my self-confidence. Why? What have I ever done to you? The whole damn world is aflame with hostility and aggression.

GIRL

(sadly)

How true, how true.

SCAVENGER

(grabbing the cop)

Oh stop your sniveling! *(She drags him near the ash can and her cart.)* Here's a little something to make you feel better. *(She hands him a torn brassiere. She begins slowly to lead him off stage.)* Take that home with you. Maybe it'll help you understand the human race.

COP AND SCAVENGER EXIT. THE BOY AND GIRL SAY NOTHING FOR A COUPLE OF MOMENTS. SLOWLY THE BOY CIRCLES THE GIRL.

BOY

Why did you want to kill yourself?

GIRL

I'll tell you . . . if you tell me what you were dreaming about.

BOY

You're a very pretty girl.

GIRL

Don't evade the issue! What were you dreaming about?

BOY

(sighing heavily)

Well, all right. But I'll tell you on one condition.

GIRL

Yes?

BOY

That you don't laugh at me.

GIRL

I promise.

BOY

O.K. I was dreaming . . . that I was in love. *(The girl starts laughing hysterically)* I knew you would laugh. I knew it! You can't trust anybody.

GIRL

It's just too funny.

BOY

(fiercely)

You know what's the matter with you? You have a cold heart.

GIRL

(after she collects herself)

Shall I tell you why I was going to kill myself?

BOY

(sulking)

Maybe I'll laugh if you do.

GIRL

I was going to commit suicide because of love.

BOY

Oh . . . .

GIRL

Do you see now why I was laughing?

BOY

Because . . . .

GIRL

Because of the crazy things love makes you do. It turned you into a sleepwalker and me into a potential murderer.

BOY

Were you in love?

GIRL

I had a lover.

BOY

Did you love him?

GIRL

I loathed him. And I loathed me. I wanted to murder myself.

BOY

(He walks around the stage for a couple of moments thinking—)

I used to think about death . . . I really did . . . then I discovered sleep, and dreams. Oh, they're wonderful! They allow a person to really live, unmolested!

GIRL

It sounds so lovely. I wish I could dream.

BOY

(falling at her feet)

I'll teach you.

GIRL

Oh you adorable boy! *(She embraces him)* Teach me now. Teach me now.

BOY

First of all, you must lie down and relax. *(She does so)* Now you close your eyes. *(She does)* Next, you have to clear your mind of all distracting elements . . . elements that disturb you . . . elements of reality. *(There is a long pause as he walks slowly about and the girl clears her mind.)* Are you all ready?

GIRL

(sleepily)

Yes, I am ready.

BOY

Good. Now let's see . . . what should you dream about. *(pause)* Ah, I have it. Dream that you are the prima ballerina of the Ballet Russe de Monte Carlo. You are onstage at the Metropolitan Orchestra tuning. You have just finished dancing in *Swan Lake.* And the audience is madly shouting Bravo! Bravo! because you were so brilliant, so divine. You curtsy and blow hundreds of kisses. All right, now let's try it.

THERE IS A LONG PAUSE, THEN THE GIRL SLOWLY GETS UP.

GIRL

It didn't work.

BOY

(aghast)

It didn't work? What do you mean?

GIRL

(shrugging)

I got only as far as the stage. Then everything stopped.

BOY

Really?

GIRL

Yes, That's the absolute truth.

BOY

(puzzles for a moment, then has it)

I know what the trouble was. That wasn't your kind of dream. We'll try another. Lie down again and do just as I told you before. *(She does)* All set? *(rubbing his hands)* Good. Now then . . . You are a shop girl . . . very poor . . . you live with your old mother and father in a tiny basement room. Your life is completely miserable. You have only one dress, and it's torn. One day you make a three-penny bet on the national soccer lottery. And . . . you win! You win three million dollars!

THERE IS A LONG PAUSE. THEN THE GIRL SLOWLY SITS UP.

GIRL

No, that one didn't work either. I got as far as the torn dress . . . and I couldn't go any farther.

BOY

Could go no farther? *(Screams in anguish)* A wonderful dream like that and you couldn't have it. Oh, you horrible girl! You monster! The wonders of the world are wasted on you! You can't dream! *(He pulls the pistol out of his pocket and hands it to her.)* Take this back. You don't deserve to live. *(He slowly gets back into his dream stance and begins to glide offstage.)* I must get away from you immediately. People like you are dangerous.

THE GIRL WATCHES HIM, THEN SLOWLY LIES DOWN, DRAWS THE PISTOL AND SHOOTS HERSELF. IN A FEW MOMENTS THE SCAVENGER AND THE COP RETURN. THE COP IS DRESSED AS A BROKEN DOWN BUM. THE SCAVENGER HAS HIS HAT ON AND IS SWINGING HIS BILLY CLUB. THE COP BEHAVES LIKE AN ANIMAL. HE WHIMPERS AHEAD OF THE OLD WOMAN AND IS PUSHING THE BABY CARRIAGE. SHE PAUSES IN FRONT OF THE GIRL

Bless you, sweetie. Sleep tight. *(She blows her a kiss. Then she pushes the cop toward an ash can.)* Go on now, you little dog. Pick me something real nice.

HE BARKS AND WHIMPERS AND BEGINS TO PICK MADLY. THE OLD LADY
LAUGHS AND TURNS TO THE AUDIENCE.
    SCAVENGER
Lordy! What would life be like without a trash can or two?
CURTAIN

III "YOU MUST BE CRAZY OR SOMETHING,"
Sylvia said, standing over me as I lay on the bed with an ice pack
on my head. "Getting beaten up in a stupid peace demonstration!
You really are slipping back into childhood."

"I wish I could," I mumbled. "Those were my happiest days."
My head was a boutique of strange pains.

"Did you burn your draft card too?" she continued in characteristic form.

"As a matter of fact I did. My 4F classification from the last
war." I lifted the ice bag from my eyes. "Caught you on that one,
didn't I?"

She snorted. "Mr. Smart Ass. You're so clever you're going to
end up in the pen. How are you going to explain your moronic
behavior to the judge? Just tell me that if you can." She sat down
on our big black canvas bedroom chair and sipped a scotch and
soda. Her slax-fitted legs were folded under her with dreadful ease.
What a swell picture of bitchiness, self-appointed power, and
disengaged sexuality. She was wasted in this apartment with me.
She was meant for a world-wide audience. Movie screens in London, Paris, Anchorage, the Congo should be flashing her impeccable image in ganster plots, murder mysteries. I tried to think of
some way I could arrange for her to achieve her true status, but
my head hurt too much for anything that massive. Some other
day.

"Simple," I said, shifting to my side to ease the pain. "I'll
explain to him my profound interest in saving the human race
from extinction." I rubbed my stomach to make myself feel better.
"I'm sure he'll understand."

Sylvia laughed and I thought of a Karloff movie. "You're off your rocker!" Then she stopped chortling and stared at me, a smile stunned and paralyzed in mid journey on her pretty and viciously inhuman face. "No. No. I'm wrong. You're not off your chump. You're sane—in a way. That's the terrible thing about it." She looked mildly disgusted now. "There's something obscene and unnatural about you. You're sane but completely out of this world." She drank off the scotch, to give herself courage to go on, and to numb her feelings at being legally connected with anything like me. "You're like a strange fungus from another planet." She looked me up and down as if seeing me for the first time. "Or a germ that nature has no antibodies to fight." She fell back in the big bat-like chair and shook her head. She looked for a second like an insect that had been caught by a huge bat or spider. I shifted myself again and put the ice pack on the side of my head. My head and neck were almost totally wrecked. I could only feel the vibrations of the pains, their dirty noises.

"On the contrary," I said, trying for my best English accent and delivery, "I have never felt more like a member of this globe's population. I think, futhermore, that I have gotten closer to the true heart of man than at any other time of my somewhat diverse career as a human being. In fact," I went on, raising myself up to get a better look at her, "I feel like Everyman himself."

She began filling up her glass again (she brought in the bottle and ice to save wearing herself out in frequent trips to the living room medicine chest.)

"You can say that again," she sang out, "I sometimes think I'm living with a dozen different people." I honestly do, I could feel she was thinking. I'm not being funny. He's the strangest man I ever met, and I had to marry him. He even looks completely different at times. What did he look like when I married him? Can't remember. But I think his nose was smaller. He wasn't so strange then, otherwise I'd never have married him. He was kind of amusing. I even liked sex with him. Then everything turned cold inside me. That's funny because I feel very sexy most of the time. It's like something didn't get delivered to the right place. When he comes near me I feel like kicking him. It isn't that he's repulsive. My sister is always telling me I've got the best looking husband around and how marvelous it must be to rassle in the hay with him. Why does he want me to do all those weird things? Is he a degenerate? Or do all men want these bizarre things and are too shy to ask? And why do some men like to be teased? George liked for me to fuck him in the shower, and Jackson liked it upside down, but that's nothing compared to twinkle toes here. He wants a circus. Maybe he'll get one some day, but I sure won't be in it.

Because I want out. And when I do I think I'll go and live in Italy again. Saved enough money in this crummy publicity job to make out for a year. Had a damn good time there with George. If only he hadn't gone to pieces drinking wine and writing that bloody goddamn novel.

"If it gives you so much agony, why do you do it?" she asked him one day.

"I can't help myself." George said. He had brownish green eyes that flecked up mysteriously when he was feeling something. His mouth, shaped by others' desires, was a playground of ingenuous kisses, and it was always a bit moist, as if it had just completed that mouth-to-mouth loveliest of all trips.

"Does it make you happy sometimes?"

The answer that came out of that angelic but so often pained face—the simplest things could disarray its fragile serenity, a knock on the door, a casual remark, then you could see it flee over the slopes for its life—was more of music than language. "Happier than I could ever tell you. It isn't like anything else in the world."

"Is it better than screwing?"

"Yes."

"Are you all alone then?"

"Exquisitely."

That bothered her. She didn't want anyone to be alone and apart from her. It made her feel small and like a helpless child in a huge suddenly vacated building. This apartment looked out over the Spanish Steps in Rome and often when they talked George liked to stand at their small balcony and watch the people in the long, wide old steps. He looked like someone poised on the deck of a boat watching a new country come into view. He was so beautiful in that stance.

"Is it hard to write a novel?" she went on, afraid that he might drift away from her if she didn't talk.

"I don't know what it's like for other people," he replied without turning his head toward her. "It's difficult for me if I lose contact with the characters. I mean, if I ever stop feeling that they are really extensions of me and me of them. Then they become strangers and very surly and unreal."

"Oh." She wished he had given her a simpler answer. She decided to ask another writer they knew what it was like with him. She was sure he would not come up with something so peculiar. Still, George was so very yummy, and he always looked so clean, even when he was drunk. Their favorite eating place was a trattoria in the Via Margutta, where the sensuous colors—umber, orange, red, even yellow—of the houses and shops made you wonder why intelligent people persisted in living in frigid withdrawn countries where the buildings said no to you instead of yes! yes! Their restaurant was called Maria Piccola, little Maria, the tiny, unbelievably active old woman who did all the cooking and who, Sylvia was sure, slept in the oven when the place closed at night. They met their friends here, and during and after dinner George consumed stupendous amounts of Frascati wine. Two of their chums were Anthony and Virginia Hampden. He was a cultural affairs officer at the American Embassy and a dedicated anti-semite. She was a well-mannered, small-nosed vestigial error of his youth. He had married her in his college years when he was convinced, erroneously, he later discovered in Italy, that women did not care for him.

"Have you heard about the Mafia's latest gimmick?" Anthony asked one evening while they were gorging on baby goat and fried artichokes.

"I adore the Mafia," Sylvia heard herself say.

"No," George replied, drowning some meat with half a glass of wine. "What've those rascals done now?"

Anthony started laughing before he had even started the story. Crime against the establishment always delighted him. "As you know," he finally said, his laughter having floated out into the courtyard and joined the ivy, "one of their biggest sources of loot is narcotics. But they've been having a problem getting large amounts into the States. Well, they came up with a real winner recently. They injected seven-million dollars worth of pure heroin into a huge shipment of Sicilian oranges! Once they were delivered there, all they had to do was squeeze the damn things and the heroin came out in the juice. Can you imagine!" And more laughter swept and shrieked out of his mouth. Everyone else was very pleased too.

"What a wonderful game, " George said (he was getting high now and his words no longer leaped ballet fashion across their mutual stage but rather walked), and plunged a moldy chunk of gorgonzola into his mouth followed by far more than the necessary amount of Frascati gargle. "What would the Mafia and the American police do without each other. They would go to pot." He poured more wine around. "The Mafia is the only big business with a true sense of humor. We should be gratified for them."

Sylvia never knew whether he was joking or not when he talked this way, he often seemed to be having a conversation with another part of himself, and this required her often to tread so cautiously that she found herself in the reluctant and unstable role of part intruder and part fool, hardly herself, unless, in his perversity, that was the way he wished it. "Grateful?" she ventured. "But they seem terribly destructive to me. In fact, they do everything they can to create chaos." Anthony and George were looking at her with ghoul amusement. "Think of the thousands of people they turn into animals by selling them dope."

"Oh dear," Anthony muttered.

George responded with his usual wined-up laugh and shook his cherub curls over his plate of green cheese. "Sylvia baby, sometimes you make me positively despair. Your moralistic outrage makes you miss the point of the great world game." More wine. "All those good chaps are doing is encouraging the survival of the fittest. It's very beautiful."

Virginia peeked out from behind her bush. "I must say I agree with Sylvia. Things like that disgust me."

Anthony patted her on her milky unblemished right forearm. "Of course they do, sweet pie. That's why you are you."

George smiled at Virginia's puckering embarassment. "Virginia, honey, have you ever thought how much more degradingly people are treated by their very own governments? In the way they are manipulated and lied to and often led off to the battlefields to be killed for the most absurd reasons?

"The difference is that the Mafia action is much more honest. They don't try to appeal to anybody's emotions or ideas. They don't lie to their customers."

"A very good point, George old boy," Anthony said. " A very good point indeed. My own thoughts to a tee."

Sylvia took George's hand under the table and reestablished contact with him. He squeezed her hand in return. She was not entirely sure whether the squeeze was an I am with you response with all the lovely implications of his awareness of her as an important human being in his life, or merely a muscular reflex action. In any case, it was much better than no squeeze or vibration at all. A girl has to live howsoever God allows her to. In a safe and mellow corner across the room, under a rococo ceiling panel depicting the endless delights of eating and screwing—a couple of the shameless models were doing both at the very same time—sat a bald, muscular pre-middle-aged man with a lovely beard which did not, to Sylvia's surprise, interfere with his eating a bowl of fettucini. With him was a half-caste girl of delicate but total beauty plucking at a salad. When the man spoke it was with a slow richness and Sylvia could make out nearly all the words. He—his companion called him Zachary—was talking about a tenth century Zen master of very stern methods of teaching.

His other-worldly companion seemed to understand everything he was saying because she was smiling. The man was wearing a tasteful cashmere sweater without a shirt underneath. In the opposite corner, having a go at dishes of mussels marinara (Sylvia learned the recipe from George, who happened to be a very cultivated cook on some things), were a chic and angular and very much New York City couple. The man had a patch over his eye. The woman had blond teased hair and beautifully self-confident half-exposed breasts. The woman was saying something about the number of certain kinds of people who could stand rubbing out. The man's one eye (the left one had a patch over it), sky blue, was amused and deadly at the same glint. A few simple feet to Sylvia's right was a most handsomely degenerate looking man with long gray hair and a nose that was unquestionably Roman and unquestionably had seen a lot of this wild world. A mustard colored silk tie proclaimed him a man of boundless taste. He was making short work of a dozen Portuguese oysters. His companions were clearly not sufferers either; two heavenly brunettes attired in the latest homosexual dress designer fantasies, and they too were eating very well (snails). Sylvia knew immediately that they were in the movie business when she heard him say, with an accent she wanted to cuddle, "Ve vill go into produgshun in vun veek in za heart of teeming Cairo." The girls smiled happily at each other and one of them, with unconscionably full lips, leaned over and kissed the man in his ear.

That's just the beginning of the goodies he will receive, Sylvia thought, and to her own surprise, for she was basically an envious woman, found herself wishing them the finest of fun.

" . . . so I give the non-communist countries twenty years at the most," George was saying (he was very wined up now), "and I think they know it too."

"My advice to everybody is to learn Chinese immediately," Anthony stated, and had a drink of brandy on that exceptional thought.

Sylvia didn't like the drift of the conversation, so she delicately stomped it by asking a large dumb question: "George, would you tell me again what your novel is all about?"

He looked at her with a sudden seriousness, glanced at Virginia and Anthony, as if mutely pleading, Why would anyone want to know my secret?, stared again at Sylvia—he could have been asking, What could such information possibly mean to you?—and began to laugh. "The whole of western civilization," he gasped in a few seconds. "Contemporary man in all his follies and false whiskers." He drank off the four fingers of wine left in his glass and histrionically wiped his wet mouth with the sleeve of his gray doeskin jacket, "and guess what, Sylvia old sweet spot, you're in it like everybody else."

I guess that's better than not being in it, she thought. God only knows what he's having me do in those nutsy pages of his. The bearded bald man and his girl shuffled by. "Knock on infinity and hear a cry," he was muttering to his still entranced student (what beauty!). "Strike wood and hear nothing." There's no accounting for taste, Sylvia said to herself.

The remainder of that night was filled with wonder, then washed with madness, and reprieved by the infinite flexibility of the human soul. No less. The four of them ended up at an oversize party in a studio at the top of an old palazzo off the Piazza Colonna, a gamey, quick-witted place populated by small criminals and second-class prostitutes who strolled as if in a reverie, not completely in tune with the immediate street scene and the direct demands of the flesh. The studio was the living and working and playing quarters of Martino Villarubia, a shamelessly well-heeled Italian (his family manufactured an addictive soft drink) who projected his dreams of creativity onto sculpture and whose other hobby was cultivating an exotic social life as some less energetic humans nurture herb gardens. Sylvia, standing on the curtain of these whirling phenomena, feared she might be swallowed up by it. "Now don't you be afraid, Syl honey," her mother had urged at her first big school dance, "everybody here feels just the same way you do. And just remember, hon, nobody here is any more than human." None of such advice had ever done her any good. She had not been there ten minutes before George and Anthony and Virginia somehow vanished into the seductively vibrating mass there. Many of the guests were frugging, while an equal number were standing about making conversation; and this combination, or contrast, of frantic motion alongside—or in and around—non-motion gave her the momentary sensation of having lost a piece of her mind that took care of balance; she felt she was moving and standing still at the same time. The ecstatic, or enraged, music was infiltrating her muscles and joints and was beginning its assault on her central nervous system. Her attention was caught momentarily by a red haired, wolf-grinning man—and could that be his nose?—who was frugging madly with a long haired woman whose breasts were going to leap out of her dress at any moment and whose tight blue skirt was well above her tanned bare knees. He seemed to be experiencing a vision or something, his look was so entranced. But this did not interfere with his dancing. (Nor did his friend's huge whining dog at his knees). He wore a white sweat shirt with the words God is Gay printed on both front and back. At first Sylvia thought she might be going insane, because the words were like neon signs. She reassured herself when she realized that they were glowing because they were in luminous paint.

"I'm being born again, Daddy!" the woman shouted to him.

"Sing it, Countess!" he shouted.

They're crazy, Sylvia told herself. Or in drugs, hallucinogenic drugs, and they're trying to have interplanetary awareness or something. I'm only a little tight from the wine. Where in God's name did George and the others go to? Goddamn them. I exist too. I'd like them to know that. Grabbing herself by the lapse of her psyche, Sylvia dragged herself off that rutted brightened spot and toward a cluster of talking people who were not dancing. ("How can these lovely children get to know you unless you say something to them?" her mother said, pushing her forward. "Speech is man's highest accomplishment.") A pair of fathoms-deep wet black eyes surrounded by soft-tanned smiling skin engulfed her at the human oasis. "Isn't it absolutely marvelous," he said, "They're making a movie of it."

"It?" Sylvia puzzled.

"The party," he replied, making a half-sweeping gesture with his arm. "Look," he continued, and pointed to the balcony overlooking the dinosaur-sized room. "That's Memo up there with his movie camera. And over there somewhere," he pointed to another part of the writhing room, "his friend Victor is recording all the sounds—people, music, finger and foot sounds, everything. *Che bella!*"

"Wow!" Sylvia exclaimed. "I'm in a movie and a novel at the same time."

"And in real life too!" the man shouted. "Three different realities."

A woman next to Sylvia—she had the greenest eyes ever—said, "And then one dreams too. So that is four." Her voice was raised high so that it could rise above the rock and roll.

"Oh me oh my," a skinny chap with a polka dot tie and a sweet button nose murmured, "all these realities. What does one do with them?" He had a French accent.

"Wish I knew," Sylvia confessed. His face is familiar, she mused. He's a celebrity of some sort. Artist? Criminal? I think they're really the same thing.

"Have some of my drink," this man said, extending a tall glass with milky looking stuff in it. "It's very good. It's absinthe."

"Mm, never tried it." And she took a big swallow. From that point on, she entered still another reality. Far in the distance, surrounded by countless bobbing human facial masks and expressions, some frantic, some barbaric, others smooth and serene, George's face appeared, for just a second, then disappeared.

"You know," the man named Memo said softly, "the real party is going on downstairs. Why don't we pop down?"

"Why not? I've been abandoned, haven't I?"

She seems to be all right, George said aloud, though he wasn't speaking to anyone. He was quite drunk. Strangest damn feeling. This party isn't a party. It's something I wrote about and it's come alive and I'm in it. Does that mean that I invented myself along with all these others? Or that fiction really does exist and isn't fiction at all? That it's a world that's just waiting underneath until some odd bastard like me scratches a pen which opens a door and out they rush? And if I were to tell them I invented them, or at least sprung them, what whould they say? Maybe they would say that I don't exist without *them*. And it is they who sprung me! Oh, luvvy! What a ring tailed bowl of spaghetti that is! Those two girls over there—I wrote five pages on them just last week. They were at this very fandango. And that little lunch mouthing pederastic peccary under the chandelier—burbling stuff about pop art—he was in a short story I wrapped up in that constipated week in Capri. One of my classier items too. Triumph of talent and trickery. Having to do with transvestism and the suspension of disbelief. And now I remember the creepy thing was that I felt like a drag queen after I finished it. Christ! Is that me over there? Are those two cunts over there me too? Oh mamma! I'd better check the fingerprint bureau before this thing goes too far. God, yes, I was under that rich Greek squid instead of the girl, the bone doctor who liked to bite and pinch because it made him so hot. I even ached for hours when he'd twisted my arm after tearing my dress off. And that Negro boxer who killed the boy in last year's story about Harlem—nobody would publish it because it was anti-Negro they said. I was ill with remorse for days because I'd killed somebody. Him too—is that me? My knuckles ached from hitting him. And yes, oh Christ yes, I talked like a Negro all the time I was writing it. Oh circus within a circus!

A wavering floaty deep underwater Italian girl's face appeared softly in front of George's. "You look very English, but English men don't look sad as you do. *Perche?*"

Before George could concoct a localized answer, a deep chested princely man materialized and took her gently by her glowing naked arm. "You must excuse Melina," he said. "She is always trying to invade the privacy of another's despair." The girl smiled at him, slow motion under water. A squeal of indeterminate pleasure skittered from the balcony and spent itself hysterically in the big big room.

After awhile George just disconnected himself and got out. All over Rome he tried to find himself in looking at others. He went to the Club Tritone to hear Lucia sing, and hung around there until he had quite a load on. Some of the movie crowd were there, too—DeVito and Hedda, an American director and a well-known refugee American actor, and a French actress named Denise something. He had a drink with them—they were all at the same table with De Vito—but he got bored after a bit because all they talked about was themselves, the movie industry and money. Jack wasn't around. Lucia said he was in Naples on business of some kind. He stumbled out of the place just before it closed. For some crazy reason, he decided that he didn't want a cab, that he wanted to walk all that way back to his hotel.

He might have asked somebody the exact directions, but he didn't. He pointed himself in the general direction of the Tiber and set off. It seemed that as soon as he left the immediate area of the Club Tritone he was swallowed up by darkness and confusion. Not a soul was in the ancient streets, and a quietness prevailed that he had never known before anywhere. It seemed to be the accumulated quiet of Rome's three-thousand years. He thought he was on a street that would eventually lead him to the avenue that ran along the Tiber, but at the moment when he expected to emerge into a recognizable place, it suddenly took a turn and became a tiny, cobbled, dead-end alley, where the shuttered windows of the houses and stores confronted him with an implacable, unmoving stare. He turned and started out again in a slightly different direction, reeling as he went because he was as drunk as could be, though he did not want to understand that fact.

The futile search continued. He was walking in circles or backtracking or getting farther and farther away from his objective, the slow-moving, mud-colored Tiber. What had started out to be a simple walk had turned into an increasing descent into a vast labyrinth, terribly complicated by his being a stranger and very drunk. He could not even give up the idea of walking and get a cab or bus because there were none to be seen anywhere. And there was nothing open where he could go to ask for help. On one tiny, foul-smelling back street he tripped over a broken wagon wheel and fell on his stomach in the gutter, and on another street, whose only sound was the lunatic, penetrating tick-tick of someone's alarm clock, he was suddenly threatened by a huge, mangy dog who, thinking he was a thief, chased him for a block, barking madly. He was beginning to lose all hope when finally he stumbled out of this part of the labyrinth and onto a street bordering the Tiber.

Now he thought everything would be all right and he would be in bed shortly. But he was wrong. This was a part of the Tiber he had never seen before. It looked like a strange lost estuary of it. The main part of Rome rose darkly from the opposite shore. He stood there for a few seconds, pulling himself together and looking wearily up and down the long emptiness of the avenue. Then his hopes jumped, for coming toward him out of the distant gloom were the headlights of a bus. He couldn't see any stop around, so he ran out into the middle of the avenue and frantically waved his arms at it as it bore down upon him. But it didn't slacken its rushing speed. He stood bathed in its headlights, waving and waving. For a terrible moment it looked as if the bus would hit him, but it suddenly swerved, missing him by just a few inches, and roared past.

"Wait for me!" he shouted after it. "Please wait for me!"

But it vanished down the darkness like some phantom express. He shouted violent curses after it.

Looking around, he saw that he was close to an old bridge. He walked over to it. It was roped off, and a sign said that it was being repaired. He didn't give a damn. He climbed under the rope and walked onto the broken-down old stone structure. It looked as though it had been half bombed out, rather than just fallen away with age. He hopped onto the side railing and slowly, carefully maneuvered himself across it. Every few seconds dislodged fragments of broken stone splashed into the sluggish Tiber below. He finally was crawling under the rope at the other end, thinking he was now near the end of this awful, nightmarish journey. But again he was wrong. He searched around for some landmark to guide himself, but there were none, so he just followed the first street that opened up to him. By this time his grip on himself had begun to slip, and between the drunkenness and the fatigue and the surrealistic sense of being lost in the oldest big city in the world, his mind felt slightly unhinged.

Halfway down the street—he couldn't even find its name printed anywhere, which only deepened the feeling that he was the victim of some cruel and insane dream game—he came to an ancient palazzo that was now a tenement. He pounded on its enormous wooden doors, but no one came out. Somewhere inside a cat mewed eerily, but that was all. It could have been a house of the dead. He wasn't getting anywhere, and his hands hurt from the pounding, so he pushed on. The end of the street opened out into a sort of square, moonlit and unreal-looking, at one side of which was a huge Romanesque monastery with many arches. He thought his salvation lay there, and he joyously ran to it. He couldn't find any bell, but there was a large iron ring for a knocker. He banged and banged on the door with it, and he could hear the heavy echo of it sounding strangely in the room behind it. Nobody came to the door. He was in despair. Was this house of God going to be unheeding too?

He circled around it, and on the second floor he saw some windows that were not entirely covered with that ubiquitous shutter. He scooped up a handful of pebbles from the ground and hurled them against the windows. After three barrages of pebbles, he was rewarded by a window opening. Three shaven young monks—or novitiates—leaned out of the window and looked down in amazement at him.

"What is it?" one asked in his high, girlish voice.

"I am lost!" he yelled up to them. *"Sono perso!"*

"Lei ha perso?" they repeated in those strangely high, unbelieving voices.

"Si, perso!"

"But why?"

"I don't know why, but I must find a place to rest."

"That is too bad. Who are you?"

"Sono Americano."

"Americano?"

"Si."

Then they looked at one another and giggled. It was too funny. A lost American, in Rome, in the middle of the night. What a funny thing it was.

"Where are you going?" they called down to him.

"I can't find my way home. But for the love of God stop all this talking and let me in. I must rest. I'm not well."

"Let you in? *Non e possibile.* There are no beds here."

"I'll sleep on the floor," he screamed hoarsely. He thought he was going a little crazy with all this.

"We're sorry, but it is against the rules to let people sleep on the floors here. It is too bad, *Signore Americano.*"

"You can't turn me away! Don't you understand? I'm lost and cold."

They whispered and giggled among themselves. "Have you been drinking, *Americano?*"

"*Si,* but . . . ."

"Ah ha! Then you are just having a good time. *Un Americano ubbriaco.*"

"*Non e vero!* Please help me!"

They laughed and waved goodbye. "*Buona notte, Americano.* Good luck." And they closed the shutters.

He wandered on. He lost all sense and reality. This was truly a nightmare. He staggered in and out of streets and alleyways, searching blindly, hopelessly, for something that would pull him out of this terrible experience, but there was nothing. Soon the streets ended and he suddenly found himself among some ancient ruins. They were all around him, bathed in the cold light of the moon. Huge pillars of stone standing alone, acres of broken stones, crazy half-archways. It must have been the old Roman Forum, where Caesar had been stabbed, where Mark Antony roused the mobs to furious vengeance. Then he heard voices and the soft crying of babies. They were coming from caves and hidden rooms among the ruins. He remembered dimly that it was in places like this that the beggars of Rome made their desolate, primitive homes.

He called out into the ruins. "Where are you? Help me!"

"*Via! Via!* Leave us!"

"Let me stay with you. I will give you money. I am lost."

"We don't want you. Leave us alone. Go away," they called back from their hiding places.

"But I will die out here."

"Then die out there. *Via! Via!*"

"Have mercy! I'm not going to harm you. I want to lie down."

"You are crazy," they called back like some doomful chorus in a ritual play. *"Via!"* And now they began to throw rocks at him. A fragment from an ancient tile floor hit him on the arm. "You don't belong here!"

He retreated into a part of the fabulous ruins where there were no voices. His body ached, his head tingled oddly, his mouth was dry, and he was very cold. In this insane dimension he had fallen into, he half-thought he was being attacked by an ancient, lost tribe of Roman cave dwellers, not by people who were his contemporaries at all. He pushed on, stumbling over chunks of marble, passing under huge arches, climbing Caesar's broken stairs. Soon he found himself in a different area of dreamlike, historic ruins. He was trudging along a weed-covered walk flanked by mammoth pillars when he began passing a long row of broken statues. He looked around and saw the skeletal remains of a temple, and it dawned upon him that he must be on the grounds of the Temple of the Vestal Virgins. He paused there to collect himself, and into his mind drifted pictures of thinly clad young girls kneeling before pagan altars filled with burning incense and devout offerings. Then he sat on the grass-covered steps and put his reeling head on his folded arms. He couldn't go any farther. He thought he was finished. He didn't care what happened. He was on the verge of slipping into a kind of coma, when suddenly church bells began to ring out in the distance. He raised his head. It was most remarkable. With the ringing of the church bells had come the sharp, clear light of dawn, so coincidentally that it almost seemed as if the church bells had magically summoned it. He began to walk through the grotesquely beautiful ruins toward the church bells. In a matter of minutes they led him out of the incredible maze he had been staggering around so helplessly in, and landed him on the wide Via de Fori Imperiali, from where he managed, though almost dead with fatigue, to return to his hotel. He could hardly believe it when he finally opened his door and collapsed into his bed.

FOR TEN CENTS EVERY MORNING I PURCHASE my ticket to the greatest spectacular since the earth separated itself from the sun and set up house on its own. A sea of black oil is discovered under the Polar ice cap. Four nuns set fire to themselves to protest death: Saigon. A woman claims she was abducted by a flying saucer: Maine. A Russian spy is discovered in the White House: Washington. A child slave market is uncovered: Mombassa. Ancient scrolls reveal that Jesus was a member of a whipping sect: Jerusalem. A shark is caught with a bag of diamonds in its stomach: Greece. (Don't tell anyone, Nichos. I won't. We'll split them. Okay? Stop? I saw you hide that one in your ear? Pig!) Who said you only dream when you are asleep! I do my newspaper reading in the park, after Sylvia has gone to work. I often fake sleep so that she will not question me about my life plans. My only answer would be, What plans does life have for me?

Zachary is supposed to meet me soon. Some of our best dialogs are experienced out in the open, where our environment is natural and in complete tune and oneness with itself. The trees, of course, have ears, but that does not mean they are tattle tails. He is bringing along a young negro psychiatrist who has become a student of Zen. "He wants to experience the Dharma on all levels," Zachary explained. "His couch often breaks down from its burden of confessions." Seven benches away, near a sycamore, Cedric is chatting with a clean cut sailor boy. We wave and leave it at that. I know that Zachary always gets hungry when he gives lessons so I have brought some salami and cheese, and some cold wine for myself. I am more of a gourmet than he is. But then my life is considerably more superficial than his. I hope to change. A group of pigeons are fighting over some salted Spanish peanuts dropped by an old lady in a wheel chair. I don't approve of such corrupting gestures. After you've queered up the birds, what's left? The loss of World Light, that's all. From where I sit, I can just make out Blaster's sleeping form on our favorite stoop. He is clutching an empty wine bottle—muscatel, of course. I'd better get him some vitamin pills. He doesn't eat right.

"How now, brother!"

It is Zachary. With him is the very soul of the white man's fantasy, a man so profoundly, immeasurably black that the night must shrink in his presence. Huge, muscular, and so very negroid, so African that for moments all I can hear are tom toms and wild spear dancing and the roars of hungry jungle beasts. I want to throw myself into his arms and be wondrously comforted and cured. His tongue is pink and thick when he smiles.

"Doctor, I've got a dream in the balcony," I say, giving him my most self-confident hand.

"I'll be right up." he replies.

"Now, now," Zachary cautions me, "we mustn't tire our guest with psychological problems. Jomo has been up all morning trying to locate a psychotic patient who escaped from the hospital."

"Oh?" I wish I could get out of this idiot verbal habit, but it is deep in me. Society's fault.

"It's a very unusual case," the marvelous Negro began, taking a seat on my right and lighting up a savory French whorehouse cigarette. "Very. She's a schizophrenic."

"Extraordinary," I murmured. (See what I mean?)

Zachary, who had helped himself to a piece of salami, leaned over and whispered in my ear, "Remember, the Dharma Wheel must keep revolving."

"I haven't forgotten."

"Anyway," the psychiatrist went on, "this girl—she is white and has an abundance of talent and sensitivity—is a tragic victim of both her family and society. Abandoned and deceived by Society, that eyeless beast who produces guilt without a conscience of its own, sets up the impossible rules, and the parents, aided by their own twisted minds, carry them out. What can a poor babe do against such powerful antagonists? Go insane, of course. What surprises me is that all of western civilization hasn't cracked up. But then," and he turned and gave Zachary a lovely, sad smile. "I'm not so sure it hasn't. Eh, maestro?"

"We must help man escape from his nest of abstractions," Zachary replied. "They are crushing him into small pieces."

"Yes," said Jomo (I felt I knew him well enough by now) "the fruit of Western logic. Separating man's heart from his mind. A divine temple divided against itself."

"Tell me some more about that girl," I said. These philosophical ruminations were all right but I wanted some facts. No matter how hifalutin' I may sound at times, I am basically a meat and potatoes man.

"To be sure," he said, blowing out a thin stream of saucy smoke. "This exceptional and quite beautiful girl—she's really a knockout, class and sex, a rich combination—has been having breakdowns for a number of years. Her family—name of Katz—regards these as acts of willfulness on her part. Can you imagine! They think she's doing it on purpose just to make their lives miserable. It goes without saying that both parents are very sick themselves, only they don't know it. The father is a wealthy crooked businessman just reeking with paranoia, and the mother is a case of gargantuan infantilism. She is a combination of little red riding hood and the wolf. Her greatest dream, unfulfilled of course, is to be the lead in a children's revue. The father secretly wishes to destroy the world before it destroys him."

Zachary dropped a small piece of cheddar cheese into his unhurried mouth. "Another distressing example of a human not being at one with the world."

"Maestro," Jomo said, flipping his cigarette out into the street (I had to restrain myself from going after it), "the best thing that could ever happen to this country would be to have all the churches torn down and replaced by Zen Temples. Because that's where all the trouble starts, in the churches. The groundwork for mass insanity is laid at the feet of Christ."

Zachary looked at me sadly. "You forgot the cream cheese."

"Factories of guilt, that's what Christian churches are," Jomo continued. "No other world religion has done so much to make man hate himself. And persecute others. Those spikes weren't driven into the messiah's hands, my friends, they were driven into the very psyche of western man. Every tenet of the church is calculated to separate man from nature, and thus from himself." He selected a piece of sausage. "This brings us, unavoidably I'm afraid, to the Jews. Because Christ was their idea. Pagan man was doing very well without him. He had his tree gods, water gods, sex gods, his magic rituals, everything. In other words, he was having one hell of a good time. Until the Jews came along and threw a monkey into the works. They just couldn't stand seeing the pagan having so much fun. They hated him because he was as full of natural joy and juice as a mountain stream. They absolutely wrecked him with the idea of one god. And the Virgin Mary and the Holy Ghost. Lordy! How sick can you get! But those Jews were sicker, and I don't mean maybe. They gave neurosis to the world, and that was the end of man's harmony.

"The Jews," he continued, rolling a piece of mortadella around a chunk of bread, "what a delicatessen of a people! You know, I've always felt that their monotheism wasn't so much religious, or spiritual, but a wily political strategy. One king or ruler, one god, the god being the ruler only in different clothes. It is so much easier to rule with one ruler. Can you imagine the confusion of one god and several rulers? And to go further, the concept of a re-deemer, or messiah, was still another political development. The Jewish lower classes were being so put upon and screwed by the middle and upper classes, that they naturally began to wish for and fantasize about a magic man who would set things right. A sweet, asexual avenger from the lower classes. So they dreamed up the Naz. And even managed to produce him, or several of him. What he did to the hard-assed stiff-necked middle and upper classes is history. He smashed them and dashed them, that's what he did. And all the underdogs were very happy. Yessir, that Jesus baby was pure and simple a social revolutionary fantasy. Religion was merely the sauce those cats put on the barbecue."

Zachary began combing out his sunbeam-reflecting chin locks. "It took the Chinese mind centuries before it could completely grasp the Buddah. The Chinese are a very down to earth people. They do not soar. They trudge. They wanted a very practical religion."

Jomo wiped his mouth and went for a Tab chug-a-lug. "What gives with the Jews? Ha! That is one of the fine fundamental questions of our time. My own humble views follow. First of all, they have abstracted themselves almost out of existence, and they have done the same to western man. They have torn man from his pagan and natural self and thus set him adrift in a new world of so-called ideas and goals. They have made him lose the simple pleasure of everyday living. Something cannot be enjoyed for itself. It must be connected with a life plan, it must get you somewhere. Ambition! The keystone of the abstracted Judaic system. Materialism! Judaism's greatest vice. You cannot control the world by owning all the objects in it. Superiority! God's chosen people. Oh the arrogance of it! It has separated them from their fellow men for centuries, and they lay the blame at the gentile's feet, accusing him of a baseless anti-semitism. How absurd of them!

"They are always preaching brotherly love and tolerance, and all that jazz, then they turn around and contradict it with this chosen people crap. And of course they plant and cultivate—oh Daddy how they cultivate! even in their sleep—this diseased germ in their children. And I ask you, are there children more monstrous and shitty in this gaseous world than Jewish children? Ach! They make sissy fat asses out of the boys and barracudas out of the girls. And talk—all they do is shoot their mouths off to show you how bright they are. They absolutely do not comprehend silence. They think it's defective. That it's against nature and should therefore be eliminated. What they don't know—and this is why I believe a Jew could never become a Zen Buddhist—is that silence is the mother and father of us all, The Great Intelligence! The Great Nourisher! The True Self! The Infinite of the Finite!"

Zachary held a cold bottle of Löwenbräu in mid air and looked happily at Jomo. "You are experiencing a moment of illumination, a sartori. Splendid," and he took a long pull at the beer.

I was getting pretty thristy too—philosophy and religion tend to take the juices out of me—so I opened a beer for myself and one for Jomo, who certainly looked like he needed refreshment after such an exercise into the inner workings of the Jewish mind. His face was sweaty and he was staring into space, as though he had just seen three horses tie for first at Belmont. He took the cold bottle with a robot gesture and drank it empty chug-a-lugging. I had always heard that black people were good drinkers.

"We must not fight the knowledge of the body with the trickery of the intellect," Zachary murmured. He had assumed a lotus position on the grass. A couple of old ladies who had been sunning their bare legs looked at him with apprehension, then moved two benches farther away. They were afraid he might go off like a hand grenade or something.

"I'll buy that," I said, "Tell me some more about the girl, doctor."

"Ah yes, that poor bedeviled girl." He grabbed another bottle of beer. That first bottle had relaxed him quite a bit. "Her sweetness had been contaminated by madness. Oh dear, if only I knew where she has fled."

I tried to help him by imagining where I would run to if I were schizophrenic and a girl, with ghouls like that for parents. I decided that I would head for a sauna in Helsinki. Short of that, I would very likely head for Bergdorf Goodman and buy up a big supply of jazzy underwear—but nothing with words on it—and several pairs of very expensive and fragile Italian shoes. I must confess that I can get very elated over a naughty foreign shoe. Yes indeedy.

"April baby! Where are you?" Jomo suddenly shouted. "Come back to Daddy!"

Hmm, I thought. A little counter transference here if you ask me. There are worse things, however.

"I know what you're thinking," Jomo said, putting his powerful hand on my shoulder. "But it isn't true. I love all my patients equally. And I don't prefer one kind of illness over another as some psychoanalysts do. Paranoics are just as attractive as schizophrenics." He stood up. (A low-flying pigeon who was cruising for peanuts just missed his head.) "They're all sick. They all need me —their big black Daddy. Or Mommy."

Zachary lifted his head and smiled very sweetly at us. "A beautiful paradox, Jomo. To need the very thing they hate—the black pariah. You are both there and not there." And he bowed his head again in universal oneness and tranquility.

This black man was vibrating so much I could feel my skin tingle, and it was the same as if the vibrations and words were coming from within me; there was nothing separating us. "They return to my milk sea, and wish to drown and be reborn in it. They cling to the terror of my staff, hoping to be smitten and yet given strength. It has lightning and love in it."

He paused again, searching the bushy park where scores of hungry, shy psychotics might be hiding, just waiting their chance to spring out screaming their particular menus. Now Cedric left his bench and strolled toward us. He was in regular men's clothes today, but his girlish swish was as fetching as ever. I knew exactly what was going to come out of his mouth as he passed us and threw me one of his more complex, left out in the cold, nobody desires me today, looks. "You girls talking about something real deep, aren't you? Well, take it from your sister Cedric, you don't know your ass from your elbow. And that's the truth."

Poor old ninny. I knew him so well. If he could only accept that, and stop trying to hide his true feelings from me, perhaps his closest friend, closer to him than he was to himself. He minced on down in front of the line of benches, hoping for a responsive glance from one of his kind, a glance that would say take me in your queer embrace and I'll do anything you want me to do, things they would put us in jail for twenty years for, only don't leave me alone on this unthinking, self-centered bench that doesn't care whether I live or die. Take me or I will surely go back to my jock strap apartment with its girlish decor and put my head in the oven and become a casserole of human garbage. Oh. Cedric, maybe you know where poor driven April is. People in hiding are your speciality.

"Chaps," Jomo said, "while our unconscious is working on the problem of April's whereabouts, I want you to glance over a little book review I'm thinking of writing for *The Guardian*, having to do with the black problem."

I believe I grabbed something from his hand and, while the others went on doing what they were doing, more or less read away.

"These are most creepy times. The leering stench of insanity floats happily through our streets. Screams of agony tear at the night, and star-spangled giggles pour from the television. Blood drips throughout the land, and our improbable leaders call for more plumbers.

"Words become bloated and mornoci and squat on our brains like circus freaks. 'Freedom,' 'loyalty,' 'decency,' 'democracy,' 'communist,' 'identity'. . . . Ugh. But the dreadful thing is that the people who utter them behave as though these words were star performers doing dazzling things in the sky. The more sensitive users feel somewhat awkward and guilty about employing such terms and words, and we must agree with them that, by and large, until a meta-lauguage goes into mass usage, we are all stuck with the traditional gibber.

"How is the ordinary Negro different from the Negro 'intellectual?' Is it that he doesn't think and feel quite as humanly? Is his 'crisis' on a slightly less classy level than the intellectual's? What is a 'Negro crisis' that Cruse can think of as such, as against the crisis we are all in at the moment? But what is an intellectual? Perhaps it is merely a person who reads a lot of books and who acts superior. 'Original thinkers.'

"To be specific: how would the demeaned, angry, hungry Negro in the street feel about a statement such as this by Cruse: 'With a few perceptive and original thinkers, the Negro movement conceivably could long ago have aided in reversing the backsliding of the United States toward a moral negation of its great promise as a new nation of nations.'

"Or this: 'The farther the Negro gets from his historical antecedents in time, the more tenuous become his conceptual ties, the emptier his social conceptions, the more superficial his visions.'

"Surely the ordinary Negro (and isn't this the collective human about whom the whole revolution is centered?) would laugh at it, if he were not offended by its patronizing pomposity. Throughout this massive and enervatingly 'intellectual' book, Cruse sounds like an aggrieved ancient psychologist telling his patient that he cannot possibly come to grips with (much less understand) his neurosis because he, the dreary patient, is not familiar with the history of phychoanalytical theory.

"It must be quite clear by now that I found Cruse passionately wrongheaded. Furthermore, in his opinions of the desperate current scene, he sounds disturbingly like a lot of white liberals who are peeved at the Negro (activist and just plain shouter and destroyer of property) for his lack of structured purpose. This irrelevant, and weirdly genteel, response to what is going on on the simplest human level, makes me think (and with real apprehension) of the use the IQ test is put to in the South to discredit Negro children and their right to an intelligent life. In this instance, unfortunately, the white power moderator is being joined by the intellectually outraged Cruse, a Negro.

"Cruse is completely hung up on 'culture': the concepts inherent in it, the purposes of it, its goals, and what he perceives as its *a priori* merit. He is as self-consciously predetermined by it as the 'rational' western mind is by Aristotelian logic. And like the acutely addicted Aristotelian, he sees human life in terms of it. He says, for example, 'Cultural nationalism must be expressed by all possible organizational and educational means that might further and equalize the status of the Negro artist as creator, interpreter, or critic. Such an aim is certainly in consonance with the cultural development of the Negro community.'

"That statement is not too remote from the one about how well the Negro can dance and sing. . . . "

I would have gone on had I not been interrupted by Jomo himself.

"I've got it!" he shouted, slamming his can of beer into an azalea bush. "I've just had an illumination. Oh, the sweet unconscious processes of vision! Oh, how miserable, how feeble is the conscious mind, my friends. Harlem, that's where we'll find April. Hiding in the forbidden but forgiving catacombs of Black Town."

Zachary was up from the grass in a moment's petal. "Another satori, Jomo."

Jomo hugged him. "Zachary, every moment is a moving tribute to the Buddha's wisdom. The Dharma Wheel is humming. We're off to Harlem, the very heart of America's shame."

I felt very happy about it too. The light downtown was too glaring, too prissy and abstract for me. It made flowers ashamed of themselves and squirrels too guilty to fornicate. We tumbled into the first free yellow bug and, giving our destination to a mottled thing at the wheel, settled back in our plastic-covered seat, happy with the way things were turning. I looked at Jomo, then at Zachary, who was smiling most deeply, and this smile made me feel less like my disenfranchised self than I had in a long, long time. It became a gentle ravine into which I fell with oh such lovely sensations, my complete, unreserved being merged into it as it fell, melting like snow flakes that are for a few seconds themselves, quite distinct from the landscape, then in a moment they have entered secretly into the landscape, smilingly, softly, as in lyric night conspiracy.

Sat in a cave for three years cleansing himself of absurd and useless thoughts so that he could see the simple truth of the Buddha's life and teaching. Why can't I, Zachary, do that? Sure I went to India and squatted in the mountains with those hairy gurus who chewed betel leaf all the time and went into hunger and drug trances and I lost twenty-five pounds and nearly all my western vices except for a few eating quirks, and I did get a toe hold on the Buddha, but only a toe hold. Man, it was tough. Thought I was going bughouse more than once. And no booze nor pussy. That was the worst denial of all. You've got to be a two-toed sloth to get along without those crucial items, no kidding. Both compounded, and compounders, of sixty percent fantasy, but then what isn't! Just tell me that. If you think that tree-happy park we're whizzing through isn't a fantasy, you just aren't in the lifegame. Bet the old man was glad I stopped asking him for money, at long last, a lifetime at his reluctant executive's tit. Cost two dollars a month to exist in that cow-shitted village. Could have made it on fifty cents less had I not insisted on a little fruit from time to time to take the taste of the germs out of my metamorphosing mouth. Dear oh dear, how a man's mouth can make demands on him! And before that, three years in Europe wandering around like a demented census taker of cultural positions and experiences, but still building toward the Dharma, going forward, going backward, one a crawl, the other a slide, greased by what traditional-and song-immortalized weaknesses. Man drowns his inner life with external things: Renzai, a ninth-century master, gentle like a rock, he was. Oh, that stretch in Munich!

How can one human being open his mortal pores to so many devilish stimuli!

"Darling," said the German countess with the animal eyes and half-exposed giant breasts, "You know very well it won't be at all difficult for you to arrange."

"No," I said, lying there half-dressed on that red velvet couch that had belonged to the Emperor Franz Josef. "Arranging it will be easy. It's just that I could get caught and do ten years in Sing Sing. That's all."

She smiled and caressed my bare chest and delicately ran her carnival tongue between my spectator's lips. "Don't be silly. What makes you think you will be caught?"

I began playing with one of her breasts, partly from pleasure, partly to calm myself down. "Because when you get involved in crime you also get involved with the police. And as much contempt as I have for cops, both military and the German over here, I still don't think they are completely stupid."

She discovered my ear with her tongue as an Elizabethan discovered the harpsichord, and no part of that quite uncynical organ of mine went unplayed upon. "You Americans! How you worry! Like children. And it's all because you are brought up with so much guilt. You are fed on it at your mother's breast. Life can be so simple and wonderful if you would only stop feeling guilty."

I began stroking her sun-tanned thigh. I had never seen a thigh so timelessly rich and sensual and female. I had dreamed about such measure-resisting thighs since I was a child. Thighs that hungered and smiled even in their sleep when other thighs have numbed out and have become loaves of bread in a darkened bakery. "Okay, Okay. I'll take the penicillin from the medical supply closets and turn it over to you. And then you sell it to your contacts, those two headed trolls, Klein and Wolf, and that's that. We're free. Loaded with dough and all that. But what about when they discover the stuff gone?"

She put her hand right where every nerve is gorged with lust and beauty and madness and possible murder, and I could feel my blood beast, my both light and dark soul, rise with consummate muscularity.

She laughed—laughter that is not heard anywhere in the world —not in streets or stores or living rooms or churches or at dinner tables, no—but in the giant grin of the bed. It is the laughter of the loins. "Oh darling. Who would ever suspect an officer of such a miserable crime? Poof. Even if they do discover it's gone, they will think an orderly or watchman did it—that's logical, isn't it? Stop being such a puritan, expecting punishment as the inevitable consequence of every act of pleasure or gain."

"What about my loyalty to my uniform and position?" I asked as she slowly took my throbbing beast, my Apollo and Prometheus, my symphony, out of my pants.

Those animal eyes, bred centuries ago in a forest, as her ancestors, covered with fur, growling and slavering instead of forming words, tore a bleeding stag to pieces, those eyes lit up in cunning amusement.

"Those are abstractions that have been used to manipulate you and make you a slave of a monstrous hoax and system."

And now my beast is raging in her hot mouth, and I can see the fragile flowers fold up in terror, and the other animals have lain still and stopped breathing and only the giant trees are strong enough to absorb the knowledge of this deep animality and the frightening consequences of its meaning. For nothing alive can stand in the way of its furious essence. Blood is its taste, and screams are its music.

The Countess and I are in the Marquis Bar celebrating with

champagne. It is two weeks later. The deed is done. The soft rustling in my pocket is the whispering of the bank notes and they are telling each other of their various powers and beauties. What a conversation! A thousand-mark note is bragging of the liquor it will soon command, and a ten-thousand note is chuckling over the number of people it can bribe and corrupt and ruin. Another bloated note is telling about a fur coat it recently obtained. They are indifferent to me, their presumed master. They don't care whether they are distracting me or not. Though they are in my employ, they know so well who is the real ruler in this land. I don't know what keeps them all from drowning the place in their ironic laughter. Not manners, certainly. That is the tearful and stiff prerogative practiced by their temporaty possessor. Empty rooms bring out loud voices.

"I simply adore this place," she says, looking cruelly chic. She wears a sweater with the pleased arrogance of a racing-car driver. "No one can afford any pretensions here, consequently they allow you to be yourself. Most places put such a burden of disguise upon one. So exhausting."

I examine my English suede shoes that cost thirty-five dollars. They look most contented next to my soft gray flannel Daks. They are not being mismatched, nor their class betrayed. "They've brought official charges against two of the men at the base."

"Marvelous! Let's drink to it." And she raises her glass after clinking mine.

"They will very likely be convicted," I continue, drinking to my own good health and position, "because they were somewhat involved in some black market operations before."

"Didn't I tell you it would all work out?" She smiles, and her teeth—such whiteness and sharpness—are imperturbable in their savagery. They have been repeatedly, and over the centuries, sweetened and cleaned by human bone marrow. "For an esthete, you don't believe as much as you should in the logic of poetry," she goes on, rubbing my hand.

"Maybe you're right. Maybe it would make me feel less like a son of a bitch because two guys are going to prison for something I did." I smile, a hospital smile, with the corners of the mouth only, the soul quite rigid. "Of course, that's a different kind of logic, isn't it."

She laughs and a couple of people turn around because it is so openly a bestial sound. "No, darling. That's still part of the poetry. Surprise and contradiction and injustice—all that is the poetry." She raises my hand and, aristocratically indifferent to the presence and looks of those she considers beneath her, sucks on my fingers. The radish-nosed, jelly-cheeked waiter tries to take this sucking in public in his stride, but he fails. He is immobilized in mid-errand and stares at her mouth swallowing my finger. "Living poetry." She sucks on my little finger and a tingling sensation claims my body. "One must not confine poetry to books, *liebchen*."

"I agree with you." I look around the gabbling, happily evil room. "We need all the living poetry we can get."

"Kiss me."

I lean over and her tongue leaps into my mouth like an assassin from a hiding place. It possesses my mouth for several ravened moments, then, out of embarrassment, I lean away. I ask myself what would all my dear ones say to this?

I look around. This room is a garden of depravity. The flora and fauna here should be in a museum. Thieves, prostitutes, pimps, murderers, traitors—and all of them so gay, so handsomely dressed, celebrating the success of their black arts. A tall, skinny American soldier, his arm around a very blond and stunningly sexy German girl, walks by out table. He winks at me. He knows the scene completely. At a nearby table an elegant German Nazi aristocrat talks softly with his made-up boyfriend. On my right a bloated man with a scar on his cheek is flanked by two very young greedy whores eating caviar sandwiches so fast you are sure they spent the war hiding in a basement. At the bar an American captain is drunk and loud. "I'm tellin' you, those fuckin French make me sick to my stomach. They're yellow, yellow and stinky as mustard. I just don't know how those bastards can live with themselves. If it was me, I'd shoot myself outa humiliation." He is a public relations officer. He has never shot a gun in his life.

Another Nazi comes into view. He is slapping someone on the back. He is full of good cheer. I study his pocked sly face, and terrible words pour into my ears.

"I estimate that at least two and a half million victims were executed and exterminated at Auschwitz by gassing and burning and that at least another half million succumbed to starvation and disease, making a total of about three million dead. This figure represents about seventy to eighty percent of all persons sent to Auschwitz as prisoners, the remainder having been selected and used for slave labor in the concentration camp industries. . . . The total number of victims included about a hundred thousand German Jews and greater numbers of citizens, mostly Jewish, from Holland, France, Belgium, Poland, Hungary, Czechoslovakia, Greece, and other countries. We executed about four hundred thousand Hungarian Jews alone at Auschwitz in the summer of 1944.

"This final solution of the Jewish question meant the complete extermination of all Jews in Europe. I was ordered to establish extermination facilities at Auschwitz in June, 1941. At that time there were already three other extermination camps in the Polish government—Belzek, Treblinka, and Wolzek. I visited Treblinka to find out how they carried out their extermination. The camp commandant told me that he had liquidated eighty-thousand in the course of one half year. He was principally concerned with liquidating all the Jews in the Warsaw ghetto. He used monoxide gas, and I did not think that his methods were very efficient. So at Auschwitz I used Cyclon B, which was a crystallized prussic acid dropped into the death chamber. It took from three to fifteen minutes to kill the people in the chamber, according to climatic conditions. We knew when the people were dead because their screaming stopped. We usually waited about half an hour before we opened the doors and removed the bodies. After the bodies were removed, our special commandos took off the rings and extracted the gold from the teeth of the corpses. Another improvement we made over Treblinka was that we built our gas chambers to accommodate two thousand people at one time. . . ."

A shrill redhead appears at our table and kisses the Countess. "Freda darling! You are looking so fabulous. How do you do it? How do you look so young and healthy all the time?" She smiles at me and darts to another table.

"Who is she?" I ask.

"A perfectly lovely girl. She was an informer for the Gestapo. She made a living out of executions." And she laughs.

"Let's go someplace else."

"Of course, darling. I know just the place. It is the most amusing bordello in Munich." She grins. It is a gesture comprising sexuality and violence, pain and exultation, degradation and some peculiar form of sublimity that is still beyond my talents. "I should say the most imaginative. Because the people there—I should say the performers in the theatre—are artists. They use their minds where others in their profession use only their bodies.

Our cab driver is an unusual one. He has escaped from a small touring repertory company, and taken only temporary refuge in this senile smelling taxi. He is red headed, his eyes seem focused on something immensely interesting in his past life, and his nose is ill-timed. I want to pull it. Also, my stomach tells me he is an American, although I am sure he would like to pass as a German sausage.

"What is an American doing driving a cab in Munich?" I ask him, though not with the sternness of a disappointed uncle.

He doesn't turn around; just cab driving the dying cab.

"Well?"

"*Ach*"

"Come on now, Herr Strudel. Out with it."

"Well, Governor, the fact of the matter is that I am in very deep at a local card house, and by driving this terminal case I am slowly working my way up out of that gaping debt."

"Good lad. I'll tell your mums when I see her," I say, and give my beard a few strokes, proprietory and sensual. The Countess puts her hand on my cock (this woman goes to the heart of the matter without any folderol) and it springs up in full gasping delight. The red-haired confidence man, the world-wide traveler, gambler, and double identity artist, and long nose, winks at me in the rear view mirror. Such cameraderie! Such presumption! Immediate intimacy is his goal; he wants nothing less than to be right inside one's skin. I am sure he would even assume my disease so as to identify himself more delicately with me. Who is he? Is he a mirror? An echo? A shadow with delusions of body?

The bordello is the unconscious come alive and decorated with lewd chic. It is a raging, ecstatic hydra with its faces painted and its body sheathed in black silk. It is a metaphor that is happily devouring itself and its maker. The madam, a black-haired, wide-hipped woman wearing mesh hose and an open-bosomed dress that demands immediate obeisance, exchanges a few sly and savory remarks with the Countess. Waves of heat vibrate out of her. Not an inch of her bonzai body has ever known a moment's normalcy. Her mother's milk was an aphrodisiac. She leads us through a baroque and heavily gorgeous salon that is writhing with her girls, her young artists. This is the casting office for a twenty-four hour sex festival. The entire history of western pleasure-vice —the inexhaustible art of the tongue, the positions and contortions, the melodies of the inner thigh, the power and subtlety and exquisite virtuosity of the hand—all is assembled in this cultivated orgasmic room. I have never seen so much exposed voluptuous cunt—so many breasts, thighs, asses, so many varieties of wild unrestricted beauty and willingness, walking about, sitting, lying down. I am no longer in the world of the excise tax and the public works program. I have entered Greek and Chinese mythology. I am myself among the cavorting figures in the bas relief who are for all eternity deaf to the cries of time and space and lusting and human frailty. I am in every museum in the world being stared at by school children and spinsters and old men who are telling themselves they are looking at us for academic purposes. Only a blind man could view us in such a way.

"These darlings are the cream of Europe," the madam is saying (Her name is Eva.) "They are the culmination of my life's work," and she wags her tongue at them in pure admiration.

"We want something very special, Eva darling," the Countess says. "We are gourmets, you know. No peasant concoctions."

Eva laughs, deep and heavy, the laugh of a winner. (Losers have funny vocal chords.) "Everything that goes on here is *haute cuisine.*"

She leads us upstairs to a large heavy-lidded room with a giant-size—it must have come out of Homer—bed in the center. This bed is the stage. There is nothing that cannot be performed in it. Its dimensions are infinitely plastic. It is the theatre of lust. The performers will do anything you like; they are all yourself. Rich colors and fabrics, designs and clever arrangements join to create a frou frou vortex that sucks your mind from you. Two fat, smiling chairs await us, the audience. I feel I am really sitting in a huge perfumed woman's lap. I sink into her downy thighs and forget about who I am. Perhaps, of course, there is no exclusive me. Perhaps I am all these other people, perhaps I am really all that

I observe. Therefore what I am watching at all times, whether here or in the streets, are actually projections and parts of myself. I am the observer and the observed. Who knows?

The Countess holds my hand, not out of affection but to keep from drowning in the swirling waters of her desires. In a few thick moments we are watching a strange show of genitalia on the stage. Two men and two women glide out from the wings. Their nude bodies glow and vibrate as they receive the full charge of my mind's fantasy orders; my energy is pouring into their nerve cells, my energy and the Countess', who is painfully gripping my hand with lustful force. The men—they are truly faceless, all expression is gone, as if drugged away, but this is quite right, because the real face is mine—have enormous cocks, the biggest I have ever seen. I can see children chinning themselves on those iron-bar hard-ons. The women . . . one is small, with tons of black hair and very pointed breasts; the other is endowed with sleepy undulant thighs that belong to some prehistoric period in the earth's evolution. Layer upon layer of civilization is contained therein. Tribes of hunters and warriors have for thousands of years roamed those swelling valleys and hills. They hold hidden in them the cry of the dying, the wild shouts of war and drunken fireside reveling. The hair between them (what plunges they have cushioned) is exuberantly insane auburn. Careless hikers, drunken picnic groups have been lost in its denseness. Attila the Hun and his great-grandfather still snooze there in contented oblivion. They smile in their sleep as they think of the glassy-eyed, student searching parties looking for them in school history books. *Ach!*

They are arranging themselves in delightful positions (I have an irrational fear that the hard-ons may snap off.) The small dark girl is sitting in the lap of one of the men. He is biting and licking her back and pinching her nipples. His fierce rammer protrudes between her thighs. The other girl is on her knees with her head between the dark girl's legs swallowing his flagpole. The other faceless fellow has his storm machine in the wildly hungry mouth of the seated girl. They are performing all this on the floor and on a low chair. Such a feasting! I don't know which part of my body is getting the most thrills. I am merging with each one of the performers, I am all of them, I am even the Countess who is still breaking my hand and breathing heavily as small diamonds of sweat appear on her face and neck.

They have rearranged themselves, and the girls are beginning to moan and whine in real bestiality. They are back there in the caves with the animal skins and blood-stained clubs and the glistening bones of their dinner on the ground around them. One of the girls is licking the other between the legs while one of the men —he has a head covered with blond child's ringlets which are superbly incongruous—is plunging into her ass from behind, and he is spurred on in his effort by the very muscular other one who is whipping him with a short but quite significant black whip. This darling of the tormented flesh has been handed down from master to master, through the ages. It wakens only to sounds of needed pain. It is an instrument of divine chamber music. Their orgasmic spasms blend and become one in an inimitable tangle of yells and whip sounds and flesh. Next to me the Countess has closed her eyes and is emitting short cries of pain and joy as her body writhes in consummation with the others.

Now we all rest. The performers are stretched out on the huge bed in crazed positions. The Countess has her eyes closed, and her hand has given mine back to me. The madam, who has stripped to her working uniform—a black bra with holes cut in it so the nipples can see, long black hose supported by a red garter belt, and high stiletto heels—is serving me champagne. She puts a glass in the Countess' hand, and this brings her to: the promise of another kind of pleasure, something bubbling down the mouth and into the belly and bloodstream.

"We have a splendid American black man who performs with us on weekends," Eva said casually. She laughed wisely. "He says he does it because he needs the money. But I know better. It is his heart's desire. He is gifted with the largest and most brilliant liverwurst I have ever laid eyes on. Utterly amazing."

"He must be completely untouched by the class struggle," I observe, sipping the sharp champagne. "How lucky he is to be a Negro."

"You talk very odd for an American," she says.

"I am odd."

The Countess smiles. "He is studying to be a Zen master or something, Eva. He is full of unusual ideas—and desires. Aren't you, darling?"

"You said it." She wouldn't understand even if I explained the whole matter to her. The deeper needs of man are beyond her reach. What she knows, she knows extraordinarily well—the woman's a genius in her way—but the action ends right there. From the tangled bed the red cunt smiles at me. I blow it a kiss. I watch it as it glides through the spermy air and lands softly on the pink and sated clitoris. The kiss and the clitoris, they are ancient friends. Nothing will ever come between them. They need each other too desperately.

"Don't you adore Lola?" Eva asked me.

"Which one is that?"

She points a finger, smothered in rings. "The small one. She came all the way from Mexico. What exquisite qualities she has. She must have inherited them from her mother, who was a nun."

"I used to know a most unusual priest," the Countess says. "But he hanged himself one day in the bell tower. He left a note saying he had betrayed God. Can you imagine!"

"Yes," I say, but mostly to myself.

A few more drinks—I am stoned—and another performance begins. It involves another member of the animal kingdom. A Great Dane has appeared. It is black and almost the size of a pony. "It was used as a guard at Belsen," Eva whispered. The men sprawl on the floor. They are classical Greek statues, eternal in their psychology and place in life, leaving the bed to the two girls, whom the presence of the animal has excited and yet frightened. A feverish smile has crept over the faces of the girls. The animal majestically surveys them. Its heavily muscled body glistens. Slowly it approaches the bed, its breath coming heavier now, and its mouth is open wide, exposing a powerful, insatiable red tongue, a tongue that is accustomed to getting what it wants. Grinning, Lola reaches out and pets its face. The beast begins to twitch. Lola runs her hand down its awesome body, strokes its heaving belly, then slowly begins to play with its balls. The beast whimpers and growls. Next to me the Countess has gone rigid with fascination. Her face is a staring mask. I cannot tell whether she has become one with the girl or the animal. For myself, I have become the animal. I feel the girl's hand on me. My haunches tremble. My throat is thick with growls. My tongue is wet and aching. My fangs are bared fiercely. I want my quarry!

Its great cock has emerged, and its growls have increased in depth and hunger. Carefully—her face has gone demonic with this descent into the beast world—Lola now kneels on the bed with her backside to the animal. It puts its front feet on her back and she guides his thrusting, burning cock into herself. A shrill cry excapes her. A veil has been torn from a part of her being by the dog's savage entrance into her. He slavers and barks and pumps into her and she is beside herself, shouting demands and instructions at it as though it were a human being. Huge bleeding scratches appear on her back from its ripping claws. My ripping claws. The agony and sublime sensation overwhelm me. I bite her, and her scream is one of infinite gratification. The taste of her blood is sweeter than that of any animal I have ever torn to shreds and devoured. It makes me feel human, I have partaken of the communion. I swoon into velvet oblivion.

HARLEM! (I FELT STRANGELY DIZZY, AS IF I HAD just wakened.) You stink so good. Nothing fastidious and nervous-making about you, Momma. You don't shave your armpits. You don't hide the saliva in your mouth. No girdle suppresses the lovely hello daddy shimmy of your ass. Thank the bon dieu for your existence. One day I'll endow a high class college in your honor. Studies in Black Twat.

"I just know we'll find that troubled girl up here somewhere," Jomo said, looking up and down the street and at the ghetto windows.

"I feel that way myself," I chirped. (I sometimes sound like a bird.) "What about you, Zachary? Does your belly say yes to that intuition?"

Zachary made me a gift of a first class eleventh-century Zen smile. "When water is scooped in the hands, the moon is reflected in them," he replied. "When flowers are handled, the scent soaks into the robe."

Jomo embraced him. "You put your finger right on it, old buddy."

I knew of course that Zach was referring to a revealing exchange between a questing Buddhist monk and the great master Kon, who lived in Pa-Ling, down the valley. According to the best sources, this naive monk said to Kon, (also known as Chien), "Is there any difference between the teaching of the Patriarch and that of the Sutras, or not?" And Kon had lobbed back with that poetry about the water and the moon. I hope the monk got it. Some of those guys could be awfully thick.

We stood amidst the swirls and eddies of that nourishing black mainstream and sent out our signal vibrations in every direction. April, April, April—and waited for that tiny girl vibration in response—I'm here, I'm here, I'm here. God's entire gimpy show swept around us: slow-motion drunkards encased in their interminable soliloquies; blind beggars tapping on the nerve center of your conscience with their white sticks and their huge rolled-up eye balls; water-melon-breasted housewives in tidal waves of blubber, embracing groggy bundles of pigs feet, chicken backs, chitterlings and/or tails; rubberband-faced pimps leaning continually against the fenders of their purple Cadillacs and fondling sheafs of orgasm money; lewd smiling high-heeled mulatto undulations named Lurleen and China Doll; half asleep, stoop-loving junkies; screaming children in relentless pursuit of one another's vulnerabilities; white-haired runaway slaves muttering to themselves, answering the plantation owners in Swahili. And the smells! A symphony of odors: Odors with sounds! Odors with colors! Odors with souls!

"You boys lookin' for anything in pahticulah?" A sly man with spaniel eyes asked, swaying a little in his run-down heels and keeping his hands secret in his baggy pants.

"No, Gramps," Jomo said with a tribal smile. "Everything is copacetic. As you can see, I'm black too." "No you ain't," the man replied, turning to go down the street, "you jus painted yoah face, man," shuffled away, singing a hand-me-down ballad about the sufferings of men and the undoubted second coming of Christ.

"Let's go into the Baby Grand," I suggested. "That place knows everything."

Jomo agreed that a trip to the Baby Grand bar-restaurant-cabaret would surely help us in getting oriented. One thing I really liked about him is that despite being a combination of father-mother substitute, God, and, as a doctor, an authority image, he was not loath to take suggestions from others. Any time he decided to give up medicine, he could make a living as a human being. A lot of people I know who are very successful, would starve to death at that job. There are people who have trouble even dreaming right, which will give you an idea of the kind of trouble they're in. We headed north in our quest. Zachary was in fine shape, smiling at all the other exotics who were smiling at him. His sheet robes and long beard seemed most natural up here.

"They caught two missionaries trying to cross 110th Street last week, and they castrated them on the spot."

It was the Boy Killer, Blaster. He had appeared, as they say, from nowhere. It's possible, of course, that he had been with us all along only I didn't notice him until now. His goofy eyes glistened with alertness, his breath had only the faintest whiff of the sauce (I guessed it was sherry) and despite his 49 years, he could have passed for a twenty-year old. It was a marvel how that man defied the machinations of time. His youthful bloodbaths must have permanently altered his chemistry. Maybe he ate his victims, like a cannibal, and rejuvenated himself with their human essence.

"Serves them right," I said.

"You can say that again, pardner."

Hunger overcame us enroute to the Baby Grand, so we all stopped off at Lady's Place for some simple traveler's nourishment. While we were stoking in chittlin's, black-eyed peas, and a few pigs' feet cooked with hot peppers, Zachary kept our minds alive with an account of the growth of Zen Buddhism in China. How the Chinese were puzzled and stunned by the Indian metaphysics and poetry, both alien to their own pragmatic imagination, and how they gradually accommodated it to their unique character. Zen Buddism in China became a simple, direct way of handling one's day to day existence. All the fancy analytical and conceptual shenanigans, so dear to the literary and intellectual members of the Zen Buddhist sects, were finally cast aside. The Sutras had to go if Zen were to take root in the totally different soil of Chinese reality and necessity. You cannot sing *The Star Spangled Banner* with a mouthful of Greek retsina wine. All that far out Indian symbolism and pyrotechnics would have driven the Chinese plodders crazy after awhile. Also, the Zen masters had nothing to do with the classical Chinese modes of expression; they preferred to use colloquialism, the living language of the streets, as their medium of getting across their inner experiences. They wanted no part of back talk.

"I promise you that very soon I will introduce you to Yu-lu or

Goroku, the collected Zen writings," Zachary said, wiping up his black-eye pea pot liquor with a piece of cornbread.

"Zachary," Jomo said solemnly, "you have changed my life. I was a frustrated child before you brought me to the Buddha. I was mooning in the darkness."

"The lake never overflows," said Zachary, and in a few moments our little searching party had hit the road again, after thanking Lady. (Her smile was a South African gold mine.)

"I used to eat at the Palmer House everyday," said the Boy Killer. "Lunch never cost less than fifteen dollars, and dinner, I always had that at the most elegant clubs in Chicago. Picked up the check for everybody too."

"You took very good care of yourself," I said in a very friendly and comforting way.

"I had to. I lived hard."

"Worked hard too."

"You betcha."

I looked to see if there were any tears in his eyes, but there were not. Memories of great times can make the toughest of us cry —which is very odd, when you think about it. Great anything should make people smile. Something made me look across the street to the doorway of a baffling senile tenement. Just in time to see Sylvia, her black, sad-story laden briefcase under her arm, and an expression of both zeal and futility on her face, trot up the stairs. I wondered if she any longer went to the trouble to write down the myths she heard from those petitioners, in their underwear and stockinged feet. I think you would have to be Homer to do that.

The Baby Grand was a veritable depot of knowledge. Every underground pursuit or profession was represented there. Pickpockets, drug pushers, strongarm men, prostitutes, faggots, pimps, informers, plainclothes men, lesbians, con men, and begging nuns who weren't nuns. I believe you could have located Jesus Christ there if you had looked hard enough.

Jomo circulated among these apostles—some stretched out at small tables, others leaning on the big circular bar—looking for a lead as to April's whereabouts, while Zachary and the Boy Killer and I made ourselves comfortable in a reasonably dark and certainly uninquisitive corner under a light so that we could see each other, for the place was indeed on the cave side. The Killer and I both ordered shots of bourbon—we had one set up for Jomo too —and Zachary consented to a Seven-up.

"She is not really hiding," Zachary said softly, "She is merely escaping her tormentors. Quite a different operation."

The Killer nodded his handsome young head. "I know what you mean. I've experienced some of that myself. No fun, I'll tell you. No fun at all."

I said it was a wonder that half the world wasn't doing the same thing—and as soon as I had said it I realized that this was exactly the case. One half bent upon destroying the other half. No wonder that it rains blood and tidal waves wash away entire cities. Judgment Day can't be far off, I'm convinced of it.

Zachary began peering intensely around the place. "I sense there is a Zen brother here somewhere. But for his own reasons he is being extraordinarily quiet and self-effacing. He has found something here that is tranquil and nourishing. I wish he would make himself known to me," and he kept searching the shadows and the possible disguises.

"I used to know the crowd up here," said the Killer, talking more to himself, really, than to us. "Honey Johnson, Big Boy Harold, The Slider, Baby Fats, all those fellows. You couldn't want a finer bunch of men. They were wonderful to do business with. You always knew just where you stood."

"That's the only way to have it," I said. "Keeps the air clean."

Two relentlessly gorgeous hustlers—one with a cyclone of platinum hair that was breathtaking against her hot brown skin; the other with the most sublime and richly self-contained ass I have seen this year, an ass that could provoke a Congressional uprising any time it wished—these two lovelies, sipping shots of gin at the bar, had been glancing our way and smiling in wide open comradeship, now sauntered over to our table.

"How you boys doin'?" the platinum lady asked, putting her hand on my shoulder.

"We're just paddlin' along," said I.

"How 'bout a little party?" the other one said, bending over slightly so we could get a tastier view of her dark lunch.

"We could sure give you boys a good time. All kinds fun. An it wouldn't cos' you uh million dollahs eithah."

"I regard recreation as a form of health," the Killer said, smiling sweetly. Zachary had his mind on other things, for he was beaming at the ceiling, as if he had located one of the Fourfold Truths swinging up there.

"Ladies," I began, as one of them caressed and aroused my ear, "I would like nothing better than to devote the next forty-eight hours to having a topsy turvy, slam bang and no holds barred party with you, but the fact of the matter is that we are on urgent business. A human soul is missing and we must find her. She needs us, we need her. But I can assure you that when our search is done, we'll have a party that will absolutely astound the natives. My word on it."

Platinum gave me an unmitigated, unstunted wet kiss in the neck. "Okay, honey, if that's the situation, then we'll just have to congregate our talents and appetites some other time. History will hafta wait, thas all." And they wafted back to their main office at the bar. If only half the white women downtown could move like that, General Foods and Revlon would go broke, and vanish from memory. Archaeologists five-thousand years from now would dig up a shard of eyebrow pencil and break their poor hearts trying to figure out just what caused the collapse of our civilization.

"How goes it, Zachary?" I inquired, putting away some of the local gargle.

"Lovely. I am reclining on a dyhana. This place would be perfect for a Zen monastery. The walls are made of truth."

The Killer leaned over and whispered in my baby left ear, "I've been meaning to ask you: is this guy on drugs?"

"No," I whispered back, through the years of his incomprehensions. "He is with the Bhodi Dharma and everything is more than all right."

His voice made its way through Chicago, President Roosevelt, and Glen Cunningham. "Because I've known some dope addicts in my time and I can tell you they do nothing but queer up the action."

"Be at peace, Killer. He is realer than real."

"Okay. If you say so."

"Just put your mind where your money used to be and you will see it all as clear as a newborn raindrop."

Jomo's earnest but very trustworthy voice came to me from a

shady glen far to my right. It was a rich voice, experienced, trav-
eled, accustomed to secret areas of barter and dialectic, to twining
itself around other voices in life and death lashings. Now it was
offering flour and whiskey for ivory tusks; a few minutes before,
in a clearing in the forest (wild orchids were there and water
buffalo droppings), he had been offering guns and love potions for
two of the chief's nubile daughters who were watching the whole
thing from the limb of a eucalyptus tree and giggling. He was both
the Great White Hunter and the Great Black Hunter without a
novella of conflict. His cool was the size of Cheops. It was difficult
for me to tell what language he was speaking in. The words I
swallowed tasted like English, but once in my stomach they darted
about more like night language, which one understands only in
sleep.

An escaped convict materialized at our table and I ordered
another round of juice. A big razor scar enjoyed complete occu-
pancy of his right cheek, and his ankles and wrists still gave off the
faint but unmistakable sounds of chains and manacles, "Pain or
pleashuh, thas what it boil down to," he said, wiping the table off
with his long-suffering apron. "This worl' doen change century
frum century cept et gettin coldah, an thas cause all those atom
bombs been wakin up all dat ice in de Arctic."

A wild melody of forbidden laughter escaped and danced from
a woman's throat and enhanced every nook and cranny for moments. The waiter chuckled. "Oh, de delishus wondah of black
pussy." He scratched his chin and examined me carefully with
huge bloodshot eyes. "Yoah coluh is white, but ah think you a
niggah like me," and he gently rubbed my head.

"You're not far from the truth," I said. "How about another
round? Anything . . . scotch, vodka, aquavit, brandy—you name
it, brother."

"Bell's Twelve," he said, "a man mah age got to treat himself
good."

A loud and heated exchange broke out (it really did give you
the feeling of having been imprisoned) at a nearby oasis. Two
middle-aged elegants, one with black mutton chops, were shouting about the fighting merits of a lion and a gorilla. Weaving in
and out of their areas was another voice, coming from a hidden
loudspeaker, and it was singing-talking about first love; so that in

the same breath you heard gorilla powers, virgin sex, and lion blood lust. It was impeccable stuff. Byzantine gold thread tapestry work. Don't make it like that anymore. Faraway I saw Jomo get in a bark canoe and head out for a small bushy island. A great, unflagging searcher. His guide, a mere boy, was sucking on a piece of sugar cane.

"I wonder if you can help us," I ventured when the waiter brought the drinks back.

"Trah me."

"We are looking for a runaway white girl."

He just had to laugh, rich rolly laughter. "You white boys sho have trouble with yoh women." And he laughed some more. "Sumpin wrong somewheah."

"I wouldn't contest that for a second, Colonel. But it's a topic that we'll have to set several days aside for. Meanwhile, this runaway is an adorable blonde who is called April. Does that ring any chimes?"

A woman's voice behind me: "Man, it gonna cost you money to put yo' hand theah. I ain't no charity organization."

The Colonel (I don't know how I learned that was his name) pulled up a chair, and sipped thoughtfully on his straight twelve-year-old scotch. "Yeah. Ah can help you all, ah think." He closed his eyes and sank into his semi-conscious grab-bag. He was like a medium getting signals from Over There. In a few velvet moments he opened his eyes. "Uhuh. Thas the girl all right. She's lyin' down in an apahtment on a hundred-an-twenny-secon' street, two-twelve, an the flat numbah is 5-a. Name of Washburn." He grinned warmly. "An she ain't got no clothes on neither. Mole on her right knee."

"Hot damn!" I said, and clapped him on the back, an act I ordinarily stay away from. "Colonel, you are a living miracle."

He smiled and drank off that scotch joy. "It came from mah muthah's sahd. She was the worl's greatest possum trackah."

"We going up there right now and save that girl."

"Tell huh that Colonel Applebaum sens huh his very bes'."

In less time than it takes to be in a fight, the four of us were fudged into a darting yellow menace piloted by a reformed Latvian long distance swimmer who managed to get us to our destination by contradicting only two one-way streets and a red light.

"You could use a little therapy, old chap," Jomo told him when he was settling the meter. "Your driving is a classic example of a strong death wish."

The driver gave him a Bronx cheer. "It may interest you to know that I'm an analyst myself, moonlighting, and that Freudian death urge bit is a lot of fennel seed."

The Killer shook his head as the cab sped off. "In the old days we would have let him have a hole in the belly for that. There's no respect anymore. Nobody has the good breeding to be afraid."

A loud explosion, and we were spattered with water. A child's wild giggle from a rooftop. A paper water bomb had been dropped at our feet, meant for a head. A garden of giggles from child mouths and brains. "You de enemy!" a voice shouted. "We gonna destruct you!"

"Let's get upstairs and save that tormented child!" Jomo shouted.

The door of apartment 5-a was ajar, so we walked right in. It took me a couple of moments, at least, to locate April, among the bodies. Four nude human forms were sprawled about the place, on the floor and on a large bed. Two black forms and two white—two white women, two black men. April was one of them, on the bed. They were in a half awake trance. April's eyes were closed, and she was smiling. After staring at them, Jomo said,

"They're all on a trip. Everybody here is juiced up on LSD." He kissed April's left ear several times, "Oh baby, what country are you flying over?"

The thought of violating this poem with a crass prose triad disgusted me (can you imagine a flower being struck by a stone?) so I immediately, but with no crude jerky notions, just slidy ones, took off all my clothes (Zachary and Jomo and the Killer followed suit as they got the idea) and wafted over to April; deepest meditations on the bed. My nakedness and calculated vulnerability became intermingled with hers. I disappeared into a sigh, and the last words I felt coming out of me were uttered in alloyed metal by the Boy Killer. "This sure as hell ain't like the old days in Chicago. The kids then just got drunk and passed out dead. But this bunch . . . Holy blue Jesus. They look like they're in what the scientists would call suspended animation. No pain here at all."

Except in me, in my stomach. Could it be the old pains from

when that slippery tongued wop bastard Santelli clipped his shoe into me in that alley off Wabash when I was carrying all that dough meant for The Kraut? Need a long sweet drink of Thuringen. Mm, Baby, is that sweet and hot and soothing. Better than any doc's medicine. Numbers money. Low down dirty job. Luggin' numbers money. Me, the kid blaster, with a .38 tucked in my belt that has a kiss as sweet as any in the country. Got my tenth man with it by my twenty-first birthday, a squinty-eyed, rat-nosed fatty who ran the bakery rackets. Fellow named Feigenheimer. He was very obstinate with The Kraut about a small partnership deal which The Kraut had dreamed up, and he also called The Kraut something quite dirty. So I blasted him. While he was in the men's room of one of his bakeries. I was dressed up like a delivery boy so I could get in the place without a lot of suspicion. Made me feel funny as hell with that kid's jacket and hat on. A big doughnut on the back of the jacket, and the words said Wake Up with Feigneheimers. Yeah. Go to Sleep with Feigenheimer now. He never said a word, went down without a whimper. Like plugging a jelly doughnut. Boss gave me a raise for that one. But then he made me carry the money because big Phil Noonan was sick with pneumonia, or bursitis, I can't remember which. Either way, it all came from drinking too much bad whiskey.

"You sure pud avay a lot of dad sauce, Philly boy," The Kraut told him one afternoon as we were sitting around "the office" at the Palmer House.

"I got to," Phil said. "If I didn't, I wouldn't be able to face it."

"Faze what?" the boss said, looking like he'd just opened the bathroom door on a little old lady.

"The craziness of life," Phil said, and had himself a slug from a flask he kept in his jacket pocket.

Phil was okay though. He'd been a real first-class second-storey man until a cop shot him in the foot. Blew two of his toes right off. "I think the bastard used a dum-dum bullet," Phil told me. "But I got even with him. While I was in the prison hospital I had a friend of mine fix the brakes in his wife's car. Oh mother of Jesus! Killed the driver and put the old lady in the hospital for months with a broken neck. Made me me feel a lot better. Justice, that's what it was. That cop had no good reason for shooting my toes off.

Just dirty damn meanness. And besides, it turned me from a first-class burglar into a damn money messenger." Jesus, could he put the booze away. He must have had 90-proof blood coursing through his veins.

Santelli must have been following me all morning. Maybe several mornings to know my collection route the way he did. I slipped out of the side door of Conlon's Bar and Grill, made a left turn into the alley, and there Santelli was. Smiling like he'd just had a big bowl of his mother's spaghetti, dressed in a real loud striped blue suit and a polka dot tie. Christ, those dagos sure come on loud in their clothes. Must be that hot climate they're raised in.

"Let's have it, Killer," he said, with that spaghetti smile, and a switch blade was in his dark hand.

I went for my gun, and that was when he slipped it into my stomach. Oh mother of God. It hurt and made me sick at the same time and when I felt all the blood oozing over my hand when I grabbed at myself I thought I was going to die. "Fuck you, Santelli," I said and slowly fell down. He just stood there and laughed. Then he reached his hand into my inside pocket and lifted the dough. Just like that. And left. Not running. Walking. He knew I wasn't going to chase him. My Mother's blood was pouring out of me into that alley dirt and I was trying not to scream. Sticky and warm and had a funny smell. They finally got Santelli and dumped him in the lake for fish food. But he killed two of ours before going down. He was a tough wop all right. Good with his hands too. Used to be a prize fighter I think.

My mother couldn't stand violence. That's why she got rid of the old man. He liked to shout and fight, but he pushed her around once too many and she had him put away. Hanged himself in jail. Poor bastard. Mother couldn't stand my friends either. And she was always warning me about dames. "Babylon isn't the only city of whores, son," she would say. "The world is full of evil women. They'll take all your strength and goodness from you, then throw you away like garbage. Just be careful. Remember, your body is a sacred temple." Lived with her till the day she died. In that flower-wallpapered upstairs bedroom where I was born. Toys were all there too. Big teddy bear sitting right on top of my dresser. Christ it was strange waking up with a hangover ('course,

I came home late and sneaked in light so I wouldn't wake mother; she thought I was a teetotaller) and seeing all those toys and animals looking down at me!

Mother thought I had a desk job with Armour and Company. Meat Packers! I was one of those all right. And I told her I belonged to a lot of clubs like the Y and the All Christian Bowlers so she wouldn't ask me why I was out every night. Never forget the time we were at the breakfast table (she made me eat cereal just as I did as a boy) and she read in *The Tribune* about two guys I had blasted just the day before. She was trembling like a humming bird she was so upset. "This poor city has become a murderer's lair," she cried. "Human life has no meaning or value. Blood is being spilled like water. And the police aren't doing a thing about it. Oh, angel boy, what a pity it is that you aren't a police officer. You would catch and destroy these mad beasts in a matter of days. Hours perhaps. What a desperate shame it is that men of courage and character like you, angel boy, aren't protecting our streets from the madness that rages in the human soul."

Poor Mother. What she didn't know, among other things, was that I didn't feel at all mad when I was blasting. Didn't feel one way or the other except that it was something that had to be done. Only time I felt angry and crazy was when I had to kill Carola and that lousy punk she was putting out for behind my back. One of the boys, Toots Hauser it was, tipped me off about it. "Killer, I don't wanna seem like a squealer or anything, but I think it would innarest you to know that your girl friend ain't exactly dying of loneliness while you're out earnin a livin' wage. At this very second she is having a party in the Hotel Ansonia with a character name Chuck Madden. Room 14a. It's to your left when you get off the elevator." Listening to him telling me this is a slick Jewish guy named Katz. Real dude. He handles the shakedowns for the Boss.

I am feeling all empty and cold inside like a barn when nothing and nobody is in it, no birds or mice or anything. Cold and empty and afraid, but I don't know what of. Because I am not the afraid kind. I am now in that awful hotel. I nod to a couple of the fellows in the lobby, but no conversation. They saw me a lot with Carola. I took her everywhere. I am in the elevator and I can barely stand that long ride to 14. I feel like screaming. One of the old cleaning women is coming toward me with a floppy mop in her hand.

"Mother," I say, slipping a ten spot into her old fat hand, "I want to play a little joke on a friend in 14a. Would you give us the key?"

She smiles. Old ladies love my young boy face. A lot of them can't keep from patting it. "All right, angel face," she says, touching my cheek, "just for you, I'll do it." She looks like she's going to kiss me or hug me. "You sure must be a joy to your mother."

"You're an old sweetheart yourself."

"Give me the key back on your way out," she says, and winks.

My hand is shaking so much I have to try twice to put the key in. I hear them laughing inside. It's the worst sound I have heard in my life. I feel just like I felt when I was real little and I can hear my mother and father laughing and screwing and making all those moaning and fighting sounds, and I would cry then. I feel just like that now. I open the door softly and quickly and close it behind me. Carola and this guy are on a big Hollywood bed and really going at it. I have never seen anybody look so naked as Carola does. She is on top of this guy screwing him. Her big tits and long hair are hanging down in his face and he is sucking on her tit and rubbing his hands all over her ass and she is saying "Oh Chuck baby I just love this, I love it this way, baby." And they see me and she screams. "Killer! Please! Please don't! Don't shoot! Oh my God!" I am blasting her and then him. She falls off him and screams some more and he is crawling out of bed shouting, "No, Killer, No!" Blood is rushing out of Carola, from her face too.

"You no good fuckin' whore!" I yell. Chuck is crawling to me on his hands and knees dripping blood all over. I put one blast right in his head. It is all over. Carola isn't making any noise. I look at her all sloshed in blood and so naked, and something is happening to me. Feeling weak and dizzy, and I am falling. Awful darkness. So soft. Oh God.

IV

THERE I WAS, CRINGING IN A ZURICH phone booth, minding nobody's business, least of all my own, when this carnival off-scouring appeared (out of nowhere, of course, where else?). I had been trying to dial a number, furiously and with an occasional slap in the face of the phone mouthpiece itself (naughty little gossip that it was), and when I realized that my difficulty was due to the fact that I had forgotten the number, I began to cringe. This deliberate nothing, this marmalade of rejection, whose least piercing gaze came barely to my crotch, carefully opened the door of the booth and asked, "Have you seen the bumptiousness of the evening otter?"

"Yes," I replied. "And without any help from you, I might add."

"Does one know the cravings in the unbent knee?" he went on, his lips not moving even slightly.

"Not in this lifetime." I gave him a careful and stern look. "What happened to you, my friend?"

"They accused us of exchanging intimate juices," he explained, lowering his gaze, and from this I realized that poignancy was never meant to be a substitute for self-castigation.

"Good Lord! How much can a fellow get for that?"

He doffed his little brown bowler—which reminded me of nothing so much as a dishonored acorn—and whispered, "Far more than he can use, that's for certain."

Pointing at his subtle jowlings, I asked, "What are you munching? Secrets of the Danish Sea?"

He nodded his head. "No exaggeration on your part." He gulped some down. "Parsimonious revenge at my only ancestors." I must have kept watching him, because how else can I explain his allowing this: "Of course breeding forbids my commenting on those shifting glaciers called your eyes." He then did something with his body that I would rather not go into (unless there is a responsible threat involved). "We are saving immense quantities of time, you know, by not examining each other's nail clippings, bad breath, and forged passports."

I nodded. "I can honestly say that I'm also grateful, but I promise you never to display it."

We touched extremities to seal this ascetic moment.

Then he instantly considered my facial possibilities. "Your nose," he began, and rolled his eyes and gasped, "For the first time, the Inquisition comes into complete focus."

"I made no promises," I replied, "So I refuse to defend myself."

He beckoned with his finger. "there are better places than this to exchange our jewels of history," he said. We maneuvered ourselves down a street and it was not long before I had adjusted myself to the outraged stares of the Zurich citizenry at my new friend's quite unreasonable appearance. Had I been in their place I would have had me arrested for indulging in such a clear-cut descent into the nether world: It, or I, showed so little regard for social cohesion by such an act!

We made it to a cobbler's shop which had not fixed a shoe for easily a lifetime. We eased ourselves into the cobbler's old bench and my friend softened things by opening up a small bottle which we sniffed from time to time. The vapors were a co-mixture of christian ecstatic and raped young mother. Any given whiff put a chap in a splendid bargaining position.

"There are tender moments in this town," he said, "but they will never be released."

"Why?" I asked.

"How can such things feed the steel machine of progress?"

"Hmm, a good point. So what do the inhabitants do?"

He laughed. (Have you ever heard distant animals amusing themselves in the forests?) "They tell lies about how happy they are. They write stories, tons of them every year, about heroic human acts that took place in the good old days." He grinned. "But of course no one has the courage to sign his own name to such myths. Each one is attributed to some other citizen."

"Transferred guilt," I said.

"Among other things. They have another quaint praxis here. On the first day of winter, every year, each member of the community acts out a fantasy of one other member, he is of course rewarded accordingly. Usually punished, because who has fantasies that are nice?"

"Indeed. And what is the overall effect of this . . . uh . . . praxis?"

"Just what you would expect—it keeps the community together." He patted what I can only imagine was his belly. "One year a special edict from the Pope forbade their doing it, and the result was catastrophic. The crime rate was beyond count and definition—unspeakable things were done that had not happened since the birth of Christ, and a good third of the population suffered nervous breakdowns besides." He thumbed his nose at an imaginary passerby. "And more. All of the children conceived in that year of repression—incidentally that period has been known since as The Year That Vanished—all those children are freaks. But not physically. Mentally. Each one has something the matter with his mind. One, for example, is unable to deal with anything that involves numbers. Another cannot understand the meaning of tomorrow. One cannot tell the truth, another cannot lie. One goes into the deepest depression when he observes a thing of beauty. Another thinks that nothing exists unless he is looking at it."

"Were you conceived that year?"

"How perceptive you are!"

"And what is your defect?"

"I cannot dream. I mean when I am asleep. I have them, instead, when I am awake. All during the day I am weaving in and out of them."

"Then how can you separate reality from unreality?"

"In your terms, I can't. But who, after all, can prove the categorical qualities of either? Just tell me that, old poacher."

"Oh dear. It was just a small inquiry with no presumption of immortality."

He patted me on the hand (to comfort me, I suppose). His hand, by the way, was a tiny chubby dimpled baby hand and I noticed that on one of the of the fingers was a smear of jelly. "Enough," he said. "Now for some definitions. A taxonomous excursion. What is in?"

"That which will not regard out as its opposite."

"What is up?"

"A bird that has not yet been shot out of the sky."

"Down?"

"A suppressed peasants' revolt."

"Perfection?"

"A cream puff eaten suddenly in the middle of the night."

"Courage?"

"A mirror that refuses to reflect."

"Truth?"

"A whale coming up for air."

"What is one's unique and authentic self?"

"That voice which says to one's name, 'I await your claims with resolute indifference.'"

"Deception?"

"A soccer ball lying quietly on an empty playing field."

"Pleasure?"

"The realization that one has been there before and will go there again."

"Agony?"

"Proof that our Lord was just another Jew."

"Give me an example of incorruptible communication."

"The frozen Arctic seas do not lie to the waddling penguin and the snow mountains are a testimonial to stimulus and response."

"What is the basis of 'societal organization?'"

"Nonsense that works during the time you are waiting to go back to bed."

"Splendid. Your form today is tip top." He sniffed the bottle and fields of poppies bloomed on his body. I sniffed (a bit more than he did, because, you see, I was still young to the stuff) and the Great Wall of China began to whimper for forgiveness. "I have the feeling that there are animal presences in this room," I said. "Can you explain that?"

He smiled. (Boy! His lips were as self-congratulatory as a baker's dozen). "Of course. They are my pets, those fierce beasts Pause and Listen."

"I see. What do you feed them?"

"Possibilities. Meanings in the making." He lifted his bowler and scratched what I imagined to be the top of his head. "Now then, I would like to ask you a personal question."

I made a quite cavalier gesture with my arm (one of the many things I have learned from watching the movies). "My vulnerability is at your service."

"*Merci.* The question is this: are you at all interested in the position of the creative artist in our society?"

"Hm. I could be. Tickle me a little."

He looked at the wall above my head, and I could not discount the possibility that he was reading from it (but writ in what and by whose predetermined finger?). "First off," he began, "do you agree that logic is the vice squad of the imagination, that its purpose is to destroy the anti-societal human?"

I listened to my interior vibrations, then said, "I do not feel uncomfortable with those propositions."

"Excellent. Another question: Do you sense the scream imbedded in the taut fragility of the crystal glass?"

"Uh, yes. Yes, I would go with that."

"Would you, therefore, say that, in essence, crystal is scream, scream sublimated into form and texture? With the implicit contract social of your awaiting apprehension?"

"I don't see why not," I replied, sniffing from our tribal bottle (and thereby sinking even further in debt to my nose).

"Now then . . . Here is an irony: that in the beginning art, or ritual, brought together, had a communal-common experience— function. Now, art, the artistic creation, seems to be the artist's defense *against* a commonality, a statement of his apartness and at times an extreme and perhaps expensive defense against being absorbed into a common experience wherein he would cease being himself. In other words, art today, high, original art, is anti-ritual, and the artist becomes his privacy and his defense against the loss of it." He paused to pleasure himself with the sniffer, and his eyes glowed in a lovely Byzantine triptych way. "In fact," he panted, "it might be possible to say that all art primarily is an extreme device for protecting one's uniqueness and separateness, and this is the reason it is both not understood—shared in the communal sense—and even hated. To understand it is to share it —for one cannot grasp it without becoming part of it—and thus stop being part of the community. This is the root of both the attraction and the antagonism: the artist represents a threat to the very fact and idea of society." He raised his teensy hand and I could pretty well hear western civilization grinding to a halt. "Society must therefore kill the artist."

"In that case . . . " I began.

"Shut up!" he shouted, kicking me in the calf of my leg. "I'm not finished, you inconsiderate happenstance." He adjusted a gas pain and resumed. "Thus the artist's creations—his characters— can be understood, or seen, as his invented society, his own populated community, which organically functions in place of the other real or normal population (or presences) except that they are all himself. This is the central difference between fiction and literature. Literature is the property of the real, or exterior, community

—or that benign, familiar fraud passion for the imaginary, or re-lease, art invention in the other world."

He made a sound with his eensy rear end, but I would prefer not to go into its exactitudes. As if to excuse himself—or perhaps I am wrong, and it was a gratuitous gesture—he slipped me several salted macadam nuts that he had plucked, I would imagine, from the interior possibilities of a bygone trip. "Therefore," he went on (his voice was engaging my respiratory system and cerebral waves quite as much as my ears), "isn't culture the language or politics or ritual of that which one hopes to have happen and not an actual thing or series of things of the past—a thing about to take place. So—is it really in history? And can it be regarded as having happened?"

I sat up finally, perhaps to ward off another of his sudden rages at my intrusions. "Naturally not," I said. "I would even go a bit further" . . . and I jutted out a good deal of my jawbone as a sign of my irremediable confidence, "and say that esthetics is simply the rhetoric of hoped for, projected conspiracy or community agreement and not at all a science of sensitivity and codified con-structions."

I waited haughtily for him to wham me with a bagful of apple cores or a rolled sheaf or ancestral incantations. But he just looked at me with a quiet amount of restrained familiarity. "Humph! The arrogance of momentary illumination. Don't let it blind you to real scholarship." He yawned, and from that entire gesture was released one of the many imprisoned afternoons of his elliptical childhood. "I have a great deal more to say on the subject," he confessed, "but I'm going to keep it to myself for the time being. I can't trust the origin of your responses." He patted my nose without moving a hair. "Let's get out of here. I'm beginning to feel like the arch of a fallen woman."

We scurried happily along the street—quite high, really, on that combo sniffing—in the southern and neglected part of this good Swiss city. "One thing," I ventured, "do you think that before the evening is over we could go into intuition? Lay about us as to its hues and cries and coerced recapitulations?"

He pinched me with utmost intimacy, and without any provo-cation, on my bottom. "Of course, but don't expect it to lead to anything in particular."

"I am not an opportunist and I resent any winks in that direction."

"Oh fiddle!" he suggested. "Stop acting as though you'd been written about already in some chastely incorrect little history book that even the dumbest noodle will nod over." And he dodged a successful pin-striped banker without any strain on my part or his. What unconscionable style he had! What indifference to difference!

He could have been an informer for the Zurich Dowsers Society and I would not have cared a whit. Or a fragment from the Apocrypha that the auctioneer was asking too much for. It just did not matter to me. He and I had a lot in common, if nothing else. Some things have got to be sacred.

"Where are we headed?" I asked, praying that no hint of supplication was staining my question. "Perhaps to some secret rites?"

"Nope," he replied. "Secret wrongs."

For the first time that day I had the savory feeling that I might truly get to know myself. Before it was too late, that is.

V

SYLVIA WAS A TELEVISION ADDICT. SHE put in at least five hours a day in front of the Zonk Box, and I don't believe she moved a muscle. Trance is the word. And in trances of course you don't hear or see anything. You just absorb. The babbling flotsam on the screen and you become as one, flow in and out of each other, a real Zen awareness. You become it and it becomes you. Whenever Sylvia was in the osmosis state, I didn't have to watch the TV set; I just looked at her and got the whole program. What in Christ's name is this woman thinking? I ask the air. And before a moth can drown itself, Sylvia is saying "Tell me you love only me, Giulio, and I'll do anything you wish." Her eyes are transfixed space ships. I could declare war on Japan and she wouldn't, or couldn't bat an eyelash. That's companionship for you.

"There's only one trouble with talking to you," she told me one time, when I was dying for a little communication," "and that is, there's no conversation. It's like being in a Shakespeare play. All you get is a bunch of soliloquies. You don't need a partner. You just need a mirror."

She would go on like that, demeaning me as a human being, building a case for my inclusion in a horror museum, until I went to bed and pulled the sheets over my head, or stalked out and joined my buddies on the corner stoop and became plankton in the Sea of Gallo. I sometimes wonder about cannibals like Sylvia. I suspect that if they were isolated, but totally by themselves, for, say, three weeks, they would starve to death. They live on human blood and tissue. Is it possible that types like Sylvia are the answer to the population explosion? Perhaps this is a matter for the United Nations. Anyone of you can bring this up at the next meeting of the General Assembly. I don't want to hog all the credit.

Anyway, let's forget cannibalism for a moment. What I want to talk about today is of another stripe—or is it? Holy yogurt! It's the very same thing! I was going to discuss why two people who hate each other go on living together. Now, what is that but mutual cannibalism! Sylvia and I ate each other up, without stop. The daily taste of blood, the nerve-charging pain, the renting of flesh—all this gave form and substance to our existence. Love would have been as absurd and disruptive as a naked baby in an armament factory. Is that what life is all about—destruction? Even our sex (our fucking I'd rather call it: sex is something experienced in textbooks, it is the prose of the living poetry), even our lust grapplings seemed motivated and sustained by anger or rage; certainly nothing tender and sweet. The orgasm itself, that sudden chrysanthemum, is obliteration, of oneself and the partner. I have found myself driving and storming into Sylvia to make her come with the same passion as a murderer swinging an axe. I have little if any concern with my own consummation, or pleasure, as the genteel would put it: it is her death cry I am seeking. Of course the Spaniards, who have an utterly different life plan going from our friends in Quaker City or jolly old Britain and Florence Nightingale Square, know all about this. They call it *la muerta chicita*, the little death. It is as profoundly different—nay, opposed—as a

shroud from a sunbonnet. What about those blood-thirsty obscenities and character put-downs that Sylvia and I yell at each other
during our lustful confrontations? Eh? "Mother fucking madman!
Dirty rapist! Cock-sucking murderer! No-good cunt! Nut-crunch-
ing bitch! Whore! Lesbian!" Aren't these provocative fragments in
the same family as the challenges and insults smilingly hurled at
each other by Greek and Trojan warriors whose very souls are
poised by the first cut of the sword? I don't see how this point can
even be debated, it is so clearly, so undeniably true. And just as
those chaps are invariably depicted lying in each other's arms in
some kind of sublime, shared climax, some reason-transcending
cameraderie, as their life's blood oozes out, so it was with Sylvia
and me after screwing, collapsed onto the unexhausted naiveté of
those pink percale sheets.

I was very interested, really curious about, Sylvia's work, her
expeditions into the uncharted marshes and rain forests of this
world's eternally underprivileged, and frequently—when I was
refueling after one of my own innumerable field trips, that is—
attempted to get her to tell me about it.

"Are you just looking for voyeuristic kicks," she asked, "or do
you really have a normal, decent interest in sociological problems?
Which is it, Mr. Confusion?"

"Both," I replied, trying, as was my characteristic urge, to be
both honest and cute. "Is there anything the matter with that? I
mean, is that an outlawed combo?"

She sighed, like one of Jesus' close friends at the cross scene.
"In you it's so natural, it defies challenging. How can one find fault
with the fact that mushrooms must live in caves? Right?"

"Right, mother. Your scientific attitude impresses me. It's
something quite new. Are you by any chance spreading for a
biologist these days?"

Her look was a Roman soldier's spear covered with cow dung.
"Thataboy. Reduce all human endeavor to a screw. You know,
your mind isn't small, it's just paralyzed. You can only see up and
down. Fifty per cent of the world is a dark mystery to you. But
of course you wouldn't accept that, would you, Rumpelstiltskin?"

I gave her a dry cracker laugh. "You clearly don't understand
my method. I try to seize the essence of things. The before and
after don't concern me. It's the moment of unavoidable self-iden-

tification that my instrument responds to." I looked at her over my tuna fish sandwich. "Think about it."

She made an unusual expression with her face, an expression probably found often among chicken farmers whose hens neurotically insist upon laying rotten eggs. "Whenever I think very much about anything you tell me, I get the terrible feeling that I'm drowning. It's really unnatural. I mean, somebody ought to study me. Maybe an oceanographer who is also a psychiatrist."

Her statement wasn't totally unusable. At times she did seem like a drowned body floating with tragic softness among the dainty nibbling sea animals, and at these times I myself was a grotesque rubbery shape lusting flaccidly in the shadows of a coral reef, a half-devoured carp in one paw or tentacle.

"Anyway," I continued, breaking surface and emitting a great vapor stream, "what's new in povertyville?"

She smiled sly and cold. "Okay. But let's get something clear —which is that you want to hear about this raunchy stuff for simple sick voyeuristic reasons—and the sociology angle is for the birds. Right?"

A marshmallow sigh from me. Anything to get the ball game on the road. "Okay. It's a deal." Christ, the things a man has to concede for the sake of scientific inquiry.

She sipped her black coffee and puffed on her Salem. She looked like a harlequin in her tight-fitting diamond-checked slacks and lovely hugging red sweater. Her make-up mask was arch and elegant, her eyebrows swooped and darted with evil intent and her mouth held Babylonian memories. "My beat is one Pandora's box, and I don't mean that in the sexy sense either," she began, and my veins swelled and throbbed as the opening words sank into them and mixed with the blood cells, and I could feel the sea change talking place in the farthest corners of my whole self. "I get involved with species that should have died out with Cro-Magnon man. It wouldn't surprise me if half of them flew around the ceiling or went to sleep in the mud." She rubbed her chin and slowly shook her head in disbelief. "There's one man, a Jamaican Negro, who is a fake basket case beggar, named Churchill Downs. He lives with his sister who is a beggar also. A fake nun beggar. She calls herself Ophelia of the Morning Light. That's her honest to God legal name. With their combined efforts of begging and fencing stolen goods and running classes in draft dodging and growing marijuana on their building roof and selling whiskey and wine after hours, they must be millionaires, but there they are drawing down four-hundred-and-ninety dollars a month from the Welfare Department. Plus medical care. And I can't prove they have a single penny income. I can't get a shred of evidence showing that they are the General Motors of Harlem even though it's as well known as the Civil War. And these two criminals, brother and sister and lovers of course, are laughing up their sleeve morning noon and night because of the various cons they are getting away with.

"And besides which, they aren't peasants in from the fields. Far from it. They're Negro aristocrats. They were adopted by a well-to-do, guilt-ridden Jewish family and sent to the very best schools. Ophelia went to Chapin and Radcliffe and Churchill attended Exeter and Harvard and did graduate work in anthropology at Cambridge. They are doing what they're doing not out of need or desperation or lack of training, but out of the exuberance of their instinctive, natural-born fathomless criminality. They are termites destroying western civilization and values. There isn't anything they wouldn't do if they thought they could get away with it. Child kidnapping, robbing graves, spying for the Russians —anything. They start their day in incest and impersonation and end it with perjury and felony.

"Every time I go to see them I actually tremble because I'm afraid they'll swallow me up—drug me and put me to work for them in the streets or take me prisoner and use me for themselves or put me in a box and ship me to Arabia to the slave market. You can't imagine what it's like."

But I could. As if I were inside her very pores. Wearing her make-up, bra and panties, rubbing the mole on her right cheek when she was nervous. My mole, my nervousness, my selfish nippled breasts tingling with excitement-coated apprehension. Oh, how clearly, how deeply I could feel her, climbing those piss-smelling iron stairways in the yowling, jumping half crazy leaning towers in Harlem, dodging flying chicken, or terrified bodies, dodging obscene curses thrown from naked black and tan throats that were still caressing the vestigial chain sores on their necks, the last welts on their bottoms.

"Miss Lovely Lady from the Welfare Department of the City of New York, welcome to our humble but not bowed abode." And Churchill Downs, majestic, lordly in his silver wheel chair, his gold enriched teeth glowing triumphantly, led her into the rebuttal to white middle-class society that was his and his sister's apartment. "You are as a flower to our desert, sweet, blue-eyed, gentleborn and endowed lady. An orchid of hope and forgiveness, a hyacinth of non-violence and brotherly acceptance."

He was a condensed gypsy carnival, an instant bazaar. He wore a monocle on a thin gold leash, a black velvet beret with a red wool ball on top, an orange sweat shirt with the words "Vote for the Marquis de Sade" painted on the front and on the back, just below the neckline was the inscription "Hold Tight"; black patent leather britches ending at his knee stumps were capped with huge eyes painted on white cloth. He was holding a long gold cigarette holder stolen from the second reel of an early Garbo movie, and sending out foreign and tabu fumes from the tip of it was an Egyptian cigarette flown in by jet from a whorehouse in Tunis. Sylvia thought, as always when she was led into this chi chi lair, (red curtains, deep white carpets, colored lights, abstract paintings, and burning incense) that she had turned a page too fast and fallen into the travels of Sinbad. She could not prove she hadn't. She felt no provable, tangible or psychological connection t all to the world from which she was sure she had come. She felt like a little girl. She fought this regression, and she hated herself for it, but she was powerless against it.

"All that is very well, Mr. Downs," she began, trying to keep her voice firm and official. "But you and your sister and I absolutely must have a serious talk."

"But naturally!" Downs almost shouted, like an opera star on stage, "I couldn't imagine anything superficial or shallow passing among the three of us. Such an experience would demean the very air around us." And he took her child's hand and led her to a love seat upholstered in zebra skin. As if to forestall any offensive remarks about how do people collecting relief checks from the city of New York. . . . this grinning Caliban who had clearly devoured Prospero, announced (again from somewhere in the beginning of *Traviata*),

"A gift from a cousin of mine who had white man connections

down on Seventh Avenue. Lovely, isn't it? There's nothing like the real thing," he went on, stroking the skin near Sylvia's insecure thigh, "straight from Mother Nature herself. I can't tell you how those plastic imitations of reality offend and depress me. Looking at them is like waking up in the gutter instead of one's own bed." He looked deep into Sylvia's staring, numbed eyes. "Don't you agree, Miss Wonderful? Doesn't it just make your skin crawl to be within ten feet of an imitation?" And he shuddered, a black shiny shudder.

Sylvia, her deepest molecules doing the puritanical battle against disintegration, attempted a stern expression, and said, "We can discuss nature some other time, Mr. Downs." Her body was turning into a thin soup, her mind was vaporizing, and her voice barely contained vowels and consonants. "My visit today has to do with, uh . . ." she faltered, a bust of Plato grinned at her from a pedestal across the room, ". . . uh, your claims of . . . of . . . uh poverty . . . and . . . ."

Churchill Downs nodded his head. "Poverty. Yes indeed. My sister and I are swimming in it. Life has been unconscionably mean to us. We are innocent victims of the worldwide power struggle. Ophelia and I are ethnically expendable." (A beige colored maid dressed in the strictest and classiest of Oyster Bay uniforms materialized and put down a plate of half-shell clams and a bottle of Pernod for Downs, kissed each of his stump eyes, and vanished in a hip motion.) "We must scrounge in life's garbage cans in order to survive. We must crawl in alleyways to stay out of the way. We must breathe the air only after the white rulers have exhausted it of nourishment. We are left only with each other and a few loving friends." He worked down a couple of clams with a long swallow of his milky Pernod highball. "In short, Miss Pearly Teeth and Lively Ankles, we are not exactly in a top dog position. Would you say?" He unwinked his monocle, gave his ear a fine twiggle with his cultivated little finger, and grinned opulently at Sylvia. "What we need at this moment," he said, not taking his glistening gaze from her face, "is a little baroque music. Flute and mandolin." The music barely waited for the words to depart his mouth before it was galvanizing the hypnotic atmosphere.

I am a prisoner here, the small girl in Sylvia was saying in a tiny whisper. I will never be seen again by white people. I will disappear into another universe, of lust and madness and primitive sounds. I will be totally beyònd the reach of anything clean and good and reasonable. This legless black man is Evil Incarnate. There is nothing he is not capable of doing, absolutely nothing is unthinkable to his depraved vicious mind. I am going to ask God for help. He is my only hope. I can see myself ravaged and bleeding, and, uh . . . .

"Now Mr. Downs," she began shakily, summoning every last ounce of moral and physical strength, her hands clenched in fierce struggle, "I don't want you to think that I am insensitive to the unhappy lot of the Negro in . . ." The words, which had been so carefully selected and briefed before this mission, checked out for security and stress endurance, given special pre-flight diet nourishment, scientifically planned, these words were slipping back, losing their speed and guidance, were failing. ". . .white person in Negro's clothing . . . no . . . what I mean is . . . uh . . . we all have to share and share alike . . . I mean, common ancestors . . . basically God's chillun . . . worship under the same welfare check, true . . . no . . . what I mean . . . ." Wetness in her face. Lack of sharp focus in her eyes. Distant quality to her maiden voice.

An embracing black cotton voice surrounded her. "Miss Soft Skin and Finely Boned Hands, what I think you need is a drink. I fear that awful climb up those narrow stairs to our little bird's nest here has tired your frail self somewhat. Yes indeed. That sound you are now hearing, tinkling and shaking, is the lovely music of a Pernod highball being created. Here, Pride of Your Father's Well-Mannered Agony, put a little of this in the old cashmere. By the way, did you know this was Madame Du Barry's favorite drink? Helped her through many a sticky wicket. Good, isn't it? That's it. Take another big swallow. I can tell you are feeling better already. Your face is losing that transplanted quality. That licorice taste is very nifty, isn't it? Dates all the way back to one's childhood and the exquisite frenzy of penny candy. Licorice sticks and jawbreakers. Wonder who's on the bassoon in this recording. You wouldn't know, would you, Mother's Joy? Some cat from Bologna, I believe.

"Boy, he sure got his lips around that one. Trust those seventeenth-century guineas. They gave us lip culture full blown. No pun intended! But all inadvertent rewards gratefully received."

Bing, bing, bing, The phone.

"Yes? Oh for God's sake! You don't mean it. Well, doll, if you can't join em, lick em! Bye now." He returned his self to Sylvia. "That was General Custer. Seems that an awful lot of Indians are forming a big circle around him. Poor guy! He should never have gone to West Point.

"Thata girl. You're handling that drink with real style. Nothing puny and pecksnifity about you, Gardenia Girl. I'll bet your splendid lineage goes right back unbroken to the third line in *Beowulf*. Here, let me freshen that up for you. Mm. The upperclass coloring in your tight cheeks is certainly picking up. That's the big drawback to being a blackie. No skin shade delights. However, our pimples are not as conspicuous. A small but comforting compensation."

The Pernod helped Sylvia adjust to her defeat. She no longer felt like resisting her fate. She licked the sweet taste on her lips and said, penitently, "What do you plan to do with me, Mr. Downs?"

A great shout shriek from that impudently variegated entity in his silver wheel chair. "Do with you? Oh sweet Jesus! Shades of Uncle Remus! Do with you? What do you plan to do with me? That's the real, actual, and breathing question here, Rosalinda of the High Towers."

She knew, in her new Pernod-induced adjustment cozy, that Churchill Downs, the Black Machiavelli of 127th Street, The Legless Runner, The Dark Moment Before the Truth, was putting her on. All he had to do was snap his fingers and she would be aboard a small steamer bound for Mozambique and a short lifetime of orgiastic servitude. She sipped off the rest of her drink, and did not feel the least bit embarrassed or guilty about the slight slurping sound she made in the tradition of a child finishing off a tasty soda. "Oh, Churchill—if I may be so intimate—you toy with me."

The red velvet curtains and the gold candelabra had clitoral titterings with his next explosion of surprised delight. "How you do go on, Princess!" He gave his seemingly legless self over to chuckles and twitches and unbelieving shakes of his orange red black and mustard-capped head. Finally he righted himself. "We really must get something clear. You seem to misunderstand our roles in this revue. You may think that you are the victim and the manipulated, but that just isn't true. I am the real victim, the actual puppet. Don't you understand, Baby? You are the one with the fantasy, not me. I am something you invented out of some deep and very kinky need. You couldn't possibly accept the real me. You deny me my reality and thus strip me of everything. I am the one carrying out the orders given by your neurosis, howsoever otherwise it may seem. Only your guilt refuses to let you accept this, so you shift the responsibility to me. Sweet Bloom of the Heavenly Desert, I am your id, your magical nightshade. I am the culturally appointed servant of your unthinkable plots." He spooned down some black fish eggs and expedited their wondrous journey back to stomach living with a draught of Baudelaire's finest. "And man, I mean to tell you that's one motherfucker of a job. Yeah." He suddenly looked at a heavy gold watch hanging at his side. "Mercy, it's past the stroke of three!" He turned his head in the direction of a partly concealed door at the north end of the room and shouted, "Ophelia? It's time for your dancing lesson! Get a move on, girl!" He turned to Sylvia (whose past, before she entered this red carpeted womb, was now lost except for some graffiti on a cave wall). "We must keep our muscles moving. Right?"

Bing bing bing. "Hello. I have unqualified happiness here. Who's this? Who? Why, hello luv! How're you doin? No stuff? You have? Well, don't be too ashamed of yourself. We all got to live. Each to his own device, you know. Uh huh. Okay. Cool it. And I'll dig you later."

He scratched his velvet colored belly, "That was old Galileo. He just recanted. Because the town fathers were going to give him the boiling oil scene. Now then, the big thing is we've got to get the circle to replace all those futile straight lines. The circle of every returning life urge and reality. Yes sir."

Sylvia giggled. She had a nice little bag on. "I always hated math in school."

Churchill, ever grinning, patted the thigh nearer him, squeezed it a bit too, and lingered, but not insistently (because that was simply not his style).

"Understandably, Essence of Anglo-Saxon Euphoria. Straight

lines start from nowhere and lead nowhere. One end of the end is forever a stranger to the other. Can you imagine being a stranger to oneself? Frightening thought, isn't it? Well, that's what happens with all such symbols of modern men's thinking. Constant estrangement. Modern white men's thinking, that is. Leave us simple-witted but richly right niggers out of it."

Sylvia giggled happily, really as a delighted, somewhat retarded child would do it. "I love niggers. I used to play doctor with a little nigger boy named Tickle Britches out in our garage. Boy! Was that ever fun!"

The mandolin and flute shenanigans had been unnoticeably followed by some eighteenth-century French provincial wedding music including a few naughty songs covering wedding night logistics; the Greek statues of big athletes and armless, or legless, firm-tittied women, which, soft measureless moments before, had seemed somewhat distant and cold in this remarkable room, now were closer and glowing warmly in flesh tones, and Sylvia was secretly positive she could feel them breathing (and trying to conceal this fact about themselves); and Churchill, who had (when was it?) been perched (like Humpty Dumpty) on the outermost rim of his credulity, was now as in as a member of the family, cozy, lovable, thoroughly understandable, and even (though she well knew that this sort of thing frequently was regarded by the tribe's elders as incestuous and therefore not unqualifiedly okay) attractive. Yums.

An appearance—an epiphany—a flesh and blood denial of sound and space and third-dimensional logic. A pecan-colored, cobalt-eyed (bright like a ten-cent store ring) black, black haired (how could it be flowing, as it certainly was, if there was no breeze in the room?) mystery-mouthed (ooh, how thick and heavy and knowing?) high breasted woman stood not six feet from Sylvia and Churchill, clothed Indian fashion in a transparent black and gold mesh sari with nothing underneath it but the breathtaking actuality of herself (and wafting of the divinest of Chanel's perfume provocations). "I hope you two slugabeds are ready," she said most musically. "Because we've got to get going."

"Ophelia of the Morning Light!" announced Churchill, reaching out for her hand. "Sister of mine and gift to the universal aging modern man. God damn but you look good!"

Ophelia wafted over and patted Sylvia's baby cheek. "Miss

Sylvia, what a delight to have you here sharing yourself with me and my humble brother."

Sylvia gave Ophelia an unequivocal solid gold smile. "I'm all yours, Ophelia, lock, stock and unfulfilled whimpers."

"Sylvia, you're zonked, baby."

Ophelia looked at her brother. "Isn't it a pity that this big rich country with all its natural resources and accomplishments in the stratosphere, doesn't have a few more white angels like Sylvia down here? A national tragedy."

The phone binged. "Love and understanding here!" Churchill shouted into it. "Cedric! How's it hanging, baby? No, you're wrong. We're not abandoning you. We're on our way. You're always interpreting delays as rejections. There is no logical connection. No, I am not trying to con you. That's another of your neurotic hang ups. I can see that you and I must have a long and clarifying talk, Cedric. Is Katz with you? Good. Okay. Just keep all your marbles together and we'll see you shortly. Blue skies!" He shook his head like an old rabbi: "Homosexuals. They are as sensitive as a newborn lie. The withdrawal of their momma's titty, the first big shock and putdown—has made them antagonistic toward interpersonal reality. Ah well. . . ." and he scratched himself where it felt the best. "If Robespierre calls," he shouted to listening ears beyond the crimson room, "tell him that I'll meet him and Danton and that cold motherfucker Saint-Just at the Hotel de Ville Friday! We've got to get this revolution on the road. The masses are restless."

My God, Sylvia was thinking later as they sat outside at the Henry George Café in Zanzibar, what strange sounds this place has. I've never heard sounds like this before in my entire life, not even in the movies. Voices, slow moving old cats, music coming from doorways and crawly side streets, birds in the sky and hopping on the ground, animals—cats, dogs, and others not easily identified—all these emanations seemed eerie to Sylvia. How can a barking dog sound different here from in New York? she asked herself. Or a cat meowing? Or a child crying? But God help me it is different. The smells, nothing like them had ever crossed the Atlantic. They had the cunning and evasiveness of old memories. In the street directly in front of this table a twitchy, furtive Arab with a long, slithering nose, loony blue eyes, and red hair in ringlets was broiling pieces of strong-smelling meat over a brazier.

He pointed to Sylvia, then to the meat, then to his mouth, but she shook her head indicating that she didn't want any of the illicit stuff. But he was not to be put off. He scurried to her side and whispered in Arabic to her.

"He says you'll never get anything this good back at your hotel." Cedric translated. He was in a gorgeous desert robe and a fez. . . . "He says he'll even give you a rain check on it."

"Tell him absolutely no." Sylvia no longer felt like Sylvia. Someone else had rented the apartment.

Cedric barked an oath in Arabic at the offensive odd little fellow and helped him back to his smoky stove with a kick in the side. "They have no pride, no dignity," he said, now using a normal faggy voice. "But that is the wonderful thing about them. They have no position to maintain. Consequently they have infinite mobility, and they'll outlast us eight to one. You can bet on it, dearie." He looked around the steamy, jostling street, and said, really to himself, "I certainly could use a nice oily survival type Arab boy. I'm starving for affection."

Churchill and Ophelia were whispering to each other, mouth to ear, nose to ear. They were not at all conspicuous in their exotic clothes: they blended right into this breathing Mesopotamian mural. Of course, Sylvia and Cedric did too. (Actually, when you get down to it, nobody seemed out of place.) Churchill looked at Sylvia a couple of times and gave her a comforting wink. Sylvia smiled emptily back at him through light years of lost identity and nonmeaning. She was totally filled with velvet brainlessness. Cedric was staring at her in a cold, amused way. All of the fun had scurried from his smooth white face. "I just realized something, sugar doll. I forgot to give you your typhus shot."

"Oh?"

"This city is jumping with disease," he said. In a moment he had pulled up her billowy Arab skirt and penetrated her thigh skin with a suddenness of hypodermic needle pain. "There now. That'll take care of you for quite a while." He smiled knowingly. "You haven't got a thing to worry about. Old mother Cedric, she's taking real good care of you. Received her medical training in the war against communism in the swamps and highlands of Viet Nam."

"How nice."

"That's exactly what I said myself when they suggested I go over there and help those poor misguided people who were sick enough to want to live their own way in their own sweet time."

Sylvia was becoming so drowsy—not really sleepy but wierdly disengaged, or disembodied, incapable of will or decision, and her muscles were ceasing to obey—she could barely finish the honey almond cookie she had been nibbling abstractedly on. She tried to think of something that would tell her who she was, but it was simply no use. She watched a shiny Rolls-Royce glide to a stop at the curb in front of their table. A mahogany faced old Arab with a goatee and wearing a white robe stepped out, walked to the table, took her by the hand, and led her back into the waiting car. They purred away. The old man kept her hand in his. His diamond and ruby ring delighted Sylvia. The car moved effortlessly in and out of the stream of wagons and robed people and ambling camels. Palm trees and ornate iron grill work flashed by them. The two Arabs in the front seat remained completely motionless. She could only see the backs of their heads. Their faces were hidden by their burnooses. Big shiny black eyes stared at them from the swarming street. Expressionless gaunt faces. The man took the rings from his own hand and one by one slipped them on Sylvia'a pale fingers. She laughed with pleasure, the high floaty laugh of a child. He chuckled deeply and gutterally and kissed each of her jeweled fingers, running his tongue over them as he did. Tingles of odd delight and fear went through Sylvia's tummy and down along the inside of her thighs. He muttered in his strange language, and chuckled some more. Soon they were driving into barren desert through the cotton of her drowsiness. Sylvia thought how dreadfully hot it must be outside; the crackling heat was almost visible. Inside the Rolls it was cooly air conditioned and even one grain of sand was unimaginable. Just before she melted into unconsciousness Sylvia became aware of an unusual smell in that otherwise purified soundless back seat, a subtle, suggestive herblike smell, a sensual presence she had enountered way back in her other life. A dutiful border guard at one of her many experienced crossings, quite deep in her, an untouristed province, a ghost place but still preserved, made a notation which he sent to his superior: Hashish. In her journey through darkness Sylvia passed dozens of herself, dressed different, talking different, looking somewhat similar but still different; her high school self, her girlhood self, right into her round baby self. She waved slowly at all of them; they merely stared at her. The hashish-radiating old Arab began raising the skirt of her robe.

A woman was talking briskly to a man. She had a not unpleasant German accent though her voice was heavy for a female, and something about her voice and the way she spoke was definitely cultivated, upper class. "The Americans continually astonish me. Your left hand is always asking your right hand why it is doing what it is."

"Save the culture talk for later, Countess," the man said. "We've got to check the new arrivals."

Sylvia opened her eyes. The heavy, pulling, exhausting drugged feeling had disappeared from her mind and body, but she still felt that she was somebody else, or that she had shrunk to a molecule size inside herself and was watching what was happening with and to the physical frame of her. The man and woman were seated at a small table a few feet from Sylvia, who was lying in a bright green silk covered bed. The room was a sort of bed room. On the wall behind the man and woman was painted a huge mural that was so familiarly ancient and classical that for a disconnected moment Sylvia thought she might be lying down in a room at the Metropolitan Museum. The mural showed some ancient Egyptians—or people like that—hunting with bows and arrows and dancing and sacrificing naked women on altars, before huge gold statues. Sylvia now examined the man and woman. He was dressed in a blue sport shirt and khaki shorts. He had an auburn mustache and sideburns and kinky hair, and Sylvia thought, he's kind of good-looking. He was watching her. The woman was a big-breasted blonde. She was dressed in black riding pants and white blouse that bulged with her big bosom. She had high cheekbones, long black eyebrows, agate eyes, and she was beautiful in the same way as a tiger. She too was watching Sylvia, except that she was smiling and her companion was not.

"She's awake," the man said.

"Katz, you have a positive genius for the obvious," the blonde said without taking her gaze from Sylvia's stretched-out body on the shiny green bed. "I must say, she's not unattractive. Where did they bring her from?"

"New York."

"New York. A lovely city. Such tall buildings. I lived there for one year."

"Was that when you were working for the CIA?" the man asked, smiling.

"Yes."

"You sure get around, Countess."

She laughed slightly. "You could say that. I love to travel."

"That isn't exactly what I mean."

"I'm quite aware of that, Katz. Why is it that you Jews feel you must explain everything? Is it part of your general genetic vulgarity? Or is it something you are taught at your mamma's knee?"

Now the man chuckled. "We sure bug you German bastards, don't we? Jesus, what a vice to have—hatred."

"Don't knock it, Katz. It is very, very exciting at times."

"So is murder—I guess."

"Oh yes, murder has a supreme excitement, Katz. But then you would not understand. You are only a criminal, not an artist. A tradesperson."

The man laughed joylessly. "That's a beautifully paradoxical religion you have. To create is to destroy. That's very gymnastic logic. Very impressive."

"You wouldn't understand, Katz. Life to you is merely a series of economic exchanges." The woman poured herself another drink from the scotch bottle.

"Perhaps you're right, Countess. Such upper-class abstractions have always puzzled me. I have always preferred a simple knife to the torture rack. But I guess that is almost the same as saying that I prefer a nice polka to Beethoven."

Sylvia now listened distantly to the self between her legs. It spoke of fingers, tongues, thrusting male organs, of heavy drownings, exquisite paroxisms, of swampy exhaustion and aloneness. No names, no dates, no places. Merely within muscular memory. For no reason, she smiled, a smile of light years, attached to nothing but the universe, to immeasurable emptiness. Now another voice spoke to her; hunger. She wanted to put a lot of warm delicious things inside herself.

"I want something to eat," she heard her new baby voice proclaim to the man and woman.

"Yes, of course," Katz said. "You will be fed very soon. There will be lots and lots of food."

"And you will have much company," the Countess elaborated.

"Visitors from all over the world," Katz continued. "All walks of life." He stood up. "We're going to check on the other guests right now." The Countess got up too. "You will be anything but lonely," he continued.

"It will be very interesting for you," the Countess said. "You can exchange experiences with each other." She smiled and tapped her boot with her riding crop. "Oh, it will be most amusing, most educational. Believe me." And they disappeared through a clicking beaded curtain.

"Don't go away," Sylvia said, to the empty room. She thought her statement should have been a whimper, but it wasn't.

Eerie music from somewhere far away, and singing, or chanting, high voiced, in a strange language. Like a person crying. People muttering and padding about outside the room. A curse and a face slapped. But no outcry of pain. Had that person turned off his sound? Who were these people? And where were they? Did it matter at all? Why doesn't it matter to me? Female laughter. Two fat black women came into the room. They wore long flowing almost transparent white nylon robes. Ominously large breasts. Nipples like saucers. Glistening skin, oiled. Faces painted elegantly and wickedly. They looked at Sylvia for a few obscenely inspective moments, laughed and poked each other with delight and secret knowledge, then gently but efficiently each one took an arm and floated Sylvia off the softly infinite bed.

"You're nice, I know," Sylvia whispered.

They giggled appreciatively at her incomprehensibility, and exchanged a few strange-tongued words.

"I'm nice too." Sylvia said. She was quite terrified but all the avenues of expressing this were somehow denied her; a great emptiness held her prisoner inside. "I really am. I wouldn't think of doing anything bad to you. Honestly."

They were wafting down a corridor, skirting sleeping robed bodies, shaven-headed men squatting at card games, now and then a solitary oblivious musician loving his odd instrument out of which came those human sounds. The hidden power in the guiding hands of the black women was undeniable. Sylvia knew that if she tried to run for it—an idea she had considered, not truly for herself, but as if for someone she happened to be reading about in a novel, someone else, that is, because that's who she felt she was —these women could snap her gentle white arms right in half. Rounding a pure white corner, they passed a dough-faced Arab-robed white man who was polishing a rifle that had a telescopic lens attached to it. His youngish face held no expression (except perhaps the faintest sign of meanness about the mouth); his eyes were dead black pebbles. He glanced at Sylvia without the faintest interest. The two Negro guardians whispered something to each other once they were by him, and amusement was totally absent from their resonant foreign voices.

"Who is he?" Sylvia asked them, but of course they didn't answer her.

Now they came to a doorway guarded by two half naked, enormously muscled Negro men. The sight of them awed Sylvia —she had never seen men of such stunning beauty and serenity —and she paused. Either because they interpreted this move as reluctance, or because they were possessive about the extraordinary black men (perhaps those four black people had nothing else in the world but each other), and were miffed that Sylvia (who was, besides, in a captive, non-choosy position) should presume to partake of the privilege of admiring them, the women yanked her through the doorway and threw her contemptuously on the tile floor inside. They had brought her to the harem baths. At least twenty naked women of various hues and cries were soaking in the swimming pool sized bath or lounging around its edge being attended to by black women similar to those who had just dumped Sylvia onto the floor. All of the female types in the world seemed represented here. Chinese, Japanese, Balinese, Hawaiian, Nordic, Mulatto, Indian, big breasted, small breasted, heavy thighed, delicate boned, long haired, boyish bobbed—not one type or ethnic group was missing. A true connoisseur's fantasy conglomerate. A lifetime of desire at the fingertips. Just a snap of the fingers.

Heeding a mysterious logic, Sylvia slowly arose from the floor, stepped out of the robes, and naked in a way she had never before experienced, walked toward the pool where some of the women had begun playfully to splash and chase one another. Is this me? Or is this the very real me? Why don't I feel terrified and degraded and try to protest and run? Has that other life been the illusion? Have I just returned to my home from an absurd and long visit to that country of trial and boredom and conflict? I could be an Aztec princess. How do I know? She stepped into the scented bath and gently sank into it up to her confessedly untormented neck.

"No matter what anybody tells you to the contrary, this scene has an awful lot going for it."

Cedric was speaking to her. He was lying on his side at the edge of the pool, eating dates and drinking from a large glass of wine. He had a good deal of make-up on; his skin was darkened by some kind of stain. "You merely have to get with it, that's all." He helped himself to a long drink of wine and licked his lips, it was so delicious and welcome. "People struggle too much. That's what makes life difficult."

"Do you work here?" Sylvia asked, giving her body up to the wonderfulness of the bath.

"I am merely a part of the machinery. I help keep it going."

"This is a palace, isn't it?"

"Indeed it is. One of the finest in all of Africa. Belongs to the fifth richest man in the world. He has a very long Arabic name, but we all call him Daddy Abdul. An absolute charmer, believe me. He follows the innocent dictates of his heart."

"Is that the man who was in the car?" That seemed a dreadfully long soft time ago.

"If it wasn't, we're all in trouble."

Sylvia was rubbing her hands over her breasts and stomach and legs. A few feet away a woman, a girl, with swooping pointy breasts was washing the back of a voluptuously delicate Siamese girl who giggled with pleasure from time to time. Near them, a golden-haired, rich-lipped, round-breasted woman was sitting perfectly still with her head serenely tilted back and her eyes closed. But she was not out of it; she was smiling. Sylvia, getting many sweet feelings from caressing her own belly and tender, vulnerable breasts, thought how nice it would be to kiss her and to play with her hair. She now smiled a little herself. But with no clear naughtiness in the back of her mind. On the other side of the bath a strong looking Negress was giving a pedicure to a full bottomed redhead, whose hair was being slowly combed by another black woman, wearing huge, gold earrings. The woman was singing a private song.

"What's going to happen?" Sylvia asked.

"A carnival of complete and unqualified pleasure," Cedric answered, grinning. "An international festival of physical joy."

"Oh how nice."

"More than that, dear heart. Smashing! The primitive spirit will reclaim its birthright."

She watched an Indian girl with a floral tattoo, in color, on her back and a diamond between her eyes, being massaged and pummeled. Sighs and squeals of pain and enjoyment escaped her intermittently. "Are we prisoners here?"

Cedric gave her one of the most significant smiles of his career. "Only you yourselves can answer that, doll."

A turbaned eunuch padded up to Cedric (stepping daintily over a café au lait nude with spacious thighs who was having her rich forest of black pubic hair brushed out) and whispered in his ear.

"I've got to go see my boy friend," he announced. "He can't stand to be alone more than twenty minutes at a time. See you around." And he vanished off with the gelatinous eunuch (who gave him a slap on the behind just as they reached the beaded curtain barrier).

Where have I seen him before? He smiles familiar. Oh well. Who cares about all those things that happened before? Not me. She smiled to herself and turned over on her stomach for more of the lively floating sensations. A sparkling-eyed, short curly haired woman with a turned up nose and a compact behind sloshed over to Sylvia.

"You're an American, aren't you?" she asked, her accent sharply English.

"Yes. How did you know?"

"Oh just a guess. You have that American look, like you've never wondered where your next meal is coming from. You know."

"Hmm. I guess you're right, I never have."

"I was plucked from the heart of London. Where did they grab you?"

"Grab?"

"Well, didn't they?" The woman looked at her as though she were talking to a child. "All of us here have been snatched from all parts of the world. Lured here or outrightly kidnapped."

"Oh of course," Sylvia said, admiring this woman's flat untroubled belly and her perky firm breasts that tilted up like her nose. "I didn't quite understand. . . ." But before she could really go into the matter, she was being helped (taken) out of the bath by her two black guardian attendants.

"And you know something else," the woman almost shouted after her, "this place is a spawning ground of violence and rebellion! Plots and intrigues. Really! It's quite incredible."

"Yes," Sylvia said. She did not know exactly what other word to respond with.

"See you at the dinner festival, luv!" the woman shouted, and waved just like a little girl. "Great goings on! Wouldn't miss it if I could!" And she joined two other bathers in washing each other's parts.

They stretched Sylvia out on a pad, dried her with bright red towels, and gave her an amazing scented oil rubdown. Amazing because of their infinite skill and subtlety and because of the heretofore dormant and desolate continents of feeling opened up in Sylvia. Feeling? No. People—continents of personalities brought to life. Each new sensation was quite like a new person. The women did not work on her only with their hands. They employed their feet and tongues and teeth as well. Every inch of her body received the most detailed and exquisite attention; her ears were brushed and fingered and tickled and delicately licked, and so tuned up that she heard sounds dating back to her childhood, light lovely sounds that need one's sincerest attention if they are to have any confidence and existence at all (what happens to a bird call that is not heard?). Her nostrils, lips, eyebrows and eyelids were delivered up from their shy withdrawal from feeling, breathed up, tongue tingled, traced by touch of musical finger. How is it possible for my armpits to be so fabulously sensitive and articulate? Her buttock crevice and her secret loin preserve were worked upon as a Florentine jeweler would bring form and joy out of a little gold and a few stones. Her toes were twiggled and patted. By doing all these splendid things the women not only relaxed Sylvia but brought her gradually and fully to orgasm three times. Her pleasure, its totalness, was almost unimaginable. She wept with sublime joy. The women liked their work.

Sometime later she was eating hot spicy lamb and chicken and watching a man being tortured. His moans and pleas entered the very food and were thus absorbed (taken into the stomach and bloodstream and very self) by Sylvia and many others there—dancers, magicians, women, shieks and servants. Two Nubians were holding him while a Syrian attended to his human frailty and endurance limitations with a red hot steel instrument.

"He was caught just this morning," explained Daddy Abdul next to her at the long copiously stocked table they were all squatting at. "An agent provocateur sent by the American government."

"I see," she said. She looked across the room at the man long enough to notice that he had one brown and one blue eye and that even in anguish his expression seemed dishonest.

Daddy Abdul sighed, "This evangelistic self-deception! Will it never end! They want to destroy anything and everything that goes against or is even different from their own system of values and ideas. Oh, how disheartening!" And he absentmindedly fondled Sylvia's naked breasts for a little comfort. Sylvia liked this too, even though Daddy was about seventy years old.

"Don't forget me," whispered someone next to her.

She merely glanced at him. It was the same funny looking man who had tried to interest her in his home-cooked meat pies back at the outdoor café. He was dressed quite elegantly now, but Sylvia wasn't interested. Though his nose . . .

Way down at the far end of the festive table (a couple of blue painted Arabic male dancers—transvestites—were wheeling wildly in artistic competition with the howling now bleeding secret agent) George and Cedric were deep in dialog, or conspiracy.

"You think the best place is Texas?" George asked.

"Without any question," Cedric said.

"All right then. I'll take your word for it. This sort of thing is completely new to me."

"Oh no, it isn't," Cedric said, amused but very serious. "You've been thinking about it all your life."

"Murder?"

"Of this nature, yes."

"I would never have thought so."

"Self-deception is the world's oldest profession, sweetheart."

The dancers became wilder and wilder. And so did the agent's screams of pain and remorse.

"I hope nobody catches us," George said.

"Don't worry. Everybody is in on it. In one way or another."

"Hmm."

Cedric had majored in murder for one whole year in Vietnam. But reluctantly.

"Murphy," his commanding officer, a ruddy brush-cut chap, said to him one afternoon in the little hamlet of Ding Hao, "I am afraid that you are not giving our effort your fullest American enthusiasm."

"That's putting it mildly, sir," Cedric confessed. "I mean, like the whole business makes me puke."

The captain snorted. "The army would be better off without men like you."

"That's what I told them at the induction center, sir, but they wouldn't listen to me. Just couldn't have been deafer."

"I'll bet you're the kind of guy who would make broadcasts for the enemy," the captain said, smiling dirtily.

His legs ached from the brutal hike through the jungles, and the shrapnel wounds in his back still hurt. He had not been able to wash his body in a week and he smelled awfully crummy. Bug bites covered his scratched arms, and the memory of the leeches sticking on his skin in the filthy streams make him shiver and feel degraded. The breeze brought them the lingering smell of the burned-bombed village down the road. He thought he could detect the terrible odor of rotting human flesh in the smoke smell. A deep boredom and uselessness came over him now and he slumped to the ground in a cross-legged position. The Vietnamese in the flimsy thatched hut behind them stood in the doorway and silently stared.

Cedric's platoon were scattered here and there in the mud streets, trying to find something to amuse themselves with, or just resting from the hike. People in rags were begging from the soldiers. Cedric watched a heavily muscular Negro boy he was in love with give an old man—crippled, bent, drying up—some cigarets, and then, smiling at the dumbness of it all, hand a young boy a few pennies. The boy, wearing only a shirt, darted away like a terrified scavenger who might have its prize taken from it. More children came now and watched Cedric and the captain.

"I don't regard those people as my enemy," he said.

"Even though they try to shoot you?"

"Right. Even though they try to shoot me."

The captain squirted a stream of tobacco saliva into the air. "Jesus Christ. You sound like a fucking Red yourself. You're a fucking security risk. That's what you are."

"Why don't you get me sent back then, Captain?"

The man looked at him with complete disgust, and for a moment Cedric fantasied that he spit in his face: "You'd like that, wouldn't you?"

Two naked little boys were standing a few feet from them, just on the fringe of their electrical tension field. One of the boys— they were about four or five years old but the tender sweet shoots in them had been blighted forever—had a bandaged left arm held in a sling. He was holding the other boy's hand. Even the inalienable right of pain seemed to be missing from the child's presence; perhaps at this level of inhumanity, of experience, of total expendability, hurt was an outrageous luxury as unthinkable, as irrelevant as a Cadillac in a rice paddy. Neither child, Cedric speculated, can blink his eyes. Kids I've seen in America are always blinking their eyes, or picking their nose, or scratching themselves.

Not these kids. They are like spent fragments of an exploded hand grenade. They are timeless and unreal and if I blow hard they will disappear. I'll bet they have never smiled in all their lives. And I'm sure they sleep with their eyes open. A scrawny absurd chicken stepped skittishly around the four of them looking for pieces of food, or whatever. From the skies now came the soft whistle of American jet fighter planes. Cedric mechanically looked up. Four tiny shapes of death, unthinking, heartlessly innocent, moved serenely through the measureless blue. They shit murder, he thought, and a breath of amusement escaped his mouth. He watched the outraged Captain stalk away to join those of his men who were less disgusting than Cedric. Fuck you, Mac, Cedric said to himself. More kids had materialized by now. Most of them were all naked or barely covered with a shirt. They all stared in the same complete, motionless, almost dead way. Behind the simple bamboo and thatch houses, stood the lush, green, fearfully dense jungle.

"Hey man. You ain't seen any good lookin' Cong girl spies, have you?"

It was Timmins, another very attractive and—oh how fortunate—irrepressible Negro. Cedric just smiled.

"Cause I'm very much in the mood to be worked over for my military secrets. Plied with liquor and sex. Yeah." He strode on, blowing Cedric a see you around baby kiss. He is a beautiful and strong man, Cedric thought. Beautiful, clean.

Into his consciousness came—"Mr. Robinson, isn't it true that you had Mr. Doyle in trouble in the fourth round?"

"Yes sir. It's my business to have people in trouble." He had run across that white man-Negro dialog years ago, between the boxer Sugar Ray Robinson and a dumb district attorney at a hearing after Robinson's opponent had died after their bout, and it just stayed with him because it summed up the whole racial philosophical scene so neatly. He watched Timmins' broad easygoing form disappear around a house on stilts. He and Timmins and Bosworth were very effective in the Saigon black market.

"You kids are hungry, aren't you?" he said, knowing they couldn't understand a word of English.

But his incomprehensible statement did arouse the hidden child in them, and they smiled or giggled at him. Two girls of about ten were so lovely and fragile he could have embraced them even though homosexuals aren't supposed to do that sort of thing. Maybe I'm bisexual, he thought.

"I'll bet I really am as strange looking as you think I am," he went on. "I sure feel funny as hell."

They all looked at one another some more, savoring the oddness and possible surprise therein. Cedric sighed and slowly got up off the ground, his whole body, his soul, aching. "Okay. Come on. We'll go get some chow. There's some extra food because four of us got killed back in that smelly jungle." It didn't matter that they couldn't understand.

How did I get to be a faggot anyway? At my mother's breast or at my father's knee? He didn't have much of a knee though to sit on; he was always using them himself, to crawl on because he was too fucking drunk to stand up.

Hated him but felt sorry for him. Afraid of my old lady. She could say one word, or look at me, and I would be scared or ashamed. She made me feel dirty, that boys were bad and should be punished and all that. And how sick can you get—I actually felt better—cleansed and relieved—after she had whipped or spanked me. She had hands made of cold iron. Why? Christ if I only knew why.

"Did you know that Soustelle is in hiding here?"

"Who?" This Arab music really gets you.

"Jacques Soustelle, the former French Minister of Propaganda who turned against DeGaulle in the North African colony crisis."

"Oh."

"Quite a guy. Typical puritanical French intellectual. Lives completely by principle."

"He doesn't sound as though he has much fun," Cedric said.

"You never know."

"No, you don't, do you?"

"He's supposed to be directing the Algerian terrorists in France."

The village smelled faintly rotten. Suddenly a warm and slightly moist delicate thing was in his hand. It was another hand. A little Viet boy had presented it to him as their group stood at the makeshift chow and interrogation table in the village square —if it could be called that. Cedric liked the feeling of this small hand. It was somewhat like the time he had found a crippled sparrow and had held it in his cupped boy hands until it died, pulsing, pulsing, barely and then no more. Silence and no movement whatever. He hoped the child would live longer than the bird, but he didn't think he had too much chance. Did this child ever think about living to be an old man? Or did he simply feel that life can end at any moment, and one has nothing to do or say about it and that's that? Perhaps it's better, here in this jungle madness, not to plan anything in the future. The monkeys swinging and chittering back there in those cuckoo trees have a more predictable life.

The tenderness of the moment stole through layers of here and now and more recent experiential acquisitions and reached a sweet pocket of lovely, untouched by the smell or even idea of gunsmoke, flute, mandolin and oboe sounds, hanging in his memory as in virginal space. The words about them were there too.

"I'll bet Charlie is watching us right now," a soldier with a plate of stew said. "Just waiting for the right moment to drop those Czechoslovakian mortars in and blow our asses to pieces."

"Some guy told me the Russians are sending them the fastest fighter planes there are," a kid named Dolan said. His carbine rested on his shoulder.

"Them Cong gooks aren't smart enough to fly 'em right, so there ain't a fuckin' thing for you to worry about."

Far away, miles in the hills, mortar explosions. The sound that reached them was soft and round and harmless, and because of this, comforting in a peculiar way, like a nice down pillow. (The sound made other people nervous and afraid.)

"Christ," a deep voiced southern kid said, or moaned, "I sure would like to get laid. I'm gonna turn queer soon if I don't, and then you cute bastards just bettah watch out."

Some of the straightest guys go for it at times, Cedric was thinking with some amusement. Just depends on the circumstances; and the guy-girl they happen to be with. I'll bet I could lay half these guys if I put my mind to it. They'd like it more than they would be willing to admit. Just too awful a thing to find okay. Of course, they don't realize that it wouldn't stop them from screwing girls. Oh no. This would just be an additional pleasure. First time I had my cock sucked and then sucked his—a very sweet sissy boy who was majoring in political science, preparing himself for the diplomatic corps, he said—I thought for sure I would be found out and whipped and then put away in some wretched smelly prison for a few years. Among other things I was punishing myself for liking it so much when I had been told, by everybody of course, that it was absolutely the foulest most disgusting thing that could happen to a human being. Plus the fact that it would make you physically ill. Oh my oh my. When I think of the gallons of sperm I've swallowed in my time. Billions of human souls ending up in my stomach.

"You know something," a boy named Smitty said, as he came by with a tin plate full of food, "if I were in my right mind I would say this is inedible garbage. But I've gone war crazy and I'm actually eating the stuff, feeding my entire body with it."

"You ought to see what these Viet gooks put in their stomachs," another said. "I mean wow! You can't believe it."

Cedric got the little boy a loaded plateful of G.I. food. The child held the plate solemnly and looked at Cedric for a few moments, no expression on his small face, turned slowly around, and walked away, in the direction of a cluster of huts. Cedric felt funny watching the kid. I thought he might eat with me. That would have been very nice. Oh well. He looked around the clearing, saw Smitty, Parker, and Timmins squatting together, hungrily scooping the food into their bearded, absurdly bored faces, fathoms deep in disengagement, and slogged wearily over to join them. A large cockroach crawled from under a leaf and occupied the space Cedric planned to use. He stared at it. His complete weariness and frustration directed him to concede defeat and leave the field to the bug, but a deeper survival mechanism—partly man versus insect—made him kick it out of the way, and he sat down, crosslegged.

"You got to fight the fuckin' bugs in this place too," Timmins said, scraping his plate. "It ain't fair."

"You know anything that is?" Parker asked.

"Parker," Cedric said, chewing a piece of some kind of meat gristle, "you are becoming a philosopher."

Timmins laughed. "Yeah, but it ain't getting his ass outa here."

Cedric swallowed. The stuff was at least warm. "You aren't against the life of the mind, are you, dear Timmins?"

Timmins smiled beautifully and scratched himself. "I'm against anything that don't pay off."

More pillowy mortar explosions in the distance. Awful fierce whistling sound of machine gun fire closer by. Filthy bitchy sound. He could feel the hot bullets tearing into the dark flesh of the half naked Cong soldiers. And the stunned expression of death, as the soul falls through that endless abyss. When a Cong cries out, does a buddy hold him? Now the food tasted cold and sullen, and Cedric just stared at it as the sounds continued.

The music and dancing at Daddy Abdul's big dinner party had completed itself and now the entertainment was a fire eater. Big shiny muscled man, naked except for a red silk loincloth with black polka dots. Many of the ornately dressed women at the table were drunk on palm wine and were uninhibitedly playing with the Arab princes. One prince was pouring honey on a naked girl's belly and breasts, as she lay on the rug, and was happily licking it off. The girl was a gorgeous redhead with black, black unusually arched eyebrows. She was giggling and writhing with tease and pleasure. Now the prince poured it between her legs, on her heavy white thighs and over her golden pussy hair, and as he furiously worked his tongue over this trembling sweet, sweet field, the girls's giggles turned to soft moans and whimpers and delicate sharp cries.

George graciously poured some more of the pungent, fast working wine into Cedric's glass. "You know, I have this theory about modern man—that he substitutes fantasy for reality in his relations with other humans and with the world at large. And with himself too."

"Hmm," Cedric murmured.

"Most of his life is composed of these awake dreams which he exchanges with those of his various neighbors in a worldwide conspiracy against true meaning, true reality."

"Jesus!"

"Exactly."

Cedric giggled like a little girl being tickled in the back of the classroom. "What a gas! Oh I love it. I really do."

George allowed a servant swarming with happy clothes and blue tatooes to pour him several fingers more of the no nonsense local wine. Unlike many European mainland wines, this one made no bones about being anything other than what it was, with a particular mission in life which it went about with scope and precision. It really hit the spot. "Not only is it a gas, Cedric, but it's true." He licked his already wet lips. "Damn, this is a sweetheart of a wine. Tell me, who is the joyful maiden so happily making out under the prince's tongue over there?"

"Divine, isn't she? She's the cook's daughter and she also lends a hand in the royal nursery. Very handsome family all right. Migrated from Malta after the British hanged the father, who was a cop fighter. He looked at George and, organizing every inch of suggestion and implication in his yourhful face, added, "And she's got a brother too, thank God."

"What's her name?"

"Lola—short for Eulalia. Pretty, wouldn't you say?"

"I sure would."

Lola had taken her prince's clothes off and was doing to him what he had so exuberantly and with real front-line style been doing to her. She poured the honey over the prince's cherished royal dick and then dove on it, but not savagely as if to raze it (destroy it as a landmark). He went wild, sounding like both the keener and the instrument in an Oriental bazaar performance. Out of this world.

"That girl is really with it," said George.

"And as I pointed out, she's got this brother."

At a highly publicized Vietnam tour, President Lyndon B. Johnson standing in an army hospital, said, "I give you my pledge. We shall never let you down, nor your fighting comrades, nor the fifteen million people of South Vietnam, nor the hundreds of millions of Asians who are counting on us to show here in Vietnam that aggression does not pay, and that aggression does not succeed." Cedric had been three beds away from his leader at the time, recovering from a shrapnel wound—actually one shrapnel tear and one bullet penetration, in his right arm—when he said this. He was immobilized by conflicting desires—to laugh hysterically and to scream—to leap out of bed and kiss the President's ass, and to scream "General Westmoreland told me that no armed forces anywhere at any time, commanded by any commander-in-chief, were up to the group we have in Vietnam now. This great soldier thinks that you are the best prepared, that you are the most skilled, that you know what you are doing, and you know why you are doing it—and you are doing it. No American Army in all our long history has ever been so compassionate."

Or hung up, he thought, rolling a gravied piece of potato around his tongue. Or stoned with confusion.

"You know what I would like to know," Smitty began, lighting a cigaret and drawing in a great amount of smoke, like a man who hasn't had any air in a week, "and that is what the fuck goes on in the mind of Charlie when he's making those filthy fuckin' booby traps."

"What everybody else is thinkin'," said Timmins, "and that is, when am I gonna get laid?"

"I mean," Smitty went on, "do you think he's a little bit

ashamed of himself, knowin' what awful disgustin' things they are and the dirty fuckin' way they hurt a man?"

Parker shook his head. "Man, you are innocence herself. Those cats like what they think is gonna happen. That's why they do it. They hate our fuckin' guts, don't you understand that? They want to do anything to make you wish your ass was back home. It's called lowerin' your morale. Man!"

Smitty turned to Cedric. "What you think?"

Cedric thought about it for a few moments. "By now, they probably don't think anymore about what they're doing. Just like us."

He watched a soldier who was trying to talk to a pretty Vietnamese girl who seemed about sixteen, and whose skimpy shift allowed her bosom to be seen, somewhat. They were standing in front of a small thatched house. An old, extraordinarily wrinkled woman squatted in the doorway eating a bowl of rice. From time to time she looked at the soldier with a permanently puzzled expression. The girl was smiling even though she could not understand a word of what the soldier was saying. But she surely knew what he was getting at, and Cedric disinterestedly wondered if the boy would score and where? In the hut? And what about the old folks, what would their feelings be? Or did they have any feelings at all any more after the bombings and raids and killings and no food? He thought about all the hookers back in Saigon. He had been there a month ago on a rest and recreation leave after having a shoulder wound fixed up. How many hustlers had he turned down? Did any of them suspect that he was homosexual? Or did they just assume that he had other, tastier, irons in the fire? That's what he helped his buddies to believe. They were too preoccupied with their own urgent needs to devote much investigative thought to his lust patterns. Cedric discovered that Saigon catered to the gourmet as well as the glutton. He found a number of dark-eyed, lovely skinned young men who would let him do what he desired to them for a reasonable sum of money. Though they themselves were not queer, they all seemed to enjoy being sucked by Cedric. Usually, they wanted a little more money to be buggered. Vietnamese boys giggled a lot.

Oddly, Cedric's quest for love objects in this swollen suppurating city had been aided by a most remarkable young lady, a smashing blonde zippo of a girl named April who was a sort of nurses' aid and sexual fantasy No. 1 in the army hospital. Cedric just knew that the remarkable recovery rate there was due in large part to the soldiers' mad hope that as soon as they got better they could persuade April to peel off that tight and achingly provocative uniform and lay for them. Winning the war against communism took a very decided second place to this plan. Through simple primitive divination, April had spotted Cedric as a gay girl.

"We are all children of God," April said to him one day as she straightened his lumpy, kapok filled pillow.

"Exactly," Cedric agreed. "But what I want to know is if he's such a great father, why did he leave my mother?"

"We must live and let live," said April, ignoring his anthropomorphic question.

"An absolutely soaring sentiment."

She wiped his brow with a Kleenex. "Love will heal men's wounds and bring an end to all massacres."

"I'm voting for you for President."

She began rubbing his bare chest with alcohol.

"I know some people you would simply adore meeting. Nonviolence practitioners."

He sighed. "My kind of people."

"A band of young Zen Buddhist monks who have turned their backs on the destructive world around us."

"Lead me to them, baby."

She was doing some tension-relieving things to his leg muscles. "They are at peace. They are not tortured by visions of hundreds of naked women."

"I'm ready to take my vows right now. Show me the way to my brothers!"

And she did. Led him by the hand right up to the delectable temple itself on Roosevelt Avenue, where a beaming, quietly vibrating, shaven headed young monk greeted him and held onto his outstretched hand. Cedric knew he was in for one of the truly overflowing times of his entire homosexual life once he entered that cool secret temple. (Whence came the smell of Gauloise cigaret smoke and the sound of a Bud Powell record.)

"Give up all dualistic thoughts!" April shouted from her departing bicycle cab. "Enjoy! Enjoy!"

Now for a Beefeater martini and a club steak at the officers' club, she said half out loud. And a few choice military secrets. God, give those crew-cut captains a few drinks, a little cutesy chitchat, and the hope of a hot blond fuck, like their wives would never do it, and they're ready to cough up every piece of intelligence they ever heard. And furthermore—the driver swerved just in time and only grazed two Negro GI's who were staggering drunkenly down the small, crowded, slanty-eyed and stenched-up Saigon sewage canal that was supposed to be a street—I really believe they feel better after they've done it. The wonders of confession. That cute psychologist from Harvard said the fact is the American soldiers, and particularly the officers, feel ashamed and guilty about being over here, and giving out military information is one way of easing their guilt. What a smart man he was. Too bad he was so fat. I would have fucked for him except for that. Afraid he'd squash me. Funny how a guy that smart would let himself get that fat.

The driver was an absolute marvel at maneuvering out of disaster's insistent reach. Nothing in the conscious mind worked that fast and that subtly; instinct alone guided him. Insane trucks, lurching drunkards, sleep-walking, pregnant peasant women, demonic, playing children, bent, creaking death-indifferent oldsters —not one of these natural hazards fazed his awesome talents. In fact, he seemed predesigned for crisis tests; his heart beat properly only in situations of terror. He must be a Vietcong, April was thinking. He's too with it to be a fascist puppet. That prick Ky systematically discourages ingenuity in his slaves; it's a threat to his foul dictatorship. The little genius screamed at an outrageously fat, aristocratically dressed woman with a pink parasol who, his intuition informed him, was about to attempt a sneaky move into the traffic from her launching position on the curb. The look of astonishment, nay, dread! that seized her face was really something for the book.

April grinned happily. She just couldn't contain herself any longer. She had to find out if this furiously pedaling magician was, like herself, an agent in the National Liberation Front. So she leaned over and whispered the secret words into his ear: To be or not to be. Sure enough, he was a co-worker, for without missing a beat or turning around, he whispered back the secret response:

Fuck fascism. And to top it off, he plucked an avocado out of his lunch bag and handed it back to her (still watching the road, of course). Oh what a delight! April wanted to shriek with appreciation. This lovely green product of Mother Nature's bounty and brains was actually a bomb, with enough explosive power inside its skin to demolish any sizable GI-inhabited restaurant in Saigon. April returned it to him and in the act simply could not restrain herself from giving him a kiss on his hard-working no-nonsense naked coolie shoulder. The royalty of this world, she well knew, does not always sit on thrones. And for a couple of moments she felt warm all over with love and dedication emotions.

In a few slanty-eyed moments they arrived at the American Officers' Club. As April was paying the adorable driver—counting this illusory money was absurd, so she merely grabbed a handful of the silly hysterical stuff and handed it to him—she took the opportunity to look into his face. And as she and the man smiled at each other, April noticed something a bit odd about his face. It took her an intense, totally plugged-in second or two to realize what it was. My God! He wasn't Vietnamese at all. His face was just made up that way. A Rembrandt of deception! She saw that his eyes (surrounded with Asian eyebrows and slants and folds and all that yellow-hordes stuff) were tinsel blue and that the fuzz on his neck was not black—as was his really top drawer coolie wig —but reddish. And his nose was. . . . She was thinking of something to say—anything—but he was grinning devilishly and shoving off.

"Don't forget to put your diaphragm in," he said, and away he went, pretty much like the wind.

"Well, I'll be darned!" April said aloud. "How do you like that?"

But before she could slip any deeper into the delicious waters of speculation, a very healthy, Anglo-Saxon type with colonel's wings on the shoulders of his uniform raced down the stairs of the club shouting, "April honey! We've been waiting hours for you. General Parkinson is so stoned he can't tell a North Vietnam Regular from a hole in the ground."

"He can't when he's sober either, can he?" she said sweetly.

"Shh! Nobody's supposed to know that, and I want you to stop saying those unpatriotic things, baby doll, even if they are true.

You don't want to give aid and comfort to the enemy do you?"

"Who? Me?"

"All right then. Now give your Josh a little kiss. Thatababy. Did you get that case of perfume I sent you?" He put his arm around her and escorted her into the club. He managed to get a not so bad nudge feel of her sizable left breast in this action. April let him have it. She regarded that sort of thing as strictly penny candy. Throwaways. It was the big action she made them pay for.

"I sure did, Josh baby. Tell me, is that terribly attractive air force major going to be at the party today?"

"You mean Severn? The guy who runs the new air base at Dang Wong?"

"Is he the one who knows all about those simply amazing new airplanes our side is going to get? The ones that are faster than the ones those Russians are giving the VC?"

"If Severn doesn't know, then nobody does."

"I like him. He's so homey and relaxed," and she gave Josh a smile that made him want to push his small-breasted, civic-mined suburban wife in front of a New York subway train. VC Intelligence had told April that Severn had once lived in the Village and had written music.

It certainly is funny, April mused to herself as she felt good old Josh warily move his hand up a couple inches to get himself a little more breast feel, that I should have the sensation of pedaling that bicycle cab I just got out of. I mean I feel like *him.* Creepy. Not disgusting. I don't mean that. The main trouble with this clown here, who thinks I am unaware he is getting half a free feel, is that he has already told me all he knows and we have made use of it. Otherwise I'd lay for him like he is dying for me to do. Don't suppose he ever connected me, or himself for that matter, with the ambush of that jeep full of brass heading for that special and secret powwow with Ky's men in the Mohong Delta. Or the blowing up of that rocket dump near Panang while all the soldiers were having a big party which I was at with him. No, I suppose not. Maybe very deep down inside he might have wondered how the Cong saboteurs made such knowing strikes, but he surely didn't speculate on it to any uncomfortable degree. It's possible of course he forgot he told me those things, because he was absolutely blind when he did. I mean these guys get drunk like there's no tomorrow.

"My God but it's hot!" April exclaimed, and unbuttoned the top button of her wonderfully bulging white blouse. She knew full well that the sight of a little breast cleft, especially if you had a pair like April's, was a far more morale-building sight than any number of we're-with-you-honey letters from home. And very much expedited early friendship feelings—breaker of ice and all that.

"You are going to be angel cool in just another minute," Josh said, giving her a squeeze. "We've got the best air conditioners in the whole of Saigon here. There's just nothing we don't have to make our guests comfortable. And that's not to mention the more than abundant charm of our officer membership," he added, winking merrily.

"I can't imagine a better way to fight a war," she said. "I really can't."

They entered the club patio now and Josh just couldn't resist giving her a hospitable pat on her well-rounded, finely jiggling, ungirdled ass.

WHEN I SAY RELAXED AND HOMEY THAT'S EXACTly what I mean. This Severn makes those other boys look like they're all competing for the soccer team. When he smiles at me, the way he's doing now, I can feel it all the way down to my knees.

"What brings a girl like you way out to a gangrene sore like this?" he asks me, tasting at his glass of bourbon on the rocks.

"Patriotism," I say. "I want to help my country."

"But this isn't your country."

"That's quite true," I reply quickly. "But a lot of my fellow Americans are here and I am trying to lighten their load."

He laughs. A rich laugh. No crack or dryness in it at all. "You're wonderful. You're right out of a Broadway musical." He swallows the rest of his bourbon and smacks his lips. "You sure the publicity office of the Red Cross didn't dream you up?"

I am playing this very careful because he is by no means dumb. So I giggle. "In a way, you're right," I say. "I mean, I sometimes do feel somebody dreamed me up."

He lightly pinches my cheek. "Whoever did, he sure has a hell of an imagination. No question about that."

Over the mantle in this lounge—this whole situation is just like a fraternity club at college after a football game—is a barn-size picture of General MacArthur. He sure looks happy with himself. "Do you think he would have won the war by now?" I say, hoping to get the conversation off me.

"Oh indeed so," he answers, grinning right down into my belly. "There wouldn't be one living Viet Cong or North Viet left. In fact, there wouldn't be anything left. No trees, leaves, or even blades of grass. Those atom bombs don't fool around."

"Sounds positively awful."

"More awful than any of us know."

Three Sigma Epsilon types over in the corner are replaying a bombing mission. Just kids.

"Got myself three sampans," one of them says. "Man, you should have seen those babies divin' in the water when I started shootin' em up! It was wild!"

"That's nothin'," the hawk-faced one, who is very crocked, says. "I hit three of those big oil tanks last week and you could see the flames as far away as Cleveland. And I'm not kiddin'."

Half a dozen other female patriots like myself are dedicating their chatter and sex appeal to the general gaiety here and I don't think there is much doubt that before the evening is over, every single one of them will have a star spangled screw. I wonder if that low slung cutie over there knows that martinis have alcohol in them. However, I don't think a dignified front is one of her problems. She's laid everybody here at least twice.

"I hear we have some simply wonderful new airplanes," I say to Severn, who has been smooching the back of my girlish neck.

"You thinking of taking up flying?"

"Well, I will be flying after another of these drinks."

"You know what I think," he says, his big strong face not three inches from mine.

"What do you think?"

"I think we ought to go someplace where we can really talk and get to know each other."

"I love real talk. Let's go."

Six blocks away a bomb exploded in a servicemen's bar, killing four GIs, two Vietnamese prostitutes, and an old man selling aphrodisiacs. The saboteur got away.

VI GOT ME A FRUIT AND VEGETABLE

stand. Zucchini, artichokes, yams, pomegranates, Idahos, parsnips, Indian River grapefruit—you name it and I sell it. Down on Bleecker Street, next to a fish store—it's got more snails and squid than you could count in a lifetime—and a comic magazine store on the other side. I couldn't be more happily located. Nothing frivolous or cheap about my neighbors. Nothing as dumb and lifeless as shoes or hats or long brass screws being offered the public by them. No sir. They deal in basics. Children's fantasies and revenge hallucinations; sea animals, squirmy, slippery reminders of our ancient past. Real class operations.

My new line of work beats office slaving by several hundred miles. There is nothing secretive or sick or spiritually enervating about the relationships between me and my customers. It is all good clean animal fun. Our tactics are all above board. Our goals are clearly defined and within reach. No underground stuff. No sir. We attack and counterattack with exuberance. No holds barred. The only thing not allowed is judo. The women of the neighborhood regard my place as their gymnasium.

"Don't you dare try to give me that rotten bunch of finnochio!" one shouts, raising her fist as if to smash me in the face with it. "That stuff has been laying around here months!"

"What are you talking about? I got it in just this morning."

"Liar!"

And she picks the stalk of finnochio (fennel to you) up, spits on it then throws it at my feet.

"Gimme two pounds them string beans," another will demand, "and don't try to cheat me."

"These scales are perfectly balanced," I shout, "they get tested every week by a city official."

"Yeah and you bribe him so he'll let you go on cheatin."

"What kind orange is this?" yells another, holding up a perfectly innocent if not overlarge fruit.

"Looks like it's got cancer," and she hurls it into the street garbage. "Jesus!"

"That orange is full of sweetness!" I cry, hastily retrieving my goods.

"I told my priest about you!" an old crone screams. "How you been takin advantage of my bad eyesight. He says you're headed for hell." And before I can stop her she has stuffed a hand full of seedless grapes into her maw.

"Why you charge so much for the dandelion greens?" a black-shrouded bloat demands, holding up a bunch of the stuff with such fury I think she is going to choke it to death instead of me. "You can pick the lousy stuff for nothin' in the fields."

"Why don't you do that then," I suggest, and make an unsuccessful grab for the suffocating delicacy.

"Get smart with me and I'll take my business to Pinelli up the street."

She knows that I know that Pinelli refuses to trade with her. He said he would rather go out of business and commit himself directly to the county poorhouse. These constantly outraged women and I understand each other. Beneath our aggressions (actually, I am quite gentle, all things considered) lies a deep stream of rich brotherly love. Like the Harvard and Yale football games. Of course, I am quite guilty of what they accuse me of. I'm no fool. I wouldn't have a business at all if I played it straight. The women come here for our games.

Sylvia doesn't know about my new venture. She thinks I am still employed by the scurvy capitalist establishment. (In one of my many doomed attempts to validate my views with Sylvia, I read to her, the other evening, I think, a forceful statement of Freud's vis a vis the dreadful condition the universal middle class is in. "The common (or middle class) man," he said, "cannot imagine Providence otherwise than in the figure of an enormously exalted father. Only such a being can understand the needs of the children of men and be softened by their prayers and placated by the signs of their remorse. The whole thing is so patently infantile, so foreign to reality, that to anyone with a friendly attitude to humanity it is painful to think that the great majority of mortals will never be able to rise above this view of life.")

You'll never guess who I have as a backstore helper. Albert Schweitzer? No. Nelson Eddy? No. Charles DeGaulle? No. The Boy Blaster? Right! Came to me complaining that he needed a vacation from the stoop uptown. "My muscles are getting flabby, chief, and my shootin' eye is losin' its meanness." So I took him on. He can rassle a bag of potatoes like an expert. And he is very good at maintaining status quo too. Let a lettuce leaf wither, a grape rot, and he's on it like a tiger. Even when the produce is all spic and span, the Blaster still listens for the first sounds of organic decay. Another of the Blaster's assets is that he isn't always munching. A lot of helpers in the food business can't go for more than a minute without popping something into their mouth. God help you when the new cherries come in.

The fish man, name of Petrocelli, and I are good buddies. We exchange our wares. I will take him over some firm luscious eggplant, or some fresh, springy escarole, and he'll treat me to a rich tuna steak or some butter fish. He has a little kitchen in the back of his store and he often makes us lunch there. Add a wedge of gorgonzola, fresh Italian bread from the Fugazzi Bakery up the street, and a little red wine, and you've got yourself a damn cozy eating scene. Petrocelli isn't a bad conversationalist either. He's been around. He fought with the partisans in the north of Italy during the war and he became a headstrong communist. "But I got tired shootin' people," he said. "They were dirty fascist bastards. But a man can get sick of killin' even bed bugs. *Capito?*"

I said I certainly did. Death can be a bore like anything else. It becomes impersonal and engages you only technically. You might as well be working on an assembly line.

He quit the communist scene and opened up a combination bar-restaurant-bordello, in a small town south of Bari. This business was much better for his personality. Dealing out pleasure has a definitely enriching effect on one's mind.

"Nobody ever left my place unhappy," he told me one day over a striped bass and some sauteed mushrooms. "In what other kind of business can you satisfy a man's stomach, his spiritual needs, and his lust? And provide a good living for half a dozen pretty girls?"

I told him that the operation sounded like a truly noble institution. In fact, I said that that sort of package deal would be a perfect replacement for the church, which had been teasing and leaving man empty long enough.

He sucked on a section of the fish spine and dropped it in a corner to be choked on by one of the churlish rats that bothered him when his back was turned. "We were all comrades, the girls, the customers, myself. We were banded together against the falseness and misery of the outside world. We even went on outings together, picnics in the country, a day at the seashore." He speared a fat mushroom. He had cooked them in a little marsala and they were exquisite. "Why, once we spent a whole day in the art museum, sharing the glories and mysteries of culture!" He wiped his mouth with a nice white napkin and sighed. "Where are they now? Adrianna of the slow smile and the heavy breasts, Guilietta with her wolf's teeth and black stockings—where are they? I hope they haven't married salesmen. They were meant for the better things in life."

Why, you may ask, did he leave such a lovely deal to come here? The answer is simple: the Mafia. Those jolly chaps opened up their own whorehouse in the town and, like good businessmen, they made it abundantly clear to him (an abundance of threats, I like that) that what they had absolutely no patience for was competition. You can tax the patience of God with more success than you can that of the Mafia. So Petrocelli closed shop and got himself smuggled into this country. Cost him five-hundred dollars. He was part of a shipment of olive oil. (Why is it that when we flee we must change our identities?)

"That's the one business we don't have represented on our little street," I said. "Sex. Everything would be complete if we had a good whorehouse. It would balance all the tensions nicely. Such an enterprise, besides taking care of the health of the community, would add a certain *je ne sais quoi*, don't you agree?"

"Without reservation. There's nothing like a girl's bare ass to liven things up."

We agreed to give the idea more thought. Perhaps we could get a government grant to get it off the ground. Present it as a community rehabilitation project, part of the Great Society. Down with juvenile delinquency and ugly billboards! Up with neighborhood whorehouses! Dozens of smiling, complicitous, rich-loined rooms, juicy Byzantine or thin Finnish modern, take your pick—totally oriented around, motivated by, directed exclusively and exquisitely toward—skin contact! Uninterrupted, unsneaky, proudly brazen human skin contact! Oh, I feel like sobbing with joy when I think of the aurora borealis of health that would burst forth from all this. Even thoughts of social injustice, trachoma and worldwide hunger flee from my mind.

But I must return to my fruit and vegetables. Some people return to the womb, or some other crippling starting point, but not me. I always live four jumps ahead of myself, and even then I cannot be narcissistically obligated to be me, whoever that myth may be. We all know about those millions of sorry humans who fiercely—some froth at the mouth—devote their entire existence to being only themselves. They insanely fight off the intrusion of other perfectly marvelous identities. They delude and deny themselves most tragically. Speak to any child, and he will tell you how absurd it is to perform the play of life with only one character. The stage refuses such a madness. The very boards pucker and puke. If you don't believe me, then listen to our friend Heidegger— "Guilt is the call of Being for itself in silence." *Capito*? Do you know what the awful trouble with those I-am-only-Me people is? They live only with their mouths.

Ah, the customers I have! The appetites I serve! The tall black man with eagles in his eyes. A psychiatrist, an intimate of the forbidden. The things he has heard! The human ooze bubblings. Yoicks! But none of it has stained him. Sweet as a breeze off a mountain lake he is. He has a passion for artichokes. I save him the finest that come my way. A single blemish, no matter how innocent it may seem, is enough for me to disqualify an artichoke for this dark messiah's palate. Of course he doesn't know this. He would only laugh at me for thinking like an old Russian granny. My neighborhood peasant women are awed by him. They stare at him and sometimes stiffen up, as if he were some extrordinary thing loosed by the Bible. When he touches a pear or a bunch of grapes, they fully expect it to wither on the spot. (To tell you the truth, I've got the same feelings myself; but I've got more sophisticated ways of handling them. That makes all the difference, believe me.)

"If they only knew how much I loved them, they'd stop all that," my friend Jomo said, just the other day. "Love—the biggest hangup of our time. The giving of it and the receiving of it." He shook his superb astrakhan head very feelingly. "Especially the latter. The majority of human beings—western men I'm talking about—react to a gesture of love as it you were attempting to lay a batch of fresh toad venom on them. Vile. Obscene. All that, you know. And the awful damage suffered by those people carrying around huge loads of unacceptable, ungivawayable love. Lordy! See that chap over there?" He pointed to a lean, deep looking middle aged man who was more or less limping across the street. "Do you suppose he's suffering from gout? A pulled tendon? Not at all. Backed up rejected love—that's his injury. It's wrecking his leg. Poor dear fellow. If I didn't think he would misunderstand, I'd go right over and throw myself at his feet and beg him to pour his love into me. Bet you his limp would clear up on the spot. Yessiree Bob."

"Sing, Daddy!" I said, watering a box of gasping watercress. "Tell me what the whole aching thing is all about. Turn the lights on for me. Don't spare my delicate retina."

He collapsed his towering blackness into a flatulent overstuffed chair behind a sweet-smelling barrel of kale, tossed down several fat muscatel grapes (a man needs nourishment on these voyages into the tunnels of the soul), and lit up a crooked Italian cigar. "Engulfment. Suffocation. Death. That's what being loved means to most people. The total loss of their identity and independence. The very thing that enables them to achieve life and human status is regarded as their deadliest enemy. What a terrible paradox, my friend." And he inhaled several cubic feet of raging cigar smoke.

"How did this dreadful situation get started?" I asked, wrapping up twenty cents worth of dandelion greens for Mrs. Collucci of the piano legs.

"In modern society's womb, that's where it all began" Jomo said. "The entire structure of religious, philosophic, and moral ideas, all of them utterly inhuman, molding men into a monolith of lunacy. And the president of the whole smelly business. That's right—our friend Mr. Big. I can assure you that pre-Christian man was the sweetest little bundle of unity you ever laid eyes on. Not a neurotic or psychotic nerve in him. No guilt. No separating himself into compartments and identities. No sexual nonsense. If he wanted his mommy, hump! hump! he had her and it was a jolly day indeed and give us another bowl of that mastodon stew. None of that competing with daddy and hating yourself and him too for the awful naughtiness of it. Then came the one God scene and all its inhuman rules and punishments, and man has been out of his mind every since."

He vigorously scratched his leg, the ancient memory of a tiger bite. "And that impenetrably brainless notion of heaven and the angels! Turning death into a lie, a child's game of self deception! Oh dirty, dirty!" And he grabbed at a winesap apple to stifle his groans.

"I too long for the good old days," I said, putting a comforting hand on his distressed shoulder. "But how can they be recovered? Aren't they lost forever?" I was trying to sound reasonable and yet not removed.

"Revolution!" he shouted slamming the apple against a huge pumpkin, and startling the Blaster out of a snooze he was having behind the potato sacks. "A complete physical and spiritual return to paganism. Every garment of Christianity and modern morality must be ripped to shreds. Ladies and gentlemen, call your nearest tree god! Sacrifice a goat to the Cloud King!"

Inside his skin—I know, I could feel it as my very own—were crawling the mystery-charged insights of this knowledge. All the votive offerings that have been laid on the alter of my ego so that I would not harm their supersensitive defenses. The false confessions to make me think we had finally broken through to something meaningful in their psyches; rich rewards for all my sweating efforts to help them stop being sick and crazy. And all along I was being maneuvered, they hoped, away from something really good that would have scared the living shit out of them to have exposed. The keepers at their secret gates shout He's coming! The black dragon is coming! The doors slam. Bolts are shot frantically into place. And those various selves scurry into ingeniously constructed hiding places. But they don't know that I can become as disembodied as they can, and walls and doors and disguises cannot keep my being from finding theirs and entering there. The childish fools! They cannot escape. Only by being them, becoming them, can I hope to help them become themselves. And isn't this the first law of humankind anyway? Sick or not? We are all each other, floating in and out of each other's dreams and fantasies and everyday acts even the most intimate moments being crowded with dozens of others. No man is alone. If that cat only knew the half of it! I have been Hector on the Trojan barricades and will be the first woman on the moon, four months gone with a homosexual night club singer. Moonblood, moonooze. Not an artichoke here that doesn't call me by my first name.

Jomo! Jomo!

As if I were hearing my name for the virginal first time, because the name was blended—was one with—love, itself, not just a casual use of symbol to say hello to. (What if he had called out "Nigger! Nigger!" instead of my name? Would have responded anyway, I'm sorry to say.) That deep and kooky but very human boy George who was going to be a writer, bless his soul-driven sweet ass. Wading in the Mediterranean, not in some secretary's hard-earned European vacation where without any luck at all she would be laid by some curly grinning eyetalian—no baby, wading onto the beach at Salerno where the welcoming committee wasn't a pomaded travel agent with his pockets full of tourist traps but loads and loads of completely unjoking, nothing-to-lose-because-there-is-no-place-to-go-from-here kraut boys shooting guns, of all kinds, and they were not making birdsong either but vicious sounds that drew blood. George, hit in his shoulder, and side. He was flopping in the small soft Italian waves yelling my name, "Jomo! Jomo! I'm hit!"

"Coming baby!"

One of my first feelings—actually running a close second to fear—was, how strange to be a nigger boy and have a white boy call you for help, instead of for you to bring him something on a tray. I dragged his bleeding body out of the water where he most assuredly would have drowned his life away and onto the dry beach where I lay next to him while the German bullets were hitting all around us and lots of poor bastards were yelling in pain because they'd gotten hit too. "Those fuckers are in bunkers," I said, and began to do some shooting myself with my fine American Garand. Very different from the possum-hunting scene of Virginia hills fame, to say the least. "Just hold yourself together,"

I said, firing at something on the ridge up there, "and I'll get a medic over here. Okay?"

"Okay," he said.

He was doing his best not to moan but I knew he hurt like a bastard. I'd been shot, in Sicily, and when you come out of the shock of it, you hurt, and you are afraid you are going to die.

"Oh Christ, oh Christ," he groaned, and his blood was on the sand.

"Medic!" I yelled. "Medic!"

One of them saw us and started running over, bent over, as if he thought he could dodge the awful bullets that way. There were bodies all over the beach. Some of them were moving and alive and shooting, and others were dead, some with blood you could see. A few feet from me a boy who had been lying on his stomach got up on his knees to run and a machine gun burst tore his face away. I could feel it, almost, on my own face.

"Oh Jomo!" George moaned. "Oh God."

I cradled him in my arms. Cradled the blood onto myself that was coming from his terribly hurt body. The sounds of death surrounded me.

"Easy, George," I said, "You're going to be okay. Here's the medic, baby." Just in time too. An awful lot of him was on me and that beach.

But Rome—now that, ladies and gentle asses, was a story of a different color. I mean just looking at those buildings and fountains and long tasty streets gives me a hard-on. I could screw the city if I had to. Luckily, me and my buddy George didn't. They ought to change the name of that town to Cunt. Because that's what it is, or was, in every way possible—the food, the air, the atmosphere, the sounds, everything. And the women—they were made to fuck, that's their complete function, fucking, both in form and content and existential purpose and all that. A final point in their delectable favor: they think black men are the most. How do you like that, granny! Isn't that the goddamndest most supreme thing you ever heard! Every single one of those spaghetti mommas is a humanist, right down to her last pubic hair. Those Italians, they share themselves, they don't regard other humans as exploitable objects, none of that inter-commercial shit. Nobody gets used up like an automobile. Unlike in some cultures I could name.

Cannibalistic inhuman culture where the kids are brought up to hustle each other and real human emotion and contact are regarded as some awful disease that must be stamped out by crash programs to develop a vaccine against it if life is to be lived to a ripe age. Even sex, that ultimate diamond, is tarnished into human commercialism and thus is turned into a crummy zircon to be worn around the ankle. Savonarola, you got out just in time, man!

"Jomo, do you know what these two beautiful sisters suggested to me while you were away heeding nature's call?"

I smiled at George. We were in a cabaret of some kind, down in a Roman catacomb it seemed; in fact I had been looking for early Christian messages on the wall just to keep from thinking too powerfully about the disturbing amount of gash surrounding us, and in the company of two richly round and fun-oriented Italian girls who only two days previous had been aching under German occupation. "No, baby," I replied. "What?"

"They've suggested that we come home to their place for a real Italian feed with their mother and father. How does that strike you for hospitality and friendliness, when all is chaos and inhumanity?"

"All I can say is," and I took one of the girls' arms and kissed it up and down as though I were going to have dinner right there, "that I am overwhelmed by the mere thought of it and I will do everything I can not to make them sorry they asked us."

My girl, her name was Franca, giggled and patted me on the cheek. "You are beautiful black man. I like you so much all over."

Real great tits, more nourishment in them than milk ever dreamed of. Medicinal too—cure schizophrenia as well as sore gums, and body in general. Perfectly wonderful belly and slope area, the kind of country a boy longs to curl up in for great stretches at a time. To get his strength and courage back.

"You kill many Germans?" her sister Angelina said, smiling real big.

"He is one of our most famous German killers," George said, and swallowed down about a quart of the red. "Feel his muscles." He took her hand and put it on my thigh. "Go ahead. Feel that black iron, sweetheart. Rub your hand up and down that stretch of American youth and integrity, and you will know why your enemies shake in their pantaloons."

"Mm," Angelina murmured, "Yes, you are formidable. If I was German I would run from you." She smiled, "But I am not German."

"I know what you mean, baby," I said, and returned her a very friendly pat on the leg. Thank the good Lord we were all sitting bunched up together. Little things like body contact at a table get to be quite important when you are spending most of your time shooting people.

I poured some red wine into my increasing sense of well being, and the girls excused themselves to go to the john before we hit the road for the home cooking scene. This catacomb was saturated with quite a few other fun-loving, hard-shooting GIs like ourselves who were pouring every loving ounce of their wonderful personalities into making out with a variety of occupation-happy Roman girls, despite some very serious language problems. How George and I managed to get two who had studied English I can only put down to fate, which was long overdue in its benificence. And they all seemed to be doing very well in the consumption of the local juice. In fact, more than one was stoned out.

"Things are working out nicely, wouldn't you say, Jomo old man?" George remarked, grinning like he's just won a school spelling contest.

"I would be the last to gainsay that, comrade George. So forgive me if I ask you one thing: how do we know these nubile chicks got a mother and father?"

"What do you mean, old buddy? Everybody's got a mother and father."

"In the beginning, yes. What I'm suggesting is, what are the possibilities of their being some kind of trap?"

George just had to shake his head. He was certainly a nice looking boy, a bit odd, to be sure, but nice. Nothing ziggy about him.

"Jomo, dear Jomo. You shock me. Why in the name of Garibaldi would these splendid young ladies wish to trap us? We who have risked our valuable lives to liberate them from the foulest of fiends."

"Gain. This world is run for gain. These sweeties could be working with a gang, and we could be set upon by ruffians, who could even now be lying in wait for us, and rolled of everything except our American identity."

George put his hand on my shoulder. "You have been at war too long, old tulip."

The girls returned to the table—I had forgotten how utterly marvelous a girl's ass is when it is not constrained by a girdle—and George and I laid out what seemed to be several thousand dollars for the vino.

"You are the great American victors," our piggy-faced waiter said, scooping up the dough like he was the gardener in a grove of Rothschild trees. "You will win in heaven."

"That's what we get paid for," George said, "We are victors for hire," and he gave a little bow that he had picked up in a von Stroheim movie.

On our way out we passed one of our buddies, a soft as silk chap who was a real Indian prince. Old Bosworth. He was drinking real whiskey in the company of a dangerous looking blonde and a Great Dane.

"Make us proud of you, Jomo," he called out. "Give it the old tiger."

"I plan to claim the entire country for my queen."

Outside, my girl, putting her arm around me, said, "That woman, she scare me. More than her dog."

"Yeah, wonder what her story is." Way back in my brain cells I had an inkling. Something in my universal unconscious. Who. . . .

George said, "I'm starving," and put his face between his girl's big tits.

Anyway, my merely academic speculation turned out to be wrong. The babes did have a mommy and daddy, especially a mommy. And I must say they seemed awful glad to see us. Effusive, embrasive, overjoyed, stuff like that. The father kissed me at least three times, that's how he felt about the whole thing (of course, he could have had a bad memory, forgetting each time he'd bussed me; but I don't like to think of it that way). He was an ancient olive tree but the momma was a real mozarella who could have passed for one of her daughter's sisters. She wore her shiny dark hair down to her exposed shoulders, like one of those divinely turned-on cookies in Courbet. Uh huh.

"I want you to know that I hate fascists," the old man announced during dinner. Really out of the blue, because the subject had been studiously avoided, at least by me and George. (Incidentally, I am not reproducing this conversation as they really said it, half in English, half in Italian, because it would be too much of a drag. Besides, we all know how fake that kind of talk sounds.)

"Yes," Franca said, spearing a morsel of stewed rabbit, "Pappa fought the Black Shirts with every ounce of his energy. He forbade us to even speak to one of them, no matter how handsome and powerful they might have been."

Angelina gulped down some wine. "Exactly."

George did the same—he was one of the most enthusiastic wine heads I've ever seen—and smiled understandingly. "Now that the *fascisti* and the Germans are gone, I guess you people can start living like human beings again."

And how is that? I wanted to ask, but of course I held my tongue. This was too nice a scene to start sprinkling a little shit on, and besides the script had been agreed upon many thousands of years ago. But my point is that no matter what they do, people are always living like human beings. All those moral rules are created for play and self-delusion. I mean, naturally you've got to think you are different from the others. Right, Pops?

"Yes, it will be so wonderful," the mother said (she was sitting next to me). "It has been so terribly long I've almost forgotten what it is like."

My thoughts were making me feel like an outsider, so I thought of something to say that would be in the genre. "Life sure can be tough."

The old man loved that. He grinned sloppily and raised his glass. "A toast to our beautiful black philosopher!"

"Bravo!" the chicks said, and we all drank to my nonsense.

"I feel almost guilty, sitting here enjoying myself so much when there is all that misery out in the world," I went on. Man! The shit certainly can pour out once it gets started.

That one scored bingo with mamma, and unable to contain herself, she leaned over and gave me an enormous kiss on the cheek.

"Jomo," George said, fairly drunk now, "you are a genuine Christian"

That was a lot of buffalo dung too, because he knew damn well that I had joined the Moslems when I was seventeen. I was using myself as a study in comparative religions. I was as porous as cornbread in those days; one of my favorite voices was William James. Anything he said was music to my tender black ears. I was a pearly nautilus in the ocean of his mind. (I have nothing good to say about his eunuch brother Henry. His reedy tunes about the pirouetting of the opportunistic and spiritually bankrupt middle class went right by me and on into the thickets of gentility. Those characters of his, why, it's like listening to a faded tapestry talk.) But Willie. Ah, there was a stout fellow indeed. Like he said in his book on religion:

"... Our normal waking consciousness, rational consciousness as we call it, is but one special type of consciousness, whilst all about it, parted from it by the filmiest of screens, there lie potential forms of consciousness entirely different. . . . No account of the universe in its totality can be final which leaves these other forms of consciousness quite disregarded. How to regard them is the question. . . ."

After the coffee and dessert I just had to go to the head. Franca gave me the directions. Man! That was one big mother of an apartment. Down the hallway, take a left at the first oak chest, then a right, and three doors from that on the left—I mean Christ. "You ought to get a map made," I told her.

"You are so cute, handsome black man," she said, and patted me significantly on my side, just under the arm where it is sensitive and somewhat of an erogenous zone. She certainly had proud firm tits, that Franca, and she wasn't at all queasy about rubbing them against me—gently, teasingly, because too rough a rub would have dulled the delicate nerve endings—when the opportunity, developing out of its own mysteriousness, a flower unfolding, materialized. A fellow, particularly a coon like me, accustomed to snuggling under mushrooms, and often inedible ones at that, sure got a morale lift from such niceties, I can tell you, dear friends out there. In the dreadful and inhuman context of war, please keep in mind. Don't mean to sound sour grapes, but . . . who is the cook in the kitchen that is handing out the gravy in such a fashion? For some reason—Oh! Your damn questions! —I think of Nietzsche: "Every valuation, every instinct that is translated into action is today anti-Christian. . . ."

Where was I? Seem to have lost my way . . . no . . . I was feeling my way down the long dark corridors heading for the john . . . right! . . . . Smell of Italian cooking . . . that must have been their Easter dinner we just ate, probably saving those tasties for months, and then we came along instead of the Babe, ah well . . . maybe the Naz was a spade after all. . . . I opened a door, expecting to see a toilet bowl but what greets my eyes instead is a young guy lying on a bed and he is cleaning a rifle with a telescopic sight. "Oops," I blurted out. "Scusi, please." He froze in mid motion, and I closed the door and walked quickly down to the right door beyond it. Something very definitely creepy about that chap. Looked like he hadn't been outside in his whole life. And that pursed old lady's mouth on him . . . Is he the son? But they told me and George back in the café that their brother was captured with the Italian army—ha!—in North Africa. Hmm. Could be he's just a roomer and instead of going out looking for snatch at nights, he cleans rifles with telescopic lenses. Everybody to his own kicks, of course. I did get into the john on the next try and had myself a long reflective piss, examining the old bishop with what I must confess was a certain amount of pride. Remembered the time, oh what a howl that was, when brother Johnson and little Charlie Bunker and me were comparing cocks out in the shed, and we all had hard-ons, mine seemed easily to be a foot long at the time, and glory be to Jehosephat, all of a sudden a perfectly normal seeming chicken wandered into the shed looking for feed, glanced up, saw my gorgeous member all exposed and vibrating, and goddam if it didn't let out a crazed screech and leap for it! If I hadn't jolted back in fear, I would have lost my poor young cock right then and there. Imagine having your cock bit off by a mad barnyard hen! Old mother nature sure gets her laughs in naughty ways.

Now the big question in everybody's mind is—did you or didn't you get laid? I may be black but I'm not crazy: Yes, we did, and all hands are reported safe and sound after what was certainly one of the rippingest shipahoys recorded on Roman sex seas since Hadrian's circus. And it all took place in the apartment directly below the family hearth, a very relaxed and totally unstructured love nest that was free because its tenants, relatives of our divine hostesses, had nipped off to the hills until hostilities and such cooled in the Eternal City, and I can't say I blame them. Those sisters! I swear to God they must have done postgraduate work in a pretzel factory. No wonder the United States government has such fearfully low immigration quotas for Italians. Let more than five such girls as this enter the country in a year and they'd wreck our entire society. Ford would be lucky if it could get one car finished a week.

"This certainly beats bunker storming," George remarked as Franca, caressing his back under his pulled out shirt tails, guided him down a painting lined hallway and into a bedroom.

"Oh your lovely back is so smooth," Franca murmured, pushing him into the room. "I am going to handle every inch of it."

"Look under the bed, George!" I shouted after him. "One of those S.S. perverts might be hiding there!"

My giggles were silenced by the longest and most athletic tongue ever to leap from the rafters of the colosseum into a black boy's mouth. I grabbed her by her gorgeous, straining plump ass in order to anchor myself, and for a few very close range moments we put in a performace of bumps and grinds and tonguings that were little short of Salome at her demented peak, and I don't mean by the time toad-faced Wilde got his half-melted hands on a shred of her bikini either. But all this was merely the caviar before the storm. (I certainly hope that nobody under 18 is listening in on my confessions because the things I am about to detail are hardly meant for bamboo shoots. I could go to jail for violating the family's most cherished prerogatives.)

We broke for a minute while she undressed me. I mean pulled my clothes off. And at the same time executed intricate and passionate tongue and hand ballets on my increasingly bare body, making very sexual animal sounds as she did this—deep short pants, whining noises in her throat and nose. She licked and fondled and worked her way down to my ankles, then she began taking off her own clothes, and I sort of coiled onto the edge of the ancient baroque bed.

"Your body tastes like black honey," she said, pulling off her dress, under which there was no slip, that imbecile deputy of the superego, just a red bra holding in the insurgent wildness of her large breasts, breasts that could storm the barricades of the entire middle class if necessary, and drive its male members into mass whimpering defections, drooling, and a red mesh pair of bikini panties that precariously clung to her superb ass for dear, titillating life, almost begging for mercy and sanctuary because just one twitch of an ass muscle and those panties would have skulked off into the fathomless reaches of nonfantasy sans identity. She stood there with her hands on her wide boldly confident hips, her heavy legs apart, and smiled at me, oh lewd! lewd! lewd! no absurd disguises or distant deployments of her true female self—*cunt!* My forever dimmed (nay, forbidden) boyhood eyes made the agonizingly wonderful trip of her empire (every black eyed pea, every yam and pigs foot I'd ever eaten engulfed her magnificence, and every lynching and burning I had ever feared I would be in crawled over her in its panic), and I mean Jesus Christ there just isn't anything, anything in this whole wide bellevue world that remotely compares to that moment of symphonic, juicy pre-fuck lust. You will never get closer to God. In fact, the trinity is staring you right in the face: mouth, tits, pussy. And then you get into all that and thus you become Him!

I had planned to make my move when she had taken off her underwear, but I just couldn't stand it another second. I went ape. "Gimme!" I yelled, and, grabbing her ass, pulled her right into my face and tore off those skittish lace bikini panties with my nigger teeth. And ate right through the springy black watercress and into the Holy Ghost cooze. You would surely have thought I was raised in a pigpen, so gross and unmannerly was my etiquette.

"Oh black soldier!" she cried, holding my kinky incorrigible head and pumping her cunt to give my greediest of mouths seconds and thirds. Oh primal human juiciness! "You got the most wonderful appetite! Oh Holy Virgin yes! Your hot tongue is all the way up in my belly!" Oh sea taste!

In one great whisking motion I threw her on the bed and ripped off her unsuspecting red bra, spilling those unreconstructed mountains of tit joy and nourishment against the smouldering reality of my swollen balls and jibbering coon cock. I must confess that I had only heard vague rumors of the art of Roman ball swallowing. Now I was to see it practiced right before me. Her hot swarmy mouth turned them into roaring satellites. She then imprisoned my black dalliance between her breasts, rather as if she were concocting an Italian hero sandwich, and delightedly massaged it as I pumped. It was only a few inches and a few seconds more before my heavenly hammer was tickling her tonsils. She couldn't bear seeing it outside her body for another moment. She was like a high priestess who sees a rich votive offering, say a squealing piggy, placed outside the temple instead of inside, at the very altar, where it belongs. Such inefficient gestures can ultimately wreck a religion, no matter how sound its claims may be. However, before plunging her salivating crazed mouth over it, she rubbed it delicately (with controlled fierceness that is; as a violinist in a chamber music piece artistically holds back his passionate fury) all over her face, mumbling semi-coherent special things to it, and even put it in her ear for a second, where for all I know it may have whispered a few things to her. Then with a deep moan, she wolfed it in. For just the teeniest of moments, I thought I would never see my prick again; but this was merely a reflex fear traceable to my childhood and the terror that my father would cut my penis off, along with my testicles, for the thoroughly unimaginable crime of wanting to possess my heavy-lipped mother. But after that chilly moment I sank back into a truly eiderdown of an angel flake bliss. Such divine sucking! It was indeed the mother of all blow jobs. Deep never before tapped wells of ecstacy in my groin were awakened, pulled up into a swirling, by her powerful fervor.

Roiling moiling body and soul waters, melting me, dissolving the edges of my self aware identity and I felt her sucking sounds enter into my deepest, and I was entering and merging with them, gently, they were coming from me; I was feeling myself in my own mouth. Oh this man's lovely meat in my mouth. My breasts rubbing over him. Oooh I am dying with the wonderful hot of it. My skin is all on fire and I want to scream but I can't with him in my mouth filling every sensation of it; I can only moan and whimper. My cunt is drowning in its own poetry while it waits for him. Wait! Wait! He will be in you in a few star-smashing moments. I can hear the strangled sounds of its drowning. Wait!

His blackness is racing all through me. If I opened my eyes I know I would be black all over like him. I want him to spurt himself into my mouth and I would swallow it, every little baby droplet of him, and this god's juice would become part of my blood and me forever. But I want to save his leaping nectar for my pussy because if I didn't it would hate me and scream that my mouth had cheated it of the very food of its cathedral existence.

When he was eating the spaghetti you were watching him and thinking that he was eating you, weren't you? And don't think I don't know what you were thinking yesterday in church while young Father Flianno was lighting the candles at the altar. You ought to be ashamed of yourself. A holy priest. And the things you were having him do to you while the Virgin Mary and our beloved Savior watched! Oh what a scandal you are! Aren't you afraid of being punished by God? When I think of what you were whispering to me as I was trying my very best to recite those lovely prayers—you were reciting yours—you were having Father Flianno drop holy water on you and at the same time he was to try to balance a piece of the holy wafer on his—oh what a naughty you are!—palpitating prick. And you didn't stop there, you epic of insatiability. At your utterly wild commands he ravishes Holy Mary Mother of Christ, assaulting her not only with his driven maniacal body, his crazed tongue in her most sacred parts, front and back, as well as his divine prodder doing its own fascistic impieties, front and back too, and his bum, where you were having him put his bum! With her shining nose right inside it! Oh mercy! —and the perfectly outrageous, blasphemous utterances you were having the poor sweet man make to the mother of us all. Ravings of depravity, any one of which, had they been overheard, could have fetched him a public flogging to say nothing of several years behind cold black bars in the Coeli Prison, that stain house of human error.

And after the mass, out in front of that simply exquisite fountain bubbly and stone angel floated Church of Our Lady of Transference, the bestialities you were conducting with that berserk man, naked except for his shoes and socks, and the innocent-faced nuns. Whoops! Whoops! I actually had to cross myself, not only to gain forgiveness from Our Father, but to separate myself from you as well, I thought I would die with shame when you commanded him to say those very, very dirty things to them—"Sister Faviola, we are going to conduct a special service right up that bulging Bologna ass of yours. Prepare to take communion!"—and while she stood there paralyzed, completely unable to utter even a small scream, (but the others began to howl in terror)——your naked holy man leaped upon her, tore her habit right down the middle from behind, exposing all her carefully, devoutly concealed sex goodies, flung her to her hands and knees and rammed his flaming cock right up her obedient, stunned nun's ass. Her huge breasts swung like martyrs from a gibbet. "Sing the Twenty-Fifth Psalm, Sister Faviola!" you made him shout, you bad, bad girl you, and sure enough, that poor woman did exactly as she was told while the other nuns ran shrieking about and grabbing each other and just not knowing what they should do about this end of the world madness, this circus of hell upon the very skin of our Father Who art in Heaven. Mercy! I should make you say a hundred Hail Mary's. Sometimes I don't know what is to become of you. What if our nice neighbors knew what you were really like?

Oh, he is making me ride him now, while he pulls and sucks at my breasts and then grabs my ass and manipulates me this and that way, rubbing his lusty black hands up and down the back of my legs. He is making them feel so sensitive and excited. I have never felt them belong to me that way. It is as if he were bringing them to life. He is creating another person in me. Oh they are so hot I think I'm going to come with them too, come from my mouth and cunt and ass and the back of my legs!

"Ride it baby! Ride it!" He shouts right into the wet gasping hotness of my wild-tongued mouth. "That's the way. Hold it there. Now slam it down! Yeah baby yeah. Tease it. You are the greatest fuck! Give it to me momma!"

I should have a little horsey whip in my hand, like the one Pappa has. He looked so beautiful riding in his black uniform in the Villa Borghese. We always lie now and say he was never a fascisti. He is so afraid. Poor pappa. Poor . . .

I'm coming! And coming! and biting his black shoulder and screaming! "Ohhhh!" I am disappearing, floating, fainting. Into his blackness.

"I'm still drifting somewhere . . . you've floated me into the stars," and I kiss his armpit softly. He smells of cinnamon, like a madrigal or certain kinds of stories. Why are white American people so afraid of these Negroes? They are so delicious and they make you feel so soft. Is this heavy happy breathing black soldier someone else when he is in his own country? Or are the white Americans insane? Like Pappa's Black Shirt friends, some of them anyway. The ones like Colonel Romanelli who were always with the German S. S. crowd, smiling so much when they were around those filthy bastards, their impossible mouths almost dripping with fear, and behaving so rude and important when they were not, sometimes even having people pushed out of their way.

"You must help me, Franca my darling," Pappa said to me that awful day, walking along the Via Gregoriana on our way to meet Mamma at the Piazza di Spagna. He was wearing his freshly pressed uniform. "This is extremely important to me. Extremely."

I shall never be able to eliminate that moment from my being. As soon as the words "you must help me" journeyed from his mouth, my stomach hurt and I was frightened. Whenever something is truly serious, Pappa has a way of talking, of pronouncing his words, that is cold and without feeling, without the soft slur that is a hangover from his youth in the south. It is as if the formality of his style is somehow holding things together and providing him with a courage he does not really have. When he talks that way, and it makes me feel strange and very worried, I have always played a little trick with myself: I make believe I am someone else listening to the hurtful words, and the real me, or my emotions, stands a few feet away and just watches, and when they are over with, I return to myself, so to speak. I did that then.

"Yes, Pappa," I replied, or my substitute self replied. "What is it?"

He did not answer right away. The two mes waited in pain. But his long pause was understandable: His first statement was a precipice and he had to gather his strength before leaping to the next, most important one. A silly looking young matron with the face of a spoiled child was coming toward us, leading a tiny snobbish black dog. Pappa waited until she had passed us before speaking. This immediately, and uncomfortably, made it clear that his message was too secret and critical to be overheard even by a stranger.

"The Germans want Alberto," he finally said, looking straight ahead.

The substitute me collapsed, and it was I who was sucked into the vacuum there, and it was a frozen desolation. Alberto was my lover.

"What do you mean, Pappa?"

"The S.S. has found out something that even I did not know

—that Alberto is one of the leaders of the partisan underground. They know he is your boy friend. He has disappeared, because he undoubtedly knows he is being looked for. They want you to deliver him to them." He was still not looking at me.

My head felt like a rock that was going to fall from my shoulders. It seemed that for those moments Pappa and I were completely isolated in a tear drop of insanity.

"You are mad," I whispered, for my strength had heartlessly abandoned me.

"It is Alberto or me," he said.

"What?"

He stopped abruptly and turned to me. His normally small and somewhat womanish face was now so contorted with fury and despair that I had the feeling that a demented child was looking at me. "You idiot!" he screamed. "You don't seem to understand!" I thought he was going to hit me. "If they don't get Alberto, they will take me! I will go to prison or be shot! Do you see?"

Oh my God. My father or my lover. I could not speak, only stare at Pappa's grotesque face. Now Mamma appeared at the top of the Spanish Steps. She waved, and walked in her young girl way toward us. She was so lovely in her yellow knit suit. "I just saw Olivera Danezi," she said, "and do you know, she's having another baby. Can you imagine it? Only twenty one and having a third child. Madonna mia!"

I died. I had to die in order to do what Pappa commanded. I could not bear to be near him during that time, and for weeks afterward. We did not look at each other. And the most peculiar thing, he began to smell very bad. Every day it got worse. I don't know why Mamma and Maria never showed that they were aware of it. He smelled of fresh shit. Perhaps in his preoccupation with his uncertain life he did not attend properly to the wiping of himself. Or perhaps he developed one of those peculiar psychological diseases you read about. Neither Mamma nor Maria knew about my assignment. Once or twice they asked me why I was acting so strange. I lied and said that my boss, the German Colonel Heinz, was being more than usually obnoxious. Yes, I delivered Alberto to the Gestapo to save my father's life. It was the same as if I had given them myself.

"Meet me at the west side of the Piazza Colonna, next to the sweet shop," I told Alberto on the telephone, "at six o'clock."

"Is anything the matter?" he asked gently. "Your voice sounds funny."

"I think I have a cold in my throat," I lied.

"I'll cover it with kisses," he said. "That's an old Florentine cure."

"All right," I managed to say. I wanted to cry and to tell him to run for his life.

"You aren't pregnant, are you, Franca?"

"No. But I wish I were." We did not say anything for a moment. Then I couldn't stand it any longer. "I must go now, Alberto. Someone is knocking on the door of the booth. Goodbye. I love you." I hung up, and ran down the street, ran from myself and my father and my love for Alberto whom I would never never see again, the one person who made my heart want to beat every moment of the day. And I went to stay with Aunt Orianna in Frascati for several weeks because I broke down like a crazy person. Even then Maria and Mamma did not know how Alberto was caught by the Gestapo. I have never told them.

What did Alberto think when he was grabbed by the Germans instead of me in the Piazza Colonna? Of course he must have known how they got there, and the terrible loathing for me must have run through his whole body like a mountain stream of hot poison. Or is it possible he did not think he was betrayed by me, that the Germans just caught him on their own? And when they were torturing him to death . . . Oh God!

. . . bloody mother fuck cops beating my old man to death in front of me and my mother and brother Jackson just because he wouldn't step down in the gutter to let them stagger drunkenly by on the sidewalk. Huntsville, Alabama: On that day I vowed I would someday kill every white mother fuck living in you and then burn that pus-filled town down to the very ground while all those little white kids watched and screamed. Oh shit, what a time to be thinking of a mass auto da fé, when I've got an armful of Italian fuck joy.

"Honey," I said "I've decided to become an Italian citizen. No kidding."

VII

THERE I WAS AGAIN...IN A SMALL TIME street in Guadaloupe, ferociously searching for some people— "types," they might be called—who didn't have the faintest notion that they were fugitives. (When will these clucks wise up and begin to understand, if only too well, the nature of my self castigations? I ask you: when?) I was slyly taking the measure of a smoked sausage, presumably dangling in a butcher shop, when a tug on my sleeve brought me about. That amalgam of underground minutia, that eternal pensioner of freak shows that were not hiring, that smudge . . .

"Persistence in itself is not necessarily a virtue," he suggested, apropos my mission, I know, and the amount of familiarity that he secreted was not to be denied. Not by me, anyway. (And certainly not in such an unpromising alley). "It must be related to something that will reward it with response and change."

"I am not entirely unaware of that," I indicated with a few well chosen twitches. "That is, if you are referring to soliloquies in action."

I shifted our focus somewhat and at the same time noticed that my gnostic friend was sporting a red tie. Where, I asked myself, could anything so tentative, as physically and psychically fluctuating as he, where, as I said, could he have laid his teensy hands on anything as central as a hot red cravat?

"Well, that's one way of looking at it," he allowed, and scratched himself in a place that most decent mothers have placed permanent sentries around. "But before we go a step further, in either direction," he continued, putting both his little hands against my stomach, as if I personified all progress that must be halted before any cultural regrets set in, "I must make two firm observations."

"Why not?"

"First," he began, tossing a quick handful of raisins into his mouth," I wish to state that structure is its own reward, no more, no less."

"Quite acceptable," I said, dodging quickly to avoid some stuff heaved out of an upstairs window.

"Second. Your, uh, nose. My Lord! No wonder Liebnitz never went in swimming."

I patted him tenderly on the head, but he got the message.

He said, "Regarding our previous dialog in that cobbler's stifled skill. . . . A few more points have overtaken me and since there is something that binds us, some ineffable and savage glue, I plan to share them with you." He sat down quite unostentatiously on a public bench next to a patisserie. The least I could do was sit next to him (all other things being equal, of course.) An unimpaired and wholly decent anisette cookie passed between us.

"Fair game," I murmured. "That's what everything seems to be"

He lowered his lashes at me and his eyebrows (I suppose). "Hmm. Well, let's see. . . ." (Jaysus! There he was reading from somewhere again. This time it had to be written in the sky.) "The position, or lack of it, of the artist in society. And not only contemporary but I suspect from the first human groan on."

I put my finger up. "Pardon. But that last bit. . . . I'm afraid I'll have to contest it. My understanding is that in those very early times the artist was very much integrated into his community. And not only that. . . ."

He noiselessly encountered his bowler with my mouth. "Your time is up. As I was trying to say. . . . Isn't the artist always inventing himself vis a vis his fiction (dream) and therefore is he not to be more dimensionally understood, or seen, as his characters and not 'himself,' or the person-artist apart?"

He blew the fragile hand of an aging black beggar off my shoulder, then resumed his prophecy. "And does he not, therefore, literally and mythically, die—cease to be—when he cannot create himself? That is, when he can no longer invent characters? Hence his secrecy regarding his art—his ideas, his magic, that is. He can be killed if his secret, or magic, or self-life inventing force, is discovered or uncovered. And aren't his neurotic artist behavior antics really frauds, by which I mean very clever devices for luring away the attention of The Others, the seeker, the common man, from his real self and his counterfeiting factory deep underground?"

We sighed into each other's measureless expressions. How perfectly staggering that we should be having such a perfection of intermingling in such a fallen fruit as Guadaloupe. Oh tourism gone berserk!

"I understand everything you're not saying," I informed him. "I think it would have been a damn good thing for everybody if you had written the Old Testament instead of those hired old hands who did. And I mean it."

He settled a digestive dispute the only way he could, being more or less human, and leaped to it once more. "The horrifying dilemma is that in order to exist, one has to work toward separating oneself from The Others. Therefore one is continually 'mediating' oneself rather than an I-Thou situation. The artist is I-Me, or anti I-Thou. Crisis occurs in the artist when he can no longer invent characters, or substitutes for the outside community, and-or does not sustain a dialogue or 'mediation' with them (himself multiplied, that is). When he uses the language of public conventions and absurdity instead of reinvigorating them with a private speech that thinks and breathes as it is uttered. Setting up another stage as it exhausts the one it is on, you see." He let me reflect on that for a moment, then carefully, in a manner to which I could easily become accustomed, whispered, "Words think."

The honesty of the noonday sun required that I unequivocally buy us a couple of ices from a lingering illness half asleep at his cart there. As I was handing my friend his, he grabbed me by both lapels and put his complete face so close to mine that it was no longer a question of comfort. "You must understand and absorb every word I am bequeathing to you!" he whispered, and meanly too. "Because if you don't, we're both dead ducks."

"I'm here!" I shouted. "I'm with us! Simmer down, for the love of it, eat your ice cream like a good fellow."

He did, but I do not wish to relate the details of his eating style. All I can say is that it was a considerable advance (if you want to call it that) over the more conventional mouth and tongue route.

"Before I forget," he said, wiping himself with the remains of a martyr's recantation, "I have to go on record with a couple of statements about dreams, as those experiences are rebuked by the scoffers."

He lifted his bowler to scratch his head and a morning dove

—whether it had just been visiting there or leasing the space under a more or less permanent and decent arrangement with the owner, I cannot, of course say—whirred off and into a nearby tree.

"I have a few ideas about trans-schematic experiences myself," I began, "and particularly their relationship to that part of the individual I shall call The Required Schemer. You see. . . ."

In another moment I was brushing my ear where he had kicked me with his midday slipper.

"Blabberfroth!" he howled. "Soulless tongue! Phew! It licks the very meaning out of meaning. It presumes to know the secrets of speech before they even take place. Oh greed! Oh violated silences! Grafitti on gravestones!" He adjusted his queasy cravat. "I suggest you sit on the naughty thing for a bit. Might do you both a lot of good." He spat on his baby hands and rubbed them briskly together. "so. . . .dreams. . . .oh yes. . . .Dreams are counter-reality creations, one's own sanity inventions against the unbearable but required daily living in communal insanity. One has his nightmares only when the dream breaks down and is no longer nourishing, serving as counter reality, and the other, or daily working reality, rushes in; either the imagery breaks down or the super-ego feels the dream is too successful and the dreamer may vanish into the dream—be totally insane or die, as far as the super ego understands it. It is not a sign, nightmares, that is, of unbearable revelations. It is the paradox that the dream is succeeding only too well and is becoming The Only Way, not that it, the dream, is malfunctioning. One is one's own myth and mythology. The artist and dreams are the same thing: he is his own dream. He breaks down only when he can't dream anymore and the other so-called reality roars in. But why?"

I stared straight into us. "Why what?"

"Why is it that he can't dream anymore?" he replied, and wiped some tropical sweat off his chin (to give him the benefit of the doubt, that is.)

I scrutinized my own horizons, then suggested, "Perhaps because he, too, is afraid of vanishing into his own creation or dream." I was not afraid; I would pursue this. "Fear is the thing that holds him to this world. It is the price he pays for coming out of the same womb as everybody else. What I mean is, a fellow can't give himself a transfusion with his own blood."

My friend began to scribble in a little notebook. "Hm. I'll take this up at the committee's next meeting and let you know. But don't hold your breath. If you get an invitation to a truffle hunt, grab it."

We conspired our way down to the yawning public square. We crept there in a most arrogant way, and I'm honestly surprised that we got away with it. We did not have to bribe a soul. The action on the square was hardly bloodcurdling. The inhabitants had been listing over their espresso and vermouth ever since the last arms embargo, I'm sure of it. I was about to suggest a trip to an internationally famous cat house when my friend suddenly plucked a shred of paper from his pocket and read the scribble on it. "Oh mercy!" he shrieked. "I'm late for an appointment with Voltaire!" and he virtually vanished in an explosion of apprehension. But before disappearing into a cab, he turned and yelled back to me. "Let me tell you something! This place"—he slowly waved his arm in a gentle arc—"has been forged in a silence of uproars."

There was, of course, no way of telling when I would see him again. Obviously, whether one understood it or not, he came and went as he pleased, accountable only to the sweet nudgings within himself. Carefree as a spanish pocket.

VIII

GEORGE WAS IN THE CENTER OF AN epiphany. The big piece of fresh buttered bread was dunked into the mug of India tea, his mouth was soppily filled with the previous bite, the English plaid tweed cap felt firm and uncomplaining on his long haired head, the madonna-eyed girl at the table in front of him in the snatch-high mini-skirt opened her sweet mouth in amazement at something that her boyfriend said, and a male voice from behind him at the beer soaked bar announced, "That bloody bahstud coshed me for five quid!" And the moment, with its special London sights, smells, sounds and all else, suddenly bespoke itself in a ping of perfection. No specks of wrong fly, no green sneaking around like blue. Diamond, all diamond. Love tea was what he then resumed dunking his sturdy buttered bread in.

Behind him the splendid clank of half crown coins, an exchange of metal symbols for the tasty and anything but symbolic beer. The monk-haired blue-eyed lad with the mini-skirted glee touched his sausage to a bit of mustard and rewarded his soft twenty-two, or -three year old mouth with the morsel.

And where is that morsel, April? Late again. Why? Is it that she is not able to appear until something epiphanies her? That she doesn't exist yet, and is waiting there, in the air possibly? Or in someone else's mind? Or is she in fragments—a gesture, a word, her hair, lips—in scores of places around the world, Hong Kong, Nairobi, Cleveland, and each element of her is having a little trouble connecting with the other elements? That must be it— either one of those possibilities. Hurry! Hurry! We've got things to do. The stage is waiting! The audience is getting squirmy, coughing a lot.

The money is the stage—all that crinkly boodle trembling there in the pickup van with those delicious football minded limey lads, pistols on their hips that never want to be shot because it simply is not in the English mind, that sort of sound, more or less mothering the stuff to the bank. And the rich part is that it really won't be a surprise to them. That's what their fantasies are all about (when they're not on that sweaty field scoring with the dirty ball), the day of the great robbery. They have run through it so many times, playing both sides too, that the real thing will actually come as an after the fact documentation. "Sorry I'm late, luv, but we was robbed today. Bloody truth."

And then to . . . and then to . . . where? What Shangri-La will we lam it to with the bread? They tell me Rio is a veritable Eden of safety and sensuality. Rome—buy ourselves a villa and guzzle wine and watch the gladiators tear each other apart in the Colosseum. Helsinki—load up with reindeer skins and spend our days steaming and twigging each other's par boiled nakedness. Oh, the places we'll gobble up! There won't be a fun city left that won't need intensive shock therapy after we're through. Bet your granny's asshole on that! Ah, here is my peaches and cream happening. Christ! This girl would have turned Billy Goat Gruff on.

"I was going to take a taxi," April said, slipping in close by George and putting her hand in the inside of his grey flannel thigh, "But I thought of all the men I could give joy to in my new clothes. I feel positively dangerous in them," and she laughed a bower of roses.

"Baby," George said, kissing her ear, "you're dangerous even when you're asleep. Your dreams become other people's realities," and he rubbed her marvelous stomach, feeling nothing between the sly mini dress and her always alive skin.

"Is everything all set?" she asked, smiling so nice that George could have disappeared forever down her wet pink mouth.

"Everything, baby, everything. This thing is so beautifully set up I sometimes have the feeling it was constructed in Switzerland."

"Tic toc?"

"Exactly. And how is your watch, April love?"

"Set for everything."

He put his hand on her stockinged thigh. "You are indescribably the hope of the western world, sugar baby. Millions and millions of people have no days, much less hours, and consequently exist completely outside time which is to say they don't exist at all. But you *are* time. The essence of moment. April," he said, squeezing a soft area of girl meat, "I sometimes feel that you are a complete world unto yourself, so help me."

She smiled a morning rising of the sun and leaned over his small scotch and gave him a kiss that contained just the right amount of French, considering where they were. "I try," she said, "I always try my best."

George caressed her knee some more. "Children all over the world should be saluting you instead of their national flags." He had to kiss her fingers now. "It would increase their human potential and cut down on wars."

April grabbed the bald ole luvvie of a waiter by his white jacket as he passed their table looking straight ahead because of good breeding and a quite satisfying afternoon fantasy involving a youngish aunt of his in Cornwall, and said gently, "Clive, darling, I desperately require a sausage and half a pint of ale. My health is in jeopardy."

"Immediately, Miss April, immediately." And of course off the dear chap went. Miss April was in his sack in place of Auntie, and she was munching. . . .

George began to chuckle over his own pint. Small chuckles barely enough to fit into a cavity.

"Having a daydream are you?" April asked.

"I was just thinking what a beautifully clever idea it is of Zachary's to use his Zen as a diversionary technique," and a tumble of chuckles came to life.

April observed him for a couple of moments—her order had appeared and she was delicately touching chunks of sausage to spots of mustard—before saying, "Do you feel you could share the details of this delight with me without in any way compromising its secret integrity?"

George pulled his fragmentations together. "While the guards from Lloyds are loading the money from the bank onto their truck, Zachary is going to disengage them and the passers by with a demonstration of Zen archery! Can't you just see it—all those crazy arrows flying down Bond Street! Zachary and his beard wrapped in white robes as if he were right at home in the mountains of Tibet. Oh dear! Everybody there will think they're in the middle of a dream!"

"As indeed they might be," April said, washing down a piece of sausage with the ale. "I'm so happy that we'll have Daddy Katz driving the get away car."

"Me too. Couldn't have a better man for the job." He watched a boy with hair completely covering his face maneuvering a glass of beer into his mouth. "And the lovely thing is he doesn't want a penny for it. Says the work itself is reward enough."

"Oh yes. He's completely work-oriented. Keeping busy is his very life drive. When he's not engaged in a business operation he might as well be a patient in a funny farm. That's Daddy for you."

"Not much fun for a growing child, I imagine."

"Indeed not," and she patted his full-lipped, implicitly berserk mouth with a napkin to absorb a little ale dampness.

"But he's an awfully good driver. He's in absolutely perfect rapport with all the springs and valves. Very Zen. Studying under Zachary has done him worlds of good."

"Hmm. Bit late for him and other people, though, wouldn't you say?"

"Ah yes. Afraid I must agree with you there all right." And George licked a deposit of ale foam from his thin upper lip. At a small table to their right a young man with innocent cod eyes was telling a vibrating lass with fine hair all about the brutality of American foreign policy. "Genocide," he said. "They plan to wipe out the entire population. First the Indians, now the Vietnamese."

"Someone ought to drop the bomb on New York City," the girl said. "That would show them."

A gleaming swollen silver Bentley murmured up to the curb and with the most genteel gasp discharged an exuberantly fleshed black couple—man and woman—whose massive, central essence smiles were garbed in yards and yards of madly patterned materials. Around their gold slippered feet, sniffing and trembling, were half a dozen little dogs—pugs, poodles, terriers, chihuahuas, junk like that. They gave you the feeling that they had breakfasted on creamed chicken and truffles, lapped down with Dr. Pepper. The man's smile was a million dollars worth of ingratiation.

"Black African nobility," observed the girl with fine hair.

"Yes," said her lover. "Here in London to betray their people with the help of our foreign office and the American CIA."

One of the two little gray poodles began to jump up and down and bark peevishly. "Now now, Hector," the big Negro woman said, turning around and wagging a jeweled finger at the dog. "You promised me you would be a good boy if I brought you to London. Now you don't want Mummy to lose faith in you, do you?"

The complaining little beast whined some tiny response and scurried quietly to the back of the dog cluster.

"Shall we nip along?" George said, patting the fat rich mustache he had pasted on this morning.

"Smashing idea," April replied, brushing some imagined bread crumbs from her scant mini-skirted lap.

"It's very odd," George began, once they were outside and heading for their souped-up Simca—it would do a hundred-and-seventy miles per hour in a sneeze—"but every time we are just beginning to caper, I get an enormous hard-on and I'm almost overwhelmed with the desire to give you a big bang."

April put her arm around him and hugged. "Oh that is lovely. Why don't you do a paper on the correlation of crime and the sex drive?"

"I'd rather ram you."

"Let's do it in the car then. A quickie."

"That's just it," he said, putting his arm around her unforgettable waist and gently rubbing the skin just above the elastic of her panties. "I'm afraid it would sap my criminal effectiveness."

"Sounds like the age old artist's fear."

He sighed. "Does, doesn't it. Ah well, we can have a big party after the score. Fuck for days. Every imaginable position."

"You're making me hot now."

"Sorry. Let's concentrate on money then."

"Yes."

Funny thing, George said to himself, this fake mustache is giving me a reality. I'm beginning not to feel like myself. A London hovel, that's what is creeping over me. The other me, the one I'm talking to, is slipping off into the bushes. I can feel myself growing up in the slums of south London. Lots of slaps and kicks and bad food. A mum who drinks straight gin in the pubs and yells at the old man all the time because he's such a no-good failure. All he can do is lift second-hand furniture onto trucks and dream about winning the soccer pool.

"Don't have any bloody get up and go about you!" she yells, bringing the pot with the smelly cabbage in it.

"You're bloody lucky I don't," he says, sucking on his smelly pipe and turning the sports pages. " 'Cause if I did I'd get up and go out of here, that's what I'd do, you old camel's fart."

Smash. A glass bounces off the floor of that deranged kitchen. I jump up from the table and run out into the alley. As I'm going through the door I hear a slapping sound as the old lady lets him have one across the face, and his shout of rage and horror tells me —my whole dirty skinny little body—that someday I am going to kill someone.

"What's the matter, Georgie boy?" the penny-faced kid leaning against the warehouse wall asks. "Your mom and dad bashin' at each other again?"

"Bugger them," I say. "Let's go over to old Simon's and steal something."

"That's the ticket, old Georgie."

Had a lucky streak there in the reformatory where they sent me after I got nabbed breaking into Weston's clothing store with little Jimmy Barnes, a triple-kneed lad with at least one tic to his young credit. Very lucky indeed, because life in those bloody children's jails can be quite thoroughly shitty, what with their

making you do all those absurd exercises and then working in shop
to give you a trade so you won't return to a life of crime when they
spring you. Both the headmaster and his wife took a shine to me
and I was spared the dignities of punishment. Beddoes the gym
instructor tried to get me on the wrestling team but I was too busy
learning boudoir judo from the Millbrooks.

"Move up on the bed a little, George sweetie, so that Tom
won't fall off. That's a good lad."

"Now you sit backwards on George's lap, Jane love, and I'll
stand on this little footstool in front of you. That's the girl."

The whole bloody place smelled of moldy bread, even the
swimming pool if you can imagine that. Every last lad there had
the sneaky pained look of someone who has just pissed his pants.
I was totally rehabilitated there. I came out fully prepared to take
my place in society—a master lock picker. Quite as good as gradu-
ating from Harrow.

"Hmm," murmured April. "This car has such a very cozy hum
to it—just like it is all over me when I've had a big come. A lovely
soft hum starting from deep inside my cunt and vibrating warmly
all through my body. Mm."

Peregrinations needed, the car was saying to George. The
street ahead now seemed very sweet. Nothing was bothering it
any more. Several yards away—though he really seemed to be in
the distant future—a young man wearing white jockey shorts was
smiling and blowing kisses to them. At first George thought he
was an old army buddy, but when he stuck his hand out of the car
to touch him on the cheek, the young man said, "How silly of you.
We've always been strangers, you and I," and George noticed that
he had been crying.

"You heard that in a movie," George said, feeling a strange soft
anger. "Puzzling statements amuse you."

But the young man was no longer interested. He was eating
an old sandwich, and he seemed now very much like George's
mother. "I gave up my beauty to bring you into the world," he
seemed to say, but George was not really sure he had spoken.

"Oh well," George whispered. "There will be other times."
He felt mature and philosophical as he made this gentle statement.
He noticed that the brown tweed jacket he had been wearing was
gone from his body: in its place was an old blue striped suit that

had belonged to his father. This did not upset him, though. The stores that bordered both sides of the street sparkled beautifully. Over one of them, in the slim door of which a nude girl was standing, was a sign which said "keep lying in cool places."

"Naturally," George said, more to himself than to anyone else.

Then he was in a stadium where thousands of people were yelling. There was something vaguely familiar about them, but George did not feel like making anything out of this. "Some things are not worth pursuing," said an old lady who was all swollen in her face. George merely patted her head and moved away. Really, floated off. He knew he was looking for someone but he could not quite tell who. This bothered him but without anxiety. Down below on the field scores of people were fighting. Some of them were covered with blood. One of the bloodiest was April. George rushed through the bleachers to her side. He could feel pain all through his body.

"Please stop doing this to yourself!" he shouted to her, and put his arms around her bleeding body.

"You have not been invited here," she said, and threw him off and to the soft ground. "Besides, you're really worried about yourself," and she made a sly obscene gesture at him. He began to sob like a young boy.

"Oh," he sobbed. "The things a nice boy can't do."

April giggled as she hit another young girl in the face. "This is the finest day of your life."

George got up and brushed himself off. "I wish you hadn't said that," and he felt quite removed from everything there. An old man with a baseball cap on his head was climbing onto George's shoulder and making silly sounds. George merely whispered a warning in his ear and the man slid off him. "I don't really need you," the man shouted. But George was far, far away now. Up in the sky a plane was writing "Impetuous fools."

However, George was suddenly overcome with fatigue and did not want to do anything with that information. "I'm too old for that kind of stuff," he murmured, and smiled to himself. He felt safe for the first time. But was also aware that this feeling was not guaranteed to last forever. An old fashioned taxicab with a big hole in the roof stopped right in front of him. The driver was a woman with sleek black hair and George was positive she was his mother. He opened the door of the taxi and put his head on her lap.

"Tell me how it all happened," he said, as nicely as he knew how.

But the woman didn't say anything. She lit an English cigarette and began to study a road map. Suddenly a man got up off the floor in the back of the taxi. He was quite drunk and George wanted to hit him.

"You're not wanted here!" George yelled.

The man giggled. "Neither are you," he said, and began drinking out of an old dirty bottle.

Then George was driving the taxi as fast as he could and trying to avoid all the cars that were heading toward him honking very angrily.

THE AFTERNOON CROWDS IN PICCADILLY WERE just right: heavy but not clotted, and very much absorbed in the pursuit of nothingness disguised as somethingness which put upon each person an obligation of seriousness and inaccessibilty, otherwise the whole thing might just explode into thin air. A definite feeling of thin sandwich was everywhere in the air. No one in the streets looked gorged with overgoodness of life.

Katz and the Boy Blaster were seated in the serene upper class security of the front of the Rolls. Katz at the wheel on the right.

"I hope to Christ that April and George are on time," Katz said, looking straight ahead. "Like a good business, these things must be perfectly organized if they are to be successful."

The Blaster caressed the submachine gun hidden under the jacket on his lap. "I trust those kids. They're quick and hungry. Yessir."

"That's all very well," Katz said, his eyes tightening like an executive in a think tank. "But the entire operation must be synchronized perfectly. That's the key to modern industry. You can be assured of that, my friend."

"Al would like this kind of set up," the Blaster said more or less to himself, and smiled slightly. He watched the doorman of the bank, a squiggly red-haired chap with a nose that was clearly outdated.

"He won't give us any trouble. I can tell."

Katz gave the man an examination. "I would never hire a man like that." And he turned his gaze away, still squinting executively.

George and April were an indistinguishable part of the human moil on the street not far from the entrance to the bank. They both were now wearing huge stylish dark glasses, very mod. If people around them had thought about it, they would have remarked that George and April, in those glasses, had mistaken Piccadilly for Venice, but they were too enmeshed in their own fantasies. A block away, Zachary stood happily in a doorway, a bow and a container of arrows over his right shoulder. Across the street, at the wheel of a bulging vegetable truck, sat Bosworth, the Persian Prince. With him, dressed in the politely insane clothes of a vegetable farmer's wife, was Lola. She was peeling an orange. Bosworth was smoking a Players cigarette and trying to feel agrarian. He was imagining himself on a farm in Devon examining a fat cabbage for leaf worm. The smellfeast in the truck made him feel natural and happy and a bona fide member of the animal kingdom. Nothing could be wrong in the world if things smelled that good. Lola put an orange wedge in his mouth.

At exactly four minutes after four, a decently black bank delivery truck drove up the human street and stopped right in front of the bank. Three red-faced men in uniform got out of the truck. Two of them began unloading large canvas bags of English money onto a little truck, while the third man, whose calm made you feel he was either superbly sure of himself or quite dumb, more or less stood guard. All three wore pistols in holsters on their hips. When the little truck was piled high with the bags and the men turned to start walking into the bank, Zachary and his hunchback went to work. The hunchback began beating his drum as though it were a mad dog, and Zachary began shooting the balloon arrows into the street. The crowds and the cars immediately went berserk. The cars honked and stalled and the crowds yelled in delight and fear. The three guards with the money stopped and watched, and in that disoriented pause April and George went into action. April jostled the guards and at the same time—she and George had slipped breathing masks on—sprayed big clouds of ammonia in their faces. The surprised, blinded guards went to pieces and started hopping about, screaming and clawing at their faces. Father Katz meanwhile had tooled the Rolls right to that spot. In the same synchronized gesture, the Blaster opened the back door, and April and George, working with the ease, speed, and precision of two trained dolphins, flung the money bags into the car. Now, finally, the red haired guard came out of his trance of bewilderment and ran toward the car, waving his gun. "Stop! Stop!" he shouted. Blaster pointed the submachine gun at him and smiled. The man stopped, dropped his gun, shouted, "Oh No! Not me!" and scrammed back into the bank. April and George threw the last money bag into the car (the guards had been ruined even more by being pushed about by the crazed crowds, who didn't know whether to watch the robbery or Zachary's insane balloon-arrow act or the drum playing hunch). The cars were beginning to ram each other in their traffic jammed frustration. Now Father Katz shot his car away from the curb and down a tiny prim side street. A wailing siren was heard. Two police cars, summoned by some unique human still in control of his senses, sped into the big intersection. But their journey was doomed, for the Prince, exhilirated immensely by the produce smells, pulled his huge old truck into the center of the street, pulled a special lever, and spilled tons of fruit and vegetables into the path of the two squad cars. The sanity of the first car was seriously impaired when it was swallowed by a suddenness of cauliflower. A new young officer name Cedric, who was driving the police car, slammed on the brakes and cried, "Blimey! A cabbage storm!"

"Isn't that a sonnet?" Bosworth sighed, sloshed by the sight.

"It sure as shit is. Let's get out of here," said Lola, and grabbed his soft brown hand and pulled him into the protective chaos of the crazed street. Half a block away Zachary was experiencing one psychic breakthrough after another.

THAT EVENING ALL THE HAPPY PARTICIPANTS were together in a self-conscious but lovely studio in the West End. Several agonized action paintings hung on the white walls, but the gang there were in no way distracted by their cries of suffering. This artistic nonsense was redeemed, however, by an exquisite porcelain figure study—executed in the 20th century—

of Dostoievski going down on Joan of Arc (tied to her burning cross) which perched on a pedestal next to a long couch where George and April were holding hands and giggling. The source of delight to George and April—and of course to the others as well —was a bully-sized pile of English bank notes in the center of the floor. And two thirds covered by the lush green of this pile was the hunchback, beside himself with glee and gin.

"You were never so splendid, Esmeralda," Zachary said, for the hunch was very much a faggot. "Your drumming was all heart."

Esmeralda flung some money bundles into the air. "This beats sex!"

"An understandable but sick point of view," observed Bosworth, and had himself a scotch refill poured by Lola who was passing various refreshments around.

Looking at her in her gold lamé shorts and wispy halter, which was merely playing the violin to the stunning percussion of her breasts, Father Katz did not know what to concentrate on—incest, money, or booze. After a moment he chose booze. The Blaster was cleaning his submachine gun and wondering whether the newspapers would give the robbery a decent writeup. "They usually leave out the best parts," he muttered. "They just don't understand what it's all about." He looked deep into Katz's glazed eyes. "How could they know about the beauty of it?"

George softly snatched a concise bundle of ten-pound notes tossed into the air by ecstatic drunken Esmeralda, (who by this time was back in some crazy old English novel from which he had been dragged, somehow, in the first place). "Did you see that doorman!" George said, puckering with delight. "That red hair was too much. Insane! Can you imagine such a guy working for a bank? Oh no," and he grabbed April in a spasm of laughter.

"The poor dear is still running, I'll bet," said April, kissing George's ear and sipping off the remainder of the Piper Heidseck in his left hand.

Zachary strolled over from his spot under a particularly angry painting—angry and self-pitying—and dipped his sandled foot into the pile of money. "Consider all of the human vanity that is contained in this glowing heap." he said. "What does this green currency buy? I will tell you—oceans and light years of desolation and apartness. Every pound spent upon an object or a worldly pleasure is a step away from oneself."

Lola paused in the offering of a piece of smoked eel to George. "I know a lot of people who could regard that step as a very good thing."

Esmeralda shrieked under a hail of paper power. "Money is friendship! Money is food!" He kissed a bundle of fives, and reached out for his drink on the floor. "This is more money than my entire family has had in ten generations." He swallowed the champagne quickly, spilling some of it on his chin and chest. "More times than I like to remember, a lousy shilling in my pocket would have been a gift from God." He sighed, then belched—it was like a distant underground explosion—and threw approximately a thousand pounds into Daddy Katz's lonely middle-aged lap. (The touch of the money produced an instant erection—as if a soft jade's hand had done the job.) "Daddy Katz, do you remember when we were stranded out in that asshole of the world, Pocatello, Idaho, just after the show had folded due to indifference to the performing arts?"

Katz shook his head at the recollection of time past. "I still bear the scars of that dreadful act of managerial naiveté."

"Top level jerk-off, you're right. Anyway, there we were, not a stone's throw in time from the California gold rush. . . ."

"The discovery of the steam engine," Katz corrected.

"Sorry. And not a bagel between us. Jesus! I can still feel the snow drifts of my infinite despair. It was such a desperate situation that Cedric the lion tamer gave up the business altogether and married a Mormon widow who ran a sugar beet farm." Lola inserted a sedge of caviar wafer into his memory-watering mouth and just laughed when he touched her swinging tit with his nose. "Daddy Katz and I would have starved and frozen had the local saloon keeper not taken pity on us—I reminded him of his dead mother, it seemed—and let us sleep in the back room in return for cleaning up the joint. That seemed to be the end of the world for us—two of the finest low comics in show business, until one wept-out day. . . ."

"I came along," said Lola, sitting on Bosworth's brown-lap, and giving him a French type kiss in his upper-class Iranian ear.

"Right."

"And saved you."

"Right!" and Esmeralda kicked several thousand pounds into the air.

("Rome," George whispered to April, "We'll go there and devour that entire Nero scene.")

"I had come all the way from New York City to be married to a rich lonely rancher," Lola went on, kissing Bosworth's face a couple more times. "Through a marriage brokerage. I'd been working as a dancer in a cabaret in Brooklyn, and I just had to change my luck. My legs were wearing out getting nowhere."

"I remember those legs," Esmeralda said, smiling nostalgically into the air. "Wonderful lines, full of delicate bounce. Their beauty and imminent passion possessed me. Every night I went to sleep imagining them wrapped around me. They became part of my soul, part of my mind, part of my body. I licked them so often in my desire that they entered me. I felt them under me, I walked the dirt streets of that town with them. I touched the heavy cushion of their quiff hour by hour. They gradually pushed upward, forcing my grotesque torso to vanish, in disgust. My hump melted and the doe softness that replaced. . . ."

"Esmeralda! Get out of here! Get out of me! Stop it!"

"But Lola, I am you! I've become you! We are both inside you!"

"Stop it, you disgusting little horror. Out!"

Oh Jesus! imagine that little nightmare becoming me. I woke up one morning very upset and I realized I had been dreaming somebody else's dream. His dream. We were mixed in and out of each other. All day long I found myself doing things that were weird, because they weren't me, they were him, and then the other strange thing was that since he was me and I was seeing with parts of him, I was really watching myself all the time, and at night there were three of us screwing in that big old walnut bed, me and Mr. Fairbanks my husband and Esmeralda inside me or me inside him and we were coming every which way. Sometimes I could feel a bump on my back and when I put my hand down to wipe the dripping sperm from my pussy my hand would feel a cock instead, wet and spent and crazily strange. It was another person but it was me. I liked it though, I mean there I was a man and a woman and holding that cock was being in two different worlds at the same time. Mr. Fairbanks my bride-purchasing husband would have shit himself blue if he'd known he was really going down on a male hunchback. Oh dear.

But maybe not. Maybe he was also somebody else and himself too, so that a hunch was just the thing both of them wanted to be eating. Oh the slip and the slide of things! The nowhere and allwhere of life! Wouldn't change it if you offered me a dozen blue camels.

I bailed those two all right. Katz was becoming a charwoman and thinking very seriously of knocking himself off because of the humiliation and despair of it, coming down from one of the country's leading slapstick carnival comedians to this spit-soaked sawdust on a barroom floor in a one-eyed frontier town and the airplane yet to be invented. Installed them at the ranch as manager and assistant in charge of marketing. Katz was as happy as the fuzz on a peach. He was selling sides of dressed beef to greasy spoons and swank eateries as far away as Salt Lake City. Bargaining and planning and pacing, and adding and subtracting all those clanking silver dollars. He was back in top shape. For awhile there it looked like he might have to live among human beings. But the game of commerce saved him and took him right back to the world of scoring. Whew! And Esmeralda, how he loved the blood baths in the slaughter house! The screams of the animals and the briskets of red washed from Esmeralda all the false dirt and false face of civilization and swept him back to his terrible origins! Only then he drank the amazed hot blood, as it poured and spurted from a torn furred throat. Oh God! I can taste it! And I am leaping up and down around the thrashing beast and yelling with joy and now my blood-stained nakedness is grappling with another, and we are rolling on the forest leaves and a huge hairy cock is being rammed into me and another's teeth are tearing at my arms and shoulders in bestial human passion. But is this my hump or his, my cunt or hers? Both both oh I'm going to die with the incredible swoon come and terror of it! and the animal is bleating within me me! *Ohh! I am bleeding to death. The screams are dying in my throat. Whimpers leak out of me. My eyes stare through death gaze. I die. . . .*

"Lola, what's the matter with you, lady?"

"What?"

"You look sick," Fairbanks says, standing over the kitchen table. "You been sittin' here with your head on the table starin' with your eyes wide open. Somethin' you ate?" He pauses. Then a sly dirty kid smile comes out of his face. "You ain't with child, are you, lady?" and he touches my head.

The awful hateful touch from his hand dispels the jumbled feelings and mistiness that I had been floating in and I straighten up. Myself, all myself now. His smell of tobacco and farm hovers between us, a third presence. Not a human presence, but a living thing. Smells can hear, smells can think. They are the essence of the living thing they originate in. I know flowers that talk to each other at night. And their perfume on you is many soft whisperings of them.

"No, of course not," I say, "I'm not pregnant, Fairbanks."

He stares at me. He has never understood me and he knows that he never will, I am merely something he bought. Can one be expected to understand a product? I could be one of his cattle. Something to use, sell, or eat. He turns me into some thing. When he fucks me I am made into a thing. I am not any of the me. He does not put his prick into Lola. He puts it into a box. But he is not a bad man. He is like most of the others. Of interest only to themselves. A single song with no other listener.

"Too bad," he says, scratching his burr face. (It is really a field, weeds and thistles in it.) "I could of won a real good bet."

"Oh?"

He laughs. "Yeah. The boys at the feed store are always kiddin' me about not havin' it any more. I bet 'em a hundred dollars I wan't too old to make another baby."

"Just keep trying."

"I intend to, lady."

"I'm sure you do."

He laughs again. "That's what a man gets himself a wife for, ain't it?"

I think of all the men I have laid for. A lifetime of opening my legs, or my mouth, so that I could survive. My profession became my life though. How funny! That's all you do, your profession. A pair of black lace panties is my shingle. It isn't as though you work in the daytime so that you can be free at night. No such division. Your work is you. What a joke! Everything is, though. This me

is no worse than a lot of others I can think of. Just a question of
how much of a laugh you can get going about it, that's all. Some
jokes of course make you cry all day.

Why don't you tell him to go fuck himself?

Stop it, Esmeralda!

Esmeralda! Esmeralda! That's all I hear all day! You're talking
to yourself but you don't know it. Do I go around yelling Lola!
Lola! Get out of me? Of course not. I know better. Having a hump
hasn't taught you a fucking thing.

You're stealing me from myself. Please stop!

Whoever the hell you might be. Right? You dumb cunt. What
a silly thing for me to call myself.

Katz is yelling from the back of the smoke shed. "That son of
a bitch Indian! I told you he was a thief. Another pork side gone.
Bastard can't work but he certainly can steal."

Fairbanks goes to the door. "How do you know it was him?
Ask me, I think it was that little hunchback of yours. I wouldn't
trust him as far as I could throw a drunk nigger in a snow storm.
Never forget that time I caught him in the barn trying on Miss
Lola's new underwear. There's nothin' that little monster
wouldn't do. No sir."

"Lay off him, Fairbanks," I say. "Esmeralda doesn't steal."
Which was a lie. Because he was always making off with my
underwear, poor thing. "Ask Katz to come inside. I want to talk
to him about a money-making idea I've got."

He turns his rumpled hulk slowly around and gives me that
patronizing look for spinster schoolteachers who don't know what
a bed is really made for. "Oh, yeah? What is it? Money bushes?"

"No, dear. Box lunches for gold prospectors." Oh God. What
did I do to deserve this noodle?

Katz and I are talking. Fairbanks has gone to town. I kind of
like him. He's such an open and shut case of larceny that you
always know where you stand. He says he fought in the war of 1812
on the side of the British, and the funny thing is I believe him. But
not that he was a colonel.

"The men were splendidly trained and organized," he told me
once. "Straggling was out of the question. Honor, that was at
stake, you see. There was one chap I'll never forget. A tall very
black Negro. Fought like a lion. Never complained. Liked to be

alone. Communicating with his ancestors, I think. Told me once that his great-great-great-uncle's soul had taken residence inside him. Extraordinary, those Africans. Really extraordinary."

I knew a thing or two about black men, but that wasn't the time to go into it, one in particular, also a huge muscled one. Crazy as a bedbug. But what a screw. Ah well . . . Anyway, Katz is sitting across the kitchen table in his buckskin jacket—he has the funniest teeth—perfect small baby things—old in a grown person—and we are discussing my money-making plan. "You mean a whole field of flowers?" he says.

"Flowers is one way of looking at it. Pure gold is another. These aren't the poppies your mother planted in her garden, wherever that was."

"A seventeenth-century Jewish settlement of Sephardic aristo-crats in Delaware. My father was a rabbi, a noted Talmudic scholar. The Mendez-Katz family was a leading family in Toledo, Spain. When Queen Isabella. . . ."

"Okay. Okay. Back to opium. I happened to bring a bag of Turkish seed with me all the way from New York, it was a kind of payoff for services rendered, and the climate and soil and all that looks just as bad as Turkey to me, so this stuff is a cinch to thrive."

He licks his lips. "Well, how do you make opium from the flowers?"

"Easy. You know that Chink cook out at the Jackson ranch?" I say.

"Oh yes. Lin Ting. A well-organized fellow."

"Yeah. A hell of a worker. Well, before he came to this horned-toad country he was an apprenticed opium man in Peking. And I happen to know that he is just dying to lay his hands on some real money and drop the goulash operation. He's an unbelievable gambler and he's up to his eyeballs in debt, and if he doesn't pay up, the Bates brothers have promised to make goldfish food out of him." I pause and take in a lot of very clean sage-smelling air. "What I mean is he's really our boy."

Mendez-Katz' lips are very wet now and he seems quite a bit more relaxed. "There is the marketing problem."

"Your specialty, my dear Mendez-Katz."

Some more comfort-producing lip wet even though he has enough to carry him through half-a-dozen problems. "Yes, of course. I'm already seeing a structure. Esmeralda will be the bag man. I'm even considering inducements to buying in large lots. Maybe one free unit of opium for every package of ten. There is nothing like the thought of something free to stir up the appetites."

Every ghetto in the world is smiling greedily in Mendez-Katz' eyes. Money and profit and planning are his holy trinity. Sex is way down in the hierarchy, something like a second-class angel. Outside in that flat flat blue desert sky an eagle is soaring. God, how terrible and sexy they are. Oh I feel one fucking me! My cunt is screaming as this bird soars into me.

I have to laugh. "You must have learned that from a woman."

His lips suddenly dry up, and his tongue darts over them frantically. "My mother. . . ." be begins.

"Not your mother. Somebody else."

"But my mother. . . ."

"Forget it. I was only joking. Anyway, we'll plant tomorrow, as the sun is going down. That's the best time."

"Oh? Why?"

"So that the seeds can dream."

He looks almost scared. "What?"

"You heard me. Dream. If you plant them in the daytime they die because they can't start dreaming right away. Poppy seeds must begin their lives dreaming, because that is what they supply." I wait for a moment. But of course none of it sinks in. He thinks I'm nuts. He thinks all women are nuts. Maybe they are, but not in the way he means. He would be a hell of a lot better off if he were a little crazy. Stop it, Esmeralda!

"And Fairbanks. What about him?" He just glides on. The other is too freaky and wonderful for him to go into.

"What about him?"

"Is he going to be part of it, or in on it?"

There is a terrible thrashing and pushing inside me. It's Esmeralda. Oh . . . I can't help it . . . "That clod-hopper isn't even part of his own asshole!"

Mendez-Katz becomes a statue of amazement.

"Stop looking so dumb, Mendez-Katz" I hear myself say. "It's me. Esmeralda."

"Listen, Lola. . . ."

"Not Lola. Me!"

I summon all my strength and fight him back down. He is trying to pull my hair and choke me. But I get the better of him. Oh, how exhausted I am! Why does he have to do this when others are around? Mendez-Katz is still staring at me. Somewhere in the distance a cowbell is clanking.

"I'm sorry, Mendez-Katz. I don't know what came over me. Sometimes I get these fits."

"I see," and he licks some more. "Of course."

"Fairbanks won't know what it's all about. I'll tell him we're growing a special kind of pig feed."

Mendez-K. nods his head. We're on safe ground again. Nothing spooky. "Splendid. You'll handle that end of the operation. Now then . . . the profit ratio. . . ."

"We'll make a bundle."

"Hmm. One thing worries me. Interference by the authorities."

"Did you ever know a cop who couldn't be bought?"

"Hmm. Have you considered, just academically of course, what the legal fines and or punishment of this sort of activity is?"

He irritates me so much at times with his sniffing around at everything that I'd like to smash him. Good God! Do all hype artists sniff at the world this way? Mendez-K. even questions the break of day. "You want to get out of here, don't you?"

"Certainly, my dear. I'm merely. . . ."

"Merely giving me a pain in my you-know-what. Everything is going to be all right. Believe me."

I look him in the eyes, and I can see every crooked little street in the Toledo ghetto, and inside those dark stone houses the Jews are huddling like mice, bright quick eyes, small soft hands. And the children are clutching pieces of food. And someone is muttering in that strange throaty language, an old bearded man . . . and next to him whispering to herself is a veiled woman with rings on . . . oh my God it's me.

The smells in here are stifling. These heavy stone walls keep in the smells. Smells of body and garlic and fear, a zoo stench. The man in the beard has stopped reciting now. He turns to me. His bloodshot leaky eyes frighten me.

"Keep praying, my princess," he says.

"Yes."

"These *goyim* are bloodthirsty but not insatiable,"

"They burned my father," I hear myself say, and a moan-whimper comes out of me. The little boy cringing next to me is playing with a rabbit's foot. His name is Jacob. I am very hungry and afraid but in a way that is not real: like being hurt but having someone else feel the pain. Wouldn't it be divine if you could pay someone to feel the actual physical pain for you, while you suffered only in your head! Or if the town would appoint a person, a hunchback for example, to endure the citizens' misery. There are whores for pleasure—why not whores for pain? The smell of my father's body slowly burning or roasting at the stake was the most unearthly odor of my experience. Burned animal meat is not like it at all, although you would think that flesh is flesh and all of it dies the same.

"He died for us," this creaking bundle of sanctimony next to me intones, not as though he were speaking to another simple human being, myself, but in the manner of a rabbi delivering a sermon to the collection of impersonal bodies called his congregation.

"No," I say, "he did not die for me. He died for his own vanity."

De Sola, I can still hear the Duke of Toledo's churchman say, you have offended the church and the dignity of Spain. We give you this final opportunity to give up your life of abominations and convert yourself into a God-fearing decent Christian:

"I was born a Jew and I shall die a Jew," he cried.

Indeed you will, De Sola. Indeed you will.

And he died. What absurdity! What unspeakable irresponsibility! Leaving a wife and five children to swim alone in this insane sea.

"You cannot speak that way of your beloved father, my beloved brother," leaky eyes says. "You are a filthy little whore."

"I am not one," I say between my moans and whimpers, which I am executing merely because that is all there is to do in this dungeon of teeth-sucking food-dreaming despair and boredom, not for my outrageous father. "But perhaps with luck I shall become one, and be able to survive."

"A whore unto eternity. You shall walk the streets of self-hatred and degradation for centuries."

"You are always talking in such a big way because you do not understand what is going on around you."

"Whore!"

"Pig!"

And I get up now—the wailing and reciting and weeping in that room of smelly relatives! Oy!—and make my way through the clutter of self-pity and out into the tortured gnome street which, however, at the mouth—its stained, wet mouth—does have a sigh of a view of the green-blue river and the strong elegant aqueduct left by the Romans. The thin air washes through my black Jewish garments and through my thick cobwebby head and I feel a little less like a three-week-old soup. A whore, yes. I'll be a whore. It could not be any less amusing than to be locked in marriage to Moses the butcher's son who loves his hacking and carving work more than seems reasonable. Perhaps I will enjoy it. As for walking through eternity with a sign between my legs, well, we will see about that. Do we really live forever as they say, floating about invisible, carrying out our most uncherished human designs? Oy! What an idea! Crazier than a long Toledo dream it is. But why am I always trying to make sense of things, when I know that everything is madness on this earth, and that all talk of sanity is nonsense to make people feel a little less human. Christ! Christ! That black hawk up there in the sky may well be my grandmother wondering, in its swooping, if I might be good to eat.

"Psst! Eulalia!" a voice whispers from the window near me. "Come into my house for a minute. I have something to show you."

"All I want to see, Franco, is the color of your money."

"Ah, Eulalia. You are so cynical. Don't you believe in love?"

"Don't make me laugh. Your love is an empty belly and an aching cock."

"Lord! What language you use, beautiful one!"

"You love it," I say, still looking into the sky. That bird! That bird! What is it doing to me? Did those Roman soldiers watch it when they were building the aqueduct? Could it be one of them, the soul of the black-haired legionnaire? Oh bird! Take me?

Please! Please! Make me stop being a Jew! Take me!. . . . Wait
. . . is it possible? . . . am I the bird?

He makes that psst sound again. Snake sound. All of Spain is
that snake psst being made by men. I could cut it in pieces or break
it with my beak. My beak?

"Delicious one, come closer and see the beautiful silver coins
in my hand."

"Oh, all right." I say, dropping my eyes from the bird, and
turning around. "Let's see, you useless thing you."

I look into his sneaky-eyed anticipation, into his mustached
nervousness, into the coins whose strength is a substitute for his
magic, and smell, for the first time that reeking day. This bag of
dirty thoughts' red hair aches to be pulled by me. His long potter's
nose is almost snorting with desire. He must use it to turn the vases
on his wheel. I know he would love to put it into me.

"You have a shameless nose, Franco."

"HERE'S YOURS, ZACHARY," APRIL SAID, HAND-
ing Zachary a brown shopping bag containing twenty-five thousand pounds. "You earned every shiny shilling of it." She was very
tiddly indeed.

"Adorable girl," said Zachary, taking the money and giving
her hand a Zen kiss. "I can build two temples in the mountains
with this."

Esmeralda giggled drunkenly from the floor. "Or retrace every one of the Budda's steps!"

"His steps are in my heart," said Zachary.

April threw a bag to Bosworth. "Twenty rug plantations,
brown prince."

"Wrong," said Bosworth. "The alps. A deluxe return to the Ice
Age."

A bag flew to Katz sitting under one of the self-pitying oil
paintings. "Mutual funds," he said, a little tweedy-tongued because he'd partaken of more scotch than his old mother had told
him was good for a growing boy. "And a few nice steam baths
with rub downs. Get the old nervous system back in shape." For
a couple of seconds he thought he was Baron de Rothschild having
his biceps milked. He looked into the crystal ball of his scotch.

"Minnesota Mining looks very sound to me. Very sound."

The Boy Blaster snored heavily next to Joan of Arc's tongue-ravaged snatch. His own thing, the smooth and polished submachine gun, was napping at his feet. He happened to be dreaming, however, about a bolt action rifle with a telescopic sight.

Outside, in the Ritz Hotel ambiance of the front seat of their silver Bentley, sat Churchill Downs and Ophelia of the Morning Light, both garbed in the unbridled exuberance of darkest Africa's new kingdom robes. Churchill looked at his small diamond wristwatch.

"We'll give them half an hour more," he said. "Then they'll be so fried they won't have the strength or wits to put up any resistance."

Ophelia smiled. "A charming way to pick up a little side money. Charming." She took a .45 automatic from her enormous elephant-skin purse. "What lovely workmanship. I truly admire craftmanship, don't you, brother?"

"Do indeed, Ophelia baby. But admire money more."

She chuckled and caressed the barrel of the weapon and clicked the safety catch on and off just to check. "Don't forget. You've got that ten o'clock appointment with the CIA people in the Ministry tomorrow morning."

Churchill patted her red, black, and gold knee. "I won't, sister, I won't. My memory is tied to my conscience and my conscience is tied to reality."

She grinned. "Uh huh."

He looked out at the tidy prim-lipped Georgian street. "I sure could use some ribs . . . and a big plate of hoppin' john. Damn if I couldn't."

Ophelia smiled real sneaky. "An what about some poon?"

Churchill groaned. "Stop it, sister baby. Such talk strikes at the very core of my sweet shame. You know what your analyst said about that kind of family fun."

Inside the now quite lushed studio George idly riffled through a sheaf of high-powered bank notes. The several awarenesses of him were ambling each its own way, very comfortably. His left hand cupped the world of April's considerable titty (she had decided to take off all her clothes in order to make more immediate contact with everything). His feet were slipping into a pair of suede slippers in a shop on Rome's Via Babuino. His skin was being sea-sprayed on a surf board in the Red Sea. His eyes were staring at a half-filled page in his writer's notebook sitting on his lap in his tiny flat on the Rue du Bac in Paris two years ago. His ears were responding to the lyrical music of his philosophy teacher's explanation of the highly aerial reasoning of the Arab mystics. His stomach was taken up with an orgy of chili dogs he was having as a child of ten in New York City. He was a reclining carnival. April slipped her hand under his shirt and began choreographing delicately around his belly. He drifted and drifted . . . and drifted . . . came up out of the writing notebook pages, holding a red and black ball point pen he had bought for fifty cents in a glinty stationary store on the Boulevard St. Germain just the previous day after a cheap but cleverly balanced lunch of hard boiled egg and salad and veal knuckle in the company of no one but himself. Oh . . . wine of course, but that goes without saying.

"A good table wine," a chap once said to George, "is man's best friend."

"Hmm," George had murmured. "I see what you mean. Goes with everything. Which is more than one can say for most of one's human friends, right, Claude?"

"Very well put, sir. Very well put indeed."

Claude was Lady Jones-Stuart's chauffer and George was waiting with him, during that past exchange, in a Boulevard Raspail coffee bar, downstairs from her systematically indulged digs, while she got herself ready for the long, but completely insensate ride to Neuilly to visit the Duchess of Rheims and her new tutor, a veritable raga of a chap from the Himalayas. Cousin of the Dali Lama or something.

Anyway, there George was, pen in hand, smack in the middle of writing down a girl's thoughts, because he was concocting a novel about a mysteriously gorgeous American girl caught in the spitty whorls of the Paris underground, in just about any way you want to interpret and use that all-purpose all-weather category.

Now this phenomenon's name was the Countess Freda Smell (item: on her father's side she was Austrian nobility, and her mother was a raging [screaming] American beauty) and she hung around with (more precisely, existed with) a black Great Dane, which she (or George) had named Bunny, for reasons that could easily escape a second thought.

"Heavens! The stuff that pours out of me!" George said to the nice little room. "Some guys can write pleasant harmless, smell-less shit about everyday life. But not old George. Uh uh. The plague that I am beck and call to. Dear me."

He lit up a Gauloise filter, drew in a large amount of its para-doxically soothing yet anxiety-provoking smoke, looked out of the lovely old bubble-marked window at the spastic traffic below, and inched his way back into the Countess' exotically disturbed mind. At that particular moment, or at that place on the notebook page, she was imagining herself (which doesn't by any means mean that it wasn't really happening) arranging a very tricky, and possibly fatally dangerous if you didn't maneuver just right, down to the last kinky hair of it, deal, with the German SS in Rome, involving the whereabouts and laying hands on of a hugh sum of gold and antiquities hidden by some rich Italians who had fled over the ocean to New York City when the bloody handwriting was drib-bling down the wall. Her companion in this fandango was a young man of far more than average qualities, as they would say—physi-cally hard to keep your hands off (that goes for men too), a royal Mongol prince, and one of this world's truly great spirits. He was game all the way, no matter what kind of fun you had in mind. His name was Bosworth.

Now, the rather odd thing about George's writing, or creating, was that his characters seemed to exist outside him or his imagina-tion.

"No kidding," he told a friend once when he was engaged in one of the few literary discussions he ever allowed himself to get in. "They seem to be lying in wait for me. I'm just the agent or soul or something that they use to get their crazy act going. It works like this: I start writing every day by simultaneously cleans-ing myself of the flotsam that usually dominates it, of the bondage I hold myself in by way of my identity as George H. It's almost as though I am losing my identity, freeing myself of me, and, as that process of purification goes on, let myself sink into a sea of silence, or a silent sea, just sink down and down, not moving any part of my body or mind, and pretty soon things begin to happen. Sounds, shapes, smells, colors, animals, plants, and people, a really different world from the one we happen to be talking in at the moment, these people begin to emerge, sometimes shyly, sometimes ferociously, and we're off. I mean we because they drag me into whatever it is that is happening, their world. They create me as much as I create them, if you know what I mean. I am no longer George H. at that point. I am someone else, or several people as we go on, and boy do we go on. It gets so marzipan at times that I honestly don't know how I make it back to my chair and this-world position. Sometimes I don't all at once or at times completely. For about an hour or so after I come back, I'm in a funny way, I have to recollect myself. And every now and then, I don't return intact. Parts of me—or aspects of me—remain down there; and until I go back the next time, I wander around up here feeling half human, not all there in a way. They can be possessive, like all good friends.

"George! George! Where the hell are you?" they will cry. "Come back! Come on."

"How does all this get on paper? I just don't ask that one any more."

"It isn't like this at all," he went on to the friend, "when I write fiction for money, which I do under another name or names, incidentally. I really do make up the characters in those books, and do you want to know something? They don't have the slightest idea who I am. And I might as well tell you that I plan to keep it that way."

His friend said he understood some of what George told him and the part he did not grasp he did not care to go into, and had another Pernod on the rocks.

George closed his notebook. His descent was over for the day. The SS colonel who was supposed to meet the Countess and Bosworth couldn't make the appointment that day because he had to look into a niggling matter involving the killing of two of his lads by the partisans, right outside Rome too. So Freda and Bosworth said let's go over to Zerina's whorehouse and watch the fun. George wasn't in the mood, so he cut out, making a date to see them the next day at the Piazza Colonna. "Watching Italian whores going down on German soldiers makes me feel awfully lonely," he explained. "One of my many limitations."

"Oh you and your mock humility," the Countess said, joking of course.

"I'm going home for a nap," he said. He didn't want to tell them the truth because it was too mixed up. Some of which escaped even him. For example, that peculiar little story that he must have written but couldn't seem to remember the act of, about somebody named Eli Katz which he had discovered (or something like that) next to his typewriter one morning. There it was, complete unto itself.

Eli Katz lay hunched up on his left side, nervously half asleep, and watched the luminous-faced clock on the chair. It was 4:25 a.m. The alarm was set for 4:35, ten minutes before Eli had to get up, so that when it rang he would still have a little while left to doze and stretch and dream in bed before getting up. But this trick was not necessary. He always suddenly woke up ten or fifteen minutes before the alarm went off.

He was taking over a different newspaper route this morning. Every day for the past week he had gone with the boy who was leaving the route and had learned it. Compared with Eli's old route, which was small and ran through a poor section of the city, the new route was a very long jump in the right direction, the right direction being ahead. He had waited a long time for a route like this. The new route had a hundred and fifty customers and it ran through the Kalorama Circle section where the people with money lived.

Eli planned to collect the subscription money once a month from the customers on the new route, instead of once a week as the other boys did on their routes. This way he would make his profits all at one time. And he planned to charge seventy cents a month for the paper instead of the usual fifteen cents a week.

Now, waiting for the alarm to ring, Eli thought about the quart of chocolate milk he was going to swipe this morning. The other boy had told him about it yesterday. It was put every morning, the boy said, in the black tin milk box of apartment 7A in the big apartment house at Wyoming Avenue and Twentieth Street.

This apartment house was located in the middle of the new route. But Eli had decided to make it his last stop this morning. It would be too dangerous to carry the milk around with him while he delivered papers on the last half of the route. Then there were the doughnuts. He would buy two honey-dip doughnuts for ten cents to eat with the chocolate milk. Saving the apartment house for the last stop meant backtracking five blocks, but Eli did not mind that.

The alarm clock rang. Eli snapped to attention. He reached out and stopped the alarm. Then he lay back in the warmth of the bed for ten more minutes. He quickly got out of bed when he saw it was 4:45. He turned on the small lamp and began to dress.

In the other bed his brother Martin moaned. "Take it easy, will you. You'll wake everybody."

"Aw nuts," Eli said. "You sleep too much."

It took him ten minutes to dress and leave the apartment house. The newspaper station was an old garage that had been fixed up. It was in an alley several blocks from where Eli lived. Nearly all the other boys were in the station getting their papers when Eli got there. Bundles of newspapers lined one end of the garage. A heavy dark boy was cutting the rope around the bundles and giving each boy the number of newspapers he needed.

Three or four of the boys were shouting at each other. "If that son of a bitch of a carpentry teacher says one more thing to me . . . ." one boy was saying.

"Listen. When we were in Rock Creek Park last summer she was so hot. . . ." another boy said.

Eli looked around at them. He said hello to one boy.

"Okay, Katz," the dark boy shouted to Eli from across the garage. "Here are yours." He looked at Eli for a moment. Then he said, "Think you can handle this new route alone now?"

"Sure I can," Eli said, going up to him. He hated him for asking the question. "Nothing to it. What do you think I am, a dummy?"

The dark boy laughed, then he bent down and opened another bundle of papers. Eli got his papers. He put the papers and his canvas bag on the long wooden table. Then he filled the bag with the papers, swung the bag over his right shoulder, bending his back to let the bag rest partly on him hip, walked to the door and said so long to the station manager standing there reading, and left the station.

He walked slowly toward Kalorama Circle, the bulging bag

heavy on his shoulder. Nobody was in the streets. Eli felt he was master of this part of the city. He felt he was the only living soul around. Everybody else was dead. Eli looked at all of the parked cars and felt he could do anything he wanted with them. The streets and houses were his. He was the only living soul there.

And all the time he kept thinking about the quart of chocolate milk in the black tin box.

The new route covered eleven blocks. He had learned it very well going with the other boy and now, walking up one side and down the other side of the streets, he did not often have to look at his route book to make sure which houses got papers. On Wyoming Avenue he walked right past the big apartment house without even looking in the lobby, and went on to deliver papers on Twentieth Street.

He became excited as he neared the last houses on the route. He had forgotten everything else but the chocolate milk. He smiled to himself and looked around at the green-leafed maple trees lining the street. He threw a paper onto a porch, neatly, and started back to the big apartment house.

His excitement got stronger, but a slight feeling of fear came with it. His heart seemed to get bigger and to beat faster. His stomach squeezed up. Now he was on Wyoming Avenue. He saw the big building. He walked quickly toward it. His eyes were watering a little now and his face was warm with the excitement and the slight fear and the fast walking. His canvas bag had only a few papers in it now. His leg scraped regularly against it. This was the only sound in the street.

He walked up the steps of the apartment house. He held his bag so that it would not scrape against his leg and make that noise. He went through the empty lobby to the elevators. One was open. He stepped inside, pushed the button for the eighth floor, and then leaned against the side of the elevator. His body was tense and warm now.

The elevator slowed up jerkily and stopped. Eli got out. The corridor was long and narrow and there were staircases at each end. Eli walked down the corridor and dropped papers with a soft whop at certain doors. He was beginning to feel tired. His back hurt from carrying the heavy bag. When he had finished delivering on that floor he went down the back stairway to the next floor.

Just outside the door of the seventh floor stairway he dropped a paper on a doormat, turned, and looked down the corridor.

The small black tin milk box was at the very end of the corridor. He stood there and looked at it. His mouth was dry and he swallowed twice. Now he started down the corridor. Before he had got half way down it, delivering papers as he walked, he had the feeling that the corridor was getting smaller and smaller, and he felt he was getting smaller with it. He finally reached the black milk box. He bent over very slowly and lifted the lid of the box. He did not care that there was a pint of cream next to the chocolate milk. The bottle of chocolate milk was cold and damp. He held his hand around it for a couple of seconds before lifting it out. Then he lifted it out and slipped it into his bag and carefully closed the lid of the milk box. The corridor did not seem small now. And he felt his normal size.

Down on the sixth floor he walked fast delivering papers to the back of the corridor, and by the back stairs went to the fifth floor. He felt fine now. He kept one hand in his bag holding the chocolate milk so that it would not bump against his leg. "I've got it now," he said to himself. "I've got it now." He thought of buying the doughnuts and then sitting in a parked car somewhere and eating them and drinking the quart of chocolate milk.

He covered the fifth and fourth floors in a few minutes. On the third floor the soft neighing of a horse came in through the window at the front of the corridor. Eli heard it but he did not pay any attention to it. He delivered the papers.

He came out on the second floor at the front. He dropped a paper at apartment 211 and turned to walk down the corridor. Then he stopped.

The milkman stood at the end of the corridor, waiting for him. Eli closed his eyes for a moment and with all his might wished he could fall asleep and wake up at home in bed, safe. His body was suddenly so tired that it seemed almost to go to sleep.

The milkman walked toward him. Eli stood there and watched him coming. He had a white uniform on. He was tall and heavy. Now Eli could see the sweat on his forehead. He was in front of him now.

"Let me see what you got in that bag, kid," he said.

"Nothing," Eli said. "Nothing but papers." He felt his eyes get big. "I'm the *Courier* boy. I've got nothing but papers in my bag."

"You're lying!"

The milkman reached fast into Eli's bag. Eli felt him grab the bottle of chocolate milk. The milkman did not take the bottle out.

"You're coming with me, you little bastard," he said. "You're going to the cops. You dirty little newsboys been stealing on my route too long now."

Now he smiled tightly. "I knew if I waited around long enough I'd catch you coming in here after that chocolate milk. Didn't know I followed you from upstairs once I saw you come in, did you?"

Eli knew now that the other boy had been stealing the milk himself. He had not told Eli this. Eli's body now came sharply alive. He remembered the dime he had brought along to buy the doughnuts.

"Can't I pay for it, mister?" he said. "Please let me. I've got the money on me. Please. I've never taken your milk before. Honest I haven't."

"Pay me for it hell! Let you go and you'd turn right around and do it again. Come on. Finish delivering those papers. Then we're going to the police station."

Eli walked down the corridor with the milkman. He weakly dropped papers at the right door. They went down the stairs to the first floor. The milkman held him loosely by the arm and looked down at him. They did not speak.

Eli could see himself surrounded by big, savage policemen in the station house. They were going to put him where he belonged. They were going to put him in the reformatory. The milkman opened the front door with one hand and held Eli with the other.

The milkman's white delivery wagon was in front of the building. It was hitched to a large white workhorse. Now Eli remembered the neighing of the horse. Eli expected the milkman to take him into the wagon. But the milkman just stood there now holding his arm and stared at him.

He yanked Eli's arm and grabbed the bottle in the canvas bag and, twisting around, smashed it in the street behind the wagon. The horse jumped and whinnied. Eli stared at the broken glass and the thin streams of chocolate milk running into the gutter.

"You little son of a bitch!" the milkman shouted. "Steal my

milk will you!" He drew back and smacked Eli hard in the face. "Run!" he yelled. "Run! Before I kill you."

Everything in Eli's mind stopped working. The pain in his face became part of a terrible pain in his head, and his chest was burning hot and he could barely breathe. He whirled around, jumped a small hedge in turning the corner of the big apartment house, and ran down the quiet cool street.

GEORGE SLOWLY GOT UP FROM THE CHAIR HE had been sitting in for the past three hours—awkward in his motions and awkward in his emotions as always on returning from his trips—depending on which view you took, touching a book as if he had not seen it for months (had it been lost?). Wandered away and just now loped back in the side-door, examined a yellow and red tie as if it were not his, and then, smiling thinly, went outside, into the gamey Rue de la Université, which was always so insistently and coyly, of course, telling itself what a rainbow of a thing it was to be a French street, rather than a Cleveland or a rheumy-eyed, hairy Cairo street, phew. The palm-eyed, explosive-tittied woman who ran the smoke shop was sweeping hugh piles of imagined refuse from the sidewalk in front of her lung labyrinth and saying sharp things to herself in Parisian argot.

"Madame Lapique," George said, feeling a bit more returned, "today is a long thin cigar day. Don't you agree?" He spoke in French, a mystery he had studied in at least three schools throughout the world.

"Today is a day to plan one's escape from this stinking world," she replied, and kicked at a piece of garbage that simply wasn't there. "It's a disgrace even to get up in the mornings."

"I know just how you feel."

"You are a disgusting liar. You don't have the smallest idea how I feel, and you know it." She swept off a gum wrapper from the streets of her childhood. "Shit!"

George laughed mildly, a two-toned, classical morning laugh that could not possibly have been misunderstood by or provocative to, anybody, within earshot or not.

"You're a salty lady," he said.

"You would be too if you lived the way I do."

George followed her into her shop. Dozens of tobacco smells clamored for his nose.

"Weren't you in Carcasonne in the fall of '43?"

"Yes," Madame Lapique answered, picking at her tight brassiere, "But I wasn't doing what they say."

"We never are." He breathed in a dark-eyed smell from Cuba. "We must learn to accept our own lack of limitations, and to fight being manipulated by other persons' fantasies of us."

She began combing her exquisitely dyed light-blue hair in a small wall mirror. "You are a lot cleverer than I am if you can manage that, master George."

A fat fellow in a dirty black beret came in, plunked down three francs and left with a pack of Gauloise. The dangling cigarette in his mouth looked as spent as an old streetwalker.

"It is the principal job in our lives," George continued, and began selecting a cigar for himself from the crammed counter. "Nothing else really matters."

Finished with her hair, Madame Lapique began straightening and patting the discretely flowered dress that embraced her exuberant body. She had the finest ass on the entire block as far as George was concerned, and the Rue de la Université was known for its ass. At least twice a day he thought about her ass and did a variety of fun things with it. He wondered if she were aware of this. She suddenly giggled.

"You're thinking about my big behind again, aren't you, master George."

He grinned way back to his sneaky youth. "I must confess that I am, Madame Lapique." He grabbed at his nose as if that organ had been doing the naughty! "How did you know?" And he went off into a goulash of snorts and squeals and body writhings.

"Oh it's easy," she said, really delighted at the matter. "Whenever you start thinking about it, my bottom feels like a hot rum toddy and I am suddenly back on our farm in Normandy."

"Imagine that! Well, tell me: what about when I'm not here but am concentrating on it? Do you know then too?"

"Indeed I do. Last night when I was fixing dinner for that old onion I married, my bottom lit up, you might say, and I was whisked back to Normandy, and I couldn't peel a potato for at least ten minutes. My husband thought I was having some kind of an attack. He said I could not even reconize him." She leaned over the counter and patted his cheek. "You're a dreadful fellow, you are. Upsetting the eating habits of the petit bourgeois." And this time she let loose a goosey titter right out of the early Zola.

"Good Lord!" George muttered. "Isn't that the most edible damned thing you ever heard," and before he knew what he was doing he gave her ass a bam of a patty-cake.

She shrieked, of course, and leaped forward reflexively and knocked over two polite cartons of English Ovals. "Rascal!" she howled and made a retaliatory swipe at his rear, missed because of being slightly off balance, and struck instead his thing which, because of all this thought rapport, was standing at absolutely pole straight attention. The sudden and sailing contact of Madame Lapique's fun-loving hand with his fun-loving flagpole made George peck back, and he knocked over half a case of Bulgarian after-dinner cigars. "Whoops!" he exclaimed, his thing vibrating like an old harp. And he returned her another jolly clap on the ass.

This time the healthy-armed Madame Lapique abandoned whatever was left of her Catholic girls' school training, grabbed George bodily, and in the same atheistic troubadour tradition thrust her tongue halfway down his throat. George had wanted to say something nonsensical yet appropriate, like, "How well you play the harp, Madame Lapique," but decided not to because of the possibility of choking to death. So he just grabbed her rear splendidness, pulled her closer to his central communications system, and gave as good as he took. Life had never seemed simpler.

At that moment, her husband came down the back stairs. "Odette! What are you doing?" he said.

"I'm obviously giving this young gentleman a French smoking lesson," she replied, untonguing for a moment.

"Oh, I see," he said, and started back up the stairs, muttering something about how educational systems changed because he himself had been forced to learn smoking by himself in the attic of his grandmother's dirty old house in Provence.

"Forgive the interruption, master George," she said, grabbed his juicer and went back to work hammer and tongue.

"This is the best Gauloise I've ever smoked," George said, and still holding onto one full-bloomed Norman cheek, unbuttoned her flower pattern bodice, unsnapped with some difficulty, dexterous though he was with his right hand, her black very formidable bra, and got himself a beggar's mouthful of peasant tit. Madame Lapique's pragmatic hand had not left his hose for one second (because if the French are anything they are persistent), and now she whipped open his American zipper and extricated Mr. Charlie and began playing the French National Anthem on it. This is really living, George told himself, nibbling a bit of nipple. Boarding school was never like this.

Well, now, things went on like that for a short while (flower sounds of more than pleasure were issuing from Madame Lapique's mouth) until both participants, realizing that a fair amount of muscular discomfort was implicit in this position, began moving as one (without interrupting the fluid pattern of stimulus-response-counter response that was very much in working order) through the store and into the small storeroom in the back, where Madame Lapique had a daybed for just such swoon-outs as this. (The French also are quite practical: when the juices run, they run with them.)

"Standing up can be all right," she said, pulling off her clothes (George was too, of course, quite frantically, but he left his shoes and socks and beret on), "but there is really nothing like a bed."

"I'm in total agreement," George breathed hurriedly. "Great Zeus! What a fantastically splendid naked ass!" and he flung himself upon it with kisses, rubbings, nibbles and pinches. He drew several arpeggios on it with his maddened tool, then went back on his knees and resumed his feasting." Mother of Mary! I mean, this is four star!"

Madame Lapique who quite naturally had been crouching with her ass in the air, laughed a young tulip. "I must confess that I have had a compliment or two on it in my time."

George squealed and, running his shameless tongue right up the velvet, slipped one hand betwen her legs and into her wet treasure hole. "I should certainly hope so. Indeed!"

In a moment or two, she flipped gaga old George (whose tongue kept right on licking in mid-air) over onto the couch and proceeded to give him a first-rate French massage, accompanied by some expert breast contacts in what to most proper minds would have seemed the most surprising place. (Well, not really.)

Suddenly, a head appeared round the door. Madame's husband. "Is the smoking lesson still going on, Odette?"

"Yes," she said, raising her head out of George's armpit. "We are going into the pipe."

"Oh, I see," Mr. Lapique muttered, and padded right back upstairs. "Tell him not to inhale!" he shouted back. "It's bad for the lungs."

"He's really a dear," she explained, diving on George's fingers. "But he just doesn't know his ass from his elbow, if you will excuse an old Norman expression."

"Of course," George said, trying to sound more or less intelligible (for what reason he did not precisely know). "Incidentally, did you be any chance study this in China?"

"What?" she asked, garbled, because she had his thumb in her hot mouth.

"Finger blowing. It's an ancient Chinese art virtually unknown in the western world."

"No," she replied, filigreeing his index finger. "But I have been asked to give lessons in it, to sluggish wives."

"Ah so," he heard himself mumble. "Of course."

Before he could think of what to say next, she had licked her championship way to his usually neglected belly button, then down to his boyish tummy, then without any warning, with nary a shout of, "Here goes! Hold onto your hat!" or, "It's now or never, cap'n!" she swallowed his bishop and dived to at least fifty fathoms with it, trolling wall-eyed. Madame was no sun perch out for an afternoon's folderol. For the first time in his silly life George knew what it was like to be Jonah.

After a bit (during which salinity George had metamorphosed into an enormous pulsating thrill-saturated amoeba), Madame surfaced and, without even breathing hard, mounted George ("I must say, master George, that you are far tastier than a shepherd's pie. Upon my soul you are.") This gifted lady tobacconist was hardly one to ignore or waste a savory possibility (she used seeming blank spaces with the ingenuity of a lawyer); she bent over far enough for one of her robust country breasts to fit into George's otherwise unemployed mouth. (Had his mother's booby been half so yummy and had she been one-hundredth as concerned as the divine Madame Lapique, George would have grown up to be a happy square, instead of the eternally wandering sideshow navvy he was.) He grabbed her superbly jutting ass in both hands, and away they went. It was instantly clear that Madame also was one of the great equestrians of all time. George's zonker received its true maturity under her galvanic and totally exploitative pumpings. Up to this moment of epiphany, his thing, he realized, had been meandering in the glens of childhood.

"Your joystick feels exactly like that of a blacksmith I went with one summer in Avignon," she said, switching tits in his mouth, "It is most remarkable."

"What was his name?" George mouthed, putting her nipple in his nostril for a second.

"Good heavens! Now that you ask—I remember it was George."

"Oh, Lordy!"

However, this eerie insight, or coincidence, did not in any way violate the self-contained juiciness of their coitus. In truth, it somewhat enriched it. The fact that they were combining time past with time present was something to think about, which they were both doing, but in a gently sonorous unconscious way. George now did something he could be quite proud of; he changed places with her without missing a beat or without having to disgorge her quite simply frabjous knocker from his mouth. She too maneuvered expertly, which contributed to the success of this feat. Once on top, of course, George did not waste a moment puzzling himself about the stock market or the cost of electricity in Jordan. He poled her properly, he did (bracing himself with his elbows, which is quite within the rules.) Then he suddenly slithered off her and put his tongue to work where it would do the most good.

"Oh sir!" Odette moaned. "You play the tip of my tweety like a fine fellow should."

"So nice of you to say so," George more or less panted through the tickle of her muff hairs. And for two reels he saw himself performing this traditional good fellow act before a cheering audience of thousands.

After he had produced several howls of both gratitude and orgasmic realization from Madame Lapique (swallowing fully a pint of essential liquids in so doing), he climbed back on top of her and began thrusting deeply and fiercely into the made ready of her contracting and expanding womanhood. He was employing the Royal Canadian Mounties Improved Penetration Technique. Two jolting half thrusts, one long full thrust with a second's pause before a protracted dynamic drawback. He was coming down the stretch for all he was worth. She wrapped her legs around him the better to score. Her uncensored and full-bodied howls and shrieks carried him right back to the first performance of the Passion Play in the fourth century somewhere in the suburbs around Antioch.

"Kill him! Kill him!" she screamed. "Kill the false messiah!"

"I have come to free you!" he roared.

"Call out the guard!"

"Repent and save your souls!"

"Tear the criminal to pieces! Tear him! He must die!"

And in another moment or two they both saw Him, in one soaring roaring orgasmic revelation.

"Well," Madame Lapique began after a decent pause, "I think it's time I put some curtains in this room."

Upstairs, uncoddled husband Cedric was carefully watering the window plants, marigolds, lilacs, and some sweet basil, and talking to himself a mile a minute. Unless of course he was talking to the plants. "Imagine! Making a living out of lung cancer. I can hear their dreadful smoker's coughs even while I'm sleeping. Their urgency is so great they force their way right into the privacy of my dreams. They infect my very own inventions. The characters in my hallucinations have taken to coughing like terminal cases of tuberculosis. Tish! I should have been a priest, selling forgiveness and salvations. If you're going to be in business there should be a little dignity attached to it. Besides, your customers come to you on their hands and knees, with soft frightened eyes, and a very pleasant amount of self-hatred. None of the haughty perversity we get downstairs, the arrogance of the person who is maneuvering his own trip to the grave with a particular smart brand of smokes. A pack of Philomena tips and be quick about it! Phooey! A Philomena smack in the teeth is what they ought to get. And the way those teenage snots behave is enough to make a fellow want to blow up the nurseries. With their kiss-my-ass way of sauntering into the shop and grinning that sly grin as if they'd just finished shoving it up their own mother's behind. No wonder a handful of those Vietnamese lads kicked the shit out of us. It's a wonder they didn't decide to follow us right back to Paris and take the city. Probably didn't want the bloody thing. The days of

Louis XIV are surely gone forever. Thank God I have my night job at The Leaping Wolf. Opening doors for people and getting them cabs is very relaxing work, helps me keep my sanity, and the tips aren't too bad either. They'd be a lot better if I did not have to share them with that rotting cabbage Rastro who owns the joint. Greed pot! He's got so much money he shits doubloons. He even makes the bar whores lay him for nothing besides giving him half their earnings for working out of his club. Rent he calls it. And the lies he tells! God save us! That he is the illegitimate son of a ballet dancer and the king of Bavaria. More likely two toads in a Mexican slum. Old Grandet the garbage collector told me he got the money for the club through slave trading in North Africa. Specializing in girls under fifteen. His own mistress, that Sylvia tomato, is said to have been a payoff for a gambling debt incurred by her father who is an oyster fisherman in Nice. A fine way to do business! Part with your own daughter rather than a smelly boat. She's not a bad sort, either. Always ready with a smile too, when she's not down in the dumps or all drunk up. Stays in her apartment most of the time and writes poetry. I wonder if it rhymes. Anybody can write that crazy stuff that makes no sense. Call that poetry? A calculated hoax, that's what it is. Should be a jail sentence for that sort of thing. It's a crime against the heart and the common sense in all of us. Ah, and she has her little secret too. Nobody else knows it but me. How did I discover it? Quite by accident, of course, because if there is one thing I am not it is a snooper. Anyway, I was strolling around Montmartre one day— Odette had gone to visit her deaf sister in Orly—with nothing on my civilization-damaged mind that isn't customarily there, and I happened to pass a doorway (one of the few where a sneaky Arab or a frozen whore wasn't leaning) that had a little sign on it which said "The Art of Zen Living—Lectures and Demonstrations by Master Zachary."

Naturally I cruised right in. Catholic Living had virtually destroyed me. Perhaps Zen would put me together again.

Upstairs (past a couple of family floors that stank of dirty laundry, old beef bone, babies, and other human limitations), I entered a large room where about a dozen humans were seated around a bald, bearded chap dressed in white robes, like a nut or something. He had a pair of the most remarkable hands I had ever had occasion to observe: tiny and unnaturally delicate, like the hands on women in those ancient religious painting in museums. I got the crazy idea that he'd stolen them. Absurd, eh?

"When you cherish the notion of purity and cling to it, you turn purity into falsehood," he was saying. "Purity has neither form nor shape, and when you claim an achievement by establishing a form to be known as purity, you obstruct your own self nature, you are purity bound."

While I was letting that statement wander around in my head, trying to find a clean place to light, I looked around at the audience and there, sitting not two feet from the bearded one, a look on her face that can only be described as entranced, yes, as if she were indeed in a trance, was Sylvia. Sylvia yes and Sylvia no. What I mean is, there was something about her here in this place that made her seem quite different from "there"; maybe another personality in her was taking over. Or a different band was playing in her. The wolf that was usually poised to spring from her eyes had vanished. I sat down at the back next to a red-haired man with the nose of a one-armed paperhanger and what I guess was his girlfriend, a plum pudding whose hand he held in both of his as though it were a secret he wanted no one to see. Even though I didn't know him, had never laid eyes on him before, I instinctively didn't trust him. If you know what I mean.

The Zen master cleared his throat (is it possible that he was eating cream cheese and jelly from a small blue plate? How absurd! But actually it does make sense, because a chap can get hungry no matter what he's doing. I remember now the time I visited the criminal court at the Rue Garibaldi, during an outstanding wife-murder case, and the judge, a walnutty old geezer, while sentencing the scoundrel to twenty years at hard labor, was munching on a paté sandwich which he was holding half hidden in his left hand while painting with his right) and said, "You see, Zen has to do with emancipation, of all kinds. It is a series of attempts to free us from any type of bondage. Definitions and possessions and pursuits of definitions are binding. Clingings are crippling. The total true self is thus made into a dependent child. Very bad, very bad indeed."

The group joined in making a sound of approval, a long very

smug hmmmm with the suggestion, the eye knows it is there even if the ear cannot detect it, of a tongue and roof of the mouth tasting smack underneath. Sylvia, bless her misunderstood and much abused soul, was clapping her hands gently and silently and giving forth the new non-wolf personality I mentioned before. A few feet from her, squatting on the floor, mind you, as if they didn't do enough of that in India where there just isn't enough money to buy chairs, what with all those millions and millions of sacred white cows eating up all the profits, was a very banker-dressed fellow with wild bushy eyebrows that he could have bought in one of those freak dress-up shops, a woman whose hair style would have kept her from ever getting a job in a home for mentally disturbed children—I mean the bloody thing looked like the Tower of Babel, and their daughter I suppose, a happy-chested blonde who was upright but sound asleep. The suspicious snout next to me was whispering in a disgusting liederkrantz accent to his girl. Oh how I hate whisperers! They'll do anything.

The bearded master cleared his throat again. "I would like at this particular moment to raise the concepts of 'no mind,' or wu-nien and 'no thought' or wu-hsin. Now, the great master Shen-hui explained to a novice who asked about this subject, 'I would not say that wu-nien is a reality, or that it is not. Because if I say that it is a reality, it is not in the sense in which people generally speak of reality; if I say it is a non-reality, it is not in the sense in which people generally speak of non-reality. Hence wu-nien is neither real nor unreal.' We read in a Sutra: If you are working at the mastery of all kinds of samadhi, that is moving and not sitting in meditation. The mind flows out as it naturally enters into contact with any environment.

"Wu-nien is quite beyond the range of any kind of talky discourse. The reason we talk about it at all is that questions are raised concerning it. If no questions are tossed up about it, there would of course be no discourse. It is like a shiny mirror. If no objects appear before it, nothing is to be seen in it. Simple. When you say that you are seeing something in it, it is because something stands against it. When I tell you about objects presented and their illumination, the plain fact is that this illumination is something eternal belonging to the nature of the mirror, and has no reference to or dependence upon the presence or absence of objects before it.

" 'Seeing into nothingness—that is true seeing and eternal seeing.' "(The story of my life, I said to myself.)

Zachary helped himself to a little cream cheese and jelly. "Let's look into that item of thirteenth-century Chinese wonderfulness for a moment," he went on, wiping his mouth with his sleeve. "The first statement made by Hui-neng about his Zen experience was that 'From the first not a thing is,' and then he went on to the 'Seeing into one's self-nature,' which self-nature, being a 'not thing,' is nothingness. Therefore, 'seeing into one's self-nature is seeing into nothingness' which as anybody should know is the exact statement of Shen-hui. And this seeing is the illuminating of this world of multiplicity by the light of Prajna." He finished off the cream cheese and jelly, scraping his plate quite without shame, and said, "An endless and eternal flowing in and out, a oneness and an everythingness."

Then he bowed his head for a few seconds of high protein silence, stood up, made a sign which meant that was all for today, and padded into a back room, followed by Sylvia. I'm positive I heard him mutter, "French cream cheese isn't worth a damn. Philadelphia is the place." I remained where I was while the others there pulled themselves together and left. The tittied blonde with her queer parents floated by me as if she were still in sleep, or whatever it was she was in. As for that silly-nosed ham sandwich next to me, he presumed to give me a wink, as though we'd been friends for years. Can you imagine! If I hadn't been concentrating on the new Sylvia I would have given him a lesson in proper public behavior. But I let him and his girlie pass on. As I believe I said before, these certainly aren't the days of Louis XIV. After the room had cleared (the place smelled faintly of incense but there wasn't a sign of any burning. So how do you explain that?), I walked back to the door that this Zachary and my Sylvia had disappeared into.

Now before we go any further, I want it clearly understood that I am no peeping tom. I am just not that kind of creature. I have my Mona Lisas but that isn't one of them. By the way, did you know that Charles III liked to have a bugle blown up his ass? I read that in a true history book. You see, the bugler wrote his memoirs. My reasons for taking this action were deeply human.

As an admirer of hers, I was purely and simply interested in her development. Her spritual progress in this catacomb of catacombs, if you get my meaning.

The room looked like a secret meeting place for some of those goofy peasants in a Russian novel. Stern, no-bullshit posters of Mao Tse-tung, Ho Chi Minh, Castro, Lenin, and Garibaldi were hanging on the walls. Anyway, the door was open a crack and I looked in. Zachary was lying down on a red velvet chaise longue and smoking a five-franc Havana-Antonio Gold Medal Cigar. (The wholesalers of this item positively crucify you with their mark-up.) Sylvia was seated at his feet and upon my word if she wasn't massaging them with olive oil.

"This crummy arrangement with Rastro is unhinging me," she said. "I've got to break out of it, Zachary. I mean it."

"A bet is a bet," he said, blowing three perfect smoke rings.

"So they say. But it was a bet I never made. Why should I be made to pay for the sins of a psychotic oyster fisherman?"

"Who knows what drove your poor father to his excesses? Do that little toe again, dear girl. It's been acting very strange lately. That's the ticket. Mm. Yes, perhaps it was because he felt so guilty at being such a bad father, for not being able to provide you with all the good things, spiritual as well as physical, that a girl needs. In which case—oh, that's sublime, my sweet, you speak to my tendons in a rare and wonderful language—in which case, you, as his child and the inadvertent subject of his despair, you figure most significantly in his behavior. Oooolala! The things you do to my calves!"

Oh Zachary!" Sylvia wailed. "Why are you betraying my despair with this philosophical mandolin cantata! I need your help. I'm up the creek."

Zachary sighed and blew smoke through his nose. "Woman's ageless cry. I believe Clytemnestra. . . ."

"Zachary!"

"All right, all right. I'll try to think of something one dimensional. Let me see . . . Rastro . . . Rastro . . . Does he have any weaknesses?"

"Yes. All of them."

"I mean one in particular, one that makes him indefensibly vulnerable."

And she did something pioneer to his instep.

"Yes," said Sylvia. "He breathes."

"Ah, of course, of course! How direct and simple. It is a satori."

"I think we're getting somewhere," Sylvia said, looking up into the air.

"He breathes," repeated Zachary in fairly soft astonishment. "And that means. . . ."

"You're closing in, Zach, baby."

Zachary stared at her for a dawning second (I mean, you could really see the sun coming up over the Cote d'Azur), then suddenly sat upright.

"But that's against the law!"

"What isn't?"

Zachary began stroking his muff. "Hmm."

"Spell it out, hon."

He pulled every potentially human inch of himself together, sighing, of course, and slowly got up and began padding up and down the room as though he were a South American anteater in the Berlin Zoo. "Of course," he said, making a lovely Zen turn under the Lenin, "neither of us can have a finger in it."

Sylvia emitted one of those dry airless sounds all the fuddy old writers used to call a chuckle. "That's going to be pretty difficult." (I'm not sure whether I mentioned this before, but Sylvia was dressed in a way that was not at all typical of her. I mean, of course, typical of the Sylvia I knew. She was wearing a shameless pink sari.)

"That is," Zachary continued, "a third person must deliver the coup de grace. Someone quite unknown to the police, someone indeterminate and most unlikely."

"You mean like the Minister of Education?"

I had to fight down a titter, upon my word I did.

Zachary stopped in the middle of the room in order to think more clearly. He began making tiny sucking noises. I guess some of our cruddy French cream cheese was sticking to his gums. No, I'm wrong. He suddenly plunged his pinky deep in among his choppers, policed about in there, and extracted. . . . "Sausage!" he cried, and flicked the offender off his nail. He began pacing again. "A shadow of a human," he went on, "a person who lodges naturally between Tuesday and Wednesday."

Sylvia stared deeply at the floor. I could tell she was flipping through the dirtiest human folders in her memory. Gradually a smile thieved its way over her face. "I've got it," she said. "I know just the person."

Zachary stopped a little to the left of Mr. Castro's beard. "Oh? Who is the lucky cad?"

A giggle more than curled out of Sylvia. "The doorman at the club. His name is Cedric."

Holy Shit! They're talking about me! Mother's little helper.

"Yep," Sylvia continued to my utter chagrin. "He'd be perfect."

"Is he obscure enough?"

Another giggle from Sylvia's Medusa mouth.

"I'll say. He's as obscure as the Ping-Pong champion of southern Nigeria."

Zachary clapped his hands. "Zucchini!" and he embraced Sylvia over my murderous body. Then something stoney hit him, and he drew back a little. "But how do we get him to do it?"

Ha!

"You just leave that to old Sylvia," Miss Medusa said, "I wasn't born under Cancer for nothing."

We'll see about that, dearie.

Zachary grinned real greasy. "Mm. You are a talented girl. There's no gainsaying that." He smiled even greasier. "Now that we've got that settled, how about a little jig-jig? Hmm?" And he cradled her sari-covered bottom in his hands and rubbed her back and forth against his jutting self.

"Zen style?"

"You know a country boy never changes," he said, and put his all-purpose Zen tongue all the way down into her childhood. I took myself from the crack in the door when Lady Sylvia Macbeth began pulling his chimes from deep within the incense shrines of his robes. The last I saw as I turned away was the first academic inch of it, the eye blinking furiously as the light hit it. As I believe I've explained, I'm not one for feasting my saliva on other people's whing and ding fairs. So I tiptoed off into my own confabulation.

Boy sopranos have long played an important part in English buggery, and this aging lutenist is sure as hell going to play a nonexistent part in the bump-off concert you just heard. It's one thing to be a baggy pants doorman; it's another to be an alterer of The Great Plan. Not me, I instructed myself over a café espresso in the Deux Magots a couple of blocks away. (Hairy young American tourists of the Humphrey Bogart type are turning our cafés into their bedrooms! Mary! Doesn't that country have a military draft?) The nerve of that snatch! I can just imagine the vile scheming going on inside that dilettante sari especially now that light years of paradoxical Zen Buddhism is pumping into it. The juicy slipping and sliding must be absolutely unbearable in its provocation to insanity. How can a girl keep body and soul together under these mountains of hotness! Oh God what wildness he's doing to me! An armed revolt is going on between my legs! A peasant uprising. They're killing the animals and burning the barns. They're looting the castle! Their eyes are screaming! They're smashing in my door—Ohhh! I love it!

Yes! That's what is pouring through that malevolent cunt's head! Oh, the things a woman can do! The things she can think of! God must have made them when he was on a drunk. That crazy bastard. Fun is fun, but. . . . If she's going to run my life why doesn't she pay my taxes? Or get up in the putrid morning for me and brush my aching teeth? Eh? Oh oh. There's that unnaturally beautiful man Prevert the baker. I wonder if he knows that I have adored him ever since I ate his first roll and saw him blink those honeysuckle eyes of his! I'd rather eat him than be the Queen of England. That lovely brute sends shivers right down to the first confession I ever made to Father Gillet in the South district. I'll bet his wife barely appreciates him. Pearls before swine. Ah well. Oh, and there is that . . . "Another cafe, please, Marcel, and you'd better bring me a cognac. I've had a shit of a day, yes, you're right. Things are getting worse all the time, all over" . . . that bonbon, Legendre the window washer, having himself a quickie double white wine at the bar. Just to look at him, who would think that he positively loves it up the ass. Of course, you've got to put a dollop of pomade on first, otherwise it's like climbing the Great Wall of China without any hands. "Jam it to me, Cedric!" he cried just night before last. "All the way. Ooh! That's it. Don't be afraid to hurt me a little." That invalid sister Philomena he lives with was sitting in the front room singing to herself as usual. You could shoot DeGaulle in the hallway bathroom and she wouldn't know the difference. For that matter I don't even think she knows who DeGaulle is. He's a gentle. . . . "Ah, good afternoon, Madame Corot. Have I heard about what? The artichoke growers are on strike? They're dumping their produce in the streets? What a perverted thing to do. Yes, yes, I agree with you. I've always thought they were a queer bunch. Of course. Exactly. Normal people couldn't grow such a delicacy." Richest person in the neighborhood she is. Concierge for number 27 around the corner and an informer for the police. Shows you there's a fortune to be made telling on people. A fortune to be made getting other folks to do your murdering too. Oh that dragon's breath!

Not a muscle in her has a kind twitch for her fellow man. Her entire nervous system is a web of conspiracy against the human race. Plots race through her instead of impluses. Oh, I know that one all right. She's as clear as cyanide, she is. I can tell you what's in her mind this very second. I can feel her thoughts crawling all over my skin, that's how well I know her. She's looking into Master Zachary's sweaty red face above her own (she feels as soft as a lake of marshmallows after coming three times under his heaving and humping) and she's saying, "Oh Daddy Zachary! You certainly do have some good ideas."

"Everything I have I owe to the Bhodi Dharma," he breathes fiercely. "It is a question of living out the doctrine of Fourfold Noble Truth."

"Mm." And she moves her face slightly because his beard is tickling her chin. "I remember. You touched on that in your last lecture."

"One flower blooms and the universe rises with it." He puts his nose under my ear and breaths deeply of my Chanel No. 5 rich smell.

"One particle of dust is raised and the great earth lies therein." Isn't—ooh darling, don't pull out yet. It's so good in there I feel like a lake of marshmallows—isn't that the rest of it?"

"Precisely and perfectly." He gives me two birdseed neck pecks.

"Hyakuso, eighth century."

"The very person. Mm. You smell of summer dreams."

"I've got it all worked out."

"What?"

"How Cedric is going to knock off Rastro."

"Oh."

Jesus. What a difference—having the Master's bearded magic breathing into my face instead of that putrid moon surface of Rastro's. My old man smelled of garlic and wine and had a battlefield skin but there was something about him that was very okay. He was good-looking and masculine the way a beast is. You're scared of them but they excite you and the risk of the violence inside them. I loved to watch him in the Café Duart down at the docks, getting drunk with the other fishermen, laughing and shouting and telling those wonderful lies about his life in the French Underground when the Nazis were all over the place like vermin but with machine guns. Cockroaches with machine guns. What a disgusting sight that would be. "Shit!" my pappa would shout. "My leader, Dumas his name was, he could tell me to do the most dangerous fucking things and I would do them. Wire a hand grenade to a door knob in the German officers club, choke a sentry to death with my bare hands, ram a gunboat at night in the bay here. Anything. God but I was a wild man!" Oh pappa, what a lot of shit, but what perfectly delightful shit.

The men all loved it and so did I. And the fat-assed waitress Beatrice giggling and holding her stomach at the same time. My nipples hurt from your biting, Zachary. All those tiny sharp bites. Maybe bruises later. What will I tell Rastro to explain them?

"Yes. Cedric will drown him."

"Water," Zachary sighs, and rolls off me gently. "It is the mother of everything. It gives life to every living thing," and he sighs again at the ceiling.

"Well," I say, grabbing a Kleenex to wipe his spew from my thighs, "It's going to work in reverse for us. Boy, what a neat little plan I've got. Tricky and yet esthetic. Hand me that sheet, honey. I'm a little cold."

"Thanks. Well, you know how Rastro just loves to swim, or bathe or whatever the fuck it is that takes place. I mean he's nuts about it. Takes him back to his childhood as a frog or something. His idea of heaven, next to money, cheating, and you know what, is to float about in the soupy water down at St. Tropez. All by himself. We won't go into how creepy that is. Okay. So I act like the very good mistress and take him down there, telling him he owes himself a little rest. Barb Stanwyck did that bit beautifully in *Harm's Way*, remember? Take him there this coming Bastille Day weekend. By his chubby little hand, you know. Which he's got more rings on than the Queen of Sheba and every fucking one of them is a boyhood dream come true. Anyway, give him a real sense of security and well-being. Set him up real good (because you know I sometimes think the son of a bitch sleeps with his eyes open). Now this is where Cedric baby comes in, and I do think you'll love it, Zach honey. He's going to be way out there—that's where Rastro likes to be, way out there alone, away from all the splashing human forms—under water with an aqualung! Impersonating a fish! And what a fish. And do you know what he's going to do in the disguise of the big bad fish? Oh, this part is the real winner, sweetheart—I mean this is the frame that absolutely wrecks the National Academy Judging Committee, and ends all further festivals at Venice. Cedric is going to be a shark! Got it? Rastro is going to be eaten up by Killer Shark Cedric. Doesn't that hit you right where the chimes are? You couldn't improve on that if you were Captain Kidd himself. And the whipped cream touch is this: we're going to provide Cedric with a fake, but compleely realistic of course, shark fin to drag through the water out there so the innocent splashers will see it and tell the cops and anybody else who asks, yes, a terrible killer shark grabbed Rastro and ate him up. Wow! Hey, I got it! Rastro's going to take his last swim in shark fin soup! Oh Jesus! I just can't stop soaring today, Zachary sweetie. It must be all that lovely stuff about flowing in and out of nature thats juicing me up. I feel like I've eight different people inside me all hitting home runs for the common cause."

Zachary has been examining his creamy almost hairless body for blackheads, pimples, scabs or any other squeezable or scratchable action thereon. Now he smiles vaguely and, looking at me with those Chinese porcelain type eyes of his, says, "You certainly possess a remarkable mind."

"Oh well," I say slapping him on the belly, "It's the kind of thing you're said to be born with. I'm just lucky."

"You're probably right. I couldn't imagine learning that sort of thing at school." He squints into his palms as though they're some kind of road map. "Forgive me if I seem slow, but just what does the lucky Cedric do to Rastro?"

He's such a cutie, I can't help myself: I move over and sit on his lap, straddling him—don't worry, his pickle is quietly looking at the floor—and kiss his ginger plum nose that is good for a lot more than breathing, take it from me. "Simple, bubbie, simpler than voting a straight ticket in Moscow. He grabs Rastro by his dabbling legs, pulls him under and drowns him. Of course, he stabs him a few times so that the water gets real red and further shows everybody around that the shark is tearing away at him."

"I see," he says, blowing an imaginary butterfly off my shoulder. "And then what does he do?"

I give him a couple of kisses on his rosebud. "He carries Rastro's corpse for about half a mile under water to a little fishing boat which he ties the body to the bottom of."

"And leaves him there, like an extra rudder?"

I laugh. "Oh you are a funny, Zachary boy. You really are. An extra rudder! No, baby. That's where you come in."

He sighs with his whole body and gives me a little ride on his lap. "I knew it, I just knew it. A man with all my wonderful insights too, a truly and rarely cultivated chap." He shakes his head. "What do I do? Chop him up into fish bait?"

"Zachary! You're reading my mind. I swear to God you are. That's exactly what you do. You're on the boat, and you and Cedric—you'll love him, he's such a huggy-bear of a thing—take the boat out a few miles, cut him up in small pieces and sprinkle him overboard. The fish'll love him. Mex delicatessen."

Zachary gets up—easing me off his lap, of course—and begins walking around the room again. It's funny, but he isn't making any sound as he walks. His feet are touching the floor all right, I can see them, but no sound comes back. Am I suddenly deaf? No, because I can hear the small street sounds coming through the window. Wierd. It's like Zachary is in another world and I just happen to be seeing him like something funny happening to time and space and all that. A movie when the sound goes off for some reason. Not like a dream. Something else. Now he's walking toward me and saying something but I can't hear him. He isn't really looking at me. But at someone or thing beyond me.

"Zachary." Nothing. "Zachary," I say louder, but he doesn't hear me. "Zachary!"

Oh Christ! What's happening? Where am I? Help!

That lousy murderous slut! So she's not only turning me from myself into a murderer—one hell of a different kind of human being!—but into a fucking frogman shark! Taking me away from myself, the rightful owner of me. She'll be fucking around with the weather next thing you know. "Thank you, Marcel. You read my mind. I did need another cognac. Things are very tight ass, inside and out, believe me. The same with you, eh? I agree with you, what we all need is a nice little racket. Not anything big. Just enough to take the grit out of the soup, eh? You're thinking of putting your wife out to hustle? I don't blame you. It's just as dignified to work with your cunt as with your hands. And it pays better. Oh well, there are freaks in every business deal. One closes one's eyes and thinks up someone else. Use the old imagination. Right. It's all upstairs in the old noodle, Marcel. That's where the world really is, and I don't mean maybe. All that you see out there is just a stage prop. The play is anything you want it to be. It is entirely up to you what takes place and how and who gets the fat parts. No, I don't mean dreaming either. Dreaming is pretty good in its way too. What I'm talking about is the entire bloody shebang. No I wouldn't shit you, Marcel old boy. I like you, as you well know, and I don't shit my buddies. Other people, yes. But that's quite different. Another lamb chop entirely." Don't mention it. Mm. This cognac is a true, true friend. Like me, it doesn't deceive a buddy. It never fails to come through for you. It makes you know you're there. What else does that for a fellow?

Upon my word, if that isn't the famous Pamela Frothingcunt staggering across the street in the company of a giant baby panda. What a lovely couple.

IX

TODAY IS SUNDAY—THAT AIRLESS GRAVE-yard that the brutalized week finally stumbles into and collapses —so I am not down at my Fruit and Vegetable Stand to the World. I can use the rest. Yesterday there was a run on eggplant, the New Jersey Cranberries arrived all poisoned with DDT, and I was shortweighted on my Belgian endive. Half the queens in the Village bled internally because they had to serve their Saturday night trade iceberg lettuce in the salad. Oh Mary! It was one mad dog of a day. Today, however, I am comforting myself. I am going on a family style picnic with my dear friend Lola-Eulalia, that not-so-secret sharer of my love nest. (Sylvia is away visiting her sister—in the nuthouse—or so she said. Incidentally, she has lately taken to speaking French in her sleep. Too much Proust, if you ask me.) And a most engaging brother and sister team I have just gotten to know, Churchill Downs and Ophelia of the Morning Light. Actually, we met at a public flogging. Black and chewy as Greek olives they are. Politically oriented, too. They head up the National Liberation Front in Harlem. Direct line to Hanoi and to the heart of the Negro. As a matter of fact, I think Churchill went to revolutionary school with Ho Chi Minh in Moscow.

"He's got the patience of a willow tree," Churchill said once, over a glass of sour mash. And again, "No question about it: he understands political strategy as a bird understands the sky." Now, you're not likely to say such things unless you know the party in question pretty well, right? I mean, he doesn't exactly sound like *The Daily News.* Churchill and Ophelia have a great front. They are beggars, panhandlers (and some other things).

After massive consideration, we decided to have our picnic up at the Cloisters. All other places—Central Park, the Battery, Riverside Drive—struck us as a bit too vile. The flotsam and jetsam on those beaches is more than a person of feeling should be forced to swim through—mountains of dog shit, hordes of neglected popsicle-high children, light years of middle-aged armpit fantasies. The Cloisters, on the other hand, offers you a class experience. High type vibrations. Without even half trying, you are rubbing shoulders with the ancient crowned heads of Europe and all their well-dressed buddies. A pretty arty bunch at times, but classy.

Enough of that for a moment. Before we get into the potato salad scene I want to present some fine talk of Churchill's. In particular, a fragment of a Soliloquy on Violence which he gave one evening to a group of organized white female tourists who had assembled at the Fourth Mesopotamian Reform and Release Church. (What difference does it make if the audience had paid a dollar a head for the performance? Does the fact that it was part of a guided tour through Lost City make it any less important and authentic? The money, incidentally, was split with a progessive Bach combo that provided background music.)

"Contemporary civilization has interwoven violence and sex, so intricately as to confuse the identity of both and, to a fearfully large degree, sex in our time has violence in it either implicitly or explicitly. Sadistic-masochistic love-making (love is exactly what is not being made, of course) is a routine experience for children (through the mass media) as well as adults, and it has become part of our fantasy/reality cultural tradition. Violence, or aggression, is in fact so directly related to most sexual experience that the absence of it is often thought of as suspect, and the male partner who does not practice it in one form or another is considered passive or latently homosexual. In this particular ambience, the quality of the sexual experience itself is often gauged, nay, determined, by the correlation of violence/aggression. I don't think the correlation is natural to, or born in, the human breed, as all the 'instinctual drive' people, such as Lorenz, say. I believe it is an environmentally produced situation, originally, and it is reinforced by the confusions and values of the culture. Nobody is born with a love-hate syndrome: it is developed. In any civilization or culture where the attitude toward the sexual experience is not a punitive or distasteful one, the violence-sex correlation is virtually nonexistent. The fear of sexual contact makes a person anxious, and one way of releasing anxiety is through aggression. Since the violence-love-sex concept is so deep and widespread, we are all of us manipulated by it, forced into participating in it as we are forced into other culturally approved behavior thought patterns. Possibly, the love-makers, paradoxically, feel inadequate if they do not find themselves feeling aggressive-violent simply because their culture says this is what one is supposed to feel."

Okay. Does that give you an idea of the fine quality merchandise that Churchill's got in that upstairs store? That stuff is so good you almost have to smuggle it in. Which is in point of fact just about what he has to do. . . . One of Churchill's many hustles is as a busking seer (you might say.) He tours the streets of Harlem, and adjacent areas of course, giving out with these soliloquies on street corners. He has his sister Ophelia, and an obscure friend, play zither and hand drums for the music background, and Churchill, during his visionary spiels, does a little soft shoe or something roughly like it. People toss money onto a blanket in front of the three of them, and that's the way it goes. He recently picked up an easy twenty bucks, he told me, giving a very colorful soliloquy on the corner of Broadway and 111th Street called Lies We Live By, or What Keeps The Whole Damn Thing Together. A ten-buck concert was called Food Games For Newlyweds (Amsterdam Avenue and 93rd Street).

Now back to the picnic. I mentioned potato salad a while back, but I was only joking. I wouldn't eat that crap if the Prince of Wales gave it to me on his hands and knees. The victuals we lugged up to the Cloisters was true dream food, stuff you can assemble and enjoy only if you don't believe in mother and seriously question the sexual proclivities of Albert Einstein. Southern fried chicken—deep hot bacon grease, mind you, no crummy peanut oil—black-eyed peas with ham bits, meatballs made Italian style, which means with ingredients you are forbidden to use if you have your naturalization papers; zitti with the meatballs, cucumbers with sour cream speckled with fennel seed, two kinds of thoroughly criminal cheese—limburger and sunny Camembert, and wine from the cheeky groves of Lucca. You got all that?

Ophelia and Lola hit it off just grand. The communication between two dark-skinned women is truly deep. Those two flowers were giggling their way right back to the gardens of Mesopotamia. Being in the Cloisters helped us all to extricate ourselves from the contemporary J.C. Penny of it all. Those eleventh-century unicorns and those thirteenth-century flutes don't have one scintilla of foam rubber or plastic about them. To tell you the creepy truth, I recognized quite a few of my friends in those tapestries, and so did the others. The looks they were giving each other in their elegant gardens, with all the wide-eyed, gold-braided handmaidens about, were looks I knew from yore.

"This certainly is a lovely place," Ophelia said, looking about a romanesque, tapestried room, "but I don't see very many of my black brothers here. In fact," she went on, staring up even at the ceiling, "I don't see any—except yours truly and her more than plentiful brother."

Before I could think of something meaningless and slippery to come back with, Churchill chuckled and said, "The reason for that, sister honey, is that they're all at home busily planning tomorrow's massacres."

Ophelia just looked at him, "Uh huh, are you sure it isn't because they feel they're not wanted?"

Churchill put his arm around Ophelia. "Now sister, you must stop thinking about the revolution for awhile. There is plenty of time for that next week. This is picnic time."

Lola suggested we take a look at the herb garden. She's the kind of girl who doesn't like to mix her culture and her political anxieties, and I can't say I blame her. Race riots are one thing and gothic wood paneling is another. And if you get the two confused you might wind up shooting at a statue. Speaking of which, the statues that surrounded us at the Cloisters certainly got to you. They had absolutely nothing in common with those crummy blobs we manufacture for the shitting pleasure of the park pigeons.

That Ophelia! Do you know what she did? While we were all admiring the lovely herb garden in the patio—I must confess that my perusal (How do you like that! Perusal!) of them was somewhat confused by the air being sumptuously alive with recorded Renaissance music, so that I wasn't sure I was examining a few lute sounds when really I was looking at a patch of rosemary—anyway, while we were all bent over the herbs out there, Ophelia, that shiny squeeze of blackness, snatched up a few sprays of mint and stuck them in the bold and spacious bosom opening of her dress.

"Where the bee sucks, there suck I!" Churchill exclaimed, and slapped her on her more than gorgeous ass.

"Mother Nature's perfume," Ophelia said. "You barely get it anymore in this poisoned city."

"Strangling in its own diseased vapors," I said, and I really meant it. Churchill nodded his agreement.

"Makes me long for the sweet meaningful breezes off the Tonkin Gulf," he mused, and a true faraway look was in his eyes.

"Garlic is what I go for," said Lola.

Well, I needn't tell you that we gave the scent situation a whirl for a few more minutes. And I didn't mind a bit, really. You never realize, until you stop to think about it, how we ignore the world of the nose. Why? Have you ever asked yourself that? It's my feeling that we are the innocent victims of a conspiracy against smell. There is something dangerous and divine there and our rulers know this—have known it from the very beginning. Smelling, odors—this sort of thing is part of the natural world, and I don't have to tell you how the machine people feel about the natural world. Deny it, smash it, kill it—that's their attitude. Consequently, none of us has the faintest notion which way the wind is blowing. Listen to this:

"The Negrito is an intrinsic part of his environment, and what is still more important, continually studies his surroundings. Many times I have seen a Berero who, when not being certain of the identification of a particular plant, will taste the fruit, smell the leaves, break and examine the stem, comment upon its habitat, and only after all of this, pronounce whether he did or did not know the plant."

That item—from my boy Levi-Straus—should give you a rough idea of just how close you aren't to your environment. The next time you see a good-looking pine tree, give it a hug.

When we reached the jewelry room on our tour of the inside —Ophelia had wound up our examination of the herb garden scene by giving us a lovely ten-minute rundown on slave herb cures that was positively humiliating, it was so fine—the girls simply broke up. They had never seen stuff like that. I mean, ouch, you could spend two years in Tiffany's and never even see one fraction of such glory. This was soul jewelry. Gold that was so solid it made your balls ache. Precious stones so big and rich you wanted to sit down and have a good cry for the sheer unconcealed sincerity of it all. Ophelia lit up like a Times Square neon sign as she looked at the stuff. Her eyes flashed and her mouth hung open and her breathing was an animal in heat.

"Oh my good Lord yes," she said, staring at a caseful of earrings and bracelets. "I hear you talking. Oh Lordy my soul is melting. I feel you inside me, deep deep in there. Oh yea and more than that. . . ."

Your music is so rich and sweet and it's saying no to all the cheap and crummy and imitation things that hang on everybody's outside and inside Christmas trees. Oh the open-legged marvel of you! The hot handedness and strut in you! Oh Jesus! The truth you tell! You could make a child bride of me anytime. But that's what I was—and that old man's grey beard still tickles my legs even though it has been seventeen years and scores of bodies since. Black and white and yellow and terra cotta bodies. Little dicks and big dicks, round ones and skinny ones and some that couldn't get going anymore than a cooked noodle. And the kinky worlds that went with those dicks and bodies. That year I spent as the mascot of a Greek wrestling team. Went from place to place bouncing each other off a mat.

"You are my little black bon bon. But you are not so little, are you? Every place I take a bite tastes so very delicious."

"Uh huh."

"And more than that. You are learning things very well, very well indeed. You are becoming a good doer of the massage. That was very fine, the rubbings you gave me last night. You have such strong hands for a bon bon."

"I picked a lot of cotton with those hands," I said.

Seems we were always sitting on the balcony of that big house in Athens, never inside. Me and one of the wrestlers. The one who liked rubdowns was named Nikos. He also liked to have me clip the black hairs that grew out of his nostrils in whole forests. Had a special little pair of scissors for the job. Made in Sweden or some place like that where it's cold. Another one on the team, Constantine his name was, was always wanting me to tickle him on the belly. Drove him crazy. He was the strongest man I've ever seen. They were all strong but he was the most. Muscles on him that came out of nowhere. He could crack a walnut between his toes, and if he grabbed you, you knew he could throw you all the way across the street and then some. There were six of them, but I only had to take care of four. The other two took care of each other like the Greeks do. They were nice boys though. Never did anything to anybody, which is more than I can say for most of the human race.

"Someday these muscles of mine will get tired of games," Nikos said, "and they won't play anymore. Then what will Nikos do?"

"Get yourself a nice litte restaurant somewhere," I said. "Serve hot Greek heroes."

He laughed. He had the hairiest damn laugh. "Do you think my muscles will dream of the old fury of the combat?"

"Why not? They got a right like any other part of you."

He smiled and rubbed his arms. I looked at a little fishing boat sleeping out in the water. "When I was a little boy I saw two fishermen drown in that water," he said.

"What was the matter with them? Were they drunk or something?"

"They were mad. Mad with the madness of love. They fought

over a girl, a laughing girl with flowers in her eyes and breasts enough for twenty. She was willing to share herself with both of them, but these fishermen could not understand that generosity. They stabbed each other and drowned." He looked out over the quiet blue bay. "Their blood made the water very beautiful."

Then there was that rich polo player with the toothbrush mustache and the lesbian sister who had ears like a baby. Man, what a combo they were. The parties they threw. Wow. Like there wasn't going to be any tomorrow. You've got to be crazy and rich to do stuff life that. Night and day those shindigs went on until there wasn't a live body in the place; and I was the black rubber ball they bounced between them.

"Tell me something, Ophelia," he said to me one day, "what do spades think about?"

"Same things you do, only we think it in black."

"When I was a little girl I wanted to be black," his sister said. "I thought money could buy that too."

She wasn't a bad sort, that Monique. The only thing I didn't like was her funny ears. Her being queer didn't bother me. It wasn't my favorite sport or anything, but when you think about it calmly, there isn't any difference between a woman's tongue and a man's tongue. Fun is fun. The really kinky one in that household was the butler. Redheaded snatchhound with a bootlegger's nose. That cat had more depravities than a tax collecter has winks. He had the two maids and the cook trained like a circus act. The stuff that went on in that kitchen sure wouldn't fit in any cookbook.

"One of these days," said Jonathan, "I'm going to be forced to stop playing polo and take up something else."

"You mean besides sex?" I said.

"Says here the Pope has bladder trouble," Monique let us know.

Brother J. took another sip. "Besides sex, yes."

"Maybe gardening. I heard of a man—a millionaire like you—who said he saw God in a rosebush."

Monique rustled over in the corner. "They're fighting on the Chinese border again. Oh those restless yellow hordes!"

Said J. "But plants aren't games, Ophelia. That's the thing." He thought for a second—washed his throat with a drink—then said, "Cock fighting, possibly. Could go to Mexico and study up on it. I've always had the suspicion the Mexicans could teach us a lot of things."

He had funny eyes. One must have belonged to his mother, the other one to her old man. Blue and brown. He was pretty good in the hay. His tongue was the most like a lizard's you could want. It went in and of of me like it had been starving on some hot rock in the mountains of Mexico. A couple of minutes of that hot lizard tongue and I didn't know if I was me or you or Donald Duck. You can say all you want to in praise of ruby ramming meat but when it comes to is there or isn't there a Sanity Clause, a long fast tongue is a girl's very best. . . .

"Ophelia," said Monique, dropping her newspaper to the floor, "Let's take a hot shower together. I feel real dirty."

"I'll be in in just a few minutes," said J, "as soon as I figure out my future." More likely he wanted to have another look at a new rifle he just got, telescopic aiming sight and all.

There was one of their friends I liked very much. Real good-looking dark-skinned fellow named Bosworth. If you ask me he had a touch of darkie in him. His grandmother on his mother's side, I'll bet. Besides his skin, he had another something about him that was black, and that was his hot smartness. White men are dry smart. This Bosworth fellow was an interior decorator for rich people. Which is a pretty good racket because if there's anything rich people don't mind laying out money for it's for looking classy. They don't want anything to do with unclassy thing. Glasses got to be just right or else the drink in them isn't any good. Far as I'm concerned, you can get just as good a load on from a jelly glass as you can from one of those three-dollar art objects that come from Denmark. Gin is gin.

Bosworth was always very nice to me. I mean in a special way, because everybody was nice the other way, and why shouldn't they? They knew I wasn't going to take anything from them. I was that spade sexpot that Jonathan and Monique kept for their orgies, and everybody knows that in that kind of situation everybody is nice to everybody else. The thought of having some hot fun makes everybody smile no matter who they think they are. My candidate for the universal equalizer is a big male organ. A real no-nonsense symbol of democracy. Yeah. But this coffee-colored doll-baby Bosworth and I had something special going. Like we knew something those others didn't know, just the two of us. The smiles that sneak in between the other smiles, that was us. He had a crazy streak in him too. How else could you explain the fact that he had an assistant who was a faggot hunchback name Esmeralda? Oh Lordy me oh my! And do you know what this grinning sideshow claims!

"Catherine the Great used to rub my hump for good luck. And that's not all she rubbed." His very own words, so help me Hannah. Used to show up at parties wearing a velvet Fauntleroy suit. Other times he would appear in simply outrageous women's clothes that he must have bargained for at a Chink cathouse.

I asked Bosworth how he ever got in the decorating racket.

"It's really very simple," he said, sipping a real he-man drink of cranberry juice, "I had a domineering mother who wanted me to be a homosexual. But that wasn't possible. I have an ineradicable allergy to taking cylindrical shapes into my mouth, or up my ass. I tried it and the very first contact I begin to sneeze something unbelievable. So I became the next best thing—an interior decorator. Pleasing my mother was very important to me.

He looked at me real serious and I just had to laugh. "Bosworth, you sure can lay it on, honey. You ought to work in a carnival. You'd make yourself a fortune."

He gave me a joyful slap on the can. "Give me time. I may wind up in one yet."

He wound up in one—me. And I'm a pretty good carnival, if I do say so myself. We were out in the summer house and there wasn't anybody else around except the bees and the birds, and before I could say George Washington Carver I was on my back on the chintz couch and he was driving ahead like the Rome-to-Paris express. He sure had a lovely fast rhythm, and that made me more convinced there was minority juice in him somewhere because white boys hump like they're going to be caught by the school principal or somebody, and that makes you kind of itchy, no matter what color you are, and before you know it, your own gears aren't shifting right.

Funny thing, I've belonged to so many people I sometimes think of me as somebody else. She, I say to myself when what I'm talking or thinking about happens to be me. But the she at that time, the she time, wasn't really me, I don't think, but somebody else, somebody thought up, and the me was watching her. You sure as hell got to invent a lot of other selves in order to get along in this world. There she was one day, that Ophelia, sitting in a soft restaurant and holding the hand of an old man. She did not know him, but that was all right. He was smiling and putting spoonfuls of mush into his mouth. "You're going to be all right," she said to him and touched his privates almost against her will.

"It doesn't matter any more," he said, but the way he said this made Ophelia feel he was lying.

Across the room, which was filled with sounds that did not belong there, a women Ophelia knew from somewhere in childhood was making obscene gestures to her.

"You don't have to do that!" Ophelia yelled. "We can be friends."

The woman, who now was crying, threw a spoon at her. "You're not my mother." And somehow Ophelia had to accept this. She felt light and lovely and pleasantly sorry for herself.

Then she was in the street, staring at a big sign in a store window. "Impecunious gestures signed here," it said.

A little boy stood next to her and he had his hand under her dress. But she did not feel this was bad, "Don't tell anybody you saw me," he seemed to be whispering.

She was flooded with a warm very sexy feeling and she was suddenly holding his head to her bare breasts, which he was sucking. "Secrets are important," she said. It occurred to her that this was a very important thing to say and she smiled.

The boy bit her and she threw him to the ground. But he just giggled and ran gently down the street.

"No one is perfect!" she shouted after him, but she knew the sound never got there. "I meant to say a lot more," she said to no one in particular.

Laughing, falling black people were all over the street. Their laughter was soundless and they were falling in slow motion. Ophelia was laughing and falling with them. There was nothing she could do about this. She felt frustrated but not in a painful way. Someone she knew very well waved to her from a rooftop. Ophelia tried to wave back but for some reason she could not make her arms move. She planned to explain this to the person later on.

"I won't give up thinking about you," this acquaintance yelled in a gentle way from that great distance.

"Thank you very much," Ophelia heard herself shout back. "We must not forget such things!"

An extremely vivid picture of her mother came into Ophelia's mind. Her mother was sitting on a porch snapping stringbeans and singing. The words were very special and had to do with life in the south. Ophelia guessed this because she could not quite understand the words, even though they sounded familiar enough to her. Then she was kissing the picture of her old mother.

"There are some things you can't kid anybody about," a smiling fat black man said. He was lying down naked on the curbstone.

Panic seized Ophelia. "I'm not trying to! Please."

The man just smirked and wagged his finger at her. "Just remember where you are."

She wanted to go on with this conversation, and as she began moving toward the man she realized that he wasn't there anymore.

A deep, meaningful voice was filling the entire swarming street now, "We must not let ourselves be enticed by the statement of strangers."

A great relief and happiness swept through Ophelia, a total sensation that was mixed with strong sexual yearnings, "You're so right!" she shouted to the presence. Her good sensation was heading toward an orgasm and she wondered, with some guilt, if anyone could tell this. She put her hands over the area of her genitals as if to guide what was going on there. However, she could not stop herself from smiling very openly. "Ah well," she stated, more to herself than was really proper.

Then she was sitting in a clean and conspicuously chic room in somebody's house. Her clothes were not her own; they belonged to a rich person who had loaned them to her. Ophelia could not quite remember this person's name or why she had made such a generous gesture. She looked at her skin and discovered that it wasn't black and she began to kiss her own hands softly and repeatedly while tears rolled down her face.

"If you can understand that," said a gruff old man sitting on a couch across from her, "you can understand anything." He laughed mechanically and without any expression crossing his face.

"I don't owe you a thing," she said, and went right on kissing her new skin.

The next thing she knew the old man had taken a mask from his face and there was her brother Churchill Downs. He had never looked more radiant and acceptable. A very large thing was in his hand. When Ophelia leaned forward to get a better look at it, the thing extended across the room and into her mouth. "It's you all right," she said. She was surprised that she could speak so clearly with it in her mouth. Somewhere a band began to play a sophisticated march. Churchill had closed his eyes and was singing most beautifully. Such a good taste was in her mouth. It was coming from far away and it was never ending.

"BOSWORTH, HONEY," I SAID TO HIM ONE DAY after a pretty crazy game of tennis—theirs, not mine, because the very thought of black on that tennis court in one of their own games would have been just too insane, and I don't think I have to explain why—"Bosworth, let's you and me cut out of here."

"What?"

"And go someplace where we can meet some real people."

"I don't think I heard you right."

"Get something going that has a future," I went on.

"Have you been taking any thing?" he asked. "Like visionary drugs? Or grass?"

"Because the game of crazy chairs here is getting to repeat itself something awful. And if you arrange many more Lady Hamilton rooms for any more rich feebs you are going to end up in the laughing academy."

"Can't you see I'm reading the sports paper?"

I said, "Baby, you haven't read a newspaper since you were a cotton pickin' child."

He raised himself up on one arm. "Young lady, I wish you wouldn't besmirch my character. And besides, if there was ever any picking of cotton in my childhood, it was very likely in the Nile Valley. Long-strand stuff that makes the very finest of English shirtings."

I just had to go over and wrap myself around him. He was the cutest little pig's foot I'd seen in years. I knew he was hanging around with some German countess, but I didn't care. Nobody could know him the way I did. I knew the secret him.

"We could go to Paris or Rome. One of those places. I hear that London's pretty groovy too." I kissed him a couple of times behind his ear. His skin always tasted so good. Sweet like a good child. "No telling what good things could happen to us in those fine places. Hmm?"

Bos turned a little to get more comfortable. To put it clearly, he wasn't exactly resisting the situation. "Any good philosopher will tell you that the real journeys are inside your head."

"I never said they weren't. But anybody can tell you you can fake it better in some places than in others."

"Hmm. I'll have to think that one over."

"Okay, and while you're thinking it over, why don't you move over a bit. I'll hold you while you do your thinking. There. That's better." Mm. He certainly smells sweet. I'll bet his mamma gave him a lot of love when he was little. Not a bad, or sour smell in his whole body. You can tell that he's been held by lots of women.

We went to London. Esmeralda went with us. In spite of all my protestations. He said they'd been together so long that it would be humanly impossible for them to separate. He said the little hunchback had come right straight out of one of his childhood dream games. Materialized, absolutely. He was very serious when he said this too. Came right out of a dream and was standing there in his bedroom the next morning. My God. That means he's as much Bosworth as sweet Bosworth is himself.

"Maybe more."

It was Esmeralda. Standing at the end of the sun room, smiling.

"Jesus, Esmeralda. You've got the quietest feet in the whole fucking animal kingdom."

Bosworth just laughed. Actually, it was something between a giggle and a chuckle, the kind of sound that comes from a kid, not a grown-up. Usually, that is.

"Esmeralda! You naughty fellow!" he shouted. "Can't I have a moment away from you!"

"You wouldn't be anywhere without me," Esmeralda said, and he grinned like he had a mouse up his sleeve.

Anyway, back to London. That was some scene, believe me.

You can listen to all that put-down about tea and crumpets, if you want to, but I'm telling you that if that's what's at the root of it, why, I suggest that every government head make t & c required eating at least once a day for all citizens under seventy-two. That place jumps like the Congo on a hot summer night. Dukes and duchesses, street cleaners and chimney sweeps—those cats can never be accused of fucking off anytime, anyplace. After spending a few months in that I can now understand why Willie Shakespeare simply had to be an Englishman. Yogurt and goulash just don't go into making madness like that. How does his line go—

> "When to the sessions of sweet silent thought
> I summon up remembrance of things past,
> I sigh the lack of many a thing I sought . . ."

and as for being black, why those limehouse swingers took to me like I was royalty. Maybe it was a good thing after all that my parents were born in the suburbs of Nairobi.

"We're going to a castle tonight." Bosworth announced blithely one day (as the English would put it). "Lord and Lady Cliveden, if you please."

"Coo," I said.

"Quite." He mixed himself his by now usual three o'clock gin and bitters—pink gin to those in the guzzling know. "Just about the poshest of the posh, that's all. Brains, beauty, and bread."

"Mm. Just my kind of doodle," I observed, downing roughly half a finger of the booze. "What'll I wear, Bosworth old fig?"

"Nothing, absolutely nothing."

"Oh shit! You mean it's going to be another one of those daisy chain routines?"

"Oh come on, Ophelia baby. Just because you're studying medieval philosophy under old Tom Hibbs doesn't mean you have to go square on me, does it? I mean, darn. It isn't as if we were back at old Leslies'. This is an entirely different experience, new context, honey baby. Consequently, everything you do here has a different meaning vibration. You grasp that, don't you, Ophelia baby of the Morning Light? Say you do and make me feel good."

"And what's Esmeralda scheduled to do at this fandango? Play the tambourine?"

"Come on, sweet girl. Be nice to Daddy."

I thought about it. I walked around the room and listened to the sounds of the horses drawing the carts outside, and the funny honk-honk uhoo-gah sounds of the automobile horns. Maybe he was right. Back at Leslies' the only thing doing was the circus. Upside down, backwards, forwards, hands and knees and the three-layer cake that the cake itself, or themselves, excuse me, was eating. Same cake. But here, well, here it was different. Here we were really up to things, not just standing around waiting for the gong to sound and away you go, lickety, yeah, split and all that. I was becoming part of the in and out of it here, and I suppose that that's what life is supposed to be all about. At least that's what Churchill was always saying. Where is that raunchy honey bear anyway?

Last time he wrote he was special tutor to a rich Arab sheik's son in some place like Iraq. But that was a year ago just before Franklin Roosevelt was elected to live in the White House. Imagine, sixteen years old and already a teacher? Damn but that Churchill is a smart cookie. "The boy is really quite decent," he wrote. "No bad habits other than those you would normally associate with the depraved, half-blind twenty-eighth son of a billionaire loon who lives on lamb, rice, and Rolls-Royces. I am in the process of introducing Karim to the Roman philosophers, Seneca, Cato, chaps like that. I can't imagine, however, what worldly good it will do him to know these men and their minds, except possibly to arrange a cleverer type of dinner conversation than his guest of the future can come up with. It seems reasonably certain that he will never have to work for a living; having delved into these fellows won't effect his job chances much one way or the other. He doesn't know what he will be missing. Working does make a person more human—and that is something to be avoided at all costs! When we tire of intellectual activities, we go bowling—(pin boys here have a cinch scene) or ibex hunting. Ibex are antelope-like animals that look like unicorns. There are about seventeen left in the whole world, and the Arab hotshots are determined to wipe them out completely. Why I don't know. These people develop quite exotic obsessions, due perhaps to the total lack of humility. Saw a perfectly exquisite Swedish number auctioned off the other day at a local slave market. She had been Miss Stockholm or something. Breasts on her like ski slopes. Karim's uncle bought her, so maybe we'll be seeing more of her. An absolutely top drawer neck, too. If that's what Stockholm does for girls, then all I can say is, what am I doing here? Incidentally, my boss says he is sure he knew you back in Cairo at the time of King Tut. Why haven't you told me about him? I thought we kept no secrets from each other. Well, take it easy, sister honey, and you'll hear from me again after the big harvest is in. *C.* P.S. Do you know what I did with my white Keds? They are nowhere to be found. I leave you with some lasting words from the revered Okbar El Fed, poet-juggler-rapist: 'Art and nothing but art—we have art in order not to die of the truth.' "

Cairo? King Tut? Me? Good Lord! How I do get around. Without my even knowing it too. But maybe that's the best way. Because otherwise you meet yourself coming around a corner in Hong Kong or someplace like that.

Bosworth had taken off everything but his jockey shorts and was going through his daily pushups while waiting for me to answer. He really was in fine condition.

"Okay," I said at last. "You can count me in."

"Lovely," he grunted, pushing up. "You are developing a fine sense of participation."

"You don't have to joke me, Bosworth."

"I mean it," he grunted again. "I wouldn't kid you."

He certainly had lovely pushing muscle. I can tell you that from more angles than one. too. Bosworth makes a girl a real nice friend that way. Deed he does, as they would say in potato fields.

"Thirty-one, thirty-two," he panted. "Thirty-three, thirty-four. . . ."

I just remember something. "Hey. You know who called me today?"

"Thirty-seven. . . . no. Who?"

"Lord Alfred Katz."

Bosworth rolled over on his back now. His chest had a lovely dew of sweat all over it and the black hair on this chest made me think of something in the forests, an animal after it had done something real good for itself and was just resting there on the ground breathing heavy and looking satisfied. With a special heavy look on its mouth.

"What did that old herring want?"

"Wanted me to go riding in the park with him and his daughter April."

"I see. Did you know that he personally owns seventeen thousand six hundred and twenty-one Malayan peasants?"

"That so? What does he want with all those people?"

"They squeeze rubber trees for him. Half the tires you see in London come from those squeezings. That is probably a safe estimate, too." He looked at his lovely self in our seven-foot mirror. "His grandfather made millions in the African slave trade. Millions."

"Well, what do you know about that." I said. "Maybe he captured some of my kinfolk."

"Wouldn't surprise me in the least."

"Well, history to the contrary, I kind of think it might be fun to go riding in the park."

"You ever been on a horse?"

"No. But what's that got to do with it?"

"Nothing. Nothing at all. I merely ask out of academic curiosity."

"Since when does a person have to know about horses to go riding in the park?" I asked.

He put his arms around me and kissed me a few times on the neck. "Honey, if you ever get tired of being a sensational black girl, you could get a job as court logician without any trouble. Believe me."

"Mm. Do that to me some more. Yeah. Like that. Just like that."

The party at the Clivedens was a great success. Parties, I mean, because there were several of them. These English sure do like their fun. In between, I had a lot of conversation with April Katz. Wow! Is that girl ever something. When you're with her you think for sure you've run into a one-women theatre. The characters inside that girl's head! What I mean is, is this cutie for real?

NEVER FEAR. I HAVEN'T ABANDONED YOU. WE didn't miss one room at the cloister. (I am not the sort of fink who would start you out on a cultural experience and then disappear into the latrine until the snows fly. Not my style.) I especially dug the armor. Those studs didn't take any chances. They didn't expose one inch of their highly respected selves. The only way you could hurt them was by throwing a hand grenade into their basket. And even then I'm not so sure you would have accomplished very much. They had enough steel protecting their privates to make hot plates for half of Formosa. That's the sort of thing I should be wearing when Sylvia starts bombarding me with those exploding insults. Of course, I don't kid myself that such a uniform would afford complete protection. That Sylvia is a master of bombardment. She has taken special courses in assault at MIT. She has devised and developed anti-personnel explosives that can penetrate not only the proudest steel plate, but time itself.

A fellow with a red head and a floppy black hat with a feather in it is smiling at me from a fifteenth-century Gobelin tapestry. Smiling did I say? Positively grinning! His beard is rich and kinky like a primeval pubic forest. What loins has it commingled with? What female fluids have nourished it? Tell me, you writhing leek lover!

He—Know your secret, don't I, smellfeast?

Me—Haven't got a secret, you nipple napper.

He—The whole of you is a secret. You are a secret.

M—What do you think you are? A public proclamation?

H—The awful thing about you is that you deny this essential fact about yourself. You whip yourself into frenzies of exhibitionism to hide this. Oh, poor flute nose! Don't you know what you are doing?

M—What, if you're so smart?

H—You are inventing other people to be you. These other souls are the secrets of you! Hirelings to do your own work. Do you think people are deluded into thinking these creation truly exist?

M—They breath and move, don't they?

H—That has never proved existence—even you know that, carnival master that you are.

M—I don't know what you're talking about. I'm an honest greengrocer trying to make a decent living.

H—Ha! If you're an honest greengrocer, Charles the Bald is a muffin monger.

M—I never said he wasn't.

H—Speaking of the king, do you know what he's taken to doing lately?

M—Cooking one-legged marmadukes.

H—No projections, please. No, that divine man has acquired himself a hunchback.

M—Oh goosey! Where'd he get it? From a traveling carnival?

H—Quite the contrary. This fellow is a Moorish prince.

M—A Moorish prince? How did he get all the way from Africa to where you are? Did an eagle carry him?

H—He came in his own caravan. By way of Italy—where he spent a year studying the mandolin under the great Botto and also mastered in tickling, under a Sienna mystic. Quite a fellow, to say the very least. He's making the king very happy. He no longer has those dreadful fits at the dinner table. He's been extraordinarily decent to me too. Gave me five Norman peasant girls as a birthday present. I barely have time anymore to chase the stag. You see me on a rare day, rootnose.

M—You ever run into a big-shouldered, outrageously boobed blonde with a Great Dane? (I was just kidding, of course.)

H—Outra—boobed . . . mm . . .Dane? Upon my God! The Countess of Grotz!

M—Among other things, I suppose. Anyway, what's she up to?

H—Oh, the Countess—we call her Three Times, by the way, because she requires three times what other women need, in the way of everything—she's up to just about everything. It is rumored, you know, that she's the daughter of the Pope. Yes indeed. Look at the eyes. Look at the mouth. The Pope's very own.

M—And I ask you, what is this bawd up to?

H—A truly amusing thing, my friend. She's organizing an all-girl tumbling team. Zooks! But they are a jolly lot!

M—I'll bet they are.

H—All of them delectable young upper-crust types, you know. They put on the most original performances for the court. The tricks the Countess has taught them! And the inspiring joy she has infused in their performing hearts! They go at their games with true passion. My word! It's a good thing their shows go on after dinner. Not a morsel would get eaten otherwise.

M—As it is, the performing morsels get eaten later, right?

H—Well, of course.

M—What are you giggling about?

H—Oh, just a little something about the king.

M—I can't stand secrets. They make me feel lonely.

H—Well, it's a thing he does with one of the tumbling girls.

M—Stop laughing and get it out!

H—He drinks his champagne from her! Oh what a royal rascal he! First he shakes up a bottle of the stuff, then he puts the bottle in her cunt and gives her a foaming bath, and then he puts his raging mouth down there and drinks it as it comes out.

M—My God! What a capital idea!

H—Yes. Can you think of a more delightful way to get drunk? Now all the other tasty tumblers beseige him with requests to do it to them also. The champagne makers are heading for a bonanza season, believe me.

M—I'll have to give it a try. 'Course, I don't see myself making it with the Mumm's. More likely Seven Up.

H—Always selling yourself short. Well, that's your problem, rain nose. Listen, I have to take a piss. Why don't you come along and I'll show you some of the sights along the way. Might broaden you, who knows.

M—I'm on.

H—All I ask, now, is that you keep a civil tongue in your head.

M—Roger.

H—Ach! The only thing wrong with Chablis is it doesn't stay in you long enough to nourish you. See that iron-eyed chap over there? Well, that's the infamous Chumly Hotsuck.

M—Why, I'll be be basted! And that's my good friend Marmaduke Peddleshit.

H—He's very busy plowing the public fields. And when he's not doing that, he's out selling fake land grants to the local malcontents.

M—Maybe that's what he does here, but I can assure you that in my world he is a writer. A wierdo, to be sure, but not a bad sort. Why he wrote the Gettysburg Address, among other things.

H—Fiddle! Anyway, over there, leaning against his horse and picking his nose, is the King's second cousin, Romney of Drinkpiss. He's a most remarkable debater. Fought Erasmus to a draw just the other day.

M—Blimey! Who's the fatty goosing the girl?

H—Fie! You are pointing out my dear friend Harold the Finger, the finest gooser in the kingdom. But enough of this. Drag your silly ass in here. Good.

So here I am in the land of crossbow and codpiece. And you should see me! Yoicks! You'll never guess what I'm wearing. Black tights. A big yellow velvet hat with a feather in it—from time to time it brushes my nose, but that's a small thing considering the chic of it. A billowy jacket that's so petunia I do believe it was produced by slave labor virgins in a frenzy. I mean I can feel their filigree fingers tiddling me all over the innate respectability of my chesty. 'Strue. Haven't had a drop yet. But I plan to do something about that soon as that bulbous chap in front of me gets his big ass away from the buffet jug. You can hear his gurgling noises of sluice joy all the way across the Duke's own tent. Chap's got no pride, clearly. Ooff! A fart! The lousy bastard just let go a fart that blew my feather near off my poor hat! What a stink! It's blinding me. A toad must have crawled up inside him and died. He's poisoned the air. Three starlings have just dropped dead from a nearby willow tree. And do you think he is turning around to apologize for this fetid gesture?

"Stop pushing me, sir," he says out of the blue, breathing memories of fried kidneys and old punishments into my delicate face. "There's plenty for all, I can assure you."

"I didn't push," I reply, taking a stance of reasonable umbrage. "I can assure you."

He looks me up and down, (Oh what a mug he has! A forest of wens crisscrossed by streams of broken blood vessels.) "Sir, you clearly are unaware of whom you are directing your impudence at."

"A farter and and a guzzler," I say, squinting my eyes in a meaningful way taught me years ago by my Uncle Clyde.

"Blatherskite!" he screams. "Devil of infamy! You traduce the House of Bourbon. You shite-tongued pig! I'll run you through." And with that he pulls out his snee.

Who is in the mood for friction? Not me. No sir. Why come all the way from Limoges for a stabbing? Answer me that. How was I to know that underneath that walrus exterior was a tormented wire of aggression? "Oh good sir," I whimper, "little did

I realize the majesty of the man before me. May my parrot bite me for a mongoloid! Please, kind noble, allow me to extend my most infinite of self-hating apologies," and—you'll like this—I lean over and kiss his red velvet sleeve (grease-stained, of course).

This takes him aback. He looks at me—oh those eyes! River mussels from polluted beds—like I've just admitted having an affair with Judas Iscariot, "Oh! Well . . . really."

"I'm not myself these days," I go on, and I brush a particle of what seems to be pigeon crud from his shoulder. "Trouble at home, you know. Trouble trouble. My wife's been whoring about with the stable hands, my son's taken to pilfering from the church poorbox . . . and after all I've done for him too—and my vineyards are plagued with grape lice." A couple of tears leak from my eyes.

"Oh you poor man," he says, putting his arm over my shoulder. "You are in the mud, aren't you? I do indeed forgive you. Heavens! If I had half your worries I'd be laying about me with a Saracen sword. Poor bugger," and he hugs me to his very own chest.

"You're very kind, sir. I thank you from the bottom."

A couple of lads walk by us carrying the carcass of a newly slain stag. At least four arrows are sticking out of its body, and the blood, well, I won't go into that.

"Now I don't want you to worry about a thing," he says. "You have a friend in me—Henry of Navarre at your service. You and I are going to have fine times together."

"Pierre du Bac," I say.

"Pierre du Bac and his buddy Henry. Yes indeed. You and I are going to do all manner of splendid manly things together and you're going to forget all those wretched things at home."

"I'm beginning to feel better already," I say, and give my nose a good blow.

"First off," he says, "we're going to have a drink together. Some of this really sturdy Norman calvados. That wine the others are drinking is simply cat's piss by comparison. Come now, old Pierre, tilt that jug and drown those dirty grape lice. There! That's the fellow. Now then, don't you feel the teeniest bit better? Ha! Ha! Thought so. Best damn juice ever put together. I confess to you, I wouldn't be able to make it from dawn to dark unless I had my calvados to mother my terror. Grab yourself a piece of that roast quail and we'll jolly over to the Duke's tent to have a bit of fun. Always something stirring around the Duke. If it isn't whoring it's plotting, and if it isn't plotting it's cards. Many's the time I've picked myself up a brace of percherons with the one-eyed fellows." He nudges me. "Most of them are so drunk they can't tell a jack from a fairy queen."

"Serves them right," I say. That calvados is already colonizing the peasants in my knee joints.

"That's exactly the view I take, Pierre. I can see that you and I are true brothers."

I give him a hug, half a hug really because he's so abundant a repository of French cookery that my arm only half makes it. He lets go with another fart but this time I don't mind. A buddy's blast is something else, as we all know. A stranger's fart is a thing of woe, a nightsong of debasement. Trumpets. Flutes. Tambourines. Aristocratic laughter. Handmaiden shrieks. Counts. Experienced chuckles. Growls of superiority from the fastidiously bred hunting hounds. Galloping (and an occasional horseturd dropping plump!). Whirrings of pigeons in free country flight. These are the sounds surrounding me and my armful friend Henry. Gallant smells are in the air. No diseased corruptions are at work in this atmosphere. I've never felt so good (my crotch is a bit light, but you can hardly say that's the end of the world). A fat brown hare scampers past us, but I am not in the least amazed. Why shouldn't a hare scamper by if it wants to?

We arrive at the Duke's tent.

"You'll like him, Pierre," says Henry. "He doesn't have a single bad habit that you wouldn't have yourself, given the opportunity."

"Is he squeamish about Loire valley farmers, such as myself?"

"Oh indeed not. He loves the smell of a good honest farmer. It's the pushy upper middle class that he can't stomach. People asking him to be their child's godfather so they can go about lording it over their relatives. Things like that. If there's one thing he can't grasp it's people wanting to get up in the world."

"Climbers are the worst. Their brown noses disgust me."

"Delighted you see it that way, Pierre," and he gives me a fine slap on the back. "We're going to get along just fine, we are. You Loire valley chaps are all right."

The Duke is stretched out on a divan talking to a falcon sitting on his wrist. At his feet sits a roseate conglomeration of blue eyes, large breasts, long blond hair, heavily ringed fingers, a mandolin, and a voice of spun silver. My senses swim a bit. She looks at me for a moment, with her delicate mouth open while continuing to sing, and I immediately become a part of her song. Oh the transvestism of my silly soul! Lord! If that foul artichoke heart back on the farm were only this wide-eyed poem!

"Navarre!" The Duke rises. "You old shuttleprick! I haven't seen you since the stag was brought down this morning. Killed one of my dogs before it went, too." He shook his head and sighed (quite poignantly, I thought). "That dog simply could not be taught the art of fear. Oh, well, such is the price of breeding."

A small-shouldered man who is snoozing in the corner of the tent wakes up and shouts, "Bloody blasted right I won't!" and goes back to sleep.

I giggle, just to show that I'm a responsive, fun-loving, undangerous, willing to do anything to be liked, generally delighted type of French farmer. Absurdity is my dish.

"Poor Harold," says the Duke, nodding in the snoozer's direction, "He's never been the same since they burned his mother for a witch." He drinks off a bowl of wine. "I told her, Maggie, I said, just tell the judges that you've never talked to toads much less departed demons and they'll let you off, believe me. But that leaky old jade would have none of it. 'I'll deny myself sooner than deny my voices,' she said. 'All the faggots in France can't take them from me.' Can you imagine that? Shades of Gomorrah! All of us hear voices—why, I heard one just the other morning as I was having a shit in the palace—but who is mad enough to burn for them?" He hiccups and shakes his burly fine head.

Navarre has handed me a cup of wine which I put away in two manly swigs. Lordy! The joy that swims in the juice! Makes you wonder why anybody in his right mind ever goes near the soggy mug of beer. Outside a trumpet sounds. Horses gallop. Shouts of loving combat. Do I hear the deer? And did that fuckable girl wink at me? Is that lout of a Jacques mending the pig sty railings back home on my farm?

"What do you hear of the Swiss, my lord?" asks fat Navarre, scratching himself inside his thigh.

"What one always hears," he says. "More money. That is their national anthem. The next thing you know they'll be charging us à la carte for every wound they inflict."

"It's those Alps, sire," I hear myself announce as though I've been in the conversation since yesterday. "People who live in the mountains aren't quite human."

He smiles at me. "By the hind of my uncle's trotter, you're right! Mountains are for goats. We'll have to talk about human nature one of these days. I can see you're a man of feeling and wisdom. France needs men like you. Don't you agree, Navarre?"

"That's exactly what I told the Duchess just yesterday, my lad," he says, smiling at me through his brambly bush. "Feeling and wisdom—what is a country without them? An empty wine glass, that's what."

"Navarre, I want you to remind me to take this up with the bishop as soon as we get back to Rheims."

"Forgive me, my lord, but that randy rascal won't know what you're talking about."

"That's exactly why I want to discuss it with him."

"Peculiar sort, the bishop," Navarre says to me. "Likes to play with himself during mass."

"Sounds dangerous," I say. "No telling what sort of diseased ideas jump about in his head. Bears watching, if you ask me."

The Duke is smiling unequivocally at me, the way the morning sun smiles at the forests. "Your nose," he says lovingly, pointing his long jeweled finger at me, "what a nose. It reminds me of a sheep herder's ball."

"Thank you, my lord."

"I just knew you chaps would get on," says Navarre.

Sounds came from the small-shouldered snoozer. Whimpers. Moans, Squeals—in a high woman's voice. "My voices! My friends!" he shouts. Something has taken possession of him. "The king shall hear of this. You can't take them from me! Let me go! Take your filthy hands off me! I'm a duchess of the realm. Louts! Buggers! Apes! I'll have your souls for this; mark me. You'll bleed in hell for eternity you will. What do you greasy filthpots know of otherworldly things? You are dumb as stones, all of you. Does the wind speak to you? Do you know the secret of the spider's web? Do you know that the unicorn you speared to death in the forest is St. John the Baptist? Oh you vile idiots! You unspeakable moments of emptiness! Golgoth! Wek! Pandred! Help me! Kill them! Kill them!"

And a scream comes from him that freezes my heart beat. We are held in an awful silence. No one in the tent can move. The Duke rouses himself. A spindly serving man approaches Harold's small awry form on the couch and stares at him. "He's dead," the man whispers. "The poor mad count is dead," and he slowly covers the staring-eyed body with a black and gold velvet coverlet.

"Oh dear," the songstress says.

The duke drinks off a cup of calvados, "That was his mother, so help me sweet Jesus."

The girl begins to play her mandolin and sing. Navarre and another serving man, their faces ravaged with fear, are carrying the shrouded body from the stricken tent. "This is the day of the black bird," Navarre mutters. "Beware."

A blue-eyed young tentboy begins to pray rapidly in Latin. The duke's great wolfhound growls softly in fear. I tip toe out. I am wandering in the thick forest. It is very quiet. All sound seems sucked out of this place. A deer leaps by me but soundlessly. I watch a big black squirrel fly from a high limb to another tree. A bright-winged quail pops up in front of me and its beating wings brush my cold face. I stumble into an opening. What are those dark, hairy things? A family of wild boar? They are rooting about, eating stuff they are digging up. Suddenly they look up and see me. Their tusks glisten evilly. Red tiny eyes. Bleeding? Two huge bristling ones rush at me. I can't move. They must be making terrible snuffling grunting noises but I can't hear them. Why can't I hear them? I am clawing at myself to get away. I am ripping the gold and blue and red threads away. A terrible pain shoots through my leg. I had been gored. I madly claw the heavy threads. I shout my own name. Me! Me! I am not Du Bac. Me!

I am tearing myself to pieces out of the tapestry. . . .

SYLVIA—(COMING IN FROM KITCHEN, LEFT OFF-stage) Phew! You smell of mulch and mushrooms. And your pants are torn. Where the hell have you been?

Me—(flopping down on bed, center stage) I might ask you the same question.

Sylvia—(mixing herself a drink from cabinet at right of bed.

She is wearing her hair in a very different style from previous one we are familiar with. She is affecting a manner that is both snide and mysterious) You know the miserable details of my life. It would degrade us both to tick them off like some suburban train schedule. But your crazy secret life, now there's something we never seem to go into. Right, daddio?

Me—(sighing and crossing my knees on the bed) You know goddamn good and well that you've got as active a secret life as the next skirt. And we both know goddamn good and well that you haven't been spending the last three weeks visiting your sister Mary in Girls' Town.

Sylvia—(laughing as she struts across stage in front of bed) And as if you've been down in Baltimore for the last three weeks researching the first Maryland Catholic families as you claim. Come on now!

Me—(slowly getting off bed and going to liquor cabinet) Okay. Okay. Have it your way. You're right. I never went near Baltimore. All this while I've been on a bender in a Paris joss house.

Sylvia—(in amazement, but we are not sure it is not faked) My God! So have I!

Me—(toasting, with my drink) Just think of it! We've finally synchronized our fantasy lives!

Sylvia—(still vibrating her amazement but still such a good actress we don't know if she is putting us on) But honestly, I meant it.

Me—(drinking down a good one) Why not, baby? Why not? I mean, Emily Post never wrote a book on the etiquette of reality, did she? (Doorbell sounds real loud).

Sylvia—Oh dear! The dinner guests. They're half an hour early.

Me—(smiling like an old movie star at audience) That's okay, Sylvia baby, I'll go to the door. You get some ice cubes. These drunks are probably having withdrawal symptoms. That dry subway ride must have been all of ten minutes long (I exit to left, still carrying my live new drink. We hear a great giggle of joy from Zachary.

(He comes onstage with an absurdly long black coat and a small round hat. A long red scarf is wrapped around his neck and dangles down both front and back of him. He is reading from a book and being pushed by drunken George as he does.)

Zach—"Neolithic, or early historical, man was therefore the heir to a long scientific tradition. However, had he, as well as his predecessors, been inspired by exactly the same spirit as that of our own time, it would be impossible to understand how he could have come to a halt and how several thousand years of stagnation have intervened between the neolithic evolution and modern science like a level plain between ascents." (George shrieks wildly, drunkenly and pushes Zachary to the floor of the stage, where he too begins to whinny drunkenly.)

X I DON'T SUPPOSE ANYBODY IN SUCH A classy audience as this could be interested in hearing about the childhood of a hunchback, but I'm going ahead anyway. You can't live on cream puffs and self-deception forever, as Hegel would say. My mother was a six-foot dyke and my father was a freelance flute player. I think they met at a beerhall *putsch* in Schleswig-Holstein right after the Moors were routed. Or was it at Sinbad's circumcision? I'm a little vague on details, but absolutely certain on the outcome. I mean, if a hunchback dwarf doesn't know that he exists, then who does? My earliest memories involve a behemothic Great Dane named Harry, who was my mother's idea for a baby sitter, and an insanely beautiful agate-eyed little blond girl who lived next door to us. Next door meaning in another part of the forest, for the area we lived in could hardly be called a housing development. Eagles, wombats, wolves, and witches. Stuff like that floated all over the place, and on a rainy day you thought you were in a giant's armpit. And speaking of rain, I hardly need tell you that what fell in our forest, while it was indeed wet, had nothing at all in common with the sort of thing farmers pray for and outdoor ballet dancers curse. Oh no. Our rain, my mother explained to me when I was very young, was really the tears of all the world's animals, from the beginning of time. When this rain fell even the wind's presumption was quelled, and the mammoth trees withheld their usual creakings. For a day or so after such soul-lettings our forests looked quite insane, and I was afraid to leave the house. I stayed close to the beast Harry, whose size and stench made me feel more or less secure.

My father spent a lot of time away from the house. He and his flute were in constant demand at troll festivals, gargoyle weddings, public flayings, black masses, cannibal dinners, and peasant fuck fests. There is something about such occasions that absolutely requires the sound of the flute. The old man didn't have very strong family type instincts, so getting away like that undoubtedly kept him from going off his chump. Besides, the pay was good, considering the more or less agrarian, noncapitalist economy we lived in, and the fringe benefits of his job were not to be scoffed at. I will leave the enumerating of them up to your imagination. My mother of course had her own needs and art forms, and when my father wasn't around, and their energies were not being consumed in endless howling and grappling confrontations, both of the spirit and the body, she devoted all her time to the pursuit of them.

"What I can't stand," she often complained to me, "is a man breathing down my neck all the time."

Nobody ever breathed down my neck, I wanted to say, but then she would have accused me of self-pity. How utterly crazy! Accusing a dwarf hunchback boy drag queen of self-pity! My mother's reasoning was understandable only in terms of Gothic poetry. If I were in a bad mood, I would go farther and say that all of life is understandable only in such terms. But I realize that what I think isn't going to change the way the leaf falls, so there. Your Friend the Smiling Shit Machine was rigged up a long, long time ago and none of its parts will ever need replacing.

I think my old lady was president of Lesbians International. She was to the dyke movement what Rousseau was to the French Revolution. She was its theorist, organizer, fund raiser, and father image. She lobbied for dyke bills at our government's legislative houses. Her pen was the fountain of its literature. Her slogans plastered the world.

Put a Bull Dyke in the White House! Save Water. Shower with a Dyke Friend. Dykes are Part of Our Natural Heritage! She conceived and almost singlehandedly put over the International Dyke Exchange Program, and built Be a Pal to a Dyke Week into a national habit. Her publications were countless: *Seven Easy Cas-serole Dishes for the Dyke Living Alone, Setting Up Exercises for the Dyke Fighting Middle Age Blues, Are you Making the Most of Your Homosexuality?* And her weekly newsletter was in a class by itself. Tidbits, phone numbers, pet exchanges, job opportunities—I mean, it made Reuters look like an underground mimeo-opera-tion. She made me the headline writer of the newsletter when I was ten. My own twisted sensibility added an almost unbearably delicious element to these news summaries. Hardly the sort of thing you would pick up in a journalism school.

But this lesbian thing was only one of her many pursuits. She ran an international orgy booking agency, which truly explored and expanded mankind's forbidden sexual fantasies; and then she was executive director of a worldwide counter-revolutionary oper-ation. She knew at least a thousand fascist gunslingers by their first names. (A genealogical curio but fact—I have seen papers which clearly establish that one of my mother's aunts had a hand, a big scummy one, in the burning of the Maid.) In this last mentioned position my mother naturally had to be more than conversant with all the latest models of firearms. Samples were all over the house. You couldn't open a cookie drawer without a gat tumbling out. Mom's own personal delight was a sleekly tooled self-possessed Springfield 30-30 with a telescopic sight. That thing was so human you could hear it plotting at night. Oh what schemes of death possessed it! You may find this hard to believe, but that gun had plans for knocking off God himself.

You are undoubtedly, at this point, saying. "Okay. Enough of the geodetic survey. What about the hunch himself?"

All right then. The song of me. I hope you don't mind if I have a liverwurst and onion snack. I'm starving. Haven't had a thing to eat since five o'clock this morning when I began editing seven thousand feet of a dirty movie I shot with the agate-eyed kid and a handful of local lumpen proletariat children from the village. What I have in mind is a real spicy underground film movement for the emotionally deprived young. Smut for small fry. I've never understood why pornography should be reserved for grown-ups. Pain isn't, so why pleasure? (I'm trying to work out the distribu-tion kinks. My mother has suggested that I work through the already established pornography underground—she has top

drawer connections in Berlin, Rio, New York, Paris—but I don't
trust the honesty of those people. I want to work directly with
avant-garde schools, on a nice clean 50-50 basic.) Umm. Good
nibble, that liverwurst. It's homemade. Old granny Schmidlepp
from the Black Forest puts it up, along with sausage and the
tangiest head cheese you ever ate. Onion a bit strong, though.
How long can a sweet Spanish onion stay sweet?

Anyway, more of me. I wasn't born Esmeralda. That's a name
I gave myself after it became clear to me that I wasn't all boy. My
given name was—is?—Maxwell, and to hell with it. I wouldn't
have stayed with that bumper sticker even if I hadn't been one of
God's mistakes. And here is another thought to put in your bean-
pot; who would ever expect a hunchback dwarf to play it straight?

In the words of my favorite skull tapper, "The self, as long as
it is 'uncommitted to the objective element' is free to dream and
imagine anything. Without reference to the objective element it
can be all things to itself—it has unconditioned power, freedom,
creativity."

Sweetheart words, right? The kind of stuff you ought to get for
Christmas, instead of that cheap aftershave lotion. Hope they don't
give you any ideas, because this is my story. Your time'll come if
you behave yourself and kiss the right ass.

My family, as you can see, had a most relaxed economic orientation. Whenever my mother needed a little extra scratch (the
dues money from Lesbians of the World were not all that abundant, no matter what her jealous detractors may have said. Research, public relations, and operational expenses ran very high),
she grabbed her sneakers, rubbing alcohol, and terry-cloth bath-
robe and toured the provinces as the champion lady wrestler who
will take on anybody. Other times, I was rented out—dressed in
a variety of costumes, of course—to side shows, medieval religious
plays, visiting royalty (our village had for centuries been a vacation
spot for the faded aristocracy, for we specialized in delights that
were unavailable elsewhere in Europe. Normal Christian experiences and taboos stopped at our gates), and as a legal witness to
public floggings. Maxmilian the Kind, back in 1243, decreed this
necessity on the rather humane-poetic grounds that by seeing me
before him, a stark naked example of the extremest possibility of
human misery and misfortune, the guilty person being flogged

will realize how lucky he is and will thus not feel so much pain. ("Stop screaming. You could be this execrable wretch! You've never had it so good!") People who have accused our village of degeneracy and pagan animalism please take note: I can think of half a dozen big-name towns where the guilty don't get anywhere near as good a shake. My official title, court-given, is Hunchback-in-Residence. I receive forty pelks, or ten dollars your money, for my work. And that buys a lot of turnip pie in these parts.

Just a sec. There's a Belgian hare here that wants to say hello.

"Greetings, folks! Remember me in that fraudulent little bag job involving the tortoise? Well. . . ."

That's enough! Begone, you greedy little spotlight stealer! Back to your cabbage patch! Jesus! Give those furry little fucks an inch and they'll steal every plot in hour head.

Our village . . . oh, what a delirious twelve-tone, third leg of a place it was! The town fathers were fugitives from the Dead Sea Scrolls. Our buckoes were men of substance. If you think they'd be satisfied with a dram of water and a tasteless wafer, you're dead wrong. They were meat eaters to a man. Try to slip a symbol over on them and the garbage collectors would be scraping your remains off the town walls for weeks. None of that abstraction shit for them. No sir. The head man of the council of seven is a shiny black giant named Jomo the only nigger in the entire country. It is said that he was the Shiek Ahmed Bel Suduan's chief executioner in Zanzibar, until they had a falling out over time-and-a-half for overtime. Also, there was something of a problem about his cooking in his room. Then there is Cedric the Merry Woodsman; Blaster of the Bloody Crossbow; George the Sneaky Penman; Zachary of the Unholy Grail; the one we know only as Nose; Katz the Tight-Lipped Usurer; and a woman, Lola the Singing Cunt. A most delicious gourmet of a lady whom I shall discuss at greater length some other time. Suffice it to note, she was a runaway nun, Dominican Order, St. Jean de Luz (in the south of France—French Basque country) at which nunnery she was known as the Singing Nun. These seven fabulosities guided the destiny and parsed the whims of our village. I need not tell you that the agendas of our council were hardly crowded with such yawns as teachers' salaries or the fluoridation of our drinking water.

Which brings me to our school system. Jump, Dick, jump.

Run, Sally, run. Farmer Brown had a cow. Three Chinamen had seven kilos of rice. How many quarts. . . . None of that sort of pus went into the minds of our children. We may have had our faults but premeditated stupidity was not one of them. Our schools trained the young to be artisans in the daily realities of life. The pursuit of "culture," the reading of books, the reciting of doggerel, all that was conceded only to the clearly defective children who would have been destroyed in the pursuit of anything healthy and realistic and in the very truest sense imaginative. (I cite at this juncture your own Alfred North Whitehead anent the idiocy of "cultural" education: "What is the next subject in the education of the infant minds? The acquirement of written language; that is to say, the correlation of sounds with shapes. Great heavens! Have our educationists gone mad? They are setting babbling mites of six years old to tasks which might daunt a sage after lifelong toil.") We prepared our children for life! Our school gave courses in such life trades as Lying, Stealing, Informing, Copping out, Scrounging, Forgery, Fucking, Sucking, Mugging, Knifing, Gunning, and Poisoning.

Of course, the general trades had subdivisions, so that the child could become a specialist among specialists and be in a strong job and life bargaining position anywhere in the world. For example, within the overall discipline of Lying, a child could specialize in betrayal of friends of family (one of our most heavily attended seminars was in how to betray an identical twin); of lovers; of one's own country (some of our most ingenious children attended this class, partly because of the sheer delight in compounding the initial betrayal of oneself by one's country, and partly because the instructor, an awfully engaging chap with an exquisite ear tic, had been one of the three nationalists involved in selling out Indo-China, their mother country, to the Dutch). To go on. Within the quite rich category of Fucking the school offered such sub-categories as Positions for Girls: 1) lying on one's back—making the most of one's hands and fingers and legs, contrapuntal heaving of the pelvic area, rotating of the ass; 2) the top position—the delicate relationship of pacing, plunging and titillating, use of the tongue while leaning over, lowering of the breasts to just the right mouth level for the man, and of course striding backwards; 3) fellatio—gentle nibbling of the cock, tickling of the tip with the tongue while caressing the balls or inserting the finger up the ass, pacing of immersion in mouth, total immersion at point of orgasm; 4) ball licking and half immersion. For the boys: 1)the demanding but rewarding art of cunt lickery—the three principle tongue motions relating to the clitoris, clockwise and counter clockwise, up and down (the vertical stroke), which takes in the entire cunt, in all its bushy breadth; and the concentrated pin point juggling of the bud of the clit itself; 2) dog fashion—humping, both in bending the girl over (a chair or a bed for example) and when she is on her hands and knees and the proper manipulating of breasts and clitoris while in this position; 3) lap fucking; 4) sidewise fucking; and 5) fucking under water. The art of buggery, which seemed to disappear for a hundred years or so after the Crusades, was also explored and systematized.

Our courses covered every sexual possibility, in the same way that the students of the great Cordon Bleu are instructed, nay, grilled, in the infinitive varieties and secrets of food, right down to the use of goose honkings in gravy making. A graduate of our fucking course could produce orgasmic delirium in any corner of the world, with any member of the human race, (as long as this person was alive, that is).

To proceed in the curriculum: flagellation and the inducing of pain-pleasure in general (there was even a course in the subtleties of whip making); homosexuality (both lesbianism and faggotry) three-way deals, and orgies—all this rounded out our sexual expertise instruction. It goes without saying, of course, that each teacher and student interpreted and performed these arts with his or her own particular flair—just as no two cooks make exactly the same cup of low country she-crab soup, in spite of the fact that the basic ingredients are the same. We had one truly gifted young lady, for example, Mimi, the daughter of Magda the Well Woman, whose genius for cock sucking and scrotum caressing-licking carried that art into absolutely new country. Mimi gave concerts throughout the land, and if my memory serves me, she wound up as the Director of Oral Pleasure for King Dai's court in Bangkok. Her concerts were truly transporting and all the seats were sold out weeks ahead of time. You were lucky if you could get tree space. (I shall never forget the afternoon when a huge old wabash tree suddenly collapsed and one-hundred-eighty pleasure-crazed spectators had to be treated for broken bones.)

Incidentally, the ground under these spectator trees was so

enriched with jerk-off droppings that gardeners willingly paid incredible sums for buckets of it as a flower mulch. Mendicants also eagerly sought it to be used in powerful poultice mixes, along with unicorn shit and eagle screams.

One of the many crowd-pleasing aspects of Mimi's weekly concerts was that she chose her subject from the audience. She did not, as other great concert performers do, travel with an accompanist. Her method, therefore, created that most sought after of dramatic goals, audience participation. A parade of hard-ons by hopeful candidates was indeed a delightful warm-up before the main event. (Which reminds me . . . as soon as I get a free moment I'll tell you about our annual Flogging the Bishop party, at which was crowned the town's most effective masturbator.) The subject who was selected for the concert by Mimi was known thereafter as winner of the Hard-On of the Year Award. Higher status you could not achieve.

Well now, I hope that gives you a good idea of the educational programs in our village. As you can see, we loved our children and therefore tried to do right by them. This is, of course, the one true moral responsibility the older generation has toward the younger. All the rest is a crock of yak doodoo. Other cultures handle their own children in a quite miserable way, and as a result these children grow into very farty people who, unlike our children, haven't the remotest contact with reality. I quote the well-known psychologist and anthropologist, Dr. Gordon Allport: "What does our style of child training do to a child? For one thing, it puts him on guard. He has to watch his impulses carefully. Not only is he punished for them when they counter the parents' convenience and rules, as they frequently do, but he feels at such times that love is withdrawn from him. When love is withdrawn, he is alone, exposed, desolate. Thus he comes to watch alertly for signs of parental approval or disapproval. It is they who hold power, and it is they who give or withold their conditional love. Their power and their will are the decisive agents in the child's life. The effect of this is disastrous."

Let me tell you about my childhood sweetheart, April. There was no prettier tickle in the entire countryside. Her father was so busy figuring out clever and obscure ways of making a buck (he was trading in the escudo market by way of Panama City and

Zurich, for example), and her mother was totally lost in her aphrodisiacal herb garden, that they didn't have any time left for April, which was just fine. She was as free as a hair on a buffalo's ass. Our only curfew was our appetite. And April was insatiable. "You hum it and we'll play it," she often said, giving me a loving elbow in the ribs. The tragedy of life is that there are not enough people around who talk like that. "You hum it and I'll run for my life," is what most of the human race would say. When the human game is gone, what do you have left? Petrified forests.

Just a moment. An Indian lady in the audience is raising her hand.

"Yes, madame?"

"One question, sir. Did you allow the children of your village to smoke marijuana?"

"It all depended, Mrs . . . Mrs . . . ah, yes. Madame Pandit Gupa."

"On what, sir?"

"On whether there was enough to go around."

"I see. Thank you very much, sir."

"You're absolutely welcome, I'm sure."

Hmm. Wonder if that broad works for the CIA. That red dot on her forehead doesn't look completely kosher to me. Didn't I see her at one of Perle Mesta's blasts? Anyway, as I was saying . . . April. Mm. That kid was strawberry jam on a hot buttered biscuit. Two hundred per cent okay. I've got the hots for her to this day. She never made me feel like a hunch, even though I clearly was, am, one.

"Es, honey," she would say, tucking one leg under her, "This day has got the makings of something or other."

"I know just what you mean."

"Now it's our job to put those makings together come up with a real prize-winning zabaglione."

"We've never failed yet, April baby. And I don't feel the funny stirrings of a setback. No sir."

And she would lean over—we sat on a tree stump in the forest, a huge thousand-year-old fir tree that had been used in many an ancient pagan ritual—lean over and kiss me. "You and me," she would say. "Me and you. There's nobody like us." Her eyes saw birds that were miles high and her ears heard the flowers moaning in their sleep, and deep, deep inside her were dances that men and women and children dressed in animal skins had performed around the steaming inflammatory blood offerings to the gods of nature. She danced these ancient blood poems for me from time to time, in the secret parts of our forest, and in those abandoned naked moments the colors of the plants there deepened and glistened as if suffused with human passion. The animals of the forest, summoned from their lairs and prowlings by April's soundless ecstatic throbbings, observed her from foliage-hidden vantage points a mere breath away, and their musky smells gripped one by the throat and the groin. Their soft whining of bestial exultation was the rarest of music. I myself was transfixed, and barely breathed. She was dancing in the intimate corridors of my soul. In fact, in those episodes of ecstacy, she was my soul.

We had a variety of games and ingenious activities to keep us from ever being bored. (But I must point out here that since our community was in no way typical, boredom was not a major threat to our way of life.) Whenever we needed a little spending money, for example, we carried messages between lovers, or spread rumors for those who would profit by them, imitated ghosts for seances, provided alibis for liars, or made walking announcements through the village streets when the town crier was too drunk to move. Our favorite game at night was sneaking into people's dreams. This was a trick that my adorable April had been born with, and she shared it with me.

First we would eat a special candy made of taffy, sunflower seeds, and a ground-up page from a Shakespeare play. Then we would be next to each other in her wall bed, lock arms, concentrate in a very special way on someone in the village, and before you knew it, we were characters in their dream. Part of the trick was to imagine we were the selected dreamer. Holding each other tightly, so as to merge our powers, we envisioned this person in a scene we had actually observed, buying artichokes from the greengrocer, or drinking in one of the pubs, perhaps the Perfunctory Abattoir, or playing cards in the park; then we imagined ourselves speaking with his or her mannerisms, making the characteristic gestures, and if the person had a big belly or a limp, we imagined being the limp or the belly. In the case of the ravishing town whore, Tulip Openlegs, whom we selected often for our adventures, we imagined ourselves in the wildest of sex games, and there was not a jammer in town that we didn't handle and caress and cajole as though it were the Messiah itself. The only hazard in our game was the possibility of April losing her magic, or being prevented somehow from using it, and thus being unable to escape from the dream when we'd had enough. What a terrible way to vanish from this world. At least that is the way I felt. April was quite philosophical about it. "Think of all the fabulous people and creatures who live in people's dreams." she said. "Don't they make real people and things look silly? Besides," she added with that grin of infinite suggestion, "how do you know we aren't in a dream anyway?"

I had to agree with her. I could not think of a way to prove otherwise. Can any of you?

One blowy night, when the forest outside was raging and the skies were being ripped with white hot lightening, we slipped into the dreams of one of the town fathers, The Insatiable Crossbow. Oh, the frenzy of it! He had apparently gone to sleep stoned out of his mind with wine, and we all know what that does to flood gates.

Oh shit! I've lost the piece of paper with the man's name and address on it. Did it fall out of my pocket? Oh Christ! I'll bet it was in the back of the receipt the town clerk gave me when I paid my hunting tax. I didn't have to pay the stinking thing. I could have poached like a lot of lads I know and nobody would be the wiser. Lad gets caught he just gives the warden a hare or two or maybe a fat partridge and that's the end of it. Ah, here the bloody thing is. Be damned! Wrote it on the back of the map of the man's house here in Florence—Gaetano de Fillipi, Piazza de Margherita Cervantes. Beware of large dogs guarding both front and back doors of house. Me afraid of dogs? Silly idea. Never saw a dog yet that I couldn't make eat out of my hand. You've got to be born with a gift like that. Not a soul in the world can teach it to you. Well, Signor, I am sorry to say this, but you must die. Yes. That is correct. Die. Pfft! I myself have nothing against you. To kill a person for personal feelings is the worst sort of nonsense. It is a contract, Signor de Fillipi, a very simple and clean contract. I have already received 100 florins for the job and I will receive the other 100 after you have been dispatched. This is my business, my chosen profession, as the professors would say. I have been hired by your brother-in-law in Rome, Paola Romanelli, with whom, I am informed, you are in a variety of commercial enterprises. The making of bricks, tiles, wagon wheels and the tanning of hides, the weaving of fine fabrics, and the concocting of certain rare dye stuffs, the ingredients of which are closely guarded family secrets. Well, now. It appears that you are a dreadful thorn in his side, an ache in his belly that will simply not go away. He knows that you have been cheating him of his share of the profits and that you will go on cheating and lying, because you are a devilishly clever chap, until you are dead, and that is exactly why I am in this arrogant, smelly, but admittedly beautiful city of yours. Because you see, until you are dead he might as well be. As an intelligent human being, a fellow with all his senses in good order, you certainly can understand that. I understand, incidentally, that you are a friend of the painter Raphael. Good. Perhaps he will do a lovely portrait of you in your memory. Or a nice bust if he does that sort of thing. Wait! I have it! A death mask, yes, a death mask for your family to keep in the dining room. Perhaps even put it in your accustomed place at the head of the table. I know this tradition exists in many places, so you must not be afraid of doing anything out of the way, performing an act that has no place in the community experience, as a result of which the neighbors might take to spitting whenever your family goes out in the street.

As soon as I finish this litre of wine I'll be on my way. The night will be quite heavy with us by then and our little business should go unseen. Daylight and blood do not go together any way. It is an insensitive arrangement. My lovely knife is so sharp and quick he will never know any pain nor will he know what brought about his death, it will be so quick and quiet and painless. Perhaps he will not even cry out. They usually do though. Not because it hurts but because they are afraid. Ah, that cry of fear! That gasp of amazement! How many times have I heard it, brought it about? Three dozen? Four dozen? And think of it. All of those cries have become part of my good right arm, my business arm, as I call it. And sometimes when I am not feeling so very good, at a distance from myself, their cries run up and down my arm, possess it, become it, and nothing I do can stop this, striking my arm, biting it, grabbing and shaking it, covering it with a pillow, even plunging it in a pail of water to drown it and the sounds, nothing. They must go away by themselves, and then my arm becomes my own again.

That farmer and his wife sitting over there in the corner eating hot chestnuts, what a fine pair they are. Thick, strong people. Lots of work and rassle in them. Like the beasts on their farm. They've had a good day in the town market. Sold all their foods at a nice profit. They will certainly sleep well tonight when they return to their barnyards. After they have ravished each other in the bed of course. That woman of his must give a magnificent account of herself. She doesn't have those legs and that great hot bottom for nothing. Her breasts! My Lord! He must leap into them like great haystacks. Just listen to her laugh! Making me all hot all over just to hear it. She'll make my dilly jump out of my pants if I sit here much longer.

Oh, how the cold out here in this street bites the blood! A bitch! Back to my beloved Rome on the morrow, so help me. These northern jobs age a fellow. My bones are talking to each other most bitterly. I should have brought some of that wine with me. I do indeed owe myself a rest. Those two chaps stumbling along ahead of me. They don't have a worry in the world. Clearly. Oops! One of them has fallen. The other one is just laughing. Going to let him get up by himself while he takes a piss. Great Christ! The man's got a cock the size of a grown cucumber! He could crack a skull with it.

"Good evening, sir. Watering the streets to keep the dust down."

"Good fellow."

"Dust gets awfully bad here at times."

"Gives you the sneezes. Ah, must have a gallon of the stuff in me. Hey Giulio! Wake up! Here. Have a little drink. Ha ha ha."

There it is, there's de Fillipi's house. On the corner. Wall around it with a garden inside. First the meat for the dogs. Toss it over the wall and let them feed on it for a few minutes. Their last supper. Hope they believe in God. This stuff the chemist Giufreda put in the meat will lay them low for good in a fart's time. Over it goes. Just listen to them whine and slaver! Just can't wait to die. I'll stand over there in that tower for a bit while they destroy themselves. Ooh. Bells! Jesus Lord! Scramble your brains.

Eleven o'clock. Our man should be returning from his gaming club very shortly.

Black dogs. They are thoroughly and beautifully dead. Look at them lying there in the flowerbed and under the lime tree. Not a soul can see me in here. Stand right behind the door. The light in the upper window. His wife? Break wind but softly. Much better now. No bloat pain in the belly and bowels. The servants are in the back there playing about. I know it. I can feel them playing at each other. Good rich kitchen smells. I'll have to talk to our Beatrice when I return. Her soups have been very thin lately and she has spoken to my wife and my dear mother in rude ways unbecoming . . . He's here. The gate moves. My hand over his mouth. The shiv right in the beating heart. He turns and falls, gently . . . .

Oh my God! It is my brother! My brother! Oh help me God!

XI   BOSWORTH, FEELING REASONABLY HAPPY and drunk (his shrapnel wound was healing okay), leaned back in his chair, took a long drink from his glass of scotch and water, and examined the scene before him at the Café Happy Times bar in Saigon. The place was jumping with slanty-eyed whores. Some were sitting together at tables whispering. Some were sitting at tables with GIs who were talking loud while they giggled. Several were standing at the long bar with their arms around GIs who were patting their asses and getting drunk. Two whores—quite young, maybe seventeen—were dreamily dancing together to the music of a juke box. None was sitting with Bosworth. His sole companion at the table was another American Soldier named C.W. Cox. Cox had passed out with his head pillowed in his arms and he was snoring miserably.

Standing in the entrance—or rather, occupying space in a curled, willowy way—pulling out a cigarette butt was the delicate old waiter. His oldness reminded Bosworth of a statement by Jean-Paul Sartre about a boy child, "The world still seems to be inhabited by savages stupid enough to see reincarnated ancestors in their newborn children. Weapons and jewelry belonging to the dead man are waved under the infant's nose; if he makes a movement, there is a great shout—a grandfather has come back to life. No wonder, after that, if he speaks of himself with the greatest precautions, half under his breath, often in the third person; this miserable creature is well-aware that he is his own grandfather."

A young whore with breasts unusually large for a Vietnamese passed by his table and stuck out her tongue at Bosworth, wiggling it more than suggestively. He did the same thing for her. She shrugged in puzzlement and authentic indifference and walked on.

Bosworth had been screwing every day for the last week, so he was not tense and hungry out of his mind and was thus in a position ot exercise preference and timing in the sex bit. He had two more days of R & R—rest and recreation—before returning to his outfit in the Cambodian jungles, where just about all their waking hours were taken up in pursuing and killing and being pursued and killed by North Vietnamese troops. He took another drink of Scotch and rubbed his shrapnel wounded leg. Sad to say, he would no longer be admired for his beautiful perfectly proportioned calves. Those endless compliments on the fashionable beaches of the world. "It must be because you have royal Cherokee blood," everybody would observe, "because calves like yours just aren't found on farmers or basket weavers."

He would have to live with it. But it was going to be awfully hard to live with the fact that the wounds had been caused, not by the enemy, but by one of his own GI buddies. A shaky-handed, easily panicked Alabama redneck, Albee Clay Oglethorpe, who, in the heat of an enemy ambush near the border, had thrown the grenade short, very very short, of where the enemy was supposed to be, and it landed at Bosworth's feet. Oglethorpe really had thrown it just to be throwing it, just as he, and so many of the others in the outfit, fired their automatic rifles into trees and bushes just to relieve their own fears and then perhaps to make themselves feel strong.

"I'm real sorry bout that, Bos," Oglethorpe said later as the medics were giving him transfusions in a tent. "But you know, just as I was throwin' that mother—there was four Charlies just in sight—this guy next to me accidentally hit my arm. That's the truth."

"Fuck you," said Bosworth and watched the strange blood flow into his body from the plastic bag held by the sweaty young Quaker medic.

"Aw Bos. That ain't no way to be, man."

"Fuck you, and your mother."

Cox snorted in his sleep and in a spastic gesture knocked his hat onto the floor. A tall red-faced Green Beret boy smoking a cigar swaggered over to the juke box and played "The Yellow Rose of Texas" for the third time. His face made Bosworth think of nasty and brutish phys-ed teachers in high schools. Those who would always gleefully egg kids into fighting one another in front of all the others, and if one of you hung back, he would call you a sissy bastard and tell you that you stank up the place. On one occasion a phys-ed instructor had forced Bosworth to beat up another kid who, at the end of the no-contest, threw up all over the gym floor and then ran into a shower stall and cried. The teacher just laughed and laughed. Bosworth spent the next day at home, hating himself and the gym teacher. The boy he had beaten up transferred to another school the next day, so Bosworth did not have to avoid him for the remainder of the semester. He was immensely relieved when he learned this and he wanted to write the boy a letter of thanks.

"You know something, Bos," the gym teacher announced later, "you're not much better than that little yellow prick who just threw up. You don't have much tiger in you. You're too classy for the real manly rough and ready. I sure hope this country never has to call on the likes of you to defend its freedoms. Shit no."

The other boys looked at him funny, their expressions reflecting an ever-growing adjustment to and approval of male crudeness and brutality particularly when it was exercised by the man in charge. They had the repugnant slyness and moist eagerness of the monastery novice, who after the days' rituals and self-debasements in the glory of the church, jerks off under the sheets into his handkerchief. Bosworth had no difficulty, no difficulty whatsoever, in imagining them stomping any dark-skinned infidel into a bloody dead mush.

One of the whores at the bar suddenly shrieked.

"You bad Yank!" the girl shouted.

"Oo baby," said a round faced red-eyed soldier, swaying

drunkenly and grinning, "Ain't you never been goosed before?" He laughed. "Hell! That's a favorite sport back where I come from."

"Yank hurt Lin Go," she said, and rubbed her behind.

"Ain't you heard?" he said, all grinny. "This is war. Total war," and he slapped her on the ass.

The girl angrily walked away from him and, talking furiously in her own language, sat with two other hookers whose smooth faces displayed a porcelain of tranquility.

"These gook broads got no sense of humor, that's their trouble," the soldier said, returning to his drink. "They don't know how fuckin' lucky they are they ain't gettin' the livin' shit blowed out of them like their Charlie brothers."

Bosworth thought about his own sister. She had just graduated from Bennington, was packing her things to sail away to Nairobi, Africa, where, subsidized by a Fulbright grant, she would do postgraduate work in intertribal communications systems between the Swahili and Kickaya peoples. His mother and father had come all the way from their reservation in Oklahoma to spend a few days with her in New York City. His parents were pretty comfortably fixed. They had invested their share of the tribe's oil revenues in General Motors and Du Pont stock as well as Dow Chemical. These investments gave Bosworth a certain amount of moral discomfort because they clearly indicated support of the very companies that were raining death upon dark and yellow skinned people all over the world.

"The white man isn't happy unless he is killing people," his father said once when Bosworth was discussing moral positions with the old man. "He does it even if I don't support his companies. For me to get away from his madness, I would have to starve to death. There is an old Cherokee saying. 'The prairie dog shits cleaner than the white man feels.'"

"I can't see your Indian forebears being very proud of you, Bosworth," a boot camp officer had said to him one day. "Those Cherokee babies were real great lovers of violence and killing."

"No sir. They were peaceful, nice people."

"Don't give me no back talk, you little fuckhead."

"I'm not giving you any back talk, Mr. J. I'm merely telling you that my ancestors were peace-loving people who didn't do anything to anybody until the white men came along and began to cheat them and kill them."

"You could get your smart ass kicked right out of this place talkin' like that."

"I'm in this bloody shitbag because I made the mistake of joining the ROTC in college," Bosworth now informed the sleeping Cox, "and I got called up. If I had said no they would have put me in the penitentiary, where I would have had to associate with extremely low types and eat food not fit for human consumption, exactly as I am doing now."

A girl with a heavy red mouth and a sleepy style sat down next to Bosworth.

"You like make fuck fuck with me?" she asked.

Bosworth smiled. "Well, uh, I'm not sure."

She took his hand and guided it up her bare soft thigh to her heavily matted cunt, where she held it. "Gung ho good. Many tricks and fun," and she moved her pelvis around under his hand.

"Yeah, I'll bet. But I have to give it a little thought. I've never liked to rush into things."

The girl stuck her tongue out and made it do very agile and suggestive things. "Very fine tongue. Quick. Also, make good suck" She put one of his fingers inside her cunt and smiled slowly and sleepily. "Not much money. Two, three hours fun."

Bosworth thought for a second or two, then, for reasons he could not entirely pin down, returned his hand to the table, but not rudely. "Sounds like a great bargain," he said. "It really does. The sort of thing a fellow can't afford to pass up." She reached over and rested her hand on his crotch. "Uh, yeah. Well, I'll tell you what. Why don't we have a drink and get to know each other a little? Okay?"

"Okay, Joe," she replied, and squeezed his now quite stiff cock. "The general," she said squeezing his thing again, and laughed.

"Oh, yeah. He's the general all right," and Bosworth laughed too. Laughed and sort of twitched or writhed, that is. He thought of something crazy. "You don't happen to be a Vietcong girl spy, do you?"

"Vietcong?" and she giggled. She nodded her head, very amused, a caricature, so to speak. "Yes. Very big Cong girl."

"Just thought I'd check it out," said Bosworth. "Don't get me wrong. I'm not a Charlie hater. It's just that if you're a Cong spy, I'd like to know so that I can reshuffle my inside cards. You know, make adjustments and all that."

The girl's whole expression and manner and vibration suddenly changed, subsided. She looked at him with a gentle sincerity. "You nice. I not hurt you. True." And this time she put his hand on her heart.

Bosworth was touched by this gesture. He had been sort of joking up to this point, but now he felt straight and serious. "Okay," he said, "and I won't hurt you either. Let's have that drink." He motioned to the thin old waiter who was floating serenely about the place like a feather in the breeze.

"Coca-Cola," the girl said.

"Scotch and a Coca-Cola for the lady," Bosworth told the man (watery eyes, tiny goatee) who bowed, smiled, and floated off to the bar. The sound of a big jet plane disturbed the sky outside.

"Dragon," the girl said, and made a face of disgust.

"You're right. Very bad dragon."

"Kill crazy." She examined his face carefully. "You no like kill, yes?"

"I hate it," he replied, swallowing some of the new drink the old man had almost silently put before him. "I tell you the truth when I say that as far as I know I personally have never killed anybody. I always aim very wide, sometimes even into the trees, when I shoot. And on several occasions when I had my gun on Charlie, I let him run for it." He smiled and put his hand gently on hers. "If the other guys in my outfit knew this they would say that I was very sick." He laughed. "In fact, I could probably be court martialled and put in the pen at hard labor. Wow!" And for a couple of moments Bosworth saw himself crushing stones with a big sledgehammer while a fat man with a long rifle watched over him, occasionally spitting tobacco juice in a big stream.

"You very, very nice boy," she told him. "Your name?"

"Bosworth Horn."

"I am Duc Sun Lin."

Later that afternoon Bosworth, happier than he had been in at least two years, sweetly and feelingly kissed both Lin's breasts, kissed her endlessly lovely belly, and said, "I'm going to defect."

She kissed him several times on his face and chest and Bosworth's skin felt that a small flower had opened on it each time. Then she got up off the bed. "I love you," she said, standing naked over him and putting her hands on her hips. "I make food now."

"First class idea. I don't understand it. Every part of me is being satisfied today. I couldn't beat this if I were back in my mother's arms on the reservation. Let me kiss you again," and he leaned over and kissed her on her thighs and cunt while she smiled totally. "Anyway," he continued, knowing, without being bothered by this fact, that Lin's very limited grasp of English allowed her to get very little of what he said, "I'm going to turn my back on the United States Army and give myself to the National Liberation Front. That's a pontoon bridge I don't in the least mind burning."

Lin (she had slipped a shift on for some reason) was puttering about in the tiny kitchen area, chopping things up and heating oil in a pan. Bosworth smelled shrimps and Chinese cabbage. "Have many good friends in Liberation Front," she said. "Maybe you meet them? Tonight?"

"Great. I'd love that." He put on a blue man's kimono that Lin had placed at the foot of the bed. He considered it for a moment, then could not help himself from asking, "Who's is this, Lin? Boy friend?"

She looked at him in an almost pitying way and, smiling a little sadly, said, "Was my father's. He was killed by American soldiers."

Bosworth suddenly hated himself. "Oh Christ! I'm sorry. I'm really sorry," and he quickly went to her and kissed her hand, "Forgive me."

"Of course. How you know that my father's? Don't feel bad. Okay?"

"Yeah. Okay."

Rare food smells and tiny cooking sounds filled the room like exotic atonal music. Lin went about her tasks with flawless motions and natural ease. Bosworth, who had witnessed many girls prepare supper after screwing him, had never seen such lyrical efficiency and non-confusion. All of the girls in his life somehow had been in a jumpy quarrel with this primitive experience. Food seemed hostile to them, and they to it. The meals that wound up

on their tables more often than not seemed defeats, or subjuga-
tions, not mutual victories.

The telephone rang. Its shrillness seemed to still the rare musical melange of food smells and cooking. Lin stiffened, and stared
at it as if she were trying, through extrasensory efforts, to divine
its message without picking it up. After four rings, she picked it
up and in a moment was speaking rapidly and happily in her
magical tongue, which Bosworth, when he had first heard it a year
ago, was immediately convinced conveyed very rare meanings.

"My brother," she said when she finally hung up. "He come
here tonight. Brings a friend," and she returned to the meal.

"Uh huh, that's fine. What does your brother do?"

"He tell you."

"Oh. OK. I guess it is better that way."

"We eat now," she said, and the food materialized on the
unobtrusive little bamboo table at the window looking out over the
crowded Saigon street.

"Lin, you're incredible."

"Yes. Thank you. Oh! You know chopsticks? Very nice. Yes,
very nice."

"You know something?" Bosworth said, chewing down a
piece of shrimp and some rice, "In this kimono and using these
chopsticks, I don't feel anything like an American anymore."

She laughed. "You never American, Bosworth."

He considered this for a moment. "Yeah. I guess you're right."
He stared out of the window and thought of something an Indian
friend of his, a college chap like himself, had told a sociologist
visiting the reservation on a field trip (with his asexual wife who
wore baggy blue jeans and a man's fishing cap "to keep the darn
sun out," she said; also, she frequently shouted "Hi there!" to
people she had never seen before in her life): "What frightens me
most about white society is the terrible loneliness. What I mean
is that you never seem so much alone as when you are gathered
together. . . . What you call friendships are usually what we would
call exclusive alliances of two or three or half a dozen against the
world. Tribal people have an inclusive social sensitivity which no
white person ever experiences. . . . It is funny to hear the isolated
white man advocating integration for Indians. To us, he seems to

be saying, 'Come, join us and be lonely.' It is dishonest to use the
word integration. You have never wanted us to integrate, but only
to conform. Why is it that any cultural difference—not only Indian
but anywhere in the world—is an aggravation to white people?"

"You can say that again," Bosworth murmured to himself.

He returned his look to the table and to Lin Duc. She was
watching him the same way she had watched the ringing telephone before picking it up. Bosworth reached under the table and
rubbed his wounded leg.

LIN'S BROTHER DINH WAS TALKING RAPIDLY AS
he paced the room. Curiously, though he was thin, he glowed
richly and suffused the room with an enormous, but not in any way
oppressive, presence. "It is a terrible thing the Americans are
telling themselves. Their fears have completely corrupted their
minds. They tell themselves they are killing my people because
my people are evil Communists who want to enslave the world.
They tell themselves that the world can be free and beautiful only
when all the Reds are dead. They are convinced that the masses
of North and South Vietnamese are being duped and deceived by
their evil masters in Hanoi, and that they would make the most
of any opportunity to throw off this yoke of slavery. They think
that without the North Vietnamese soldiers the National Liberation Front would collapse or be easily destroyed by the superior
fighting men of the South Viet government's army.

"Well, it is quite obvious that the Americans are driving themselves insane with such lies and nonsense. They are not fighting
an army, my friend. They are fighting the entire population of the
North and nearly the entire population of the South. Every man,
woman, and child. And every single one of these will gladly die
on the battlefield fighting the Americans and their friends. Surren-
dering or giving up is a fantasy invented by the Americans in their
insanity. It is unthinkable to the Vietnamese, believe me. Unthinkable."

He paused to drink some tea at the table. Bosworth and Lin
and her brother's friend, a young Buddhist monk, waited silently
for him to go on.

"The Americans are exterminating religionists. The only way

275 | *Wake Up. We're Almost There*

of life that is tolerable to them is their own, and in one way or another, outright killing or indirect suffocation, they want to destroy every other way. Purely and simply because they profoundly fear a different way of eating, sleeping, walking, thinking, even a different way of making love. They have been brought up with this fear, from the cradle. They are not aware of this. They seek high sounding rationalizations for their feelings and acts. They cannot face this basic truth."

The young Buddhist monk made a deep sound of agreement and, with a faint smile, nodded at Bosworth. "The whole thing is horribly stupid," he said, feeling an authentic (not a sentimental, strategic) shame.

"No," said the monk, *"vicious.* The destruction is quite self-conscious. They are not doing it inadvertently."

"Oh, I agree," Bosworth said. "Just about all the way. But not all the way." He looked around, expecting the conversation, or whatever it was, to be taken over by one of them again. But they just watched him. "I mean, there are a few Americans here who hate what they are doing."

Lin and her brother and the Buddhist looked at one another. "Then why don't they stop doing it?" asked Dinh.

Bosworth said. "Uh. . . ." but nothing would follow that sound. He thought for a few seconds. "I just don't know," he finally continued. "And they don't know either."

The monk chuckled, more or less. "Indeed a very odd people. They are not involved in the very acts they commit. I wonder. Do they invent someone else to do their eating and drinking for them too?"

Bosworth laughed, because this really did strike him as funny. "Maybe they do. Maybe they really do. I know I've done that lots of times, before coming here, I mean." He paused, "I hated one class in college so much that I used to imagine I was an East German digging my way to freedom, so I could take it." He looked at his nails. "Damn if I don't still have the dirt on me to prove it."

Lin's brother came over and sat at Bosworth's feet. "My friend," he said, putting his hand on Bosworth's knee, "the Vietnamese is not like that. He is completely the person who is doing the things the person with his name is doing. But I am afraid the

Americans—perhaps all westerners—do not understand or quite believe this. They do not understand our... our lack of split within ourselves. For example, let me read something to you. Most revealing." He took two newspaper clippings from inside his light cotton jacket. "These news items from your own American press, show exactly what I am talking about." He held up one clipping (which had obviously been handled many, many times). "You remember about three weeks ago there was a considerable encounter between your forces and the people's army near Gio Linh? Well, our men, yes, *our* men, fought with supreme bravery and many were killed, as of course many of yours were killed. Well, here is what one very important American newspaper had to say about this: "About 400 green young Communist troops, *many apparently hopped up on heroin,* were in the battle. Most of the enemy troops were around 17 years old. Packets of heroin were found on the bodies of some of the dead. 'The only logical conclusion is that they do take this stuff before an attack,' said Capt. James D. Oenbrink, an army doctor from Palm Beach, Florida. 'It makes them like a drunk person. They don't know what hit them, and they don't care.'"

Dinh, finished reading, smiled wearily and slowly shook his head. "So absurd, so terribly absurd. Do you see, friend Bosworth? The Americans cannot conceive of unqualified bravery, of unqualified identification of one's ideals, passions, and physical person. So they explain this by claiming the brave young men were on drugs—which, as we know, has the function of separating one from oneself. It creates an operative illusion, so to speak." He laughed a little. "But one's common sense would tell one that heroin puts you to sleep, not into battle." He held up the other clipping for Bosworth and Lin and the Buddhist to savor the damning delicious sight of. "This appeared in another major American newspaper about a week after the other absurd nonsense appeared. But as you can fully see for yourselves, this second news story is very tiny and received its shy exposure in the next to last page, among the shipping news." He giggled and was immediately joined in this pleasurable gesture (one that Bosworth, prior to his Viet visit, had observed almost exclusively among young women in his own country), by Lin and the monk. Bosworth wanted very much to giggle with them, but it was too new and much too different a thing to do at this point in his life. All he could summon was a real grin. Perhaps six months from now, he thought rapidly, I'll be giggling quite naturally. Not, of course, as good as they do it, but certainly better than any cornball American. "I read it. 'An investigation has determined that enemy soldiers killed in fighting north of Saigon last Sunday were not carrying heroin, as reported after the battle, a spokesman for the United States First Infantry Division said today.' "

Now the young monk, whose face was alive with a constant inner sunshine, cracked up. He curled up and for seconds disappeared into a wild giggle-laughter, clapping his elegant small hands as he did. Dinh sensitively, and appreciatively, too, waited until the monk had completed his delight before proceeding. " 'He said that small packets of white powder found on the battlefield had been analyzed and found to contain potassium permanganate, a disinfectant and fungicide; calcium hydrate, used as a water purifier, antibiotics, and ordinary soap.' "

Bosworth was visualizing the entire scene (very easy for him because he had been there for the past year, so it was rather like visualizing one's own pennant-and-nudie-plastered college room), involving the slaphappy, raunchy, very dirty GIs, the mysterious white packets on the torn, bloody, dead young Vietnamese men, and the terrible, moronic, and comic-strip urge to come up with a bizarre thing like heroin. He could see himself standing on the edge of the corpse-cluttered jungle scene, watching the men through a lens of remoteness and puzzlement. They were all muddy and stubble-faced and their sweated shapeless green uniforms seemed more like still another form of jungle growth than official issue that had been stitched together by a whirring machine in a mindlessly clean American factory.

"Hey, Lieutenant! Look at this fuckin' stuff. What do you think it is? Opium? Boy I'll bet it is, or some kinda drug. Guy I know who was in Korea said those gook fuckers always got themselves all hopped up on opium and stuff before throwin' their crazy asses into battle charges. Man, they couldn't feel a thing. Sure smells funny. So do they. Ha ha."

Lin poured him some more tea. She smelled gently wonderful. There was something about her that was so totally different from the girls he had known back in the states—so diametrically opposed—that she herself might as well be a character in an ancient song. They smiled at each other and her hand touched his.

"Sometimes I wonder if all of western civilization will have to vanish—or be vanished—before mankind can begin to be truly himself in all his magnificence," said the monk. "This is something I consider very much of the time." He looked at Bosworth. "One might say the dream is ending and the nightmare of reality is under way." He bowed, smiling. "A rough translation from Tric Doc Nygen a great Vietnamese poet. One of my favorites, needless to say."

Somewhere outside a radio was sending out news broadcasts in Vietnamese. Next door a mandolin was being plucked. A vender was calling out the types of food he had in his little cart. The long hrrrpp of a Honda motorcycle suddenly obliterated the other sounds. Lin sat next to Bosworth and put her hand in his. Her brother, who had been staring out of the window and drawing deeply on an American cigarette, turned around and stared at Bosworth without speaking. Then he said, "What do you think?"

"It's pretty awful. Pretty awful and very crazy." He drank some tea. "You're right. Something, or somebody, maybe everybody, has got to go." He turned to Lin, then to the monk. "How many people are victims of other people's hallucinations?"

The monk gracefully threw open his arms. "Three-fourths of the human race." His face gave up the smile and was deeply almost sullenly serious. "And all of them live outside of the continental United States."

Dinh went to the small kitchen area, opened the bottom part of the refrigerator, and, from the back of the motor, took two US Army Colt .45 automatics. He put one in his own belt and gave the other one to the monk, Thich Nhan Ho, who slipped his inside his robe.

"You will join us?" Dinh asked Bosworth.

"Yes. Yes, I'll join you." he looked at Lin.

"Even if I had some other choice, which I don't, I would join you. I guess that's what some of the animals must have said to old Noah."

Lin's lithe hand seemed to absorb his.

That night their lovemaking was more connected and satisfying than any sex Bosworth had ever experienced. Always before he had felt, after it was over, washed up on a shore. This time the shore was far, far distant: he was part of the sea.

The following sunny afternoon, showered, shaved, freshly uniformed, walking erect, and unquestionably looking like a thoroughly okay member of the American military machine, junior officer branch, Bosworth headed down the street of Inner Peace toward the newly renovated American officers' club. His leather heels made a crisp, mean sound compared to which the sliding-pattering of the passing Vietnamese seemed sneaky and weak and somewhat unreal. He shifted his overnight satchel from right to left in order to return the salute of a couple of cruising GIs. They looked like Eagle Scouts. At the white marble entrance to the club (where he gave some change to an urgent young Viet boy who wanted to shine his shoes) he checked his watch. Satisfied with what the watch told him, he mounted the steps and entered the building.

A smooth and bowing Viet in a white jacket immediately offered to check his handbag, but Bosworth declined his offer. "Thanks," he said, "but all my shaving stuff is in it."

"Oh yes," said the very eager gray-haired man. "Shaving."

Bosworth passed under a large color photograph of President Johnson and went into the john. He was in the middle of an unnecessary pee when a fairly drunk air force colonel came in. "Man oh man," he said, taking the urinal right next to Bosworth. "I got enough in me to drown half the pigs in Peking," and a giant stream confirmed his claim. Bosworth had always been made uncomfortable by another's nearness in a toilet and now he tensed up so his water stopped altogether. He strongly hoped the colonel wouldn't look over and notice this. He deftly slipped it back in and moved away.

"You hear about those North Koreans seizing one of our ships?" the colonel asked, still pissing.

"No. Can't say I have."

"Well they did, the little fuckers. I'll tell you what I'd do. I'd drop the bomb on 'em. I mean it. Wipe 'em out. Then they won't pull that crap anymore."

"Maybe you're right," Bosworth said, picking up his khaki canvas bag and moving for the door.

"Bet your ass I'm right," said the colonel, shaking his penis to get rid of all the piss drops. "Let 'em know who's boss once and for all."

"I see what you mean." Bosworth quickly and furtively checked his watch. He had to be moving.

In about a minute he was sitting in the large lounge ordering a scotch and soda from a shiny-faced Viet in the usual white jacket. The lounge was crowded with American officers, both sitting in groups and standing at the long walnut bar. Bosworth estimated about fifty. They all seemed quite happy and in excellent health. Clean and strong and fitted out handsomely in their tailored uniforms. Bosworth felt his handbag with his foot. When he had finished giving his order he asked the waiter where the phones were. The man told him they were outside in the hall. Bosworth thanked him and said he had to make a call but would be right back.

"Very good, sir," the man said in flawless English. "I will see that no one takes your table. Please be assured of that."

"Fine."

Outside in the hall Bosworth checked his watch again, and looked around apprehensively (he was really nervous now). The two main guards with automatic rifles on their shoulders were chatting amiably a few feet away. They paid no attention to him. Bosworth walked toward the door, not too fast, not too casually either.

"Sir," the old man said, suddenly appearing from nowhere and freezing Bosworth, "Going so soon?"

"Coming right back," he said, squeezing out a grin as he suppressed a terrible desire to smash the man and run. "Getting a shine."

"Oh yes. Nice shine," said the man. "But you get shine downstairs barber. Yes?"

"No. The boy outside," he replied sharply and quickly walked outside and down the marble stairs. Just as he reached the sidewalk where he saw the car waiting for him with Dinh at the wheel, and the motor running, an immense explosion blew out the side of the club and jolted Bosworth. He slipped into the car and they sped away.

"That new German dynamite is very powerful," said Dinh, steering beautifully through the now panicked traffic.

"Good God!" whispered Bosworth, looking back. "Burning bodies are hanging in the trees!"

"Excellent."

Five army jeeps, their sirens screaming, raced past them going toward the club. The faces of the American soldiers sitting in them were contracted with rage and fear.

Two days later Bosworth appeared at the large military police station on President Ky Avenue. It was a new building and a couple dozen American and South Vietnamese MPs, heavily armed, were lounging, working at desks, and standing guard on the shiny, efficient, antiseptic-smelling first floor. The ruddy sergeant at the receiving desk saluted him. "Good morning, sergeant," Bosworth said, relaxed and appearing comradely as he returned the salute. "I wonder if you could give me a little help."

"Certainly will try, lieutenant. What's on your mind?"

"Well, I'm trying to find one of my men. He's been knocking around Saigon on leave and he hasn't showed up for a couple of dates we had. So, you know, I thought he might have gotten drunk and knocked a few people down in a bar and been picked up by you guys."

The young sergeant laughed. "That's been known to happen all right. What's his name?"

"Kosinsky, Michael Kosinsky."

"Okay. Kosinsky. Let's see now." And the sergeant began looking through the big hand-written book in front of him. Three big MPs began to laugh at a dirty joke being told by a fourth. Half a dozen South Viet MPs walked, or marched by, looking very grim. In their midst, handcuffed, was a Viet prisoner. He was bleeding from what Bosworth supposed was a rifle butt wound on the head.

"Nope," said the sergeant after a couple of moments. "We don't have your boy Kosinsky, Lieutenant." An amusing idea occurred to him. "Hey! Maybe he defected to Charlie." And he guffawed exuberantly.

"You never know, sergeant," said Bosworth, quite genuinely amused by the other's fantasy. "Well, I guess I'll have to look elsewhere. Sorry to have bothered you." He checked his wrist watch.

"No bother, Lieutenant. We're all in this bout together. This is my job."

"Thanks anyway." Bosworth began walking away. Then he stopped and turned around. "Say," he began, "do you have a mail pickup soon?"

"Matter of fact, we do," replied the sergeant. He looked at the wall clock. "In about ten minutes a jeep is going down to the PO."

"You know, you could really help me. I've got to get off a big bundle of stuff some of my men are sending back home and I just won't have time to get there today. Could your guys drop it off for me?"

"Be a pleasure."

"Great. I'll go out and get it."

Bosworth was back in a couple of minutes (Dinh had parked his car just across the street from the compound), carrying a large box wrapped in manila paper.

"Let me give you a hand," said the sergeant and grabbed for the box. "This baby looks heavy."

"Thanks. Christ, these guys must be sending back an entire VC village."

"Wouldn't put it past them." They deposited the box in a corner near the corridor where all the MPs were gathered. "It'll be okay there," said the sergeant.

"That's great, really great. Man, you don't know how glad I am to get that off my hands and mind."

"It'll be on its way to San Francisco in an hour."

Dinh and Bosworth drove a couple of blocks away and parked in front of a big sidewalk café on the Street of Many Memories. Both looked at their watches.

"Shall we have a drink or a coffee?" asked Dinh.

Bosworth made an amused sound. "I sure wish I had your cool, Dinh."

"You are doing wonderfully well, Bosworth my friend. You are getting the tranquility of the committed."

Just as Bosworth's eye was caught by an extravagantly beautiful and chicly dressed European-looking woman sitting down with a very fat, heavily decorated South Viet army officer, the explosion went off. It was twice as big as the previous one and it

had an otherworldly quality, like an eruption on the moon's surface.

"A perfectly timed mechanism," observed Dinh, checking his
Swiss watch.

The blonde European-looking woman began to scream.

BOSWORTH WAS IN A LARGE ROOM AT THE BACK
of a Buddhist temple on the fringe of Saigon. He was one of fifteen
people, many of whom were sitting on the floor. He and Lin were
seated on a low couch and they were holding hands. Dinh was
there, and so was Thich Nhan Ho. Everyone there, Bosworth
guessed, was in his twenties (or her twenties, because there were
three girls present besides Lin. Smooth, taut but not tense, quietly
elegant young women whose sincere loveliness made Bosworth
feel all of a piece as a man). Incense was burning, somewhere in
a corner, and the smell of it bound them and the statements and
ideas that were to follow in an immediate kind of sensuality.

"I will speak in English," Thich began, "because our American
friend does not speak in our tongue, and all of us here have had
the advantage of being schooled in his tongue. I say advantage
qualifiedly." There were murmurs of amusement.

"English is not in itself an evil tongue," said a young girl with
small silver earrings, "It depends whose tongue is using it."

A general laughter wreathed the room.

"Yes, of course," said Thich, slightly bowing in the direction
of Bosworth to include him in the good-tongue group.

A crewcut boy whose right ear was missing (Bosworth later
discovered it had been cut off by a police chief who thought his
answers, during an interrogation, were not spontaneous enough)
stood up. "I must argue that point." he said.

"Ah yes?" responded Thich. (That slight smile played about
his face like the song in a spring afternoon, always present, sometimes clearly manifesting itself, other times hovering just beneath
the skin.)

"Yes," the boy continued. "I say that it is the very language
of evil."

A murmur in the group, and some people looked at each other

in amused surprise. Bosworth wanted to laugh with delight.

"Would you care to tell us why?" asked Thich.

"Yes. I would like that." The boy drew a deep breath and began. "I state the following as a basis: the feelings and ideas that exist before the language are evil ones. The Anglo-Saxon attitudes toward life are in a condition of paradox because they are against life. Yes, anti-life in its great possibilities. So you see the problem."

"Yes, yes," several of the group said.

"All right. There are more explanations. English is a language of power. Life for the Anglo-Saxons has always been this power struggle, not a struggle for tranquility and meaning and richness of man and nature. There we are. The deepest implications of this language, this tongue spoken by our enemy—wait! I mean the people who are attempting to annihilate us—the deepest implication is power and separation of man from man. These things are the essential fabric of communication."

He stood there silently for two or three seconds, then he said. "That is all. Thank you." And he sat down.

"That was a most interesting disgression," said Thich. "And illuminating. Now I wish to talk about why we are all here and also of course to welcome our new friend, the American soldier, Bosworth. . . . " He bowed to Bosworth, and the group clapped hands in praise of his being there.

"Thank you, Thich," Bosworth said. "But two things. I'm an Indian, a Cherokee, not an American. And I *was* a soldier. I'm now something else. I'm not sure just what. Maybe a novice revolutionary. Maybe a half breed, mestizo-Vietnamese."

A few chuckles. Polite delicate Asian chuckles. Some from Thich. "Of course," Thich said, "Now we have you freshly identified. Very good. So. Our purpose. Beginning a week from this day, the National Liberation Front will begin an organized assault on the American positions and forces around Saigon. We have known about the possibility of this for some time, so it is really not a surprise idea. What we must do now that this campaign has been definitely put on a program basis, is the following effort: We must arrange to take care of the valiant soldiers who will be coming into the city. I am given to understand we are to have in our midst a strength of two thousand guests. Now then. Each of you here in this room must alert and make ready the citizens in your specified areas. The citizens whose houses will be accommodating our dedicated visitors and also the citizens who will be giving not their homes but spiritual and psychological assistance and understanding." He turned toward Bosworth. "The psychological is a very favorite expression in the programs of America, is it not?"

"A very big favorite back home," Bosworth answered. "An essential part of anything is the psychological. It even gets into the food."

A few semi-stifled giggles. Lin leaned against him affectionately.

"You are very fine." she whispered back.

"Crazy too," he whispered back.

"Very good crazy."

Thich cleared his voice, sipped some tea, and went on, "The time of the visitation will indeed be a great one but a very trying one. Very trying, and requiring every ounce of our strength and effort and love of our principles." He paused. "You are to keep coordinated through myself and Dinh. One of us if not the other. Will there be any questions, please?"

No one raised a hand. Dinh stood up. "I would like to take this opportunity to show our gratitude and comradeship to friend Bosworth for his very splendid work in the last few days in the freedom fight. Besides almost total destruction of the buildings housing the fascist invaders, the two very splendid explosions killed thirty-four American and seven puppet soldiers."

Everyone stood up and clapped. Bosworth stood up and bowed his appreciation. He had not felt so good in a group way since a day in his childhood on the reservation, when he had passed the intensely arduous manhood initiation rites, which included leaping into the lake through a big hole in the ice and fanging a rattlesnake barehanded—while the elders of the tribe (including his expressionless father) quietly looked on.

"Thank you," he said, "Thank you all very much. But what I did was really, and I mean this, really very, very little, compared to the quite horrible things the Americans have done to you." He sat down. Against his will, tears came to his eyes. But he did not try to hide this, because he was not ashamed. In his mind he saw his father watching him, and he was smiling. A few minutes later, after most of the young revolutionaries had left, Dinh and Thich came over to Bosworth.

"Let us go for a little walk in the temple garden," said Thich. "Dinh and I would like to discuss a mission with you."

"Okay. Can Lin come too?"

"Oh yes. She is part of everything we do. She is the leaf to our tree."

Out in the garden Lin's hand became part of his. Orchids, mimosa, dwarf willow, cumquat, palm trees, coldgrass absorbed their presence in most lyrical loveliness. It was a natural, and perfect, ambience for meaningful and confidential things to take place. The delicately attuned, never obtrusive, plants collected and fed on secrets; not a scrap of anything said there could possibly escape their benign omniverousness. Bosworth responded in kind; never had nature felt so intimately human and participant in his destiny. He and it were unequivocally breathing together. As lovers.

"My dear friend," Thich said, strolling next to him and Lin, "we want you to assassinate General Westmoreland."

As Bosworth heard those simple words containing ultimate clarity, he knew that the old Bosworth, the person that he had been, was completely no longer. Just who he had become he would not know for some time.

The Amalgamated Press office, on the third floor at 14 Rue de la Paix, in downtown Saigon, was a tomb of dead smells—cigar smoke, carbon paper, typewriter exudations and human sweat. Two teletype machines were clattering away. Charlie Manger, the man in charge of the bureau, was having a drink with John W. Appleby, one of the AP correspondents. Appleby was sitting on Manger's desk. Manger was at the typewriter.

"Somewhere in this crazy fuckin' town," Manger was saying, "is an American who is posing as a bona fide GI or who really is one and who, whichever way you wish to skin it, is somehow connected with those two recent bombings of the officers' club and the military police headquarters. Is that what you are tellin' me, Appleby ole boy?"

"Keerect," replied Appleby, putting away a finger of straight bourbon.

"An' that's what you have written in this story you are filin'?"

"As you can clearly determine by reading said story now in your very hands."

Manger gulped a hefty amount of his drink and leaned back in his chair as he looked at Appleby's copy. "Uh huh. Well kiss my ass."

"I am sorry, Mr. Manger. But that is not in our guild contract."

Manger rubbed his chin, took another drink, and rubbed his chin some more. "Uh huh. An' that is completely all you know?"

"I am not the sort of man to withhold vital information from the American people," Appleby replied, shifting a little on the desk for more comfort.

Manger blew air through puffed cheeks and stared out of the big window for a few seconds. Then he looked at Appleby's copy again. He put the copy down and slowly rolled a fresh piece of paper into the typewriter. "Appleby, we need each other in this struggle against worldwide madness."

Appleby dropped his deadpan and smiled for the first time. "I know what you mean, sir, and you can count on me all the way."

"That bastard must be insane and brainwashed and just about everything else," Manger said, looking at the expectant white paper.

"No question of it."

Manger began slowly to type out a new story.

"Allied military forces in Saigon today were putting their heads together for a solution to the latest war threat—an insane American 'soldier' who is suspected of leaving time bombs recently in an officers' club and the new military police building. Fortunately, authorities say, the bombs were defective and did very little damage. Two civilians were killed, however. It is the considered opinion of these authorities that the 'mad bomber' is an AWOL Negro civilian who was employed as a truck driver by a civilian transportation unit here and who has obviously stolen a GI uniform. This man, whom authorities have declined to name for security reasons, is known to have been corresponding with communist-controlled 'black power' groups in the United States. One army psychologist close to the case, has said that the man is suffering from 'a severe white-man persecution complex.' "

Manger leaned back to read what he had just concocted. Finally he smiled. "Yessir," he said, and resumed typing.

"I knew you would work it out, chief," said Appleby, his own smile turning to a conspiratorial grin. "I'll have a drink on that." And he did.

THOUGHT YOU'D LOST ME, DIDN'T YOU? FAT chance. You could sooner lose congenital dropsy, the way we got things rigged in this place. My kindest advice: just stay real loose and everything will wash out fine. Uptight people always lose out. You know it and I know it.

My fruit and vegetable store has done so well that I've turned it over to the Blaster and Shoeless Grogan, one of my former drinking buddies back in the days of the brownstone stoop. (We haven't blown that scene, by the way. We make it on weekends.)

This gives the boys time to scuffle for a little dough and also to catch up on their health and correspondence. (Mich, for example, had not written to his Mum in thirty-three years.) They've got the hang of things beautifully. Grogan is a wizard with chicory, celery, watercress, and escarole. He really knows how to keep that stuff living and breathing and looking saucy as you please. What I'm doing with myself is something else again. Right down the street from my old place I've opened a two-way business: a nadaria, a store for nothingness; and a fantasia. I have erected a fine plywood partition between the two to keep them apart in a most sanitary way; also, I've sealed the baseboards with a latex putty to prevent seepage.

To forestall any accusations of arrogant commercialism, I want to say right now that I did not go into these enterprises primarily to hustle a buck. You could almost call me a pragmatic romantic: I made this gesture to satisfy a great public need, or needs that were, in all truth, not being taken care of elsewhere. All right? At my nadaria you can buy pure grade A nothing, or no-thing, if you prefer. Think what this will do for your already massively assaulted contemporary soul! All your life you have been lured and dragged into stores and made to purchase something. You have been shaped, against your will, into a buyer of things. The madmen who run this materialist world have cruelly subverted your human need for nothingness, for the very simple reason that it terrifies them. In your need for nothingness lies the seed of their doom. My nadaria is very simply done. A few completely empty shelves and a small freezer, in the event that you may wish to purchase some frozen nothingness. Another thing: You may spend as little as five cents in my place. "Please, sir. A nickel's worth of nothing." That's the sort of customer statement that would not in any way distress my ears. And one thing my customers need never live in dread of: running out of merchandise.

Now for my other store. The world we live in has become so cheesy and thick-witted, so fascistically intrusive, that even our fantasy life (yours, that is) has been eaten away. More than that, I understand there are plans afoot in Congress (specifically in the House Internal Security Committee) to severely legislate fantasy! Think of that, and weep. In my store you can buy fantasies outright. And you need not be ashamed of this. Does a diabetic feel shame when he is provided with insulin injections to cure a deficiency? Of course not. You can rent fantasies (by the day or week, any longer would wear them out). You can have your own fantasies adjusted or retooled. (Even a Rolls-Royce needs occasional fixing.) You can subscribe to my Fantasy a Month Club, or you can arrange for an entire fantasy program. This program, I must admit, is a real sweetheart. It makes those 30-day package tours of Europe look ridiculous. In fact, I spit on them. What have you got when the tour is over? I'll tell you what. You've got sour stomach from bad wine and greasy beef stew. My fantasy program gives you an entirely new world, with infinite variety. Fantasies for the morning, afternoon, and evening. Fantasies to have while showering, waiting for the long distance operator to wake up, standing in line at gin sales, watching the woman across the hall fumble with her door key, listening to the boss present as his own one of your finest advertising schemes. And so on. I have developed programs to fit particular people in particular situations. Women who live in the suburbs and are married to paraplegics. Negro shoe shine boys who are former lightweight boxing champions. Middle-aged stockbrokers doing time for fraud. Young Irish-American girls whose fathers are alcoholic bus drivers. Now then . . . does this give you a rough idea of the scene? If it doesn't something's the matter with you, and you'd better go see a husky Finnish masseur.

By the way, if things go well at my new shop, I may very well take in an apprentice or two, in the style of the old master artisans. If you know of any likely youngsters, boys or girls, whose imagination and ballsiness are making them unsuitable for life in Shit City, why, jot their names down on a piece of wrapping paper and mail it in.

Guess who I ran into last night in front of the Electric Circus? The Countess! Oh Whiffenpoof! She was in the company of a bunch of uptown swells and they had just snickered their way out of a two-block long Lancia, chauffered by a giant hippy with a great cocked eye and a red fez. The Countess was in rare form, I must say. For one thing, she was sporting an outfit that must have alerted our planes at the Dew Line. It was an authentic southern jailer's uniform, plus a shiny black hat.

"Hi, you makin' it, poppa?" she asked, slapping me on my overburdened peddler's back.

"Touchdowns every day," I replied. "How did you come by the redneck accent?"

"Whatsa mattuh? You prejudiced?"

"Not old me. No sir. But when I last saw you, you had a limey thing going."

She shrugged. "Ah frazzled it, hunney. Lef it whumperin in tha groin." She looked at me real close. "You ain't playin' it straight, are you, Daddy?"

I shuddered in disgust, "Heavens to Betsy no! What a thing to suggest to the last of the great dissemblers."

She scratched her ass and spat, just as we would both imagine the southern screw would have done it. "Well, ah certainly ayum glad tu heah that. 'Cause ah wuz afraid you mighta gone crazy or somethin'."

"One thing I haven't lost, old fruit, is the talent for survival," I said. "A man's best friend is still his make-up kit."

"A-men." And she chucked me under my Hamlet's chin. She grabbed a fat little millionaire (don't ask me how I know he was a millionaire. I just did. I can spot real money a mile away). And they tumbled into the waiting joy spot. But not before a shimmering big-eyed bawd in the menage looked closely at me and said "Good grief! Your nose! It should be a home for wayward children."

Sylvia, who had gone into the Electric Circus ahead of me to see if the place was too creepy for her consumption, came out now and said, "It's a pretty nutsy scene. A lot of people there are turning into blobs of colored light."

"Why on earth are they doing that?"

"Don't ask me," she said, shrugging in that fake Lebanese way of hers. "Maybe they've got personality problems."

I took her arm and guided her toward the door. "There's got to be a scientific explanation for this," I said, putting on my best Danish scientist's tone.

"Why?"

"Why do you hate meaning so much?"

"Ha! Look who's talking."

Well, I soon got to the bottom of it. This middle brow debauch house contained an elaborate array of multicolored lights that kept flashing on and off over the assembled pleasure seekers, and the effect was a benign kaleidescopic hallucination. I immediately ordered an Albert Schweitzer—gin, rum, champagne, wildly homogenized—and a double Johnny Walker red on the rocks for Sylvia. It's silly to stay sober in a place like that.

"You haven't taken me out for months," Sylvia began. "Why tonight all of a sudden?"

"Guilt," I said, downing half my drink as soon as the topless waitress (medium tits) put it before me. "And unbearable love."

She snorted and guzzled a bit herself (the music was Chinese rock and roll). "Huh. You're really hung up, aren't you? You can't have one without the other. Sick."

"Each of us reaches out to God in his own way."

Several hundred humans were swarming all around us, writhing and jerking and turning into sudden blobs of red, green, yellow, purple.

"You're full if shit," she said.

"We are discussing the relationship between love, neurosis, and religion. Not organic chemistry."

She drank down some scotch. "You're still full of shit."

I sighed. I mean I really had to. "Oh Lord. What ever became of objective analytical inquiry?"

"You buried it."

I drank some more to numb my despair. Sylvia is one of those creatures you see depicted so fearfully on Egyptian friezes. They have evolved, and persisted on this earth, by processes that are totally outside the experiences of the normal animal kingdom. In those early days man tried to deal with "things" like Sylvia by incorporating them into their art forms and by giving them top billing in their temples. But today, unfortunately, we cannot handle the problem quite so effectively: Christianity just won't have it. This is another reason to mourn the disappearance of demonology. Modern man is insanely boxed in.

I glanced around this hall of the mountain king hoping to find a proper device for changing the subject (I know when I'm beat). And I did. Sitting not five yards from us was the Countess, surrounded by (or should I say festooned with?) her little mob. "Upon my word," I said "There's an old friend of mine. The Countess of Liederkranz.

"Where?"

"Right there," I said, pointing to her eminence.

"Good grief! You mean Captain Bligh?"

"Oh, that's just a camp."

"With a camp like that, who needs a penal code?"

I finished my Schweitzer and beckoned to Round Tits for another round. "Actually, she's quite a beauty, in her rather oversize way."

Sylvia looked at me very meanly. "Oh, I see. Another of your furtive bang jobs?"

I smiled as humanely as possible. "You know, I'm not the sex maniac you imagine me to be."

She presented me with one of her demon creature, flappings in the moonlight, smiles. "Poor man. The most pathetic thing I know of is your need to palm yourself off as a normal human being. I mean really. It's as ludicrous as Himmler trying to tell the Jews he's interested in urban renewal."

I could feel the gin and rum and champagne holding secret meetings in my toes and fingertips and I relied on them to come up with plans to save me from my mortal harassments. The multicolored dancers were contorting and going to pieces all around us. A tall Negro girl in a minishirt up to her quiff (I swear to God, she had dyed her black pubic hair white) was having a spastic reincarnation while a madonna-faced boy with blond hair down to his shoulders held one of her hands, swayed back and forth, and grinned from ear to asshole. From a glowing green bandstand four crazed young men dressed in animal skins were sending out cries of joy regarding LSD and the interior world. Hard-pressed, I could not have proved that we were not lost in the stomach of a deranged dinosaur. My own center of gravity, admittedly an ingratiating sensorium (all right! known to be on the make at the most unlikly hours; and with a police record) was beginning to have second thoughts about itself and its whereabouts. I turned to say something to Sylvia. She had gone. Sitting in her place was the fat little millionaire. I started to scratch my head, and, oh dear, my hand discovered this was impossible because the slick black patent leather of a jailer's hat was on my head. My hand fell in dismay and in so doing brushed against my big breasts.

"Countess," the bottle man was saying to me as he puffed on a huge cigar, "have you given my offer any further thought?"

I laughed, "I must confess, Poochie, that I've forgotten most of it. Please. Give it to me again, like a good boy."

He shook his sleek little head. "Oh Countess! If I were not so much in love with you, your casualness would drive me mad. Really it would. Well . . . the offer. It is simply this. Join me in Ecuador and take over our fabulous playground in the lake country. Our elite retreat needs your fantastic talents." He smiled through his cigar smoke, a tiny-toothed doll smile that reminded me of my Uncle Hugo, who was a barker for a sideshow in Prague, before the Nazis came and killed him and the others. "Name your price, my darling."

Helena turned to me and shouted through the wonderful noise unnecessarily, "Don't sell yourself cheap, Freda!"

"I never do, darling," I replied, winking at her. "I have many weaknesses, but that is not one of them." I returned my amused, haughty gaze to little Poochie. "And who comes to this remote paradise of yours?"

He chuckled and beamed like a piggy who had just trussed the farmer up over the smoking barbecue pits. "The cream of the cream, from all over the world."

I took a drink of champagne and puffed on the long Russian cigarette that I had taken from Henry Du Pont who was getting drunk next to me and clapping his hands to the music. "Very interesting. Tell me. Who are the owners, besides yourself? Who would be my employers?"

"Some people you may know, as a matter of fact. The Baron de Sousa, Max Longenhoff, Prinz, the Swiss steel magnate, Lily Puegot, the Paris designer, Nino Martinelli, the Italian yachtsman. A lovely and very very wealthy group."

"Ah yes. I know them all, more or less. Except for Longenhoff. Never heard of him."

Poochie leaned through the cigar smoke and the crazy flashing lights and said in a half whisper, "That isn't his real name. His real name," and he looked around to be sure no strangers were listening, of which, of course, there were legion, "his real name is Martin Bormann."

I was stunned. And by so many things in the uttering of that name. While the Negro waitress with adorably long pointy breasts (is she smiling at me? I must get her name and address) gave us more drinks, I thought about Martin Bormann, and Martin Bormann and myself. The last time I saw Martin was the night of Hitler's death. He was running through the bombed-out gardens of the Chancellory above the bunker where we had all been with Dr. Sax. The sounds of shooting and bombing and sirens swept madly around us like an abominable hurricane. The city was burning like something in a Bosch vision. The sky was streaked with streams of tracer bullets. The perfume of explosives strangled the air. Fire was devouring the city.

"Hurry Freda!" he shouted, turning in his running. "Come with me! This way. Hurry!"

Something made me stop, I don't know what. A shell exploded near the Chancellory, blowing a huge hole in the wall. I was suddenly terribly confused and afraid. Part of me said to run with Martin and escape death in Berlin. He had planned his escape weeks before. Every foot of it, all the way through Germany and France and Spain to South America. The other half of me said no. I knew that I had to get to my father as fast as possible.

"Hurry, Freda!"

I began to run out of the garden in the direction of my father's basement apartment in the Gartenstrasse.

"Where are you going, you stupid little bitch?" he screamed.

I did not answer. I just kept running. Far down the street two

Russian tanks were rolling and firing their guns at the apartments.

"Bitch! Bitch!" he howled, and just as I was turning a corner he fired his pistol at me. The bullet hit the side of the building a few inches from my face and splinters of stone cut my face. But I did not feel a thing.

So many people said that Martin was killed in the streets by the Russians who were killing everyone. But of course I never believed those official stories. Martin is almost impossible to destroy. The only way you can do it, I am sure, is to drive a stake through his heart. He is not quite human. Those insane weeks that followed! What I went through to cease being Freda Schwitters to become the Countess. The forging of documents, the burning of records, the plastic surgery from the little Czech doctor on the Stuka Platz. The money and the unspeakable depravities I had to perform with him to get him to change my face just a little. How happy I was to kill him—the man who literally created me, the only person who knew that I was not me. The absurd noise he made as he died: a little fart.

Do I miss the thrills and the dangers of those days with Martin Bormann? I was just a girl, fifteen, and Martin gave me the power of life and death over anyone in Germany. Anyone! Except Der Fuehrer and Eva. No one could touch them. The only ones who could destroy them were themselves. And they did that, of course. We burned them later, and now they are ashes in the winds. I myself poured one of the cans of petrol on their bodies. I did this at the request of Goering. He felt it was the personal touch. The soldiers represented the Nazi touch, I suppose. He was so terrified that the Russians would get his body and keep it on exhibit in Moscow for all eternity to spit upon. It amused Martin to give a young girl like me—his "baby marzipan" he called me—the power of my whims. It was not, as many people said, that Martin was insane. He was not. He simply did not care about human life.

"I thought Frau Hofer and her husband the Prussian colonel were very rude to you at their party, don't you?" he would say.

"Well, yes, I suppose so."

"For no reason at all. Just because they do not approve of you."

"Ach! Who cares what they think."

"And of course that is a way of showing disrespect for me."

"Yes. You are right, Martin."

296 | *Chandler Brossard*

"You do not like that sort of thing, do you?" he would say.

"Not at all."

"And you want them punished, of course."

"Yes. I demand that they be punished."

"Ah, good. Your orders shall be carried out immediately, my little darling."

And he would pick up the phone, call his special police—more special than even Himmler's—and order the immediate arrest of Colonel Hofer and his wife on charges of disloyalty to the Third Reich. They were never heard of again. All of the people I had ever disliked, who had ever been bad to me since I could remember, I had taken care of. Eliminated. Pfft! The swine who made me cry in my elementary school history class, Buder. The fat-faced social worker who made me get a job as a kitchen worker, Liza Kampf. The greasy butcher who always cheated my poor old father because he did not understand how the weighing scales worked. My uncle Horst because he would never give us any money to get along on. All such people got paid off all right and they never knew what it was all about and who had arranged to have them sent to the concentration camps by the secret police. And that was not all. Martin always asked my advice about procedure if he had the slightest doubt himself. He relied on the strength of my innocence, so to speak.

"That young officers' club in Helsinki," he said one evening. "You know, the homosexual elite of our SS in Finland. They have been worrying me."

"Yes, Martin my darling."

"Such degenerates are a security risk. What if a Russian agent were to pose as a homosexual and get vital information?"

"I see what you mean."

"I think they should be taken out of commission right away, before something very bad happens. Don't you agree?"

"Without a doubt. You are very right in your suspicions, my wonderful Martin."

Within the night a dozen men were arrested, dragged out into the falling snow, and executed for "treason." No trial. No questions and answers. Just the sound of the firing squad. Martin was always immensely pleased when such a purge was carried out after getting my backing, and I was swamped with fabulous presents.

Leopard-skin jackets. A Mercedes coupe. A genuine pearl neck-lace. (Which of course had simply been taken from the neck of some unlucky rich woman "in the interests of the Fatherland." But I did not care whose neck it had been around. It had belonged to a family of oysters once, so what difference could it make?)

Martin was so funny. As an "upholder of the dignity and purpose of Hitler's Third Reich" he could not bear other people's sexual amusements, but he saw absolutely nothing wrong with having his own outrageous sex parties. How wild and ingenious they were too! I can still feel them all over my body, to this very moment. In my mouth, on my tongue, in my cunt, up my ass, biting on my breasts, fucking in my armpits. Ohhh heavens. Lots of people. Martin would invite a handful of his own secret police force buddies—the only humans he could trust, more or less—and I would round up some of my girl friends—all of them were very gay and ready for any kind of sport; for what else was there, really, in those crazy days?—and away we would go. The longest party lasted for a week. We held it in Martin's place in the Alps, not far from Berchtesgaden. My God it was something! What utterly fantastic things humans can do!

"This is an indoor nudist camp," my friend April said one jolly evening. "I have never seen so many naked bodies in one place. Just look at them!"

"Yes. It's so wonderful," said Colonel Weigand, who was stretched out on the rug with a bottle of champagne not five inches from his huge dangling prick. He looked like a great white pan-ther. "Just like my childhood on Lake Garmisch. Hilda over there on top of Kurt looks very much like my cousin Maria except that Maria would never let us suck on her big breasts that way. Great God! Look at her ride him! Oow! It slipped out of her. Now, she's got it back in. Bravo. What a beer barrel of an ass. Excuse me, girls, but I must have some of that."

And he fairly leaped across the big room to get at Hilda, his big pink penis, now stiff and raging, pulling him like a magnet. Hilda shrieked as he grabbed her from behind. Holding onto her breasts, but not moving her from her position above Kurt, except to lift her off his cock, the colonel slammed his monster in her from behind, deep into the living room where Kurt had been such a well-behaved guest, and amidst her squeals and Kurt's delighted laughter, gave it to her good. They thrust and writhed like that for a couple of minutes and then Kurt, who was not to be satisfied with merely watching, guided her willing head down to his own still erect emissary, which Hilda seemed almost to swallow, and none of this in any way interfered with her screwing with Weigand. Oh she was a very agile partner she was. She was not one of those dumb cows who can do only one thing at a time.

"Ah, Ernst!," April murmured from her chair behind me. "You devil!"

I looked around, and there was Major Ernst von Hassler, an ordinarily very correct and even forbidding chap, when sober, that is, on his hands and knees licking April's legs. Someone had painted a big swastika on his bare back with a red lipstick. April giggled and drank her champagne. His curled mustache was tickling her a bit. "Delicious, Ernst," April said. "I wish you would teach this to my masseur."

A Marlene Dietrich song came on the phonograph now, and wreathed in and out of the laughter and giggling and occasional shrieks in this room and the big bedroom down the hall. Ilsa and a plumpish but very attractive girl named Bettina were dancing in front of the big mirror and it was amusing to watch their unreal nonexistent reflected selves moving in such crazy harmony with the live humans. They were kissing and playing with each other as they slowly danced. They were both quite drunk but this did not effect the kind of dancing they were doing. Bettina began to put her tongue in Ilsa's ear. On the fur-covered couch near the big portrait of Hitler, Martha, who has the most marvelous long black hair, had passed out, or perhaps just fallen asleep from fatigue, while Iggy Schultz, *ober lieutenant*, excuse me, was busy licking her thickly pelted pussy. His work, or pleasure I should say, was a bit complicated by the fact that she was curled up on her side, but he was maneuvering very well from the back in an upside down position. His feet almost knocked over a lamp on the table near Martha's head, but it managed to right itself. Across the room George, who was a writer for that little garbage Goebbels, was eating a big sausage and drinking beer while Rosemarie, who was wearing her high heeled black boots, and nothing more, stood over him and massaged his neck. Her long swooping breasts brushed his head from time to time when she leaned over to caress his hairy chest.

I couldn't see Martin anywhere in the room so I decided to look for him. I wanted very much to have sex again. Once I get started, particularly in one of our orgies, I must have it half a dozen times or I feel strange and hungry and very angry. It takes a lot to satisfy me. I am very animal and I am proud of it. None of that nonsense of gentility or niceness ever got its hold on me thank God. Perhaps this is because my mother died when I was a baby and I raised myself on the streets while Pappa was out working. Those polite and fragile women I see everywhere make me sick, positively sick. I would like to slap their faces, hard, slap a little animal passion into them. Then their poor husbands might have some good times for a change and would not have to look for tavern girls to be naughty and abnormal with. Yes, a good beating is what those prissy proud bitches need to get their blood up and their woman juices bubbling. Right now those juices are dead, like the streams in underground caverns, dead and stinking.

"Hans! You are hurting me!" Hilda shouted.

"Be still," he said. "You'll get used to it."

"My behind is still sore from last night. You should put more cream on."

In the corner Martha began to moan with pleasure as Iggy progressed in his dedicated licking.

"George, darling, do you like that?"

"You are marvelous, absolutely marvelous. Pour me some more beer."

April, that naughty thing, began to giggle and poured her champagne over poor Ernst's head. I walked down the hall looking for Martin, truly aching for pleasure. The others having theirs was driving me to distraction, I can tell you. I was so hot and jumpy between my legs. My God, I wanted to bite a piece out of a body, so help me. Laughter was coming from our bedroom. Martin's and a girl's. Then another voice. Zachary. He has a voice that sounds like a dirty beerhall baritone. It's so funny. Zachary is an unfrocked priest. He was booted out of his parish in Silesia for drinking and whoring and stealing church monies. Nothing halfway about him. He would have picked a saint's stone pocket, I do believe. But of course he still might have loved God. Life is so very funny. "It is a crime what they have done to the image of Christ," he once told me. "He was a fine gutter chap and they've made him look like a pansy. Phew!"

I opened the bedroom door. Oh what a sight! The three of them looked like a tumbling act in a carnival. Really! Kosta Berne, a red-haired girl who worked part time as an informer in the SS office, and a wolf among wolves if you know what I mean, was sitting on Zachary's lap being screwed with her back to him, while he played with her breasts, and at the same time, in the same motion, you might say, she was sucking the cock of Martin who was standing in front of her. He was holding her bushy red head while she was holding onto his muscular buttocks. You could not have asked for a tighter physical performance. Many people go their entire lives without half that nice an arrangement. Their coordination was excellent (naturally, because these people are not Johnny-come-latelys to the orgy stage): Kosta's bobbing head was completely timed with the thrust of Martin's cock into her mouth, while Zachary's lap pumping was so understandingly managed that Kosta never received any sudden out-of-proportion, unsynchronized hot pleasure jabs that would have distracted her from her mouth fun and made her suddenly pull back in a one-sided ecstasy. Yes, it was most admirable.

Suddenly from the kitchen below came the radio news. It was Goebbels. "Gentlemen, in a hundred years' time they will be showing a fine color film describing the terrible days we are living through. Don't you want to play a part in that film? Hold out now, so that a hundred years hence the audience does not hoot and whistle when you appear on the screen."

All his words, so long familiar to me, with their rage and insinuation, floated to a special place in my brain where nothing happens. I did not feel they were happening now. The radio was suddenly turned off. Oddly, it was as though I had not heard that snarling voice at all. So many things like that happened then and they did not seem real. The others there acted as though the voice had not been heard. So perhaps it hadn't.

"Martin," I said, "what a sly rascal you are. Disappearing with your playmates without telling me. Shame on you."

He laughed. "You were so busy when I last saw you, Freda my love. You were in the showers with Kurt." A look of sudden bliss came over his face as Kosta changed her technique and began to tickle the tip of his cock with her tongue, very dainty little touches full of electricity. "Ah that is just splendid, Kosta darling. Your tongue is a master. Mm. It really deserves a commission. A colonel in the interior security force. Full rank. Yes. That's what I shall do."

I stood there thinking of some way that I could participate in their joy game, but as I was considering various ingenious possibilities including rimming Martin's behind, a delight he is quite fond of and calls "tipping the velvet," I saw that they were approaching the fever peak of pleasure. What an artistic triumph if they all came together! A Beethoven chamber piece! Zachary began to pant, Martin's face turned red and he closed his eyes, Kosta suddenly plunged her mouth over his cock and her nails tore into the flesh of his buttocks. Then, as one person, Zachary howled and bit into Kosta's back, Martin let out a great sigh like a martyr giving up his life for Christ, and Kosta, her stuffed mouth stifling all but the fringes of her screams, stiffened in a great spasm that shuddered over her body. Before I was even aware of it, I too was contributing a sort of moan to their sounds. The entire room seemed to leap out of itself and come alive as the three of them exploded with supreme sexual joy. Like a huge man-eating flower in a burst of blood ecstasy. Plant and animal became one. That is strange, because it means a kind of dying. But that always happens when a person becomes part of something else. They stop being the thing they were before. A strange death to be sure. Very strange, and beyond understanding.

Kosta and Zachary and Martin, the three drunken acrobats, collapsed to the big mink rug and lay there for a while in a seeming stupor of satisfaction and spentness. I lay among them. The fur felt so eerily delightful on my naked, hungry body. All those little animals—did they not die in order to become this rug? Of course they did. They were squealing little rodents; now they are a fabulously rich rug caressing me. It is all very simple.

"You know," Martin murmured, his head on my belly, "we killed seven thousand Russians yesterday. In the Crimea."

"Only seven thousand?" mumbled Zachary sort of sleepily and woozy.

"Yes," said Kosta without opening her eyes, "that isn't so very many, Martin. There are millions of those dirty swine."

"I did not make myself very clear," Martin said, fondling Kosta's foot that was plopped on his chest. "That was in just one engagement alone, with our Fifth Panzer Unit. You understand. There are many, many engagements."

Zachary turned over on his stomach now and reached for the champagne bottle at the foot of the huge bed. "Ah well," he said, taking a big drink, a good deal of it spilling down his beard. "That is different, dear Martin. Very different. Burp! Indeed."

"Mm," Kosta muttered. "Quite. Much much better, Martin."

"You should not think our Panzer boys are losing their touch," said Martin, drinking from his big bowl of brandy and handing it to me. "That would be most unpatriotic."

"Unthinkable. Burp!" said Zachary.

"What happens to dead Russians, Martin?" I asked, the brandy burning my tongue so very beautifully.

He chuckled. "They become fertilizer."

"That's good. At least they serve some purpose."

A throaty cave sound came from Zachary. "It is about time, that's all I can say."

Now Kosta giggled softly. "Martin, do you know what fat General Hochmuth told me last week?"

Martin now began caressing my furry crotch. I opened my legs a little so he could put his hand in deeper. "No. What did fat old Hochmuth tell you, Kosta?"

She giggled again, still keeping her eyes closed. "Well, Martin, he told me that the Russian Army was killing many more Germans than we are told officially and that we are losing the war. That's what he told me, Martin."

I felt Martin's body stiffen with anger. "Hochmuth is a filthy liar and a traitor!" he shouted, sinking his clutching fingers so hard into my thigh that I cried out. "And he will pay dearly for spreading such disgusting lies. Yes, very dearly."

Kosta sat up now and leaned over Martin, her rich red hair falling in front of his face even down to her heavy sullen breasts. "But Martin . . . other people have said the same thing. My cousin Ramina got a perfectly dreadful letter from her husband who said his soldiers are freezing to death by the . . . ."

Martin leaped up like a giant spring and yanked Kosta to her feet and slapped her face, bang! bang! "You are a rotten little lying whore!" he shouted. "I could have you put in a concentration camp for talking such garbage."

Kosta began to sob. "Please, Martin. Please. I am so sorry."

"Pig!" he yelled.

He picked her up and kicked upon the doors of the balcony and carried her out. I was terribly afraid yet I was thrilled by what he might do.

"Martin!" she screamed. "please don't!"

"See how you like this, you piece of trash," he said, and heaved her off the balcony. She screamed a terrible scream. In a couple of seconds there was a big splash as she fell into the lake two stories below.

"Oh my," I heard myself say.

Martin stalked back inside and called his special office on the phone. He angrily threw a pamphlet to the floor that he had been reading. He was always reading to see if he could discover cleverer ways of doing things. It fell half open at my feet. I picked it up, it was written by somebody named Hebb. I read a line Martin had underlined. "The restricted dogs haven't the brains to be bored." Then Martin was shouting in the phone. He instructed his man to pick up General Hochmuth immediately and to hold him incommunicado until tomorrow morning. "I've always hated that fat son of a bitch," he said, hanging up. "He can't be trusted at all."

I held out my arms. "Come here to me, Martin, darling. Let me hold you and comfort you."

He drank off his bowl of brandy and lay in my arms, muttering all kinds of fierce things—loyalty and dying and Hitler.

Zachary sighed. "Poor silly Kosta. I've told her to curb her little tongue. Ah well, once a grocer's daughter, always a grocer's daughter." He guzzled and slopped more champagne. "Breeding always shows, believe me."

Martin began sucking on my breast, just like a baby that wants a little comfort from mommy. At night Martin couldn't go to sleep without having my breast in his mouth first. I know of many men who need this. But I am sure that none of the other powerful Nazis around Hitler would have dreamed this of Martin. They just knew him to be a fiercely and cunningly efficient brute. I glanced up at the big portrait of Der Fuehrer over the bed. Every night (sometimes in the day too) our leader watched as we did our little tricks to each other. He was such a prude. I did many disgusting things just to shock that picture. But a funny thing . . .

One of Goebbels' mistresses told me that Eva Braun had confessed to her once that the sort of sex Hitler engaged in with her was positively depraved. I remember one thing in particular that centered around her menstrual pads. Oh dear. Also that he likes to dress up in women's clothes. All this behind those big double locked doors of course. There was absolutely no chance of anyone surprising them in one of their strange scenes.

Our reverie was interrupted by the appearance of April. She was very tipsy, and she was wearing Kurt's Air Force hat cocked on the side of her beautiful golden head. She had a simply divine body. White velvet. Heavy jutting nipples that were always so red and alive you thought some one had just finished nibbling on them. And the sort of bottom that makes all men turn to watch her walk down the street. Sway really, because April did not walk as if she had to get anywhere. She strolled to bring joy to the day. If only I had five dollars for every fantasy that April's behind had provoked. I would be a millionaire several times.

"Goodness gracious," she said, with that mocking smile. "You haven't all gone to sleep, have you? To come all the way to the Alps to have a snooze. Really!"

"April darling!" cried Zachary. "Come here at once and let Father Zachary give you a big kiss."

Zachary's idea of a kiss was just as unorthordox as an upside down crucifix. Instead of standing up to kiss her on the mouth when she came to him, he simply rose up on his knees and buried his face in the sunshine hair between her legs and kissed her pussy. "Mm," he said, falling back on the fur rug, "you are an infinity of good tastes. If there had been nuns like you around my parish, I would never have left the service of Our Lord." He turned to Martin. "You know, Martin, old chap, the only reason the church has lost its hold on the modern imagination is its outlawing of sexual participation in the glory of Our Lord."

Martin grunted. "The church is a pot of old lady shit. We are going to dump that pot on the Pope's head one of these days soon. Mark my words. Der Fuehrer told me just the other day that if the Vatican does not hand over to us that bunch of diplomats who are hiding there, we will go in and get them." He chuckled. "I wonder how his Holiness would feel with a German submachine gun up his fat Italian ass. Hah!"

"Oh dear," April said, "if you're going to talk politics, I'm leaving."

"No! No!" I shouted, and pulled her down on the rug. "Pass that champagne, Zachary you old glutton. Whatever became of your manners?"

April took a big drink, then another. She leaned over Martin, put her mouth on mine, and squirted the champagne down my throat. Adorable funny girl! Perhaps she got these charming ways from her mother, who was a famous movie actress and for years the mistress of the big coal tycoon, Kepple. April was their illegitimate child. It was whispered that the old man shared her bed as well as her mother's. And why not? I mean, if you can make guns to kill people, why can't you sleep with your own daughter?

"I have a marvelous idea," April announced. "Let's make a movie. A crazy wonderful movie."

Martin clapped his hands. "Bravo! I will show you what a splendid actor I am."

"There has never been any doubt of that, Martin," Zachary said, but Martin didn't catch his meaning. Martin was not too intelligent with humor. Perhaps because he thought that witty people were weak.

April's movie—what a movie! She had such a freaky sense of fun. Our movie, which Helmut the manservant shot (he had been a projectionist in a movie house before spending time in prison for blackmail) was about the real story of Helen of Troy. Oh that April! She played the lead role—it was her movie, wasn't it?— Martin played Hector, Zachary played Paris (Paris with a bald head and beard!) and I played Hector's wife Andromache. April had gone to good schools for awhile (her mother wanted her to be a lady of refinement, you see), that's how she knew about such historical things. Martin got to play Hector, who was really more of a hero than Paris, because his cock was bigger than Zachary's, not because of his superior acting ability. I later discovered that many acting roles, in Paris and Rome as well as Hollywood, are awarded on the grounds of genital abilities, and why not? Many times I was to hear an actor characterized by such standards. "Magnani is marvelous. She acts with her cunt." Or, "The exciting thing about Richard Burton is that when he is on the stage you feel he has a hard-on. This makes the stage pant." Zachary's cock, by the way, was fatter than Martin's, which threw us into a heated debate about what makes the man's tool more effective, its length or its width. April decided the point, in her usual unexpected way.

"A fat cock is better for sucking," she said, holding Zachary's in her hand as an exhibit. "A long cock is wasted in a girl's mouth because there is nothing back there for it to tickle. But inside a girl's box there is."

Martin beamed. "Well, put. A good German cock gets to the heart of the matter. Zachary, my friend, your manhood was foully betrayed by your maternal Hungarian ancestry."

Zachary, looking at his now stiffening plunger in April's small hand, said, "My boy, you have heard the verdict on your destiny. You must stop peeking up women's dresses and address yourself to their faces. Do you understand! You have been going about life the wrong way."

Of course, my own experience is that it doesn't matter how long or fat the item in question is. What counts is whether it is quick-witted and can use its imagination at just the right moment. My cunt is heavy with the memory of the tons of dull-witted meat that have gloomed its succulence.

Our movie was the greatest of fun. The others—eight satiated nudists in various stages of drunkenness—assembled in the rose garden to watch our performance, eating and drinking and yelling just as the crowds in Shakespeare's time did, before audiences decided they must be refined and well-behaved. Oh, you have no idea what those mad Greeks did behind the walls of Troy! To put it mildly, you do not get the true story in your schoolbooks, not by a very long shot. For example, did you know that the real quarrel, the nitty gritty, as my dear friend Sartre would say, was not about Paris and Helen but about Helen and Andromache. They were having a passionate affair and this was driving Hector insane with jealousy, to say nothing of what it was doing to Queen Hecuba, King Priam, and other members of the royal court. No one seemed to mind that Hector and Paris had their little incestuous bisexual business going on the side, or that Cassandra drew pictures, pornographic of course, of the enemy Achilles all over her bedroom walls. But then, has life ever been fair?

It was not surprising that the scene that ran away with the production was a bedroom action between me and April, Helen and Andromache, that is. It was a triumph of tongues.

Helen: Tell me again, Andromache, that you think of nothing but me. (She bends Andromache back.)

Andromache: I do! I do! Dearest Helen of my heart!

Helen: Do you think of me when you are in Hector's arms?

Andromache: Yes! Yes! I could not bear a moment of his foul touch if I did not imagine that it is you.

Helen: Good, good. Tell me once more what your life was like before the gods dragged me to this scene.

Andromache: Oh sweetest Helen! Savior of my mother's dreams! I was the dirt beneath the camel's foot, the scum the maids washed from the kitchen pots, the lonely wind that blew across the rooftops at darkest night, the staring eye of the dead fish that washed up on the desolate beach.

Helen (pulling her back up and very close to her): What would be the most divine thing you could wish to take place with you at this moment, lovely trembling woman?

Andromache (running her hands up and down Helen's bare back, and moaning without restraint): To feel the exquisite poetry of your tongue rhyming itself in the waiting tenderness of my woman's secret chamber.

Helen: Splendid, dearest Andromache. Such words do make my own body a shrine of a thousand harps. (Andromache lies on the couch and Helen moves her legs up and widely apart, thoroughly exposing her parts. Helen kneels on the floor and puts her head between Andromache's thighs.) Ah, honey-stricken Andromache! Flower of Troy's royal garden! A thousand downy delights whisper their secrets to my throbbing skin! The taste of your clitoris is spring's promise unsheathed! (She dives back to licking Andromache.)

Andromache (writhing and curling her fingers in Helen's long blond hair): Ahh! Priestess of pleasure! Nightingale in my unrequited silence! My soul is rising to your song.

Helen: Now we shall be as one, a double-headed love of single purpose (and she climbs atop Andromache in the 69 position and they eat furiously away at each other. Enter Hector and Paris, arms around each other, staggering in happy drunkenness and singing a bawdy song about a siren who had a blind passion for an aging octopus).

Paris: . . . and he wrapped an arm around her . . .

Hector: . . . so that he could better sound her . . . (sees the girls going at it) What ho! Zeus! What manner of monster is this?

Paris: By Jove! (He tilts one head up, looks at the face, puts it back in crotch, then does the same to the other head.) Helen here and Adromache there, or vice versa, dear Hector, or both. Joined in love's low labor.

Hector: Unnatural women! Gorgons of degeneracy! Lash them, Paris! Lash them! Let their blood wash away their vile stain.

Paris (picking up a thin whip from the floor): So be it, Hector. My whip shall be their conscience and their guide. (Begins to lash Helen and Andromache. Shrieking, they leap off couch and run around stage. Paris chases and whips them. Hector howls with rage and pleasure and joins in with his sword belt. Women are responding to whipping as much with fierce sexual pleasure as they are with genuine pain. Men also are having their strange passions inflamed. Suddenly Queen Hecuba [nee Ilsa] appears on stage. Whole scene amazes her.)

Hecuba (pointing first at Helen then at Andromache): Our garden become a snakepit. Vile bodies! Oh madness! Oh treachery!

Helen (frantic): I can explain! It's all very simple.

Hecuba: Zeus! Punishment! Thunder and lightning and destruction! (And such does descend upon the stage.)

But dear God in Heaven, the weird thing was the coincidence of our stage fun thunder and an actual bomb explosion in the house and garden, an assassin's attempt to kill Martin and his Nazi friends. And this explosion, which for a few minutes wiped out the present, in which present my identity as Freda was rooted, wiped that identity out too, leaving me as Andromache in Troy and April as Helen, my companion, caught prisoner, you might say, in our own rearranging of time and place and person and doomed to wander in this artful conceit until released and returned to our true selves, if such a thing truly exists, by a similar act of freak coincidence, or the hand of God, or someone's crazy imagination run rampant in history, as when everyone assumed the earth was flat and behaved accordingly, or when the police create out of their own strategic necessity an assassin of the prime minister, who escapes and is the object of international manhunts and civic fantasy, when all along the police themselves did the dirty job at the bidding of another political faction. But we all know that the mythical man does assume reality nonetheless and takes his place in that ever-shifting dimension between what is and what isn't and what could just as logically be.

Suffice it is to say, all of us scrambled for our lives. I don't know what happened to Paris and Hector and Hecuba, but as for myself and Helen, we ended up living for a while in the belly of that fantastic wooden horse the clever Greeks built to fool the lazy Trojans. Along with dozens of other Trojans (and some beat Greek soldiers too) who had taken all they could from the outside world. How extraordinary! Escaping from outrageous fortune by squatting in the belly of a metaphor! Helen and I—or April and I, or all four of us—simplified, and yet of course complicated, our lives by assuming the identity of simple Trojan housemaids. Life in the horse's belly would have been unbearably sticky otherwise.

"It stinks in here," she said to me one morning, looking about at the strange encampment of refugees.

"Yes," I replied, "but it stinks out there too."

She made a face. "How long are we going to be holed up here?"

"Your guess is as good as mine."

She rubbed her behind. "That crazy bastard Paris ought to have his head examined. He didn't have to lay it on so hard. Ooh. I'll ache till I go to the grave."

Several yards away from us, near the opening to the horse's giant leg, a young mother gave her squalling child her breast, while her weary bearded husband, his toga in rags and his sword missing from his belt, dreamily gnawed a goat bone.

Suddenly I realized that my dog Thor was not there with me. I looked around. Nowhere. "Has anyone seen a large black dog?" I shouted into the tattered rabble.

"A frothing beast with an iron cross around its neck?" an old woman answered from afar. "Yes."

She cackled, a sound that should have come from cracked stone. "You'll never see that animal again. Ulysses took him on his ship."

XII

MISSED ME, HAVEN'T YOU? WHERE'S the crazed little dumpling been—that's what you've been asking youselves, right? In jail? In somebody's freezer? Nope. I've been in another play. A real knockout. We opened in a new theatre: The Missing Link Playhouse. And this time I'm going to help you out a little. I'm going to let you in on the fact that I play the part of the secretary. No candy wrapper noises, please. Here we go! *The Test of True Friendship!*

Oops! I just remembered something that may make things a bit more comfortable for you. It is a statement made to me just the other day by that splendid scholar G. Wilson Knight. We were gabbling about Shakespeare and he said, apropos a new field theory of his own, "His hero is not an isolated 'character' rigidly conceived, but in direct and living relation to his own dramatic environment . . . it is precisely such a 'relationship' that lies regularly behind Shakespeare's use of symbolism as distinct from persons."

Okay. Now we'll open the saturnalia.

SCENE I

SCENE IS THE OFFICE OF LUTHER WATSON. HE IS AN EXECUTIVE. HE IS SURROUNDED BY PHONES AND THE PARAPHERNALIA OF HIS STATION. HE IS ON THE PHONE, AND WAITING PATIENTLY IS HIS SECRETARY, MISS BEDERMEYER, PENCIL IN HAND.

WATSON

(into the phone)

No! No! You're absolutely wrong. I can assure you that the Argentine pork market is as steady as it ever was. What? Don't be absurd! The Brazilians couldn't raise a pig if they had to! *(Other phone rings and he picks it up)* Hello? Ah, Briggs. I want you to build me six air tankers instead of three. Why? Because water is passe! *(Another phone rings)* Amalgamated Alloys? I want to report a flaw in your last shipment. The beams were all one-sixteenth of an inch short. No, I'm sorry. You'll have to melt them all down again. *(Grabs another phone.)* Philbrick and Morgan? Good. I want you to buy me fourteen thousand shares of AC&C. That's right. I've decided to corner the market. No. Just for the fall season. *(He hangs up and pauses in a moment of transitional awe. Then he turns to his secretary.)* Where was I?

SECRETARY

You were in the middle of a letter to the Philippine Daughters of the American Revolution.

WATSON

(leaning back)

Ah yes. "I am sending you herewith my check for five thousand dollars to help you keep up the good work. Don't ever stop believing in what you believe in. Keep your colors flying! Good health! Amen."

SECRETARY

Any more for today, sir?

WATSON

(sighing deeply)

No, my dear. I'm a bit fagged out. Besides, I'm expecting a very important visit from my old friend Jonathan Weeks.

SECRETARY

(smiling happily)

A most delightful and attractive human being.

WATSON

Indeed he is. And a chap who absolutely lives up to the full responsibilities of friendship. There is nothing he won't do for you! *(Slams his fist down on the desk)*

SECRETARY

(almost swooning)

I understand—I understand.

WATSON

(smiling dreamily to himself)

Friendship and belief—my two favorite qualities. *(They dream for a second.)* If only the world had more of it.

SECRETARY

Even just a *little* more of it.

WATSON

(almost weeping at the thought of it)

Yes—even just a *(makes pinch gesture)* pinch more. *(After a moment he returns to exec role.)* Miss Bedermeyer, before you go would you see if you can get Mrs. Watson at home.

SECRETARY

It would be a pleasure. *(She gets up to go to the phone.)* How is Mrs. Watson these days, sir?

WATSON

(fearfully)

Mrs. Watson is always in tip top shape, being the type of woman she is.

SECRETARY

(as she dials)

I'm *so* glad. *(They both listen to the phone. They hear the busy signal.)* It seems to be busy.

WATSON

I wonder who she's talking to.

SECRETARY

(jokingly)

There's only one way to find out—and that's to tap the wire!

WATSON

I've thought of that . . . uh, that is, I know that people do such things.

SECRETARY

(still gaily)

The police do it all the time.

WATSON

Lucky fellows. *(Thinks about that for a moment.)* Well, I guess that'll be all for now, Miss Bedermeyer.

SECRETARY

Very good, sir.

AS SHE REACHES THE DOOR, JONATHAN WEEKS RUSHES IN. HE IS THE HANDSOME GOOD FRIEND.

WATSON

(holding out his arms)

Jonathan!

JONATHAN

(holding out his arms)

Luther! *(They embrace.)* My old buddy!

WATSON

My old pal!

SECRETARY

(as she leaves)

It's so wonderful to see two friends together.

SHE LEAVES

JONATHAN

(breathing deeply)

It's certainly good to be alive.

WATSON

(his arm around Jonathan's shoulder)

Isn't it, though? Look outside—at the clean, healthy way nature goes about things. The golden color of the leaves . . . the birds sailing so happily through the brisk air . . .

JONATHAN

Gosh! It reminds me of our old college days . . . the beginning of the football season.

WATSON

Ah, yes . . . a clean, healthy life. *(They begin a football skirmish of old times)* Tackles forward!

JONATHAN

(rushing by)

Touchdown! *(They fall into each other's arms again, laughing)*

WATSON

Friendship! What would life be without it.

WEEKS

(straightening his clothes)

A mockery. A Sahara Desert.

WATSON

Exactly. Jonathan, you're my closest most beloved friend . . .

and I am going to take advantage of that fact to ask a favor of you.
            WEEKS
There isn't anything I wouldn't do for you, Luther, old buddy.
Name it.
            WATSON
(putting his arm around Weeks shoulder)
Thank you, dear friend. *(He pauses)* Jonathan, I want you to
become my wife's lover.
            WEEKS
(after a stunned moment)
Your wife's lover?
            WATSON
(nodding his head)
Yes.
            WEEKS
But you must be joking.
            WATSON
I wish I were. But I am completely serious.
WEEKS MAKES A GESTURE OF ASTONISHMENT.
You see, I want to prove something.
            WEEKS
What, in God's name?
            WATSON
That my wife doesn't really love me. That she is playing a cruel
game with me. That she is really a whore at heart! And the way
for me to prove this once and for all is to catch her in bed with
another man.
WEEKS POINTS TO HIMSELF
Right. It would take far too long and be much too messy if I
waited around until she betrayed me spontaneously, so to speak,
without my help.
            WEEKS
(rubbing his chin thoughtfully)
Yes . . . of course.
            WATSON
(slapping him on the back)

I knew you would understand. So you'll do it?

WEEKS

(shrugging almost helplessly)

Why not? Friendship is friendship.

WATSON

Wonderful! *(Rubs his hands gleefully)* Ah, will I fix that bitch!

WEEKS

But how do you know she will fall for this? After all, to betray your husband with his best friend.

WATSON

(tortured and pleased)

That will appeal to the truly base part of her. That very fact will give the whole business a most deliciously perverse twist.

WEEKS

Hmm . . . perhaps you're right. Well, when do I start?

WATSON

This very evening. Ah, I can hardly wait to get your progress reports.

WEEKS

You want me to give you progress reports?

WATSON

Of course. I want to savor every step she takes toward her self-destruction.

WEEKS

Won't this . . . uh . . . upset you . . . I mean, hearing about how we are betraying you?

WATSON

Not in the least, dear Jonathan. I'm not at all involved in this emotionally. I feel rather like Socrates, proving out a problem.

WEEKS

Like Socrates? . . . Well, so much the better.

WATSON

Yes, it's really the most unemotional thing I've thought of in years. *(He pats himself on the tummy, smiling. Then he looks at his wrist watch.)* What ho! It's lunch time. *(Puts his arm around Weeks)* You're going to be my guest for lunch, old friend.

WEEKS

That's very generous of you, Luther.

WATSON

We'll go to my club. The special today is creamed finnan haddie.

WEEKS

I suppose that's as good a dish as any to start a betrayal with.

THEY START, AND THE PHONE RINGS. WATSON DARTS BACK TO HIS DESK.

WATSON

(on phone)

Hello? Oh, Simpson and Wainwright . . .

AS FADE OUT BEGINS

I want you to buy up every can of Algerian sardines on the market. I'm going to bring the delicatessen people to their knees!

FADE OUT.

SCENE II

WATSON'S OFFICE. HE IS BUSY SIGNING LETTERS, ETC., AS HIS SECRETARY MISS BEDERMEYER SITS BY. HE IS IN FINE FETTLE.

WATSON

(handing secretary a sheaf of correspondence)

There we are, Miss Bedermeyer. Seven corporations have just had their faces lifted.

MISS BEDERMEYER

(with awe as she looks at the papers)

And three simply staggering mergers! Oh, you're in such splendid form this morning, Mr. Watson. You must have had a most restful, satisfying evening.

WATSON

Indeed I did. One of the best I've had in years.

MISS BEDERMEYER

(dreamily)

Homelife . . . connubial bliss . . .

WATSON

I spent the night in town, at my club.

MISS BEDERMEYER

Poor Mrs. Watson. I hope she had something to keep her from being lonely.

WATSON

(grinning triumphantly)

I wouldn't be at all surprised.

MISS BEDERMEYER

Such a lovely woman. I don't imagine she ever thinks of anything but pleasing her husband.

WATSON

(beaming as he thinks of the betrayal)

You are so right, Miss Bedermeyer. Pleasing her husband!

MISS BEDERMEYER

(sighing dreamily)

She must be like Florence Nightingale.

WATSON

(sighing likewise)

Yes. Taking care of the needy.

AS THEY ARE STARING OFF INTO THEIR SEPARATE FANTASIES, THE BUZZER IS HEARD. MISS BEDERMEYER JUMPS UP AND RUSHES INTO THE OUTER OFFICE. IN A MOMENT SHE RETURNS WITH JONATHAN WEEKS.

WATSON

(jumping up and holding out his arms)

Jonathan! My comrade!

WEEKS

(less exuberant)

Good morning, Luther.

WATSON

(turning to his secretary)

That will be all for now, Miss Bedermeyer. And please—I am not to be disturbed for anything while Mr. Weeks is with me. Not one single corporate demand!

MISS BEDERMEYER

(retreating backwards)

As you wish, sir.

WATSON

Now then . . . tell me the good news, Jonathan.

WEEKS

(shyly)

The good news?

WATSON

(impatiently)

Yes . . . you did betray me last night, didn't you?

WEEKS

Well, not exactly.

WATSON

Not exactly?

WEEKS

Luther, it isn't as easy as you think to make a fool out of you.

WATSON

What happened, man, what happened?

WEEKS

(embarrassed)

Well . . . I . . . I laid . . . *(embarrassed)* the groundwork.

WATSON

(exploding)

You're crucifying me! All I want to know is specifically what took place between you and my loathsome wife and all I get from you are figures of speech. *(He holds his head.)*

WEEKS

I'm sorry, old friend. Forgive me. *(He pulls himself up.)* All right. Your wife allowed me certain privileges.

WATSON

(delighted)

Ah! That's more like it. Go on. *(He rubs his hands together.)*

WEEKS

(tenderly)

I measured her foot.

WATSON

(dumbstruck)

You . . .

WEEKS

We were having a pleasant conversation and I bet her that I could guess what size slipper she wore.

WATSON

(feverishly)

How was she dressed at the time?

WEEKS

Completely. Anyway, I made a guess, and I was wrong. Since I couldn't believe the size when she told me, the dear thing allowed me to measure her foot myself.

WATSON

And just how did you go about it?

WEEKS

(matter of factly)

With a tape measure from the maid's sewing basket.

WATSON

(getting up in exasperation and striding about)

Jonathan, are you pulling the wool over my eyes?

WEEKS

I don't know what you mean, my friend.

WATSON

Surely something more . . . conclusive, more incriminating, more satisfactory went on . . . didn't it. My God—a handsome fellow like you and a born streetwalker like my wife. That's a combination that should produce results under any circumstances! *(Weeks shrugs)* Now then . . . what took place after you got through with her foot?

WEEKS

(shyly after a moment)

Well, to tell you the absolute truth . . .

WATSON

(delighted with the prospect)

Ah! That's what I want, the truth!

WEEKS

I kissed her.

WATSON

(jumping in the air with pleasure)

I knew it! I knew it!
WEEKS

I kissed her . . . right here *(He points to his thumb)*
WATSON

(awed)

You kissed her . . . *(Raises his own thumb)* here?
WEEKS

Yes. Right here. *(points to his own thumb again.)*
WATSON

(approaching Weeks menacingly, holding up his thumb)

You kissed my wife on her thumb?
WEEKS

(drawing back in fear)

Yes . . .
WATSON

(grabbing him)

You madman! You can't go on this way! You're wasting my time. *(He throws Weeks toward the door.)* Do something! You fiend!

WEEKS RUSHES OUT. THE LIGHTS BEGIN TO FADE.

WATSON

(like a disappointed worshipper)

Friendship—you can't even count on that anymore.

FADE OUT.

SCENE III

HIS OFFICE AGAIN. WATSON IS ALONE AT HIS DESK. HE IS WORKING WITH HIS PAPERS. HE HAS CHANGED SLIGHTLY. HE SEEMS IN A PHYSI-CAL AND PSYCHOLOGICAL WAY TO BE WEAKENING. HE LOOKS FRAYED. THE PHONE RINGS AFTER A MOMENT.

WATSON

(picking up phone)

Yes? Oh . . . Cheelcroft and Rogers? The coffee bean situation? you say? I should grab them all up? They're going for practically nothing? Well . . . if you want to, get a corner on them, and then

exchange them for those Algerian sardines. I've developed a distaste for small fish.

HE HANGS UP AND STARES OUT INTO SPACE FOR A MOMENT. MISS
BEDERMEYER RUSHES IN. SHE IS BRINGING A ROSE IN A VASE.

MISS BEDERMEYER

A rose from Picardy!

WATSON

Picardy? Where's that?

MISS BEDERMEYER

Where all lovers live!

WATSON

(startled)

Lovers . . . yes, of course. A hot bed of depravity! A sanctuary
of betrayal! Picardy!

MISS BEDERMEYER

(startled)

Mr. Watson!

WATSON

(subsiding)

I'm sorry, Miss Bedermeyer. Forgive me. A case of nerves. I
haven't slept well lately.

MISS BEDERMEYER

Are you still at the club?

WATSON

(slowly)

Yes, still at the club.

MISS BEDERMEYER

(after a moment)

Well, on to our work. There was some correspondence with
the Boys Club of America.

WATSON

Yes . . . Send them a check for ten thousand.

MISS BEDERMEYER

(writing)

And shall we say a few kind words?

WATSON

Give the poor lads my love, and bid them beware . . . of chippies on the make!

MISS BEDERMEYER

Oh sir!

WATSON

(leaping up)

Get Jonathan Weeks in here!

MISS BEDERMEYER

(leaping up in terror and rushing around the room)

Jonathan Weeks! Jonathan Weeks!

IN A FLASH, WEEKS RACES INTO THE ROOM, PUTTING ON HIS JACKET.

WEEKS

At your service!

MISS BEDERMEYER HURRIES OUT IN PANIC.

WATSON

(grabbing him)

There you are! Where's your report?

WEEKS

(pulling away)

My report? Of course . . . We had a most delicious evening!

WATSON

None of your lies now. None of your folderol.

WEEKS

You look for lies like a dog smells for fireplugs.

WATSON

She came through, did she not? She revealed her true self! She wallowed in her knowledge of my weakness! Say it!

WEEKS

She was divine.

WATSON

(screaming with delight and pain)

Oh thank heaven! *(He prances about the room victoriously)* Confirmation, thy name is woman!

WEEKS

She said things of a most extraordinary nature.

WATSON

What? What?

WEEKS

(proudly)

She talked about things that interest her.

WATSON

Things that interest her? Pah! Did the bitch give herself?

WEEKS

She promised . . .

WATSON

(lighting up)

She promised.

AS THE LIGHTS FADE

WEEKS

She promised to give the matter serious consideration.

FADE OUT.

SCENE IV

THE OFFICE SHOWS THE DECLINE OF WATSON. IT IS DISARRAYED AND
MESSY. MISS BEDERMEYER IS BUSY CLEANING AND STRAIGHTENING.

MISS BEDERMEYER

(clucking)

The way he's letting things go lately . . . I just don't understand
it . . . he used to be so fastidious.

SHE CONTINUES FIXING, ETC. IN A MOMENT WATSON ENTERS. HE IS
VIRTUALLY A CHANGED MAN. HE LOOKS AS THOUGH HE HAS SLEPT IN
HIS CLOTHES. HE IS YAWNING. HE IS CARRYING ONE SHOE IN HIS HAND.

Good morning, Mr. Watson

WATSON

(yawning and scratching himself as he heads for his desk)

My back is killing me.

MISS BEDERMEYER

Oh, I'm so sorry! Did you strain it while playing squash at the
club?

WATSON

(picking up mail, glancing wearily at it, and tossing it over his shoulder)

I got it from sleeping on an old cot in the attic.

MISS BEDERMEYER

The attic?

WATSON

Yes. I've taken up temporary residence there . . .

MISS BEDERMEYER

But there are so many beautiful rooms downstairs . . .

WATSON

(woefully)

I can't go into them anymore . . . they've become impenetrable to me . . . *(The phone rings. Watson slowly picks it up)* Hello . . . Standard Oil? . . . No thank you. I am no longer in the Arabian sand market. *(Hangs up)*

MISS BEDERMEYER

(worriedly)

Have you had breakfast, Mr. Watson?

WATSON

I bought an apple from a blind man.

MISS BEDERMEYER

Goodness. You must be dying for a cup of coffee.

SHE RUSHES OUT TO FETCH IT.

WATSON

(holding up a check and looking at it)

A dividend of twenty thousand dollars . . . What good is it to me now? Who can I share it with? What will it buy but more horrifying revelations? *(He slowly tears up the check and throws it over his shoulder.)*

MISS BEDERMEYER RETURNS WITH A STEAMING CUP OF COFFEE AND A BAGEL.

MISS BEDERMEYER

Here you are, sir. This should certainly life your spirits.

WATSON

(taking her hand and kissing it)

My one true friend.

MISS BEDERMEYER

(as she returns from the office)

It's a privilege to serve a man with your character and distinction, Mr. Watson.

EXITS. WATSON BEGINS SOAKING HIS BAGEL IN HIS COFFEE AND MUNCHING REFLECTIVELY. NOW JONATHAN WEEKS SLOWLY, SNEAKILY, GUILTILY COMES IN. WATSON DOES NOT SEE HIM. HE STANDS THERE FOR A MOMENT, THEN CLEARS HIS THROAT. NO RESPONSE FROM WATSON.

WEEKS

(finally)

Luther . . .

WATSON

(slowly raising his head)

A voice is calling to me . . .

WEEKS

It's me, Luther. Your old pal Jonathan Weeks . . .

WATSON

(dreamily)

Jonathan Weeks . . . *(He turns abruptly and yells)* Jonathan Weeks!

WEEKS

(coming forward now)

I didn't mean to interrupt you at your breakfast, Luther . . .

WATSON

(the tragic, broken man)

Think nothing of it. What is a little nourishment in the face of major news?

JONATHAN NODS HIS HEAD UNDERSTANDINGLY

You have good news for me, my friend?

WEEKS

I have the news you want, Luther.

WATSON

(tragically happy)

At last . . . the whore of Babylon reveals her true self . . .
WEEKS

She promised to go to bed with me . . .
WATSON

(jumping up)

Hurray!
WEEKS

. . . because she knows that's what you want her to do.
WATSON

(amazed)

What?
WEEKS

She revealed to me that she has known all along that you put
me up to this *(Watson gasps in horror)* but she didn't really mind,
if that's the way you wanted it. She said there was nothing she
wouldn't do to please you . . . even if it meant betraying you.
(Pause, as Watson becomes demonic) Your wife, Luther, loves you!
WATSON

(screaming)

No! No!
WEEKS

Yes!
WATSON

(the animal at final bay)

This is a trick you two have concocted to drive me out of my
mind . . . the final stroke to destroy me!
WEEKS

(advancing upon him)

You monster! You are the one who has destroyed me. I fell in
love with your wife . . . and as she gave in gradually I thought she
was doing it out of returned love. Then I discovered that it was
all for you! You! Who hated her! And I . . . I had become the
victim! A cast-off man, tricked by love and friendship. *(He takes out
a gun)* You fiend! *(He shoots him. Then he turns the gun upon
himself.)* There is nothing left. This joke has had its way. *(Shoots
himself and falls upon Watson)*

MISS BEDERMEYER

Oh, sirs! *(As she gazes, the phone begins to ring. It rings loudly, then slowly gives up.)*

CURTAIN

XIII CHURCHILL YAWNED, STRETCHED,
farted, and then scratched himself vigorously under his left armpit.

"Oh God! If I read one more government report about how to control Negro riots, I'll go right off my chump, I mean it. Listen to this." He picked up a newspaper. "Mayor George Walkowitz of Cleveland announced today that a specially appointed riot panel had submitted to him a survey in which conclusive evidence is presented that black power groups in that beleaguered city have been arming themselves for barricade fighting in the coming summer months. The Mayors' Committee, composed of local government officials and community leaders, said that unless something is done immediately to improve the living conditions of the black community, there will be open and bloody revolution in the streets. The Committee submitted a five point crash plan of action: 1/ build better playgrounds for Negro children, which will include instruction in competitive athletics and body-building programs; 2/ institute adult cultural programs at local high schools wherein Negro men and women can participate with whites in drama, and music and art appreciation; 3/ open job head-start centers where Negro boys and girls who are not academically fit can be instructed in useful trades, such as automotive mechanics, carpentry, sewing, household management, and food processing; 4/ integrate black and white church groups for mutually beneficial religious expression and spiritual exploration; 5/ provide monthly examinations for those members of the Negro community who wish to obtain white-collar jobs in the city government.

"Mayor Walkowitz expressed his conviction that such a program, if carried out with vigor by Cleveland's white community, would result in a 'most significant' lowering of Negro discontent and aid immeasurably in bringing about a 'sharing of the finest traditions and values in our American democracy.' He plans to meet all this week with his special advisor on Negro affairs, Professor Churchill Downs, instructor in social anthropology at the State University and a recent recipient of a $120,000 Ford Foundation grant to study urban renewal problems. Professor Downs is here on loan from the University of Ghana. Said Mayor Walkowitz: 'Professor Downs and I will not give in to the pessimism and dark feelings that seem to be overcoming some elements in our fine city. We will not come out of our meetings without a viable solution to our problems. Professor Downs has assured me that there is historical precedent for a dynamic amalgamation of intergroup aspirations.' Professor Downs' sister, Miss Ophelia of the Morning Light, director of the Walker Street Third Baptist Egyptian Temple, is spearheading a white-Negro community action-group."

Churchill dropped the newspaper—*The Cleveland Herald-Tribune*—and sighed within an inch of his suffering, black life.

"Oh *merde*. Did you get a load of that, sister baby?"

Ophelia sipped at her tall Steuben beaker of chilled Heineken's beer, put down the book she was reading, *Sanity, Madness, and the Family* by R.D. Laing, and gave her brother a magnificent smile. "Deed I did, my shiny black brother, deed I did. All that plus ten cents will get you a hot corn muffin. But, don't get your ass up in the air about it, honey. I keep telling you that the only way you can survive in this world is to hold on to your sense of the absurd. Believe me, no other orientation will work." She quaffed some cold beer and delicately wiped away the foam mustache from her dark upper lip. "I myself find it hilarious. Here you are playing a double role, at best. The secret head of Cleveland's black power movement on one hand, and the Mayor's special anti-black-power adviser on the other."

Churchill chuckled slightly at himself. "You're right. That is something of a howl all right. But it's very difficult for me not to react to the white middle-class bullshit. Those people are crazy, from their eyebrows down to the soles of their feet."

Ophelia's heavy black gaze went to her own feet for a reflective moment. Her toenails were a portrait gallery. On each nail had been pasted a colored mini-photograph of a revolutionary hero. Smiling up at her from the nail of her big toe was Mao Tse-tung.

From the other big toe came the beatific gaze of Ho Chi Minh. Flanking them were Che Guevara, Castro, Trotsky, Tshombe, Jean-Paul Sartre, Malcolm X, Régis Debray and, finally, peeking up from her left little toe, the pure saintly face of Klaus Fuchs. Ophelia gave them all a little exercise by wriggling her toes.

"Not only are they crazy," she said, looking at Churchill "but they're vicious, which is a lot worse. Those people want to kill in the worst way. You know it, I know it, they know it, and all our black and yellow and red friends know it." She paused, sipped some beer, and went on, her voice low and steady. "The white man always has been and always will be a murderer. You must not forget, sweetie, that Jesus was a black man."

"Yeah," said Churchill heavily, looking at the floor.

They shared a few moments of silence. The only sound was the remote one of a ballgame being played by some kids in a field down the road. Ophelia finally dispelled the silence. "Let us not fall victim to gloom or unreal reflections on what might have been. We must hustle the existential present, brother baby. And in so doing, how would you like to hustle up another cold beer for your admiring little sister? Ah is dry."

Churchill was on his way to the fridge. "Could use one myself. Those Dutch cats sure know their business when it comes to a good brew."

Ophelia (flawlessly smooth and self-contained in pink sheath tight Italian silk pants and black cashmere sweater, Italian also), reached over and flicked on the KLH stereo record player, flooding the room, or rather delightfully permeating it with Buxtehude's Concerto in C minor for harp and mandolin. Ophelia opened herself completely to the music, letting it penetrate into every part of her, even the secret areas that no one knew about but herself. The exquisite contrapuntal joy worked its clean lyrical way right down into the earliest remnants of her childhood. She closed her eyes and smiled in euphoria. Moments of dearest woman bliss.

Churchill refilled his beaker. "Forgive me for violating your reverie, honey, but have you seen Cedric lately? He missed an appointment with me last night."

Ophelia returned to the moment in waves of tingly crisp mandolin. "Ah yes. I forgot to tell you. He called this morning while you were sleeping. He couldn't make it last night because the special riot police picked him up on suspicion and held him incommunicado until this morning."

"On suspicion! Violation of the Mallory law right there. But why would they pick up a white queen on suspicion of being involved with black power?"

"Perhaps they thought he was passing. I don't know."

The harp and mandolin music filigreed around them, played on their faces and skimmed the surface of their black and white eyeballs.

"Damn. I hope the cops didn't squeeze anything out of him. He's a key man in our May Day blitz."

"That so? What's he going to do? Lead a faggot uprising?"

"Now sister. You must not be unkind about the third sex. Cedric is a highly intelligent and committed fellow, a thorough revolutionary. He is on our side against the white oppressors."

"All right, all right. I was just funning. Mm. That man's harp is the very epitome of nonoppression. Listen to it."

Churchill did for a few moments. "Yes indeed. Unfettered harp supreme. So, back to Cedric. He is our contact man with the air power scene."

"Air power? What do you mean? Have you figured out a way to harness the oxygen?

Churchill drank off the last of his chilly beer. "It's really a stroke of genius, both tactically and psychologically. In fact, it will be the beginning of a completely new dimension in the revolution." He lit a large black Cuban cigar and exhaled a most truly pungent and billowy smoke that was immediately finessed by the music into its own thing, thus producing sound that had an aroma. "We are going to employ whitey's methods and instruments against him in our blitz. We are going to bomb him from the sky. Cedric has a boy friend who is an air force pilot stationed at nearby Fort Blair. On the morning of the big day he's going to steal a fully loaded B-52, fly it over the city and drop bombs on the city jail, town hall, and the headquarters of the Cleveland vigilantes." He inhaled some Cuban flavors. "When whitey talks about a dialogue between whites and blacks he's just turning on the jack-off machine. The status quo doesn't change. He's got all the power and we've got none. So anything that goes on under such circumstances is a meaningless ritual that even the most disaffected aborigine wouldn't buy." He licked his lips appreciatively. "The only thing the white man truly understands is the dialectic of obstruction."

"Mm," murmured Ophelia over her beer beaker, "nice point." Churchill unloosened the side belt buttons on his gray flannel Daks, got some respite from fat belly squeeze, sighed gratefully, and resumed talking. "Bombed rubble. Can't you just see those shocked sons of bitches. I'll bet the first thing they think is that the Vietcong has attacked the United States! Oh Jesus! I can hardly wait to see those terrified pig faces. You know, it will be the first enemy bombing attack in the whole history of this baby-faced country."

"Unfortunately," said Ophelia, "I'm afraid it won't change their understanding of what it's like to be on the receiving end of bombs. So I hope you aren't counting on instilling any compassion in them, for the suffering of others, that is."

A grunt from Churchill. "No, sweetie, nothing as naive as that. We just want to scare the living shit out of them. But the unavoidable thing is that by employing their own methods, the only methods they dig, our people are of course being corrupted and degraded. This is a terrible paradox and a dilemma."

Ophelia stood up and stretched, a splendid blackness of animal sensuality. And a resounding, full-bodied Nigerian yawn. "So is just about everything else in this whacky world."

"Yeah, I suspect you're right. I've been dipping into Herbert Marcuse, and he had a few disconcerting things to say about the general situation." He reached over to the mahogany and white marble coffee table for a paperback. "The efficiency of the system blunts the individual's recognition that it contains no facts that do not communicate the repressive power of the whole. If the individuals find themselves in the things that shape their life, they do so, not by giving, but by accepting the law of things—not the law of physics but the law of their society!"

"Sounds inescapable, doesn't it?"

"The answer is activism on the most basic street level. Period."

The record ended. "Buxtehude, I love you!" Ophelia sang out.

The dark green Princess phone rang, a muted non-jingling ring, a very civilized and reasonable summoning. Really, it was like having a rather nice girl whisper to you.

"Revolt of the masses," Churchill said clearly and firmly into the feminine instrument. "Cedric sweetie! Where you been? Oh . . . those lousy cops. They didn't do anything to you I hope. Oh really? Well, they'd probably do that sort of thing to anybody. But they didn't get anything out of you, did they? Good, very good. Contacts OK? Great. Ha ha. Yeah, I guess that could be a pun, not intended though. A person's private life is their own, far as I'm concerned. Everybody to his own style. Right. I agree. Who is to say what is normal. Sure, sure. Read them all. Kinsey, Masters, Sacher-Masoch. I know. Even animals? Really? I didn't know that. Wow! That is amazing. Polar bears? You're kidding. You've seen documentaries? Made by Russian scientists? An entire generation hooked on bestiality? Boy that is something. No, I didn't see *Son of Lassie.* I don't go to many movies. What? The kids watch this stuff all the time and that message is gotten across subliminally? Wow! Well listen, let's talk about it some more when you get here. Okay. About three thirty. Right. So long."

Churchill relit his cigar and puffed it back to life. "That Cedric. He's something else. He really is."

Ophelia looked up from her book. "Does he still work for the Y?"

"Uh huh. He runs a night drama class for delinquents and high school drop-outs. They do a lot of Elizabethan who-struck-John stuff." He helped himself to a little of Ophelia's beer, and made mouth-happy sounds afterward. "Speaking of night, are you going to be here for supper?"

"I can't, sweet brother. We're having a little buffet do at the church, then I'm going to lead the ladies in a discussion on the future of integrating black and white feminine culture."

Churchill reflectively fondled his goatee and looked out the window into the yard where a dogwood tree was half in bloom. "What's that mean?"

She laughed, got out of her chair, and gave him a kiss on the cheek. "It's the same old baloney, only sliced different."

"Are you going to exchange black and white make-up secrets? Recipes—a blending of spade cooking with suburban Cordon

Bleu? I've got it: six ways white female aggression can be used in the black boudoir."

She slapped him on his kind of fat behind. "You've got it. You ought to go there instead of me."

He hugged her. "It's a good thing the city's paying you to do this. I mean, that kind of nonsense can be hard on the brain cells."

"It gets to be pretty funny at times. One of the group is a very uptight WASP girl who has been begging me to come to her house so I can help her children out. She wants me . . ." Ophelia began to howl uncontrollably, holding onto her brother to keep from falling to the floor. "She wants me . . . to teach them . . . how . . . to sing . . . Negro . . . spirituals!"

Churchill began to howl too. For a few culturally timeless moments they embraced and lubricated each other with subversive tribal laughter. Every sand castle that white Christian fantasy had ever built on the shores of this world's reality were flooded over and washed away by their black mirthful tears. Watering, effusions, ducticities, lachrymal precipitations that have nothing at all in common with the white man stuff that is so easily, so very easily come by on any white cheek. White tears are to black tears what ginger ale is to vintage wine.

Consider: how often have you seen Negro tears? Exactly. They are a rare phenomenon. And an even rarer phenomenon is the white person who has observed them. It is against Negro law and for a very good reason. The Negro regards his tears with respect and even awe. They are magic, and they are thus not to be wasted, for example, on such infinite nothings as hangnails, bad haircuts, broken lunch dates, unfortunate love affairs, lumpy mattresses, or crummy shakes of the dice. That would be like putting airplane gasoline in a lawn mower. Black tears are to be used on the death of a child, for bringing down the walls of China, or for stopping snowstorms in the spring planting seasons. Incidentally, the punishment for misusing this powerful stuff is very severe: no more tears. Imagine yourself driving a new Porsche in the Alps, a soft gray cashmere turtleneck sweater hugging your torso. Lovely clear weather. Tasty firm roads. Cold squab and a pint of Neuilly-Boeuf in a bucket. The young Princess de la Griory waiting in a chalet. You make a turn at sixty-three miles an hour (you are smiling). Suddenly there is a sheer drop of several thousand feet (the road has not been completed). You slam on the brakes. But the brake fluid has leaked out! You keep right on going. . . . Got it? (Years go by and there come into being second generation searching parties, but still no body is found.)

"And to think that such people run the country," Churchill said, after recovering himself.

"It's just too much," said Ophelia, "It really is. History sure has its freaky humor."

Later that night, over a quart of iced 140 proof Polish vodka given Churchill by a buddy of his at the Polish consulate (blond Vassily Wysniski, with whom Churchill had studied revolutionary fighting tactics in Moscow and whose involvement with Christine Keeler and Profumo had escaped exposure in the great London sex scandal of 1962 which affected European politics more than people like to think). Churchill and Cedric checked out various parts of the May Day Revolt. "Did your students put together the three hundred stink bombs?" Churchill asked Cedric.

Cedric smiled widely. "Yes indeedy they did. Those night kids of mine are workers, and I mean workers. Especially when it comes to getting back at the bastards who've been pushing them around all their lives." He swallowed a jigger of vodka and after catching his breath, said, "Our stink bombs will contaminate Cleveland for the next twenty years, they're that great. We tried one out the other night in a movie house out in Shaker Heights and cleared the place in two minutes."

"Excellent. Now what about the fire alarm detail?"

Cedric winked. "We've got that operation worked out like a Swiss watch movement. One hundred and fifty teen-age foundlings at the city shelter, one hundred and fifty fire boxes. My connections at the shelter are very good inded. There won't be one piece of fire equipment left in any firehouse. Seven hundred and ten fire trucks, engines and ladders raging through the streets with their sirens going full blast."

Churchill chuckled. "Beautiful, Cedric honey. Just beautiful. Let's see now. Oh yes, fire boxes in department stores."

Cedric pulled a slip of paper from his tweed jacket. "They're all covered. Ottinger's, Kahn's, Bamberger's, Ludlow & Janney's, Goldheimer's. Our janitor brigade is ready and waiting."

"Good. I certainly hope they can restrain their acculturated impulses and not do any looting, as we have instructed them."

Cedric's face lit up again as he downed another shot.

"We can expect a couple of violations at least. The example set by us whites can't be that easily transcended. Honesty will take time." He blew air through pressed lips. "Foo! Is that vodka hot?"

"Cedric old tulip, you have an unusual grasp of our problem, and I drink to the beauty of your intellect and the strength in your balls," Churchill hoisted his jigger and downed it. "Aye! Mother? Yes, dear friend, the first great problem after the revolution has obliterated the past and the presumption of the present, is forging the black man in his own mold. At the moment, he barely exists, in the authentic psychological sense of that concept. He is an operative illusion, a projected political fantasy of white which he has given life to in order to exist in the white man's world. And then to himself and his family, the black community, he is a reaction to this dreadful role he has been playing all day, and this reaction identity is inauthentic because it is rooted in the white man's myth." He shook his head sadly. "I sometimes think the only self he has is his black skin, and the irony there is that this skin color, which is nature's way of helping him physically survive over the ages, is the very thing that has undone him." He sighed heavily. "Life, what an insane bitch she is."

Cedric, who was now high on the vodka, giggled. "The mood of your story is devastating. The only way you can make it is by not being yourself. Existence and survival are mutually exclusive. I mean, wow! That's the heart of the artichoke."

"Yes. I believe this is usually where God comes on stage." And he poured Cedric and himself another drink.

Cedric grinned as he watched the colorless stuff fill his shot glass. "Whose own credentials aren't exactly unquestionable."

"No, I don't see him getting much of a security clearance."

"Ha! Ha! Then of course as the man in the joke said, 'First of all, she's a nigger.' "

"Love it. Absolutely love it. My kind of chuckle."

Cedric excused himself to go to the john, and while he was gone Churchill, feeling fine and loose on the vodka, ready for just about any interesting possibility, metaphorical or otherwise, now that his own societally imposed defenses were down, let his mind rove and ramble, into a country of soft feel and curry smell, a terrain of gentle, knowing vibrations and unrestricted slyly mellow hues. No frigid geometry, no thin straight lines that insisted you concede their length. He was back in Kampala, where he had gone to school, primary, run by the White Fathers, and where his father, Afu, held a job in the kitchen of the Hotel Speeck, where his mother, Kula, was a maid for the British government family named Davis-Hobbs (the daughter had braces on her teeth, and a funny way of looking at you out of the side of her pasty face). Not back there in returning down time's slippery steps, but over there and back, and something else too. Not dreaming either. Funny sounds, sounds that stretched and curved as well as made a noise in the air. Smells that laughed.

The beggars in the little park in front of the hotel were lying about in all kinds of positions, positions that Churchill knew were not approved. Their rags covered only parts of their bodies and the other parts were left to fend for themselves. Two or three of the beggars did not have all their arms or legs.

Churchill was trying to decide how to feel about this—he felt very soft, almost boneless, but that did not seem too bad—when a thin beggar with a half-eaten banana in his hand said, "What a silliness you are."

Churchill reached out to touch him but he did not quite make it. "My mother knew yours," he said in a voice he immediately realized was not his own.

"Your memories are all lies!" The man screamed and hurled the banana at Churchill's face.

The beggars now began to laugh and giggle obscenely and to scramble casually all over each other. None of them seemed to pay particular attention to this. Their thoughts were elsewhere.

"Why can't you forgive a little human error?" Churchill shouted. He had begun this shout in true anger, but by the time it had completed itself all that feeling had gone, and he began to laugh foolishly and caress his own face.

He saw now that all the beggars had gone and this produced a sensation of fear and loneliness. Standing alone under the big fountain was a tall bony man who was completely naked. He was holding his immense stiff penis in one hand. Churchill knew that the man was not just a show-off. He was there for a purpose. A clean strong urge to state this rushed at Churchill. He wanted his face to look like an advertisement he had seen of a community leader. "We must never stop fighting for our ideals," he whispered to the man, even though he was several yards in the thin distance.

"I don't want things to make any sense," the man replied, and began furiously to jerk off.

Churchill rushed toward him, panic stricken. "Think of your family! Please!"

The next thing he knew his entire body—which no longer had clothes on it—was covered with the man's sperm. He knew this was not a proper thing and he hoped no one of any significance and power could see him. He looked furtively around at the park and hotel, then began to wipe the sperm off and put it in his mouth. It tasted like strawberry jam, just like the jam his father used to steal and bring home from the hotel. He suddenly wanted to cry a little about his father, but he decided to save that for later. "Thank you very much, sir," he said, but the man had vanished. Two white lady tourists were standing where the man had been. They began shouting and pointing but somehow he could not hear their words. He suspected that they had bad breath. "You will not be here long," he said of the ladies.

Then he was a little boy in his parents' bed and his parents were whispering about him. The warmth of their bodies made him feel sexual and weak, and he felt that at any moment he would wet the bed. He did not know what to do. He thought of crying. "Don't bother me with your small needs," his mother said grinning, and gave him a slap in the face.

"I didn't say a thing to you," he said. "Good boys know their place." He noticed that the bedroom was not really their usual one. He wondered if he should bring this up, but as the thought deepened, he grew afraid, and tried hard to forget about it. "Possibilities have no meaning," he said, but not to anyone in particular. Now his parents began to do naughty things, and he was flooded with shame. Suddenly he began striking at their naked writhing bodies. The strength he thought he had, however, was not in his arms, and his blows became like soft rubber bands. His parents paid no attention to him. So he grabbed on to his mother's large breasts—she was on top of his father now—and held on very tight.

"Why aren't you at work?" he heard himself ask his father,

who at that moment looked like a friend of his in school, about whom he had very mixed feelings. Then he realized that it was his sister he was holding on to and he screamed with terror. He began to disintegrate.

Now he was walking in the jungles. A great deal of time had gone by and the sensations in him were wise and soft and very generous. Two naked children were playing with a dog on the tiny jungle footpath. A splendid sweetness enveloped them. He could taste this atmospheric sweetness in his mouth, like a candy. "We all start from here!" he announced to the children, his voice coming out much louder than he had hoped. "Our roots are in each others' hearts."

"That's what you think," a silly voice said. Churchill looked up in the huge green banana trees. Sitting on a giant leaf was a small woman with gray hair all over her body. She exuded an extreme remoteness yet at the same time an intimacy that was difficult to apprehend.

"Self-examination was never your style," he replied, and made a defiant, classically obscene gesture with his finger. The old woman cackled and began eating a large piece of red fruit.

"Big fat nigger!" she yelled, and spit fruit at him.

The children now turned around. Their faces were an ecstasy of smoothness, their teeth untouched by troubled foods. They began to sing in rich, meaningful voices about a variety of things. The words floated out of their mouths with a great, slow beauty. Even though the precise meaning of their words escaped him, he nonetheless loved the thought of them and was grateful that the children were bothering with him at all. As he looked closer at them, he became aware that one of them was himself, when he was young. Before he knew what he was doing, he was hugging and kissing himself.

"How did I know I would find you here?" he murmured, fondling and kissing and absorbing.

In the distance, perhaps in the gentle mountains beyond the trees that were now suffocating, explosions began going off. Boom. Boom. Boom. Churchill knew he had to leave soon, and with the boy who was entwined in his arms.

XIV

ONE PIERCINGLY LOVELY AFTERNOON in May, a young Spanish lad of sixteen or seventeen was strolling on the beach just outside the City of Palma, in the Balearic Islands. His name was Miguel. He worked as a bellboy in the new Hotel Jaime V. He worked very hard six days a week. Older people were impressed with him.

"Miguel," José, the aging bell captain, told him once, "You are a good boy. You don't present rich people with funny looks, and you don't stand around with your hands always in your pockets. Life will play ball with you. Yes."

For three years he had been studying English and French at night school (run by the lay priests). He wanted to get ahead, to become a first class hotel desk clerk. Miguel was lean and springy, from hunger and work and a certain amount of anxiety about life in general.

The beach was clean and deserted. This was fine by Miguel, because he wasn't in the mood for any clutter, animate or otherwise. Especially, he was relieved that there were no half naked girl bathers around, because then his mind would have abandoned him and concentrated its powers instead on the action between the legs. He knew that that sort of thing had prevented many men from achieving greatness in their thinking. He wanted to think a few things through. The hot sand felt nice beneath his bare feet. He kicked at a shell, an insignificant act involving an insignificant shell that had long since served its worldly purpose. Then a dark effect on the beach caught his eye and made his breathing change. It was a bottle, a wine bottle with a cork in it (the label of course had washed off in the sea). He approached it almost with stealth. Always he had dreamed of finding his magnificent destiny and fortune tucked inside such a sudden mystery bottle. His hand trembled slightly as he picked it up and pulled the cork out ever so gently. Oh, how beautiful! How perfect! The message was there, a large rolled up sheet of paper. He extracted it, grinning wildly, and began to read its elegant handwritten words.

You poor unlucky bastard. You are going to spend the rest of your dumb life wishing you had not opened this bottle.. I am an atheist and therefore cannot avail myself of the comforts of confession. So I am making of you my secret sharer. I am herewith presenting you with the dreadfulness of myself—the crimes I have committed against my own humanness and that of others.

Item: I am a thief. I steal other people's ideas, hearts, possessions, illusions. Just last week I stole another man's integrity and with it his wife. I had known him since our school days.

Item: I am a liar. I lie even when it is not necessary. I feel physically uncomfortable with the truth. Yesterday, for example, I told a lie about the weather to a perfect stranger.

Item: I am a degenerate. No member of the animal world is safe from my lust. I am sought in six countries for crimes against human decency. Tonight I plan to do my best to lure a large Irish setter into my cabin.

Item: I am a hypochondriac. I complain constantly about imaginary ailments. At this very moment I have a bandage around a cut that does not exist.

Item: I am vain. My apartment in Helsinki (I have one in Budapest also) contains no fewer than ten full-length mirrors. I frequently get up in the middle of the night to look at myself. I save my toenail clippings, and I have a chart recording my bowel movements for twenty years.

Item: I am a slave to gold. I will do anything for money. When I am making love I think of rooms full of money, and my love-making becomes bestial without qualification (of course, it goes without saying that I have never confessed this to any of my mistresses).

Item: I am a disbeliever. God is a hoax. So that is it, my curious and now forever burdened friend. I cannot tell you how relieved I am —how thoroughly buoyant I feel physically—that you have assumed, by your simple gesture, the responsibility of all this crime. My innocence has returned."

Your inseparable new friend,   Judas the Nose
(Yes, 'twas I whose lips did kiss Him low)

Miguel slowly stuffed the paper back in the bottle and resealed the bottle with the cork. Then he hurled the bottle back out into the sea. "I shit in the milk of your mother!" he screamed.

He stood there for a couple of moments and stared after the bobbing bottle, which the outgoing tide was gradually carrying off. Raging strides took him back down the beach toward the town. His mind now was flooding the sand with voluptuous naked female bodies smiling smiles of unspeakable complicity.

XV

SYLVIA IS LYING ON HER BACK. SHE has been staring at the loaded bookshelf on the wall in front of her for at least five minutes without saying a word. She wets her dry lips with her tongue, starts to say something, then decides not to. It is such an unimportant thing to bring up. An exchange yesterday between herself and her brother involving his crummy little wife, Margie, and silver salt cellars that had belonged to her mother. She hears her analyst behind her begin to write in his notebook. This upsets her. "What are you writing?" she asks, turning her head to look at him. "I haven't said anything."

"Why do you think you haven't said anything?" he replies.

"I asked you first."

"Do you think your silence is connected in some way to the dream we examined the last time you were here?"

"What dream?" Sylvia asks, fingering the buttons on her gray cashmere cardigan.

"You know. The one where you and your brother go on a — your words were 'happily kooky'—trip with a man named Zachary, 'a very important stranger,' you described him as."

"Oh that dream," Sylvia says. "Yes, well . . . the thing is I've never known anyone named Zachary. In fact I've only seen the name in novels, and then there is that actor, Zachary Scott, but he'd dead. And I don't care for Hollywood types anyway. They're so vulgar."

The analyst, a very large blue-black man, clears his throat. "Why do you think that dream bothered you so much—or our examination of it—that you did not want to talk this session? And if you recall, in the dream your brother was called George, not Willie, his true name."

"George?"

"Yes," the analyst replies, "and he was a writer, a novelist."

"That's a joke. My brother couldn't write a thank you note, much less a novel."

"Something is there, Mrs. B., something is there. Do you suppose you feel shame or guilt for having invented this man Zachary and made of your brother a novelist named George?"

Sylvia chuckles. "In dreams begin responsibilities."

"Hm?"

"Yeats. Anyway, maybe I didn't really invent them. I mean, maybe they do exist but in another sort of world, a world within a world. Something like that. You know what Jung says about the universal unconscious. Everybody has it and we all know each other there, in all kinds of shapes and scenes. What about that, Dr. Jomo? For instance, maybe you and I here in this room are just one reality. How about that?"

Dr. Jomo clears his throat again. "All that sort of thing may well be, and it's interesting as a speculation, but it isn't going to help us help you here and now. So let's talk about George and Zachary."

"Oh all right. We'll do it your way for a while. But I want to get back to those other possibilities the next session and, as you yourself have said on more than one occasion, 'It's your money, Mrs. B., it's your money.' OK now. Zachary and George . . . hmm . . . maybe." She twists on the couch and puts her hand over her face to concentrate. "Maybe Zachary could be my father. Throw the sack away, my father used to say every time he wanted us to forget something. Zachary . . . sack away, Zackaway. Yes. And in the dream he was leading us away, me and my brother . . . away from my mother . . . which was like throwing the sack of my mother away. And I was very pleased we were doing that and I guess that's why I couldn't talk, because I was afraid that I was a bad girl because I was pleased. I hated her. And my brother being this George person, a writer. . . . Well, I've always wanted him to be something, I mean something better than average . . . exceptional, creative so . . . oh, wait! I've got it! So that he could create a story for me and my father and himself. He could do that if he were a creative writer . . . and writes . . . to make right . . . that which wasn't right . . . our real family story. George the Righter. Oh boy! And if that's the case, then in the dream Zachary's—or

my father's—leading us was just a screen for my brother who was
to do the real leading . . . because it would not be acceptable to
my conscience to allow that project so directly, that would be
showing my contempt for my father's ability to right anything,
and the taboo against such a feeling is too strong."

She pauses, but does not take her shielding hand from her face.

"That's very good," her analyst says, writing away, "I think
we're getting someplace."

"But does that mean that I really also want my brother to be
my father, if he takes my father's rightful place as leader?"

"Well, we don't know. Let's explore that."

"I wonder why I selected the name George. Why not Charlie
or Maxwell?"

"You tell me."

"There you go again. You sound like that spooky husband of
mine, the Helsinki Hustler. Pins you against the wall as though
you're some kind of butterfly."

"Has he been doing that lately?" Dr. Jomo asks, his chair
creaking as he shifts his huge frame.

"When he's not involved in some loony scheme, that's his
favorite sport."

"Loony schemes?"

"To put it mildly. Can you imagine a store that sells nothingness? Christ! What will that nut do next? Head-start programs for
mermaids, I'll bet."

There is a soft pause. "By the way," he says, "do you realize
that you have never referrred to your husband by his name? Today
you call him the Helsinki Hustler. Last week you spoke of him as
Rumpelstiltskin. What the devil is his name?"

She sort of sniggers. "Well, today he can be known as, uh,
Gelb. OK?"

"Gelb? Why?"

"Why not?"

"Did you ever know a Gelb?"

"There you go again."

Dr. Jomo lights a cigarette and inhales deeply, and the heavy
white smoke floats softly over Sylvia's head. "Well . . . so we were
wondering why you selected the name of George for your
brother."

"Oh God. I'm so tired. My brain is used up. Why don't you

do the exploring now and I'll just lie here and listen."

He chuckles slightly. "It's my job to keep myself out of your explorations as much as possible."

"What's it called when you don't exactly succeed? Counter-tranference?"

"That's right."

"And when that happens, what?"

"Well, I project into you, and this situation, my own problems and life experiences. I respond to your fantasies with fantasies of my own, I am absorbed into you and you are absorbed into me." He clears his throat and puffs on his cigarette.

"Hmm. Sounds kind of great. A festival of fantasy. Give me an example."

"This really isn't . . ."

"Aw come on, Dr. Jomo. Be a sport."

"Well, all right. Suppose you bring up something about a Ne-gro, either a real or an imagined thing. Since I'm a Negro, and quite aware that you are aware of this, my own sensitivity, fears, and experiences as a Negro might well be provoked, or at least elicited. At this point, what has been taking place between us as doctor and patient, would very much change. I would, in a sense, lose my identity as the 'objective doctor.' I might become the black antagonist and view you accordingly. Do you see? Then I might go even farther and as you are weaving your own web of fantasy, start weaving mine onto you and also onto myself. I might go very far away, taking you with me or leaving you here.

"Start reliving experiences of my own—as they perhaps au-thentically occurred or inauthentically in my wishfulness. I could be lured back into, say, a terrible trauma in my life when I was the victim of a white woman's madness. Where I allowed my own needs and vulnerability to be used and manipulated by a demon white goddess who happened to be the only link available in that small town to the world outside which I felt I must get to or perish. This woman was the wife of the richest man in town, who hap-pened to be a part-time homosexual, and she was mad and cruel, beautiful beyond measure and sensitive as a young wasp. She introduced me to the life of the mind and to the song of the lark, the fathomless world of the creative imagination, and the unbeara-bly measurable moment of the specific humiliation. I started out as a houseboy on their country estate in Madison, New Jersey, and I wound up as her number one boy in her satin bed, with five generations of silky soft inbreeding wrapped around my lowly black body. We used to sit around the big kitchen and discuss poetry while her husband Jasper was out in the stables trying to make out with one of the raunchy exercise boys.

"All right, you dreadful heathen, she would say, "tell me how Marvell employs metaphors in 'To His Coy Mistress.' "

"Marvell," I would sigh, "I love that man."

"Yes, yes. Aside from that. The use of metaphor, please."

"Okay, Okay. He employs the metaphor of time—For at my back I always hear time's winged chariot hurrying near—to deepen the perspective of the immediacy of his need to get laid."

"To have sexual intercouse."

"To have sexual intercourse. The metaphor of the chariot, and the other line, *Had we but world enough, and time*—is used to make this girl understand that she's just a moment in his life and her life depends upon using that moment. Marvell surrounds the individual with metaphorical reflections of his humanness." I poured and sipped a coke.

"How's that, Mrs. Twimbly?"

"I'm very pleased with your progress, young man. You are coming right along. Someday you will amount to something. Just keep using your brain. Now would you be a sweetheart and mix me another of your incomparable daiquiries."

"Amount to something," I said, doing my mixing magic at the sink. "Does that mean I will stop being a nigger and become a white man?" The frosted glass felt lovely in my hand as I carried it across that spic and span upper-class kitchen.

"Not on your life," she said, sipping the drink. "But it will make people stop treating you like one, even if they don't think any different." She looked at me with those mad Shirley Temple eyes and smiled.

"I wouldn't want them to love me," I said, munching on a potato chip.

She snorted, "They have a hard enough time loving their own kind."

"Someday I'll get out of this cheesy little town and live in a place like Paris, or London. The West End."

"Step by step, you beautiful bright black thing. Now let's get back to Marvell. Tell me how he compounds and extends an image in metaphors in the 'Mistress.' " She sips a lot of the juice up. "Mm. But before we do, I just want to tell that your love-making last night was simply super. My breasts still hurt a little but that's okay."

"Thank you," I said. "I kind of lost myself and bit them too hard. So . . . Marvell . . . well . . . he keeps hammering away at how everything is perishable, with all kinds of images, like the vegetable and worm images . . ."

The doctor clears his throat. "So that's the way that sort of thing goes, Mrs. B."

"Wow," she says. "Who would have thought that's the way you got your start as a big psychoanalyst."

"You, Mrs. B."

"Me? I don't understand."

"That wasn't the real story of my background at all."

Sylvia sits up on the couch, almost angrily. "What?"

"Just that. I was presenting you with my version of what I guessed might be your fantasy about me. As an example of a really rich counter-transference. Now do you see how that works.?"

She gets up and walks around the book-lined study. "Let me see if I get this right. As the seemingly objective doctor, you are forced out of your objective position, perhaps by something I say which touches on a so-called touchy part of you, and that sets you off on counter-transferring one of your own fantasies. But that fantasy—or real story maybe—happened to be a retelling, or re-shaping, of one of my fantasies about you. Not one of your own at all. Right?

"Exactly."

"So that what can happen here can be just an elaborate exchange of transference and counter-transference, fantasy and counter fantasy, and the real thing, I mean real events, simply goes by the board."

"Very often that's what happens. Of course, there is one thing you missed. The necessity for creating reality out of counter-projected, or reified fantasy."

"Oh dear," Sylvia says, like a surprised little child.

"Here's what I mean. I think you set things up so that I would validate your fantasy by assuming to make it my own. Give it back to you as reality. Thus, we have a perfect example of the manipulative power of fantasy."

She stares at him, puzzled and amazed. "You mean that's the way I planned it all along?"

"Yes. You can control me, or castrate me really, if I agree to live out your fantasy about me. Because I don't really think you have any interest in either my own reality or my own fantasy about reality. That would be too complicated for you to handle, with me or with anyone else. But if you can maneuver this other deal, you can handle it very well. You have all the power and you never have to connect with the other world. Incidentally, in that production I gave back to you, you of course were the domineering rich lady."

His chair squeaks. "And of course there is the possibility that, without even knowing it, I could actually incorporate your material into my own wishful reworking of the past, and live out the past quite aside from any connection with you."

Sylvia sits weakly on the couch. She is bewildered and a little frightened. She is watching her smash hit disintegrate right on the stage. "Good Lord. What a crazy mix-up. But tell me: why would I want to do all that?"

Dr. Jomo sighs heavily. "In this case, you cannot face the fact of being in a terribly new situation with a terribly new human being. You came to me for help, number one, and number two, I happen to be a Negro, a member of a race you are not only not accustomed to coming to for help, but have always treated as inferior. These two things are simply too much for you. Now outside this office, you very likely do the same with everybody else."

Sylvia starts, "You mean invent them—and deal with my inventions?"

"Precisely. Everyone does it all the time. It is the human way of dealing with life because the human is simply too frail to face real reality. How do I know, for instance, that this man you describe as your husband really exists?"

Sylvia jumps up. "Of course the little bastard exists! Why, at this very moment he's probably trying to con St. John the Baptist into a lecture tour."

"Please, Mrs. B., don't get so distressed. I am merely trying to show you how people twist, distort, and create life in order not to have to confront that most incredible of all things, Being. Let us assume your husband does exist. But how do I know that everything you tell me about him—his characteristics, his exotic doings, those freaks he calls friends—how do I know that this is really he?"

Sylvia is aghast. "But my God, Dr. J., then how do we know that the whole world isn't an invention?"

Dr. J. smiles and makes a carefully philosophical, imploring gesture with his huge hands, "We don't."

They look at each other, Sylvia amazed, Dr. J. amused. Then he glances at the clock on his leather-top desk. "Well, I see that the hour is up. Until Friday, then."

Sylvia begins walking out, slowly. "Until Friday—if there really is such a thing." She closes the door behind her.

Jomo gets up and stretches his immensely tall black frame and rubs his face with his hands, as if to restore life to it, or wake it up. "Oh my," he says to the room. "What a life. What a life."

The phone rings. He lets it ring twice, smiling as he watches it, before picking it up. "Yes? Ah, Genevieve my squeeze! Where have you been? Ah, I see, I see. Well, I've missed you something awful. A little gathering at your house? Sounds . . . uh huh . . . why, of course. Be delighted. I could talk on, say, the ritual of alienation. A paper I've just completed for the *Existential Psychiatry Quarterly.* Fine, fine. And what . . . oh marvelous. You certainly know my weaknesses, Genevieve. Promise me a *pot au feu* and I am a slave at your feet. Philip won't be there? Oh, too bad. Well, I hope he has good business in Spain. Right. See you at 7:30 Friday. Bye, bye, you shimmering thing."

He rubs his hands with pleasure. Genevieve Palmer. Genevieve Novodny Palmer, that is. A pink-skinned blue-eyed horn of plenty, sprung right from the upper-class gluttony of Budapest into this current scene. Mm. What a dish! If Franz Kafka had known the likes of her there would have been no need to pen *The Trial.* Money to burn. Her husband owns half of every car produced in America. That marvelous farmer's market of a woman. Her very accent represents a thousand years of stylized depravity. Not a healthy bone in her opulent body. She's the mamma that every boy wants to lay and kill daddy for. When that woman laughs her middle European laugh, fifth-century monks cry out in pain. Ah, Gen—the things you and I are going to do with each other! They haven't even appeared in the psychiatry books yet. Damned good thing I'm in shape.

He suddenly falls to the floor and does ten quick pushups. "Yessir," he says, getting up, smiling. "Very good shape indeed. Not one in fifty analysts in this city can do that." And he bows to all his books. "My soft fat castrate white colleagues. May the memory of your mother's apple butter serve you well."

His watch tells him that he has fifteen more minutes before his lunch date with Dr. Charles Blye, director of the Interstate Committee on Teen-age Drug Addiction. He picks up the newspaper on his desk and reads the headline stories: "Gen. William C. Westmoreland has asked for 206,000 more American troops in Vietnam, but the request has touched off a divisive debate within high levels of the Johnson Administration." He sighs. "That poor idiot psychotic." He scans elsewhere. "Archbishop Terence J. Cooke paid a surprise visit to his old friends at Misericordia Hospital in the Bronx today. 'This,' whispered a patient, 'is the most wonderful experience in my life.'" He allows an enormous fart to vent itself. "Oh Christ. What a dreary fraud. Old repressed homos filling in for God." He looks at another story: "American radio astronomers during the last week have been recording radio signals from beyond the earth that they and their British colleagues believe could be from other civilizations."

He chuckles. "Why not? There are civilizations all over the place. New ones are springing up every moment. Every one sending through signals that just aren't appreciated. Those science boys have developed an unhealthy dependence on their reality boxes. Us poets never get hung up that way."

He is walking through the park to his lunch date. The weather is light and full of pizazz. Ready to play ball with you. He breathes in deeply, noting to himself that nothing beats real fresh air and sunshine for spiritual nourishment. He begins to think that the weather has gotten to the automobiles in the streets, because they are not behaving in their usual demented manner. His thoughts race over his immediate and contemporary terrain. (He smiles at a bum sleeping, full length, on a bench with one shoeless naked foot dangling and an empty wine bottle nestled in his arms.) This woman Mrs. B., what am I doing for her? Is any substantial change really taking place? Or am I engaged in an endless conspiracy of supportive therapy? Has she become an analysis freak? Afraid so. The crutch that stretches into infinity. She's been with me for a year and the only changes have been very small change indeed. She doesn't have as many headaches and she can sleep seven hours rather than five. Oh yes, and she says she is nicer to cab drivers who try to talk to her. This is not what I became a psychoanalyst for—to rearrange the minutiae of the urban woman. I dreamed of breakthroughs, character changes, visions springing up from dust-bowls of despair, blocks removed from great talents. Stuff like that. And the imaginings in this poor woman's brain! Great Heavens! (He smiles at a jaunty old woman in tweeds who is being vigorously led by two lean afghans.) Does she for a second think I believe all that stuff? Why, she's living the lives of every heroine in every cheap novel she's ever read. Unless of course I'm crazy. Mm, that young man coming toward me with those high-wire eyes certainly could use a few sessions on the couch. Have to tie him down of course.

Direct therapy. Now is that the answer to it all? Wrestle them physically to the floor of their—and mine too—neuroses? Shock them out of their lairs and their intricate guile, that's one way to force them into the sublime of true existence. Destroy their categories of existential apprehension . . . and thus put them on that awesome threshold where their categories are about as adequate as a flashlight in Hell. All these words and exchanges become real-life substitutes for the things they are supposed to be describing, and away we go. Peculiar and fascinating form of strategic inauthenticity. As if when we were asleep our clothes walked about assuming our identities and prerogatives. Very much worth doing a paper on. Have to make a few notes tonight, which means I can't have too much of that superb cognac Sister Eulalia serves. The hippest nun in the country. The Madame Pompadour of the Church. If only the Pope knew what he's got in her. A fourfold humdinger right out of the Old Testament.

"The arts festival building? Right down there, three blocks."

"We're going to see two new Godard movies."

"Splendid idea. Those French lads certainly have a nose for fun."

Oh my. Two homosexuals living their lives through French culture. Oh well. Why not? The very nature of that culture is asexual. But then, so is all culture. Make a good paper. Maybe I should have a stenographer accompany me on these walks. Lots of good stuff. Sister Eulalia . . . yes . . . odd way to meet a nun . . . through her sister Mildred's breakdown. Poor tortured thing. Took off all her clothes and ran screaming down Fifth Avenue shouting obscenities at the motorists. Three squad cars filled with red-faced Irish peasants finally trapped and subdued her in the fountain in front of the Plaza. Was making my rounds at Bellevue on my one day a week hospital stint when I came upon her strait-jacketed body in the big ward with all the Puerto Rican and Negro derelicts and loonies. Talk about snakepits. The place absolutely did smell like the reptile house at the zoo. Crocodile oozings and python sweat. Can still smell it. Terrible! (He whips his white silk handkercheif from his lapel pocket and vigorously blows his nose). Ugh! And those dank defectives who were the guards. All of them look as if they grew up in a German beer hall. Where their mothers were crooked-eyed waitresses. Makes one wonder if euthanasia is such an inhuman idea after all. That's another one I'll have to give closer examination to, close and unsentimental. "Get all those people out of my playroom!" she demanded of me first off. "Of course," I said. "I'll do that right away," and I had the attendants immediately take the strait jacket off her. "Glory be to God in the lowest!" she shouted when that was done. She looked like a newborn Biblical baby. She had gone crazy in order to return to both herself and her historical origins. My duty was to assist her in that return and make her want to reconsider her re-entry into this world with all its richness. That's where I sometimes feel I'm lying. At best this world is a temporary abyss. Freud knew that better than any of us, and we knock the old chap for being so dark in his insights. All these latter-day saints . . . hmm . . . delicious whiff of Chanel No. 5 from that haughty red-haired vixen . . . who preach adjustment and environmental negotiation are euphonic masturbatory falisifiers, if not downright fools and mountebanks. Horney, Blanton, Menninger, Adler, and those others. Drug pushers just as felonious as the ones up in Spanish Harlem. (He steps back to the curb quickly to avoid being struck by the fender of a white Cadillac driven by a woman with dark

glasses who does not even look at her almost victim. "Watch out!"
he cries into the thin air. "Crazy bitch.") Let's see now . . . oh yes
. . . all of them are pushing the ritual of being, not the reality. The
reality of being . . . maybe it is just too frightening to be experienced. Man needs ritual to take himself away from himself.
Hm. Interesting thought. Another paper? Start at the beginning.
Prehistoric and primitive man. Fantastic things going on both
inside and outside himself. Couldn't really tell whether those extraordinary and terrifying goings-on in nature, like thunder and
snow and lightning, weren't somehow part of the world of crazy
and wonderful and terrifying feelings and thoughts inside himself,
including dreams, nightmares, hallucinations, and visions.

So it would only be natural and logical for him to want to
mediate this fantastic show . . . or have it mediated, taken out of
the immediate and overpowering and placed at a safer distance.

So he invented ritual, all kinds. He made a ritual of himself
(kind of like turning yourself into a corporation so that it and not
you will be liable for all kinds of bad things like law suits and bad
debts, all of such things of course incurred by you and not the
ritualized corporation) and how did he do this? Simple. He invented the shaman, the magic man for the tribe. This shaman was
of course a projection of, and a surrogate for, himself. Kind of like
personifying one's unconscious. So primitive man could thus carry
on a dialogue with himself, particularly with the crazy part of
himself, by way of his self surrogate, the witch doctor. What an
incredibly clever strategy! Talk about survival instinct! Wow. And
all those other rituals . . . the same purpose . . . to take him away
from himself. To eventually communize and politicize himself.
Because the more you are you, the less you are them and without
the them of you, you just don't have anything like a group with
all its advantages and power and so on. Rain dances and conjuring
rites and the religious institution itself . . . all rituals to make it
easier, and thus of course, less authentic, to be yourself. Take God,
or the Gods in general. . . . every one of those amazing half
animals, half humans back there a half a million years ago must
have felt like God. How great. But what kind of a village structure
are you going to have if everybody thinks and acts like God?
Chaos. But only as far as the political structure is concerned, not
the individual. So you agree to take God out of everybody and put

him in the sky, actually and figuratively. Then you suddenly have the institution of the church, which is nothing more nor less, in its original form, than the collective projection of all the individual God-feelings of every member of the community. Hm. Love it. Then you can worship yourself and at the same time not cause your neighbor to fear that you are going to devour or overpower him in your respective Godness, which of course makes The Man from Nazareth you and me. (He smiles at a beautiful dribbling child who is being wheeled by a thin-nosed young mother with a distant expression.)

Now of course we come to the fatal rub. The ritual, which was invented by man to save himself, has taken over. It has become The Machine. And it dominates him, and it will go on dominating him and keeping him from ever again becoming himself and his own master. What a paradox! It is The Paradox. The very thing man devises to allow his human experience to become tenable turns out to prevent that very thing from taking place. The entire Ritual of Life moment by moment kills life. And . . . here's where psychoanalysis comes in . . . isn't this too an aspect of The Ritual and doesn't it compound it? To begin with, the classical surrogation of the patient . . . having his dialogue with himself by way of me instead of directly confronting his unconscious . . . I am his unconscious. There is the Ritual of Self right there. Second . . . the Ritual of the Past . . . the reliving of the past is a flat impossibility, no matter how recently it occurred. So we ritualize it, and call it the present. Then we get the dreams . . . what is more removed from real participation with self than creating all those whacky people to function for oneself during sleep? It would be impossible to beat that for self-splitting. Wonder if primitive man did that? I mean used his dreams that way, or did he use them more magically or did he even dream? Hmm. Good thought. Dreams are certainly connected with the rise of a repressed society, and if man does not live in such a society, perhaps the very need to live his so-called real life in dreams would thereby by nullified, since there he is presumably able to be himself in his waking hours. Think I've got something there. Damn! Wish I'd brought a notebook with me. Must really look into bringing a quick meaty secretary on these scintillating promenades.

Anyway . . . . now we move in on the central spot . . . and that

is the entire concept of illness and cure in our society. The ritual
of sickness and the counter-ritual of cure. These people aren't
really like a wolf leaping in the woods or a bird falling out of the
air. They are sick only in regard to the conventions of health, or
the ritual of contemporary being! So what happens? We come up
with this other ritual, psychoanalysis! Holy Jesus! What a situation!
An abstraction fixing an abstraction. A machine to repair another
machine. Wait . . . am I thinking myself right out of a profession
and a living? Oh, I'm getting so hungry, so suddenly hungry.
Have my thoughts aroused anxiety which I am converting into
hunger? Isn't food a substitute for being, in a solid way? (He
reflexively rubs his stomach and licks his big lips. A loud after-
dinner fart escapes him. An old lady in a French cut gray flannel
suit, passing him at that momemt, makes an undisguised face of
distaste. A dart of shame shoots through him.) Upper-class fastidi-
ousness. That's what destroyed Rome. Ah well. A nice omelet,
ham and cheese? No. Not enough. A club steak with lyonnaise
potatoes and a dish of tart endive. Maybe a wedge of soft camembert after. Yes. Much more like it. Prepare me for the preposterous
talk about programs for fighting pot smoking among the young.
Why not an all-out drive to abolish greed among the rich? Or a
radio campaign to cure advertisers of lying?

That Mrs. B. What fantasies must she be having about me right
at this moment? Am I on top of her ramming it in? Or underneath
her? Am I a black African chief bartering for her in a slave market?
Maybe I'm her husband Gelb. I know some chaps who really do
fuck their prettier patients. They believe it is much healthier to let
the patient live out their sexual transferences. However, she could
be imagining something entirely different. We would be in a
strange city together. Surrounded by all manner of weirdies performing all manner of odd human acts. The atmosphere would be
most peculiar. Unusual sounds. Soft insidious breezes on our bodies. The crowds are shouting complicated and disturbing things to
us. A man whose nude body is painted blue is dancing wildly in
front of us and banging a tambourine. A half-naked girl wearing
large gold earrings and a wicked smile is cooking meat over an
open fire and singing to herself. A huge strong man is wrestling
with a bear and making fierce growling sounds. Sylvia grabs me
in fear, yet she is fascinated. I say comforting things to her.

"These people don't mean us any harm."

"Then why are they carrying on so?" she asks.

"It's just their way," I explain.

Good heavens! Who is that coming out of the wild crowd? Sister Eulalia! She is wearing her nun's habit but for some reason her hair is not hidden under her cap. It is falling in long black heavy waves over her shoulders. I have never seen her looking so radiant. Does she have a great secret inside her? She is carrying an enormous sign. She stands in front of us and I read the message printed in large letters on the placard.

The Last Message of Our Lord Jesus Christ—As It Was Whispered To One Of The Faithful Standing Under The Cross:

"My poor weeping supplicant, your tears fall wasted upon a tragic error. I am not the man you think I am, nor would I want to be. None of this would have happened had you been sensible and confined your urges of immortality to the graven images you inherited from your pagan ancestors. Please. Hear my song, such as it is, and try to understand it.

"The thrust of the Roman spear drove the swallows from my tree and made the wolf in my wood cry out in pain. The rivers choke and writhe with my blood. I who sought to bring peace to my people brought pestilence to myself, a simple man weighted with the mad dreams of others. My every act, from first to last, from the fond touching of a blind man to throwing a few crumbs into the sea, a song of innocence misunderstood as a battle cry against the golden-eyed authorities. Your frenzies of hatred, your need to overthrow your envied oppressors, used me and corrupted my oh so measurable humanness. Day and night the whispering waves of our sea of Galilee will remind you of this, and you will sooner turn back the tides than undo this fait accompli. Believe me, I never wanted anything to do with being a God. I was a simple chap who was doing his best as a citizen, an honest man trying to help his fellow man get a decent break in all this venal madness, not at all a revolutionary as they would say. And then everyone lost his sense of balance. I was made into all kinds of things that had no connection with the truth. Judas' group of wild revolutionaries maneuvered me, the Roman rulers used me as a scapegoat, the rich rabbis secured their foul bourgeois positions by choosing me as a distraction from their own now visible corruptions, and you, you miserable crying lady, did me and the rest of the world for all time, the worst injustice of all by making of me the Son of God. Things will never be the same again. I die with this thought: I could have had a good life, perhaps even have gotten married to the baker's daughter, a splendid full-breasted girl whose charms and devotion would have made my life a little less lonely. With my last breath I curse you. The man you really are looking for is asleep this very moment at an olive farm outside Damascus."

I ask myself: what am I doing in this absurd place? And where is that sick Mrs. B.? Gone, of course. I was on my way to a luncheon appointment. "Mrs. B! Where the hell are you?" Oh Christ! That shows you what can happen when you let your guard down and show a little trust and willingness to participate. Interpersonal psychiatry can clearly get out of hand. No wonder those Freudian chaps play it so distant and hard to get. They want to make it home for dinner every night. Business after all is business. It used to be dentistry they went out for. "Mrs. B! Come back!" I'll bet she's gone off to her childhood in Milwaukee.

"Why, Dr. Jomo," exclaims Sister Eulalia, putting her hand on my shoulder, "What on earth are you doing here?"

"The result of excessive psychic generosity, Sister. But it's too long a story to go into. However . . . what are you doing here, dear Sister?"

"That's exactly what I've been asking myself. I just don't know." She looks around at the milling crowds and the gamey old street in general, as if expecting an answer to appear osmotically.

"Well, we'll figure something out, don't worry. Just a little imagination and some muscle, that'll do the trick."

She smiles. "Don't leave out prayer, Dr. Jomo."

"Never fear, Sister. I thought we'd split up the workload. You handle the prayer and I'll throw in the muscle and mind."

She puts her hand in my arm, gently. "Lovely, just lovely."

"Glad you agree. Now then . . . do you see that little street turning to the left? Where the man with the monkey is standing? Well, there's something about that street that vibrates possibility. Purely on an intuitive level, mind you. I have the feeling that the street is saying something to me. That street is going somewhere and it's going to take us with it."

She puts her hand in mine. "Mm. I'm beginning to feel it myself. Sort of like velvet moving inside me."

"Fine. Now start praying and we'll run for it. Pray that we're going someplace else. And put a little English on rematerializing, or whatever it is that we need. Okay? Let's go!"

THE FAT RUMPLED IRISH CLEANING LADY LOOK-ed up from her scrubbing position on the rectory floor. "Sister Eulalia, you are workin' too hard. The demands of the church is eatin' you alive. You can take that from me as a fact. With all due humility, of course."

Sister Eulalia laughed and signed two more letters at her desk.

Mrs. Kavanagh scrubbed off a floor smudge. "If that dear lady were here and not in Dublin, I'm positive she would exercise her mother's love and require you to take a health-givin' rest."

Sister looked through all the papers on her desk, finally found two stamps under an old invoice regarding seven new high school English textbooks, and licked them onto the freshly inscribed envelopes. "The work must be done, and it is my job to do it. Our parish needs pulling up, as you well know, Mrs. Kavanagh."

Mrs. Kavanagh went to work on the white wall near the door where someone had scrawled his name in crayon. "Pullin' up is it? And where is the good Sister Margaret when this is bein' done may I ask? I'll tell you where. She's every sweet minute of the day over at the library doin' research for that new young priest Father Perez who is writin' the true history of the Franciscan nuns from the very beginnin.' Yes indeed she is." She put more Clorox on the rag and rubbed it away. "Fine work if you can get it, I say."

"She and Father Perez are doing serious work. A benefit to the church and its intellectual tradition."

"All that may be, Sister, and I myself would be the last one to throw a cabbage at a fine and glorious tradition such as that. But you and I both know that the desperate humans in this neighbor-hood barely have time in their struggle to wash their filthy feet, much less read a history work."

Sister got up from the desk and went to the big green filing cabinet where she kept dossiers on all her needy parishioners. She began looking for the file on the Hernandez family. "Yes," she said, half absently, "Our people are sorely pressed all right. Their fight for survival is our fight."

Mrs. Kavanagh made a funny mouth sound. "Others may not notice it, but it's as plain as the hole in the doughnut that Sister Margaret is possessed by funny and unreligious thoughts and feelings regarding young Father Perez, is what I'm sayin', Sister. If you'll forgive an old biddy for the natural honesty of her tongue."

She found the file and began looking through it. "Ah, Mrs. Kavanagh, I'm afraid you've been watching too much television."

The old lady breathed on the brass door knob and rubbed it into a mirror. "It may be that the telly is full of baloney, Sister, but so's the world." She got up and opened the door to leave, her rags and brushes and pail and ointments decorating her like a lunatic Christmas tree. "You'll know what I've been sayin' all right when those two run off together and wind up livin' in Miami Beach," and the door clicked firmly behind her.

Sister Eulalia sighed heavily, shook her head in amusement and resignation, and sat down with the folder of the problem-contaminated family of Hernandez. The father, Luis, was debauched, epileptic, a petty thief. The mother, Theresa, was a part time prostitute. The two older boys, Juan and Carlos, were both in the reformatory awaiting trial for murdering a Bronx grocery store owner during a holdup. The older daughter, Finestra, had been kicked out of high school for peddling marijuana in the playground. The seven-year-old girl, Margarita, was mentally retarded, and the baby, Francisco, had an upside-down stomach that needed fixing. They had been taken off the city relief rolls because the mother and father had thrown the social worker down the stairs of their ghetto walk-up last week when he asked them too many questions about their efforts at securing gainful employment. Luis at one time had been an automobile mechanic and Theresa knew how to make plastic flowers, having learned this trade as an inmate of a girl's correctional home in San Juan, run by the Little Sisters of Mercy.

She stared at the appalling record. A pyramid of evidence made her brain feel like a grain of Egyptian sand. For the hundredth time this week, she was made aware that the tools of reason are inadequate to deal with a large segment of human life. But since all of her education, except for that centering on God, had inculcated into her the view that man's goal is to define and categorize and then master the mysteries of this world, she found herself fighting the rising urge to use absurdity and metaphysics in order to deal with such as the Hernandez family. Furthermore, any intellectual effort that opened up the possibilities of nonreason that is, wildness and solo soaring, rather frightened her because of that living, screaming example of nonorder, her sister Mildred, who at this very moment was singing to daisies in the gardens at Rockland State. Mildred had been at odds with God's Kingdom on earth ever since she could remember. She had refused to learn to read and write until she was ten, preferring, instead, to paint pictures. She had refused religious instruction of any formal nature and had thoroughly mortified everyone concerned by hanging around those storefront churches where the Puerto Ricans and Negroes sang and danced and rolled on the floor. They thought she had changed when, after two years of college (Goddard), she joined the Peace Corps and went off to the Philippines to help the Huk peasants in their presumed struggle for the better life. They discovered how wrong they were three months later, when Mildred turned up in a cargo plane tied to a stalk of rare bananas which had been shipped from the Philippine Agriculture Minister to the Philippine Consulate in New York. She had successfully camouflaged her humanness under a remarkably deceptive papier maché copy of another stalk of bananas. Her escape from the Peace Corps had taken twelve days altogether, in the air and on the ground, from Manila to San Francisco to Kennedy Airport.

"I wish mother had kept her in Dublin," her brother Kevin had said at the time.

"It amazes me," said Kevin's wife, Meaghan, "how a family with two fine people like yourself and Sally could include a defective thing like Mildred. It certainly shows you that we know very little about genes, doesn't it?"

Kevin, now he had never given anyone a moment's bother. (It was true, though, that the old man, who had since vanished into the wastes of Cork, had, for some strange reason, openly despised Kevin, calling him "that penny-faced little shitpants.") He was a member of the New York City Police Vice Squad, and his record was indeed a glowing one. He was relentless in his work. It was Kevin who had almost singlehandedly broken up the most elite and expensive vice ring in the city, referred to by the newspapers as the Diplomats' Retreat, because of the fact that easily half the male clientele were foreign diplomats attached to the United Nations and various consulates. Half a dozen of these emissaries were immediately recalled by their home offices, and the affair threatened international fraternity. Four millionares were divorced by their wives, and five-thousand-dollar-a-week call girls, among them the notorious international beauty, Diana Harrod, the Golden Girl of Vice, who was playfriend to notables from all walks of life, were sent to Women's Prison for several weeks.

Also, several high-ranking members of the police force were demoted when Kevin's sleuthing revealed they had been protecting the ring in return for large sums of cash.

Another thing about Kevin was his puristic refusal to allow his sacred authority to be challenged by members of the criminal world. Within the five years of his police service, Kevin had shot and killed no fewer than five criminal recalcitrants—one a woman —who had resisted arrest by assaulting him. This was a department record, as was his list of vice convictions. He had been cited twice by the Mayor for distinguished service over and above his normal call of duty.

Even the church had become aware of Kevin's devout public service. "My boy," Cardinal Spellman had said to him at a Police Benefit Service, "the Department's gain has been the Church's loss. You would have made a topnotch priest." Kevin could not keep himself from crying upon hearing the words. When the Cardinal died, Kevin spent the entire day kneeling in St. Patrick's. He did not come out of his funk until, two weeks later, he arrested two former Playboy bunnies and a famous lesbian jazz singer misbehaving in a suite at the Plaza.

Knocking on the door. "Come in," she said. The hunchback dwarf who was the sleep-in caretaker entered.

"Am I disturbing you?" he asked, grinning slyly.

"No, not really."

He sat down in the big black leather chair next to her desk. It seemed to swallow him up. "Well," he began after a moment, "we need a few repairs to this old shack. The top floor plumbing is leaking again, the wiring in the basement nursery is on the blink, and somebody threw a brick through the big bay window looking out over the garden."

She sighed and shook her head. "Oh dear. The endless minutiae of the Lord's work."

"This place wants to die, Sister. Why can't you face that fact? And the people in the parish, they want to kick the bucket too."

"Now, now. You must not give in to despair."

A high laugh came from his strange form. "Despair my foot! I'm just reporting on the true story, Sister. This place and these nutsy people have had it. You're fighting a lost cause."

"You have no idea what wonderful things a little faith can accomplish. One must never, never give up."

"Listen. If a race horse keeps losing, you don't keep putting your money on him. You're not going to make the dumb thing run any faster by giving the guy at the window a sawbuck. I mean, that's basic. People have lost fortunes thinking that crazy way." He carefully peeled the cellophane from a long black cigar, licked it all around for moisture-grip, and lit up. The smoke had a leisurely other-culture arrogance in that chaste office.

"You haven't been playing the horses again, have you?"

"I never quit. But you're changing the subject, Sister. I'm trying to find out, and maybe help you do the same thing, why you are throwing yourself every day of your young life into a losing proposition."

Sister looked at him for a moment without responding, then she laughed. "Ah, you devil! You're teasing me again. I know you."

He poured cigar smoke from his nostrils, and for that moment resembled an ancient demon. "I don't tease that way, and you know it. I'm serious. I really am." He tapped his cheek and smoke rings floated toward Sister. "You've got a lot of class. You shouldn't be wasting yourself on this dung heap. If you're going to be in this business, why not go where you'll be appreciated. The upper-class sufferers, for instance. They deserve just as much help as these slobs. I mean just because they're clean and rich, doesn't mean they can't make a deal with God."

"I feel more at home among these people," Sister said, a slightly odd ashamed feeling coming over her. "I was a girl of the streets, so to speak. My parents were lower class, as you probably know. Truly, the upper classes make me nervous."

He chuckled. "You make them nervous. You're a lot better than them and they know it. Tell me something. Why did you get into this racket in the first place? Ooops . . . I mean profession."

Sister thought for a few moments about this. Should I continue this conversation? she asked herself. Can I trust him? Can I trust myself? What is happening here with this twisted little man and myself? He should not be talking to a nun in this familiar and unusual way. Why am I allowing this? Have I set up some peculiar bond with him? Then, an involuntary process began in her, really a deep organic and gentle unmeshing. Sister Eulalia was no longer thinking and feeling just as a nun. This here of her, in a way the final personal achievement, moved aside from its dominant position, (or in any event, withdrew its many lines of control) and the normal woman in her, with its own history of experience and development, made its presence felt. The nun personality observed this pluralism with distress. I knew that things like this happen, especially in women. Oddly, the strong male smell of the cigar smoke seemed to facilitate this. It had an inescapable everyday reality, a hereness. "First because my mother wanted me to," she finally replied.

"That's what I suspected," he said. "But why did your mother want it?"

She cupped her head in her hands. "That's a very good question. Well, first of all, every Irish family wants one of the children to be a priest or a nun."

"Or a cop."

"And the reason, I believe, is that the children who do so are assured of food and lodgings and a job for life. That was very important, particularly among the lower and middle classes, where there was a terrible shortage of both. Then there was the strong desire to be a member of the thing that was so powerful over your life, the Church."

"I like that," he said, puffing away in pleasure. "Very tricky."

"But I'm pretty sure my mother wanted a nun for other personal reason, besides those." The church bell began to toll the half hour, giant sounds, blind dumb sounds that belonged someplace else, in a distant farm country, a small donkey-walked village. She waited until the gonging had finished. "I think she always hated the choices she had to make in her own life, because they were degrading, or so she thought, and the choices that life forced upon her. Being a poor farm girl. Having to marry a man whether you liked him or not. Marrying my father who turned out to be a drunkard. Being abused by people because of these things, being treated like scum almost. Having to have sexual intercourse which she still thinks is bestial. And the work and responsibility of giving birth to children you never really asked for." She smiled. "In other words, my mother was a classic victim, and she wanted me to become a nun so that she could undo all that by living through me. In her mind, you see, she is me. Every day, rocking in her old wicker rocker, she imagines she is me running this parish." She suddenly laughed, a lovely lyrical girl's laugh. "Do you know that I have to write to her every day, telling her all the things I have been doing. It's like a daily script."

He slapped the arm of the big chair. "It's beautiful!"

"More than that," Sister continued. "When she writes me, at least twice a week, she instructs me to do certain things. How to talk to a particular bad child. Or what to tell a young girl who is planning to get married. The sort of food the cook must prepare for the nuns and priests who live here. Everything. Even thoughts I should be thinking when I go to bed every night. Can you imagine?"

"It's fantastic, Sister. It really is. Even kind of crazy. Doesn't it get to you at times?"

"It did in the beginning. But it doesn't anymore. I've developed a technique, a removed personality, that takes care of it. It has become automatic, a routine, like so many other things. You know."

He looked at her with amusement and affection, and then his expression softened into a seriousness. "What about the church bit, and God? Is that a routine too?"

"It certainly is for some. Just another profession."

"But is it for you?"

She looked inside herself, and then said, "At the best moments, no. Something else happens then. A true union. And then I am something other than myself. In another human, maybe divine place." She smiled totally. "It's exquisite."

"And that's God? That place or thing?"

"Yes. I think so."

"Hmm."

"It's impossible for you to imagine, isn't it?"

"Maybe. I sometimes feel the same thing when I'm drunk. It's pretty great."

She laughed. "That isn't what I'm talking about at all. Mine is very, very different."

He examined his cigar, then looked up at her. "Can you prove it? That yours is different, or better?"

She shrugged. "Well, I suppose everybody finds God, if you can call it that, in his own way."

He wagged a finger at her. "Come on now, Sister. You're pulling rank on me, trying to patronize me. That's a cheap cop-out. And you know it."

Embarrassment and anger waved over her. The idea of anyone talking to her like that, particularly a hunchback dwarf, was absurd. She did not know what to do. She struggled silently with her confusion. The nun and the normal, the past and the present, writhed and groaned. Fear and strength met face to face. The simple commonsense of her, that loveliness without the protection of particular clothing, emerged, finally. And she was relieved, she was lighter. "You're right. That was a cop-out." Smiling gently, she shook her head. "No, I can't prove it. Maybe we're talking about the same thing after all. Ecstasy."

"It's real good, Sister, no matter how you get it," he said.

"You're very hard on me, do you know that?"

"Maybe. But I'm not trying to kid you or hurt you. I wouldn't want to hurt you. I like you." He puffed luxuriously. "Maybe I love you."

"I know you don't want to hurt me." She looked around the imperviously polished Mr. Kleen-smelling office to gain a few moments, to create a new, perhaps neutral, zone of their being. The oddness and disparity of this confrontation had ceased to occupy a place in her political awareness. Buber's message, which she had read so many times, but which, like so many other messages from outside oneself (despite their pure quality), had nearly always remained in its niche of art form, now made warm sense, was now being lived more than planned or conceptualized. "The primary word I-Thou can only be spoken with the whole being." Of course. But there were light years in that of course. Verbatim the words from Buber tiptoed into her now clear mind-presence. "He goes out with his whole being to meet his Thou and carries to it all being that is in the world, finds Him who cannot be sought."

"I am seeing you in Africa," he said.

"Oh? Why?"

"Well, I don't know just why that came into my mind. But you were in Africa at one time, weren't you? I read that in the diocese newspaper."

"Yes," she said. "I was in the Congo for a year."

"Must have been rough."

"Mm. It was very rough indeed. I barely came out alive. But you know, that was the most amazing year of my life, and I really and truly met God there."

"In the nigger jungle?"

"Yes, in the black man's native home." She paused and began summoning that year back. She was smiling to herself as she did, yet including the dwarf in her smile. More, he was as much a part of the smile as she was. He was something like her Thou at this moment in her search through the world. "Perhaps that is the only time you do see Him, when you are about to die. And I think that is because only at the point of dying does a person truly cast off all his pretensions and civilized defenses and thus become human. Then God has an opportunity to reach you."

"I don't believe in God, Sister."

"Oh yes you do. But you think it is weak to admit it."

A chortle came out of the dwarf. "You don't know me very well."

"Better than you think, my friend."

"Okay. Have it your way. So what happened in the Congo that brought you and God together?"

She could smell and taste the unbridled air of that scrambled village of Konmora. And the always slightly troubling sounds, of black voices, of animals, of birds. Utterly at odds with white sounds. The very opposite. White sounds were a rejection of those black men sounds, were the terrified denial rather than being a thing positive and absolute unto themselves. Those black sounds stayed in your skin like breathing things. White sounds were merely that, and kept right on going. Those black vibrations were on her skin here in this office, now. "I loved it and was afraid of it," she said, and then she was back there. Ah yes.

Kimo, the young chieftan of the Kula, talked very straight to her that trembling January night, "Sister Eulalia," he said, his voice as rich and soft as hot velvet, "You and the other nuns must leave this place immediately. Your lives are in peril."

"We can't go, Kimo. We can't abandon our work here. The mission school, the hospital, all the villagers who have come to depend upon us. We sould be betraying them, and ourselves, to run."

He put his strong black hand on her shoulder. "You must forget all those things. They are of the past. The past does not exist anymore in my country. But you do exist, Sister, and so do the other gentle loving sisters. And this is what you must understand: the Bwaki are madly rampaging. They are burning and killing and destroying in every way possible. You do not understand these people and what is in their hearts at this time. Hatred and insanity is what consumes them. And much drunkenness. You cannot sit down and discuss things calmly with them. Calmness is completely outside them. They want very bloody revenge upon the world that has oppressed them. What I am trying to say, Sister, is that you and your lovely nuns will not only be killed, but you will be ravaged and raped and tortured before you are completely murdered." He paused. "Forgive me for being so direct but there is no other way."

They were sitting on the steps of the white stucco mission building, in the heavy darkness. Several half-naked Kula were gathered in front of the building, speaking softly among themselves. From the dirt road farther down came the whining and barking of one of the many village mongrel dogs. A radio inside the mission was alternately announcing news of the Bwaki uprising and playing old American dance-band records. The short screeching of the wild flying toga bats intermittently came from the tree area behind the mission. The surreal juxtaposition of these sounds, compounded by the Oxford accent of Kimo, was creating eerie feelings in Sister Eulalia. Ordinarily she felt herself to be all of a human piece. But now each sound, both in its absoluteness and in its rich autonomous implications (then working against other disparate sounds), each sound was attempting to break down her official and personal unity. To separate her into contradicting identities. Kimo's accent was making a singular demand upon her in this remote African bush village, taking her back to her school days in Britain; the dog sounds were summoning up the identity in her that had served in the ghettos of Harlem; the gentle night mutterings of the natives a few yards away were the here of her; the American dance music was uncovering her lost, or chastised, normal womanhood; the frantic news statements of warfare were creating a new frightened person of the future. She tried to subdue all of these personages (each of which was demanding to be let free and go its own way) and at the same time to concentrate on her immediate problem as head of the imperiled mission of Our Lady of Mercy. But those various members of her life, with those different countries of their experience, were fighting back. She tried to call forth a special power and energy, not from within herself, because that energy had been split up by those others with their quite authentic claims, but from far, far, outside, up. From, perhaps, the infinite remoteness (yet of course nearness) of the new Sister Eulalia, who was, in a sense, a divine abstraction, a star beaming signals and light from outer space.

From the distant jungle now came the ancient drum sounds, the native communications system. Endlessly subtle, enduring, penetratingly round soft messages.

"I'm not afraid, Kimo," she said at last, clasping her white smooth hands in her lap.

His sigh was so deep that it was almost a moan. "Sweet lady. I know you are not afraid. You have God on your side, and all the history of the Christian martyrs comforting your traditions and intellect. I am aware of that. But those splendid things, very splendid like Bach and those Gregorian chants, do not make the central nervous system change its simple habits, I can assure you. God and history books and all the chanting monks in the world will not stop it from screaming out in unbearable pain when the drunken raging Bwaki tribesmen are tearing off your fingers and cutting off your breasts." He bent his head. "I cannot bear the thought of it. I have seen it happen and it is not only your body they want to destroy and desecrate, it is your soul. They want to obliterate your infinity. I will not permit it to happen to you, dearest lady. No. I won't."

She took his hand and held it in both of hers, as if it were the child of his concern and anguish. "All right. I'll tell you what I will do. I. . . ." She was interrupted by a loud news broadcast coming from Stanleyville. "Government troops have been forced to withdraw from the village of Detroce after a day of heavy fighting against a force of Bwaki rebels estimated at three thousand. General Oto reported three hundred of the rebels slain. General Oto stated that the government has undeniable proof that the uprising was instigated by foreign Communist powers. The government repeats its order that all foreign peoples in the northwest province of Kotu evacuate immediately. The Bwaki rebels are committing wholesale atrocities in those Malu areas."

She drew a deep breath and continued. "I will take a vote among the sisters whether we should stay or flee. What ever decision they make I will abide with."

A very old and bent man, using a walking staff, appeared from the breathing aromatic darkness. He said something in Kula, and gave Sister Eulalia a present of three mangos wrapped in a banana leaf. Before she had time to thank him he had bowed and disappeared. "That sweet old man," she said.

"Will you please discuss this with the other Sisters tonight," Kimo implored.

"Yes. I promise you. But what about you? Aren't you afraid that the Bwaki will kill you and the rest of the villagers?"

He stared into his hands for a few seconds. "No. I am on the side of the Bwaki."

Everything inside her came to a stop. She was a stunned moment that had been disconnected from past, present and future. "You are what?"

"I have thrown in my lot and my people's with the cause of the Bwaki. We have secretly become part of their revolt against the white oppressor."

The moment that had been her now returned to a time and touch center. "Oh, I see."

"The Bwaki only wish to destroy the white, and their black puppets. The day of the white bloodcells is over, dear Sister. We are on the threshhold of waking up. Up till now the whole business has been a seriously bad dream."

What he was saying was much too rich and tricky to be assimilated and dealt with in these steps. Simple action, that would have to be the extent of it for the moment. She stood up, brushing off the back of her habit. "I'm going in now to have that discussion with the others. I'll let you know immediately what is decided."

Roughly three hours later, the Bwaki orgy of burning, raping, torturing, and slaughtering of all the Americans and Europeans and their property, began. An armed and hashish-high and drunken, half-naked force of about a hundred Bwaki did the job. The screams of the white victims—they numbered forty-one, including ten members of the Peace Corp—mixed absurdly with the pleasure yells of the Bwaki and the wild laughter of the Kula villagers, most of whom got drunk too and joined the spectacle as delighted observers. A few of them, strange young people, added weird dimension to the festivities by writhing and howling in imitation of the hapless white victims, all of whom, including the seven nuns, were dragged out into the flame and moonlit street and stripped-ripped nude by the rampaging ecstatic Bwaki. Their white bodies, amidst all that blackness, seemed more grotesque than human and therefore something repugnantly unnatural that nature itself (the all-covering and embracing black of the night being part of it) must eliminate in order for balance, or sanity and unanimity, to be restored.

The whites were simultaneously beaten, tortured, and sexually assaulted. The wild flames of the burning buildings gave the scene an end of the world quality. Each white was swarmed over by several shrieking Bwaki. Four men from the Peace Corps were buggered by a dozen Bwaki who, when they tried of this, chopped off their genitals (and later their arms and legs and heads) with machetes.

"Oh please!" one young boy, covered with blood, screamed. "My mother in heaven! Help me! Oh Mother!" Two staggering Bwaki dragged him to a burning building, hit him in the head several times with their gun butts, then threw him into the flames.

Another man whose ears had been cut off and whose rectum was bleeding profusely, shouted: "Let me go! Oh please let me go! I'll give you money, all the money you want." A laughing Bwaki dressed in a leopard skin promptly cut off his genitals and shoved the bloody things into his mouth, and began jumping up and down on his stomach. A naked little boy standing in the crowd a few feet away clapped his hands with delight and, howling wildly, stomped the ground as if he too were destroying a hated white.

Two big Bwaki, splotched with blood from other encounters

there, were wrestling on the ground with three of Sister Eulalia's nuns, Sister Margaret, Sister Theresa, and Sister Mary, who looked even fatter with all of her clothes off. Sisters Mary and Theresa wept and cried out as the men hit and bit and beat them, but Sister Margaret did not utter a sound as she fought the raging black giant of top of her. Her unthinkable silence enraged the man even more and he slapped her face several times to bring sound from it, but nothing issued forth except blood. Her body suddenly relaxed and the Bwaki jammed his sex into her and began violently to hump and bite her and lick the blood that was pouring from her mouth and nose. The crowd yelled its approval.

"Kill her sex!" someone shouted.

"Yeah yeah!" several chanted. "Yeah yeah!"

A great piercing scream of pain was loosed by fat Sister Mary. The man assaulting her—he had pulled her on top of himself—had bitten off one of her nipples and was rubbing his face over her huge bleeding breast. "Save me Jesus!" she howled. "Oh save me!"

Another Bwaki joined them. He kicked her enormous rump, knocking her over on the blood-sucking man. "Jesus shit!" this Bwaki shouted. He pounded her rump and back with this club he was carrying and kept shouting, "Jesus shit! Jesus shit!"

The man underneath her began penetrating her from that position, savagely pulling her huge buttocks apart as he did. The second Bwaki then dropped his club, fell on her back, and rammed his member into her spreading anus. A chorus of pleasure went up from the crowd of natives around them. A crazed mongrel circled them, barking and snapping and whining.

Sister Theresa too was being ravaged now by two sweating drunken warriors. She was flat on her back. One warrior was sitting on her face and rubbing his genitals over her, while the other was furiously licking and biting her sex. Her writhings became weaker and weaker. One of the burning buildings collapsed in a huge roar of fire. Billowing smoke was obscuring the village and the howling, berserk crowds. Burning flesh reeked through the other insane smells. Kerosene cans stored in one of the Peace Corps sheds exploded, and the whole scene was for moments illuminated with millions of splintering flaming wood fragments. Loud cheers from the demonic crowds.

Directly in front of the flaming mission house, two of the

Sisters, Anna and Catherine, were literally being devoured by the crazed warriors. And crucified. Two laughing, blood-stained warriors were holding the struggling Sister Anna while a third waving a machete first hacked off her large breasts. "Ayyy!" she screamed, and the blood gushed all over her twisting white body. "Mercy Jesus!" Then the machete man, beside himself with excitement, plunged the machete into her belly and slit her open completely. A torrent of blood spilled from her. The man dropped his machete and, maddened by the sight before him, began tearing out her insides—her entrails, her lungs, her heart, and throwing them behind him into the leaping, yelling Kula villagers and Bwaki killers.

"Yes! Yes!" a woman shrieked. "Fine thing! Much blood!"

The two men holding Sister Anna released her gushing rent body, and two more warriors, shouting things in their own language, began hacking off her head and arms and legs, and throwing these dismembered bleeding pieces into the air.

"Bad sister!" a woman shouted, catching an arm. "All gone. Oh yes!" Quite carried away, she began hitting a fellow bystander over the head with the bloody arm. The native being hit reacted with wild laughter.

Near the dry goods store (which had been one of the first buildings to be looted and burned and into whose flaming madness the Indian and his wife who ran it were thrown after being machine gunned into bleeding rags), a beleaguered young Peace Corps fellow, being alternately flogged and forced into a variety of sexual acts, among them sucking two stoned warriors' genitals from a kneeling position, during the act of which a little boy very much amused stepped out of the crowd and pissed all over his back, suddenly broke away from his tormentors and ran toward the edge of the jungle about fifty yards away. Instead of upsetting the Bwaki, this development pleased them. They used his fleeing white body for target practice. Two expertly and powerfully thrown spears brought him down for good, generously penetrating his body from back to front. The spectators clapped and shouted their appreciation of such fine throwing skill.

A very special thing, a ritual of a sort, was taking place with Sister Bertha several yards away, under the ancient spreading branches of an enormous eucalyptus tree. She was tied to a huge cross made of two building boards that had been in a stack along-side the mission building. This crucifix was leaning upright against the trunk of the big tree. A great bonfire of furniture and beds and papers from the mission lit up the proceedings. The crowd around this spectacle was very large and noisy and the black sweating bodies glistened in the light of the bonfire. Many gourds of homemade beer were being passed around in this excited drunken swarm. A couple of drums were being thumped and some in the crowd were swaying back and forth to the rhythmic sounds. About fifty jubilant warriors—most of them wildly drunk —were shouting and leaping and shaking their spears and guns and clubs at the naked nun on the cross. Several of the Bwaki had passed out on the ground. The blood of their white victims stained their snoring black bodies. A long skinny warrior, who was com-pletely nude except for a nun's beads and crucifix around his neck, was lying on top of the unconscious, dirt and blood smeared body of a Peace Corps girl. Every now and then he stirred himself and made weak pumping sex motions (her legs were lewdly spread wide), then collapsed back into half consciousness himself.

The ecstasy and fury of their raid had clearly not pre-empted the Bwaki's sense of humor. Two of them—one a muscular giant, the other a short fat fellow with a silver ring in his nose—had dressed themselves in nuns' habits, starched white hats and all. On the naturalistic comedy level, their transvestism was an enormous howl to the orgiastic crowds as well as to themselves. On the deeper identity level it opened up a mind-breaking surrealism. The sight of two demented black nuns dragging a squealing naked white woman along the ground—that was truly a reality of an-other order.

"Me nun!" the giant shouted. "Me nun. Nigger nun!"

"Mister nun!" the others yelled, laughing. "Mister Sister!"

Machine gun and rifle fire came from the other end of the village.

Hanging on the huge wood cross, Sister Bertha looked both obscene and sublime. Her shaved head, for example, made her seem, at first glance, a peculiar man; her voluptuous white body —rich, pointed breasts that swooped boldly out rather than sagged; generous curving hips; elegantly smooth and mellifluous thighs—shockingly contradicted this. So in a way it seemed that two humans—a strange man and a woman were joined there in the crackling flame light. Her head hung to one side, and on her face was an expression neither of agony nor disgust, but rather, of sublime, permanent, ageless open-eyed vacuity, exactly the face and feeling of a marble statue from the Renaissance. Not a tear, not a smudge, not a mark interrupted that infinite smoothness. Her heavy black pubic hair was the very poem of immediacy and humanness that has always been missing from the otherwise splendid representations of the man from Nazareth on the Cross.

The ceremonies began when a gray-haired old Bwaki, their chief, emerged from the writhing, leaping group and solemnly approached the cross. He was wearing a shimmering zebra skin; gold bracelets covered his arms. He stopped a foot from Sister Bertha's legs, and began to speak, or really intone, to the hanging figure. He was reciting some kind of ritualistic prayer. The crowd had become suddenly quite silent, and the only noise in that immediate area came from the crackling, sensually roaring bonfire that was ravenously consuming the effects of the mission. The chief's melodious, unhysterical recitation lasted for about two minutes. At the end of it he pointed at Sister Bertha's face, suddenly shouted three or four words, then made a final horizontal gesture with his hand flat. (A long scream of unbearable pain came from somewhere in the villlage, but no one around the cross and bonfire was distracted by it.) At this point in the ceremony a young warrior stepped up to the chief, bowed, handed him a long dagger, and then bowed away. It shone elegantly in the fire's orange-red light. The chief kissed the dagger, pressed the kissed side against Sister Bertha's forehead (her smooth staring expression had not changed at all, nor had her body twitched or trembled in fear or awareness of what was going on around it; she was in a trance state) and plunged it between her full, firm breasts, and with a minimum of effort, cut out her heart. The blood that squirted and splashed over her (at the thrust of the dagger her body writhed for the first time but no scream came from her mouth, merely a long gentle sigh) somehow did not have the effect of making her look disgusting and frightening (as the gore had besmirched the others' loveliness.) Instead, it contributed to an other-wordly sensuality that permeated her.

When the chief plucked her still throbbing heart out, a collective gasp-moan came from the crowd, a sonorous exhaling of breath and awe. "Ahhh!" He held the bleeding heart for everyone to see, said several words very loudly, then, with a suddenness and ferocity that were more characteristic of a beast than a human, bit off a piece of it, and, his face splotched with blood and blood running from his mouth, began chewing and swallowing. He said something else, and passed the heart to a beaming, rifle-holding warrior near him. The warrior took a bloody bite, and passed the living heart on. The chief began licking Sister Bertha's blood off his hands and arms, savoring its taste and immortalness. Thus was Sister Bertha devoured, thus did a dozen warriors take her flesh and her essence into their own flesh and essence. And each one, after passing the diminishing heart on, carefully and thoroughly tongued her blood from their hands and mouths. As the heart was passed reverently around, the natives and swarms of Bwaki warriors danced and sang to the beating of the small skin drums.

Two native boys threw a yelping village mongrel into the bonfire. Several still unsatiated warriors ran up and down the dirt streets firing their automatic rifles into the buildings, both the thatch huts of the blacks and the more solid buildings of the loathed nonblacks. Several native women, swept up by madness and the hashish and home brew, were fornicating in the streets with the warriors and laughing hysterically. The stench of burning flesh, both animal and human, wafted mercilessly through the gorged polluted air. Out in the bush a hyena, attracted by the flames, barked insanely. An Artie Shaw dance record began playing very loudly.

SISTER EULALIA WAS SEATED IN KIMO'S HOUSE, a large round thatched hut situated on a slight rise at the north end of the village. Seated in a semi-circle around her were the two leaders of the Bwaki, Benda and Luku, and Kimo. Benda was a young man, in his middle twenties, and his face, elegantly featured and Egyptian rather than Negroid, was a consortium of angelic contempt. Around his neck hung a heavy hand-wrought silver and turquoise necklace that featured several large bleached animal fangs. He wore thick silver earrings. He was bare to the waist; his skirt was a bright red and yellow madras. Luku, who was in his early forties, was a being of pure and incorruptible energy, the born hunter. His glow, his deep emanation, was not vitiated by the nonsense of intellectuality. An S design had been cut into each side of his face, and his teeth had been filed into points. He wore an ocelot skin.

"Quite a bash those chaps are having out there," said Benda, smiling archly. (His speech was English public school.) "I would imagine that it is most revolting to you, Sister Eulalia."

"Unspeakably loathsome," she said. She had removed her mind and feelings to a rational remoteness in order to keep from disintegrating with horror.

"It is ironic," Benda continued, "because this sort of thing has been practiced for centuries by your Church. The Inquisition, the Crusades, the war against the Walloons—those episodes come to my mind. We could even dip into the Bible."

"You are insane and inhuman to be enjoying this," she said.

Luku chuckled. "This Sister is a very tasty one," he said, his speech also English accented. "She would make a good wife to play with." He swigged from the scotch bottle and handed it to Benda. Kimo looked pained but philosophical, and often stared at the floor (after looking from face to face for some sort of answer or promise or new dimension of reality).

"You cannot make a case against my historical facts, can you, Sister?" Benda asked, sipping from the bottle. "Oh well, I am not surprised. All of you white Christians are the same. You absolutely refuse to share your monopoly of power. You are simply, and crudely, unwilling to allow us the right to perpetrate what you perpetrate. Your entire conceptual system is predicated upon domination and superiority. Any violation of this a priori vanity turns your stomach but does not reveal anything to you."

Sister Eulalia felt that he was the force of Evil Incarnate, that he was infinitely more than just the taunting savage sitting in front of her planning her physical obliteration. "Why are you going through this absurd interrogation?" she asked, gripping her chair. "Why don't you kill me and have done with it?" She looked toward Kimo. "What are they doing, Kimo?"

He spread his hands in perturbation. "Dear Sister, I am not the architect of their thoughts. They are their own masters."

"You know," Benda said, grinning his dry-ice grin, "it is a pity that you poor idiots did not prepare yourselves for our obscene missions with a little reading. Allow me to read the words of someone you should know, Frantz Fanon." He plucked a pamphlet from his folds and began to read. " 'In decolonization, there is therefore the need of a complete calling in question of the colonial situation. If we wish to describe it precisely, we might find it in the well-known words, *The last shall be first and the first last.* Decolonization is the putting into practice of this sentence. That is why, if we try to describe it, all decolonization is successful.'

" 'The naked truth of decolonization evokes for us the searing bullets and bloodstained knives which emanate from it. For if the last shall be first, this will only come to pass after a murderous and decisive struggle between the two protaganists. That affirmed intention to place the last at the head of things, and to make them climb at a pace the well-known steps which characterize an organized society, can only triumph if we use all means to turn the scale, including, of course, that of violence.' "

He put the pamphlet away. "That should cast a little light on the situation, my dear absurd Sister."

Smiling, Luku slowly got up and came to her. He lifted her black nun's skirt and exposed her bare white thighs. She acted as though he did not exist. She knew he would be pleased if she struggled like an ordinary woman. She would not give him that recognition. Concentrating on a particular afternoon in Dublin, when she was being instructed in singing by a fat priest named O'Toole, helped her maintain aloofness. "Ah! Fine thighs. There are many splendid games in them." Still holding her skirts up, he turned to Benda. "Brother, let us stop this jabbering and have our sport. This tasty lady needs to be christened." He groped her privates. "Yes indeed. She is all there." He smelled and licked his fingers. "Mm. Honeysuckle."

Kimo hung his head at this incredible brazenness, and his act made Benda laugh. "Poor Kimo. The white Catholic teachers of your youth diseased you with their kind of guilt. What a pity for you. It prevents you from completely and truly being a black man." He paused and looked patronizingly at the distressed Kimo. "I do hope it does not prevent you from completely giving yourself to our cause. That would be a very unpleasant failure." He drank some scotch from the bottle. "You know, dear Kimo, it is quite possible for your head to be in many different places. But your heart can be in but one place, and one place only. Please try to understand that most crucial fact."

Kimo nodded his head slowly. "I understand."

Sister Eulalia, her remote cool collapsing, suddenly shouted, "Scum!"

Luku slapped her face hard. "Stupid bitch!"

A mirthful sound came from Benda. "All right, Sister, that's all from you. Now for your cleansing and rebirth, as your Church would say. Please be so kind as to take off those holy clothes."

She felt both strength and fear, and for the first time in her life as a nun she had an unavoidable apprehension of the challenge of her calling. "Nothing you do to my body could possibly affect my spirit. You are wasting your time."

Luku roughly assessed her breasts. "Hm. Some nice stuff there too."

"Please, Sister, the clothes. We will now investigate the spirit and the flesh relationship."

In order to deal successfully with the approaching ordeal, she made a quick but complex personal change deep within the who am I and where am I and what is happening to me areas before rising from the chair to do Benda's bidding. She became a young girl convert in an old religious play she had once seen in London. The God-loving girl was beset by Protestant village brutes who hated the power of the Pope. So this foulness she was in now became a play, and no matter how awful the things that took place, they were still theatric make-believe—but with a moral, of course. Firmly rearranged in this play, she took off her nun's habit. What otherwise (in the real here) would have been overpowering shame and disgust, now, in her new reality and identity, became transmuted into glowing pride and superiority pleasure: she could now fully throw herself into the debasing experience, absorb it instead of fighting it, participate without restraint, joyously in fact, in the sensuality and pain and mental assault, because she would be converting it into something else. What to these three black men would seem to be shocking compliance and enjoyment in this game would be, in her role, passionate joy in her courage and convictions as the beset seventeenth-century maiden. To cringe and fight and deny would have made of this maid an unworthy athlete of Christ and therefore there would have been no triumph and no play. The greater her sensual response, the greater the other reality was being brought alive; it was its profoundly paradoxical fuel. These black men had to fall before such reasoning. As Sister Eulalia stripped herself of her elegant, yet ascetic, black garments she thereby divested herself of the person and representation about which the imminent vile program was oriented, and also (as in a metaphor) made her more the maid who in the play was forced to suffer her indignities without benefit of garments.

"Look, Benda! The lady smiles!"

"Ah so!" exclaimed Benda, rising and stepping up to the now naked Sister, and looking her over. "Don't be deceived by it, Luku. With this smile she is conveying her contempt for us."

Luku, caressing her stomach and full thighs, then her breasts, said, "You're wrong. This smile is passion, man, female excitement. Can't you tell? Look at the hot color coming into her face and most meaty body. Feel the skin swell all over her need. Look! Look at the eyes, Benda! Those are the eyes of a woman in the bed. Man oh man!"

Benda stared unbelieving into her glowing, smiling face, seeking the deceit. He touched her heavy redolent lips, and slapped her hard twice. "Pig! Liar!"

His blows were delicious gusts upon her Christian martyr's fire. Her spirit was rising with rich sweet volume.

"This woman is magnificent!" howled Luku, and he grabbed her breasts from behind, poised himself urgently against her firm buttocks and bit her lustfully in the shoulder. She moaned with her love for Jesus-pleasure. "I am dying for her!" Luku yelled, and threw her to the dirt floor of the hut. She offered no resistance; on the contrary, in her now total transformation of identity and reality, the most natural and logical response was one of cooperation. Thus, she spread her legs and arched them back the more to facilitate this indignity-turned-glorification. Luku plunged his black member into her reddish black forest, squealing with amazement, passion and primitive delight. He put his tongue deep in her open sighing mouth and Sister Eulalia nearly swallowed it in her own soaring. At this point she was in the first act of the seventeenth-century play, was completely the God-chosen maid, and she knew that with every harassment and obscenity, she was getting closer to sainthood. She cried out and wrapped her legs around Luku, who was thrusting into her like a maddened beast and licking and biting her face and lips and neck. She saw his skin as the white skin of a seventeenth-century village poltroon and in her ears—now the ears of the simple maid destined for Heaven—was the roar of the audience witnessing this purifying performance.

"We'll teach you!" screamed the incensed, still bewildered Benda. "We'll bring down your wretched vanity!"

At that moment the transported Luku (who had managed to pull his native skirt off, revealing a shiny black mass of writhing muscle) rolled over and maneuvered Sister Eulalia on top of him. She was now participating in this sex as wildly as Luku, biting at him and panting as he had and pumping and rubbing alternately on him. Her excitement-conversion was totally consuming.

Benda, his elegant features now twisted with confusion and rage, suddenly lashed her buttocks with his short lead-tipped whip. Fire shot through her. She screamed ecstatically and slammed her pelvis against Benda's. "Repeat after me!" Luku commanded, lashing her again. "God is filth!"

"God is filth!" she shrieked, twisting and humping on top of Luku, whose eyes were closed in bliss.

Benda's whip came down again on her back. Another scream of joy from Sister.

"God is vomit!" he yelled.

"God is vomit!"

More lashes, up and down her back and heaving buttocks and sweating legs. "Christianity is an abomination against human life!"

"Christianity . . ." Her joy was threatening to drown her conscious senses. Sweat was pouring down her reddened face. "Christianity . . . is . . . an abomination . . . against . . . human life!"

Luku's black strong hands grabbed at her welted buttocks so savagely that his sharp nails drew blood. Animal grunts and roars were coming from his mouth. Benda was shaking with fury and spittle was oozing from the corners of his lips. "I piss on the Infant Child!" His whip snapped across her bottom.

"I . . . piss . . . on . . . the Infant . . . Infant . . . Child!" She was on the verge of consummate grace. The world, and herself, was become formless sounds and colors and sensations of unbearable physical and spirtual euphoria.

The whip struck her neck. "Death to all white men!" Her back was striped with vivid welts.

She now reached climax. Her entire being soared into millions of symphonic bits, and a high long scream of infinity contact began rising from her throat. Luku too howled his own coming. Benda, now totally demonic, dropped his whip, flung her over onto her back on the floor (she continued expanding into heavens of saintly climax), and yanking a statuette of the Virgin Mother holding the Baby Jesus from his clothing folds, rammed it all the way into her inflamed vagina. Her second climax exploded around this sacred object. Every tissue, nerve and brain cell in Sister Eulalia was in an aurora borealis of incredible vision. Then she was floating on a plateau of momentary gently vibrating quiet. Delicate space sounds were surrounding this astral area. And then she saw Him . . . the whispering vapors and colors began to assume the grand visage of God Himself. An immeasurable wisdom and fatherly presence. His face was unspeakably intimate in its familiarity and at the same time oceanic in its remoteness. He smiled and spoke and Sister Eulalia felt herself gently disappearing into His words and omniscience.

"Come unto me, my beloved daughter," God said, His voice a vast cloud of softness, and absorbed her utterly.

XVI GEORGE SCRATCHES HIS HEAD, RUNS

his hand over the three-day weedy growth on his thin undeniable face, and looks across the permanently obtuse oak table at his fellow flower, Pierre Montand. "This smelly inn is getting on my nerves, Pierre. I am beginning to itch on the bottoms of my feet."

Pierre laughs and his fatness giggles—the entire business more suited to a bubbling, roiling, hissing pot of leek and kidney stew than anything you would want to put a first and last name to. "You are a funny one, my dear friend. You complain about this life as though it were all new to you." He bubbles and oozes again. His breath is insane with onion. "You should have been born a prince of the blood, not a bastard and a thief and now a murderer." He swallows off the rest of his wine and bangs on the brain-damaged table for more.

George sighs, picks his nose, and flicks away a gob of yesterday's poetry. "Pah! I didn't mean to kill the old jade. If she hadn't screamed out, nothing would have happened to her." He suddenly chortled—not a laugh, not a giggle, but an old lone Andalusian chortle, such as was first imported into England in the fourteenth century by a rich Suffolk family—the Baillie outfit to be exact— that had run out of its own sounds. " 'Twas like skiving a jelly doughnut!"

"Fair enough," says Pierre. "She was the baker's wife." He sucks on a chicken giblet, as though he had gone to kindergarten with it.

George mouths some wine and looks around this pig's lair of an inn that is also, of course, a public tavern, open to anyone with the price of a drink and a covering for his loins. Knaves from every English garden are flopped about the place, largely in arrogant disarray. Not a moral there, nor the slightest respect for God, country, or mother. Mostly males, but here and there a bawd of raging indecency and a farewell to the middle-class minuet as they have all known it (from hearsay and outside observation, naturally). Business half exposed in the manner of King Henry VIII's time, codpieces nestled poignantly between tightly sheathed thighs, waistcoats stained with all of life's dribble, some presumptuously ruffled blouses or shirts. Hats to make an actors' troupe squeal with recognition, and even a couple of flutey feathers from birds who had their say but were not listened to. A rabble chorus of body smells and foods and spirits and one fallen chimney sweep.

A saucy lady with something of a flush about her pinchable cheeks winks more than openly at George and he wearily waves his long-fingered hand, not a turndown so much as I have other things on my agenda and my body and mind can only do so much; perhaps later, dear thing. In a corner of the room two chaps are arguing over a split of some sort of booty. Getting bitter too.

George emits a quantity of mournful air. "I think I've got the scurvy."

"Hmm. Maybe you need a good bleeding."

George shakes his head. "No. You're thinking of gout. Scurvy is different. What I need is a hot climate and some nice fresh fruit."

An old man who looks like an intimate companion of goats and sheep drifts in playing on a flute. He is followed by a raggedy seducer of a child who goes from table to table with a hat.

"Did you know that our good king Hal writes dancing music —when he's not chopping off his wives, that is?" says Pierre, a chicken neck in his fingers now.

"And why not?" says George.

A pause from Pierre who sort of stares at George. "Yes. Quite. I see what you mean."

George does it with his wine and says rather much to himself, smiling smally (a soft crack in the world's ramparts) "We used to practice Latin together, we did." Shakes his lovely golden head. "Those days are past using."

This cheeky flounce comes up, grinning from mole to mole. Nice bottom and the sliver of cunning in her eye. "What about it, gentlemen? A toss for a shilling." She chucks Pierre under his overhang. "Do your outlook a world of good, y'know."

"Indeed," says Pierre, and takes her fingers in play.

George penetrates her with a gaze of direct poetry. "You could be my sister."

A giggle and a laugh and a clutching of her ripe bosom from the girl. "Blimey! That would be a pickle, wouldn't it!"

"Indeed," says George, "but not mine."

She looks at him with grown interest and amusement. "Quite a cod, aren't you?"

"Mm."

Pierre gets all of his juicy levers and hoists going in his corpulosity and gets up, still in possession of girlfinger. "I'm going to lighten my soul and you know what with this lass, George. Leave you to your visions for a bit. All right?"

A brotherly smile from George. "There's something very natural about you, Pierre. I like that."

The girl twirls herself with a guffaw, and they grapple off. Pierre's right hand is already staking out a choice plot on her untrammeled rump. George watches them disappear up the groaning old stairs. "Latin wouldn't have been his dish. Not at all."

Quite a bottle of noise from the two divvying up in the rear. Smashed glass. Oaths and threats. A firm-sized crashing and thudding of body hitting chair and then floor. Some routine scurrying and pattering sounds of management and house lackies hopping to the clean-up scene. A wild laugh of triumph. Resume normal sounds of tavern lowlife. The beggar boy approaches George, his sweat-compromised old hat right under George's decent nose.

"You look well enough fed to me," observes George to the lad.

The boy makes a pained face. "Me arse. Don't be a smellpot about it."

"Hm. Yes, you're quite right. That has nothing to do with the situation, does it?" And he gives him a couple of ha' penny pieces.

The boy pockets them, then grins directly from his own little cesspool. "Not queer for starvin' lads, are ya?" Runs off into the forest of stained tables.

"Not so far," George says to his vanishment.

He muses over the outside sounds. Carriage-wheel rumblings and squeaks. Horse whinnies. Shouts of local merchants about their wares. "Feathers here! Fine goose feathers!" A cock crows, then a flutter of panic wings. Anvil clangs. A child's voice calling to its mum. She answers from afar. A high nasal voice cluttered with deprivation, love, diminishing youth. George makes up her face. Bad teeth but succulent cheeks and lips of evening's promise starting around noon. A bugle blows. The postman with absurd announcements from out there. He remembers another time he had come to Exeter, with his Dad. They had journeyed all the way from Southhampton to visit his crinkly old gran who was giving up the ghost cough by cough. The Dad had fallen off a farm roof in the gurgling, groping explosion of very human relief after the final pointless sigh. Ah misery! Why did I have to run the red of that barfing pastry!

The bar bawd's face and naked bosom appear over the balcony railing. Her pink face is a breeding ground of short-term spurty pleasure. "Sure you won't join us, luv?" she inquires.

"It isn't that I don't like you," he says raising his voice to be heard above the tavern raunch, "Because I do. I mean, you honestly are an arm and mouthful." He sips some wine. Throat dry. "It's just that I've got these other things on my mind. And I've only got one imagination. Do you see?"

"I guess so." Her hair is a song of wanton disarray, the sort of thing that makes magistrates summon the stockade just at the thought of.

"Besides," George continues (a silliness of afternoon light keeps tickling his face) "there's that thing about you and my sister."

"So you said. What's her name?"

George permits a grin to sneak through. "I don't have a sister. I said that for quite other reasons."

A mirth happening is experienced by the bawd. "Oh dear! You are a jokey one."

She is suddenly yanked away by bare-chested, heavy-handed Pierre.

"Hm," murmurs George to his own presence, "the humor here is sleepy."

Nothing to do but accept the bowlegged tavern lackey's offer of another tumbler of the sauce and a small bowl of river mussels. The poor bum's face is scarred from a flashing shiv. "Thrupenny," mutters the man.

"It's a cheat," says George, tossing it to him.

"I know," says he, "but 'tisn't my place."

George lays out a rounded, three-point fart, but no one around cares about this at all. None of these particular Englishmen are very polite themselves. Too hard-pressed by life's small-change requirements. A vaguely familiar-looking chap with a high cheekbone and a well-read eye, comes over from a near table, sits down, puts a clean hand on George's shoulder, and says,

"You've a secret in your face."

George's hand rubs his own features. "Wouldn't be at all surprised. I didn't wash this morning."

"I've been observing you, and I think I have a plan for you."

A careful but not hostile scrutiny of this one by George. "Haven't I seen you somewhere before?"

"Possibly," the visitor answers. "But I wouldn't bet on it too heavily."

"I'm not a plunger."

"Wise of you. Well, you're not blissful here, and we both know that."

"Continue."

"For you to not be here, that's our problem."

"Do you do this sort of thing for a living?" asks George.

Man shakes his cared-for head. "Pater has money."

"Good."

"Had money, that is. Died last year of bee sting."

"Oh, too bad, What was his jib?"

The chap swallows a couple of times. "The cut of, you mean? Well . . . a decent sort, really. Very careful about himself personally, if you know what I mean."

"I rather like an old party who's careful about himself." George reveals. "Shows, uh, pride."

"Oh yes. You're right about that." He looks out of the doorway for a couple of velvet moments. A dove flies by. Then, "Say, do you chase after the fox?"

George shakes his head. "Absolutely not. The shedding of beasts' blood is completely against me."

The chap's face morning glories with pleasure. "I can't tell you how much it pleases me to hear that. Really." A felt pause. "My plan for your immediate salvation . . ."

"Excuse me," interrupts George. "But what's in this for you?"

"Nothing. Nothing whatever."

"Then . . . uh . . . why are you doing it?"

The man thinks for a few moments, then shrugs, "I don't really know. I seem to be pushed from outside myself."

"Hmm. In a magical way, would you say?"

"Yes. Quite."

"I see. All right. The plan."

The other, the Chosen Helper, smiles and bobs his head. He opens his mouth to let the jeweled stuff come out, then sees the bowl of black river mussels as if for the first time, stares at George and says, "Your black river mussels. You haven't eaten but one!"

"Yes, I know," says George, without the slightest display of shameface.

The other puts his hand on George's somewhat beseechingly. "But my dear man, why? These mussels are the pride of the valley."

"Well, they just don't seem to have the proper air about them." He looks pensively, but not at all accusingly, at the objects in question. "They look as if they're dreaming. Wouldn't you say?"

Short eyes grips the mussels in undivided interrogation for three moments. "I would never have thought of it just that way. But I certainly grasp your implications. Yes."

"Excellent."

The other shifts back in his chair (very oak) removing his soul from the mussel snooze. "So there. The plan at last. Simply write to the Sheriff of Gloucester and tell him the whole thing was a terrible mistake. That you absolutely did not mean it. That such an act is utterly outside the tradition of your desires. You see?"

George considers. His foot itches but he refrains from doing anything about it. "Mm. Then what takes place?"

"Precisely the following. He reads your letter, is most moved by it, says to himself 'By Jove! Here's a chap of high quality who has been short-handed by Fate. Must not allow that.' And he forthwith sends you an official pardon."

"Oh?"

"Absolutely. In fact, I can assure you." He dips into his jacket's secret interior, "I have his pardon right here." He hands George a scrolly thing.

George eyes and fingers its immediacy and even, because he's not an easy one to turn inside out, sniffs at its regal edges. "No doubt about it, I suppose. Tip-top handwriting, I must say."

The other almost drowns the area with such a smile "I knew you would approve!"

George clears his throat. "Does he do it himself? Or is it the work of a hired finger?"

A shake of the head from the other. "That is something I am not allowed to discuss with you."

"Oh. Sorry."

"Now then . . ." He does the interior dipping thing again. "Here is your letter. If you will append your name to the bottom where I've put a tiny x, the whole business will have become a fait accompli, as my tutor would say."

George does as he is so tastefully bid. No silly country questions this time.

"Splendid. Here is the Sheriff's exoneration of the unfortunate unhistorical act performed in Exeter against the untimely baker lady. And History once more swallows her pride." He gets up (our very old oak creaks at this suddenness, of course). "You are a free man now." That table-devouring grin of his again. "That is, as free as your own imagination and circumstances allow you." He shakes George's more or less willing hand.

"Awfully nice of you, old fruit," says George.

"Don't let's go into it, please."

"Oh. All right. Say, I wonder how Pierre is doing." A wink from his benefactor. "That one's in clover."

"Is that her name?"

A shake of the other's head. "You should fight that sort of low humor down, my dear friend."

"Sorry about that."

The other leaves, by the front door, squeezing past a besotted, belching, unmoving lump with a nose that would have played "God Save the Queen" had it been given the opportunity. George goes back to his winebowl and ruminates. The tavern roiling has slightly increased in expansive gestures; arguments, chair bumpings, and even solo singing by a blowsy young thing with the marks of pock upon her early debauch and decline.

"She made a puff sound when it went in," George says to nobody. "A cloud of powder issued forth from her. Was that lady make-up? Or was it sugar-dust? Dear Lord! That could have been an enormous jelly doughnut I stabbed, not the baker's wife at all. I mean, the shriek could have come from somewhere else completely. Must admit I was quite beside myself with heavy drink at the time. Hmm. That death-of-a-jelly-doughnut possibility certainly does open up one's mind, doesn't it?"

Of course, no one says a thing to him, not even the heavy-jowled, cock-hatted smellies muttering at the next table. So George beckons the lackey and orders himself a jellied pig's foot. A fellow's got to eat, no matter how things are going.

He is stared at for further character understanding.

"Very well, sir. The foot of a pig it'll be." He's off through the tavern jostle. But then he does deny this by returning.

The tavern servant—graying muttonchops on his drooping cheeks and teeth that nobody would want under any circumstances—avoids George's decent gaze and looks instead at the dirt under his own nails. "Lark pie, sir," he finally says. "That's our special pride here."

George shakes his head. "No. I absolutely cannot eat anything that flies."

The servant scratches his old belly and shifts uneasily in his footing (looks bathroom-bound). "We put mushrooms in it."

Another headshake from George. "No sky life for me."

All right. George is doing quite a lot with the pig's foot. Into his mind, which was not engaged in the immediate shameless bodily salivations, and which, in point of fact, very considerably had its own requirements and ways, without limit (and of course placeless), like a bird with a full belly, well, into this timeless freedom comes a remembrance of something he'd read in the priest's library in London when a few years younger. "Whence comes to all sovereign nobility? From a gentle heart, adorned by noble morals . . . No one is a villain unless it comes from his heart." That had been written down (first sung, he knew) by one of those melancholy troubadors a couple of hundred years previous, in the middle of the thirteenth.

(A certain amount of time passage required, and of course understood.) Slurping, sucking, groveling, giving no ground yet no offense either, putting himself on the foot's level, no nonsense about class superiority or patronizing noblesse oblige, entering fully into its juices and tendons, and not ignoring or otherwise cold-shouldering one iota of its fat, so that his face gets a good pig smearing. So complete that he doesn't even notice until it is all over that a dancy-eyed wench with more than ordinary earrings has sat down at his very table.

"Go right on eating," she says, straightening her skirts. "I merely thought I would take this opportunity to make a few statements about my life as a member of the Jewish business community here in rural England."

George nods his approval and noisily sucks a tiny soft bone.

"Thank you," she continues. "My name, by the bye, is Mrs. Cecelia Katz, wife of the local silversmith." George nods his assent to this fact. "We deal in the vanity of others, but we are good people."

"I've heard that before," George says.

"The life of a Jew is a hard thing indeed. We try our best to perform as people ask us and at the same time keep our dignity."

"A feat of the gravest desperation," George allows, and sucks a tiny round piggy bone.

She nods. "Aye, that it is, make no mistake about it. What is a man if he satisfies the world but cannot greet himself in his own mirror? A shadow among shadows. So what does he do? He conjures up the past, which denies the present and makes of the future a stillborn babe. The private evenings in our abode become rituals out of the Bible." She blows her nose. "The Jew is History." She crosses herself, takes a mussel for sustenance, and continues, "And that is why we are so put upon and hated. The Gentile cannot look back for fear he may disappear into the dreams that made him. I can't say that I blame him, but that does not mean I forgive him. He will not share the living moment with us, he devours it in his terror and is puzzled because he remains so famished. Oh dear. When will it all end?"

Heady wine trickles down George's morseled throat. "Maybe never," he says.

She looks softly out through the doorway. Her red lips are full and freshly licked. Glistening. "But we keep on trying, nevertheless. There is absolutely nothing we town Jews don't do to make you Gentiles feel a little bit better about things. The list is as long as the road to Shrewsbury and it's getting longer every day. We walk about looking sensitive and apprehensive so that you can feel strong and confident. We wring our hands, dart our eyes, slurp our words, and in general seem sly and dirty so that you may feel clean and straight. We amass wealth to encourage you to think we are not concerned with the spiritual things in life. We force our children to become artists and intellectuals in order for you to feel inferior to them and thus have an immediate object for the hatred you have for yourselves and must continually direct against others, if you are not to be destroyed in an instant of self-confrontation. Our women develop a coquetry of mystery to excite the wildest secret passions of your men in order to keep them going, for your own women in their primness forbid their bestial dreams. Your wanton stiffs are the leaping poles to your primeval sanity, but of course it would be beyond you to accept that they flutter with our accommodating eyelashes. And finally, we even deny the Messiah to even the score for our being the Chosen People. Can you imagine what a hell on earth this life would be if we took Him from you?"

George wipes his hands on his breeches, permits his thirst a mild reprieve of wine, half succeeds in cozzening a belch, and says, "I don't want to think about it, Mrs. Katz."

She smiles and avails herself of a second mussel. "I wouldn't either if I were you."

"My entire future depends upon the authenticity of the Holy Grail. Among other things."

She purveys to his philosophical position the beamings of a Jewish mother, "I understand. A lad must make his way as best he can."

A cheroot is lit by George. "Precisely."

She points to the inner pocket of his waistcoat. "You got the paper, I gather."

Smoky fragrance around his face. He taps his pocket. "Oh yes. Yes, indeed. This crisp lovely resurrects the morrow."

"By gibbetting the day before."

"Of course."

A tavern table crashes in a scuffle not far away. Oaths and sounds of clattering pewter dishes and ale tankards. One man calls another a boldy lying swine. A curlicue of laughter from a bashed bystander. Undeterred by such low stuff, a mandolin plays.

Mrs. Katz rises. "Well, Master George. I've said my piece."

"So you have," he acknowledges (almost in the manner of his Uncle William).

"I wonder if you heard a word of it."

"I promise to deny everything."

She violates the propriety of others by chucking him under his chin. "Good boy." Halfway through the doorway she turns. "Do you know of Erasmus?"

"He's on everyone's lips if not in their drawing rooms."

"Well, he's coming over for cow's udder and parsnips tonight. Complains he hasn't had a good home-cooked meal since landing on this lisp-lipped island. Poor man. Why don't you join us?"

George considers, "Hm. I've heard more outrageous suggestions in my time."

She leaves those lovely words trilling in his immediate air, "Let's say about eight."

He speaks after her (her skirts are visible in their fading billow). "Aren't you going to tell me that I probably have a Jewish granny?" He looks back at his solitary table. "Truth is, my mother's maiden name was Rose." An inoffensive chuckle. "How absurd. A Christ-killing flower. Me own Mum." He considers the activities of his mother at this moment. Decides she is singing in some church up north of here. He can see the gold in her teeth as her throat gives forth (breast rising too).

He sighs heavily and gets up. "I do hope that lout Pierre is not soiling that wench's dishonor." Money goes from him to table. Decent tip too. "Think I'll walk about the town," he lets anyone know. "Wouldn't mind seeing a good cockfight, or hearing a rousing metaphysical debate on a corner. I could use a little head jostling." He sneaks a look around. "Now that I'm no longer a murderer on the lam."

Once outside, and on the horse-manured dirt street, he remembers, suddenly and for no acceptable reason (a canny white goose twats by noising, as if anyone cares. It is not as if he were the mayor, George muses), word by word the small mouth change, word nothings, between two bumpkins back there.

"You 'eard bout the King's new law?"

"Noo. Is there?"

"This mornin'. Every man over fourteen must bear arms for one year."

"Oh shyte upon it!"

"Ha! Ha! That'd be a sight!"

The air about him is thin and quick and unpresumptuous. More blown places like London and Southampton tyrannize one's lungs. Many singular actions are around him. This village, he says to himself, is beside itself with small happenings. But there is no desperation to it, and that is very human indeed. You could bring up a family here and be quite sure that that is what you did. Deception is a street game here and lies become flowers. A wrong wink tickles the village mulch heap and the whole place grows in it. The silly sounds here fall upon my body without anger, and my visible mortality says yes to them. Anvil strikings. Horse clatterings. Cock crows. Child shrills. Vender shouts. Market bickerings. And those starlings on that slanty roof know very well that I see them. Black rascals. They don't know what it's like to fall. How lucky. Bless me! How many times have I wished I were a bird as I fell.

"Lookin for lodgins, sir?"

"Um, not at this moment," George says.

"Me name's Tom Yost and I'll be next to the horse trough when you needs me. Tyke ya time."

"Good enough, Tom."

Obliging old Tom is rather bowlegged, he is. But I shouldn't think that would interfere with his taking care of an unindentured lad's night needs.

A bustle of juicy-jowled vegetable farmers in front of him, their wagons groaning with splendid nature stuff. If I knew what I were going to do with myself, George says to himself, I suppose I could just as easily do it here. If what moves this worldly show allowed me to, that is. Who or what does move the bloody thing? Is it something in everybody's brain, something strange that we just can't get to? A chimera like the mystics draw? He mutters this, under his breath, and for no provoked reason, "Would be a very sticky thing if it were known that I am the youngest offspring of the Duke of Kent."

He pauses in front of a mendicant's shop. Three men there chuckling about in proximacious leisure. "Is there by any chance a village event planned for this particular day?" he inquires.

"Yes," replies a chap with a clean blue vest. "There is that. A flogging, at four chimes."

"Oh? Who? And why?"

A fellow whose mouth is a swamp of tobacco dribble (obviously he has foresworn many mouth delights in obtaining this condition) spits splats and says, "A dip. Took the purse of one of our better citizens."

George feels distress and some revulsion. "Good heavens!" he splurts.

The third—a winker and a smirker (and a part time snuffler) with a mushroom cap for a face (almost)—squeals and rocks on his square heels. "This way the poor bastard won't have his toes eat off by the jail rats."

"Is the poor culprit young?" inquires George.

"Oh no," replies swamp mouth. "His hands are very old."

Nothing more to exchange, actually, so George floats on. He

smiles sadly to himself as he considers his own paper (quite safe in pocket) and the poor beggar who is soon to get ten on the back. The pigs foot begins to make itself heard from the inner reaches of his stomach. "Easy on," he cautions it. "Someone might hear you."

Halfway down this winsome street, which is clearly meant for dancing in at expected moments, a girl makes her presence (and of course more than just that) known, in the doorway of a hatter's shop. She herself is gotten up in a tasteful blue frill of the era. Long-braided blond hair, too. A chap could lower himself from a castle window with such braids. She cannot help smiling in George's direction. Which delights his entire masculine growth.

"Upon my soul, but you are indeed the loveliest lass in sight," says George, very close to her now.

"We were meant for each other, wouldn't you say?" she says, and puts her mouth up close to his.

"Good Lord yes," says George, and . . .

"Cut and print!" shouts a man, a skinny man in dark glasses sitting near a big rolling camera. "The whole thing's terrif."

"Beautifully handled," agrees a chubby man wearing a turtle-neck shirt and holding a script. "The mood was like the young Olivier. Better, don't you think so, Mel?"

"Yeah, this kid is great. Hey, George! We've shot the scene. Relax, baby."

George, holding the girl in his arms, turns disdainfully. "I beg your pardon, sir, but I don't believe we've met."

The director stares at him, "You must be kidding, George. Or have you gone off your fucking rocker?"

The fat assistant seems very confused.

"George, baby!" he squeals. "Stop it, will you? You too, Debbie. What's the matter with you kids anyway?"

The girl, cuddling George, says to him, "Tell me, darling, who are these silly clods? And what are all those queer-looking devices?"

"Have no idea, dear thing," he replies. "Balmy rude bunch. Must be a group of players up to tricks. Let us be gone," and he walks off with her, arms about waists. Drunken fools. Disturbing the peace of a decent country village.

A girl in a mini-dress holding a make-up kit begins to

shriek. "Oh Jesus! They've gone nuts or we have! Wow!"

The director jumps up, his small hands waving. "George! George! Come back! Please! Let's talk. For the love of . . ."

XVII
ZACHARY AND I HAD A LONG RAP last night, in his new apartment, which is a metamorphosed loft with a view of the river. He took on a part-time job recently and he needed a little moral support. Also, he changed girl friends. He simply couldn't go on fighting with Alma about politics. He's a radical and she's a virtual John Bircher. The girl he switched to is a most flexible and giving type whose interest in politics is nonexistent. She's a waitress in a midtown restaurant, a place called the Blue Duckling. Zach is now teaching two days a week at City College, in the humanities division.

"Most of the students are pretty funky. They've learned how to go to sleep with their eyes open," he told me. "I don't blame them, really. If they had listened to anything their grade-school teachers said, I mean listened consciously, they would have gone crazy." He stretched out his legs and yawned. "The demoralizing thing to them and me was that they were there only because they wanted to hustle the system better. Whatever you want to call education wasn't involved at all. The system says, if you're a nice kid and put four years into this thing called college, you will be rewarded with a nice job and people will trust you as though you're human. If you don't, then you'd better be prepared to run an elevator."

What did he attempt to teach? Anti-culture. A careful, analytical debunking of the concepts and methods of western civilization. "The whole thing is a big lie," said Zach. "My particular concentration is on certain kinds of sociological thinking. The kind that reinforces establishment of societal views, in the disguise of furthering man's understanding of himself and his destiny." He got up and went to his tape-recorder. "Listen to this. A lecture I may give tomorrow. I call it 'The Function of Rhetoric Within Contemporary Power Politics.' While you're listening, I'll take a quick shower. I need freshening up before that dinner tonight. I'm covered with school gibberish."

That dinner being the monthly get-together of our old Seventy-Seventh Street Gentlemen of Personal Freedom Club. While Zachary was in negotiating the hot and cold water, I listened to his lecture (or his possible one).

"Rhetoric—or a calculated stylized nonsense—has come at us from all sides, and usually from the mouths of people we have learned to perceive as hungry types: politicians, healers in carnivals, 'educators,' movie propagandists, religionists, to name a few. We know that such as these are up to no good and are to be ignored. Now it is in just this connection that we do ourselves harm: we tell ourselves that rhetoric is a device peculiar only to 'hustlers.' And this positions us to be damaged by the equally nonsensical utterances, and politics, of 'high types' and serious investigators of the human condition. We are duped by those very people we have all along been assuming shared our own need for illumination and meaning. This can, of course, precipitate despair.

"The rhetoric employed by many psychologists and sociologists these days is very rich, and that which characterizes Erikson and his followers is indeed among the richest and most effectively delusory. A dimension or two needs to be added to the definition of rhetoric. For rhetoric represents not only a language style but a life style and a political commitment as well; that is, as it relates to one's power relationship with other humans. Erikson's work, in this volume, must be viewed in terms of its contemporary relevance rather than in the confines of clinical psychology (though that would be worthwhile too, since rhetoric must be a dubious clinical tool with which to cure the sick). Otherwise, it is outside our interests as ordinary human beings.

"Erikson's work has influenced a great many other 'serious' investigators who have then 'understood' and manipulated human experience and data by means of it. In other words, they have been guilty of making life a lot tougher. Let me first quote a series of his statements:

" 'One may note with satisfaction [!] that the conceptualization of identity has led to a series of valid investigations which, if they do not make clearer what identity is, nevertheless have provided useful data in social psychology.'

" 'I spoke of a loss of *ego identity* . . . we have recognized the same central disturbance in severely conflicted young people whose sense of confusion is due . . . to a war within themselves, and in confused rebels and destructive delinquents who war on their society.'

" 'We have learned to ascribe a normative *identity crisis* to the age of adolescence and young adulthood.'

" '. . . . I would call a sense of identity . . . a subjective sense of an invigorating sameness and continuity.' "

"The above selections are self-validating statements which defy and discourage any cognitive response. 'Invigorating sameness and continuity . . . .' is bad poetry and patently illogical. Sameness and continuity have never in my existential experience been invigorating. But I do not wish to niggle. What is more important than this bad logic, and Olympian disengagement from human reality, is his apparent unawareness of the profound difference between, and mortal conflict of, Identity and Being. And this reveals the totality of what I feel is his conservatism; that is, he regards as basic that which is superimposed, and the rejection or lack of this as, *ipso facto*, a sign of sickness. (This is equivalent, and I am not being funny, to Secretary Rusk saying that the peace demonstrators are injuring our organic political body and ought to be either straightened out or punished.) Further, it indicates Erikson's crucial flaw as a seriously engaged observer: he has no grasp of (or sympathy for) the political-power matrix of contemporary life. He seems to be looking at our society from a secluded upper-middle-class nineteenth-century country home. My thesis (and response to Erikson) is this: Identities are political superego forms placed upon a person in order for him not to experience his unique and nonmanipulative Being. Insofar as you have 'successful identity,' and survive the 'identity crisis' (Erikson's most popular concept re today's youth), you have abandoned your *self* and become some *thing* else. This is the essence of To Be Or Not To Be, and what the social revolutions all over the world are about.

"Erikson's peculiar naiveté (not really; it is the essence of his strategy, as I hope to show later) moves on. He is able, for example to say this: 'The responsible Negro writers continue to write and write strongly, for fiction even in acknowledging the depth of nothingness can contribute something akin to a collective recovery.' This single statement is paradigmatic of the total Eriksonian *way*, or rhetoric, and can rewardingly engage our scrutiny. 'Responsible' is a key word-view. In his middle-class *Umwelt* it can only mean 'nice.' He clearly suggests that there are some *irresponsible* Negro writers who cannot be taken into serious account, either as artists or members of an acceptable community. What I would like to know is, who are they? What is the nature of their irresponsibility? Are they artists and not middle-class puppet propagandists? Would Céline or Miller or Joyce be considered responsible? Erikson sounds like the white principal of a disorderly Harlem high school recruiting fink hall monitors. More. Does he really think that any kind of fiction—good, bad, responsible, irresponsible—is going to 'contribute to [the Negro's] collective recovery'? Have the novels of Baldwin and Ellison and Richard Wright made the slightest dent (assuming, absurdly, that the Negro in the street has read them) in the average desperate Negro's life on the tenant farm and in the ghetto? Has it made him 'recover' himself, whoever he may be? This borders on the preposterous and, as I have said, reveals an awesome lack of contact with the very reality that Erikson is presuming to generalize about.

" 'Youth' is something that engages Erikson (rhetorically, of course), and it is in that invented country of psycho-social academic ritual that he is a figure of prominence; that is, he is an expert. It is interesting to note the projective revelations of his style and tone: 'Whereas twenty years ago we gingerly suggested that some young people might be suffering from a more or less unconscious identity conflict, a certain type today tells us in no uncertain terms, and with the dramatic outer display of *what we once considered to be inner secrets* [italics mine]; that, yes, indeed, they have an identity conflict—and they wear it on their sleeves, Edwardian or leather. Sexual identity confusion? Yes, indeed: sometimes when we see them walking down the street, it is impossible for us to tell, without indelicate scrutiny, who is a boy and who is a girl. Negative identity? Oh, yes; they seem to want to be everything which 'society' tells them not to be: in this, at least, they 'conform.' "

"I do not know any young person (who has not been scared out of his intelligence and his right to react negatively to authoritarian figures such as Erikson) to whom this would not clearly be a hostile, contemptuous, and *irrelevant* response to them and their personalized way of exploring themselves and their possible Being. Such 'views,' ritualized, rhetoricized, and proprietary, have degraded them for generations, in families, in schools, in institutions, which decided whether they should be 'included' and rewarded. It would be silly, therefore, to expect such authorities to even vaguely understand the contempt, and sometimes hatred, the young have for them (unfortunately too often expressed only in secret and among themselves in futile disenchantment).

"One searches in vain throughout this book for any authentic relevance to the actuality of our time, for any views or concepts that understand or take into consideration such humanity-molding features as loneliness, power, class struggle, boredom, credibility, conscience, good or bad faith (in Sartre's sense), the emergence of style to replace sensibility (a critical gesture of defeat among the mass population). Where is his acknowledgment of Fromm, Sullivan, Schachtel, Buber, Friedenberg, Camus, Marcuse, Laing? Where is his awareness of the new languages of intergroup communication? His strategy, or perhaps his anxious professionalism deny these men and realities their validity and existence. But surely, without an awareness and an assimilation of their significance, no explorer into the world around and in us can be understood as having passionate substance, no matter how hallowed his image in the academy. He can only be regarded as a rhetorician. And the function of rhetoric is based upon the necessity for disengaging the audience from its simple street-corner intelligence so that it does not question a position of presumed a priori superiority —the very essence of a power structure.

"Erikson's *status quo*ism, and his operational co-optism, are stunningly expressed in this paragraph: 'The possibility of a true polarization of the new specialized-technological identity and the universalist-humanist one must be allowed for the simple reason that such a polarization is the mark of the over-all identity of any period. A new generation growing up with and in technological and scientific progress as a matter of course will be prepared by the daily confrontation with radically new practical possibilities to entertain radically new modes of thought.'

"Technological and scientific progress, by their very nature, eliminate any kind of true polarization and any true dialog.

Just read the newspapers, daily, if proof is needed."

"Zachary," I said upon his newly cleansed return to the front room, "I think you've got it by the short hairs. I do indeed."

He laughed. "The Sociology Department boys will blow their balls when they hear it."

I thought for a moment, looking at my sandaled feet. "Why did you become a teacher, knowing what a fraud the college system is?"

He began brushing out his great red beard before the mirror. "I want to see if I can reach a few kids, who then might be able to live a bit more like human beings, instead of mindless zombies. I've almost given up making contact with anybody in the so-called adult world." He smiled at me. "Except of course our small group of demon angels."

I laughed too. "Fugitives from history."

"Maybe the last such around," he said, sitting down to his cigar and Pernod.

"Or the first."

"Depending on how one views the world story."

"Exactly," I said, grabbing at an itch on my toe.

"You know," Zachary began, "that's the basic hoax of education, all the other deceptions merely being decorations on its centralness. I mean, what is taught in school, especially what they like to call higher education, is purely and simply western culture —or the lie about mankind as perpetrated by a minority with a limited and corrupted view." He watched the cigar smoke. "The real life of man is too rich and mad for the culture-history auditors to deal with." He looked at his watch. "As you and I know," he said rising because it was time for us to go, "none of it takes place the way they say."

On the old creaking stairway going down, I said, "I suppose the only thing to do is let your imagination take over."

"The best advice I could give to anybody who didn't happen to know it already. All the rest out there is negotiated self-deception."

I sniffed the air. "The best thing about the old buildings is the smell of the air."

He nodded his bald head in agreement. "The fragrance of memory. Yesterday's answer to Descartes."

"Why, Zachary," I said, joking in my style, "That's poetry. I didn't know that was one of your dishes."

He held the old oaken door open. "There's a lot you don't know about me." And he winked and nudged me in the ribs.

"Here's a little something that might amuse you," he said, slipping me a piece of paper. "Francis Bacon."

I read it in the cab going uptown. "Now the idols, or phantoms, by which the mind is occupied are either adventitious or innate. The adventitious comes into the mind from without; namely, either from the doctrines and sects of philosophers, or from perverse rules of demonstration. But the innate are inherent in the very nature of the intellect, which is far more prone to error than the sense is. For let men please themselves as they will in admiring and almost adoring the human mind, this is certain: that as an uneven mirror distorts the rays of objects according to its own figure and section, so the mind, when it receives impressions of objects through the sense, cannot be trusted to report them truly, but in forming its notions mixes up its own nature with the nature of things."

OLD CEDRIC WAS IN FINE FORM THAT NIGHT. He could make a fortune on the dinner circuit any time he wanted. The stories he told us! Gadzooks! Particularly the ones about the days when he was a C.I.A. agent. He really got around. Don't ask me how he got there in the first place. That's his business. If he wants to go into it, he will do so, but on his own time. I'm not going to press him. What the C.I.A. didn't know was that he was always working for the other side. Haiti was a scene he made in all his passionate duplicity.

"Every time Duvalier had a bad dream, he sent the Ton-Ton Macout out to machine gun a few people," Cedric said, "National security and his neurosis became one and the same thing."

I saw the Blaster in the back of the room and waved to him. His baby-blue eyes were as crazy as ever.

"And of course we were working hand in glove, or finger in trigger, with him keeping the country free of communist aggression. We complemented his own secret police, and our job was to find out about any revolutionary types with funny ideas of overthrowing Duvalier. In reality this meant about five million people, or the entire population of the island. My particular assignment was to infiltrate the organized activists' groups, discover the identities of the individuals and the plans for action, and then pass this information on to both Washington and the Haitian secret police. The latter were to take immediate action—which meant to apprehend, torture, and murder."

A member of the group, brandy in hand, asked him, "What did you actually do in those circumstances?"

A: Kept the underground groups appraised of all government plans.

Q: How did you satisfy the Duvalier government's need to make arrests?

A: The upper-class mulattoes. The rich bourgeoisie. Even members of the ruling army clique.

Q: Didn't they find it quite simple, and logical, to prove they were anything but revolutionaries?

A: That very logic hung them. The more reasonable their protests, the more Duvalier interpreted this as a perfect cover for subversion.

Q: What were the actual commitments of these people?

A: Self-advancement, greed, power over others.

Q: Were they in reality pro- or anti-Duvalier, politically speaking?

A: Pro-Duvalier insofar as he helped them maintain their elitism. Any fascist rules would have satisfied them.

Q: Were these people truly against the socialists?

A: Any action involving intelligence, honesty, and self-determination threatened them. Mechanization of the human spirit was and is their central orientation.

Q: What happened to these people?

A: They were tortured and killed.

Q: How do you square this with your conscience and your presumed morality of anti-violence?

A: The machinery they kept in motion tortured and killed thousands of innocents.

Q: What happened to them after they were dead? I mean, were they given proper Christian burials?

A: After they were dead their property was confiscated and

their immediate relatives were thrown out of the country. As for their corpses, they were hung in public squares as reminders to the people of what befalls those who do not love and fear Papa Doc.

Q: Could you tell us how else you aided the underground?

A: I was able to channel arms, medical supplies, food, and money to them. Quite openly, because they were supposed to be anti-guerrilla groups. I gave them moral support as well. I relayed to them messages of solidarity from international revolutionary groups who were similarly engaged in overthrowing their own fascist governments. Also, I was able to obtain the release of some political prisoners from the Duvalier dungeons.

Q: What was your relationship, if any, to the voodoo scene?

A: Very close indeed. I participated in many of the voodoo rituals, in order to gain the confidence and respect of the peasants. And I eventually became a voodoo priest myself.

Q: Wasn't that a pretty tricky impersonation to bring off? Considering your double roles in the first place?

A: Everything in this life is tricky, some human efforts more so than others.

Q: Exactly why did you become a voodoo priest?

A: On a political level, to use the magic, both the agreed upon and the true, in orienting the peasants around the revolution against Duvalier. On a purely personal level, for my own education.

Q: Could you be more explicit on that last point, please?

A: I would be happy to. The peasants of Haiti worship the power of voodoo magic because they are so totally powerless themselves. And because their condition of powerlessness is so degrading and enraging, the voodoo they cultivate is composed of hatred and revenge—all the murderous emotions and wishes which they cannot realistically express as members of the body politic against the forces that degrade them, and make of their lives excremental and unbearable denials of human evolution. I imagine that the government encourages their voodoo practices in some conscious knowledge that these wild and bloody practices afford them a pacifying outlet. They pretty well know that if the millions of hungry desperate peasants did not have such an outlet, they would literally go berserk and tear the country apart, bush by bush, arm by arm, eyeball by eyeball.

So . . . in order to fully gain a position of power and credibility with these people, as a counter agent whose purpose and goal was to organize and politically redirect them, I became a voodoo priest. That is, I became them—the personification of their fantasies, their magic-power wishes. I was several things simultaneously— myself, a C.I.A. agent, a counter agent, a particular voodoo priest, and the projection of their personal and collective wishes. They gave themselves unto me and I rewarded them by magically carrying out their darkest desires. Of course they themselves were the entire operation—object, subject, and recipient. I was able in this very rich role to politicize them and their needs. Together, we developed a political consciousness, under the disguise of unconsciousness, and many new horizons and many anti-government episodes were the result.

Q: Would you give us an example or two, please.

A: Gladly. But on which level?

Q: The first, that is, the nonpolitical.

A: Very well. Two instances of individual hex magic. I arranged for the death of two pigs owned by a bad neighbor, a Mama Tricot, and a midnight fit suffered by a thief named High Boy. These traditional feats involved the transmigration of the victim's souls via finger nail parings, hair combings, fecal matter, and photographs.

Q: Did you, as the magic agent of this liaisoned hatred, have to enter into any peculiar states of being?

A: Yes. Trances, frenzies, and visionary hallucinations.

Q: Did you employ any drugs to induce these states?

A: Yes—that is, to a large degree.

Q: What were they?

A: Alcohol, hashish, peyote, and an herb composite known to the mountain peasants as *loup grand,* or the Great Wolf.

Q: What did you mean when you said to a large degree?

A: I meant that I employed my own imaginative resources as well. Unverbalizable magic. That thing we are all born with.

Q: Would you care to explicate that?

A: I would prefer not to. That sort of thing is better left unexamined.

Q: Why?

A: It is the point at which we all of us both begin and end.

Q: The other levels, please. You spoke of new horizons experienced by the degraded peasant.

A: He saw himself for the first time as a human being with possibilities far beyond his immediate surroundings and despair. He no longer felt that he would live out his life helplessly drowning in that swine muck.

Q: And the anti-government episodes—what precisely were they?

A: Destruction of military outposts, sabotaging of telephone and electrical facilities, killing of soldiers and members of the dreaded Ton Ton Macout.

Q: Can you tell us what your relations were with the various United States officials in Haiti.

A: Well, I knew them all. The Point Four representatives, for example, who were supposed to be administering agricultural and developmental aid to the Haitians. Those puritanical, officious flops and rejects from our own economy. Those aging boy scouts. Then there were the embassy people, the Marine officers, the United States Information Service group, and my own C.I.A. and F.B.I. contacts. My relations with them were officially chummy, and in the case of the security people, operationally intimate. I went to their parties, played tennis and snorkled with them, and shared their peevish complaints about the lousy life in such a hell hole for such refined and superior Americans as ourselves.

Q: Didn't the other security people ever suspect you?

A: Of course. But mutual suspicion is a professional group trait. It is systematically inculcated as a survival defense. In fact, one is even trained to suspect oneself. This last acculturative introjection is of course a basic factor in our civilization's defense—power system. As obedient members of the society we must continually undermine our effectiveness with self doubt. If we were not taught this, democracy could not function as manipulation, and every man would be a God. I need not tell you what anti-societal mischief would follow from such feelings. Society as we know it would cease to exist.

Q: Were there any occasions when these professional suspicions manifested themselves in a way that was menacing to your safety and or effectiveness?

A: Yes. Two different such manifestations come to mind. A

secretary in the Embassy who was having an affair with one of our boys, my anti-government cadre, who worked as a gardener there, discovered through him my true role.

Q: What happened then?

A: Expediency took over. I had to eliminate her—I personally saw to her accidental drowning on a swimming party at Cap Hatien. The boy, who was a fine chap with a weakness for white middle-class girls, was sent away to the Dominican Republic, to work underground there.

Q: Who was the girl?

A: Not that it is important, for all such people are the same—anonymity crises. Her name was Doreen Watson, aged 23, a native of Uniontown, New Jersey. A Civil Service employe, rank G 7.

Q: And the young man. What was his identity?

A: Luku Mohit. A mulatto.

Q: Was there any personal connection between you and this chap?

A: Ah, our old friend suspicion.

Q: Yes and no. But you do not really have to answer the question if you don't wish to.

A: I shall answer it, if only to eliminate any elements of trust and specific credibility. Yes. The boy was my lover. And I will answer the question that is now forming on everyone's lips. No, I did not kill the girl because of this. She was a serious danger to our whole operation and could not under any circumstances be allowed to live. My jealousy had nothing to do with it. That is the truth.

Q: And the other incident?

A: A bit more complicated, and a great deal more—how shall I put it?—ironic. Two American anthropologists happened to stumble upon one of my voodoo performances, back in the hills near Petionville. They were doing field work on subcultural community patterns among mestizo populations in the Caribbean. I say stumbled because they were out on a midnight search for, oh dear! for the mythical Sleep Walkers of Infinite Forgiveness. I can't help laughing. The gullibility of scientists! Well . . . these two —a man and his wife, doctors Noah and Selma Hartshorn—had been told by one of the mountain hags, Philomena Lechic, a lovable old madwoman, that the mountain region was protected and graced by a band of natives who regularly, as a band, roamed the mountains—sound asleep—pacifying the dreams of the mountain people. Specifically drawing off and unto their own fabulous selves any nightmare vapors that might be collecting in the dreams of the sleeping folk. That fantastic Philomena! She could cook up more nonsense than any ten people. Anyway, these two innocents, the Hartshorns, searching the scrubby hills for these somnambulist myths, penetrated my own sacred ground and saw me in action. They would not have gotten by our perimeter guards had not those three guards, because of the wonder of the particular occasion, been stoned out of their minds on homemade rum. The sight of a white man—and a naked one at that—biting the head off a live chicken and smearing the hot blood all over his white wild body was enough to make these two go out of their minds with anthropological breakthrough fantasies. In their minds they were already making their reports and receiving their rewards at the Cultural Affairs Office in Washington. So of course they too had to be eliminated.

Q: If I may suggest, weren't you developing, against your principles of non-violence, a very suspicious pattern of killing?

A: We did not kill them. We incorporated them into their own mythology and at the same time added to the rich folkways of the region. They were forced to eat a rare root concoction, prepared, incidentally by the same Philomena who had set them on their original bizarre course, which produces loss of memory and general mindlessness. They are now wandering through those mountains as the very mythical grace-giving somnambulists they set out to discover in the first place. The natives are most delighted with this addition to their own fabulous machinations and they take quite good care of the Hartshorns. Philomena gives them regular feedings of her drug so that they never come out of their state of no-mind and timelessness. In its entirety, a breathtaking philosophical amusement, if you think about it.

Q: Getting back to the C.I.A. for a moment. Is it true that this organization directly participates in the oppression of the Haitians?

A: Let me answer that question this way. The Duvalier government stays in power by intimidating the people and by brutally crushing anything resembling dissent. The C.I.A. abets this by aiding in the crushing of dissent, no matter whether it is communist or socialist or plain liberal. The C.I.A. through informers and second-level agents, ferrets out anti-government Haitians, turns this data over to the Haitian security police, and then participates, by permitting the torture of these people for information regarding their underground friends and activities.

Q: Did you yourself ever participate in these torture operations?

A: To my pain and disgust, yes. It was necessary in the beginning, when I first landed in Haiti as an agent.

Q: Where do these things take place?

A: In the dungeons of the Vallard Prison.

Q: Could you tell us precisely what the tortures consisted of?

A: I would rather not. I will merely say that they were the vilest performances I have ever witnessed, human pain and degradation at the lowest level. Compared to which freak sex circuses are angelic happenings of purity.

Q: Who were the people who administered the torture?

A: Some professionals, and some of the seemingly most unlikely people. Cabinet ministers and sometimes their wives or mistresses. Dilettantes of death. And of course ordinary citizens were frequently brought in to witness the horrors so that they would know exactly what would happen to them if they ever got out of line.

Q: What was the position of the Catholic Church regarding all this?

A: Its authoritarian logic required it to be on the side of the government, and therefore on the side of oppression and murder. In such countries as Haiti, the power of the church is largely based upon the ignorance, fear, and passivity of the masses. Law, order, and God hold hands in unholy grandeur. Anything that threatens this arrangement is against the power of the church, that is, God, and must be wiped out. The priests are even more savage in their way than the government murderers. The latter merely take away one's physical life. The priests threaten dissident peasants with eternal damnation. However, here and there you will find a priest who transcends his habit.

Q: What has happened to the millions and millions of dollars, American dollars, that have been given to Haiti for the building of roads, dams, water systems, harbors, and such as that?

A: The roads are half finished, the dams have no turbines, the electricity works three hours a day. The water pipes have salamanders in them. All those projects are in a permanent state of incompletion and half function. The ruins of Carthage are in better condition than the modern towns of Haiti. The money goes into the pockets of the government people.

Q: What is the health of the people?

A: Appalling. The average life span of the Haitian is 35, the infant mortality rate is the highest in the world. Fifty percent of the population has congenital syphilis. Dysentery is as rampant as the common cold. Psychosis is a natural state of being. Malnutrition makes half the people comitose.

Q: Is it true that Duvalier has millions stashed away in Swiss banks?

A: Yes. Once a month his daughter Francoise flies to Geneva with a suitcase filled with American currency. The estimates of his fortune run to fifty million dollars.

Q: Are there no islands of joy there?

A: No islands, but wooden structures. The whorehouses that are kept alive by the sailors off the American naval vessels that regularly come over from Guantanamo Bay. Each of their acne-faced orgasms is underwritten by your coerced tax dollars. The peasants starve while the whores shower in Chanel on your money.

Q: There is a slight note of peeve in that last answer. Do you find that your view of life is warped somewhat by the fact of your being a homosexual?

A: A legitimate question, but I am not sure of the answer. I am sure, however, of the general public's warped view of me and in consequence my own warped view of myself. Imagine, having one's total humane image reduced to an obscene figure forever kneeling before a grinning man's naked crotch! I cannot be myself because I will be exterminated: the price of my authenticity, my life, is my death. To be me is not to be me. So disguises become my daily game and subterfuge my habitat. Not a moment goes by that I am not prepared to be exposed and punished. The sound I hear within myself is not the beating of my heart; it is the endless running of criminal feet. When I think of pleasure I think of pain, and as often as not when my pleasure is not accompanied by pain, and I don't necessarily mean the lash, I feel that the pleasure has had no meaning, and is a vagrant mindless thing to be dismissed. While the rest of the world cruises brocaded salons and sunlit terraces, I sneak about subway platforms and loiter in bus station latrines. While those happy others bounce and cavort in king-size beds on sheets of silk, I do my furtive work against the scrawls on leaky walls and the broken slats of park benches. Let me present to you a typical liaison in my world of shadow groin.

Just last week I picked up an American school teacher on the Piazza di Spagna in Rome. He was a small-fingered chap who taught sociology at the University of Michigan. I moved in after it became quite clear to me that he was not reading his Baedeker at all. He was tingling with imagined adventure, and his tiny blue eyes, which had been permanently damaged from squinting through his mother's bathroom key hole all through his terrified childhood, couldn't keep still for a second.

"Forgive me for intruding," I said, "but I just know you're from Cleveland."

He almost dropped his little book. "Good Lord no! But another place almost as dreary—Detroit."

"All those dreadful cars," I said, easing myself next to him on the wide step. "They must have driven you mad."

"You can say that again. And the fumes! Phew! I had to get out. Any place but Detroit."

I looked around at the scene on the steps. The people, the venders, the lovers, the whole Roman-ness of it. "Mm. It certainly is lovely here, isn't it. Free and beautiful and everything."

He grinned shyly. "Oh I love it. Just love it. Rome brings out the pagan in me." He snickered sweetly.

"Mm. I know just what you mean. It does the very same thing for me."

"I'm writing a diary of my Roman sojourn," he went on. "For my class back home. I teach sociology at the University of Michigan."

"Oh? How nice."

He nodded his curly little head. "It's an intimate and totally honest journal. It's my view that if you can't be honest, you can't be anything."

"Oh I would be in complete agreement with that," I said. "Dishonesty in people makes me positively ill."

"You see, I hope to let the students participate in the living sociology of the Roman experience."

I just had to touch his knee in admiration. "What a wonderful idea! Really. I wish I'd had teachers like you when I was in school. It would have made my schooling so much more meaningful."

He gave me a wet little smile. (I still had my hand, my right one, on his leg.) "It's my guess that you're an artist or a writer. Am I correct?"

I gave his thigh a squeeze. "Right on the nose! You're amazing!" I lied. "I'm a painter. I'm here on a Guggenheim Fellowship to study the Renaissance masters."

"Oh how exciting! I just love Michelangelo. He was so, so *unfettered!* He looked furtively around, I guess to make sure nobody was eavesdropping. "I understand that he was, uh, well, one of the third sex." And he giggled happily.

"Well, yes," I said. "There is absolutely no question about it. He gave his love to men. He was utterly open about it. But in those days, you know, people were more civilized about love. They weren't small-minded and afraid and mean. They understood that love has no boundaries, it has no absurd laws."

He looked at me very sincerely. "Our society is so cruel about anything that doesn't fit into its silly ideas. Inhuman. Sometimes I get terribly depressed about it. The human spirit is hounded in America."

Very understanding and sad vibrations went between us. He was a soft adorable little thing. I wanted to put my tongue in his mouth right then and there, but I restrained myself. There were a couple of old ladies near us and I wasn't about to risk a hue and a cry. "Listen," I said, putting my hand on his, "I've got a wonderful idea. Let's go up to my studio and have some nice Frascati wine and prosciutto. And I've got some marvelous Italian madrigals we can listen to."

He bathed us both in his delight. "Oh great! I'd love to."

"I live in the artists' quarter. The Via Margutta. Just around the corner."

"Wonderful," he said.

At the bottom of the steps, I said, "My name's Cedric."

411 | *Wake Up. We're Almost There*

"Mine's Lonnie. Lonnie Beeker."

Well, that girl turned out to be a sweetheart, from all sides of the question. If I'm ever a mother, praise the dear Lord, I hope I have an issue like dear Lonnie. Pliable was his middle name. The word no just wasn't in his vocabulary. There wasn't a tune that I played that he didn't dance to. As if he had been born to the music. Ooh Mary! Tickle me for a popsicle! Here's a sampling of the scene in my studio. (Incidentally, he kept his socks on for some reason.)

"Don't you worry about a thing, Lonnie dear. You're as safe with me as you would be with your own sister."

"Oh golly! It's the prettiest thing I've ever seen. Honest. It winked at me. See if you can touch my tonsils with it. Slip it in slowly."

Or this: "Thata girl, bend over a teeny bit more, and open your lovely legs wider. Lordy! What smashing cheeks you have, Lonnie honey! Oh dear. I'm afraid we'll need a little more Vaseline."

"Try once more. I just don't want to stop now. Push harder. Whoops!"

"Darling Lonnie. I'm afraid of injuring you. I'll get the Vaseline. Stay just the way you are. Don't move."

And. "Ooh! Cedric! You're tickling me out of my mind! Where did you get that tongue? Bite it some. Mother Mary! Ohps! Your finger is setting my whole ass on fire!"

How about this part? "Is that what you call it? A 71? I'll have to remember that, you fantastic thing you. You don't leave a hole untouched, do you? Honestly, Cedric darling, I've never felt so wonderful. I've had some good lovers before, but you are the absolute end. That thing of yours up my you-know-what was like a wild sixteenth-century flute."

"You bring out the Jean-Pierre Lampal in me, Lonnie. I mean it. I thought sociologists were dry old sticks. But you're the sauciest tenderest thing I've ever had."

"Jesus Cedric! It's coming to life again! This is fantastic. After all it's done. I mean I've swallowed gallons of your juice, love. You're greater than Borden's cow. If my mother's nipple had only been half as nourishing as this red devil meat of yours!"

"I'll bet you won't put this in your journal."

"Don't be a tease now."

After it was all over, I took him out to Benno's Table, an absolute jewel of a workingman's trattoria on the Piazza del Popolo. Simple food and strong simple men. We both had a big plate of spaghetti al sugo and then roast veal knuckle. I gave Lonnie all the marrow in my bone. And I'm not being dirty when I say that. Bone marrow is a delicacy he had never tasted. Over our espresso we sang songs with the fellows. They don't kid around, those eyetie chaps.

All right. Those fragments should give you all a better than rough idea of the kind of business that takes place when such as I do our thing. I hope none of you are offended. What was that, Blaster? Did I just use him and then throw him away? Dear me. What sort of a rotter do you think I am? Just because I'm queer doesn't mean I'm a cold-hearted sadist. That's the trouble with you so-called normal people. You think that deviation means subnormal. Well, you're completely wrong. My feelings can be just as sweet and decent as yours, only a little jumpier.

But's that's not my fault, as I'm sure you will concede. Society doesn't give me a moment's rest. What? Well, all right. It doesn't give any of us much of a breathing spell, but it jostles us poor things overtime. Blaster, I've never seen you so pushy and restless. Stop worrying. You'll get your chance on the platform. Please contain your egotism for a few more moments. I just wanted to say that Lonnie and I remained the sweetest of sweeties for the duration of his stay in Rome. He moved in with me and I showed him everything and everybody there was to see in that eternal city of oomph. We cried like babies when the hour came for him to get in that awful plane to take him back to his make-believe world, that dreary fraud where everybody agrees never to wake up his neighbor. It may come as a surprise to some of you to know that we still write to each other. At least once a month, and I don't mean one of your cheesy hello how are you exchanges either. We write each other from the heart, and I mean it. Oh. I almost forgot. Besides being a teacher, Lonnie was also a four-star member of his local rifle club. His Browning Automatic was as dear to him as anything. Don't ask me why. However, I reject all those sex-symbol psychology explanations. Okay. Blaster. It's all yours. Make the most of it, you rascal.

Blaster: "Isn't it funny the way fags—no insult intended, Cedric—make us other simple folk feel guilty for the naughty things they do? Like Cedric's hogging your kind attention and then blaming me for getting nerved up about it. What I think we ought to do one of these days is have a world meeting of straights and queers and air a few of these problems. A little coexistence never hurt anybody and we could all do with a lot more of it. As these newspaper clippings I have sure as hell show. *Andy Warhol deserved what he got! He is a goddamn liar and a cheat. All that comes out of his mouth is lies.* The newspaper story goes on to say that this girl, who is named Valerie Solonas and who blasted some guy named Andy with a .38, is the founder of SCUM—the Society for Cutting Up Men. And here's another object lesson, as Miss Eubanks used to say back in third-grade civics class. Columbia University President Grayson Kirk announced today that the school has suspended 73 students for at least a year for their part in the recent rioting on the campus.

"So much for that. First of all, I want to inform you that I have been reading a lot lately, as part of my self-improvement program. I am trying my damnedest to rise up out of my boom! boom! past, and what I realize was a very circumscribed life in general. I mean, I was barely living and didn't really know it. Not that I didn't enjoy it, because I did. I know a lot of people, uppy-uppy types, would say how absurd! But I want to tell you something: If you take the absurdity out of a man's life, what the hell do you have left? Indigestion, that's what. And sometimes even boils on your bottom. Anyway, in this self-improvement thing, I look up all the new words I run across. And I ran across a real beaut the other day. Fungible. Does anybody here know what that little sweetheart means? I didn't think so. Nope! too late Zach. You didn't raise your hand in time. Well, fungible means that one thing can be used in place of another, just as though it were that thing all along. Got it. I'll give an example. Let's suppose that I go to my country club all ready for a nice swim in the pool. I'm in my trunks and thinking about my first dive off the board, when the manager informs me that the pool is out of order. He pats me on the shoulder and says not to feel bad because while the pool is out the tennis courts are in great shape. So why don't I go out there for a couple of fast sets and that'll make me feel just as good as going swimming. In fact I'll feel just the same. So what has happened?

Something very nifty indeed. The substitute thing took the place of the real thing. The tennis game was fungible for the swim. And it gets niftier. Let's suppose I couldn't make it to the club in the first place, because of a hangover or a toothache. So I call up one of you dear lads and tell you to go in my place. You do all the things I was supposed to do, and it's Okay with the club that you are there instead of me. When that happens, you are fungible for me, you are having my experience for me. So you are me. Now isn't that just wonderful! See what a little home education and a trip to the dictionary can do?

"I don't have to tell you smart folks what absolutely great and sure fire living possibilities open up for you with this winner of a thing called fungible. Your own mind is the limit, and that's a fact. As a matter of fact, I think it would be a darned good idea if everybody here bowed their head for five minutes and concentrated on all the splendid virtues lying ahead. (Five minutes were passed in bowed silence.) Okay. Now here we go again. Oh. I think it is very fitting and perhaps even relevant to tell you another thing that has been revealed to me, this time on the Greyhound Bus going to Washington, D.C. to see my old mother who is ailing with her arthritis. She still works, the old dear. Directing the kitchen help in the Fisheries and Wildlife cafeteria. I was sitting next to a very fine-looking tan-skinned fellow—and I am not trying to be refined about him being a Negro, because I'm not the cute type. This fellow had very aristocratic features and he looked like one of those husky islanders you see in the movies who dance and make love a lot during the day when they're not swimming naked in the ocean! Anyway, he was reading, a sight I always like to observe because it shows that a person is not settling for the everyday misery around him. When he noticed me sort of looking over his shoulder, he put his finger on a part of the book for me to read. This is what is said:

" 'The definition of the reality principle as a social demand remains formalistic unless it makes full allowance for the fact that the reality principle as it exists today is only the principle of *our* society. Adaptation to reality is interpreted simply as adaptation to society. The reality principle has had different contents in the past and it will change again to the extent that the social order changes.'

"I only wish I'd had time to discuss this important subject with him. But just as I was about to open my mouth, the bus came to an extremely sudden stop on the highway, almost throwing me out of my seat. I thought we'd hit something. But we hadn't. The bus had been stopped by two ladies, a girl pretty beyond human description with endless golden hair, and a very impressive Negro woman who was wearing some kind of African native costume. I don't know whether she was camping or not, but it sure was real looking. And so was the submachine gun slung over her shoulder. The blonde, by the way, now that I remember it, was dressed kind of interestingly herself. In green fatigues, along the Robin Hood style, and very nifty too. Well . . . oh, here it comes.

"We decided not to hold the meeting in Washington," this blonde said. "The heat's on."

"Oh?" he said, going out of the bus with them.

"I sure hope you can fly a Piper Cub," said the Negro lady. "Because that's all we've got to get us out of this Klan country."

"We've got two of their high priests" said the blonde. "They're going to sing a lot before their Last Supper."

"I hope so," said the man. "We've got to find out all we can about their infrastructure."

The last I heard as they were going out the bus door was the Negro lady saying, "This may sound funny, but I smell a lot of Arab money in it. The way it works . . ."

And off they went. That was just outside Cambridge, Maryland. Incidentally, I think I saw the blonde hanging around outside tonight. Or at least somebody who looked just like her. Waiting for somebody—or something, I don't know which. Funny thing, when I saw her, it reminded me of the days when I was a stage-hand in the old Hippodrome in St. Louis. The actors would hang around like that backstage waiting to go on. You know, dreamy and walking up and down. Well, I guess that's neither here nor there. Let's see. Where was I?"

There was suddenly some scufflling at the far end of the room. It was one of the private waiters and Cedric.

"You're a terrible person!" the waiter shouted at Cedric.

"Calm down," said Cedric, grabbing futilely at the young man. "You should never have struck at me."

"And you should never have said those things about Lonnie.

What right have you got to get so high-handed with another person's experiences?"

"Oh shut up!" George shouted. "Get that nut out of here."

The man leaped onto a table. "Not before I recover every scrap of my friend Lonnie that's lying around this crazy place!"

"Ah, man!" moaned Jomo the big blue Negro. "You miss the point. You're way behind us."

"In the name of Lonnie Beeker," yelled the poor chap, "I hereby exorcise his representation!"

He leaped off the table and raced out, with Cedric good-naturedly hurling a soft roll at his bobbing head.

"Now that's over with," said Blaster, "I'll go on with my bit. Let's see now . . . oh yes. Bettering myself and all that. Fighting my demons, you could say. The baser elements in my character that society and circumstance nurtured to dreadful dimensions. I know those words have been spoken before, but in my case they're the truth. As my mother often said to us, you eat what's on the table or you starve. That's it in a seashell. I mean a nutshell."

Blaster was trying very hard, very hard indeed, but it is no mere sniff to be both the guide and the tourist in one's own labyrinth. He needed a little help, and I of course decided that it was my job to give it to him—as best I could naturally (I don't want anybody to think I think I'm God). So I closed my eyes, drew in all my wandering thoughts and energies, and tuned in on Blaster's frequency—as we used to do in the Italian undergound with our secret sending and receiving sets (I'll have to tell you about those heroic experiences some day.) I had a little trouble at first, because Blaster was wandering around inside himself. You know, moving from one personality program to another. which is okay, except that you have to be in possession of powerful equipment to get away with it. Look what happened to Radio Free Europe, if you need an example. Okay. Our signals finally merged. However, Blaster indicated (I can't tell you how; that would give away our little secret, at which point the enemy could come down on us and baroom! that would be the end of us) that he wished to have me do the real broadcasting, while he fed me the stuff. That was more to his capacities at the moment. It happens that way from time to time.

All right. Here goes (switch to FM, you fools!).

"Mm," said Blaster, "That Fundador sure shoots the power to you. I could go four rounds with Philadelphia Jack O'Brien and not even feel it. Now then . . ." He reached into his jacket pocket and pulled out . . . "I want to read to you a short story I wrote last week. I'll bet none of you suspected that I went in for that kind of thing. Did you? Uh huh. Just goes to show how wrong we can be in our estimations of other folks' talents, doesn't it? I'll get to recriminations later.

"I know that there are people in this small world who have made up all kinds of stories about me based on a misunderstanding of the facts. And these stories have been taken as the real me. Now if there is any fabricating to be done about me, I want to be the one who does it. That seems only fair. I think that when people run out of lies about themselves, that's when they go to work on others. Sheer despair, obviously. Surprised, aren't you, that Old Blaster would come out and say such strong things? Old Blaster, who has always been so easy-going, who never upsets any apple carts. Doesn't really sound like me, now does it? What's come over the poor guy? you're saying to yourself. Has he been taking dope or something? You just better check out your smartbox, that's my advice. Meanwhile, here the story is. It's called "The Color of Fall," and it's a sort of fictionalized treatment of an episode in my own life. Now don't worry too much about my presentation of it. I've gone to the trouble of having copies made for all of you to take home for more intense study. That'll give you time to read into it all kinds of things that aren't there, or even absorb the real beauties that are there. Also, I'm sending the F.B.I. a copy to put in their file on me. I try to help those poor fellows as much as I can. Save them carfare and all that. Enough said. Here's the story."

Alice suddenly shouted, "Look, Daddy! The leaves are bleeding!"

They had just turned from the barren stoned street, and now before them lay the park. The trees were abruptly thrilling to the eye accustomed to the grays and blacks of the street, the leaves indeed seemed to be covered with blood. Carl held his seven-year-old daughter's hand, and stared.

"It just looks that way," he said. "That's the color they turn before they die."

"No, no!," Alice protested and broke away from him. "They

really are bleeding. Leaves bleed like people." She ran into the trees and began grabbing leaves off the ground.

Carl was immediately sorry, as always, that he had said something that seemed to contradict his daughter's view of reality. "Well, perhaps you're right at that," he called after her. But it was no use. He saw the words gasp and collapse in mid-air before they reached her.

Alice ran back to him in a moment. "Here, Daddy. These are for you to take with you when you go back today. They'll keep you company. Okay?"

"Okay," he said, and kissed her because he loved her more than anything he knew of in this world. Then he put the leaves in his jacket pocket. They walked on into the park, Alice tugging him slightly in her youngness, as though, Carl thought, she and they were escaping somewhere together and must hurry before they got caught. By whom? he wondered.

"Take me on the swings, Daddy," Alice shouted as the playground materialized, surrounded and held aloft by children's shrillness of activity and demand. Children were everywhere in it. Carl's first reaction was to turn away. He literally hated places that were crowded on weekends with desperate children having fun and one of their parents, almost always a father, who reeked with out-of-placedness at being there because, obviously, children's games could never possibly involve them, "Do you really want to go in there?" he asked. "It's so crowded and noisy, honey. And all the kids will be fighting for a swing."

"Yes," she replied firmly. "I want to go. And you're going to swing me." She ran into the madness there, and he followed, slowly.

He wanted to make it different. He knew something was wrong because he could not. The largeness and bouyancy of his feelings about the child always capsized when he took her out for his weekly visit. Where can you take small child? he asked himself as he moved toward the concrete and iron playground. To the zoo, to the park, to a museum . . .

"Swing me higher!" she demanded, and for a moment he felt connected with her play needs. And he swung her higher. Amidst the desolation—the other fathers had dressed themselves in uniforms of play, like children, and they were talking like children to theirs: "That's wonderful, baby. See, I told you that you could do it! Daddy is proud of you."—he hoped they could come to some understanding. One that would unburden both, and free them for each other. "Easy now," he said. "If you go much higher you might fall out."

A couple of fathers glanced at him, inviting conspiracy— "Christ, would I like a drink now"—they seemed to breathe but Carl did not respond in any way. This is for me and mine. We are not going through what you and yours are. There is a negative, self-enclosed world of that obligatory experience, he thought, and I will not join it.

"Daddy," Alice began as she got off the swing and took his hand toward another place, the see-saws. "Why can't we ever go to your place, where you live?"

He put her on the see-saw and then himself, unreasonably heavy against her weight, and then he raised her into the air.

"Why not, Daddy?"

He began the task of the see-saw. It hurt his legs.

"Well, because," he began to explain, "the place I live in isn't very comfortable. It's pretty small."

She came down, and before he let her rise again, she got off. "I wouldn't mind that. I really wouldn't."

"Let's wait until Daddy can get a bigger apartment. Okay?" She was holding his hand. He looked around the playground for something else to do. The shrillness of the other children now seemed almost hysterical to him, not at all happy as he was sure it should be. He hoped, shyly, that the other men there were not looking at him and Alice. "How about going on the slides a couple of times, then we'll walk to the zoo?"

"Well, all right," she said, and the weary answer of her voice made him feel like a criminal. At the end of the playground a little girl and a boy began to quarrel over the swings. Their bored father rushed over and threatened to hit them. "Why the hell can't you have fun like the other kids?" the father shouted.

Alice dutifully went down the slide twice. The first time, she waved at him before sliding down, and he waved back. But the second time, as he held his arm in readiness to wave she only sat there, then slid slowly down to the end.

He wanted to ask her why she didn't wave again, but he

was afraid of what she might say. They walked slowly toward the caged animals, through the bleeding trees and the withering grass.

"Daddy, is it true what Mommy says," Alice began, "that you live with another woman?"

"No, that isn't so," he lied, and hated himself. He wished he could somehow explain the whole thing to her. He knew that it was impossible.

"Then why did she say that?"

"I don't know, sweetie."

"Is Mommy lying?"

"She just might be guessing wrong, that's all." Why did Barbara have to do this? he asked himself.

"Is that why we can't go to your place—because somebody is there?"

"Honey, I told you . . ."

"Because I wouldn't mind," she said, and frantically grabbed his hand with both of hers. "I would be very nice to her, and I wouldn't tell Mommy. Honest, I wouldn't."

He stopped. "Please," he began, desperate because of the impossibility of the situation, "listen to me. I don't live with anybody."

"Yes, you do," she said, and tears formed. "But you just don't want me there. You don't trust me!" and before he could say anything she started to run down the path toward the zoo. "You hate me!" she screamed, running faster.

Just then a lion began to roar, and as he started running after her down that endless path, shouting her name, "Alice! Alice! Wait!" he wondered, his own tears held back, what it would be like to be mangled by such a beast.

XVIII   APRIL'S DIARY: FEB. 10.

Had a perfectly wonderful day at the zoo sketching the animals. Charcoal pencil. Absolutely adored the tigers! They're elegant and powerful. And so, so self-contained. They just couldn't care less what you do outside their cage. The coolest of cools is what they have. And the baby cub! Loved it! Wanted to take it home with me. Did three quick studies of it tearing at a big hunk of raw meat. Old Hornburger at the Royal Academy here in Stockholm will be very proud of me. He thinks I'm just a sexy girl with no talent. If he would only takes his eyes off my breasts and look at my work for a change, he'd learn something. What am I supposed to do about my boobs? Flatten them down with masking tape or something? I mean they could ruin my art career.

Saw the most beautiful little girl walking with her father near the lions' cages. She was crying. Poor little sweetheart. What was bothering her? Her father looked kind of unhappy too.

Creepy incident: an odd little man who was selling balloons and Cracker Jacks and stuff—and his nose! Dear Aunt Belinda! I mean it looked like fifteenth-century Antwerp!—anyway, this thing shuffled over to me and whispered if I would like to buy some "secret nuts."

"And what could they possibly be?" I asked.

"The kind you eat in dreams, my dear."

Yoiks! I should have called a cop.

Feb. 11:

Remember that shy beautiful boy I was telling you about? The one who keeps painting flowers in spite of the fact that the model is an adorable naked girl. Some problem he's got (or else his eyes are crazy). Well, I finally got him to come to lunch at my studio. On the pretext of having him help me with my flower arrangements. He agreed but only after making me promise that I would let him take me to his grandmother's house to see his collection of Swedish crackleware—whatever the hell that is.

Talk about seduction scenes! I had to start from scratch, literally from the bottom up.

"Mm," I said, "isn't this fresh dill superb!"

"Oh yes," he said, going at the salad. "My grandmother . . .

"They use it to make those marvelous deli pickles. I just love pickles."

"At the right time, of course."

"Exactly. How's your pickle, Sven?"

"My pickle?" He looked around his plate. "But I don't have any."

I giggled, "Oh sure you do, sweetie. A nice big one too, if I'm any judge of things."

He was really confused. "But I assure you, April, that there is not one pickle at this table."

"Positive? Not even one resting on a chair?"

He looked frantically around the chairs and even got up to examine his own. "No," he said. "Not a single pickle here."

Get the picture? All uphill. But I did not give up. (His eyes were so outrageously beautiful. Like a lynx in the jungle. I could barely stand it.) I tried a sneaky end run, so to speak, when we came to the ice cream, which was cherry, by the way.

"We're going to have dessert in the cinema style, Sven dear."

"How perfectly jolly!" he said. "Do you mean like cowboys?"

"You could say that" I straddled him in his chair. "This is cinema style," I said, squirming suggestively in his lap. "The Pilgrims ate ice cream this way. It's called bundling." (I might add, diary dear, that I was wearing very, very tight cotton slacks, so that his imagination wouldn't have to work very hard.) "Now you feed me and I'll feed you."

"Oh yes," he said, putting some in my mouth. "I think I saw this in a John Wayne movie. Very interesting those Pilgrims."

I moved my fanny up and down a little right over his Swedish whammer. But it wasn't getting at all stiff! Jeepers. "Don't you just love cherries?" I said, giving him a mouthful.

"Fruit is very good for you," he said, slurping away.

I gave it another cozy wiggle. "Especially girls' cherries, right?"

He nodded. "Yes indeed. In botany class we learned that the female cherry has all the vitamins." And he put a spoonful in my mouth.

"Sure pays to go to school. When was the last time you ate a girl's cherry, Sven baby?"

He looked puzzled, "A girl's cherry? Now let me see . . . ah yes! In my grandmother's garden, last spring."

Oh brother! No wonder Ingrid Bergman married that guinea! But as you know, diary of mine, I am not a girl to throw in the towel when things look dark. I mean, they didn't write the Old Testament about us for nothing.

"Listen, Sven," I said a little while later (over a Swedish cigar, as a matter of fact, a habit many Swedish women of the upper classes go in for), "this Stockholm humidity is something awful. I'm going to unburden myself of some of these burdensome clothes."

"I quite agree," he said, nodding that divinely shaggy head of his. "It is not healthy to suffocate the body."

"How nice it is to hear you say that, Sven sweetie," I murmured, giving him a friendly little pat on the cheek. "That's a topic I would like to probe at great length."

He just nodded, and presented me with one of those north country smiles of his. You know, like something out of Sibelius. Anyway, I was getting hotter all the time—you know—frustration is the mother of Screaming Meemies.

"If it's all right with you, dear, I'll change right here."

He nodded again. "Please do. It is not a Swedish custom to indulge in false modesty."

"Attaboy. I think we've got the makings of a good soccer game here."

So I stripped right there. At this point, I wasn't horsing around. This was the moment of truth, coming up. (I mean, Christ, I've known times when at the mere unbuttoning of my blouse, guys started climbing up the walls.) Well, I needn't tell you about what I was wearing underneath: those fabulous lemon panties trimmed in black lace, and a matching bra with holes in them for the nipples to come through. Real mind-blowing items. Half the states in America would lock you up for even mentioning such clothing.

"Mm," I said, stretching in front of him. "Sure feels nice and free."

"Here in Sweden we believe in allowing the skin to breathe," he informed me, without batting an eye.

Mamma Mia! I swear to God! I don't believe his muscle had moved even once. Honestly, he was supposed to be frothing at the mouth at this point. Was I with a Swedish faggot? I asked myself. I decided I had been too subtle. After all, there was something of a cultural difference.

"Aren't these beautifully designed, Sven?" I asked, moving over in front of him. Actually, I practically put it in his face. If he'd stuck out his tongue he would have gone right inside me. That's how close I was. At this point I was on the verge of panting, to be quite frank about it. My nipples felt like they were going to explode and start whistling *The Star Spangled Banner.*

"Indeed they are," he said. (His voice was a little muffled because he was talking through my panties. Get the picture?) "My cousin Haldeman designs clothes, you know."

"Does he really?" I bent way over and put my not inconsiderable knockeroonies in his eyes, "Isn't this bra clever? I mean, the way the holes are cut for nipple exposure?"

"Very," he said, his nose rubbing against my right nipple. "I particularly admire the hand-stitching around the edges. American ingenuity is way ahead of ours."

"You won't find me disagreeing with that, honey boy. No. sirree." And I brushed both tits against his face. The last time I did that the guy screamed. Of course, he was from New Hampshire, which partly explains it. I faked falling off balance—"Oops!" —and grabbed at his crotch to keep from falling. Well, do you know what I found, dearest confidential diary of mine? A bone a mile long? A sex-crazed throbber? A short-wave radio set? Not on your life. His thing was as calm as Bonny Prince Charlie the day he was made a Knight of the Garter.

That was the last straw. I decided to go over the top, and to hell with the local morality code.

"Say Sven," I said, adjusting my panties a bit (because they were on the tight and skimpy side) "Did you know that I studied French wrestling?"

"Upon my word," he said, looking up the white canyons of my thighs. "How charming."

"Yeah, isn't it. I learned a couple of simply amazing holds the other day. Come on in the bedroom and I'll give you a demonstration."

"Jolly ho!" he cried. "Physical fitness has always been one of my special bugs, as you would say."

"Good," I said, taking him by the hand. "I think you'll like this. In fact, it might even drive you buggy. Ha! ha!"

"Ha! ha!"

"Or me."

"Ha! ha!"

I could have kicked him in the balls. But I was determined to bring this show off. What I mean is, my entire girlhood depended upon it. Dig? In the bedroom, I turned to him and said, "First, you've got to undress, Sven baby. These holds don't work on clothes."

"Oh yes," he said, "that's quite understandable."

Well, when he finally stood there all nude, I thought I'd come right off my rocker. His body was an absolute midsummer night's dream. All muscle. Not an oodle of fat on him, I swear. And his dong! Honey, I know you'll feel I'm exaggerating when I say that it was the Eiffel Tower upside down. But that's the God's truth. Why, the Swedish govenment could build an entire tourist season around him and make millions, and I'm not kidding.

"You've got a natural build for French wrestling, Sven," I said, trying to keep my voice calm. Down below of course all hell was breaking loose. "Your grandparents must have eaten all the right foods."

He gave me five generations of modesty in a big smile. "It is clean living and snowbaths."

"A sure fire recipe for winners," I managed to say, and with truly monumental effort took my eyes off his masterpiece. "Now I'll take my little things off and we'll get down to business." I almost tore my panties and bra off, and there I was in all my vaunted deliciousness. Did he change color? Did he quiver and come to attention? Did he make funny choking sounds? Hell no. Not my Sven. "Okay," I said, my voice beginning to crack, "now for the first hold, or trick I mean. It's called the two-handed calf lock with split-section thrust." I bent my head a little to grab his joint in my mouth "and you can have it with or without French fries!" I cried, and dove on him, taking at least half of his measurement in my initial crazed gobble.

Well, sweetie pie, I'm telling you right here and now when that tower of his rose I was almost lifted off the floor. But I hung on to his legs and sucked away. A couple of minutes later, I pulled my head back, looked up at him, and said "Pretty good trick, don't you think?"

"Very interesting," he said, looking down at me. "Very interesting. Is there a French wrestling trick I can do?"

"Yes indeedy," I said, springing up (I bumped my head on his huge bone and for a moment I really saw stars). "There certainly is. This is very much a two-way sport, Sven honey. It's called the double-breasted tongue in groove. That's a rough translation, you understand. The original French words come from somewhere near Toulouse and they're in the local argot. I lie back on the bed like this, you see, bend my knees up, and spread my legs. Also, I reach back and grab onto the brass frame so that I don't fly off the bed, a thing that sometimes occurs if one is not careful. Now, you lie down and put your face between my legs, that's right. Now let me see your tongue. Good boy. A good long tongue is what we need for this one. Now grab my breasts in you hands. Mm. That's fine. See if you can't grip the nipple between thumb and forefinger. Right. I think we're all set. Are you comfy down there? Good. Now what you do is take that long pointed tongue of yours and, imagining that you are a mole working your way through a ten-foot wall of ice cream, start licking that pink top part that looks like the inside of a flower. Attaboy. Roger!"

Dear, dear diary. What a scene! When I finally came it was so great I almost broke my arm holding onto the bed frame. It's a good thing my studio is miles away from anybody else down at the market district, because my screams would have raised the dead. I'm not sure but I think I blacked out for a few seconds.

"Did I do that right?" Sven asked me, sitting up on the bed.

"Absolutely right and then some, baby." I said dreamily. "Part two of it, honey, is called the long hump. Just put that property of yours inside me below where you had your tongue, and pump away."

A look of sudden joy and understanding spread over his adorable face like a midnight tidal wave. "Ah hah! I see exactly what you mean. This part is what we Swedes call pfukking."

"Well, I'll be damned," I said.

"Yes truly."

"Then, sock it to me daddy!"

And he did. Wow and how!

The thing of it is, diary dear, that the Swedes, being a lot freer and healthier than Americans, don't go in for that indirect stuff. They don't even understand it. Right from the heart, that's them.

Feb. 14:

Went to the bicycle races with Sven. (Sorry about no chatting with you yesterday, loveliest of all diaries, but Sven and I spent the whole day in bed doing the Swedish national anthem.) The Swedes feel about bike racing the way we feel about mugging. I mean they go at it like they're nuts. I found them pretty dull, however. Except for the size of the riders's legs, which are beyond belief, they're so huge (they could crack coconuts between them like eggshells, but I'm not a masochist, so what good does such a comparison do me? Right?) and a couple of mass crack-ups, when a little gore was spilled.

Another odd episode: While I was wandering around the stadium looking for the girl's john, a smooth-faced Asian type came up to me and congratulated me on the fine work I had done for what he called the people's cause in Vietnam. Huh? I told him I'd never been in Vietnam. This seemed to amuse the dear thing.

"Ah yes," he said, smiling very big, "I quite understand your desire to remain incognito. That is the proper way for a good agent. But please accept the whole-hearted gratitude of the National Liberation Front."

Now what do you make of a thing like that? He wasn't trying to put the make on me, that's for sure, because he simply vanished into the crowds there. Oh well, that kind of thing happens all the time, I guess, even in Stockholm. But how did he know my name was April Katz? Because he did say my name when he excused himself.

Feb. 16:

Mommy has taken up her yogurt and wheat germ diet again, just because I happened to remark that smorgasbord certainly seemed to be agreeing with her. Another thing . . . she's gone in pretty heavily for social work, to get rid of 2000 years of guilt I suppose. Her pet project, as of now of course, is setting up a ski-camp for under privileged boys from Palestine. Honestly! Can you imagine a Jewish skier?

Daddy is going in for genealogy, of all things. He wants to prove that he is a direct descendant of a Count Dag von Kahtzenbog who was very big in the south of Sweden during the seventeenth century. Something of a bohemian and a wandering musician, besides being very big.

"I'm not going to take this Jew rap lying down," Daddy said. He's even started talking with a Swedish accent!

All I can say is, everybody to his own kind of game. If you take this world too seriously, you're sunk.

Feb. 18:

Try this for laughs: " 'Liturgical Arts! Offers Design For a Chapel on the Moon' The whole thing is hypothetical of course," said Maurice Lavanoux, the managing editor, "although I spoke to the people at the National Aeronautics and Space Administration and they didn't seem to think it was too far out."

I wonder when the Daughters of the American Revolution will make their moon move. Sure is loads of fun being an American citizen. And as for you, how do you feel about being an American diary? 'Fess up now, wouldn't you rather belong to somebody really exotic, like a Chinese movie star?

Feb. 20:

Another wierdo happening: Went to a hippy bash last night with Sven—I mean when the Swedes bash they go right up the chimneys!—and halfway through the evening, while the combo was at the bar wetting its collective whistle, I saw this beautiful man with sad blue eyes and long black sideburns. He was standing in a corner by himself, holding a shot glass of aquavit. As I watched him, the strangest feeling came over me. Like time had collapsed or something, like I was there in the room but also some other place some time ago. I felt I knew him, that we'd done things together somewhere, some time in the past, but maybe not in the past because as I've said straight normal time—you know, yesterday, today, and tomorrow—seemed to have gone haywire, in my head anyway. I felt myself being pulled toward him, or floating in the air.

"Don't we know each other?" I said to him.

He smiled a sweet sad way, and said with a French sort of

accent, "As much as I would like to say of course, I must in all honesty say no, I don't believe so."

I felt disturbed and anxious. "Are you positive?" I said.

"Quite. It would be impossible for me to forget anyone so beautiful as you."

"But I know we've met and . . . and been together. I just can't focus it."

"How very flattering of you. But . . ." and he shook his head.

"What's your name?"

"Jorge," he said. "Count Jorge Fragonda."

"God but you're familiar. Count Jorge Fragonda. . . . Are you French or Spanish?"

"Spanish. From the town of Burgos north of Madrid."

"What do you do?"

He laughed slightly. (A very aristocratic slight laugh. Not one of those silly-assed titters, that you get from the lower classes.) "Oh all kinds of things. Things that would probably appall you."

"Oh no!" I said. "Please tell me about them, I'm really a very hard person to appall."

At that moment Sven found me and against all my protests hustled me away to dance. Oh that dumb bastard! When I returned a few minutes later Jorge was gone. I looked all over the place for him, but he was nowhere, and I mean nowhere to be found.

Feb. 22:

Franklin Delano Roosevelt has been re-elected President of the United States. He's rich and so good-looking and according to the newspapers he doesn't put on Navaho drag like those other presidential squares. I think that's a good sign, don't you? Maybe the country will become a place an intelligent human being might want to live in. For a few months out of the year anyway. I mean, Jesus, if it isn't hot dog signs in the Grand Canyon it's bingo in the churches. *Sleazy*, that's what it is.

My painting is coming along great. I'm getting to be so damned good it's embarrassing. (Since you can't see worth a damn, to put it mildly, old diary, you'll just have to take my word for it. Right? Right.) Professor Hornburger is going to pieces, I'm afraid. He's started to drink on the job, and moon about something awful. Something must be going on in his personal life. He barely pays any professional attention to the other students. He spends most of the class time sitting on the floor near me (with his bottle of Swedish dynamite) and saying perfectly irrelevant things (as far as art goes, that is). Like the following samples:

"Tell me, Miss Katz, do you do a lot of American breast exercises?"

"Breast exercises? What for? How do you like this blue, Professor?"

"Then you must do certain special back exercises. To get such remarkable upright bosoms with such aggressiveness to them. Isn't that so, Miss Katz?"

"I was born that way. Am I doing this red area right?"

"Well, I know I am right when I say that you must have some secret formula for achieving the almost abnormally fine curves and fullness to your posterior. You will admit that, won't you, my dear?"

"I'll admit nothing of the kind, Professor Hornburger. It's all up in your head. I'm putting too much paint over here, aren't I?"

"You remind me of a girl I once knew in Oslo (guzzle, guzzle). We used to eat halva in bed together. She had the most amazing teeth. Very clean and like little fangs, like yours. Do you brush your adorable teeth a lot, darling Miss Katz?"

"Like any other decent clean person I brush them before going to bed. Gee this brush is soft, must be fake sable."

"Yes, beautiful white fangs, like Hilda's. Listen, do an old man a favor, Miss Katz, and help him recover the past. Bite me a little bit on the neck here, would you, please?"

"Stop acting like an old silly! Think of the other students, puleeze! And wipe your eyes, for the love of Pete!"

"Let us approach this problem in a different way, Miss Katz. Don't you suppose that for say five-and-a-half minutes you could imagine that I am Mr. Clark Gable?"

"No, Professor, I couldn't arrange that at all. Not for a minute-and-a-half. Sorry. Now this face . . . doesn't it look like a Poussin face?"

"Who cares about Poussin! I want to talk about pussy!"

Poor old crock. And I was hoping he would help me finish my

mural of Leif Ericson discovering Massachusetts. Oh well. Life does have its complications, no getting around it.

Feb. 23:

Went to a Carnival today with Sven. (We're always thinking of interesting, out-of-the-way things to do together.) Boy! What a bunch of wierdies those carnival people are! A giant black man—really more blue than black—with this dwarf hunchback on his shoulders. And a strange looking, short-haired blond woman with the biggest dog I've ever seen. The size of a shetland pony. Wow. I sure wouldn't want to meet that thing in the shower bath when the lights go out. Anyway, the blonde had a very tricky mind-reading act with her beast. The dog-beast was some kind of medium for her. He would stand in front of a person in the audience, sniff around them, stare at them in his animal way, and the blond lady would say things the person was thinking—picked up in the first place by this so-called mind-reading dog. You ever hear of such a thing in your life? It had to be fixed, of course. The people the dog sniffed around were undoubtedly part of her gang. Even the red-haired lady who ran out screaming after Madam Freda (the blonde's name) told her about some experiences of hers (the redhead's) as a social worker in New York City. Of course, the dumb people in the audience were taken in by this act, but not me. Look at the simple logic of it: If you've got magic like that, what are you doing in a sideshow in Stockholm, just tell me that? (Unless, of course, they are up to something that just doesn't meet the eye. But who wants to speculate on such spooky things? Not this little peppercorn.)

Feb. 26

Remember that sneaky little rag of a man who wanted to sell me the secret nuts? Well, guess where I saw him this morning? Sitting on my doorstep! And do you know what he offered by way of an explanation?

"This looked like a lovely place to have a dream," he said, "So I sat down and fell right to sleep."

Wha?

"It isn't nice to sleep on other people's doorsteps," I told him.

"How do you know? Have you ever tried it?"

"No, but . . . oh phooey!" And I came right back upstairs with my bottle of goat's milk. The nerve of some people!

Feb. 28:

Extra! Extra! Mom has joined a nudist colony! No, baby, I wouldn't put you on. My old lady, who undressed in the dark up until she was thirty-seven has gone all the way! She read in a magazine—*Sun God,* to be exact—that the body is slowly poisoned to death by all the dyes in clothes. So every morning after coffee and bagel, she drives out to this camp in the Gluckholdt Woods (G. apparently was the father of Swedish nudies), tears off all her clothes, and parades around in her birthday suit. Have you ever!

"I feel like a girl of fifteen," she told me. "Not only does my body glow and tingle, but my mental attitude has improved three hundred percent. To tell you the God's truth, April honey, I feel like a totally different human being, a different person. Reborn, that's the word for it, reborn."

"I see," I said, containing myself quite well under the circumstances. "But what about shame? I mean, there you are, with everything hanging out."

"We're all as natural as the trees," she said. "And trees aren't ashamed of each other, are they?"

"You've got a point there, mom."

"Believe me, April sweetie, you really can get to know people when they've got no clothes on."

"And in more ways than one, I'll bet."

"No deceptions, no false pride. It's totally human."

"Mm. Sounds a lot better than the other way round. And you get all those ultraviolet rays besides."

"That's right. I'd almost forgotten them. They're very life-giving."

Hooked, that's what the dear old evergreen is. But it's better than hanging around with that Swedish B'nai B'rith bunch, any day. I mean, they were getting her to see anti-Semitic meanings in weather reports.

March 2:

The big topic of conversation—or at least one of the big items
—sex, boredom, and the free spirit being the current hit parade
leaders—is the Germans. Whether they're going to take over all
of Europe and turn it into one big beery goose step. Oodles of
Nazis around town. They're dreadfully handsome but most of
them are queens. Too bad. They've got such fun-looking bodies.
One thing I've wondered: why are their mouths always wet and
why are they always smiling? What the hell is so funny? Do they
smile because they hate people so much?

Daddy is very jumpy these days. He says he's convinced the
Germans are going to kill all the Jews one of these days. So he's
working overtime on that Swedish aristocracy hang-up of his. I've
been looking in the mirror to see if I can detect any Jewish givea-
way signs in my face, but so far nothing. I could be Miss Aquavit
as far as anybody knows. I've also been looking down there but it
doesn't look Jewish to me, and Sven hasn't said anything either.
A funny thought—maybe the Nazis have special detective whangs
that act funny when they're in a Jewish girl. What a way to flush
a Jew! Oh—maybe Jewish girls taste different. I'll have to take this
up with Sven. He's very funny with his jokes about hot open
sandwiches and eating at the Y. I don't have to elaborate, do I, dear
diary? All I'll say is he is the finest deep-sea diver I've ever known
—and I've known plenty. Since we've been having our simply
tip-top body and soul sessions, Sven has stopped going to visit his
grandmother. And I didn't have to say a word to him.

March 4:

Daddy possessed me for a while yesterday evening. I was lying
around the living room after dinner (sweet and sour beef with tiny
noodles) kind of reading a magazine but not really concentrating
. . . you know, just letting my mind wander, while Daddy was
standing at the big window across the room looking out at the
sunset. He must have been really thinking hard, because pretty
soon his thought vibrations, or whatever, were coming all the way
across the room and mixing with mine. I knew something like that
was taking place when I began looking at an ad for a new kind of

face cream for fair skins. One moment I was considering buying some, in a wispy late afternoon sort of way, and before I could even imagine putting some on my face (that is, conjure up a picture of myself sitting in my room before my mirror, while at the same time there would be a picture of myself as I was, looking at the magazine, so it would have been like splitting myself up into different people anyway, you see), I was thinking about a boy named Wilcox who was explaining to me why I didn't stand a chance of getting into the Sigma Phi dining club at Princeton.

"You don't seem to understand, Katz," Wilcox was saying. "It doesn't have anything to do with you personally. It's just that the fellows think of Jews as termites in the gentile woodwork."

"Aw come on, Wilcox," I said. "You're joking."

He shook his head and drank from his stein of brew. "No I'm not either, Katz old buddy. The fellows feel that if we let you or any other Jew in, our way of life would vanish in no time and we'd all be wearing those funny little skullcaps and our asses would get fat and high up on us." He belched. "Total corruption, Katz."

"But that's silly," I said.

"I'm not so sure about that. You Jews are awfully clever people, and your Jewishness comes first before anything."

"It isn't that," I said. "It's that we don't want to disappear. So it isn't really what you could call vanity or ethnic colonialism, Wilcox."

But I knew I was not leveling with him. I've never known a Jew yet, including myself, who didn't feel, right down to the corns on his crooked feet, that not to be a Jew is to be semi-human. And that if the whole world were Jewish, everything would be all right for a change. Then there would be real understanding, real brotherhood. There wouldn't be all this group and class conflict. We would all have the same habits and nobody would miss any subtleties, as they do now because they're not Jews. And now what's taking place? Those German pig-snout-eating bastards are going to kill us all. Except me. They're not going to get me. I may have been raised as a Jew, but that was a slip. I'll find that noble Swedish ancestor if it is the last thing I do. Goddamn, that April is a pretty thing. Wonder if she'll marry some guy with something on the ball. Nice having a son-in-law I could talk to. Whose interests are wide enough to include a few things other than clothes and getting his nuts off. Kid's got the best pair I ever saw. Reminds me of her mother in off moments years ago. Certain spicy something that you can't catch in a butterfly net no matter how hard you try. Gave it to the old lady this morning when she was half asleep. Do they do a lot of that in those nudist camps? Must be hard on the men.

There I was arguing with that cop in Belgium. "You can't push an American around," I said to him. "That other fellow . . . . "

"Was hit by you when you make wrong turn. Here is your ticket. Now please to shut up and go away, Mister American."

Joe Louis would have let him have one right on the kisser. Boy that was great the way he give it to that bastard Schmeling. Broke his back with one punch. Wish I could punch like that. People treat you very nice when you're that tough. Hi Joe. You sure looked good in there. I was right there at ringside rootin' for you, man. Good to shake your fine strong black hand. Bet it is strong too. Wish I had seen him in person. What a guy. There I am on that filthy boat with my parents and grandfather Benya who kept talking to himself in Yiddish. Everything smelled like shit and dirty feet. My mother cried a lot. Father walked up and down a lot to keep his legs in shape. Now he's in Mount Hebron Home for the Aged in Milwaukee. His favorite food was kasha with chicken fat poured on it. I promised him he would get a dish of it every day. Bella certainly has gotten more responsive sexually since she started running around out there with all her clothes off. Likes it in the mornings before she gets out of bed for breakfast. She's just like a little girl then. Half asleep and her voice is high and soft like something out of a dream. Whispers daddy! daddy! when she's coming. Wonder if she even remembers it happened. We never talk about it. She never would let me watch her take a shower. She got that from her mother. Who is this Sven that April says she has been seeing? Does he really exist? Or is this another fantasy of hers? If he really is in the flesh, why doesn't she bring him around for dinner or something?

That girl can be a terrible liar when she wants to be. Like the time in Rome she told us she was going to music school every day and we found out she was hanging around with that degenerate Marquis who forged masterpieces and sold them to unsuspecting tourists. Boy, it sure was neat the way that Moranda fellow and I cornered the market in flour. There wasn't a string of spaghetti made in the whole area unless they paid our price. The thing in business is you've got to move fast. Like lightning while everybody else is sleeping. What's wrong with that? Anything goes in business. That's why it's so stimulating. Bring out the natural tiger in a man. What was that fellow Mussolini trying to do anyway? Those poor wops, he has them walking sideways. Wants to recover the glory that was Rome, does he? Throwing Jews to lions and stuff like that. Oh wasn't that a wonderful seance I had with Signora Bevelaqua! She sure knew her stuff that lady. And what eyes. Eyes that had distant voices in them. When she had me talking with an Egyptian princess from King Tut's time, that was something fantastic and scary. Just think of it. Millions upon millions of voices and presences floating in space since the beginning of time. Just waiting for a good medium like Signora Bevelaqua to enable them to break through to you and to convince you how you too are immortal and have been living all the time in various times and identities. It's overwhelming, that's what it is. The human consciousness is eternal and fathomless. That's what the Signora told me and, damn it, I believe it. So why do I let all these petty things get me down all the time? Maybe I just don't believe in myself enough. We're all victims of this day by day world, a world of petty illusions and finite grit. Just stinks. Seems I was a very close friend of the mighty Cheops. I was supervisor of internal development. I believe that's what the Princess said. We spent a great deal of our time discussing the domestication of the Nile flamingo as a source of food.

"The meat of their breast is like the taste of the evening light," he said.

"Indeed, mightiest of all rulers," I said. "It makes the mouth water with nature's joy."

"I see thousands of ships' sails woven of their soft pink feathers."

"When the enemy barbarians see our fleets of pink they will fall to their knees in terror."

"Let us not waste another day, supervisor. Make of this project a living thing."

"Exalted majesty, my humble feet are already picking their way through the multitudinous hatcheries."

The velvet touch of the Nile night was the soul of all men united in one breathing vastness.

Golly! Look at that horse-drawn carriage down in the street!

It must be the King of Sweden's. I've never seen horses that big. And so white. So powerful pure white. To have my arms and body around one. Oh, to have it inside me. All its powerful whiteness.

"Hey April! Look at this. Come over here."

XIX

STOP SHOUTING SO! DO YOU THINK I'm blind? All right then. So it will happen again. Where will it be? Some slyly uncompromising place, you can be sure. In a field of winter marzipan in downtown Tiflis, let us say. And what will I be doing there? Oh! Stop flaring your nosedrops! I'll be scabbing in a nonexistent workers' strike and damned if he won't be there (mushroom bowler and all), that bifocal nuance, that living answer to the toilet's flush, that . . . Ohh! He won't even respect the tenseness of future . . .

"Here we are again," he more than observed. "Brought together by the vices of others."

"Why is it," I began, my territorial shame producing a far-flung style, "that the unspeakable is our moment's flower?"

Of course, that sort of thing is never launched in the regular dialectical presumption, and the anticipation of an answer would have placed me at nobody's disposal but my own.

"Yonder peasant," he said, winking in the direction of severest anxiety, "is relieving himslf in the future's sweet tooth."

I was about to make amends, but I realized that I was not a guild member. (Such is the genesis of intergroup humility; the sort of illumination, really, that is later degraded, by those all too well-equipped, into a cheap noblesse oblige. But then . . .) "Collecting fragments of abashment, are you?" I could safely assume he would not dock me for the accent, Limey, that traditionally accompanied such a jibe.

"I shall go into that when your propriety has achieved a certain manhood," and he patted me where I most expected it. "Meanwhile . . ." He made one of the savagely velvet noises that so frequently distinguish him form the plant world. " . . . we have our work to do."

It did not matter in the least to him that not a harlot's throw from us a terrible political calamity would be brewing in a hundred years.

He looked me in the shiftier of my eyes (Am I to be denied a viable context simply because my Dad pounded his pud in a maid's closet?), and began. "A few unmuscled and elementary definitions for a warmup."

"My hindsights are my own," I am quite certain I said, "but my foresights are my gift to the community. Forge ahead."

A certain spasm passed over his presence, and this set me to observe the following: Self-abasement requires two people.

"Another such tropistic perfidy," he point out, "and you'll be eating gruel from the hands of De Sade, no more, no less." He accepted my apology noiselessly. "Now then. Definition uno: procrastination."

"A dead horse that still longs for the lash," I replied.

"Insincerity."

"A balloon floating in the afternoon sky."

"Loneliness."

"A greeting spoken in one's sleep."

"Fulfillment."

"The capacity to endure pain without having to communicate it."

"Friendship."

"The limb that does not break under the nightingale's weight."

"Hm," he exuded. "I can see that you have not scratched yourself in vain."

Of course I had to say something with just the right amount of mock humility. "Ah well, a third of the nation is unemployed." But did he hear me?

"Essence."

"What is still there after you have thrown up your hands."

He cleared his throat and seven hundred political prisoners in Madrid were given an extra water ration. "Not too wretched, I must say. Something may come of you yet." He fixed something around his tummy, but you can be sure that this was on the advice of his doctor. "Low utterances are coming from the surrounding field lackies."

"I never said we were alone, and the record will back me up if necessary." Now my voice dropped. "Those poor people have as much right to their finitude as we have to our alienation."

He measured my nickel and I've never felt so cheap. But then . . . Oh, sorry. His voice was yards inside my ear as he said, "You are the sort of fellow who is always hiding in unsuspecting places and whispering things that aren't secrets."

I ask you—could I be gulled by the inherent strength in such a statement? Is it always necessary to bow to the inevitable? For example, in Budapest during the . . .

"I'm starving," my inextricable accuser confessed without the faintest symbolic representation. "Do you suppose this place is famous for its mushroom omelets?"

I put my arm around the entire history of his suggested shoulders and at about the same time (thought I must make it quite clear that I am not a toady to time-space concepts) assured him that it was not.

"Hot damn!" he shouted (without disconcerting my own facial serenity). "Then let's hit that sneaky little trattoria down there near the well and have ourselves some kidneys in sherry and a plate or two of undaunted endive."

Need I say that we established pictorial history as we trudged arm in arm (among other things) through the collected boredom of the surrounding fields and into that very recently observed eatery? Post cards of our innocent, childlike journey adorn every religious household in western Europe. Generations of barren wives drink to our unfettered backsides and then smash their husbands in their impotent faces. I could go on, but there may be nothing more to reveal than that which you have least suspected.

My friend—that mulch fragment from the primeval forest floor who lived to tell his side of the story—confounded more than gravity when he leaned back, spat a fennel seed into the face of logical positivism, and laid this observation on me (nothing in my own table manners could explain such a gesture, and it did not seem likely to me that local custom demanded it. However . . .) "Lying."

"Where?" (And my ear is still ringing from the beginning, middle, and end of his immediate physical response.)

"What is the real reason for the morality of lying?"

"As soon as I've finished this gorgonzola . . . "

"Isn't it that lying is really sacred—very likely the first true creative act of the prehistoric man, fabrication, that is—and that cheap lies contaminate this sacredness, which is really a form of magic (or presumed as such)?"

"So far," I replied, sucking my teeth, "you're in the clear."

"What is needed is a science of what does happen, if esthetics is the science of agreed upon nonhappenings."

I offered myself a cheroot and he took no offense. He had his own vices. "Are you appealing to my memory?" Neat, eh?

He went on (and I could swear that he was not blowing out my cigar smoke). "Can one say this: that all communication is an arrangement, or that interpresence, that comes into being once two people or more agree to share a lie, or a hope, about the nature of what they are doing?"

The waiter, a reformed malingerer who obviously had other fields to conquer than this, brought us fruit before the urge had quite left him. But his pettiness will not become my concern.

"I have as yet no way of proving your thesis to be invalid," I let my friend know, and why not? Secrets could not grow between our abysses.

"Isn't betrayal really the violation of the treaty of nonhappening—and the shock of the void rushing in (void being the privacy or secret self, which the agreement-lie-mediation was to protect forever?) Who shall we be? is the first question that is mediated between two people. Next, where shall we go? Into what adventure or lie? Getting back is of course quite another thing. I promise not to do anything to wreck our trip, they both say."

I slipped him a sliver of apple and did not wait for any gratitude. For this reason: we were not there together involuntarily; we had no panic to ally with amenities, you see. "What you are saying has already seeped into my bloodstream."

He did the next best thing to swallowing the chewed apple, and carefully, on tip to really (which is of course merely another way of saying this: immense forces are being exquisitely held at bay and only the dullest audience will not include this in its delerious empathies), went on. "An artistic creation can be regarded as a lived-through and therefore useless system of lies; that is, the lies that worked for the time being." He made a motion in the air with his weensy hands which could not hurt anyone (but which at the same time, naturally, could hardly, because of that, be ignored). "One must keep lying."

I'm pretty sure it was a good thing we weren't on a public platform, because almost any one of his statements could have been twisted by the audience to satisfy their own personal, all too humanly suppressed desires. I would not be stepping out of character if I were to say that along about here—between our brandies and the dawn of civilization, that is—he indicated (I refuse, however, to discuss this in intimate detail) that in the past (yes, I suppose so; if not, to hell with it) he had known more than a few moments of unexcelled clarity and purpose of action.

Suppose we leave it at that. He had his work to do, and I too had something up my sleeve (without meaning to offend). I saw him off on the 2:24 to Vladivostok, where, according to my best calculations, he had been promised employment in a childrens' zoo. "One is always looking back on one's successful lies for help," he explained, blowing on his fingers as the train ooozed out of the information station. "I could call it the cannibalism that is history."

"Is there any way of finding out who the Prime Liar is?" I pretty much shouted at his blurring smudge.

He giggled (without malice? Oh well.) "Exactitude is always an evasion!" I would say he howled softly. And I must confess that I have not been let down by that floating maxim.

Howled . . . I ask you, what sort of scientific comradeship could I hope to establish if I were to say, instead, that the words emanated from his total body?

Oh . . . and here is an item: according to a lurking that is trying to ingratiate itself with my (!) memory, it is possible that my small friend (pah! amanuensis to his own impersonations would be a cleaner way to put it) said this to me: "And as for that, phew!, nose of yours . . . it is a vision corrupted by popular usage."

However, we do not have to accept this merely because it is hearsay.

XX THE CITY-WIDE PLAYGROUND TRACK meet was to be held tomorrow, and Zach Williams, who was ten, was ready for it. He had trained every day, all summer long, at the

Phelps Public School Playground, across the street from his house. He had spent a certain amount of time practising the high jump, and after that the broad jump, and then the seventy-five yard dash. It was not long before he could beat anybody his weight in the playground at these three feats.

In fact, Zach was generally recognized as the seventy-five pound champ of all the playgrounds in the Columbia Heights section of the city. He had won all the medals he could possibly win in his own playground, and in the four sectional track meets that had been held during the summer, he had won every event he had entered. The older athletes at Phelps, who guided him in his training, were quite naturally very proud of him. He was, as they often said, their boy. The finest mature athlete at Phelps was a boy named Johnny Cannon, who was twenty or so, and Zach had the distinction of being the only young kid around the place with whom Cannon would discuss the technical aspects of track. The other boys Zach's age somewhat disliked Zach for this, but he did not care.

A rule of the track meets was that a boy could enter only one event. Zach had always resented this rule because he was excellent in three things. In order to express the fullness of his talents, he entered a different event in each meet, and he invariably won. He was a thin, explosively springy boy with an astonishing amount of energy for his size.

He slept fitfully the night before the big city meet, at which the best track talents in the city playgrounds would compete. At breakfast, when he had only a glass of milk with an egg in it, his mother said, "If you don't eat more you'll starve to death. What's the matter with you, anyway?"

He did not want to go into the details of his training regimen and he said, "I'm not hungry," but for safety he added, "I'll eat a big lunch."

Mrs. Williams shook her head, muttered something about the ways of small boys, and went back to the kitchen.

It was ten o'clock now, leaving an hour to kill before the big meet started. Zach walked into the bedroom to get his track clothes. The nervous excitement in him was so strong that he felt that at any moment it might consume him, but he remembered what his playground trainers had told him about the importance of keeping calm and conserving his energy, and he concentrated hard on suppressing the excitement. He walked slowly around the room, like the inmate of a cell, looked casually at the ceiling, the floor, the bed, and whatever other objects were in sight. He kept telling himself how calm he was, that there was nothing to worry about, that he was very calm and relaxed and sure of himself. He worked his face into several expressions of boredom and uncon- cern, and even yawned, to get himself in the right mood.

Then he took his track clothes from the small chest of drawers: red track pants, a sweatshirt, a heavy towel, and an undershirt. The undershirt, he felt, was unquestionably the most beautiful under- shirt the world had ever seen. Stretching diagonally from one side of the shirt to the other were two parallel red, white, and blue ribbons, trophies of past victories. He had seen famous track stars with these ribbons decorating their chests, and he had persuaded his mother to sew them on a undershirt for him. Finally he took from the drawer two lemons. He would suck on these during the meet instead of filling his stomach, as he was sure a lot of other kids would foolishly do, with big drinks of heavy sloshing water. He put everything together in a small canvas bag, and walked rapidly back through the apartment to the door, hoping his mother would not detain him, and trying to keep calm.

He was still fairly calm when he arrived in the playground. The other boys who were going to participate in the meet were gathered in a large bunch under "The Tree," the only tree in the playground. Mingled with the athletes were quite a few boys who were just going along for the fun. These boys were talking loud and horsing around. The boys who were going to compete soon, most of whom were quietly sitting cross-legged on the ground, held themselves aloof from this horseplay. The day was glaring and hot, and the great field which was normally frantic with games of one sort or another, was now deserted and quiet.

Zach looked around until he spotted Johnny Cannon, who was sitting with some older boys a little to the side of the main group. He walked over to him and sat down.

Cannon, a good-looking blond boy, patted Zach on the shoul- der and said, "Hi, champ. Are you going to win for us today?"

"Sure I am," Zach said, and laughed, to show the older boys who were now watching him that he was half-kidding. He liked these older boys and he did not want them to think he was cocky. Cannon patted him on the back again, then went back to talking with his friends. Zach kept quiet and listened. He was relaxing easily now.

After a while, Joe Gaines, the superintendent of the playground and an ex-football player, came up to the crowd and announced that it was time to be going. The competing athletes were to be driven to the stadium in three cars. The hangers-on were taking a bus. Zach walked out of the playground with Cannon and four other boys, and they got in the car driven by Joe Gaines. Zach thought about the coming meet. He felt pretty sure of himself, the way a good athlete does, and now he began to resent more strongly what he thought was the unfairness of limiting him to one track event. He couldn't understand what was wrong with being good in more than one thing, and why he couldn't prove it. Then he decided. To hell with them. I'll enter two, one under a different name. Nobody will know, because the different events are held at different times at different places in the field.

When they had been riding for a few minutes, in a tight silence, Cannon leaned over to Zach and said, "Take it easy now. Hear me?"

"OK. I will," Zach said, and settled back in the seat. It delighted him to have Cannon, the great runner, tell him to take it easy.

While they were piling out of the car at the stadium Joe Gaines stopped them all and, putting his arms around the shoulders of two of the boys, said to the group, "Now I want you guys to do the best you can. If you win, that's swell, but if you lose I don't want you to get sore. Take everything in your stride, because there'll be plenty of track meets after this one. Understand?"

They all said yeah, then walked in through the gates. Zach now hit on the other name he was going to use: Billy Jordan. He would use this name in the high jump.

The stadium was a vastness of bodies and motion. Boys of all sizes were running and walking around in the field, some of them dressed in track shorts and shirts, others in sloppy summer clothes. Here and there in the field were officials seated at small tables, and around them were crowded the boys who were signing up for the track events. The stadium seats were filling up with spectators from all the playgrounds in the city. Each playground had its own section marked off with a great colored banner bearing its name. Zach decided to register for the dash and the high jump before getting into his tracksuit. He wasn't nervous when he registered at the table for the dash, but when he had walked across the field to the high jump table, he got scared, and he kept wetting his lips. Nobody he knew was around, though, and in a minute he went down on the books as Billy Jordan. Then he walked to the lockers.

The lockers were clogged with noisy, sweating, tousled boys. Each boy who was undressing was accompanied by two or three of his friends who were there to help him keep up his courage. Zach sat down among some boys from a distant playground and undressed. He was anxious to see the effect his beautifully striped shirt would have on the boys around him. When he had put it on, so slowly, so elegantly, he got his reward. The other boys stared at him as those he were some magnificent, formidable champion who had been sent to destroy them. One boy even stopped dumbly in the act of putting on his shorts to stare at Zach. He took his time about walking out to the field, and on his way he did not miss even the slightest, most side-long glance at the beautiful stripes on his chest and the proudness of his bearing.

He found a spot of ground which was apart from the crowds on the field, threw his towel and sweatshirt down, then lay back on the towel and waited for his name to be called for the dash. He was not too worried about participating in the two events. Each event has several heats, for the various classes, and he knew that he could be in one, rest for a few minutes, and get to the other in time. The sun was nicely warm against his thin bare legs and arms, and the warmth helped relax the small queer tightness in his stomach, a tightness of apprehension and excitement and happiness. He bit into a lemon and sucked deliberately on it.

In a few minutes his name came over the loud speaker at the track. He was in the first heat of the dash. In contrast to Zach and his fine stripes, the other kids at the starting line looked shabby and absurdly unprofessional. Zach felt that they were frightened of him. The starter was yelling at the boys to get at their marks and for the spectators to get off the track. Zach wisely chose the outside lane, and with his bare feet firmly gripping the small pockets in the cinders, waited for the starting signal.

The starter, standing just off the track, raised his black pistol, shouted "On your mark! Get set!" and fired the gun. Zach sprang from his crouch just as the gun went off, and in another moment was speeding swiftly down the track. At the three quarters mark, he was so far ahead of his nearest competitor that he turned his head a bit to see exactly where he was in relation to the others. He broke the tape four yards ahead of the next boy.

Joe Gaines ran up to him as he walked off the track. "That was wonderful, boy. Christ, you sure had that one!" and slapped him on the buttocks. Zach afraid that Gaines would accompany him and perhaps discover his secret, thanked him quickly, then hurried away. The first heat had been just a warm-up to him and, stretching on the ground, the sweatshirt around his shoulders and the lemon in his mouth, he barely panted. He got up in a few minutes, looked sharply around to see if he was being watched, and walked across the enormous field to the high jump. He was the only boy there from his playground.

Most of the boys jumped from their left leg and were, therefore, lined up on the right side of the high jump bars. Zach, a right-leg jumper, was on the left side with three other boys. The first heat of the jump began with the crossbar set at four feet. Two boys from the right side had missed by the time Zach jumped. He cleared the bar easily, taking a shorter run than is usual, and then his feet were sinking into the soft cool earth in the jumping pit. He got up quickly, brushed himself off, and walked back across the field to where he had left his stuff, and lay down. He was not very interested in the clapping that followed his jump. This is easy, he thought, lying there on the ground, and sucking on the lemon. He listened detachedly to the hysterical shrieking and whistling in the grandstands, and waited for his name to be called for the second heat of the dash. It came in a couple of minutes.

Again he chose the outside lane, and when the starting gun had gone off, he was charging down the track. He won this time too, but a dark-faced boy with clipped hair was not far behind, he noticed. Afterward, he needed the rest on the grass more than he had before, and when he walked across the big field to the high jump he did not walk so fast. There was too much lemon taste in his mouth, and he spit a couple of times.

About half the jumpers had been eliminated by the first heat, and Zach was the only right-leg jumper left. The conspicuousness of being the only boy on the left side of the jumping bar bothered him, and to get away from the place as quickly as possible, he took an almost savagely short run to the bar. He cleared it and fell into the soft earth, where he sat resting for just a second, the velvety loam covering, caressing his hands and feet. There was just one jumper in the whole crowd who interested Zach now. He was a tall, slow-running, easy-jumping boy in black swimming shorts. Zach watched him clear the bar with a slow, sure gracefulness, then walked away.

While he was lying on the grass, Johnny Cannon came by for a second on his way to his own event. "How do you feel, champ?" he asked.

"Pretty good."

"That's fine. Keep resting until you have to get up. Don't walk around like these other guys."

"All right. I won't."

Cannon winked at him and walked on.

The third heat of the dash was the next-to-last one. Zach felt a tiredness now in his legs, and when the gun went off he was slow in starting. The dark-faced boy was ahead of him by a yard or so when they reached the halfway mark. Zach pulled at all of his muscles to reach the boy, and the rest of the way down the track he tried only to keep abreast of the other boy and forgot about winning. They tied.

Zach panted heavily when he lay down. The lemon couldn't entirely quench his thirst now and he finally, but reluctantly, went to the drinking fountain nearby. He swallowed half a mouthful of water and gargled with the rest, and spat it out. The walk back over the field to the high jump pit took longer, and he had begun to look forward to the end of the whole meet.

The jumpers had been cut down to five, Zach and the tall, easy-jumping boy among them. Zach just managed to clear the bar this time, and he fell heavily into the dirt pit. He stayed around the place long enough to see everyone else upset the bar but the tall boy. The next heat would be between the two of them. Zach forgot about the beautiful red, white and blue stripes on his chest as he looked the other boy over. He wished the boy did not have such long legs. The sun seemed to be much hotter now.

In the last heat of the dash the dark-faced boy was in the lane next to him. Zach glanced at him, as they both knelt tensely at the white starting line, and decided he hated him, not only him, but all the dark-faced boys in the world. At the gunshot the dark-faced boy got away faster than Zach, whose legs ached and were now quite heavy. But Zach ran grimly, desperately after him, and he felt that his legs were some mechanical pounding things apart from the rest of his body. The boy's fresher condition kept him a couple of feet ahead of Zach all the way down to the finish tape, which he broke by sticking out his chest, and his arms were impressively outstretched. The boy in the third place, behind Zach, was very close to him at the tape.

Zach was too tired to hate the dark-faced boy as much as he wanted to, and too tired, right now anyway, to hate himself for not winning. An official grabbed Zach and the dark-faced one by the arm and walked them over to a small table, where they would get their medals.

"You boys ran a really close, fine race," the man said happily, but Zach was not listening to him. He was thinking about the silver medal and the jumping he had yet to finish. The other boy's face was covered with a triumphant smile.

They reached the little table. The official who had brought them there said to the man at the table, "Here they are, Bob. First, second and third."

The official at the table smiled, and picked up the gold medal for first place. "Congratulations, son," he said to the dark-faced boy and shook his hand and gave him the medal. "I hope you win a lot of other races." The dark-faced boy, still smiling triumphantly said, "Thanks, mister. Thanks a lot." He walked away from the stand, happily examining the medal, and surrounded by several congratulating friends.

Then the official turned to Zach. "And this is for you, son. I'm sorry you didn't win, but maybe you'll win the next one." Zach, breathing deeply and tiredly from the running, took the silver medal, thanked the man, and slowly walked to the spot where he had left his stuff. He turned around for a moment and looked after the victorious dark-faced boy who was walking with his friends across the field, his work at the meet now finished. Then Zach looked across the field toward the high jump pit, where in a few minutes he was supposed to begin jumping against the graceful thin boy. The bar would be raised higher and higher as they tried to outjump each other. He imagined the boy gliding easily over the bar and he could feel himself wearily running toward the bar, then exerting all the aching, heavy muscles in his legs to get over it. He lay down on the towel, exhausted, and dully examined the small silver medal for a moment. Then he closed his eyes; with great effort he wiped the perspiration from his face with his sweatshirt. And he began to despise himself now for losing the dash.

In a couple of minutes he pulled himself off the ground and started walking to the high jump pit. But he had not gone many yards before a terrible fatigue and futility settled over him. It was too much. He turned around and went back to his resting spot. Scooping up his towel and the sweatshirt and the medal, he plodded toward the lockers; and now he began to despise himself more and more for not winning. The fury and fatigue pressed relentlessly over him, and he dropped the medal and began to tear the beautiful ribbons off his shirt. But they were too well sewn on, so he grabbed the middle of his shirt and ripped it half off.

"I'll never go in another stinking damn meet as long as I live," he said fiercely. "Never go in another stinking one." He was too tired and baffled and angry to cry now, and his skin for the first time felt very tight and sunburned.

"OPHELIA, SWEETIE," NEUGERBORN SAID, "I THINK it's your turn to do the cooking tonight."

"Yes, I know," she said, brushing the sand off her feet and slipping her sandals back on. "But what I don't know is what that motley crew wants to eat."

Ophelia slowly walked across the big room to the kitchen area. "Maddy and Jack don't like meatloaf. Remember? They didn't eat it the last time I made it."

"So they didn't. Goddamn those two. They fuss about everything. How did they get in this scene anyway?"

She began looking through the canned goods on the shelf. "Simple. We needed two more people to share the rent on this house after the Hansens copped out at the last minute and went to Europe instead. Maddy and Jack were the first people to answer our ad in the *East Hampton Star*." She began looking through the big refrigerator. "That's the simple history of it."

"Too bad you couldn't have waited and been more selective," Neugerborn said, sipping his vodka and sour lemon.

"Too bad you keep thinking about what's done. We had to get the rest of the three thousand rent and in a hurry. You know what I think we'll have? Lamb shanks and rice and beans, and a big crazy salad. Which you can make. How does that hit your tickle bone?"

"I'm laughing already. It sounds fine. Maybe I'll substitute pot for oregano in the dressing."

Ophelia laughed as she strolled back across the living room. "You're a rascal, Neugerborn. I'll bet your mamma doesn't know what a naughty boy she's got."

The surf sound and the flat sharp sunlight made this big dune house seem physically vulnerable. Nature would come first here. A pair of sea gulls floated serenely outside the floor to ceiling window.

"Please don't tell her," he said. "I'm the last illusion she's got. Are you still working with that crazy scientist?"

"I sure am," she said, shifting in the armchair so that she could look out over the dunes. "He's really pretty great." She smiled at Neugerborn, a naughty and sly smile. "He's going to take us all into the twenty-first century." She paused. "Well, how was it?"

Neugerborn began to laugh and bang the arm of the chair. "Oh that was beautiful! We ought to do this for a living. I mean it. Oh Jesus!"

Ophelia giggled. "Living *New Yorker* stories!"

"That bit in the kitchen was a gem, baby. With the scanning of the food shelves and icebox and that line. 'And a big crazy salad which you can make'! Tell me the truth . . . did you make that one up, or had you read it in a story?"

"I saw it on TV," she said, "a perfect and crummy little play about a couple making the lovers' scene on Fire Island. But I added my own English to it, of course."

"It's a classic moment, when the girl let's the guy make the salad. Jesus, but it's incredible how people really have become the crap they read and see, isn't it?"

"I'll bet you our scene really is being lived out by eighty percent of the summer people in the houses down here in Amagansett."

"No question of it," he said, tasting his drink, "and if it isn't Maddy and Jack as the villains, it's Debbie and Mel."

"And Mel is in marketing research."

"Right. And Deb is an assistant editor in children's books."

"Just loves to talk about how many times she's read *Alice in Wonderland*," and Ophelia made a sort of la-de-da gesture with her hand.

Into being came several magic moments: silence, a sinking of their consciousness into the cultural byways that imprisoned them; glittering sand-shot sunshine; rolling frothing of sea waves; two gull cries that were anguished in a way . . . such was the submersion experience of Ophelia and Neugerborn there in the soft sifting dunes.

Finally this from him ended that delicate suspension: "Let's go to Hordon's tonight for dinner. Have a good steak and scare them with your blackness."

"Okay."

"And afterward we can talk about your days at the Sorbonne and then have a lot of sex."

"Couldn't we have the sex first?" she asked.

"Well, I guess so. But what if it drains my brain power? I wouldn't have any thing left for the conversation."

"It'll be a calculated risk."

Later, that evening, after they had screwed (a quite satisfactory scene, from all points of view) and had a good laugh about the response at Hordon's (the waiter served her duck instead of steak and brought her two desserts), Neugerborn said (he was lying on his back and one of his legs rested on Ophelia's thighs), "Did you ever go to a bistro on the Rue du Bac called The Blue Boar?"

"Uh huh. It was run by a little Algerian guy with a big mole on his chin."

"That's right. His name was Albert. Very sweet guy."

"Uh huh. And he was also an informer for the fuzz."

Neugerborn stirred. "He was?"

"He sure was," Ophelia said, running her hand along his leg. "And in return for his fine work they let him push dope unmolested."

"Dope? I'll be damned. He seemed so, uh, ordinary and, uh, you know, harmless."

"I never thought the little turd was harmless. He always smelled bad to me."

Neugerborn carressed a nipple. "You probably have better instincts than I have."

"Because I'm a spade, right?"

"Right."

"Black people don't use their brains, they use their animal senses. Right?"

"Keereck," he said, moving his hand around Ophelia's generous breast.

"Other people use their bodies."

"White people using the bodies of blacks. On the nose again."

Ophelia watched Neugerborn's pulse beat in his ankle. "What were you doing in Paris, Neugy?" She could feel the ocean frothing sweetly on her skin.

"What me mums always told me to do."

"Which was what?"

"Smile while you're faking it."

Outside this glass house two sea gulls cried to each other through the sea sound.

"Under what circumstances did you do that, Mr. Hairy Chest?"

"I had a Guggenheim."

His hand paused on her tasty black belly.

"Ah hah. And exactly what piece of fakery were you perpetrating while being underwritten by those copper gleanings?"

"A humdinger. A real sweetheart. I was researching the secret love life of Benjamin Franklin during his Paris days as the American Ambassador to France, as revealed by very unrestrained letters written by him to an Alsatian chambermaid. Such letters first unearthed by me, of course."

A sound of mirth leaped from Ophelia's throat. "Neat, very neat. Did you ever write this thing up?"

"Of course not. I devoted all of my waking hours to making the Left Bank scene."

"Making it as a baker makes pastry? Making it as a boy makes a girl? Or making it as a military academy makes a man?"

Neugy shifted his body to an ass-facing-the-ceiling position. He waited for a few seconds with his nose in the down pillow before murmuring, "All of those ways, I guess." Then he raised his head and looked directly at Ophelia's armpit (exposed in its curly dark mystery because her arms were raised) and said, "But I don't want you to interpret that statement, or the soft tone of my voice, as meaning that I am demeaning myself or my efforts."

Ophelia looked at Neugy's muscular calf and said, "There you go trying to influence my evaluations, willing the unwillable. I'll think whatever I want to think."

Neugy's head sank back into the pillow's softness, so his next words came out pretty muffled. "Trite que and pell wut."

A smile made its leisurely way across Ophelia's blackness as she gazed at Neugy's bottom. "Tell me, Neug. Were you spanked a lot as a boy?"

He turned his body and half embraced Ophelia's "No more than was good for me." He blew on her lower throat. "What about you?"

Ophelia heard a deep plaintive sound that seemed like a ship out on the ocean, which was only fifty yards or so from the house.

"Guess what? I knew the cat in Paris who wrote those chambermaids' letters. He was really a fantastic guy. He made a very good living faking such documents. He sold a friend of mine a faked letter Villon wrote to his mother." She ran her fingernails delicately up his back. "What do you think about that?"

He groaned. "Try me again tomorrow. Presents too much of a threat to my stability now."

"Okay."

"Aren't we going to have any of that Sorbonne stuff?"

She looked at the difference between her skin and and his and wondered if there were a short simple explanation of it in a book she could get. "I'm sleepy."

Out on the beach the next day Ophelia and Neugerborn sipped chilled Almaden rosé and watched the skin and social action. A fairly swarming scene, and it included two distinctly separate and clumsy games of volleyball.

"Have you counted the premature middle-aged pots on the men?" Ophelia asked.

"No. But I'll take your word for a large and sociologically interesting number."

"These white princesses certainly like to tease and strut. They're bombing those poor boys."

Neugy trickled sand through his fist. "Nothing compared to what they'll do later, when they hook them."

"Heavy legs on them."

"I used to go with that girl in the pink bikini," Neugy said. "Listen. What about some Sorbonne tidbits?"

Ophelia chuckled. "I was just kidding you, Neug. I never went to the Sorbonne. I was a dancer in a jazz joint."

"Never went to the Sorbonne?"

"Once, with a friend, just to look at it."

(Oh to hell with those two. Let's forget about them. People who don't know how to communicate with one another clearly and honestly, without distorting or suppressing the facts, can't be worth bothering with. There is enough natural sickness in the world, cholera, yellow fever, cancer, without a person having to be subjected to spiritual and mental sickies. I mean . . .)

"Neugy. What was all that strange static?"

"Damned if I know," he said, looking around and up into the sky. "Must have been some kind of electrical disturbance in the air."

Ophelia shook her head. Uh uh. It was something different, weird. Like getting a radio station on the radiator or something."

"Yeah. Well, these are strange times. I mean, nature's gone a little whacky. Testing all those atom bombs has queered everything. I read somewhere that a heavy snowfall was reported in the Amazon Valley."

"Mm. Very, very peculiar. Makes your skin crawl."

There was a shout and much laughter on one of the volleyball stretches. Two young men, neither with a pot, strolled by and just could not help giving Ophelia a very steady once over.

"Okay then," Neugy said, stretching out on their beach blanket. "Tell me about dancing in the jazz joint."

Ophelia smiled. "Later. I've got a better idea. I've been watching some kids way down on the beach playing football. And I've been making up a story about them."

Neugy crushed a sandfly on his leg. "Hey, that's a great idea! And then when you finish I'll make up one."

She wagged her finger gently at him. "There you go again, Neugy, baby. Getting pushy and aggressive."

Crestfallen, he said, "Sorry 'bout that. Have to watch myself."

Ophelia returned her black, smiling gaze to the distant boy football players. "Now I want you to look at those kids with a lot of concentration."

"Yeah."

"Clear your mind of all other things. Stop thinking about what a good lay that blond fat girl would be. Now focus your feelings on that kid in the red shorts. He's the main character, so to speak. All set?"

"Yes."

"Okay. Here we go."

Marvin's most cherished dishonesty was his love for his father: deep down, he thought his old man was a second-rate sparrow. His next most prized deceit was his shining record in his Intellectually Gifted Children class at P.S. 189: he knew that any knish who could memorize a little could get a pat on the head and not really care about scholarship at all. And finally, his third favorite tickle was that only vulgar and stupid children resorted to physical violence in a situation: nothing in this world could shake his knowledge that his was the song of the midget.

He was turning these life-things over in his mind, like an old cook basting meat goodies in the oven, as he scrunched up on the summer furniture couch and watched a Henry Fonda saga of good and evil and long suffering he-men he had seen twice before on the Late Show and more or less sympathized with. He was having a clearly uncertain oral relationship with a grilled cheese sandwich. Just a heart's thump away from him, sitting on a creaky chair trying to deal devotedly with a collection of modern French plays, was his ebony-haired mother. She was in furiously skimpy shorts and halter, fairly exposed, and even a Bantu could tell that tranquility was a country never once visited by her in this or any other life.

"You're going to go blind watching that idiot box," she said, keeping her gaze fixed on the French stage.

"Why did you buy it?" Marvin asked, placing a morsel of cheese on his tongue.

"It was your father's idea. He'll do anything to avoid reality." Her voice was a cultural spiceship loaded with tastes and tangs and intonations from a variety of countries and tribes. "Why don't you go outside and find your friends?" she went on. "Develop your social instincts or something." She flipped a page firmly and you half expected several of the actors therein to tumble to the floor. "After all, the beach is where you're supposed to explore your personality more richly, get to know people in a way denied to you in the frenzy and chill of the city."

Here was a philosophic split: he loved New York and its locked, protected life. But he got up from the couch, releasing a splendid sigh, worthy of a rabbinal conclave, and headed for the door.

"Play nice now," his mother advised him, as if she were directing a promising young actor before her French-inclined eyes. "Don't do anything to exhaust yourself. Okay?"

Marvin said um, and padded out of the cottage and into the measureless challenge of sand, water, and air. He was twelve, and he wished he were right now twenty-three and driving a Cadillac convertible along Riverside Drive.

After searching the beach and dunes for almost half an hour—in which time he knew that a city can be razed or a Leonardo da Vinci masterpiece swiped—Marvin came upon a cluster of his summer friends fooling around in a deserted, seldom-visited section of dunes and beach. He forgave the sun its unintentional cruelty and the sand its relentless goyisha stupidity (he was trying to cultivate humility at the request of his temple teacher) and prepared his heart for the delights of group play.

"Catch it, Marv!" and in another moment he was embracing a football and racing joyously down the beach toward a phantom touchdown. "You're getting better, Marv," said the thrower, a dumpling-faced boy of 13 whose name was Alan and whose parents floated in an unwavering state of grace because he attended a private school on the East Side. Marvin loved this appraisal because it exorcised the demons of his obesity and his customary non-championship form.

"I've been practicing," he gasped, in full and pleased awareness of the innocence of words. Who has ever been punched in the nose by a violated word?

The grinning young group of athletes consisted of three other boys besides Marvin and Alan: wet-eyed, silver-tongued David Pincus, whose parents were confidants of angels of the Broadway variety; Arnold Boston, thin and tortured as an Arab whose ascetic, beautiful glance made flowers ashamed of themselves; and Arthur Krause, whose mother's and grandmother's insistent culinary triumphs were pushing his behind closer and closer to his apprehensive shoulders. Arthur had an uncle Morris who lived with his family and repaid their indulgence by being an outspoken soul mate of Maimonides. These half-naked sweating five, they could have been Philistines cavorting on the shores of Galilee, held high-voiced, complete dominion over this stretch of sand and rocks and salivating sea.

"Come on," shouted socially connected Pincus. "Let's get a game going. That's what the ball is for."

"Attaboy!" Marvin sang out in a lyrically formless appreciation of friend Pincus' spirited thinking.

"My father knows Tom Harmon!" Arnold yelled to the unknowing, not totally approving world, and raced down the beach as if he were expecting a long touchdown pass.

In a few moments they were playing a kind of football game, an exercise that was absolutely and remorselessly indigenous to this particular spot and players. Falling down and dropping the ball and Nijinsky type collisions gave their game a certain intimate and yet vain-charm sensibility—like a species of woman who knows that her sloppiness and faint dishevelment, fatal to a public image, delight and seduce her lover in private. Marvin forgot all about his domestic cobwebs, including his outrageously bright little sister Deborah, as he unfolded his frenzy in this moiling game. The ocean was an audience of complete conspiracy, and the sky above showed no signs of disbelief.

"I'm going to Music and Art when I graduate," Alan announced, getting up from a fall and charging a ball carrier.

"I got higher marks than anybody on my exams."

"How do you know?" asked Marvin, more in the manner of a person wishing to share a secret device than one inquiring into proof.

"I just know, that's all," Alan replied, grabbing the ball from Pincus and flying off. "I don't have to ask anybody."

It was Marvin, extricating himself from a fantasy of conducting the Boston Philharmonic while Alan sat smally in the pits, who first saw the dark forms of the two strangers approaching from the north. He reacted with irrational surprise and apprehension, as one who is abruptly wakened from sleep. As the two strange boys came closer they were noticed by the others in Marvin's group, buy no one said anything, as though there was a blood-deep understanding that outsiders were not to be recognized. The two boys were heavily tanned and Marvin was sure they were Italian or Spanish. Their tan looked very professional to Marvin; it wasn't kidding around as was his own fickle shading which he knew would flee from him soon after his return to New York City.

They continued their game under the amused watch of the strangers, who were their same age, eleven or twelve, but their competence a fragile and private agreement at best, balanced under such scrutiny.

"You guys stink," one of the dark ones said, and slapped his companion robustly on the back.

"Yeah," the other one mocked, his face illuminated as only contempt can illuminate. "You can't play ball at all." And they both showered the group with their black laughter.

The others just looked at each other without saying anything. Finally, Pincus, the oldest, said, with dove-like uncertainty. "That's what you say." His response was almost visible as it fluttered uncertainly in that violate atmosphere.

Both the strangers, who had been squatting like natives in a primitive village, stood up and one of them walked boldly up to Pincus. "That's what I know, you sissy kid," and he wrenched the ball from Pincus.

"Hey!" excaped from Marvin's lips. "Don't."

Now the other boy strode over, a smile on his face that had never known a moment's uncertainty, "Want to make something of it?" and he adroitly tripped and knocked Marvin down. Alan's gasp of astonishment did nothing to assuage the reality of Marvin's fall. Looking up at the dark boy's bright tiger eyes, Marvin, the quail of fear whirring through his stomach and into his groin, saw himself as one of the world's strongest men and he was crushing this boy's body in his bare hands as he would a soft pretzel.

"Let's go," the first intruder said, and the two of them victoriously walked away with their prize of superiority and the football.

The five boys seemed stricken, as one hears the village of Pompei was instantly paralyzed in mid-motion by the wrath of the volcano god; they could only watch the invaders walk up the beach and out of sight around the cove bend, their pride vanishing with them. Marvin remained lying on the sand, prone as an idea that has been publicly refuted and officially banned. Finally, the five boys relaxed.

"Bastards," Arthur said, kicking the dumb sand.

"Yeah," Arnold agreed, just nodding his head blankly. "I'll bet they had knives," Marvin ventured, getting up and brushing himself off. "Those Italian and Spick kids always fight that way."

"Yeah," Pincus said, his face coming back to normal. "They don't fight fair."

Arnold rounded out the tune. "You can't get at a guy with a knife."

They were making each other feel less shat upon when they became aware of a man standing on the dunes watching them.

"Good God!" the man said loudly, and they could see his head shake. "Two kids against five," and laughing like an old Greek god, he disappeared over the sand hills.

The boys looked at one another inquiringly, as though they did not identify themselves with the five boys the man had derided and that each inquirer would come up with the real people he was talking about.

"Who does he think he is anyway?" Pincus said.

"Yeah," Marvin mumbled, "The big schmuck." His agreement with Pincus at this moment made him feel very warm toward him.

An unspoken understanding and command now moved them slowly away from the scene of their confrontation, away from the beach and inland toward an area of boulders and marshes. The light had somehow lost its brightness; a somber quality had surreptitiously seized the atmosphere. What had been pink was now gray, what had been moving was now still. In a few minutes—during which speechless time each boy had scurried deeper and deeper into the labyrinths of his own being—they found themselves at the brink of a sort of ravine. Huge oily black boulders banked this place and at the bottom, about thirty feet below the boys, was a stagnant pool covered over with nature's shameless excrescences. Stunted and twisted bushes and trees brazenly grew here and there, when they should have been hiding, and the breath of the place, like that of a sleeping giant, was fetid and most melancholy. The bleak and primeval aura of this spot held the boys spellbound for many moments. The first thought that surfaced in Marvin's mind, when he came out of his trance, was strangely irrelevant: he wondered if he could ever find his way back home.

"Gee," Arthur murmured. "This is the kind of place you find treasures in I'll bet."

"Did pirates get up this far?" asked Pincus, trying to sound like an incorruptible mapmaker.

"Pirates got everywhere," Marvin heard himself say, and immediately felt intuitive and in touch with life.

Thin-nosed Arnold picked up a large rock and threw it fiercely at the pool below. It made a soupy splashing noise when it hit, not the clean stone and water sound, and the green slime splash that followed was turgid and sick and fell upon the stony embankment with the stain of a curse.

"I'm going down to investigate," announced Alan with an authority, almost aggressiveness, that had not been in his voice all afternoon. It was said with the imperiousness of a detective about to clear up something immoral and against the law.

"I'm going with you," said Arthur, climbing over a boulder as though he had not been fat a day in his life.

The others all followed, and in seconds they were halfway down the obscene, brooding slopes.

"Get out of here!" a high clear voice demanded.

They all stopped and looked around. Down below them, to the right and next to a growth of dwarf trees near the edge of the dank pool, stood a small boy quite naked except for a pair of black shorts. He had stunningly blonde hair and the face of an outraged choirboy. "Go on." he shouted. "Get out. This is my place."

"Who said so?" Pincus sneered.

"I did," the boy answered defiantly, holding onto a branch of the demented looking tree. "I found it."

"That's tough," yelled Krause.

"Yeah," Marvin joined in. "So shut up and don't mess with us, kid." A kind of electricity, a deep vibration, could now be felt running between the five boys, something that had been totally absent back on the beach. It was closeness and strength and it was bristly as with a pack of animals.

"Find your own place!" the angelic blond boy insisted, straining his lungs with this order, and he stooped down and picked up a dead branch and shook it threateningly at them. "Beat it!"

Without thinking, as though he were really all five boys instead of his single self, Marvin scooped up a rock and hurled it down at the boy. It struck him on the shoulder and a sharp cry of pain came from him. Then, utterly unified, all the boys began to throw rocks at the boy.

"We'll show you!" screamed Arnold, and his voice, once soft and childish, now had the steel of madness.

A rock hit the boy in the face and blood began pouring all over his nakedness. He was screaming unceasingly now and the rocks kept coming with incredible fury. He was hit all over his small body and the sounds had the heaviness of death. Another rock smashed into his bloody head, and he staggered to the edge above the pool. He teetered there and when a stone flung by wild-faced Pincus struck him in the ear, he fell with a great final shriek of pain and horror into the green water.

The boys stared down into the slowly disturbed foulness of water below them, at the blood coloring the bile green, at the twisting and drowning boy, then, somehow returning to their earlier selves, began to scramble out of the ravine.

"We weren't here!" shouted Pincus, reaching the top. "Tell them we weren't even here!"

OPHELIA AND NEUGERBORN WERE WAITING FOR their cocktail guests. The radio was playing late afternoon music —Shep Fields and his Rippling Rhythm—and from time to time a news item was burbled in: Senator McCarthy flushes out two more homosexuals in the State Department, Frank Costello gets another stay in his deportation proceedings. Cheese and crackers —a Brie and some melba to be exact—and small slices of cold Polish sausage were laid out as lures on the big round glass coffee table. Ophelia was dressed in a very eye-catching silk print dress that just about scraped the floor, it was that long. There was nothing unusual about Neugy's clothes. He always seemed to be dressed in a clean white pair of pants and a blue polo shirt, even when he was undressed. His blue eyes were clean and well-dressed too: they came right off a malted milk ad.

"Who did you say these people were?" Ophelia asked, examining her nail polish job.

"The Whitcombs run a design store in Southhampton, the Millers live off the sweat and misery of the Bantu tribesmen, via shares in De Beers Diamond Co., and John Bolton and his friend Nancy both work for the Rockefeller Foundation." He put some salted almonds in his well-bred mouth and after a decent amount of chewing action, sipped off some martini.

"Ah hah," said Ophelia. "The picture becomes a little clearer. The ones you are hustling are the last two, correct?"

"You got it."

"That Rockefeller money. What do you want it for?"

More cashews went into the chopper. "My North African project. A two-year study of religious rituals as related to political behavior among the Riffs." He really had to grin. "A real fore-square sweetheart."

Ophelia began mixing herself a little something.

"Aren't these clean white people going to be knocked on their stiff-upper-lip asses when they see that you are shacked up with a dinge?"

He nodded. "Deep down inside them, yes. But on the surface, up where life's skating rink is constructed, they will be thrilled. They will knock themselves out feeling liberal, chic, advanced, partonizing, and superior. We will be directly concerned with manipulating all that, all those icy smooth and slippery lies they live. *Comprenez-vous?*"

"Indeed I do, Neug honey, indeed I do. I am torn between complete admiration and complete disgust." She laughed slightly.

"Me too," he said. "But that pretty much describes the human situation all over."

She tested the martini. "Mm. Pernod is great. Much better than vermouth."

"Oh absolutely. Vermouth is cat's piss." He slapped her on the ass as she passed him on her way to the glass doors facing the approach to this dune house. "Fine stuff you got there. Very fine indeed. Must be due to your Negro way of walking. White girls don't have asses like yours. They walk too fast. So . . . who were these white people who adopted you as a child and took you to Paris?"

Ophelia just gazed out of the big glass doors, vibrating in her silk print like an Arctic sunset. "Here they come. Oh, Neugy! For the love of God! Why didn't you tell me that one of them was a dwarf and a hunchback?"

"You didn't ask me."

"Which one is he?"

"The Rockefeller money giver."

XXI IF ANYBODY ASKS YOU, TELL THEM you haven't seen me around lately. I don't want anybody bothering me with idiot questions or proposals. People sniff and suck around too much. They can't leave a fellow alone for a minute. Privacy is un-American. Wanting a little of it is worse than being a Commie. Anyway, I'm out of circulation for the time being. I'm working on a lot of things and I need to be alone. One of my major projects is a humane solution to Sylvia. I plan to get her deported to Crete. I don't want to hurt her. I just want to get her out of the way. She can live quietly there and maybe, with a little application, learn how to press olives, so that she can fit into the community in a nice way. Maybe even meet a clean Cretan widower, and make out. I am assembling all the required proof—false, of course —that she entered this country illegally. This will take time, but it's worth it. What I mean is, my sanity depends upon it. For the past couple of weeks she has been in Belgrade, chaperoning a tourist package tour. Part of her duties as assistant of the Hi Fly Travel Agency. Dishonest work never hurt anybody. So . . . she's not breathing down my poor neck as usual. You know, asking me dumb questions about my underground activities, and why I spend so much time talking to myself in different voices.

"Is something unusually wrong going on in your noodle department?" she says. "Spanish and French accents yet. Last week you were muttering in something that sounded like Japanese faggot."

Screw her. She's so square she doesn't know the difference between a brownie and a troll. One of these days I'm going to look into the facts surrounding my marriage to her. Maybe I'll find out that it wasn't even me who did it. Which reminds me of a little something I composed the other night. Or was it the day? I'm not completely sure, to tell you the truth. All I know is it was under my pillow when I changed the sheets this morning. Here it is:

Sweet eyes that always come and go
Sweet eyes heating the fur coat of those who fall in love.
Sweet eyes of pearly clearness,
They say: I am ready when you please,
To those whom they feel to be powerful.

True huh? Nothing cheap and ephemeral about it, unlike all that stuff you hear sung in night clubs these days. Not my style. I like things that will go whispering down through the ages. Permanence, that's my bag. I wish I could remember who I was thinking about when I knocked it off. Obviously it wasn't Sylvia of the Subway Change Maker Eyes. Jesus. Lift a skirt and what do you find? Fifty years in Siberia, that's what.

My job at the World Wide Institute of Contemporary Dialogs is just perfect. (I got it through an ad in *The Daily Worker*.) I don't have a single complaint. I put in six hours a day and the work is divinely simple. I clean the floors, check out the garbage disposal units (which get stuffed with some pretty strange stuff, I'll tell you), and a couple of times a week adjust the thermostat controls on the oil and water, because every now and then the mix does go off a bit, and then our visiting Fellows start climbing the walls.

Most of the time, though, everything goes real keen. I know, because I'm allowed to sit in on the dialogs, jumping up from time to time to answer our one phone, and the door—which is at the back in an alleyway—always wild hyacinth types who claim they are dialog masters and world-famous logicians but who are really copping out on their middle-class responsibilities or trying to dodge the draft.

"I insist that you open this door and let me in! Stop trying to run this institute like a private club. Ideas belong to the world, to nature. You guys will soon start to monopolize the air at the rate you're going. Stop pushing me! I have some very crucial things I wish to discuss on the relationship between ethics and property. The whole question of violence in our time is bound up to this. Furthermore . . ." Slam!

"Pleeze, your egcellenzi, allow me to zit vor joost a vew minitz und dizguz wid you my eggstrimly berzonal gonzepts off zee nezzessity off free emozional contagt in zee racink off highly distuhrbed infanz. Und . . ." Slam!

Moochers, all of them. I can tell you from experience. I made the grave mistake of letting one of those guys in once—actually it was a woman. She hadn't been there three hours before she had set up her headquarters in the shower room, was cooking fish-cakes on her hot plate, in the director's office no less, and had sabotaged a fine dialog—on male-female power relations in subcultural Latin American groups—by throwing in some completely irrelevant crap about her childhood in White Russia. One of our finest minds, a chap from Istanbul, who had been the debating champion of that city for ten straight years, threw in the towel and just sat there at the table and cried like a baby.

But listen to this lovely exchange that bloomed just this morning up on the sundeck (officially known as the Pascal Porch and Study Area, because of an endowment arrangement with a rich Swiss), between two lifetime Fellows who also happen to be okay guys. (Unlike a couple I could name who are always asking me if I would mind running out for danish and coffee for them. I don't do it of course. I bring my grub to work and they can bring theirs.)

"I submit that the basis of authoritarianism is not political power over the masses, but a fear of the wonders, and therefore the chaos, of the human imagination."

That came from our man from Holland.

"I disagree," said Zlivianos of Greece. "It is my contention that authoritarianism is rooted deeply in religious feelings."

"You must be mad," said Holland.

"Nonsense," said Zlivianos. "I have never felt saner in my life. Absolute structures of authority are earthly, human representations of the absolutism of God. Such structures are profoundly religious, and therefore admirable, attempts to reinforce man's need to live within divine order."

"Man's greatest fear," said Holland, staring at Zlivianos with firm blue eyes, "is his infinite humanness. His imagination carries him so far beyond his immediate situation that he cannot bear it. Thus, the expression of this imagination outside immediate limitations threatens to otherworld or annihilate him. So how does he deal with this paradoxical situation? He produces, or unconsciously conspires to produce, a political order that supresses this imagination that his fears tell him could destroy him."

Zlivianos shook his bushy black head as if he were a great water buffalo about to charge a puny white hunter. "My dear colleague, your analysis reeks with contempt for your human brothers. You should be ashamed of yourself."

Holland's face tightened like a gun about to fire. "On the contrary, my dear Greek friend, I am filled with love for my fellow man and my analysis is based on this love and its hope for his immortality. It is you whose mind stinks of contempt like a huge pus ball."

Apparently without knowing what he was doing, and without taking his furious gaze from Holland, Zlivianos slowly began crushing sheets of note paper, stuffing them in his mouth, grinding them into pulp, and swallowing them. "Allow me to inform you, Mr. Edam Cheese, that in my country people like you are not allowed to walk in the same streets with decent folk," and he gulped down a pound of pulp.

Mr. Dutchboy, oblivious to the pain he must have been producing upon himself, was pushing a ballpoint pen harder and harder into his neck. "Mr. Olive Oil, I am forced to inform you that in Holland the likes of you are regarded as vermin and once a month are sprayed out of existence." A tiny trickle of blood appeared on his neck where the point of the pen had pierced the skin.

At this moment in the dialog, when it seemed that our high standards of intellectual discourse might be altered by something untoward in the lowbrow animal way, our fellow from the lake region of Zanzibar, the very large and blue-black physicist, Mr. Perkins, stood up at his end of the table (an immensely large round magnificence that had once been a tree trunk in the mahogany forests of the Philippines), and bellowed, "Gentlemen, I believe it is time for our afternoon skin-contact exercise!"

This particular part of the institute's program, which might be regarded as mere recreation by less sophisticated organizations (the YMCA, for example), was not only a pleasant change from the intense cerebral exchanges, but was also a very important component of our entire exploratory investigations. In other words, an essential part of our over-all dialog. (I can't help saying *our* because, although I am there as a mere janitor—incidentally, the latrine bit is performed by two splendid deaf mute twins sent to us by a wealthy Bolivian lady—I have begun to feel that, in my way, I contribute to the life of the operation just as much as anybody else. Of course, I would never presume to call myself a Fellow of the Institute, just as the piano would never have the gall to regard itself as a part of the sonata.)

So . . . everybody stood up and formed a circle.

"All right, everybody!" said the skin-contact leader, a fine figure of a woman named Eulalia Cabrera de la Portinoy, an ethologist from Uruguay. "Stick out your tongues."

Out sprang twelve pink organs, including my own. "Wiggle them around," Dr. Eulalia directed, and gave an exhibition with her own tongue. "Make them feel their joy and knowledge. Release them from their drudgery in the prison of the mouth! Make them dart and swoop, twist and turn! Turn your tongues into birds! Splendid!"

It sure was. Everybody there clearly was beginning to feel a new dimension of being, a new element of human dialog, emerge. Dr. Eulalia smiled with satisfaction.

"Now take your neighbors's hands. Fine. Now let all the messages in those fingers become part of your own messages. Let their deepest yearnings become as one with your deepest yearnings."

I was holding hands with a Chinese poet, Lin Wang, and the ancient emanations pouring out of his bony porcelain extremities were so rich and zonky I thought my own hands would turn into Lobster Cantonese. Holy mackerel! Something out of the ordinary garden stuff must have been zapping out of me into him because the things he was doing with his facial expressions could have been mistaken for opium addiction. A few feet away from me the blue-black physicist was sweating to beat the band as he held the hands of Dr. Molve O'Toole, the great historiographer from Dublin.

"Isn't it wonderful?" shouted Dr. Eulalia.

"Yes! yes," we all chanted together.

"Isn't it universal?"

"Yes! Yes!"

"Oh deepest human revelation and symbiosis!" she howled, swaying back and forth and holding out her own hands. "Oh total immersion in human joy and energy!"

"Joy and energy!" we yelled in unison, rocking, swaying back and forth in our ecstatic hand-holding.

"Now rub noses!" she commanded. "Don't lose each other's hands whatever you do!"

"Oh joy! Oh joy!" we chanted. "Oh deep juiciness!" Our universally activated and sensitized noses rubbed and moans of illuminations and power-release went up from everybody.

Dr. E.— Eulalia—boy! what a front-liner she was—whipped up the shirt of Professor Wills Breedlove (Biblical scholar: London) and sang out "Bellies! Rub your brother's belly!" Her eyes shining like wet black diamonds, she began a circular massaging of old Breedlove's massive Yorkshire gut. It was simply unbelievable how this belly-rubbing wiped out all false identities and self-protection systems that were locked in our bodies. I was well on my way toward early innocence, under the dissolving hand of Dr. Wang, when Zlivianos, who was being worked on by Dutch, began to sing the Greek national anthem in the soprano voice of a child.

"Give yourself back to yourself," Wang panted to me, rubbing away.

"I cut gym yesterday," I heard myself say.

"Let your navel tell the truth."

"Mommy, my bear is lost," a whiny tiny voice coming out of me said.

"I'm two fishing boats in the harbor!" shouted the big black.

"My brother is a cheating son of a bitch!" howled a deep alien voice from Dr. O'Toole, "Ooh what a nasty nibble that was."

The next thing I knew I had disappeared into my own skin . . .

" . . . and you say you have no idea whatsoever about how you got here?" the fat bald old man with a black beard and big ears is saying.

"None at all."

"Do you know where it is you come from?"

"Nope."

He scratches his belly and sighs. "Very peculiar. Are you sure you did not get very drunk and get on a plane?"

"I guess that might be possible, but from the looks of these mountains there couldn't be an airport for miles."

He nods his small old head, "There isn't. The only transporta-ton to the nearest town is camel back, and once a week someone from the compound here drives into that town, which is Elaheeb. You couldn't possibly walk that far without looking half dead. Which you don't."

"I feel just fine. As though I'd just wakened after a good night's sleep."

Several heavily loaded camels clump by this building. they are being led by a dark skinny little boy and a woman with a veil covering most of her face.

"Are you given to a great deal of lying?" the old man asks.

"I can't really say. Perhaps if you give me an opportuni-ty . . ."

He sighs again and glances wearily out into the small dirt street. "I don't know what to make of this. A total stranger, a complete alien, appears stark naked, suddenly from nowhere in a village in the Atlas Mountains." He runs his hand over his old face. "I wonder . . . could you be the Messiah?"

"I think I could probably be anybody."

He smiles vaguely. "Yes, I suppose so, since you don't seem to have any identity that we know of. Amnesia . . . no, I don't think so. I have seen people with memory blackouts, and they carry with them a strangeness, an other-placeness, that you don't have."

"I'm very hungry. Could I have a little food?"

He picks up a little bronze bell from his desk and tinkles it. In a moment a thin man wearing an ornately embroidered skullcap pads in on bare feet. He bows, holding his hands palm to palm. "Some slices of goat meat and a dish of our soft cheese. How would that be?"

"Yes. That sounds more than adequate."

He speaks in a guttural language to the man who nods and goes out noiselessly. Then he looks at his watch. "It will soon be time for our director of spiritual rehabilitation to assemble the villagers. Hon Do, a marvelous man with diamond mines of wonder in his soul. You will be very impressed with him, I hope."

"What does he do?"

"He helps these primitive Arab villagers to understand themselves in the new world that has come about."

"New world?"

He smiles and rubs his old hands together. "Of course. Being this strange neuter, this man who has no past, no participation in history or evolution, you would not know what has taken place in this world." He sighs heavily. "The old rotten world ended ten years ago. Our Chinese brothers are in charge of everything now. It took a long time, a very long time, but the white man has finally been subdued. His madness and destruction are at an end. Centuries of horror are behind mankind forever."

The servant appears with a tray of food.

"Well," begins the old man. "I guess we will have to find a place for you in this new history. What do you say? You have marvelous possibilities, you know. Your mind apparently exists as a pureness. The shit of the bourgeois world is not burying your brain. Is that not so, my friend?"

On I go . . .

PLEASE. YOU MUST UNDERSTAND. I AM NOT trying to seduce you with my solitude. Nor do I wish to shackle you with my despair. I am simply attempting to share my fathomless humanity with you. Like you, I am a wanderer in my own lost world. For every dragon I spy and slay, there is another disguised as a mouse waiting to take its place. Only your completely unashamed sympathy and fellowship can save me from becoming an anthropological artifact in a public museum.

The very first thing I do before going to sleep at night and upon waking up in the morning is to ask myself, Where do I go now? And then I ask, and who shall I be? Are we all merely extravagant compilations of aches and pains and ungovernable terrors? Are our accomplishments self-delusory attempts to give ourselves a unique human substance which we therefore do not really possess? Is there one single dot we can point to and say without hesitation, there I am? Or are we, tragically and absurdly, only that thing that others agree to say we are because we will do the same for them? And then, oh dear, does it turn out that we have invented this co-conspirator?

Well, do you know what she said?

"Darling, I don't know what you are talking about, and if I did, I think it would bore me. Now would you turn the light out and put your face down there where it feels so good."

THE SHOWER ROOM WAS CLOUDED WITH HEAVY steam.

"What the hell happened to you in Barcelona?" the heavy naked man shouted through the stream and pelting water.

"They didn't want us, that's what happened."

"What do you mean? You were told to set up an office and get some accounts."

"None of the people I talked to thought they needed us. They said . . ."

The heavy man sputtered and rubbed himself. "Goddamn it! Your job was to convince them they needed our services."

"They said the Spanish consumer had nothing in common with the American consumer, that the whole psychology of buying and selling was totally different."

The big man's body was turning pink with all the soaping and rubbing.

"Oh balls! That's defeatism, that's what that is. I've never known of a place that didn't do better with American advertising know-how. Christ, just look what Markson did in Zurich. He got us two-million billing inside a year."

"Spanish people aren't built like the Swiss. Besides . . ."

"Balls! Everybody wants to live better."

The showers went off and an attendent brought in big wrap-around towels.

"Besides, they're afraid a civil war might break out. There's a guy named Franco who wants to take over, and . . ."

"Excuses, excuses. You want to know something? You're in the wrong racket. That's right. The wrong line of endeavor. You're one of those introverts. You ought to work in a library, or maybe run a small hotel somewhere. Something real quiet. I'll put it to you straight: You haven't got any of the old touchdown spirit."

I AM IN A LARGE GYMNASIUM WHOSE FAMILIAR-ity is almost oppressive. Various smells are telling me secrets that I do not wish to know. "I must have my privacy!" I shout. But that does no good at all. A foot smell asserts itself with a terrible arrogance. I know that I should immediately put it in its place, but I am ignorant of the local methods for doing this, so I let it slide. "Our day will come," I murmur, and I hope that I have not said this so softly that it will seem sneaky and cheap.

"You'd bargain your life away," says a blubbery fellow in shorts. He is shooting soft baskets nearby.

I try to grab the ball as it floats off the board, but this sudden act is permeated with failure. I feel ashamed and a very strong wish to disappear into one of the many smells there occupies me for moments. Several fellows—they are taut and honest in jockstraps alone—are engaged in splendid tumbling formations quite a distance away. This distance puzzles me into vagueness, for something tells me that it is not in feet that this distance is to be measured. An urge for assimilating this forces me into what I think is a clear and efficient run toward them. Despite a lot of this efficiency, the splendid, trustworthy tumblers remain the same distance away from me.

"Do you get it now?" a fellow on the climbing bars asks, and with no premeditation whatsoever he lobs a tennis shoe at my face. It hurls me right back to my wet crib.

"May we please talk this over?" I beg him, and my words are betrayed by inadvertent tears.

We are suddenly holding hands. "We both have feelings but they are not relevant here," he is saying, and as we denounce our parents with a hug and tongue kissing, the uncompromising vastness is circled with laughter.

"Something's up," I say.

He just collapses gradually to the floor. His smile is his biggest asset.

Two astonishingly large young ladies are carrying me by my arms and legs. My groin is experiencing an unspeakable freedom. A rather dreadful and unmanly giggle is pouring out of me. I want very strongly to enjoy this entire business without compromising myself, but along with this powerful wish is a cozy old sensation that such things are always decided much later.

"Have we anything in common?" asks a voice which has to be mine but which somehow seems to be coming from someplace else.

They only laugh knowingly and obscenely and begin to exchange critical information whose real meaning is tantalizingly just inches away. The blond girl has more than courageously formed breasts. They are demonic in their availability. Somehow I am swarming all over them even though I am still being carried. My entire existence is wallowing in the infinite soft excitement of these breasts. I bite through a nipple, and blood pours without remorse into my mouth.

"They'll never find out," I say hugely, as if under fathoms of water.

These impenetrably sincere girls go right on laughing. They know that I am a little rascal.

XXII

BOSWORTH AND CHURCHILL, SITting at a small sidewalk café in Nice, were facing two facts: 1) they were down to their last twelve francs and 2) the man they were doing the work for was overdue by two days.

"Well, Church," began Bosworth, "what do you think?"

Churchill finished his espresso, "I was just going to ask you the same thing."

Bosworth shook his head. "I don't get it. Guys representing the U.S. Government aren't supposed to be two days late. That's the way people act when they are badly connected."

Churchill watched a donkey-drawn milk cart slowly move down the Rue Buta. "I know. It seems out of order somehow. Maybe his train got stuck in a tunnel in the Alps."

Bosworth fingered his brandy glass thoughtfully. "That could be. But I kind of doubt it. Those tunnels aren't made of glue." He sipped his drink. "If he doesn't show up by six, we'll write him off. Okay?"

"Sure," said Churchill, his gaze roaming to an old man in a beret who was tending a fruit and vegetable stand across the street. "And then I guess we just throw all this research away." The vegetable and fruit man began eating a bunch of his own grapes.

"That would be a damn shame. We've got some really great stuff here." He began to turn the pages of a large typescript. "Techniques of French Mediterranean fishing cooperatives . . . seine netting at low tide . . . long line fishing in open waters . . . the selective sharing of catches . . . structures of voting councils . . . Everything you'd want to know."

Churchill lit up a Gauloise. "Or at least all the United States Bureau of Fisheries would want to know. I wonder if this kind of stuff is really of any value to fishermen in America."

Bosworth shrugged. "Who knows? But I don't think that's the real purpose of it, do you? Like everything else those guys in the government do, this study simply justifies their own operation. They've got to think of things to do to keep their jobs going."

"Yeah," said Churchill, stretching and at the same time reading a Perrier ad on the side of . . . "And they validate it further by hiring college stiffs like us to do fieldwork. Oh it's sweet all right."

The waiter, a sparrow-faced fellow with a very serious little mustache, asked them if they wanted another round. He held a dirty white towel as a child holds a teddy bear, and while he waited for their answer he . . .

"Why don't we take a walk and come back," Bosworth said to Churchill.

"Okay. Maybe I'll drop a postcard to my sister."

"This tipping thing," said Bosworth, looking at his small French change. "I'm never sure about it."

"A nice calm looking town," said Churchill as they strolled along the Rue Passey. "I like these palm trees."

"I didn't know you had a sister," said Bosworth, stepping back lightly as a motor bike zoomed by.

"Uh huh," and Churchill returned the curiosity smile of two young schoolgirls. "I would have thought people here would be more accustomed to the sight of a black man."

"What does she do with herself?"

A newsie thrust a copy of *Le Figaro* at Bosworth and . . .

"Dreams a lot."

"Ha! ha! Besides that."

"Studies chemistry at the Novodny Institute in Kiev."

"No kidding."

They passed two old English ladies walking dachshunds in front of the Hotel Negresco. One of the dogs growled at Churchill. The old lady holding it said, "Don't be naughty, Charles."

"Did she win a scholarship or something?"

"Sort of. She was working as a secretary to a Russian-Polish importer in San Francisco, and this guy fell for her. She is a very nice armful is Ophelia. And when he made his annual trip back home . . . that glass-importing business was a cover for his government observation work . . . he was a spy . . . he carried Ophelia along with him." He gave the nod to an elegantly attired old man wearing a yachting cap. "She just naturally took to chemistry, I guess."

Bosworth nodded pleasantly at this revelation. "What did your parents think of that?"

"They don't think too much. They're dead."

An ice cream vender didn't get far with them. "Dead? But didn't you tell me when we were out on the Blue Dolphin yesterday that your parents ran a sort of medical clinic in Lagos?"

"Did I now? Wonder what made me say that . . ."

"You tell me," said Bosworth.

"Must be because I really don't know where or who they are. We were orphans, abandoned as babies and left in a Trailways station in Salt Lake City."

They paused in front of a . . . they halted next to . . . across the street from them was a candy store with a photograph of Maurice Chevalier eating from a box of chocolates, and his . . . eyes were glazed with joy.

"Well then, tell me," Bosworth went on, "how did you manage to arrive at the University of Grenoble where we met? That's a lot of doing for a Negro foundling, you must admit, Church."

Churchill laughed and slapped Bosworth, who was about a foot shorter than he, on the back. "Brains and the white man's guilt."

"I see. Well, if President Wilson has his way . . ."

"He won't. He's just a nice white sissy boy."

"Anyway, legislation is coming along that is supposed to help the Negro rise in the world. More equal rights and stuff like that."

Churchill stretched his legs, leaned back on the bench, and stared out at the greenish-blue Mediterranean. "Bunch of lies. You know, Bosworth, when I get my master's in marine biology I'm going to Zanzibar and look for the fabled . . ."

"That's nice."

"What else you plan to do with your life?"

Bosworth watched the yacht riding anchor. "Go back to Ceylon and start a school with my brother."

"Hm. Is that your caste? Parsee or something?"

"Yes. All my ancestors have been professional people."

"It's those untouchables who have to pack the elephant shit, right?"

Bosworth sighed, "Someday we will do something about those poor devils."

"Yeah. That's what that cat Ghandi is always saying. I understand he lives on a glass of water and seven peanuts a day."

"A little fruit too," said Bosworth. "Figs and dates."

The insidious sirocco that had been sulking about all day, coming from the south and picking up the ancient taste and immovability of the sea on its journey, had become, by now . . .

"Quite unbearable," said Churchill, so Bosworth and Churchill, seeing that the ultimatum hour for the American government man's allowed arrival was near, pulled themselves together and started walking slowly back to the café.

At dinner that evening—Bosworth had snails and a veal knuckle in sherry, while Churchill took on the challenge of an octopus swimming in its own ink—they had the pleasure of meeting a retired French academician who had taken his life savings out of the Bank of France and had bought into the sunken-treasure business. This fellow, who had been sitting at the next table openly listening to their conversation until he couldn't stand the distance any longer and so joined them on his own invitation, this fellow (record a guiltless lip tic, silent gray hair, down to his shoulders, and the eyes of an otter building a dam) put a fresh breadstick in his mouth and then, taking it out, said, "You two lads on the bum?"

Bosworth and Churchill looked at each other—You must be kidding, Jack—and Churchill asked, "Are you a queer, by any chance?"

"Good Heavens, no!" the fellow replied. "I'm as straight as a plumbline."

"Whatever that is," muttered Bosworth.

"Yeah," said Churchill. "You'll have to do better than that, Pops."

The man sighed very heavily, put the breadstick down, and reached into his jacket pocket. "Oh dear. Whatever became of human trust? Ah well . . . I have documentary proof here of my intense heterosexuality." He pulled out a white envelope bound with a rubber band. "Overwhelming proof, if I may say so. Just take a look at these, my friends."

Bosworth extracted about a dozen photographs, or really French postcards, totally dirty ones. Each one showed their visitor in a powerfully sexy action with a woman, or women, because in some of them the participants numbered three.

"Pretty good, wouldn't you say?" observed the man.

"Not bad," said Churchill, turning one upside down. "Not bad at all. Which one is you?"

An inch of slovenly hurt appeared on Gascar's face. "That was unkind of you."

Black-boy-scores-a-point look from Churchill. "Stay loose, daddy. Who's the broad?"

"A cousin of mine. A wonderfully game young thing named Petulia."

Bosworth shuffled throught them, making various soft whistling and clucking sounds. "Boy! Those French photographers sure know how to employ light. The tones are first-rate. Wonder what pound paper this is. And not a single one is incorrectly exposed!"

Churchill examined one of them closely. "How were you able to breath in this one, doc?"

"I wasn't," he admitted. "I held my breath."

At another place, the sporty Café Lux, over brandy and cigars, the man was saying, " . . . and among other antiquities, they have discovered priceless statues, fabulous jewelry, gold coins beyond counting, and . . ."

Bosworth tapped him on the arm. "What about those stone jars . . . amphorae . . . any manuscripts in them, Professor Gascar?"

Professor Gascar nodded. "Very much so. Poems, plays, historical writings, secret cult messages. Rich, teasy stuff, my friend."

"Good. Look. If you agree to cut the 'my friend' stuff, I'll call you Pierre."

A total relaxation of all muscular provocation took place on Gascar's face. "Of course. And how completely decent of you. But you know of course that my name is not Pierre. It's André."

Churchill put his arm around Gascar's old shoulder, "Don't get finky, dad. We're all in something together, that's the important thing. Okay?"

The United States government man hadn't shown up, of course, and for a very good reason: he had drowned in a whorehouse bathtub in Geneva. No foul play, either. Quite sweet play, in fact. It was just that he suffered a heart attack after doing incredibly clever things which he had up until then only fantasized about while staring through skin magazines in corner drugstores. When he was young.

"Where?" asked Bosworth.

"Lake Como," said Gascar. They were much closer at that point. Also, they were on their way to a naughty, naughty show on the Avenue Lupin, to be performed by a group of second-rate ballet dancers who were down on their luck.

"I hope I can remember how to find this place if I ever want to come here again."

That was Churchill talking.

"You could always ask directions from somebody."

That was straight from Bosworth with no help from anyone.

"Tell me, Professor," began Churchill as they started up the stairs of a prostrate building on the Avenue Kleber, "What's your academic discipline?"

Gascar blew complaisant brandy smells into Church's blackness. "Greek civilization and character."

"And would you believe it," Churchill said years later to a group of bourgeois shark researchers in Tokyo, "right then and there he began quoting Thucydides on the class war: 'At this, the conspirators, rendered desperate by the law and also hearing that Pithias, before ceasing to be a member of the Council, intended to persuade the masses into concluding an offensive and defensive alliance with Athens, banded together, armed themselves with daggers, burst into the Council and assassinated not only Pithias but no less than sixty other persons.' Oh, God."

"Marvelous," said a biologist from Australia. "Absolutely marvelous. Incidentally, speaking of the French coast, we've just received a report from the marine station in St. Tropez of a shark attack there. A middle-aged night club owner from Paris—named Rastro, I believe—was the victim. The amazing thing about this attack is that the shark carried the victim off."

"Extraordinary," said a man from Wood's Hole. "I've never heard of such a thing. I think this incident should be followed up immediately. Can't imagine what species it could have been."

Someone there, a fellow on the fringe, suggested a Mako. A lady researcher from London, a certain Dr. Lankenauer, said no, it was more likely a . . .

BOSWORTH WAS THERE AND THEN AGAIN HE wasn't there. In one sense, he was slogging along the bottom of Lake Como in a steel-helmeted diving suit. In another sense, he wasn't doing that at all: he was in a variety of places—in a bedroom, up on deck, in a bar in Bombay, in his mother's lap—watching this person, himself, walk through this water. It was really pretty mixed up. Fortunately, Bosworth had a good strong mind—"it's the inner strength that counts, my son," his old Parsee aunt told him time and again—so he could handle it.

"I certainly hope this air hose doesn't develop hardening of the arteries," he said to himself, and watched the bubbles rise from his steel headpiece. "What a perfectly crazy place for Bosworth to be," one of the many other Bosworth consciousnesses said. To be exact, it was the Bosworth who, at that moment in his extraordinarily active mind, was reliving a tennis game at the Bath and Tennis Club in Ceylon, where he often went in his late teens to while away the time when he got tired of planning his future, in good Parsee style.

"Something's the matter with this whole thing," he said, as a school of perch swam by him. "I have no right to be down here. This place is for fish. I'm going against nature."

Up on deck—a martyred river-patrol boat hustling a little moonlighting dough on the side—Churchill and Professor Gascar were manning the diving machinery and stuff. They were both very much waiting for Bosworth's tug on the basket rope which would indicate that he had an ancient goody for them.

"What do you think that stuff is worth that we fished up yesterday?" Churchill asked.

"An original manuscript by Pliny," exclaimed Gascar. "And a dozen pairs of third-century earrings. Good find. It staggers me to think of the money we will get."

"Well, please let me in on the stagger, old buddy."

Gascar sipped from his bottle of Courvoisier and started counting on his fingers (he was wearing an old striped sailor shirt). "Half a million, I would say."

Churchill nodded his head in appreciation. "Nice. That's a lot of economic stability, all right. Who do we plan to sell it to?"

Every sneak thief in the world would have creamed over Gascar's grin. "The classical French Archeological Museum for one."

"No kidding." Churchill shook his head. "A crooked museum. Wham."

"And a certain member of the Krupp family for another."

Churchill stared at the lines—oxygen and basket—leading down to Bosworth. He felt very gentle about Bos. He hoped he wasn't getting wet or lonely down there with the crabs and octopi. "What are these people going to do with the stuff we sell them?"

Gascar put a wedge of paté in his aging, learned mouth. He looked out over the lovely Italian lake, at the exquisite villas on shore, munched sagely, and gave the impression that he was preparing to deliver a deep, illuminating five-hour answer to Church. "Nothing," he finally said.

"Nothing? What do you mean?"

"Exactly that," said Gascar, selecting a black olive from the food spread on the deck. "They will simply have it." He spit the pit into the lake. "You see, my black friend, there are people in this world who want to own history. They think that by possessing these old things, these—how shall I put it?—these tangible moments of ancient thought, they become part of the thing itself. It is as though they were buying a substitute soul for themselves. You see?"

Fish-fellowed Bosworth was indeed seeing. But not necessarily with his eyes, because for the very first time in the conspiracy he could weakly call his life (or the lies of the demented mirror, as his weary cousin Southwick Mehta would often say), he was aware of how little one sees with one's (or anybody else's) eyes. Eyes, he was thinking, are for getting you across the street without colliding with a car, and down here we don't exactly have that type of situation. He was seeing down here with his long buried fish sense. If more people could float around at the bottom of a lake, he was saying, there wouldn't be so much strife and aggression in the world. Centuries of lake life were flowing in and out of his total being. Undulations of primeval security and allness were informing his immediacy. And the fish that were taking things easy all around him, breathing and darting in and out of the ancient wreckage there, knew this was taking place. Nobody had to tell them either.

He felt a strong urge to talk to the fish. But he just couldn't think of anything worthwhile to say. "It would be pretty stupid to throw this rare opportunity away by tossing out a lot of small talk," he said to himself. He would wait until something meaningful came into his mind, something that could form a common ground of interest and friendship between himself and his fish neighbors.

Bos now didn't feel at all interested in the exotic relics that lay about him in the mucky galleon wreckage (the countless amphorae—big pottery vases!—that were scattered all over looked beautifully like eternally sleeping humans), but he did feel a definite responsibility to Church and Gascar up above, so he began filling the basket with such poignant and no longer in-bondage items of greed as a gold goblet here, a silver and jeweled bracelet there, some blinky coins. All that. And watched that indifferent robbery of the past float upwards after a couple of rope tuggings. "Too bad I can't send up a Roman's tooth," said Bosworth. "or a case of Sicilian clap." A large irresponsible purple fish swam onto the basket just for the ride, because it was not every day that such a silly opportunity came along.

Up above, in the dry strife-torn non-osmotic world, Churchill (or that part of him that was not visibly black) was absorbing himself in his sister Ophelia's daily doings, for the fourth time (letters, like stews, get better as they sit for a few days). ". . . and I've taken to borscht like a cat to nip," she was saying in the crumply letter in his hands. "There are about a dozen ways to prepare it, and like the clever black girl that I am, I am mastering all of them. I've made a bunch of friends here, mostly young scientists, and the awful loneliness and fear that daily swamped me in the good old USA have become relics of the past. The Russians are the only non-lonely people I have ever met. And there is something remarkably sincere about them. Not only when it comes to other people but in regard to themselves. They don't cheat themselves, if you know what I mean.

"My studies are coming along beautifully. There is a very good possibility that in the spring I will join a group in Leningrad who are working in rocketry. Gregor will be transferred there too. He is busy working with some very bright and dedicated socialists from China. One can thoroughly say that the world revolution is on. I just wonder if the bourgoisie power groups know what is in store for them. The rivers of the world will run red for quite some time.

"Had a very jolly time last Sunday on the set of a great new movie called *Potemkin*. The man who is directing it, a marvelous wildman named Eisenstein, is a friend of . . ."

"Ha! Ha!" shouted Gascar, throwing his sausage into the air. "Dear Bosworth has some treasure for us," and he began pulling on the basket rope. "Give me a hand, my friend. We're going to be rich again."

"Keep calm, professor," said Churchill, grabbing the rope. "The past ain't goin' nowhere."

Gascar was a madman at the rope. "Hee hee! Roman civilization at its crowning moment is on its way!"

"Well," said Church, doing his part of the pulling, "that's one way to look at it."

It would be absurd, if not boring, to say that Churchill was not thinking somewhat greedy thoughts, because, being, finally, human, he was. But his main mind was on Bosworth, who had been down below for an awfully long time. It seemed like ages, really. Churchill had excellent and very warm feelings for Bosworth, and for these reasons he wanted things to be always going okay for Bos, on the land, in the air, and under the water. Or in whatever other dimension of nature he might be. It really had been a stroke of genius that they had met at the university. Life there would have surely been very ordinary and cloddishly everyday had this not been arranged by the Great Arranger. (No phone numbers will be given out. Sorry.) Handball, poetry, drinking, walking, esthetics (they had rassled Ruskin to the floor), philosophy, research projects (the fisherman bit), the mysteries of snatch—there was nothing they did not participate in as one. More. They were both nonwhites. Brothers in pigment, a Negro and an Indian (or Tibetan). When they clasped hands, no cultural fuses were blown.

"Whites are not only full of shit, but they're crazy besides," said Bosworth one day in Rouen. "Don't you think so, Church?"

"I don't think there's any doubt about it. Thank God I'm not one of them."

"Can you imagine the whites having enough brains or sensitivity to come up with somebody like Buddha or Mohammed?"

"Not in my wildest dreams," said Church, and he gave Bos a hug right in front of everybody in Rouen.

"Church, you know what would be simply smashing?"

"If I had a sister so that you could marry her."

Gascar was panting and pulling like an aging freight train. "Mon Dieu!" he exclaimed. "I never realized Bosworth was so far away."

"Just about twenty-five hundred years, Pop."

A small sightseeing boat appeared from perhaps nowhere about a hundred yards away on the starboard side. But their operation was in no jeopardy. Nor was their privacy. The sightseers were utterly, fundamentally engaged in taking pictures. In fact, the only attention Churchill and Gascar got from that floating carnival of narcissism emanated from a large brown Great Dane standing motionless and alone on the silly little deck. He could have barked, but nobody would have given a damn. The barking of a dog doesn't necessarily have any significance anymore, and people know this.

Gascar had put the loot safely away in a cotton-lined box and Churchill was lying on his back looking at the Italian sky. The lake was slapping and licking away at the boat in a reaction that was not particularly new. Churchill suddenly sat up. "Just occurred to me, Professor, that we have not heard from Bos in some time."

"Hm," murmured Gascar, scratching himself and yawning. "That's right. I hope that fine fellow hasn't gone to sleep down there. This Italian water is very seductive. It is *dolce far niente* water."

Churchill jerked at the rope that led to Bos. No jerk back. "Hey. Maybe he has gone to sleep." He began pulling on the rope. "Jesus Christ, he's light."

Gascar peered over the side. "Maybe he's lost a lot of weight down there. The shrinkage . . ."

In a few moments Churchill had pulled all the rope up. There was no Bosworth at the end of it. "He's gone!"

Gascar stared at the personless rope and then at Churchill. "Gone? You mean he just walked away at the bottom of the lake?"

"It looks that way," said Churchill, and without any more conversation he dived into the lake to follow his good friend Bos wherever he may be.

XXIII RIGHT NOW GEORGE IS RIDING IN

a subway in Chicago—oh, what the hell! This same George, this instant bibliothèque of worldwide self-imagery, this in of his own out, could just as easily, or correctly, have been bouncing along in a subway in New York, Philadelphia, Paris, Berne, or London for that matter. Because being in this particular subway train in Chicago did not make him any different (substantively) from his usual self. Just as Hamlet was always Hamlet whether in Copenhagen or Piccadilly Circus. Same hang-ups, same sick full lips. Chicago was just another backdrop on his life stage. Okay . . . riding on a Chicago train, and very much reading one of the many adorable little advertisements which decorated the train and which were designed to further separate the already fragmented riders from their native wit more than they already were. George is reading this: "Do you really understand people? Do you have the secret of sensitivity? Read how to acquire this uncanny ability —the key to lasting friendships and marriage—in four easy steps . . . in the October issue of *Reader's Digest*."

He sighs, crosses his tired legs once more, and notices that a young lady next to him is reading the same ad and repeating the words half under her breath.

"You don't believe that shit, do you?" George says to her.

A frightened, queasy expression paralyzes the girl's face. "I don't know you," she replies, and stands up. A few feet from him, holding onto a strap now, she turns and says, "You shouldn't say things like that to decent people. You must be sick."

George smiles in defeat and shakes his head. Too bad. Another attempt at human solidarity is lost. He hopes the girl does not go ape and call the train policeman. Why is it that some real nice-looking pieces, like her, girls with heavy rhythmic hips and just the right amount of little-girl around the mouth, why is it that they are so fucking square and jumpy? I mean, Christ. We could have had an exchange of mildly tasty sensations, but she is instantly seeing herself on a slab in the morgue being examined for signs of depraved assault, besides the simple knife wounds that did her in. I can see her puffy-handed mother whimpering into a handker-chief and telling the reporters what a fine clean girl her daughter was and how she got to be captain of the Trailways Nature Club in Sheboygen High. What crazy awful things have happened to the soul of America?

He leaves the subway at the next stop and walks to his destina-tion four blocks away. The neighborhood is quite smelly, and worn out like a cheap plastic toy, and he almost succeeds in not responding badly to it. At the dirty small brick tenement num-bered 1305 he knocks on the only door on the first floor. A woman who is surprisingly good looking, in a tough way, opens the scarred old door only partly.

"Mrs. Parks?"

"Yes. . . ."

"I'm the man from the New Batavia District Attorney's office," he says. "I called you yesterday."

"Oh," she says, "Come on in."

He sits down in a chintz-covered old chair, notebook in hand, and she, smoking nervously, sits across from him.

"You worked as a dancer in Jack Ruby's place, is that right, Mrs. Parks?"

"Yeah. Look, you didn't tell anybody my address or anything, did you?"

"No."

"Because I know they'd kill me in a second if they could find me," she says.

"Nobody knows your whereabouts but you and me."

"Thank God. And we're going to keep it that way. I'll be out of the country in a week."

"You were keeping company with . . ."

"I was laying for Charlie Bates who was a detective on the Dallas Police Force," she says, smiling.

"Oh. And Bates was investigating the assassination."

"He was in it like a lot of others. But let's get to the point. Everybody thinks that there is no record of the questioning of that poor little jerk Oswald after they arrested him. But there is a record and I've got it. Charlie was in on that interrogation and he took notes which he was supposed to turn over to the chief of police, afterward, but he didn't. That's why they knocked him off, to get those notes."

"Nobody knew he had given them to you to keep?"

She smiles. "It didn't occur to them right away, and by the time they did decide that, I was out of that place and hiding here, where my sister lives."

"I see. Well, uh, where are the notes now?"

She laughs, tossing her blond head back abruptly with the sound. "Wouldn't you like to know!"

George can't help a short laugh himself. "Okay. But I'm not here to trick you, Mrs. Parks. I'm really not." His expression becomes serious. "D.A. Pitts and I and the others feel that it is of the greatest importance to this country for the assassination conspiracy to be laid bare."

"I suppose so," she says, "but if you ask me it won't make any difference. It won't make people stop thinking or acting the way they do." She crosses her legs again and pats her hair. "Anyway, they're in a safe place."

"Good. We'll get back to them in a minute. Did you ever see Oswald and Ruby together?"

"Two different times. At the club, in the back room there. I was doubling as a waitress one night and I brought a tray of sandwiches and drinks in. Oswald was there with Jack and two guys who looked Latin. They had some kind of a map on the table, and when I came in, Jack put his arms over it to cover it."

"And the other time?"

"About a week later." She giggles slightly. "It was kind of funny. I had just finished my act. Charlie was there watching me, so I put a lot of extra oomph in it, you know, as a little private show, and this really got him hot. He grabbed me and said he wanted to get laid right then, no two ways about it. I did too. Charlie really did things to me. So I took him into the back room where there was a couch which Jack used to take naps on. I forgot to lock the door behind us." She giggles again and shakes her head, amused. "Well, there we were, screwing away to beat the band, when in walks Jack with Oswald. The look on Oswald's face when he took us in! I thought he was going to bust out crying. Then he ran right out of the room. Jack was kind of shook too but he wasn't scared. 'Goddamn you, Sylvia,' he said. 'You would of laid Christ as they were nailin' him to the cross.' "

George is embarrassed and amused and sexually titillated. He has been writing rapidly in his notebook. "That must have been quite a scene all right," he says, and fumbles for his cigarettes.

"It was. Charlie never said a word. Nothing took his mind off screwing. He was really what you would call oblivious."

George grins. "So Charlie was a dedicated screw. How come he was involved in the assassination?"

Sylvia shrugs. "Well, I guess because he was a member of the Minute Men and he always did what they told him to do. You know, keep America pure and strong. Save America from Communism."

George nods. "Yeah. I know. And revive the rack and the burning posts." They are silent.

"What about some coffee?" Sylvia says, getting up suddenly. "Or a drink? That might be better."

"Okay. A drink." George looks around the small apartment for clues to Sylvia's life, or character, or something. "Did you ever run into this guy David Ferrie?"

"That wierdo pilot who was killed in New Batavia the other day?" she says, breaking out icecubes.

"That's right."

"I saw him once in a fag joint in Dallas. A bunch of us went over to this place, the Club Adonis, one night for a few laughs, and uh . . ."

"Was he alone or with somebody?"

"Several Spanish-talking queers. Boy, when those spicks go gay they really do it up."

"Anybody else? Anybody you . . ."

"Hey! That's right," she says, handing him a vodka and tonic. "A local rich kid named Cullum. He publishes a nasty little newspaper called the *White Leader*." She is standing in front of George as she tests his drink. "He was also connected with some Kluxers who bombed a Negro minister's house. How's your drink?"

"Fine," George says, looking up at her and smiling. "Just fine." He wonders what she is like in her stripping act. She is smiling down at him and her left hand is on her hip, jaunty. "This Cullum boy was found dead yesterday under a bridge just outside Dallas."

"What?"

"That's right."

"Oh my God! They're going to kill everybody, everybody who know anything . . ."

He nods. "It certainly looks that way."

Sylvia slowly sits down next to him on the old sofa. "Oh Christ. And they ran that poor little Margerie down on a highway." She shakes her head and swallows some vodka and tonic.

"If they can kill the President they can certainly kill a lot of lesser people easy enough," he says. "And the thing is that they know they can get away with it because people really don't want to find out who does such things. Because of their own secret wishes to do a lot of killing themselves. Finding the killers would be the same as exposing them, you see."

Sylvia is watching him, puzzled and fascinated. She lets this sink in. "Yeah," she says softly. "That kind of makes sense."

George turns to her. "Listen, Sylvia. Tell me how much you want for those notes."

She sips her drink and thinks for a few moments before answering. "A hundred thousand dollars."

"That's an awful lot of money."

She turns to him and puts her hand on his leg. "It's peanuts for what's in those notes. They can blow the roof off this country, and you know it."

"They can blow your head off too."

"What you're saying is I shouldn't be difficult and hold out for a lot of money because the longer I'm in this country, the shorter my life is going to be. Right?"

George smiles with a small amount of awkwardness. "Right. But listen. I didn't come here to chisel you. I'll phone New Batavia and report the price."

She pinches his cheek. "You do that, honey."

"Okay." He puts his hand on her leg (not completely un-self-consciously). "Tell me. How did you get into stripping?"

She takes his chin playfully in her hand and looks closely into his face. "You tell me how you got into being an investigator."

"Boredom really. I was in my family's antique business in St. Louis for a while after law school but I didn't especially like it. So I tried restoring old houses. So so. Finally I ran into D.A. Pitts at a party. We liked each other and before I knew it I had joined up with him. So that's my story. What about yours?"

She rubs her hand across his knee. "Simple. I discovered that I like to take my clothes off. And if you can get paid for doing what you like, why, sweetie, that's the best kind of deal."

"No question about it. What about before this discovery?"

She is holding his hand and examining his fingers and nails. "Oh I did a lot of the usual. Waitress. Nurse in a dentist's office. I even went to college for three months. In Miami."

"Where were you born?"

"You may not believe this, but I don't know. There's a lot about myself I don't know."

"Oh?"

"Yep. I can't seem to remember anything about myself before the age of fourteen."

George looks puzzled. "Well, how did you . . ."

"I was found wandering around the business district of Los Angeles. They put me in foster homes for three years until I couldn't stand it and so I just busted out on my own."

She slaps him on the thigh. "Oh, it's a long screwy story, my friend."

"It sure sounds unusual, I'll say that."

"It's funny," she says, looking dreamily at the floor, "but one thing that sticks in my mind is that I've been to some Arab country sometime. There's this picture in my mind of me in a harem, and in the background somewhere there's this strange Negro couple." She shakes her head. "Maybe I just dreamed it though, and this dream got stuck in my woken mind." She shrugs. "Can't figure it out for the life of me."

George drinks. "I guess everybody experiences something wierd like that." He looks into his glass. "Maybe there's another dimension in life, who knows."

Sylvia crinkles up her face at him and says, "You're cute. You're not at all like an investigator."

"Thanks."

"Those guys look like they came out of a paperback novel. Listen, do you have any plans for the rest of the day?"

"I have to make that call to New Batavia, that's all."

"What about having dinner here with me? I've got a good steak and we'll have a salad. I'd really like that. I'm lonely as hell here. What do you say, sport?"

He smiles, "Sure. Why not."

"Great." She pats him on the leg and gets up. "I'll mix us another drink. Then I want to change into something a little more comfortable." She winks at him. "This is an outside dress. I want to put on something that's for inside."

"Sounds perfectly reasonable to me."

She reaches over and pinches George on the cheek again. "Maybe later on we can put our heads together and try to discover where I've been half my life."

George smiles. "You hum it, and I'll play it, as the man said."

Her expression is relaxed and pleased, no longer wary and tight, as she looks at his upturned face. "I know I'm repeating myself," she says bending down and kissing him on the mouth with her lips open and wet," but I'm lonely, and I haven't kissed a man in so long"—she kisses him again, softly and tastingly—"that my lips are beginning to hurt."

"I liked that very much," he says.

"It didn't hurt me either."

She mixes two more drinks, somewhat stronger ones, and delivers George's to him on the couch. "Mm. Tip top," he says, after sipping it.

She sips hers, smiles and nods her head, and says, "I'll be back out in a couple of minutes. Don't go away."

"I'm not crazy."

The sounds of radio dance music come from the bedroom where Sylvia is changing. George, his mind and body buzzing very nicely with the drink, watches himself maneuvering gracefully and happily on elegant dance floors with lovely, pliant women. These images give him quite a bit of pleasure because he has never been on a dance floor in his life. Much too public. He is whispering something endearing to one of the women as Sylvia comes in from the bedroom.

"You haven't forgotten me, have you?" she says.

"Uh . . ."

Sylvia is dressed in Hollywood bedroom style. A white transparent thigh-length top piece through which George sees a skimpy gold gauze breast halter and bikini panties. Her glowing naked legs end in gold slippers. He looks up and down her slowly as she sips her martini.

He whistles softly. "I couldn't improve on that one bit. No sir."

She laughs and drinks off the rest of her martini. She is a little drunk. "I thought you'd like it. Christ! It seems years since I was last got up like this." She twirls in front of him, and the hem of the filmy overgarment almost touches his hot face. "Mmm. I almost feel on stage again. I wonder if . . ."

"Your body is fantastic."

"You really think so?" She grins. "You wouldn't kid me?"

"Uh uh."

Intensity and poignance suddenly come over her. "Please touch me and kiss me. I need your hands on me so much . . . so much."

George slowly rises from the couch, on the point of trembling, his concentration on this is so great, and reaches inside the over-garment and begins to play with her delicately haltered breasts. She closes her eyes and sticks her tongue way out. George takes it in his mouth and she moves it back and forth. His hands are caressing her gently moving ass.

"Ohh," she murmers, rubbing her body hard against his. "I've missed this so much. Jesus I've missed this."

He is kissing her breasts when she says, "Listen. You're not going to try to screw me on this deal of ours, are you?"

George moans. "Oh Christ no. What a thing to think. I mean . . ." He rubs his free hand up her thigh and continues mouthing her breast.

"Okay, okay," she murmurs, running her hands all over him and undulating with his hand between her legs. "It's just that I've never met an honest person yet." They begin to exchange tongues again, and she massages him between the legs, not hard and crudely but expertly. "Oh this feels so wonderful what you're doing. I mean I've been dead here by myself. Mmm."

"Let's go into the bedroom," George mumbles. "I don't think I can take this much longer."

A throaty sort of laugh from her. "That's the kind of thing I like to hear." She has unzipped his fly and is fondling his cock. "So let's . . ."

"On the couch first. We'll do it on the bed later."

She is stretched out on the couch, grinning, and he is starting to take his pants off. "No," she says, taking his hand and pulling him toward her. "Leave your clothes on. I like it that way. It's kind of naughty, and that's fun."

"Sure."

He is on top of her, squirming and kissing, and she has wrapped her legs around him. "Don't put it in yet, honey. Let's do this some more."

"Okay."

"Oh wow. You're as hot as I am. When was the last time you were laid?"

He takes his mouth from her breast, which still is haltered. "Uh . . . I can't remember."

"I'm the best," she says, squeezing him with her naked strong legs. "You'll see. I'll make all those other broads look like noth-ing."

"Swell."

She puts her tongue in his ear and after a couple of moments whispers something to him. "I'll bet you've never done that, have you?"

"No."

She laughs, "It's my speciality."

"When . . ."

"In a minute. Mmm. You're so big. I hope you don't hurt me with it. You wouldn't want to hurt me, would you? Mmm. Now let's put it in. Easy . . . not so fast. Ohhhh! Fuck me! Fuck me!"

THE STEAK AND SALAD ARE LONG SINCE IN THEIR stomachs, George's jolting semen is resting sweetly in large quantities in Sylvia's womb, and they are both resting on their naked backs looking up at the ceiling of the small but adequate (for their fleeting purposes) bedroom. "Tell me," George is saying, "did you ever run into a blond German woman and her boy friend, a bearded guy named Zachary, in your doings in Dallas?"

"As a matter of fact, I did," she says, turning her warm nakedness more toward George's. "She had a big dog with her all the time."

"What do you know about them?"

"Just about nothing. I asked Ruby about them once, because they would show up at the club to watch the acts and they clearly weren't part of the local population, and he said they were part of the international crowd that came to Dallas to see the rich White Russians there." She shakes her head. "Christ, that dog was creepy. It was almost human. When I was stripping the goddamn thing was staring at me and moaning like it was going to leap up on the stage and rape me."

"I see," says George, and although his eyes remain on the ceiling, he is not really looking at it.

DOWN IN GUATEMALA CITY, HOWEVER, ZACHARY

really is looking at the check for his uproarious dinner in the restaurant in the Hotel Luxor.

"What's that?" he asks the dreadfully heavy waiter, pointing to a scribble on the check.

"Baby eels." the man replies through glistening false teeth. "From the lake countries."

Zachary shakes his head. "I didn't have any baby eels."

"No?"

"No. I had just soup, then that piece of baked lamb, and salad."

The man smiles almost crazily. "Golly to hell with me! The baby eels are such wonderful that I think you have them because you look like a man who knew what he is doing. Very intelligence man with a beard."

Zachary examines the Spanish-Indian expanse breathing down him. "So that's what you thought. Well, I'll tell you what. I kind of like that view of things, so I'm going to assume I had the baby eels, so I'll pay for them."

The man slaps him on the shoulder. "Señor, you sure know a good taste when you see it!"

"You said it, Pancho," says Zachary, and lays down a lot of silly-looking Guatemalan money.

"Generosity is one of my American favorites," says the waiter, scooping up the dough. "Where is your wife today, señor? Isn't she hungry?"

"My wife?"

"The dog lady, your wife."

"Oh her. She's, uh, out shopping. For Indian jewelry and stuff."

The waiter intimately nudges him. "Spending the money you broke your nice American ass for in your serious workings, huh?"

"Yeah, Pancho. All broads are spendthrifts. Well, take it easy. See you around."

Out in the Plaza Santa Cruz, he pauses to light up a cigar. He is just blowing out the match as the bloated waiter rushes up to him. "Señor! You forget your book!" and the sweating anxious man shoves a paperback book into Zachary's hand, and scurries back into the restaurant.

"My book?" repeats Zachary to the thin air. "I didn't have a book. Much less this one," and he examines the greasy old thing the waiter has foisted upon him. It is a cheap English novel with a hot jacket, and the title, *The Shame of Her Sister*. He opens it, and there is a folded piece of white paper just inside. It reads: "I may sincerely be of good helps to you in your special secrets work here. After 6 p.m. I am 267-6370. Pancho. Always at your servants."

Zachary smiles and shakes his head, and slips the note into the pocket of his white Latin-style shirt. What does he know? Zachary asks himself. He decides he will call him later and find out. He strolls into the shy leafy park, flipping through the paperback. "Emily threw herself in front of the smiling hunchback, Count Esmeralda, lord of the moors. 'Please, your lordship,' she cried, 'I'll do anything you say! But please spare my dear sister!' "

"Giggling in cruel glee, Count Esmeralda threw a handful of marshmallows at her trembling naked body.

" 'Silly nubile thing,' he chortled. 'You'll soon find out how we do things here in Umberland.'

" 'Oh for Christ's sake,' says Zachary. 'Leave the kid alone, you dirty little thing.'

" 'Who are you?' Esmeralda shouts. 'How did you get by the palace guards?'

" 'That's a secret you'll never break. I'm taking this poor girl back to her parents.' He pulls the girl up from the floor. 'The King will be told of your degenerate practices, Count Esmeralda. You can be sure of that.'

" 'Ah hah!' shouts the hunchback Count. 'I recognize you now. You're one of Suffolk's hirelings. That knave has hated me ever since the day I exposed him as a fraud. Guards! Guards!' "

Zachary chuckles triumphantly, "Your guards will never hear you. They're all dead," and he presses the girl's still trembling, large-breasted body next to his own for comfort.

Oh my, Zachary mutters, and drops the crazy worn old thing into a trash receptacle. The reading needs of the young masses! He smiles and nods at two young Indian nursemaids in white who are watching three fat kids. They look at Zachary with puzzlement. He sits on a wooden bench under a mahogany tree and (a fart discreetly escapes him, discreetly in deference to the flat-faced young Indian maids; otherwise he would have blasted out with it) reflects on life in general and specifically on those multicolored dregs of it that he can fairly call his own.

How did I get involved with this madwoman anyhow? There I was in Athens, minding my own business, winding up my stint with the Peace Corps, and along comes this whirlwind with her dog. She senses that I am down on my luck and offers me an opportunity to pick up a nice piece of change. Conspiracy money, to put it blandly. And in of all crummy places, Dallas, Texas. Had I known what it was all about, the killing of that nice man whose only fault was that he wanted his family to be the royal family of America, well, I wouldn't have done it for anything. No. Absolutely not. And then, I had to be there, part of the gang, when they killed that dreadful little policeman. Why? Oh God. I just can't go on thinking about that terrible day. And now what am I doing? Being blackmailed into further complicity. Getting guns to counter-revolutionaries. How disgusting! Here I am in this neolithic ruin, this guava jelly outpost inhabited by the dwarfed and syphilitic descendents of the Incas, awaiting the pleasure of our Lady of Evil the Countess . . . Oh Christ Almighty! Too much. Simply too much. If I had only played my cards right with those Peace Corps clods. But of course I didn't. I had to go and falsify those expense vouchers for the village well. That could have been glossed over, I think, but then on top of that my affair with the village carpenter's daughter came out. Oh beautiful incredibly fuckable Irena, why did you have to tell your stupid father about our marvelous times in the grotto? Why? Didn't I give you a joy that you had never experienced in your entire simple village life? Didn't you tell me, again and again, that the ecstasies we shared made you understand for the first time what it meant to those ancient Greek ancestors of yours to celebrate the god Dionysus? Oh God when I think of you lying there in your dark, naked, glorious-breasted beauty as the blue sea made its rushing sounds! Oh! You and I became the sea and all nature. The taste of your young cunt was the sea taste and we returned to our mortal innocence when we both came. "Oh your thing is a harp inside me. Truly!" That's what you said. And I loved it so. Christ! What am I doing in a dump like this. Ohh!

And do you remember, dearest girl, the throbbing stiff taste of me, the first time? Out in the garden of the little villa I had on the hill? You said it was like having a wild animal in your mouth. And you asked me if I thought the village women would be able to divine your secret thrill by looking at your mouth. I thought I was disappearing into you forever when I came. I wish now that I had,

I'd much rather be in you than in this deplorable state or thing called Zachary.

This little park—my word! that green monkey in that big walnut tree is flogging his bishop—this little park makes me think of that little park in New York where I used to sit, during that awful summer, and read the classified ads. Looking for a job. What a degrading experience. That time in the agency—and I was such a young man—was I Zachary then?—

He got in line behind the two men standing at the reception desk. He looked quickly around the employment office. It was crowded. All the seats and benches were taken. Four people were leaning against the wall. They were all waiting to be interviewed by the three men sitting at desks. He looked away from the people in the room and at the back of the man in front of him.

"Are you registered?" the receptionist asked him. She had a slightly cultivated accent.

"No," he said, "I'm not registered."

"You'll have to fill out a registration form before you're interviewed," she said. "Fill this out." She took a form from her desk drawer. Then she asked, "What kind of work are you in?"

"I'm looking for something in an advertising company," he replied. He could see two of the people standing against the wall watching him.

"You see Mr. Green then," she said. "Fill this out over there and wait to see Mr. Green." She pointed to a long writing table where three people were sitting.

He thanked her and walked to the writing table and sat down carefully, not wanting to make any noise or in any way attract attention to his presence. He avoided looking at the other job hunters sitting there. The entire place was filled with an insidious combination of apprehension and guilt and shame and self-hiding. Each person seemed to be going through something sneaky. He wished he were undergoing this all by himself; it only made things worse to have to be seen by others. Also, there was the thing about his clothes—they were not as chic and successful and arrogant as they could have been; a faint seediness had settled over his physical presence, making him feel decidedly on the defensive, very second-rate.

He had to check carefully over some of the jobs he had held

before he could answer some of the questions on the form. "Oh Christ," he said to himself, "how in God's name did I get here? Where did I slip up? Just having to recall his recent and even remote "job experiences" was like reopening hidden wounds. Each memory was of a failure of sorts. He thought now of all the things he had never learned to do, of orders he had refused to obey, of rules that other people obeyed in order to survive that he had broken time and again, and of all the people he had treated brutally or with contempt or with nothing more in mind than whether they could be of use to him. So painful was this journey back that it seemed he was writing the answers not with ink but with his own blood.

Half of the jobs he listed were nonexistent except in his fantasy of the moment. He tried to remember the specific people on the jobs he had actually held. Here and there an image came up from his past that did not disgust him: three or four people he had worked with for a short time—in a packing house, a stockroom, a large grocery store—and for whom he felt affection, but for some complex reason really could not reveal his simple feelings about; something made him hide his feelings and whatever human warmth he experienced. Somehow, in his mind, such feelings were the same thing as being weak: if you showed you liked people, you were letting your defenses down and you could be taken for a sucker. "I wish I could have done it some other way," he went on, to himself. "I wish someone could have told me."

He had to go all the way back in his mind to his early high-school and grammar-school years to find the himself who was warm and loving and like other people. As he thought about those days, he suddenly saw himself as a kid, and could hear his high kid's voice shouting to his friends and shrieking with unrestrained pleasure during a game of some kind. He felt almost like crying now. He wished there were some way for this whole thing to absolutely disappear and himself with it.

When he had filled out one side of the form he re-examined each question and answer before turning it over. This side was for a detailed résumé of the actual work he had done on the jobs. Sighing heavily, unguardedly, he began the tedious, anxious job of inventing details that would please the people at this cold and terrible employment agency. He could hear a woman being interviewed by Mr. Green. He felt sorry for the woman—her voice was shy and not terribly steady, and in a strange way reminded him of his mother's voice when she was trying to hide some unpleasant family thing—and he wished, helplessly, that he could do something to make her feel nicer and prouder and less afraid. Even something like just putting his arm around her and saying, "It's Okay. I know just how it is. Really, I do. I'm your friend. Everything is going to be all right." He listened on, keeping his eyes down on the table. Mr. Green was saying, "I'm the best man in the country on these positions." Now he began to write his résumé.

The people ahead of him were interviewed by Mr. Green. There was a pile of magazines on the table in front of him. He picked one up and looked through it. Once he glanced around at the other people in the room, then looked back at the magazine.

"Who's next?" Mr. Green said loudly. His voice grated. Putting the magazine back with the others, he got up and went to Mr. Green's desk. Mr. Green was big and had a mustache. He told him to sit down and asked him for the registration form he had filled out. He read the list of jobs he had held.

"I see you've had a lot of experience, Mr. Hobson," he said.

"I guess I have," he replied, keeping his voice low.

"What have you been doing since your last job?"

"Traveling in Europe."

"Did you do any sort of work there?"

"No. Just vacationing."

"Just looking the place over?" Green said, smiling.

"That's right," he said, smiling slightly too. "Just looking it over."

Green looked at the form again. "You've come to the right place, Mr. Hobson. We're specialists in your field. Some of the biggest outfits in the field are our clients."

He did not say anything. He could see a man and a woman at the writing table watching him. He did not look directly at them. He looked down at his shoe and waited.

"Just what sort of job did you have in mind, Mr. Hobson?" Green asked.

"I'd thought of something in a new advertising agency."

"Well, unfortunately there's nothing around at the moment," Green said slowly. "But something should develop in a couple of weeks. The situation is loosening up now."

"That's fine."

"You weren't in the service" Green asked, looking at the form.

"No. I wasn't in the service."

Green looked at him. "Any particular reason?"

"Medical."

"Anything serious?"

"Not terribly."

"I see," Green said. He looked back at the form. He turned it over and read the résumé, then dropped the form on his desk. "This is a terrible résumé. I could get better English from a school kid."

He stared at him. "I don't think you know what you're talking about," he said. "There isn't anything wrong with that English."

"It's a terrible résumé," Green repeated, his voice loud and gravelly. "It doesn't tell me anything I want to know."

"That has nothing to do with the English, Mr. Green." The people sitting at the writing table were watching them. "I came here here to see about a job, not to be insulted."

"All right, all right," Green said, holding his hand up. "I wasn't insulting you. The résumé isn't long enough. It's like a telegram. I couldn't sell you to anybody on the basis of this."

"Why didn't you say that in the first place?"

"Okay, okay," Green said, his voice still loud. "I'm sorry if you felt I was insulting you. Now I want you to write me a full page about what you did on these jobs. Tell me everything."

"I'll do it that way if you want," he said. "But it isn't necessary. People know what you've done by the kinds of places you've worked at and what your job was."

"Listen," Green said, leaning toward him. "I've been in this business for ten years and I know people prefer long résumés. I'm a specialist in this field and I know.

"Okay. You're the specialist."

"Now then," Green said, "I see you've left the salary part open. You were making a hundred a week on your last job. Shall we put down fifty-five hundred a year now?"

He looked past Green's head and through the window at the

building across the street, and then back at Green. "I'm pretty elastic about salary," he said now. "Let's keep the salary part open."

"A hundred a week minimum then?"

"No. Make it seventy-five. I really wouldn't mind taking a job at seventy-five while I'm waiting for something very good."

"I'll put seventy-five down," Green said. "But I never advise a client to go lower than their last salary. It isn't a good practice."

"I don't imagine it is."

The receptionist called across the crowded room, "You have a call, Mr. Green. A Mr. Shuman."

"That's Ted Shuman," Green called back. "I'll take it." He picked up the phone on his desk. "Hellow, Ted. Fine, fine. Listen, Ted. Hold on, will you?" He turned to him. "Okay. Then you send in that résumé." He smiled and held out his hand. He shook it and stood up.

"Shall I call you from time to time?" he asked. "Or will you get in touch with me when something develops?"

"Neither," Green said. "Come in here Mondays and Fridays. We're very busy." Then he said, "Remember: you're just one of a couple hundred gents we handle all the time."

"Thanks."

"Thank you for coming in." Now Green took his hand away from the mouth of the phone. "Listen, Ted. I've got just the man you fellows have been looking for."

He walked—it seemed more as if he were creeping—through the large, alien office. He carefully avoided looking at any of the others being interviewed; any exchange of glances with the other unfortunate petitioners under these circumstances would have been shocking, if not absolutely obscene. He stopped at the receptionist's desk. The girl there was quite pretty, a brunette with Irish blue eyes, and she reminded him of many conquests in his past, in high school. He stood straighter and adjusted his tie, hoping that with the smile he was preparing he would radiate self-confidence and masculinity and great charm and the girl would overlook the fact that he was not in the very best of condition, as it were. He made his voice sound very sexy and Hollywoodish as he bent over (as Gregory Peck would have done it) and asked, "When is it best to come around?"

"Early," the girl said, presenting him with a slick New York smile. "Early and often."

"Yes, I suppose you're right," he murmured. "You might say that's good advice for just about any, uh, enterprise."

The girl chuckled sort of knowingly at the complex allusion of his witticism. "I'll go along with that," she said, resuming writing.

"You been working here long?"

"About a year," she said indifferently.

"It beats working as a salesgirl or typist, doesn't it?"

"That's about all it beats."

"You looking for something else?"

"Isn't everybody?" she replied.

He put a lot of English on his next question: "Say, how does a guy get to the head of the line here anyway?"

"What do you mean?"

He smiled shyly, yet sheepishly. "You know, how does he get first consideration for the jobs that turn up?"

Her bright little smile was becoming less so now. "Priority is based on qualifications and how long you've been coming here."

He winked at her, and kept flashing that smile.

"I'll bet you hear about some of the best jobs first, don't you?"

She looked at him a bit coldly. "There is no way anybody can be made a favorite around here."

"I didn't mean that," he rushed on. "What I meant was, it would save a lot of time and all that if, you know, I could just check with you on the phone and see if something good had come up. A friendly call . . . you know," and he let out a little laugh.

"I couldn't help you," she said, and it was clear that as far as she was concerned, the conversation had come to an end.

A twist of self-hatred went through him; he just couldn't score with this chick. He'd lost his old touch. "Okay, okay," he said. "Thanks anyway," and he walked quickly through the door and down the antiseptic, inhumanly pale corridor to the black-doored elevator.

Waiting for the elevator, his hands in his coat pockets, he fingered the want-ad slips he had cut from the paper that morning. He started to take them out of his pocket, but a man leaving the employment office came down the corridor toward the elevator. He kept the incriminating slips hidden in his pocket. He and the other man did not look at each other.

Outside the building he stopped for a second, then walked across the street to a drugstore on the corner. The drugstore was warm. He sat down in an empty booth, slowly unbuttoned and took off his trench coat, and ordered coffee. When the waitress had gone, he took the want-ad slips from his pocket and reread them. He threw away the ad that had brought him to Green's agency. There were two clippings for advertising and research jobs through other employment agencies. He looked at the addresses and estimated how long a walk it was to the offices of these agencies.

Now the waitress brought his coffee. He hurriedly put the slips away. The coffee tasted good. It was hot and there was cream in it instead of milk. He drank the coffee slowly and thought about going to the other employment agencies to be interviewed.

It was near lunchtime. He could probably get to an agency and be interviewed before lunch. He though about that, drinking the coffee slowly, and then he began to think of someone uptown whom he could call for lunch. He could have an early lunch instead of going to one of the agencies right away. He could go to the agencies in the afternoon. He could probably get someone at his old place for lunch. It would probably be better to go to the agencies in the afternoon, he decided, instead of just before lunch when everything might be rushed. He could kill the time before lunch, now, by strolling along Fifth Avenue.

Now he felt more relaxed. He finished his coffee, left the waitress a ten-cent tip, and went to the back of the drugstore to the telephone booth. In the booth he dialed the number urgently, hoping against hope that he could make a lunch date with someone who was still talking to him, who considered him to be still among the living.

THAT DIABOLICAL WENCH BACK IN THE HOTEL is plotting my future. What does she have in store for old Zachary, the Boy Who Went Wrong? Eh?

Well . . .

The Countess is pouring tea for Father Escobar, a hairy-handed man who smells of old confessions and who looks like a two-act play that collapsed in the first act.

"So you see, Father," the Countess is saying, dropping two

lumps of sugar into his tea, "my friend and I will need a place to stay for a few weeks."

"Ah yes, I can indeed see that," he says. He has a German accent beneath his Spanish name. "Those American people who are looking for you will certainly be keeping a careful watch on your movements for a while."

The Countess gives the Great Dane a lump of sugar and sits down facing the priest. "There is really only one person who knows about us—a dreadful little investigator who is trying to upset everything."

Father Escobar nods his head and slurps his tea. "There is always one person like that."

"He is such a fool," she says, stroking her dog's huge head. "He does not understand that everyone, the entire American population, wanted the assassination."

Father Escobar continues to nod and slurp tea.

"The killing of the king is a deep primitive urge in the human psyche," she says, "and that man was their first king." She smiles quizzically at him. "You understand, Father?"

"Ah, yes. Yes indeed."

"It simply had to be done, otherwise the collective unconscious would have burst through with frustration, and there would have been massacres in the streets." She lights a long, strange-smelling cigarette. "Their primitive health required it. Just think, Father, how deeply the Biblical masses needed the death of Christ."

He nods on, folding his hairy hands on his big stomach.

"Just think of the chaos that their world would have experienced had Jesus gone on living," she says, blowing smoke high into the air.

"Unthinkable," he says.

"So this poor stupid little investigator and the even more stupid man he works for, are going against nature in the investigation. They are attempting to undo the blood dream. Ach! They make me so sick with their blindness!"

The big dog growls and lifts its head as if sensing a menace somewhere.

"Easy, Thor," she says patting him. "Easy." She shakes her head. "What can one do with people who do not understand their own destiny?"

Father Escobar allows a slight tea belch to escape him. "I think something can be arranged for you and your, uh, companion," he says, and what can only be described as an oily smile assumes a prominent position on his face. "You can, uh, rest up for a few weeks in some unoccupied rooms we have in the, uh, rectory. Of course, a contribution from you toward our building fund will be most appreciated."

"Naturally, Father. Would five thousand be all right?"

He apparently has a fathomless supply of oiliness in him, because more of it appears on his already almost-saturated face. "Most generous, dear Countess. The good peasants of Santa Maria will be eternally grateful to you. Your donation will be used to build a maternity ward." He shudders with the sort of humor that is supposed to seize men of the cloth. "Our poor women just can't help getting pregnant."

"Poor dears," says the Countess, radiating a smile that contains several choices of meaning, "the call of the flesh is their downfall." Something occurs to her. "Perhaps I could help them. I could set up a physical hygiene clinic for the young girls, say between thirteen and sixteen. That's a nice . . . I mean educable age."

"Hmm," murmurs Father Escobar, nibbling on a tea biscuit. "We might consider that. Tasty things . . ."

"I'm sure they are," blurts the Countess before her defense system can go into operation.

". . . these cookies."

A LITTLE LATER HE IS SITTING IN A STUDY with another priest, a paper-thin man whose blue eyes do not say anything about his inner life. On the antique seventeenth-century Spanish table before him is five thousand American dollars in new money.

"Not bad," he says, picking up a neat bundle of crisp fifties.

"I agree," says Father Escobar. "But we now have a bad space problem. We already have six guests—the bank robber from Los Angeles, the man from the Mafia, the two Nazi generals, the Swiss girl who killed . . ."

The other waves him down. "There is no problem. We will put these two new ones in the winery."

Father Escobar nods his head. "Excellent. Now then, brother, how much do we have so far?"

The tone and shape of the other's voice indicates a long tradition of unsentimental grasp of this world's dimensions.

"Ninety-five thousand. Five thousand more and we'll be there."

The other—oil oozing up from his lifetime supply—slaps his unconscionable belly and exclaims. "Then Paris! I can hardly wait. All those unspeakable sins that await us there! The rotten world of Balzac, Hugo, de Kock!"

Pale light emanates from his fellow priest. "The Garden of Eden revisited. Ah yes. But we must get one or two more guests first. I'll tell you what brother. Keep a close watch on *The New York Times* for those members of the human race who must flee their own cultures. Write to them and tell them about our little sanctuary here. And mention the clean air and home-like foods."

Father Excobar claps his hands. "A capital idea! I shall attend to it immediately." His glance wanders to the window. "Ach!"

"What is the matter?"

"That lurking fellow, that breathing piece of nothingness with the apochryphal nose . . . "

"Upon which nose the Saviour will be crucified again . . ."

Father Escobar sticks his tongue out in the direction of the shame in question. "Perhaps he heard us and our plans."

The other shrugs. "What does it matter? What if he did tell someone? Who would listen to him? No one here believes he truly exists. Everyone thinks he is the product of someone else's perverted imagination. So stop worrying." He cries, "Come with me to the Chambers. I have a heretic to punish."

"Ah yes," says Escobar, getting up himself. "I heard him screaming for mercy last night."

"Wait till you hear him today."

"Where did you get him?"

"From the Bishop of Peru. I exchanged a case of scotch and a fine chestnut riding horse for him." He swings upon the creaky ancient door to the confessional chambers.

"They're as rare as unicorns these days," says Father Escobar.

"And far more precious."

XXIV

SEX. MURDER, CRIME. WAR. PO-
litical dissension. Sports. Country living, these contemporary human endeavors presented themselves to Mrs. Katz as she read the
daily paper. She was seated in the breakfast nook which looked out
over the Potomac River. Covering her entire soft, no longer
severely contoured, patiently innocent, 49-year-old body—except
for her head and sandaled feet—was a flowered Petti robe. The
silly used remains of bagel with cream cheese and lox distorting
its original purpose lay before her.

"Honey," she said to her husband Eli, "did you know that
Emerson was upset yesterday in Buenos Aires by Gimeno in a
stunning five-set match?"

Mr. Katz drank off some coffee. "No."

"Well, did you know that the Spanish authorities sealed off San
Sebastian as the first step in quelling civil disorder in that Basque
town?"

He speared some scrambled egg. "No."

"I see. Did you know that there is evidence that polar bears
may return annually to the same spot in the Arctic?"

"Nope," he said and nibbled on a roll.

She put the paper down. "That's what I mean. You're not
interested in anything anymore except getting re-elected to Congress. Not interested in world events, not interested in animal life
on the very planet where you happen to be residing at the moment. And," she straightened her hair daintily, "very obviously I
don't interest you any more at all."

He looked up. "What makes you say that, Bella?"

An expression that could have presaged tears came over her
face. "For example, no more morning sex."

"Oh."

"That's right. Oh. Before you became the representative from
Cleveland's 14th district, we had morning sex all the time." She
wiped at her dry eyes. "I guess I've grown old and repulsive to
you. I must look like an old sock to you in the mornings."

"Aw, come on, Bella. You know that I always have the hots for you."

"At night maybe, but certainly not in the mornings. You just lie there counting votes, not caring one iota that all my womanhood is lying next to you, trembling and filled with soft warm sex needs."

He put his hand on hers, "Aw, Bella, that's not fair. You know I've got to give this new election everything I can muster."

She took his hand away, petulantly perhaps. "You can't convince me that one little orgasm, five minutes of normal, healthy married fun, is going to lose you those votes. No. I don't believe it."

He got up and put his arm around her. "Forgive old Eli for neglecting his Bella baby."

"Look at you," she said, keeping her head down, not too far, really, from the bagel ruins. "Afraid even to touch me where it counts."

"Not true," he said, and put his hand inside her robe and over her large left breast. "Mm. Real nice stuff you got there."

She suddenly moved her chair back. "You're just saying that! I don't feel any desire whatsoever coming from you." She looked up at him. "Why, I'll bet I can't even make you get an erection."

"Aw, that just isn't so. You know that when you give me that special smile . . ."

She jumped up and began unbuttoning her robe. "Let's just see. We're going to have a moment of truth here, that's what we're going to have." She threw her robe off and stood before him in all her opulent, former princess, nudity. She put her hands behind her head like a model in a skin magazine and arched her body teasingly, "Okay, Don Juan. Let's see your thing. Take your fine silk robe off and let's see once and for all what gives with that passion-filled peenie of yours when faced with the unadorned."

He did as he was bid, somewhat apprehensively to be sure. They both looked at his meat. It hung down.

"Uh huh," said Bella. "It sure is going out of its mind with desire, isn't it."

He shrugged apologetically. "This really isn't fair, Bella. You're taking me by surprise."

"That's supposed to be the spice of life," she said, wiggling her tongue in stripper style tease. "Didn't you know that, Mr. Lover Boy?" And she began to do slow bumps and grinds while they both kept watch on his pecker.

"Gee, Bella. Where did you learn that?"

She threw her pelvis at him in a fine wind-up grind. "Let's not get academic, Eli Cold Pants. What we need here is some action in the manhood department."

He stared at her undulating body and at his reluctant member, "I'm trying, Bella, I really am." He looked suddenly frightened. "What if April should come in now?"

"Don't worry about her. She's out . . . probably getting laid by some rugby champion."

She began to run her hands up and down her body, starting from the dense crotch hair and working up to her nipples. "Think stiff, Big Boy. Let your mind fly into forbidden human scenes."

"Bella! You've gone mad!"

She cupped her hands under her breasts and offered them to him, sticking her tongue out as far as she could. "Take your hand out of the voter's pocket, Eli. Stop stumping along sleazy Fairmont Avenue. Come with me to the Casbah." And she began to twist her hands above her head like an Arab belly dancer.

His forked lightening wouldn't fork. He shook his head sadly. "I don't know what could be the matter. Maybe I should see a psychiatrist."

"Don't you dare leave this room!" Bella began doing somewhat more lewd things—putting her fingers in and out of her snatch, making very clear sucking noises. "I'm going to produce an erection on you if it's the last thing I do on this earth."

"I'm with you, honey. Honestly I am. There's mountains of lust in me but they just won't move. Maybe we ought to try another tack."

Bella turned her fat round bottom to him, bent over, and wagged it, "Like?"

He took his thing in his hand and looked at it as a friend betrayed. "Well, food, for instance. For years as a kid I connected food with sex. I used to eat in my cousin Max's deli where he had two very sexy waitresses. Polish girls. You know, big thighs, heavy breasts, a little bit of perspiration on their ruddy faces. That sort of thing. So I would sit there every day and eat lots of stuff and pant after these waitresses, and play with myself under the table."

Bella, facing him now, slowly nodded her head (one hand was holding a breast, the other her snatch). "I see. You never told me about that part of your life."

"It wasn't that I was hiding it from you, Bella."

"We'll go into that matter some other time. What we've got to do is put all our eggs into the basket in this room. Okay, Mr. Dirty Memory. Let's go!" She began her belly-dance routine all over again, bumping, writhing, shaking her heavy breasts. "Kreplach! Derma!"

Eli was suspended for a moment in transition, as his interior mechanisms retooled. Then he shouted, "I feel it, Bella! I feel it!"

She increased her motions. "Matzoh balls! Stuffed cabbage!"

His weenie began slowly to rise, a prehistoric creature being aroused from deepest slumber. "Look! Bella! Look! It's coming up!"

She was a whirling dervish of sexual projection. Her breath was coming in pants, and sweat appeared on her wild body. "Chicken fat! Dill pickles!"

A cry of joy leaped from Eli. "Bella! It's up! It's up like a flagpole!"

"Don't just stand there, you dopey bastard!" she yelled pumping her thick black thing back and forth. "Sock it to me!"

Eli leaped across the room and embraced her. "It's all yours, honey. Take it all!"

"Salami!" she cried, grabbing his resurrected whammer. "Corned beef! Hot brisket!"

They fell to the thickly carpeted floor in the classic furious grappling position.

"Wow! It's never been like this!" shouted Eli, pumping away.

"Make up for lost years, Eli!" yelled Bella, hugging him and pulling her soft, happy legs way back for better entry. "Throw caution to the winds. Strudel! Borscht! Lox . . . and . . . *creeamm . . . cheeeese!*"

"AND WHAT DID YOU SAY TO THE PRESIDENT after that, daddy? April asked.

"I put it to him straight," Katz replied, looking both ways

before they crossed Dumbarton Avenue. "I said, 'Mr. President, this country is in gravest trouble. Our rivers are poisoned. There is not one creek or stream that you can drink out of without almost immediately dropping dead of pollution.' "

"That's putting it to him straight all right," said April, turning to look at a cream-colored Mercedes with a foreign plate. "Did he get the message?"

Katz wearily shook his head. "I don't think so. He's a very complicated and difficult man. No sooner had I gotten the words out of my mouth than he blew sky high. It was simply awful."

They entered Montrose Park.

"Poor Daddy," said April, and put her hand in his.

" 'Katz, you creepy Jew bastard!' he yelled at me, slamming a paperweight against the wall, 'You got the nerve to whine to me about a few lousy motherfucking rivers when you know I am up to my eyeballs in the shit of the world! If it ain't the fucking Russians taking over poor little Czechoslovakia, or them fucking Vietcong gooks killin' decent clean American boys, it's them pimply faced long-haired cocksuckers marchin' up and down the American streets demandin' I turn my country over to the crazy niggers! Katz, if I hear one more word from you about smelly rivers or giant redwood trees or the vanishin' mountain goat, I will personally see to it that you will not only lose your seat in the American Congress but you, will find your uppity ass back in the ghetto of Poland.' "

April put her arm around her father after this exhausting recitation. "He sounds perfectly dreadful. And to think that such a dirty old man is the leader of the country. Good Lord." They found an empty bench on the side of the tennis courts—most of the benches were occupied by white uniformed Negro women who were watching over cutely dressed white babies—and April eased her father down on it as though he had suddenly become an invalid.

The dark-haired young man who was serving on the tennis court double-faulted and immediately spit on his racquet in disgust.

"I hate to say it, April," Katz began, "but these United States are on the verge of disappearing."

April patted his hand, "There's no doubt about it, sweet old

Daddy, but I wish you would stop upsetting yourself so much. We can always pack up and go elsewhere."

He shook his head. "That would be immoral. We just can't give up the good fight."

A little blond girl waddled in front of them and extended a half-eaten cookie to Katz. He took it without being aware of what he was doing and munched it down.

"Listen, Daddy," April said, looking at him both sweetly and seriously, "that so-called good fight was lost a long, long, time ago. Honestly it was. So forget it already."

He looked at her with fear and puzzlement. "That's a terrible thing to say, April. What about the Constitution? The Founding Fathers?"

"A bunch of elitists who laid a great fraud on the public."

The dark young tennis player put a ball into the net, a poor service return, and shouted "Shit!" and spit on his racquet again.

"Where did you pick up such stuff?" Katz asked her. "You haven't become a communist have you?"

A morning glory of laughter spun from April. "Oh Daddy! You sound like Winston Churchill. Of course I haven't turned Red. Whatever that is. I've just never believed all that junk they told me in school, or the newspapers, or all those other dumb places." She lit up a Gauloise.

Her father sighed heavily. "I don't know. I just don't know." He stared in the direction of a clump of magnolia trees where a girl and a boy were wrestling and laughing. "To turn my back on a lifetime of public service. Why, just try to imagine what Cleveland would be like if I hadn't seen to it that the water was fluoridated and the relief plan for the disadvantaged and . . ."

She blew a furious stream of smoke into the clean park air. "I'll tell you. It wouldn't be any different at all."

"April! I forbid you to talk to your father in such a cynical way. It's . . . it's disrespectful."

"Oh Daddy," she said, taking his hand and kissing it. "You know very well I couldn't be that way with adorable you. I'm just trying to open your eyes a little. Little Red Riding Hood was a dyke."

Katz reared back. "What?"

April laughed. "What I mean is, don't fall for all that goody-

goody land-of-the-free stuff." The sound of croquet balls clicking into each other floated across the leafy simple-minded park. An ancient park policeman strolled by humming to himself. "So really, to turn your back on things, might be the healthiest act of your harassed life."

A smile of resignation and some dreaminess lightened the gray day on Katz's face. "Hmm. Just pull up stakes and drift like gypsies, eh?"

"Don't knock the gypsies, old Dads. They're still going strong after two thousand years. And you can't find a single one of them in the bughouse."

Katz stood up. "This kind of talk is making me nervous. Let's walk a little."

"Okay. Whatever you say."

April put her arm in her father's and they began walking through the baby carriages and Negro nurses toward the arboretum. Suddenly a tennis racquet sailed over their heads and landed in some bayberry bushes.

"Good heavens!" Katz said, looking up into the surprise-filled sky, "Where did that come from?"

"From the depths of that poor boy's being," said April, and she chuckled.

They skirted the croquet field and headed toward the park greenhouses (which had been donated to the city by Mrs. Robert Wiggins Lowe in 1940, in memory of her late husband, a banker who loved flowers).

"Yes, indeed, Daddy," said April, plucking a leaf from a bush, "I'd certainly do some second thinking on democracy if I were you."

"It's all we've got," he said. "We've just got to make it work."

She took his hand. "That's what I mean. It was never supposed to work in the first place."

"What?"

"It was just an interesting, amusing idea, that's what," she said, as they entered the first greenhouse. "Listen," she continued, taking a paperback book from her handbag. "I want you to hear what de Tocqueville has to say on the subject."

"Who's he?"

" 'The public, therefore, among a democratic people, has a

singular power, which aristocratic nations cannot conceive; for it does not persuade others to its beliefs, but it imposes them and makes them permeate the thinking of everyone by a sort of enormous pressure of the mind of all upon the individual intelligence.' Now how does that hit you?"

Katz leaned against a pole next to a host of South American fern. "I'm not going to think about such subversive things. It's immoral and treason. I'm a member of the legislative branch of the United States government and I know it's against my oath of office to let such stuff even enter my mind." He plucked a fern leaf and put it in his pocket. "The whole moral fiber of the country could deteriorate."

"Oh shit!" April exclaimed, and tossed a handful of heather at his head. "You oughta be in pictures!"

"Washington didn't cross the Delaware for nothing!" he shouted, and hurled an African lily plant at her.

"They oughta send you back to Africa!" she shouted and swatted his cringing form with a young rubber plant.

"This country will not stand by while the human dignity of millions is being crushed," he cried, and darted down the plant-flanked aisle.

April gave chase, lobbing dwarf Japaneses crab apples after him. "You'd sell your own mother for a profit, you heartless carpetbagger!"

Way over in a corner of the greenhouse, sitting in a patch of herbs, not unlike a leg of raw lamb waiting to be christened with sweet basil, was the dark-haired young tennis player. He observed April and her father without any visible signs of disbelief.

MRS. KATZ AND APRIL WERE IN THE MIDDLE OF— okay, at the very heart of, is that better?—a scene of upper-class niftyness. The cashmere sweater department of Garfinkel's, the only store in Washington, D.C. where any white-skinned woman of quality would ever dream of being seen, dead or alive.

"I think this one's awfully cute, don't you, honey?" said Mrs. Katz, holding up a gray cardigan.

"Simply vomitous," said April.

"April! Please. Someone might hear you."

"That's what speech is for, isn't it?" April observed. She picked up a bright orange turtleneck. "Now this one really says hello."

Mrs. Katz put her hand to her throat, a genteel gesture approved by millions of chubby genteel women since the time of William the Conquerer. "Isn't it, uh, just a wee bit bold, dear?"

"Oh shit, mother," April said, and tossed the sweater onto her shoulder. "You know, you ought to join the DAR."

"But I was only. . ."

April went into the dressing room to try the bold sweater on. Before slipping it on, she paused for a second to look at her bare chest in the mirror (she never wore a bra; she felt they were corny and against God). She smiled at her swooping full firm breasts. Just for fun, she tweaked her nipples. They rose to the occasion, stiff and pink.

A grinning Spanish-looking boy in his teens stepped into the room. Staring happily at her breasts, he said, "Boy oh boy! You sure got a swell pair of choo-choos." He certainly had a Puerto Rican accent.

April looked him over, then went back to examining herself in the mirror. "Sorry, but I don't have time for the peasant revolt today."

"I ain't got my glasses with me," the boy said, stepping up to within a few inches of her bare bosom, "so I got to get myself real close so I can see things correct." He put his nose on one of her breasts. "Yeah. I see them real correct now."

She turned slightly to get a profile view of herself, brushing the boy's face with her left breast. He followed her turn beautifully.

"The old family structure is clearly cracking up," she said, raising her chin slightly.

The boy rubbed his cheek over her breast. "You oughta be in Spanish movies. Man they are the most. They smash right through you."

She picked up the sweater and slowly pulled it over her head. "If I read the news stories correctly, you should be busily engaged in a gang rumble or shooting heroin." She slipped her arms into the sleeves. Her bosom was still quite exposed.

The boy rubbed his nose on her other breast. "Mm boy. If my cousin Alfonso could see me now." He looked up into April's face in the mirror. "Listen. You know what a medical dentist in the clinic told me?"

"I wonder what it would be like to live on an island filled with people like you."

The boy had rested his hand on her hip as if to balance himself, an indication, possibly, of an inherited vertigo. "He told me the only cure for tooth cavities was the milk from a girl's breast. You wouldn't want me to get sick with cavities, would you?"

She turned her face from the mirror and more or less looked at the boy's upturned face. (To be somewhat more exact: her gaze was in a very old human tradition; people use this gaze or expression when they are looking at distant buildings of great historical interest, or when they are reading very significant, but not inflammatory, writings on walls.) "Are you ten years old or just small for your age?"

"I didn't think you would," he said, and began sucking her breast, holding onto her hips now with both hands.

From outside the room—which had a heavy curtain for a door, came a statement from her mother. "You're taking an awful long time, April. Is everything all right?"

"Fine," she called out. "Just fine. The zipper needed fixing."

"What zipper?" her mother's voice asked.

"Any zipper. But let's drop it."

"I'm going over to the shoe department," mother said. "I'll meet you there."

April just sighed. The boy began working on her other breast, chewing the nipple with a certain amount of gusto. He was now bracing himself by clasping her round buttocks. In a few moments he looked up at her (To be more exact again: his look, a craning thing, was the kind employed by schoolchildren seated in the front row of the Met while some ballet stuff is taking place on the stage a few feet above their heads.) "Listen. You ever read much about the Puerto Rican culture?"

"I thought kids your age were busy having identity crises."

He began unbuttoning her slacks. "Well, in the Puerto Rican culture we are very strong on good manners of making outside people comfortable. That's the thing I want to do for you." He began pulling her slacks off. "Because I don't want nobody to say that Carlos Randa has the bad manners." Her pink and black bikini panties stared him in the face, "Carumba! The colors of the Puerto Rican national anthem." And he gave tham a quick kiss and a nose nuzzle. "I am going to make you comfortable." He maneuvered her over to a long foam-rubber seat. "You just lie down here and you'll see what we mean by the Puerto Rican manners. I'm tired of hearing bad things said about my people." He pulled her panties down and away with splendid smoothness. (And not absent-mindedly put them in his back pocket.)

April acceded to his manners and lay down. "Do you work here as a stockroom boy or something?"

The boy got down on his knees and pushed April's naked legs up and open. "Just the other day I read something in the newspaper about Puerto Ricans that was very untrue. That's the kind of bad stuff that's got to be stop pretty soon." He dived in and gave her vulva and clitoris a couple of exploratory, well-mannered licks. "Our solidarities can't happen no other way, and I'm not lying about it," He tongued her on both thigh approaches to the pubic grotto. "Loyalty to my race is big with me, I can tell you that." Another deeper dive, and inside the womb. "Believe me, if Pancho Villa was here that guy would be doing the same thing as me." Down again, this time on the clitoris and remaining there breathing faster and beginning to move her hips and pelvis in steady gyration.

"That's the first time I ever heard Pancho Villa called a Puerto Rican," she said. Small moans and sweet gasps came from her (her eyes were closed now) and, her body writhing gently, she twined her fingers in his thick bobbing black hair. "I always . . . ooh! understood . . ."

He began twirling his tongue. Clockwise, very fast, on her clit, "That's what I mean," he said, lifting his face up. "There is lots of real good facts that spiffy white people don't know nothing about." His quick tongue went back to work.

April's thighs shuddered, "It's certainly . . . ohh Jesus! . . . difficult to understand . . . ahh! . . . history . . ."

A fat woman holding a new young dress opened the curtain. "Oops!" she exclaimed, her big eyes doing somersaults. "I thought this was the fitting room."

And she vanished. (Well, not entirely. She went into the ladies room and had a good scream.)

DOWN IN THE BASEMENT OF THAT VERY SAME
building—three of the store's employees were seated (okay,
flopped) at a long table depositing quite second-rate food in their
mouths, Fritos, hot dogs, Merry Maid chocolate cupcakes, making
conversation, as inmates of institutions dreamily and gonkily make
defective little things like potholders, paperweights and cardboard
castles to peddle to guilty suckers on the outside. There was Mae
Walters, a cleaning drudge, whose no-good husband, Chuck, had
been faking cancer for thirty years. Charlie Boscoe and Milt
Glaser, seedy sales trainees who would always wear white shirts
and laugh at the wrong moments. (Charlie intended never to
recover from the historical fact that he had pitched on the winning
ball team of the Little League.) These glazed children of God were
also listening to a radio which was set on a chair just as if it were
a person, because who the hell ever heard of a chair that was
designed to seat a radio. And of course the radio was talking away
exactly as humans talk away. Voice-wise, that is.

Charlie, Milt, and Mae weren't really listening to what the
radio was saying (listening as done by the scientists who were
waiting to hear the explosion of the first atomic device, or by St.
John the Baptist those heavily sanded mornings in North Africa
when the Lord would speak), because if they had been listening
they would have flicked the program off. (All three, by the way,
were completely convinced that George Wallace would clean this
country up and show those dirty hippies and the niggers what was
what, and every tree in America would have at least one such
smelly body swinging from it.) It was one of those throwaway
afternoon culture programs—the childhood of Beethoven, a walk
with Jan Hadich the great Finnish poet—and this afternoon the
plat de jour was Exciting Historical Discoveries.

".... consequently what we have here is a very, very wonderful and important cultural breakthrough," the voice was insisting.
(It was, naturally, an abstract voice, in that it was the sly and small
flower product of speech classes and genteel terrorism which had
eliminated all regional and thus humanly identifying qualities
from it. It was, therefore, the perfect voice of No Man. However,
had you asked any one of the millions of aging crotches moulder-
ing away in a welfare dump, she would have said, "That feller sure
talks nice.") "Archaeologists from Harvard University have

unearthed and translated the diaries of the great fourteenth-century black philosopher Jomo Daga of Africa's Gold Coast. These diaries, which were written on specially treated palm leaves, were found in sealed clay urns which had been buried in a mountain cave in what is now Nigeria. Historians claim that Jomo who was known as the Raging Wind, was the first western man to document and systematize the use of natural hallucinogens. Specialists in the field rank Jomo's diary as one of of the great human documents of all times, on a level with the Confessions of St. Augustine, the Book of Job and Jean-Jacques Rousseau's Journal. A truly great find, ladies and gentlemen.

"Station WCAI has gone to great trouble to bring to its listeners a dramatic presentation of a part of these diaries. We have arranged for the famous Negro actor Jomo Johnson, the ancient philosopher's namesake—isn't that a marvelous coincidence!—to read from the diaries. To play the part of Jomo himself, so to speak, in Jomo's own self-drama. Ladies and gentlemen, we are honored to present to you Jomo Johnson as Jomo Daga."

Mae Walters blankly stuffed her mouth with a few potato chips; Milt examined a wax picking from his left ear; Charlie read the same baseball box score for the third time. A voice of deep rich, untampered-with black oil now poured out of the seated radio.

"My days are filled with strange sounds, my nights belong to the jackal. Oh Jomo! What is it that is taking place with you? Your mother's dream is falling away into broken petals. Jomo, correct yourself before it is too late. Build your empires inside yourself and leave the rubble of tribal power to those pigmies of the soul like Miku and Gwombo, whose infinite emptiness feeds on the genuflections of the meek and miserable.

"Do not let such as those suck you into their savage games. This innocent green land could be drowned in blood and not a hawk nor a cockatoo could fly so high their wings would not be stained with this terrible red.

"It is so strange that in this rubble of black men I feel white; the very same tongue slips in and out of all our mouths but the words are theirs, not mine; when we dance my legs are not mine but the property of the drums; the arm that hurls the spear is my father's and grandfather's, and thus the lion in its moment of roaring death is betrayed by an abstraction, and, as the animal that was supposed to be joining it in the deepest communion, I ask its forgiveness. I feel most myself, when I lie naked on the hilltop at night and feel the stars smashing their divine diamonds into my body and making me one of them, and when I walk in the sacred caves of Ogona and exorcise my consciousness with the ancient drawings on the walls. My ancestors indeed knew what they were about: they knew the concept of the Self was a lie that could destroy a man's anonymity and make of him his own worst enemy.

"Yesterday was the future: we of the thinking council discussed the central problem of man, the individual and his relationship to the group. We wish for our children the best of human conditions, and if we can arrange tomorrow's community around our solution to the problem, perhaps that fond hope will come true. How can the individual remain himself and at the same time be a part of a thing called the group? Or should we attempt to raise our future generations to regard themselves as nonexistent outside the group? Or should we, as I suggested at our meeting (held as usual in the Grove of Destiny where we were shaded from the sun by the shadows of our forebears), develop a mock community structure that would permit the individual to go on about his single and real business and at the same time satisfy the whole population's illusion that a community is essential? We have rituals of worship and rituals of magic, so why couldn't we institute a ritual society?

"That dreadful beast called Fear prevailed. Our Council decided that chaos and death would result if the community did not come first in man's life. Thus, the only place that a man belongs to himself is in his dreams, be they waking or sleeping. And if this be the case, then man as we know him, the self, the person, ceases to exist. He can be anybody, which is the same as being nobody."

"That was simply wonderful, Mr. Johnson," the cultivated announcer began, "and station WCAI wishes to thank you for being . . . Stop it! Why are you pushing me, Mr. Johnson? Oh! Stop that! You must leave! You've done your routine. Help!"

From the stricken radio box come sounds of furniture colliding and crashing. Shrieks. A body thumping to the floor. Curses in a strange ancient tongue. Rich terrible laughter.

"Oh dear," said the black velvet voice of Jomo. "That fellow was so silly and naive. He thought he could summon forth the past and then push it back again when he was through with it. You cannot put your foot into the lake without bringing part of it with you. Any good Benga child will tell you that. And now where is that fellow Jomo Johnson who acted me?" Great laughter. "He has vanished into his own past, me! And I am now his present and his past." More rolling-hills laughter.

Mae reached over and turned the radio switch off. "They sure got some dumb programs on these days," she said, and put another potato chip in her mouth.

Milt scratched himself and yawned. "Wish I was at a ballgame with a cold beer. Goin' upstairs to them empty boxes . . . " and he shook his low-class head.

It was Charlie was first noticed the tall strangely clothed black man—he was draped in a many-colored sheet or toga—standing in the basement doorway. He couldn't think of what to say, so he said nothing. All the feeling in Charlie's body seemed to stop as he stared at the man. Some blood was on the black man's hands. Milt saw him and an odd sound came out of his throat: "Ulk!"

Jomo walked toward the table. As far as Mae was concerned he lumbered ghastly like Boris Karloff. She quickly began straightening imaginary rumples in her dress and sat up very straight (because doing this was a way of bringing order into an unruly situation). "Mr. MacIntosh is in charge of the department and he isn't here." She said that in one breath and in the voice of a child.

Jomo began speaking in a strange language. In English it would come out this way: "My reason and my experience tell me that you do not exist. Your hands could not have touched those things my hands have touched. Your feet could never have served me in my walkings. Your smell is not to be smelled. My nose does not wish to join you. I do not think you understand the lion in the morning nor the crocodile in his night mud. I could not sing songs about you at any tribal feast. And your meat would not go down if I were to eat you."

Charlie had been working on an urge and a particular sentence, which sentence was to sound like, "Come on, Milt. You got to help me pack the stuff goin' to Bethesda. Let's go now." But no, this utterance never took place. Instead, this came from him: "I'm a good kid and I do my homework like you told me. Don't believe those lies the other kids tell you about me." His voice was a child's. Milt nodded his head (his face had metamorphosed). "Me too. An' you can use my mitt." Same with Mae. A clean little girl in a Catholic school. She wiggled attentively in her chair and said, "My class assignment was to choose a news event from the newspaper that was of international importance. I will now read that." She sat back primly in her chair, put her hands in front of her exactly as though she were holding a paper, and recited verbatim, as though she were actually reading, an item she had read in the morning paper: "Officials of the Army-backed Greek regime are expected to press anew for resumption of United States military-aid shipments after what they regard as the first step toward a return of democracy tomorrow." An imbecilic smile was her total face.

Jomo looked from one to the other, shook his head slowly, and took his leave of that basement sample.

Once at home he did the least absurd thing he could think of: he half drowned himself in a hot shower and then went to bed. Three hours of interior journey turned out to be all he needed. (Incidentally, there are no ticket takers in such journeys and this fact protects them from being cheap and commerical.)

He was in the middle of a fried pork-chop sandwich and a cup of java when he began thinking out loud. "I've had some pretty challenging roles in my acting career but I must confess that my most recent one, under the kind auspices of station WCAI, indeed taxed my talents in a brand new way. Without challenge an artist withers. Challenge is his very life's blood." He swallowed some pig meat, some java and said, "My ass. All I need is another part like that and they'll carry me away to the crazy house. Man, if I could only get away from these chickenshit one-shot deals! The big role! The big score! That's what this cat needs. Hamlet. Faustus. *The Brothers Karamazov.* Shit, I'd even play the President of Bolivia if the price was right." He started gnawing on the bone. "What I need is a good agent. A hustler with *chutzpah*, a pioneer in brainstorms who says to himself, the sky's the limit for my boy Jomo. Somebody like the famous Gelb. There's the baby who could put my name up in lights for keeps. He never stops working for his clients, night and day. There is nothing Gelb won't do, no place in the whole world he won't go, to keep his people working in top-drawer roles. Space and time do not defy that cat. His actors worship him like he's some kind of God. They really do. I've even heard some of them say that if it weren't for Gelb they would simply cease to exist. Now that kind of devotion is very hard to come by these days, I mean, to put it most mildly. Why, just the other day I saw an example of this. I ran into my old buddy Esmeralda, the grooviest hunchback dwarf of all time. He was standing in front of '21' and for a moment I thought he was one of those jockey statues that adorn the building."

" 'Baby, you sure lookin' sharp,' I said, pointing to his red-velvet sequin suit.

" 'Gelb,' he said grinning.

" 'Success and well-being emanate from all over you,' I went on.

" 'Gelb,' he said again.

"Our confrontation was ended by the appearance, or sudden materialization, of Miss America—a redhead of such splendid stacking, it's a good thing for the Catholic Church St. Augustine never met her because we would have lost the Church right then and there. Esmeralda naturally did not waste any of his precious time by introducing us. No indeedy.

"I must get Gelb, that's all there is to it. He doesn't know it, but we are meant for each other." Jomo threw the bone violently at the wastebasket. "Goddamn him! I need the bastard and I hate him! The fucking unfairness of this world!"

He poured himself more coffee and lit up a cigarillo. The telephone saved him from further psychic distress.

"Jomo here," he said sweetly, because you never knew if that other on the phone might be in a position to give you something and therefore would not be averse to a soupçon of brown-nosing.

"Lucius baby!" he shouted. "How you doin' honey? Yeah? The what? Artists against the War in Vietnam? Never heard of it. Oh, is that so. Uh huh. I see. And you want me to join this group and parade before the White House? Wearing a what? The costume of a skeleton? Representing . . . yeah, yeah. Got it. Like a medieval pageant. Sure, sure. I'm not totally stupid, Lucius sweetie. And you say the pay is a hundred bucks for a three-hour shift. You couldn't make that a hundred and a quarter, could you? Uh . . . well then how about a hundred ten and throw in lunch?

Fine. You got a deal, brother. Oh, by the way . . . Would you happen to have a few extra ounces of grass on you? Because my connection had to go to Richmond to see his mother and . . . Okay. Fine. You're beautiful, brother. Real beautiful. Just leave it in my mailbox, and I'll return it to you soon as my boy gets back. Okay, I'll come by your place tomorrow for the costume. *Arrivederci*, man."

Jomo decided to do a few exercises to get the deep fluids of his black body running right again, and he knew that once that took place, his mind would get the hint and, out of shame if nothing else, banish from its domicile all improper occupants, such as bats, bugs, cobwebs, digressions, funks, and low thoughts with no future. Ten fast leg stiff push-ups. Twelve knee bends. A thirty-second imitation of an upside-down English bicycle. Mm. His body was singing and his mind now more nearly approximated a clean well-lit squash court than the reeking, vaporous pen it had been. Except . . . squatting on that nifty exorcised squash court (you could have held the National Championships there without a bit of official fuss) was that leering rotten little Gelb. Jomo could have wept. "Oh you insidious ragpicker!" Jomo howled. "You sixth-rate negotiator from the Congress of Vienna!" Jomo could have gone on from there and developed a career out of such name calling and toured the capitals of the world. But he caught himself just in time (which is a lot sooner than most promising people do). He realized that under the circumstances, there was only one way to deal with the Gelb thing: he brought his actor's talent into play. He knew that unless Gelb was nothing but an inhuman rumor, a lie from start to finish, he had to have a character. So Jomo, using all he had learned from his own experience and the advice of Stanislavski, assumed the character of Gelb, just as he would have assumed the character of Hamlet, Oedipus, or the Gingerbread Boy.

He began to think such thoughts as he was certain Gelb thought, deep, penetrating, city-consuming thoughts. The conquest of Paris, the sack of Rome, the defeat of Socrates in open dialog. He began to feel Gelb feelings—icy Arctic wastes, jungles of maddened lechery. He made characteristic gestures—imperious waves of the hand, elegant stances of triumphant cunning, provocative eyebrow raisings. Gradually Jomo was left far behind.

He finally sat down at the table and on the back of an announcement of a vast Love-In, began writing an intimate Journal à la Gelb.

He had heard just enough about the man's unusual life to be able to improvise on a factual basis. He did not of course begin within quotes because that would have been an admission of separateness. Last night at the home of the brilliant young Swiss pianist, Duval Gruchek, my wife and I made utter fools of ourselves by getting stoned on Piper Heidseck, 1957. However, we were not alone in our foolishness. Everyone else got drunk too. The company was divine, and Geneva in May is simply too much to resist.

My ass! It's so difficult to resist that I wouldn't have gone there had Sylvia not practically broken my arm. And it wasn't on champagne that I got smashed but gin, good old Geneva gin, which I drank in the kitchen with the servants because my delicate stomach couldn't stand those pretentious assholes who were there to suck around each other. My pal for life Sylvia among them. That woman would eat owlshit if she thought it would get her into the Nature Lover's Annual Ball. Sylvia's season would be made if the wonderful Duval Gruchek would appear at one of our parties in Paris and play for everybody. Free of course. Boy, if that happened she would really be Queen of Suck Hill. But what can you expect from a woman whose mother testified before the House Un-American Activities Committee that Albert Einstein was a faggot? You may ask me what a pluperfect chap like myself is doing married to such a crumbled cookie. It's simple. I am being punished. For saying that the earth was flat, that oil is heavier than water, for claiming that Al Smith would win in a landslide. You think I'm laying it on too thick. Okay. Then what do you say to the fact that at this very moment I have in my back pocket a note from Dante asking permission to do my life story in a thing he plans to call the *Inferno?*

Ever since her appointment as Vice Consul of the American Embassy here in Paris, Sylvia's behavior has gotten more than normally disgusting and revisionist. I mean, it is all I can do to concentrate on my work at the National Library, where I have been knocking my brains out putting together the first true history of the family structure of the French Troubadors during the fourteenth and fifteenth centuries. (The lies and distortions that have obscured *this* subject are enough to make any honest scholar weep.) This work will be the culmination of my life's scholastic commitment to historiography and will, I hope, justify the faith of my employers, the French Historical Institute of Harvard University, which has sustained me since my graduation, long years ago. (Much longer than the trustees want to think about, I'm sure.)

Sylvia's insane need to hustle the scene has taken us, in the last three weeks alone, to four art exhibits, six plays, two ballets, two bicycle races, one opera (we were supposed to go to another one, but some student rioters blew up the building the day before), three poetry readings, and eight hundred and seventy-three dinner parties. As a matter of pathological fact, we're on the go so much that I've packed a sleeping bag in our car and a three-day change of clothes. Sometimes I can't even remember where we live.

And another thing: Sylvia's got herself a sidekick whom I would gladly kick in the head if I had an iron foot. A know-it-all pain in the ass named Lola who is married to the Finnish Ambassador, Sandor Haldok (a decent enough fellow who made medical history last year when he was recipient of the first reindeer heart transplant). This straitlaced, puritanical goody-goody is one of the social leaders of the diplomatic group, and is unconscionably active in such cons as the Lilies of the Valley Club, Women for International Peace, Care, the Girl Scouts, and the Association for Limited Motherhood. Not only does this Lola broad cozy with Sylvia about dress, hair-do, and Kotex styles, she also throws in her two cents on the subject of Sylvia's spiritual and marital life. Why, just yesterday while we were supposed to be having a quiet nip at the Crillon Bar, this hemlock root set civilization back four hundred years, and caused considerable brain damage in me personally, by saying (Sylvia was making wee-wee at the time), "Sylvia is one of the most sensitive, intelligent women I know. Why don't you treat her better?"

"Gulp?"

"Most men would give their right arm for such a woman," she continued, sipping her vermouth like a fascist titmouse, "and she has nothing but respect and admiration for you. So how can you explain your peculiar—to say the least—behavior?"

"Oh God," I moaned as my equilibrium began to crumble.

"I'll tell you what I think . . . I think you are a very sick man and very much in need of psychiatric attention." She looked calmly out over the sea of my despair. "Precisely. And I can assure you that my husband Sandor would agree with me if he were here." She sipped again. "In fact, I'll get him on the phone if you like and he'll tell you himself. Even friendship does not prevent Sandor from being honest." She daubed her wet upper lip with a pink lace hanky. "That's one of the reasons I married him." She smiled up at God. "Sandor is a deep, pure mountain stream."

"First of all," I said, as I began to bleed heavily from my ears, "mountain streams aren't deep. They are shallow and fickle. And second . . ."

Oh Christ. Why bother? Would you like to know what other activities this woman infiltrates her imaginagion with? The suppression of vice in the provinces. I mean it. She and three or four other highly placed paradoxes have been meeting with the various provincial chieftains—or warlords or whatever—to arrange for the policing of every hayloft, corncrib and wine cellar outside Paris. (She was going to do the same for Paris until the Minister of Tourism threatened to lift her passport.) Her problem is that she read Zola upside down. She thinks that chaste farm girls milk cows better and that hard-ons cause accidents in the field. Can you imagine? I'll tell you something, and I'm not kidding: people like Lola can make crops wither and hail storms come in the middle of the night.

These two have gotten so chummy that talking to one is just about the same as talking to the other. And who needs that kind of arrangement? Get a load of this (for example): "Would you kindly explain to me why you must regress to an animal condition when we go out?" Sylvia asked me this morning.

"I can't for the life of me guess what you are talking about," I replied. (Our apartment overlooks—and I don't mean by that avoids or misses—the Seine, and I was watching an old man poling for eel.)

"That's because your brain is like a watch that has sprung a leak. What I am referring to in particular is your snoring so loud in the middle of *Spectre of the Rose* that the woman in front of me called the usher."

"Oh, that. Well, the reason . . ."

528 | Chandler Brossard

"And at the preview of Picasso's new sculpture, what did you do? Locked yourself in the bathroom for two hours, that's what."

I shifted in my seat. "I didn't feel well. I . . . uh . . . had a terrible attack of *déja vu* and my doctor advised me that the only way to handle that kind of thing is to . . ."

She mashed her Lucky Strike out as though it were me. "You are making me the laughing stock of Paris. Everywhere I go people smile at each other and whisper, 'There's the wife of the All-American Spook.' " Her tone now took on a combo of whine and snivel. "Don't you care about my career or my dignity as a human being?"

The old man caught an eel. He reached out to pull it in and . . . toppled into the river. "I'm glad you brought that up," I said, a certain snap somewhere between October and stringbean coming into my style, "because I would like to discuss my own dignity and career. In the past few months I have felt a certain . . ."

Slam! Her hand striking the seventeenth-century tulipwood table (Jean of Toulouse). "You're doing it again! Moving the discussion around to your side of the story. You're positively unbelievable. You can't stand the thought that you may not be the only person in the universe."

(As I was thinking of something to say, the firm and pure words of Kierkegaard, whom I had been reading just that morning, leaped into my mind. "Generally speaking, imagination is the medium of the process of infinitizing; it is not one faculty on a par with others, but, if one would so speak, it is the faculty *instar omnium* [for all faculties]. What feeling, knowledge, or will a man has depends in the last resort upon what imagination he has." Mm. Good stuff.)

Now, as anybody who knows me well can testify, I hate a good argument. There are more important projects in this world than bile-pouring carnivals. So I immediately introduced a little cashmere into the tableau. "I'm very sorry if it seems that way, Sylvia dear. Because truly at heart I am a most generous fellow. It's merely that my work requires a great deal of concentration and . . ."

She blew her nose as if she had been crying. My words cannot penetrate or mingle with nose sounds, so I stopped talking. She took advantage of my sensitive silence and leaped in. (In the very